WYCHFIELD MANOR

S.P. HURST

ISBN: 9781729325544
ISBN-13:

Dedicated to my readers and fellow authors.

With special thanks to Spiffing Covers

CHAPTER 1

Dark menacing vultures circled outside there was no escape route, Emma Taylor was trapped! The tawdry paparazzi were surrounding the wrought iron gate, of the smart mews house she shared in London. Knowing she would have to face them head on, sooner or later, they were not going away.

Recent events were catapulting her into the glaring spotlight. Her father's scheming actions were out in the media for all to see. Sky News was ablaze with a fast noisy live scene from outside the court room. There was breaking news; the latest shameful report about his rapid fall from grace.

Emma quickly switched off the TV screen, unable to watch or process the dire outcome of her father's downward spiral. Wild thoughts were like a pendulum in her brain, swinging back and forth, ticking down the seconds like a metronome. She needed to urgently hit the re set button on her life, it was like a living nightmare.

Keeping low she peered out of the sash windows of the second floor flat, looking through the blaze of daffodils in the window boxes at the front of the house. She could see the journalists and photographers clearly, clamouring for the best photo shot of her.

They were patiently waiting for her to emerge from the Georgian town house in Notting Hill. Although the early spring sunshine was warming the air, an ice cold chill ran down her spine.

The embarrassment was total; she thanked god she had completely finished at college. So she did not have to suffer the further humiliation, of explaining every single detail of the drama to her class mates.

All was quiet now inside, in an isolated manner she continued her search for answers, what had just happened had cast a deep emotional shadow over her life. The devastation was complete, the tension within her was building, she felt sick to her stomach!

She sat quietly in her underwear carefully shuffling her tarot cards, spreading the pack onto the coffee table. The ominous death card was staring back at Emma crossed by the hanging man, the tarot deck on the table showed clearly change was imminent, and painful.

When to act and what to surrender was the challenge revealed on the cards. Urging her to do what her inner intuition believed to be right. She was franticly looking for guidance, her life had been changed forever. It would take enormous strength, and courage to survive the immense shame her calculating father had brought on the family.

She carefully laid another card in the Celtic cross spread. Yes, she would have to take a leap of faith! The lion of strength, a major Arcana card was there, with the fool at the beginning of his journey; then the lovers and the karmic scales of justice.

The bizarre notion that your thoughts could materialise, exactly what you wanted from your desires had prompted her to pursue her destiny. A belief that absolute abundance and divine timing was available from the universe; had driven Emma Taylor to shape her own future from the wreckage of the past.

Shifting her focus to what she could do, instead of suffering with her weaknesses. She was plagued with bad habits that had ruled her life, but not anymore it was time to alter her life for the better. She knew the secret! She would ask, believe and receive, pushing her forward with swift action.

As a typical Aquarian Emma was resourceful, caring and creative, a bright original thinker. Her bohemian dress sense was a complete throw back to the hippy era. She dressed in her own way, with a charming mystique which suited her personality. She was a free spirit and proud of it, although fair she was no dumb blond and followed no one. Her casual yet understated style was her own distinctive impression of timeless shabby chic, Emma had created her own unique signature look.

An obsession with reading her horoscope and tarot cards, had become part of her weekly ritual. It shaped and influenced her actions, many years before she had experienced a feeling of being guided by intuition; the feeling that her life would unfold in a way she could manifest to her advantage, toward her single personal destiny. Now more than ever she found herself at a crossroads, her father had done a great deal of financial damage, he would pay a high price for his deception.

She felt it was her duty to pay back to all those family members who were suffering from his absolute greed. Her father had let her down badly, she could never forgive him, for what he had done. She vowed she would not see him again!

However fate unfolded, her life had just been turned upside down, her comfortable existence and careful plans for the future had just been ruined. Now the time was right to change her pattern of behaviour before it became too late. Destiny had thrown a giant sledge hammer right through her business ambitions, in a way that she had not seen coming.

She knew how privileged her comfortable life had been, thanks to her financier father who had provided a generous trust fund for her. But was appalled to realise that it was at others expense, she had set high ethical standards for herself, which he had violated. He had sullied the family name once and for all, she would try hard to make amends.

Emma had spent many foundation years at catering college in London. Getting ready to start a business of her own, she had always been a brilliant cook inspired by the top chefs. As an avid fan of TVs Masterchef, she was constantly scanning cookery books and You Tube for new unusual food combinations, trying out unique tasty dishes to inspire. The only problem was her love of rich desserts was having a disastrous effect on her once slim waistline.

Having already gained top business degrees and qualifications, it seemed natural for her to work for herself in some way. In the past she expected her rich father to fund her start up career in the future. Funny how things don't work out as you plan! It had been just purely a matter of timing to find the right business niche to get started. She had been so excited to get it right, waiting for the best opportunity to come along, as surely it would. Now what?

It should have been a nice start to the day, now a complete disaster! She was startled back to reality by the shrill tones of her house phone. Emma rushed down the stairs still in her underwear grabbing her dressing gown from the back of the door in a frantic hurry to answer the call.

It was her mother calling from her home in Scotland, seeing how her daughter was coping with the awful situation unfolding around her.

"What can I do about the press? There outside!" Emma shrieked down the phone to her mother. She was being followed at every turn, she had endured weeks of feeling pursued and scared. There was no place left to hide Emma was caught in a whirlwind of frenzy.

Her family meltdown was caused by the actions of her famous father, the problem was propelling her into the limelight changing Emma's life forever.

"Mum the paparazzi had been hounding me, setting up cameras right outside the steps of the house. There are at least ten photographers and reporters, eager to catch a glimpse of me as soon as I step foot outside the front door." She was trapped like a mouse waiting for the mechanical spring to snap shut. It was something she had never experienced before and never wanted to again.

Emma knew they were pumping anyone, and everyone who knew her father John Taylor, for any juicy snippets of information regarding her father's alleged fraud. He was a financial adviser extraordinaire to the exclusive rich list, he had become notorious for his business dealings and tax avoidance schemes.

"Mum what can I do" Emma panicked, "they are drip

feeding a constant poison onto the tabloids daily. This cannot be happening to me, the worlds gone mad, I can't stand it!" She knew the relentless stress of the situation had to end, she was no closer to finding the answer to her dead end dilemma.

The tarot cards had not forewarned her of what was to come about, she was completely on her own against the odds. It was a catastrophe unfolding before her eyes, the tragedy was that there was nothing she could have done to stop it.

Mums reply came swiftly. "Keep your focus, life has ups and downs don't get rattled."

It was easy to say keep calm and carry on, but her whole life was unravelling at alarming speed. The heartbreak had only just begun, she just knew it! Hope alone was not enough.

Now it dawned on Emma that she must make her own way in the world, without her father's money to support her life, the prospect of going it alone was frightening. Any money in her account had run out as she expected, and her flat contract at the Georgian town house was terminating soon. The last year had flown by quickly, the catastrophe had unfolded bit by bit over the months, as her father's court case proceeded.

As the weeks went by the press vanished, Emma started to take stock of her life. Looking back it became clear, the father she grew up with was a liar and a cheat, he was a confidence trickster of epic proportions. She came to the conclusion that the re set of her life was imminent, Emma phoned her mother in Scotland.

"Mum I've just received your text message. What do you mean! Dad has got... life! That's unbelievable."

She said, choking back her tears. "Why have you never explained to me what exactly was going on! I am in a total state of shock." Emma's mum replied calmly.

"Sorry darling, I didn't want to upset you, the financial pressure was one of the reasons we got a divorce. You're father has confessed all at the trial, the recovery agents believe the missing money may never be found. His investment opportunity, it appears was never legitimate; trustees estimate the loss to be several billions of pounds!" Emma listened to her completely dumbfounded.

"Your father had invested money from a lot of people, money was completely lost in the financial crisis when the stock market plunged. He lost every penny he had invested, mainly in the property market in the United States which went belly up. It was pure greed."

Emma was in a state of disbelief, unable to process the huge scale of the financial loss. "Will dad be ok she asked her mother?" She replied to her quietly, trying to help by de stress her daughter.

"Actually I think your father knew exactly what he was doing, he is no fool he just didn't think he would be caught out. The sub-prime housing market was his final downfall, it didn't help the situation. It was sadly the last straw in a massive catalogue of errors." Trying her best to explain the evidence at the court proceedings, and the final verdict, she continued.

"He was always looking for the next deal he became a slave to materialism, his clients trusted him like a friend. He thought that greed was good! Making money sadly became an addiction. He couldn't stop no matter who he was hurting, or how much money he made. The process held some sort of control, a strong hold over him. Honestly he thought he could not lose, it was almost like a gambling addiction, It was an easy way of making vast sums of money."

Of course Emma knew the odds, that the gambling house always won in a casino. It was the same sort of situation just a matter of time, and time was not on her father's side. The hour glass had flipped over, the grains of sand had run out.

Stress of the family situation had made Emma revert to craving fattening and sweet foods again, she had been bingeing on high calorific foods. Comfort eating was her Achilles' heel, she knew it was completely out of control. She had put on at least thirty pounds in the last year, although she normally had an attractive slim figure with her shoulder length dark blond hair, and hazel eyes. She was now unhappy with her new stocky figure, and told her mother she was.

"Desperate to get the weight under control."

Her mother sympathised with her daughter admitting that she also had too much on her mind to diet. With her raging hormones, both admitted the need for a complete overhaul of their lives. They agreed together to get healthier and to nurture themselves with exercise, to try clean healthy eating as the best way forward.

During their lengthy telephone conversation Emma worryingly asked the question she had wanted to ask for weeks.

"Did we lose money too?" Her mother hesitated in answering her.

"I'm afraid so, we lost all your trust fund money. As you know the account was frozen when your father was accused of fraud, and now the account has been completely closed. I will have to sell the family house in Scotland, and downsize to make ends meet financially."

Her mother's house in Sterling was a large grey granite Victorian house with two large bay windows at the front. It was quite imposing with steps up to the front door in the centre. Far too big and costly for her to maintain on her own, the heating bills were horrendous. She was beginning to see the sense of moving to a smaller cheaper house to run.

"The worst thing is that your aunt Lady Mary, has lost a vast fortune. She trusted your father to invest all of her capital, which included equity in her beautiful Wychfield Manor estate in Sussex. I'm not sure how she will be able to cope, she must be in her late seventies now. It will be such a shock to her."

"Mum I think you need to talk her quickly, she will be devastated."

"I know," mum replied.

"Your aunt always mentioned the estate was worth a fortune, and would be handed down to her adopted son Stefan eventually." Emma agreed.

"Do you think he is aware?"

"Probably not. He is her sole heir, but as you know he has been living away from home, in New York for the last few years." Her mum sighed then continued.

"It's such a shame, because your aunt Mary has turned into a hermit, she became a recluse when her husband died. Stefan has not been back home to Wychfield Manor since he left to finish his fine art degree in New York." Emma interrupted her mother.

"I heard through facebook that he was married in Las Vegas last year!"

"That's right" mum sighed again.

"Such a shame! I thought in the future he would be a perfect match for you!"

"Mother! You surprise me now. I had no idea you had concocted such a strange notion. Where did that brainwave spring from?"

"I remember seeing you both playing kiss chase on the lawn at the manor when you were tiny. You always were so easy for him to catch!"

Emma chocked back a laugh.

"Even easier to catch me now! Emma replied. "I have put on at least a stone."

"You were always such a beautiful child, with your golden hair swishing when you ran, and your trim figure. Stefan definitely liked you a lot, he would rather be with you than any of his other friends. You must admit you liked him too!"

"Mum you have not seen me for a while. The comfort eating on desserts, including tubs of ice cream has taken its toll. When I caught sight of myself in a shop window, I had such a shock! I seriously thought. What the hell has happened to me!" She continued.

"Then I saw the latest awful photograph of myself in the tabloids. The headlines read, *Emma Taylor fraudsters daughter ....Loses cash and gains pounds*!"

At twenty one years old Emma was feeling that what should be the best time of her life, was now a living nightmare. She had become so ashamed of herself, too upset with her weight to be seen out socially. Which only added to the anxiety she felt about her father.

Emma had lost touch completely with Stefan many years ago. She hadn't seen him for at least five years when she was sixteen. When she was younger she had a very serious teenage crush on him. He was smart and handsome in a Scandinavian way. Very fair and tall for his age, with a striking athletic figure, he looked like every woman's dream of the ideal Adonis.

She was saddened when Stefan went to live in New York to complete his degree. She tried to follow his progress via mutual friends on face book, but was far too shy to keep in touch with him herself. Plus since she had gained weight she did not want him to see her as she was now. Hoping he had not seen the recent English newspaper picture of her.

Over the years since he had seen Emma, Stefan had gained a degree in art history at university in New York. He had specialising in the Pre Raphaelites Victorian symbolism, he was now an art expert of repute for Victoriana. He was becoming a leading authority on the subject, he was kept busy writing his first art book.

Stefan was also fond of horse riding, he had become a talented polo player in his teens, and was often seen on the polo field with the young royals. Much sought after by the clingy society girls on the polo circuit, who were eager to make Stefan's acquaintance. He had turned from a lanky teenager into a handsome man, and a great catch for any female wishing to bed him. Many had tried, and some succeeded for a short while until he tired of them, preferring to string them along while he played the field.

As Emma's mother was in the process of packing. Selling her house in Scotland having put it onto the property market, enabling her to down size. Emma suggested to her on the phone that as she was so busy; she herself would telephone her aunt, Lady Mary in Sussex.

It was a good way of keeping in touch with her

beloved aunt, they had once been very close. When Emma was growing up she often stayed with her favourite aunt. She also wanted to see how Lady Mary was feeling about the dreadful financial situation. Aware that her aunt was all alone at the manor house, Emma felt she could help her. Knowing that soon she would have to move out of her London flat.

Emma was not sure how much information her aunt had, or what changes there were in her financial circumstances. Aware it could be worst than Emma had contemplated she braced herself to make the dreaded call.

The phone rang for a long time without answering, she held on knowing it might take a while for her aunt to get to the phone, then it picked up.

"Hello aunty Mary, it's your niece Emma here. It has been a long time since I spoke to you. How are you?"

"Oh Emma dear it's so nice to speak to you again. I am surprised to hear from you. Sorry to be so out of breath." She gasped as she took a seat by the land line phone trying to catch her breath.

"Wait dear, while I take off my gardening gloves. How is London?"

"It's as busy as ever aunty, traffic noise everywhere it's so hectic, but I do like it! Hyde park is lovely at this time of year, it's getting prettier every day with the tulips all in bloom."

"Oh Emma spring is such a lovely season, summer is coming gradually. The sun is getting warmer! I was busy re potting some seedlings in the orangery when you rang." Emma enquired. "Do you still have a gardener, and cleaner at the manor house? It must be quite an up keep, how are you coping?"

"Oh no dear I had to let the cleaner go! So many small precious things were going missing, I couldn't risk keeping her on. But I have kept Brandon the gardener on to keep the lawns in order, it is far too much for me to cope with at my age. He now lives in the old stone lodge at the entrance to the drive."

Emma sounded surprised.

"Aunty Mary, you can't possibly do all the cleaning yourself at Wychfield, you must have at least a dozen bedrooms there." Lady Mary replied.

"No it's not a problem, when my husband died many years ago, I shut off all the bedroom doors, it helps to keep the warmth in." Emma continued

"Sounds sensible aunty, as long as you are ok."

"I do get lonely in the house alone Emma, but I am a bit of a recluse as you know, I'm like a hermit happy on my own. I am very grateful to have lived in this house as long as I have. Even if it looks as though I will lose it now." Shrugging her shoulders resigned to her fate, she added.

"There is no point going down memory lane. I feel very fortunate that I have never been poor, until now that is!" She tried to add a joking giggle, but could not fool Emma, her mood had changed. Emma sighed with sympathy.

"Aunty I would like to come down to Sussex to see you. Would it be ok if I stayed with you for a while? I could do with a break from the stress of London with everything that has happened recently, I would love to see you! We can catch up with everything at Wychfield."

"Yes darling, That would be great, I do miss you, it has been a long time since we got together. So do stay as long as you like, I would appreciate having time to catch up with you again. I'm sure you have so much to tell me about your exciting life in London."

Emma then asked her aunt the one question she was dying to know.

"Do you see Stefan very often."

"No not at all" she replied.

"Now that he lives in the States, he has so much to take care of in the auction business." Adding proudly.

"He is very successful now you know, busy writing his book about the Victorian Era. In truth I think it would be too boring for him now in the manor. The Sussex downs are no match for Times Square."

"He has such an exciting life now, and such a good future ahead of him there is nothing to hold him here." She seemed resigned to the fact that he would not come back home to see her.

"Oh that's a shame aunty," said Emma, sorry to see that her aunt had been all but abandoned.

"It was such a shock when I heard on facebook that he had married in Las Vegas." Lady Mary said sadly.

"As a notable family we were expecting a big society wedding when he got married. It was so sudden and unexpected. Stefan can be so head strong and impulsive he shocked the family to the core." Lady Mary then added snootily.

"A Little Chapel in Vegas is not what we wanted at all, but it was too late, the deed was done! He is now repenting!" Lady Mary continued.

"Stefan did mention to me on the phone a while ago, that he had made an awful mistake! He was sorry, he is certainly not happy, so I guess we will not be meeting her any time soon!" She added with a chuckle.

"But he has made his bed and now he has to lie in it." Emma was surprised to hear the latest news, although saddened, to hear it had not worked out for Stefan. However, quietly she was pleased that her jealousy could be resolved, he had not been taken away from her forever.

Having talked at length to her aunt, Emma had arranged to visit the manor in a couple of weeks time. Courteously giving her aunt the time to make her arrangements for the visit. Lady Mary was excited to be able to have her niece staying with her again. She had not seen her for so long, it was a pleasure she looked forward to.

Wychfield Manor was the best place to be at the moment, a special place! Emma was sure of it. She remembered when she had stayed there before many years ago, as a child. Happily playing with Stefan in the blue bell woods, running together and hiding in the trees on the edge of the Sussex downs. They playing house in the pretty stone lodge that now belonged to the gardener. She remembered the heady scent of the flowers and cut grass that filled the air, it seemed truly magical. It was the most beautiful spot on earth, looking back now, she realised it was one of the happiest times of her life.

CHAPTER 2

A few weeks later Emma was settling herself onto the fast Gatwick Express train at Victoria Station. It was another bright spring day without a cloud in the sky, she had grabbed a cheese sandwich and coffee at the station café. As the train pulled out of the dark station into the day light, she began day dreaming, hoping the visit to the manor would be a good omen. The soothing motion of the train, dispersed her tension as the miles sped by, stopping at just a few stations along the way she would soon be there.

Changing trains at Gatwick broke up her journey to Brighton, the platform was packed with a heavy throng of people as she dodged the heavy suitcases of the travellers boarding the express train back to London. She was happy to have the opportunity to stretch her legs while she checked the screen, waited for her connecting train due in two minutes on the opposite platform.

Relieved to be single with no ties to bind her to the city, her last boyfriend had been a complete disaster it was a really disjointed relationship. She had met him via an online dating agency, he worked in the city as a broker for a large insurance company. So full of himself, Dan was part of the snooty Chelsea set, which made her feel like an inferior spare part. She was thankful when it fizzled out, she could do without the stress of trying to keep up appearances with him. She now had no job, no car, with no prospects and her money rapidly running out. It was a waste of time to tie herself to anyone at the moment, she was at last enjoying her liberty to do what she wanted, it was time for her free spirit to soar.

Emma was well aware her bad eating habits had got the better of her; knowing there must be a way to alter her behaviour. She had to, if she was ever going to be happy in her own skin.

A welcome break was what she needed, to get away from the pressure and fast pace of London. But mainly it was a chance to get away from a stressful existence. She needed this break away, before deciding what her new beginning should be. She had released the flat in the rented mews house in Notting Hill back to the rental company, when the term was up. It was far too expensive to carry on renting the flat. Her few belongings and books from University were put into storage with a friend for the time being, until she decided where her new future was going.

So from this point in time her future was to be a free agent, to make a new life for herself. It felt great to know that the dodgy boyfriends, she had dated along the way in London were firmly in her past she had no plans to keep in touch. No more nightclubs and wine bars, she felt relieved the rush and bustle of London was now off limits. All she had to do now was to look after herself, get healthy and be stress free, getting back into shape was her new priority. She was determined this spring would be the turning point in her life, to launch her new beginning, a leap of faith at the crossroad and most importantly a new start!

She put down a diet magazine into her lap, and called Lady Mary on her mobile.

"Emma dear are you on your way?"

"Just leaving Gatwick railway station now aunty, I should be at Brighton on time." Excitedly she replied.

"It will be so lovely to see you, after such a long time it must be at least five years now!" She agreed.

"I know aunty it must be."

"I will grab a taxi from outside Brighton station see you soon."

Arriving at last at Wychfield Manor Emma released a sigh of relief, the weight of the world had been lifted from off her shoulders. She felt as though she was returning home after her long nightmare. The imposing wrought iron gates were left propped open wide so the taxi could enter, tyres crunching along the winding gravel drive, past the pretty stone lodge on the left.

The taxi followed its way through the towering rhododendron and azalea bushes, heavily budded and beginning to come into flower with various shades of purple, and pink. The dense high bushes casting dark shadows along the way. Suddenly from the darkness of the shrubbery, she saw the imposing mock Jacobean manor house emerging into view in the bright sunshine.

Her mind took her right back to her past childhood when she visited Wychfield. The scene opened out onto the stunning large sandstone and timber framed manor house. The manor had a sturdy Tudor oak front door, and two enormous ornate leaded pane windows on either side the door. It was a magnificent grade II listed building, set high on top of the south downs, overlooking rolling grassland with bracken hills stretching far away into the distance.

Lady Mary was waiting beside the stone porch at the front door, looking much older than Emma had remembered her. Smaller and very frail, she stooped when she slowly walked, using a sturdy walking stick. Her large chunky knit jumper swamped her tiny frame, her long white hair was whisked up onto her head in a topknot tied with black ribbon, her face was crumpled and lined yet her bright blue eyes sparkled as always as she smiled.

She hobbled forwards and embraced Emma near the door step, as the taxi drove away.

"I am so pleased to see you after such a long time. I have exciting news for both of us," she said. Gesturing for Emma to come inside into the huge hallway. "Why don't you leave your suitcase here while I get some tea arranged? You must be hungry."

The afternoon had flown past and she was beginning to get hungry again.

"Just some tea and biscuits will be fine for me." She answered not wanting to put her aunt to too much trouble. Emma went into the drawing room to wait, it was a room that was seldom used but kept for best when visitors arrived. Instantly she felt at home this was her happy place! Lady Mary walked slowly to the kitchen setting the kettle on to boil. She soon returned pushing a small trolley with the tea , and a biscuit barrel into the drawing room.

"I love having an excuse to use my best teapot!"

"You said you had some good news aunty." Emma said opening the china jar and placing a selection of assorted biscuits onto a plate, while Lady Mary poured the tea from her teapot, into the finest bone china cups and saucers she produced from the large mahogany dresser.

"Well the good news is that Stefan will be coming back to England soon. He wants to talk to me urgently about the estate! He said he is keen to get some legal documents signed quickly, in view of the dire financial situation we are in."

"That's good news aunty, you must be pleased to see him again after all this time!" Her aunt nodded as she continued.

"I do hope Stefan can be of help to you. He is so clever, he should have some good ideas! Is he aware of the full details of my father's financial involvement, and how his dealings has affected your finances?"

"Yes he is, in a way! The down side is, he is not aware exactly how precarious my finances are!" Lady Mary answered, with a worried look on her face.

"Precarious, in what way?" Emma replied looking intrigued.

"I have been a very silly old woman trusting your father, I should have taken a second opinion, better legal and financial advice. I could lose everything!" She emphasized slowly.

"And I mean everything! Including the manor house and its estate." Her watery blue eyes were staring wide in her crinkled face with dismay as she spoke.

"Stefan is not aware he will lose any inheritance that was due to him, it will be a devastating blow the worst thing is; it's all my fault!"

"I will be so pleased to see him. Then I will have to tell him exactly what the situation is!" It was not something Emma wanted to be involved in, but she would have to help her aunt, it would be such a hard thing for her aunt to do alone. The revelation would be a bitter pill to take, Emma volunteered to help her although she was not sure what the reaction from Stefan would be, it would turn his world upside down, the same as hers.

It was a double edged sword, his lifestyle had been based on his inheritance, like Emma he had a comfortable background. His financial future was now in significant jeopardy, due to his mother's lack of common sense Lady Mary was guilty of financial stupidity, and she knew it. But change had come to them all suddenly, perhaps it was meant to be! It would jolt them out of their comfort zones, destiny was shaking up their lives in an unexpected way.

"Emma let's get you settled in." Lady Mary suggested as she stood up to clear away the tea trolley.

"We can discuss everything in more detail later." Going into the hall way and up the curved oak staircase, Emma noticed a distinct smell of dampness, the amount of dust and cobwebs surrounding the ceilings and chandeliers was alarming.

Her old bedroom at the end of the long landing was the same as she remembered it from five years earlier. But it felt colder and darker, turning on the tiffany style bedside lamp and opening the curtains she let the sunlight flood into the room. She noticed the set of framed watercolour paintings on the wall, Stefan had painted them for her many years ago. Pictures depicting the manor house and gardens, he had given them to her as a keep sake long ago.

There was an strange feeling that crept over her it made her shiver; she knew then that for some reason she was meant to be here, at this precise moment. It felt right, she was not frightened by this feeling, somehow she had an awakening sensation. Something extraordinary had brought her back to Wychfield!

Trying to allay her fears and lift her weird mood, she grabbed her denim jacket, putting it on over her jeans and jumper and pranced downstairs. Excited to check out the surroundings and outbuildings. Would she still feel the same about the place?

The lawns were manicured in lines as neatly as before, the smell of newly mown grass was pleasant, after the long winter. It brought back good memories of sunny days gone by when she was truly happy. Remembering how she used to run with Stefan through the piles of grass clippings with their bare feet, shaking their feet and washing it off in the lily pond. Childhood seemed such a long time ago, yet a contented haze of friendship and laughter lingered here! Yes this lovely feeling is what pulled her back.

Emma had committed to memory that it was on this grassy bank that she and Stefan would bring their watercolour's, paints and paper. Sketching the birds as they gathered twigs, and moss, making their new spring nests. They were inseparable, like the birds they painted, she had thought those long sunny days would never end.

Brandon the old gardener spied her from a distance, he had been moving compost by wheelbarrow into the greenhouse.

"Hello Miss Emma I am pleased to see you." He chuckled.

"What a nice surprise to see you all grown up." Coming towards her he put down his empty wheelbarrow.

"I am sorry to hear what happened to your father, I've been following it on the news channel." He said taking off his gloves, and flat cap, holding out his rough hand to shake hers.

"Can't have been easy for you, I often read about it in the papers."

"Oh Brandon it's been so long since I've been here" she responded. "It's a terrible shame, all the problems my father caused, that's what brought me back! But it is so nice to be here. You have kept the gardens looking brilliant the borders are so colourful."

"It has been a labour of love really." Brandon replied.

"I couldn't leave Lady Mary, she is such a kind person, she told me that there would be problems ahead. Due to her lack of money, she may have to leave the manor, I do hope it can be avoided." Emma agreed.

"So do I, that is one of the reasons why I am here. I will speak to you later, I'm staying for a while to help to sort things out here."

Brandon nodded, putting his cap back on and resumed his duties in the garden, he hoped she could help. But he knew there was a more pressing problem! Much more than financial trouble was facing Emma, he had faith that she could cope with what was about to be unveiled.

Returning into the house through the old back door Emma headed straight for the kitchen looking for Lady Mary. As she opened the door to the kitchen she stopped dead in her tracks.

"Oh my god no!" She shuddered at the sight that surrounded her. Every surface was completely covered in mess, clutter was everywhere, old news papers, cereal boxes, tins, jars and food not thrown away was all over the place. The greasy surfaces were black with dead flies stuck with gunk on the kitchen work tops.

"What a mess!" she said under her breath, as the smell wafted to her nostrils.

Emma resisted the temptation to retch as the stench filled her nose. Running from the kitchen she then went systematically room to room opened the doors to the library, dining room, and back sitting room. Each room was a sight to behold with newspapers and discarded knick-knacks far and wide covering from floors to ceilings in some areas.

This was such a shock to her, as Lady Mary was always such a house proud woman; everything was normally kept in place always neat and tidy. Fresh flowers were usually displayed in most rooms in cut glass vases filled with her favourite blooms. Emma remembered back to her youth on hers visits, the fresh scent of honey suckle and roses had filling the air. Her aunt was normally a very smart lady, well dressed in designer tweed suits with pearls, the typical country lady.

Emma realised that when she had arrived at the manor she had presumed, Lady Mary had been wearing her gardening clothes. It now dawned on her that perhaps things had changed since she had last seen her five years ago; it seemed ridiculous how much her strict dress standards had drastically dropped.

There was something very wrong here! After checking most rooms downstairs. Eventually she found her aunt in the large oak framed orangery, adjoining the manor. It was a beautiful room surrounded by ornate antique screens which was Lady Mary's favourite spot to relax in. It was full of sunlight, and warm compared to the rest of the house. Lady Mary was busy potting up some summer bulbs in pots for the garden, this was her one and only pleasure, she had not heard Emma frantically calling her.

It worried Emma that the house was in such a bad state.

"Aunty Mary what has been going on here?"

"What is the matter, you have let the house go to rack and ruin. It's not like you to let things slide like this."

Emma slumped down on the edge of the wide oak window sill in the hazy sunlight.

"I cannot believe that you are living like this. The mess is disgusting! You have amassed such a stock pile of things, there's stuff hoarded all over the place."

Lady Mary looked up at her she felt ashamed, yet unable to explain what had happened to her, the blank stare of her water eyed bewilderment was stark.

Emma was aware that in her youth Lady Mary was considered a great beauty, conscious of her royal connections, Lady Mary had always maintained a strict image of the landed gentry. Her family had been wealthy landowners, connected to Scottish whiskey distillers; the family had once lived in a small castle in the highlands on the west coast of Scotland. Family photographs still covered walls as a reminder of past times.

Lady Mary had always been very career minded, which was unusual for a woman at that time. She was well educated and became a successful magazine publisher in Edinburgh, she had stayed single until her late forties, preferring to work rather than to settle down.

Eventually she married her long time friend Robert Hargrave from Sussex, he was in the printing trade it was her husband who encouraged her in pursuing her career ambitions. He understood her need to work in an interesting company, she was bright and enjoyed setting up and running their publishing business. He was a divorcee with no children of his own, and was not interested in children at all. Their home life in Sussex was ideal, they had such a lot in common it was a good match made even more comfortable with their vast inherited wealth.

It was Mary who eventually decided to adopt a child, as it was too late for her to become a parent naturally she was nearing fifty. They decided to adopt Stefan from an orphanage in Stockholm when he was just a year old, he was a good looking boy with a mass of blond curls. Stefan instantly became the love of Lady Mary's life, and so she gave up her career to take care of him, It became an obsession for her to adopt him. She wanted an heir to follow on, to inherit the large family home they had both set up in the Sussex downs.

It was many years ago that her husband Robert had died suddenly of a congenital heart condition. Stefan was in college at the time in New York, he came home for his father's funeral, which took place in the local church. His father was buried in the family crypt on the edge of the Wychfield estate. This was the last time Emma had seen Stefan, when she stayed at the manor. Now that she was 21, it seemed like a life time ago.

Stefan stayed home in England after the funeral as long as he could, but he had to finish his degree course in New York. He went back completed his degree then started working at an art auctioneers in New York. He had not been home to Sussex at all since the funeral. His career had become the main focus of his life, he felt settled in New York with no plans to live back in England.

Turning to Lady Mary, Emma calmly persuaded her aunt to open up to her regarding the dilapidated, grimy state of the house. She must have known that Emma would be shocked when she looked around.

"Why has this happened aunty?" She asked, taking off her aunts gardening gloves and placing her small hand in hers. Lady Mary sat down beside her in a wicker chair her face showed her inner torment.

"It became difficult for me to cope with the cleaning when I let Tessa go, she was the young local lass that came to the house to clean for me twice a week. As I said before, things were going missing it could only have been her." She wanted to tell Emma everything, but was embarrassed at how easily she had let things slide.

"I felt so lonely so many times since Robert died, it can be so very isolated here especially in the winter. I began to take comfort from keeping things safe, I felt more secure I could not throw anything away. It worried me when items were going missing." Lady Mary looked worried sharing the details of what happened to her for the first time, it was an overwhelming feeling of release to have someone to confide in about her situation.

"You know the griffin is our family crest and symbol, well I think I have become the griffin! He is an emblem of guarding treasures, well that's is me!"

Listening intently Emma was beginning to see how things had changed for Lady Mary as she explained.

"The cleaning slipped more day by day, my social life became nonexistent. I did not want any visitors to see how I was living, I was ashamed but I could not help it. I had become a recluse! Like a hermit. But inside, I am happy with the way things are now, I'm in my eighties now. I have learnt to like my own company."

"But why did you let me come then aunty?" Emma asked.

"Well it is different with you I knew you would not judge me, that you would try to help me." Lady Mary was very aware that Stefan was going to arrive back from New York any day, but he had not given her a definite date. When he had called her, he was furious that she had not taken adequate advice regarding her finances, he wanted to find out exactly what was going on.

She had secretly hoped that Emma could quickly help her, to get the place cleaned and tidied up, so that Stefan would not be so shocked at the cluttered state the place was in. The prospect of him coming home and seeing the current mess was Lady Mary's worst nightmare.

Emma quickly understood the situation, she would help her aunt all she could. It would be quite a struggle, it was a large house full of disorder, but somehow she would make difference. Hoarding was something she had never experienced first-hand, but was aware that there had to be an underlying cause, that had to be understood to tackle the problem. She wondered if her aunt may have had a nervous breakdown at some point, but she had not sought medical help. Emma could not be sure, exactly how or why, it had happened but felt it to be her duty to help all she could.

She started a plan of action for clearing the house room by room. It was difficult not knowing precisely when Stefan would arrive, but knew she must proceed at a quick pace. The first part of the process was ordering a rubbish skip to be delivered in the morning, she also rang a local cleaning company, arranging for them to send two helpers urgently with cleaning supplies, for a couple of days to clear the rubbish and to help clean up. Not having her own car was a nuisance but there was no way around it, she would have to cope.

Having done this Emma felt more relieved that something could be done. The main stumbling block would be to get Lady Mary to part with the accumulated stuff, which was choking each room on the ground floor. She had explained to her aunt that to get rid of things would be essential, as clearing the rooms had to be completed to enable thorough cleaning, it was the only way forward. Her aunt took some persuading, it had become a comfort for her to keep items that she had accumulated over the years from local charity shops, and car boot sales on her foraging trips, the many items had become her little treasures.

Time was short, as Lady Mary had received a brief call again from Stefan in the United States to say he was arriving soon in a few days. Which she was pleased about, yet daunted at the same time, as it had been such a long time since she had seen him. However she did not tell him that Emma was staying at the house, she decided to keep it as a surprise.

The race was on to see if they had time to complete the task. The next morning the skip lorry arrived unloading the skip leaving it right near to the kitchen window at the back of the house. Emma donned some blue gardening dungarees she found in the potting shed pulling them up over her jeans, and tied her hair up into a scarf. With her doc marten boots and rubber gloves she was ready for the task to begin, there was no time to lose.

CHAPTER 3

Deciding to start in the front room Emma, with help from her two agency cleaners who arrived mid morning. John and Sarah had come straight away direct from another easier job. They were astounded with what they encountered as Emma slowly showed them the huge task room after room.

"Wow this is the worst job we have ever had." They looked at each other in amazement. Emma was careful not to show them the kitchen, which was the worst room in the house. Just in case it put them off completing the job, she didn't want them to buckle under the stain.

They proceeded to tackle the mountain of clutter that rose from the floor to the ceiling. Knowing it would take many hours of clearing the rubbish, before being able to clean the surfaces. Many items were good enough to use and could be salvaged, and placed in boxes to be given back to one of the charity shops in town.

The better items were kept aside, to be valued at a later date. There were hundreds of dusty old books and records piled high, many lamp shades of various sizes, curtains with poles from other rooms. There was no way that Lady Mary could have needed any of the items which were unsuitable for the manor. It was just an obsession that had got out of hand. Emma had to tell the cleaners not to enter the kitchen, as she would be tackling the worst room herself. They both appreciated the gesture as they had enough work to keep them occupied, it quickly became a badge of honour to see who could tackle the worst job.

Lady Mary kept out of their way by staying in the orangery, while they rummaged through the piles of clutter, she felt ashamed that she had not sought help before. It came as a timely rescue for her, knowing that she was losing any sense of cleanliness. Before long she might have succumbed to an illness caused by the dilapidated state of the house, it was an unhealthy environment to live in.

Emma positioned boxes of items in piles out in the hallway, sections to keep, charity or throw. There was a mountain of old news papers and magazines that went straight out into the skip, the process was slow and likely to take the rest of the day to clear the front room alone. They had decided to start downstairs then proceed up into the many bedrooms. The downstairs took priority as the other rooms on the upper floors could be tackled one at a time.

Lady Mary was asked to keep occupied by providing them with supplies of tea and biscuits. When the front room was clear enough to see the floor they invited Lady Mary to check the progress to make sure they did not discard anything of value. It became apparent that there was a real problem with getting her to part with some of the items, that had a sentimental value. Most of the items including photographs and collectables were moved to the barn to store for now, to be checked through in more detail at a later stage.

Emma dragged the old discarded and unwanted broken items to the skip, near to the back door, which was quickly half full. She then began the task of cleaning pictures and ornaments, then proceeded scrubbing the grand ornate fire place until it gleamed. Wooden floors were mopped and carpets shampooed, cleaning them as best as possible. Heavy curtains were taken down shaken outside and sent to the dry cleaners. The many chandeliers were carefully cleaned one at a time, which took many hours of delicate washing in buckets of hot soapy water, each glass strand of crystal droplets, started to gleam again reflected by the light.

The leaded windows were washed and vases filled with fresh spring flowers, gathered from the gardens were positioned on side tables. At last it was job done, it was a pleasure for them all to stand back to admire their progress. It had taken two long days of back breaking work but worth every minute. The main living room looked fresh and clean just as Emma had remembered it, but it had taken its toll on them all, it was hard work but immensely rewarding. They all celebrated with a well deserved Chinese take away served in the newly cleaned dining room.

The tasks went on again for several more days, going upstairs cleaning the bedrooms which were luckily not as cluttered or dirty as downstairs. Leaving the worst cleaning job until last, the kitchen had to be tackled at the weekend, as it was John and Sarah's day off, it was a task for Emma to tackle on her own. Emma stocked up on bleach and cleaning materials and with her rubber gloves, set to work again early Saturday morning.

She found a nest of cockroaches living behind the wood panelling near the kitchen sink, ants had crawled in through cracks under the sink, and mouse droppings were everywhere. The stench under the sink was foul as though a rat had died there, it was a job she did not want to tackle alone, but there was no other choice it had to be done. The putrid smell under the sink made her retch, the filth was too much, she had to quickly run outside to catch a breath of fresh air.

Managing to bleach everywhere was a real chore, her arms were aching scrubbing every surface down. Thank goodness that the pest control man arrived on time to eradicate the vermin's nest as she shuddered. Emma continued her chores, conscious that her time was running out, she longed to finish the work. Covered by black burnt on rancid grease, she immersed herself in cleaning the enormous range cooker, her overalls and hair were splattered in sticky black gunk. She swept the wisps of greasy blond hair off her face, and lunged back into the enormous oven with her backside in the air, while she balanced with one knee on a bar stool, with her feet right off the floor as she plunged further into the massive waist high oven.

Suddenly a weird silence made Emma become conscious of someone watching her, out of the corner of her eye she noticed a tall man hovering in the shadows behind her. He stood still, silently watching her, waiting in the background. He leant towards her making her heart skip a beat, as her head banged against the heavy oven door.

"Sorry to disturb you!." He stooped down low to address her in the dark oven. Without turning around she instantly recognised his voice. Oh my god no! This could not be happening to her, all the years she had been yearning to meet Stefan again. Not now....Not like this. At this precise moment she felt like a complete idiot covered in slime. He must not see me like this! Her thoughts raced as she squeezed herself backwards out of her position in the oven. But kept her gaze from him pulling her scarf further over her sticky hair, hoping he didn't see her face in the darkened kitchen. She mumbled,

"If you're looking for Lady Mary, she has an afternoon nap in her room."

"Oh that's OK, I am her son! I will go and unpack my things and see her later. Don't let me stop you, I can see you are busy!" He turned and picked up his suit suitcase from the floor.

Oh no, oh crap! Emma thought, I must have left the back door wide open! Stefan had just walked straight in to the kitchen. Emma's face was a picture of wide eyed panic, thank god he didn't know it was me! Glad she had kept he face away from him on purpose. She had not even looked at him, but she had recognised his familiar voice immediately despite his slight American accent.

Stefan had disappeared up into his room to unpack after his flight back from New York, thinking he had just seen the cleaner in the kitchen. He assumed it was the his mothers regular cleaner, so didn't give her a second thought. He was exhausted after the plane journey, he had caught the early red eye flight into Gatwick Airport.

His bedroom was always kept ready for him, all his possessions were still there just the same as they were when he left to go to college. He guessed the room had been closed off as his chest of drawers and bedside table were dusty. He had always liked the tranquillity of the country surroundings, and felt instantly at home again like old times. He had forgotten how quiet the countryside could be, it was like a sleepy haven hidden away from the world.

He was impatient to talk to his mother to see what could be done to save the Wychfield estate from bankruptcy. But knowing time stood still here, he resigned himself to wait until later to talk to his mother. Gazing slowly around his room, reassured that his possessions were still as he had left them. His series of water colour paintings of the Sussex downs surrounded the room. On the shelves were the numerous cups and trophies his team had won at polo matches.

Changing into comfortable faded jeans and a loose white t-shirt, he felt relaxed at last. He lay down on his bed, closing his weary eyes, turning his head away from the sun now glaring through the window he fell swiftly asleep.

Emma was in the process of sweeping the last remnants of dust from the kitchen floor. It had been a shock to see that Stefan had arrived faster than they had expected. She was sure he had not recognised her, the kitchen was completed to her satisfaction, and the house was as good as it was going to be. She felt like a maid of all work, working from the crack of dawn, all day long without a break. She was ravenous and made herself a quick cheese and tomato sandwich, drinking a strong coffee to keep awake, holding off her hunger pangs.

Now she must make sure that there was time to get ready for her great reveal, very pleased Lady Mary had not let on to Stefan that she was here. It had been so many years since she had seen Stefan, she wanted the meeting to be memorable. He had always been so special to her, she still tingled with delight when she thought of him. Would her feelings still be the same? More importantly would he still find her attractive?

Thank heavens, she had started her strict diet when she had, at least she had lost most of the weight gained due to her stressful situation.

It was time to set the record straight with Stefan, she felt a gnawing duty to help with the situation at the manor. But there was so much else she wanted to disclose, she was sure he had never known about her longing for him; or her juvenile crush that had been almost forgotten. Emma quickly rushed to her room showered then put on her dressing gown ready to blow dry her hair. Feelings that would not go away resurfaced, with the reality that she would be with him again soon! It had been too long a wait, knowing his marriage had been a mistake gave her renewed hope for their encounter.

She wanted to unveil her real passion for him. It was an infatuation that had grown over the years, since they were young children. Emma had hidden her feelings deep inside, now it was a primal force, only a grown woman could understand. Sometimes she day dreamed about him, she had wanted to be held by him, to feel his warm body as his strength enclose her, to wrap her in his arms. He held a magnetic attraction, there had been so many women who were fascinated by him; but they did not have her special childhood connection, that only she could comprehend.

Choosing to put on her black jeans and best cream silk blouse, she was concentrating on the image she wanted him to see as his first impression of her. She took her time with minimal makeup and peach lip gloss, her blonde hair was softly blow dried, the curls bouncing around her shoulders. Looking in the mirror she was pleased, the look was pretty yet understated, it was time to use the law of attraction.

Grabbing her jacket she happily bounded down the winding stair case, she jumped the last two steps in her cheerfulness, rushing head long right in front of Stefan who was returning to his bedroom with a soft drink. Emma taken by surprise shrieked.

"Oh sorry Stefan, I didn't see you." He was so shocked to be jumped upon, he let out a cry.

"Who the hell are you?"

She had spilled the contents of his glass of orange juice all over the front of his clean t-shirt.

"I thought I was here alone."

"Sorry I didn't see you in time. It's been a long time since we have seen each other." She giggled. He hesitated, there was a moments silence then he smiled widely back at her, showing his surprise.

"It can't be, Emma." He had a vague sense of de ja vous that it was her.

"No really. Emma you have grown up to be a very beautiful young lady, who would have believed that you would turn out so exquisite. I didn't recognise you."

Her cheeks blushed scarlet as she lifted her gaze up to him.

"Oh thanks," she laughed scanning properly his grown up, manly features.

"You certainly didn't recognise me in the kitchen earlier, did you!"

"What!" He chuckled realising when he had seen her without knowing.

"Was that you cleaning the oven?" Emma laughed out loud.

"It certainly was! I fooled you! That was my impression of a Cinderella moment, I was petrified that you would see my face so I had turned away. You were always playing cruel tricks on me in the past when I was little, I just had to get my own back!"

Wiping down his t-shirt with his hand, he was completely soaked right through glaring at her.

"Well you certainly fooled me, it's just like you to use magic on me, you always were such a witch!" He said.

"Look; I had to get my own back on you, as you were my very own jailer locking me in the potting shed! Do you remember." She looked at him cheekily.

"Anyway, Stefan I think we should get you cleaned, up give, me your t-shirt I can wash it for you."

Taking off his t-shirt; ruffling his curly blond hair Emma's eyes widened. His tanned abdominal muscles were honed to perfection, his broad arms and shoulders tapering to a narrow waist, he had obviously been working out in the gym.

"Good god! I can see you have been keeping fit!" Her face lit up, whilst clutching his t-shirt. She was spellbound watching his toned muscles, she turned away as her cheeks blushed a bright crimson. Taking his top into the kitchen to soak it in the sink, she thought she might need a cold shower to cool her passion.

His many years of working out always had the desired effect on the ladies. He wanted women to fall at his feet, which they certainly did. He was an experienced player and hunter looking for his next victim; he unexpectedly wondered if it could be Emma?

While he went back to his room to change his top, Lady Mary was still fast asleep in her room. Emma made a light snack which she served in the dining room for herself and Stefan, she was glad to have time to speak to him alone, there was a lot to discuss. She served lemonade and cucumber sandwiches, while they chatted followed by vanilla ice cream which she declined keeping to her strict diet plan.

They spoke at length about their years apart, and his strict fitness regime. He was like a strutting peacock, telling her how he had entered numerous body building competitions. Showing her the photos on his mobile phone, he had won some major amateur trophies in competitions. But he was no Mr Universe, and had no delusions of being professional, it was all pure vanity.

Emma laughed out loud when she saw numerous pictures of him being fake tanned by a female competitor in her tiny gold strap bikini, she had applied a spray tan. Finishing the effect by using a small paint roller and sponge rubbing him down. She was having a good time smoothing the dark stain tanning lotion into his gluteus, while he wore his skimpy posing pouch.

"Truly erotic! Please tell me you don't look like that all the time in your posing pouch." He grinned his full white smile, back at her.

"No I certainly do not! I don't wear anything to bed just my tan." They were having such fun catching up on past happenings, laughing loudly as they updating each other on funny events in their hectic lives. However Emma needed to know more about the truth. What did he know about the financial situation at the manor.

"How much do you know about the financial situation for Lady Mary?" She asked.

"Did you know my mother is downsizing the big house in Scotland?" Emma then asked him.

"I guessed that she would have to let the house go, is she upset about moving?" Stefan asked Emma, she shrugged her shoulders.

"Mum was shocked, but not surprised it could be a blessing in disguise. The house is too big for her anyway the upkeep is so very expensive, mum is looking forward to getting a much smaller property which is easier to manage." Luckily for her mother, it was not really a hardship, as she was ready to downsize anyway treating it as a new adventure. She enjoyed decorating, so would be happy to start a new project in a smaller house on her own.

Emma wanted to find out how much Stefan knew about the situation relating to her aunt.

"As it is for Lady Mary, there's no way that she can keep on top of this house, it's far too large an estate for her to manage on her own. She had to shut off most of the rooms, such a shame! But she can't keep the house clean on her own there's no servant or cleaner now, only Brandon the gardener."

Stefan was shocked to hear what Emma had to say about his mother. He had no idea that Lady Mary had been completely alone in the house for the last five years, since she had buried her husband in the family crypt on the edge of the estate. He explained that when he left to go to college in New York everything seemed fine. Lady Mary had staff to help her as she was getting older, and gave no indication that she could not cope.

He asked Emma how long she had been at Wychfield and what was the situation she found on arrival.

"When I arrived a week ago it was obvious there was an underlying problem, Lady Mary was shabbily dressed which was very unusual. The front parlour was tidy as it was always kept for best and was unused. But the rest of the house was in complete chaos. Your mother has become a recluse, only venturing out to the local town for essential supplies, and to look in the charity shops. The more worried she was about the manor and how to cope, the worst the it all became."

Emma was aware he could not take in what she was saying, he did not understand what had happened, he had no idea things had got so bad.

"Broken possessions with no value were hoarded to start with." Emma told him.

"Then she started saving news papers, and un opened post, anything and everything was kept, Lady Mary had been stock piling things up for many years! When I arrived I was very concerned, and have been cleaning up ever since. You have no idea how bad it was here!"

It was impossible to take in what he was hearing, and yet he knew Emma would not lie to him, he believed her, but was not sure what to do. Stefan sat with a bemused expression on his face he was dumbstruck, by what he had heard. He understood finances were bad, but this extra information brought things to a whole new level. All of a sudden it dawned on him that his inheritance was at risk, he had no money of his own. He spent every penny he could earn on his lavish lifestyle. Fast cars and keeping a string of polo ponies did not come cheap. It cost a fortune to keep up appearances with his group of friends. His image as a wealthy playboy, with an upper class lifestyle meant everything to him.

Having enjoyed a luxury life, he did not want the paparazzi to mention in the tabloids that he was broke, he would never live it down. Somehow he had to keep up the facade, at all costs, he wanted to know the true facts of what occurred, and then take expert advice.

Stefan would fake it if he had to, until he could make his fortune, there had to be a way out of this mess, he had to find it. The money he was earning in New York was a drop in the ocean to the amount he needed to maintain the lifestyle he craved.

Perhaps Emma could be one of his allies, as she was involved with helping Lady Mary, he wanted to know what her plans were. Was she going to stay at Wychfield?

Would she agree to help him? So many questions to ask, he needed to see the documents relating to Lady Mary's legal financial contracts to access the damage done to his inheritance, and to his mothers fortune.

CHAPTER 4

Stefan asked his all-consuming questions. He was becoming attracted to Emma in an unexpected way, her wit and warmth of character shone out from her. The caring nature, with the commitment to help Lady Mary, was endeared. Her purpose in being at the manor was an added draw, she had nothing financially to gain. He found her to be like a strong aphrodisiac, she was an unusual woman not wanting anything at all for herself.

"With what you have just told me so far. There are two things Emma that concern me. First of all do you think your father took unfair advantage of my mother? By using excessive influence on her, when she was not of her right mind." He needed to try to fathom out what exactly had gone on.

"Grief can do strange things, it leaves such a great sorrow, has she recovered fully from her husband's death. Or could she have an underlying problem we were not aware of! And secondly, exactly how bad is it financially?"

"Could we join forces as one, like we used to! He appreciated Emma being with him, exactly what he could do on his own was an unknown element." Stefan asked.

"And what can we do about it together?"

He was trying hard to find out if Emma was planning on staying any longer, or was she frightened off and going back to London soon. If the worst happened financially he would want her beside him, to be around to help to dig him out of this hole.

They sat chatting it through, looking at different angles to the problems, and possibilities. He was so glad that Emma had a sense of responsibility for her father's actions. He felt she was doing the right thing in trying to lend a hand, she seemed strangely fearless in the face of what had happened to the family.

Lady Mary came into the dining room after her afternoon nap, happy to greet Stefan after the many years of him living abroad. It was an unexpected crisis that had brought him back, but she was delighted to see him. He was taken aback with her appearance but did not comment, not wanting to be rude. Lady Mary wanted to speak to both of them to clarify the financial situation. She had wheeled in the tea trolley into the room which had on it two box files of papers, she placed the files on the drawing room table, ready to show them the details at last.

Emma wanted to give Stefan a chance to speak to her alone first, so went to the kitchen to make a pot of tea, as Stefan was busy opening and going through the paperwork spreading the papers out on the dining table. He knew that from what Emma had told him about Lady Mary's hoarding, that at least she would not have thrown any vital paperwork away.

When Emma returned with the tea tray, she noticed that Lady Mary seemed vague on the details of what documents she had signed, and when. The contracts were all legally binding, and witnessed. There could be no mistake, she was liable to pay vast amounts of money owed to the banks. Stefan using a calculator was writing down in a note book the large amounts of cash yet to be paid. He shook his head in disbelief at the total amount, as he showed his figures to Emma and Lady Mary.

Looking at the details on the contracts Stefan noticed that the first original documents, did have an initial pay out of a small return to investors, but nothing had been paid out since.

"It looks very much like a ponzi scheme." He said.

"I am not an expert, but Lady Mary seems have to have been lured in with the false sense of a bigger return on her investment in future." He passed Emma details showing the initial payment on Lady Mary's bank statement, as he continued.

"See here," he said pointing to how much more she had put in after that first initial pay back.

"She had trebled her original investment. She signed off using the Wychfield Estate as collateral for the deal, Lady Mary will forfeit the house! If she does not pay the banks back the money owed." Lady Mary was unsure what a ponzi scheme was, so Stefan took time to explain. Emma read the contract to see if there could be any way out of the agreement, if there was a way out she would spot it!

"Stefan this looks water tight, I don't see any way out." She pointed to a clause in the terms and conditions. Thirty days was all that was allowed for the re payments.

"Oh my god," she said pointing at the small print.

The schedule for the repayments expired in three weeks time! Stefan and Emma joined heads to discuss tactics. Whilst Lady Mary looked bemused she was well out of her depth. The papers were spread out all over the table, figures that Stefan had calculated were staggering totalling many millions, they were done for and completely broke there was no doubt about it!

Three weeks until repayments were due was alarming, they were both frantic working out a plan of action. Emma was going nowhere she told Stefan.

"I will not leave you to sort this out alone, we can tackle it together head on." Stefan squeezed her hand, he was so relieved that she was willing to stay and sort things out with him, he relied on her. She had such a good head on her shoulders, her business degree would come in useful.

They formally shook hands to seal the deal, stacking the papers in order of priority Emma wrote down bullet points of her action plan to stave off disaster.

"We will make a good team." Stefan said smiling at Emma.

"Better not say that too soon, your wife might have something to say about that." She replied with a grin knowing full well that it was a taboo subject. Stefan looked at her in unsettled horror.

"Don't go there she is my worst nightmare! That was the mistake of the century! Remember what they say, what happens in Vegas stays in Vegas." They both fell about laughing at the joke at his expense, it lightened the mood for a while.

They moved to the main lounge and talked non-stop until evening, opening a bottle of white wine when Lady Mary retired for the night. It was relaxing to sit on the sofa together discussing the intervening years when they were apart. So much had happened to them as both went their separate ways to college, with Stefan off to New York.

Stefan had a few business ideas he put forward to Emma, to see what would work and what wouldn't setting out plans to go forward. He was determined not to lose the manor house, Stefan knew his inheritance was lost, but if he could save the manor and estate, he would feel that their joint effort now, would be worthwhile.

It was a strange coincidence, both had lost their family fortunes through no fault of their own; but if they could come up with a workable plan out of their cash flow problems, that the banks would agree, they could hold their heads up high.

Emma spoke softly to Stefan as they sat reminiscing about their childhood memories, and the contrast in their fortunes now. How things had turned out was wretched, and yet it strengthened their resolve. Their shared financial losses joined them together in a close bond that only they could share. The disclosure of the problems to anyone else was too painful, but when they had revealed their feelings of loss together. The effect of keeping it to closely to themselves, dissipated the unbearable pressure.

"My father caused all this mess, it is so hard to forgive him. I feel obliged to put it right. I owe Lady Mary, and you a great deal, I will try my best to make it right for all of us." Stefan took her hand as they sat together sipping their wine, looking closely at each other. He instilled an long forgotten shyness in her when he looked deeply at her, savouring her spirit.

"Emma you don't owe us a thing, you're father was a con man, plain and simple. You are not responsible for what happened, but I would appreciate it if you could stay a while to help me sort out this mess."

She was more than happy to stay, he was so charismatic and handsome she would be a fool to go now. She answered him sternly, trying to keep a straight face.

"You only want me as a cleaner, I know you're sort!" They both laughed out loud until their sides split with agony as the wine took effect.

He answered her in good humour.

"I now know you are good at cleaning ovens, what else are you good at!" She blushed bright red, sipping more wine from their second bottle.

"Getting tipsy!" She answered temptingly twirling her blond hair around her fingers.

"You will have to find out Stefan. That's my secret!" Emma knew he was a typical Leo, he was a fire sign who could ignite her passion. She knew he would want to be the centre of attention, the flames of desire were growing. He was more intrigued about her than ever before, she was enjoying his company, he had a strength in mind and body. Her red flag warning signs were heightened, as her attraction to him grew.

They were having such fun reminiscing about their lives, catching up with their experiences. The financial problems were on both of their minds but they were glad to have some light relief. There would be difficult times ahead, but it was good to be together to tackle the financial problems. Going up to her room she felt giddy with pleasure, at meeting her old friend at last. They said goodnight on the landing, as they went their separate ways to bed.

In the morning Emma woke with a sore head, she

had drunk far too much wine and was suffering. Feeling queasy, her strict healthy diet had gone completely out of her mind. Now it was time to get back on track with her weight loss. Deciding to start the day by going for a jog around the grounds to get some fresh air, to clear her head. She put on her jogging shorts and top, she was going to look in on Lady Mary on her way out, to make sure she was alright. It was odd she had seemed strangely confused when talking to them both the night before. Lady Mary was still in bed not feeling well, so Emma went out saying she would let her sleep in, and see her at breakfast.

It was a lovely day, the morning mist was rising as the sun broke through the trees casting a dappled shade on the gravel path. It was her first chance to take a look around the grounds. Feeling at home she started a slow jog up to the back of the manor house, up past the barn; jogging up to where there was a disused railway line, heading out on the path in the direction of the village.

The train line and wooden sleepers had been taken up many years ago when the line was abandoned. The gravel and dirt track was bordered with shady hedges and trees covered in ivy and mistletoe, fragrant bluebells were dotted throughout the route. It was so refreshing and magical, feeling so different from being confined to the streets of Notting Hill.

She was taking pleasure in the exercise so much, she had run further than she had expected. Up the track past low farm buildings, with cows grazing in the fields and on past the old abandoned railway station. The track was known by the locals as the Wychfield Way, a small abandoned red brick station was on the estate boundary, owned by Lady Mary. Behind the disused station platforms were fields and stables which had not been used for years, Emma guessed that the fields must also be part of the estate.

It felt good to be out in the countryside seeing right across the rolling South Downs. She felt so much better her hangover was receding, her hunger was increasing as she longed for breakfast. Emma knew that if she kept going along Wychfield Way, she would eventually come to the church at the edge of the village. She decided to turn around, back down the route she had come, there was no way she could run all the way back. She was getting too out of breath, so she ran and walked in intervals back to the manor house.

The peace and quiet while walking gave her the opportunity to work out some solutions to their money problems. Grateful that she had no job to go to, she wanted nothing to get in the way of any progress. There were a few good ideas building in her mind, but she needed to check the size of the estate on a map before working out a realistic plan that could work.

Getting back to the manor, she found Stefan was already in the kitchen boiling the kettle, making a pot of tea, she was glad to speak to him about the estate grounds.

"I had such a hangover this morning, so went out jogging. I will just have a shower, then I can make us some breakfast if you like, I'm starving." Stefan didn't want her to be waiting on him, and agreed to make breakfast for her while she showered. Emma finished her cup of tea, placing the cup and saucer in the butler sink.

"Perfect I will see if Lady Mary has got up yet."

But when she knocked for her there was no reply, Emma pushed the door slowly open to find her slumped in the bed, her face was lopsided as though she could have had a stroke, her eyes were open but she was unable to speak. Emma tried to sit her up but there was no way she could move her. Rushing downstairs she called out.

"Stefan call an ambulance, I think Lady Mary has had a stroke. We need to be quick."

The ambulance was fast arriving, the immediate diagnosis was as Emma thought it was likely to be a stroke, her face was paralysed down one side and her speech slurred. Lady Mary was taken to the local hospital, Stefan went with her in the back of the ambulance, while Emma showered. Later Stefan called Emma to let he know that tests had shown that the stroke was severe. Lady Mary would need to stay in hospital for further tests, she would be staying there for a while.

The next day Stefan had to make sure that a power of attorney was in place. He would be responsible to pay all the bills for the estate, while Lady Mary was ill. Emma helped him as much as she could by arranging various meetings with the bank manager, about the financial crisis. Funds had to be found quickly to stave off a disaster, she was aware that time was running out to get a plan of action organised.

CHAPTER 5

It was a good thing that Stefan and Emma had arrived at the manor when they had, Emma was conscious that if they had not been present Lady Mary could have died. The stress was too much for Lady Mary, it had contributed to her illness, it was obvious she had not been looking after herself properly for years, since her husband had died.

Brandon the gardener was very loyal he had worked for her ladyship for many years, he was the only help that Lady Mary had kept on. Emma walked along the gravel drive heading to the front iron gate, to the pretty stone lodge at the entrance to the estate. Advising the gardener what had happened to her aunt, he had guessed that there was something wrong with Lady Mary. Aware of her hoarding, but said he did not go into the house, so was unaware just how bad things had become.

He was taken aback when Emma told him exactly how filthy the house was when she had arrived. She explained how she had cleaned up, and cleared the signs of hoarding, filling a skip container just in time before Stefan had arrived home.

Later that day Emma and Brandon rummage through items that had been put in to storage in the barn, there were valuable things that could go to the auction house in town. He was happy to help her and they spent the afternoon going through the piles of collectables, before admitting that they needed an expert to value the toys and ornaments. Lady Mary had been collecting items so over many years, Emma presumed that some of them could be valuable.

Her laptop came in handy as she carefully listed all of the items for possible sale, and went on to various websites to check if things were of interest for the local auction house, or for private sale on line. Once a list was comprised she arranged a valuation to assess what could be sold locally. She knew that Stefan would be useful valuing any paintings she found stored around the house or in the attic, which she had yet to tackle she was dreading going up into the loft in case Lady Mary had been hoarding there as well.

The place was turning into a museum full of antiques instead of a house, it could take weeks to check everything, nothing had been thrown away for generations.

Job done, Emma sighed with relief that something worthwhile had been accomplished. When Stefan came back from the hospital they sat together in the dining room with all the documents, and contracts, spread out in front of them. Emma had compiled many lists and spread sheets including all the facts and figures. Assessing what needed to be done next was a mammoth job. But at least they had full permission from Lady Mary, to do whatever they could to keep the wolf from the door.

Although the work was exhausting and turning into a marathon rather than a sprint. They agreed to stick together, and see it through even if their precious time was running short as the days passed by. Lady Mary continued having further tests, with bed rest in the hospital expected to recover in time after therapy.

"Let's decide between us the order of what to do, and see how much money we need to hold the creditors at bay." Stefan said, holding his calculator poised with pen in hand.

"Now we can see what total is on the spread sheet we compiled." She said pointing at the columns of figures on the screen.

"We need to see the funds, and savings we each have to add in here."

"What we will need in the account in the short term for the bank, needs to go in there."

"I agree," said Stefan. Suddenly he looked angry at her, as he stressfully added.

"But I want it done my way, I have a few ideas of my own you know. It's not all about you!" He stood up his face flushed with fury his blue eyes were blazing with rage. Oh no, she must have hit a raw nerve, yet it was so unexpected. There was an underlying conflict brewing, she could feel the tension in the air, what had she done?

"Remember this is my home, don't try to take over! Don't interfere with my wishes. I won't forget it was your greedy father that lost me my inheritance."
Sheepishly she said.

"I thought you wanted me to help you."

"Yes, but not to take over!"

"Look, first we need to see what the house and land

is worth," she said.

"Is there a map of the estate boundaries? We need to get an up to date valuation of the estate?" Stefan calmed down, he was sure he had seen a map in some of the other documents in the dresser drawer. Taking a look he found what he was searching for.

"Here it is," they spread the map out on top of their documents. The chart clearly showed the boundaries and buildings on the estate, it was a much larger park than Emma had expected.

The coloured areas on the map showed that the land continued past the disused railway track, on Wychfield Way right up until the church wall, at the far end of the fields.

"Wow, that's amazing there are far more acres of land than I expected." Astonished at how much farm land was included, there were several fields that had once been used for shire horses many years ago, when the estate had been a working farm. There were a couple of fields that were rented out to a local farmer for his dairy herd, his farm buildings and milking sheds were on the other side of the railway trail.

The way forward was now clear, to raise funds in the short term, and have valuations completed for the house, estate, and valuables. They were not broke yet, Stefan knew they had a small window of opportunity, there was no time to lose. They agreed to fund what they could with their own limited savings, then they would be reliant on their own talents to make and to raise money.

"What made you snap at me earlier?" Emma asked now that Stefan seemed calmer again.

"It's just that Lady Mary seemed better today when I

visited her at the hospital, she is talking again.

"But what she said disturbed me." Emma listened intently.

"Surely if she is recovering that's good news." She said then he continued.

"I told her that the power of attorney was in place so that I can pay the bills. But she said she has seen her solicitor in her private room at the hospital, she is changing her will!" Emma was shocked at the idea.

"She wants you to take over at the manor. I don't know what hold you have over her, but I'm not happy about it!" This news had set the cat amongst the pigeons.

"Why would Lady Mary change her will to favour me, I can only think that as your work is in New York, she knew I would not desert her in her hour of need."

"Perhaps I have been hasty in thinking that you would do anything underhand." He felt bad for doubting her.

"I'm sorry it's just losing everything is so stressful."

"I know you want things done your way, I will try harder to listen to you." She said.

"Trust is something we both need right now." Stefan had always had an arrogant streak, he was like a strutting peacock. Aware of his aura of superiority, and good looks. It was a big part of who he was, but underneath she felt he had a softer side to him.

During their conversations Emma knew her attraction for Stefan had increased, now he was a man and not a boy. His inner personality shone through his posh veneer, he was a former member of the Chelsea set. But his actions now showed he was really a caring person. She was the one individual who knew him from childhood, he knew his upper class act would not wash with her. He could not get away with his superior attitude with Emma, she was going to be his equal and show him her strengths.

Whilst going over the paperwork, they spoke together about possible options for the future of the manor house and estate. Emma's ideas were setting up murder mystery weekends, weddings and conferences using the barn as a main venue. Or bed and breakfast using the surplus bedrooms or glamping using yurts in the grounds and woodland. Stefan wanted an equestrian centre using the existing stables, or holding weddings in the local church using their lawn area as a base with a marquee. They had so many ideas that they were full of hope and enthusiasm, but not sure how their grand ideas could be funded.

Stefan arranged a hire car for the next month, it would help with the various meetings that Emma had arranged with the bankers. In the evening they both visited Lady Mary at the hospital, she was still not able to talk normally but she was getting slowly better. It became obvious that her recovery would be a slow process, she was in a quiet private room for the duration.

The change to the will was mentioned again as Lady Mary wanted Emma to have control, to allow Stefan to go back to his job in New York. He agreed reluctantly as he realised she had a point, if Emma could not pull off saving Wychfield from the creditors then it was game over.

When driving through the dark Sussex countryside from the hospital back to the manor, Stefan was astonished to see a group of reporters, and photographers; staked around the tall iron gates to the drive. Emma remembered what it had been like when her father had been arrested a year before. Her flat in the mews house in London had been surrounded with paparazzi for days, she was hoping that it was all over, hoping she would not have to experience it again.

"Quick Stefan don't stop drive through the gates when I open them." Emma quickly jumped out pushing the gate as it swung open the flashbulbs went off in their faces, temporarily blinding them. Emma was sure that the photograph of them in the car, would make the news in the morning. It seemed the media were looking for an update on the their story. Not sure what could have prompted their interest, the car sped up the drive to the manor.

They both needed a stiff drink after their ordeal at the gates, not sure what action to take next, the clock was ticking there was no time to lose. Relaxing in the lounge, in the dimmed lights, both seated themselves on the sofa. Emma poured another glass of white wine, handing it to Stefan she was reassuring him that it would be alright, she had been through it all before having been surrounded by the media in Notting Hill.

He was thankful to have her support not having expected the media to become involved so soon. It seemed natural for him to open up to her with his feelings. Having known her since childhood, she was a true friend who still stood by him in his darkest hour. He wondered if his wealthy Chelsea friends would abandon him if he lost his fortune, knowing Emma would stand fast beside him.

He decided to tell her what had happened in the States.

"I expect your aunt told you about my marriage in the America. I think I should come clean with you about it." Emma had been intrigued about his wedding but did not want to ask him, as she felt sure he was embarrassed about his mistake.

"Lady Mary did tell me you regretted getting married, but she spared me the details, and I didn't want to be the first to bring the subject up." Stefan was ready to tell her, she was the only person he felt comfortable with to hear the truth.

"It was really a stupid mistake! In one of my drunken moments! We met in a nightclub in Las Vegas, I was on my way back to New York after a conference in Vegas. Staying at the Venetian it was just a fluke that we met, when I went for drinks to relax I saw her. She was a beautiful blond show girl having a few days off from her performance at Caesar's Palace. She was so radiant and funny, looking back I didn't know anything about her, but she had such a great charisma we had a good time." Emma nodded listening intently.

"Go on," she urged him.

"We enjoyed each other's company and ended up stayed in my suite for several nights, we were drinking champagne most of the time. We talked about how many people got married in Vegas, It just seemed like a good idea at the time, she knew I was single and wealthy. I was persuaded in my drunkenness to get married in the Little Chapel, the rest as they say is history."

Emma smiled at him saying.

"You always were impulsive, wanting to be the centre of attention you just never grew up!" She knew him so well, but did she really know who he was?

For the first time he looked at Emma with new eyes, she was steadfast and true. She had dazzling qualities he respected, she was gifted, intense and resilient. Perhaps it was the wine taking effect or because he was suddenly needy, he suddenly wanted to kiss her to see if she felt the same way. Stefan put his arms around her shoulders pulling her tenderly towards him. Emma responded, she had waited for this moment all her life, her fingers twisted through his thick blond hair, her lips meeting his in a submission of desire as their tongues entwined. The first kiss sealed their fate, it felt right, their bodies responded in a rushed yearning of passion as he drew her closer.

She had never felt like this before, the sensation enthralled her she was spellbound, and totally submissive as his tongue pressed firmly into her mouth tasting her from within.

"This feels so right," Stefan said.

"Let's go to bed! Emma was ready to agree, the flame of desire had been re kindled in her, she was in a state of high anxiety. Like a wound clock waiting for release, she was more than willing to give herself to him. His muscular arms undressed her slowly as he savoured the sight of her nakedness, he pulled her towards him closer slowly taking off her bra and silk panties, slipping them down as he pulled her onto the bed. He removed his t-shirt as her hands unbuckled his belt sliding down the zip on his trousers freeing himself as he wrangled out of his jeans. He manoeuvred his body on top of her, he was aroused with a great desire for her as her hands caressed him. His passion inflamed, this was different, what he had wanted all his life.

She was his willing servant, he needed to take her

slowly; sensing her highly aroused body wrap around his. Savouring the moment waiting in his heighted state of arousal. Turning her, as he kissed her neck revelling at her luscious peach behind, he cupped her breast in his warm hands, entering her from behind in his moment of sheer bliss. They spent the night in exhilaration together in each other's arms, taking their time to explore their naked bodies together for the first time. Tonight it felt right, tomorrow they would face the world head on together with no regrets. He had not only won her trust, but her mind and now her body.

"***Heir fights repossession***" Emma checked the headlines on line with their photo as headline news, an informant must have told the tabloids that the estate was in danger of being repossessed. When Emma read the article, she saw that the papers were full of details relating to Stefan and his background, that he had been adopted by Lady Mary, who was recovering from a stroke. The article included Emma's past, their family connection. Highlighting her father's financial scandal, resulting in the lengthy prison sentence was plastered across the pages, with the clear flash bulb photograph of them both arriving by car at Wychfield Manor.

The worst thing, as far as Stefan was concerned was his portrayed image as a failed bankrupt, the article mentioned that his inheritance had vanished. His friends in Chelsea would be sure to ridicule him, he felt like a ghost of his former self. Emma tried her best to distract him from his troubles by keeping him busy.

The fight was on, there was no doubt now they must continue what they had started, this was no time to hide from their troubles. A representative from the local auction house would arrive later to value the items left in the barn. Stefan and Emma had listed an inventory, hoping some items were valuable enough to be taken to be included in the auction next week. They needed hard cash faster than ever, there was no time to delay, the days were ticking by as creditors letters arrived daily. The house phone had been unplugged to stop the unwanted calls that were annoyingly constant.

Stefan remembered paintings hanging in the house from years ago, they had been taken down so he was now on a mission to find them. They were not in the barn so perhaps they were in the attic, taking a torch light he went up the stairs past the bedrooms that led to a gloomy hallway leaded to the loft stairway at the end of the passage. Putting on his torch he stepped carefully into the loft, the floorboards creaked as he progressed into the dark void.

The space all around the roof was stacked with large trunks, old mirrors and stuffed animals covered in glass domes under a thick cover of dust. Oriental rugs and old dresses were on rails with dust sheets covering them. There were more clothes and fur coats in old wardrobes, large cardboard flower boxes were full of yellowing linen and handmade lace from a by-gone era.

Emma joined Stefan with another torch, as they proceeded to check towards the back of the large attic that ran the full length of the house. Propped up against the back wall they found the paintings Stefan had been looking for, he expected them to still be in the house. He knew Lady Mary had kept them especially for him, as he dealt in fine art. The paintings had always been of interest for him, he thanked his lucky stars that they were still there.

The main painting was large and framed with a wide

deep black and gilt frame. Stefan unwrapped the first framed canvas which was covered with a blanket. This was what he wanted to see, it was an original Pre Raphaelite masterpiece. An old oil painting depicting an English country scene at lambing time, with shafts of sunlight piercing the clouds as sheep crossed a stream, to hills rising in the background.

Emma came to Stefan's side with her torch helping him to steady the painting.

"It looks like the paintings in the Tate gallery." She said shining the torch closer onto the canvas.

"Yes you're so right this is a valuable and important painting, we will have to get Brandon to help me in moving it downstairs. This is the painting that got me first interested in fine art many years ago, it used to hang on the landing at the top of the stairs.

"It's a stunning masterpiece."

"What about the others, lets uncover them all." Emma said pointing to the smaller paintings propped against the wall behind the larger one.

"These are watercolours which look as though they are William Blake's, if they are genuine they too will be high-priced. They should not have been stored here ideally but Lady Mary was obviously not aware how to look after them correctly." The watercolours had been enclosed in bubble wrap and brown paper tied with string. Stefan inspected one smaller painting then said.

"We should take these down stairs and open them up properly to check them over, luckily it is dry up here so there should be no damage."

"How exciting it's like a treasure hunt." She said putting down her torch helping to lift them out of his way.

"Gosh their very heavy."

"Wait here I will go and find Brandon to help us, the glass makes the water colours difficult to lift." After some strong arm tactics the gardener, with Stefan and Emma's help manoeuvred the large painting out onto the landing, then with straps under the frame moved shuffling it carefully downstairs into the hallway. Emma brought down the smaller paintings one by one, placing them carefully alongside the larger painting in the hall for careful inspection.

Removing the brown paper and bubble wrap, Emma was pleased that the pictures looked in tact with no visible damage. Brandon helped her to discard the wrapping intrigued to see what the paintings depicted.

Some were rare sketches and some watercolours, Stefan knew they were originals, turning to look at them he said to Emma and Brandon.

"These will have to be looked at by a William Blake specialist, It could be they are unknown originals which would be very exciting."

Brandon helped to stack the pictures in the hallway, noticing how good they looked. He remembered that he had seen books in the barn with some pages depicting these sketches, they must have been by the same artist. He wanted to show Stefan the books, so they went to the barn and proceeded checking them over. Stefan agreed the books were special but had no idea of their value and should be kept aside for the right dealer.

In the afternoon the man from the local auction house arrived Emma showed him their finds in the barn hoping for some good news. Most of the items were suitable and were taken away ready to be listed in the next week's auction. Emma felt as though they had made the first crucial steps towards their goal. A meeting at the bank was scheduled for later in the afternoon. Stefan and Emma were ready with their plans, having rehearsed the details, knowing it was something that had to be done correctly to stave off disaster.

The press photographers had disappeared, no longer waiting for them at the gates when they left the estate on their way to the bank. They both hoped that the press would leave them alone now, as they had the photo they wanted. After Emma shut the heavy gates behind the car Stefan squeezed her hand in a reassuring touch of calmness. Emma lightly kissed his cheek as they drove away, hoping it was not the calm before the storm.

It was not an easy meeting at the bank, the manager wanted clear proof of an attempt to make an initial payment by the end of the month. Which would satisfy the creditors, he was aware that Lady Mary was ill and expressed a hope that Stefan could keep the estate out of bankruptcy.

They told him that together they had good plans to keep the manor and estate solvent, and would make an initial payment during the week to satisfy the bank. Emma moved the last of her meagre savings of a few hundred pounds into a new business account with Stefan to pay the initial down payment to satisfy the bank. Along with a transfer of ten thousand pounds of Stefan's money it should help to keep the creditors happy for the time being, they made a further appointment to give the bank manager the business proposal in more detail. Emma was pleased that she had her business degree, it would be a labour of love for her to lay out a more detailed proposal for the bank, she felt confident she could do it. Wanting to impress Stefan with her business skills was part of why she felt eager to get their ideas onto paper.

Stationery was ordered on line for her purpose, a binding machine, printer, paper and ink cartridges, she would spend the next few weeks on a detailed one hundred page plan on how to get a professional business operation at Wychfield. Running through her ideas with Stefan was great, he was supportive of most of her notes. He had some plans himself that they discussed while have supper, their confidence was high, it had to work or they were done for. Every hour Emma spent tapping away on the laptop, Stefan helped by checking and editing details for her as she typed.

It was coming together nicely, slowly it gained momentum. Stefan was impressed how quick she was setting out their ideas onto her screen. Slowly their remarks took form, and took on a life of its own, it was a real plan an impressive business proposal was taking shape. The manor and estate was too important to let go, they had to succeed. The bank manager was hard core, he had insisted on half a million pounds up front, before looking at any business proposal.

Together they scraped up enough money to satisfy his demands, but it came at a cost they sold everything they could put their hands on, each of them had put all their own money into the account. For the first time they were rich in love for each other, but cash poor.

Their relationship was growing stronger every day, Emma was getting involved with Stefan on every level, she was attracted to him physically, and found his arrogant nature was a facade, he was strong and resilient. When they made love she experienced a sensory overload, as their magnetism deepened. He was as determined as she was, he would not be beaten whatever it cost him. She was getting used to his moods, which she knew were stress related, or when he was tired, then he snapped sometimes at her. But it was understandable, she had her flaws and he over looked them, no one was perfect.

They had formed a routine of sleeping together at night in Stefan's room, it had become their perfect love nest, a retreat from the stress of the day. The nights spent together were passionate, and idyllic Stefan had at last found his soul mate. Emma had the midas touch in so many ways, everything she touched turned to gold. Stefan was so bored with empty air heads just interested in him for his social standing. At last he was enjoying the woman of his dreams, she was supportive and attentive to his every need physically and emotionally.

There was something special about Emma, she had a natural aura about her, in her effortless way she had charmed him. There was nothing false about her she was spontaneous and sincere. It lifted his spirit to be with someone who truly cared about him as a person, rather than his false smokescreen of wealth. She was genuinely interested in him as a man, instead of his money, he felt relaxed in her company.

CHAPTER 6

Emma spent time typing up her notes on the lap top in the dining room. Taking a coffee break she decided to spread out her tarot cards once more, to see what the month ahead had in store for her.

Her intuition helped to channel her readings, the Celtic spread before her showed a wheel of fortune, for great change in the circle of life. Next the beautiful empress and the devil, plus the star card, which was her own unique card being an Aquarian air sign, then quickly followed by the ten of swords. The cards spread before her showed the path of fortune with sudden trouble, a back stabbing, before an ending then new beginning. It was as though she was looking down the barrel of a gun, what could it possibly mean?

Emma lost in her thoughts almost jumped out of her skin, as she heard the loud buzzer in the hallway from the front door. She was expecting another stationary delivery, so quickly went to open the door expecting a van driver to have her order. But instead of a van, there was a taxi parked on the gravel drive.

There on the front door step standing under the

stone porch, with a suitcase by her side was a fair haired woman. She was so stunningly beautiful she could have been Miss World for all Emma knew, her tight blue dress with a narrow red belt accentuated her small waist and large cleavage, she was quite tall tottering on her high red stiletto heels. The blond looked down at Emma who was clearly taken by surprise. The woman's blood red mouth was wide open with a look of surprise on her face. Then she spoke assertively with a broad American accent, as soon as she spoke Emma instantly realised who she was, but did not know her name!

"Hello how can I help you!" Emma was trying her best to be civilised, in an overly polite customer service way.

"I'm here to see my husband Stefan." She said with a haughty glare as though Emma was the maid.

"Tell him I am here!" She said not waiting for a reply, there was no please, or thank you.

Her red talons pointed to her large suitcase by her side in her very own version of Cruella de Vil's instructions to Emma.

"Pay the driver, and bring my suitcase into the manor house, I will not be leaving!"

OMG this could not be happening. Emma had no option but to oblige in paying the driver, and pulling the heavy case inside.

"If you will wait in the drawing room, I will find him." Emma said leading her through to the front room door beckoning her inside, as the Americans high heels clicked right behind her on the tiled floor. Emma quickly turned and ran to where Stefan had been working in the library at the end of the hall.

She rushed through the door nearly knocking him over in her hurry. Dropping his weighty books down from his arms he said.

"What the hell's the matter!" Stefan could tell all was not well, by the strange look on her face.

"There is someone waiting to see you," she said slightly out of breath.

"I have asked her to wait in the drawing room, she's a dead ringer for Marilyn Monroe! I think you're wife has come to stay!"

"What." He screeched in panic, the colour drained straight from his face, he had not seen his wife Becky for months, and had not expected to ever see her again. The last time he spoke to her was when he phoned her to say divorce proceedings were initiated, it was just prior to his trip to England. Her reaction was that she was not happy having been dumped by him, when he ran away. She had shrieked down the phone that he was a coward, too afraid to speak to her face to face.

"How did she know where I was," he said really annoyed at the intrusion into his life especially at this time. What Emma thought was strange was that she had no idea of his wife's name, Stefan had never mentioned her name at all. Was he trying to distance himself from her by denying her existence, well he could not deny it now, she was here!

"She must have seen the photo in the media," Emma suggested. Stefan would have to face her now whether he wanted to or not, she knew where he was hiding. Struggling with his emotions he strode up the hall to the front room, he was determined to get rid of her once and for all.

He had forgotten just how gorgeous Becky was, or

how stimulating the effect was that she had on him, she was like a temptress. He had been attracted to her in the past, like a moth to a flame. Stefan had thought he was no longer under her spell. It was absolutely the end of their marriage, he would have to face her. Their marriage was over it was a big mistake, she would have to face the truth, as far as he was concerned.

The door was open when he got there, his tall wife was standing by the fire place with her back to him. Hearing him enter the room she turned around to face him head on.

"Well here you are my gorgeous reluctant husband, aren't you glad to see me!" She said her ruby lips pouting provocatively at him, her blue eyes widened as her false eyelashes fluttered to give him the full effect of her stunning beauty.

She stepped towards him swaying her hips giving him a smouldering look, her full breasts beckoning him like succulent ripe melons. Her arms outstretched to embrace Stefan as he stood firm silently savouring her appearance. She clasped him securely to her chest like a spider, she was the most attractive woman he had ever seen in his life, there was no doubt about it. She had a feline presence, moving so elegantly, he had forgotten how magnetic her face was, her red tipped claws latched onto his shirt pulling him enticingly closer to her great breasts.

She was a diva, and had come to claim her prize, which was her wayward husband, who had escaped her clutches. She made no attempt to hide it, the strongest of men would buckle under her command, she was an irresistible force of attraction. Her hot lips held his so enticingly as her tongue chased his, he could not resist her allure, her fingers clasped through his lustrous blond hair he was an easy prey. Her magical charms were working as well as before, he was no match for her she was way too clever for him, her feminine appeal was so strong as her heavenly scent encircled him. Stefan was beyond help, his formidable erection nudged rigidly pressing hard against her, she knew at that moment that she had won!

Her caress was intoxicating, his arousal was complete he suddenly wanted her perfect body, she was willing him on. Her sexual mind-set was encouraging him on with enthusiastic perfection. He could not break free from her and didn't want to, she was his wife he was her husband, to consummate their reunion seemed only natural.

She asked him to carry her suitcase to his room, so that they could enjoy the rest of the day in seclusion in his bed. She was as suggestive as an alley cat wanting to play with a mouse, he craved her flawless body so much he forgot everything, and everyone in his attempt to satisfy his lust.

She watched him as he took her case up the stairs to his bedroom, Becky followed right behind him purring, shutting the door firmly behind her. They stood facing one another, he was like a naughty schoolboy waiting for a beating. Unzipping the side seam she slipped out of her skin tight dress taking off her stilettos. Standing proudly before him in her black lace bra and panties, she licked her finger tips, smoothing the high curve of her heavy breasts.

"Once upon a time you loved me," she said.

"I want you to make love to me again, love me hard and slow like you used to!" Stefan could not resist and pulled her firmly towards him, fumbling in his haste clutching the clip on her bra, releasing her huge breasts as they bounced freely into his hands. Slowly his tongue tweaked her nipples he savoured the tingling sensation, as her fragrant Chanel perfume surrounded him. Stefan took off all of his clothing until he was standing completely naked, firmly erect, she laid back ready, waiting patiently for him to arouse her.

Becky's blond hair tumbled across the covers as he pulled her down into the right position beneath him on his bed. She had been an exotic dancer and knew all the most enticing moves, she knew how to hold him in suspense, as he lifted his body over hers. She was a gold digger, with extraordinary powers, this was to be her finest hour yet. Now he was hers to command, she would never release him, the last remnants of his will power melted as the heat of her body increased in a fiery furnace of desire.

He turned her around facing the bed pressing her firmly down onto the covers as he snatched her panties down. The sight of her naked body made him almost weep, her firm round bottom pushed back into his touch as his fingertips caressed her gently; she was everything a man desired a lush fruit ready to be devoured.

He nudged his muscular body behind her taking his time to feel the silkiness of her skin beneath him as he rolled over her, spooning his strong body behind her. His hand cupped her abundant breast arousing her, as the other hand slipped between her sleek tanned legs, feeling that she was already moist to his touch. It lit the touch paper for him; he could not wait to be inside her as he slipped his engorged penis inside in a rhythmic pulse of pleasure riding her until they reached a climax.

Poor Emma had been waiting in the library, then hearing nothing a while later, she returned to go to find them both. Expecting Stefan's wife to be talking to him in the drawing room. Emma had a strange feeling, a feminine intuition, as she walked through the hall to the drawing room. They had both gone the door was wide open, at that moment she felt that all would not be well like an omen, she felt it!

Something had changed. There was a weird silence, somehow it was different, not how it should be. She had kept listening out for what would happen; she thought perhaps a row would erupt in the drawing room. But she had heard nothing happen, silence was all she heard. Where were they?

Turning back to the hallway she saw them in the corner of her eye, both were climbing the grand staircase to Stefan's bedroom. Emma had watched as the blond woman closed the door securely behind them. This was not what Emma wanted; Stefan had taken the woman to their love nest, the sanctuary where Emma and Stefan had shared their nights of passion. Where Emma had given herself to him unconditionally with all the years of waiting and longing, until her shuddering climax. It was Stefan's room where she had sealed their union with their love making; Emma's underwear was in his chest of drawers with her clothing still folded neatly on the back of his bedside chair.

Now the pair were both in bed together, Emma knew that his wife was now sealing her claim to Stefan, she had won. He was as weak as a kitten Emma could see that now. But where would the situation leave her!

A dark loneliness had found her again pulling her down to the blackness of despair; her mood plummeted to a new depth of desolation. It would not matter at all to Stefan! He was under the woman's spell, the peroxide bitch had enchanted him. All of his manly desires and fantasies were being fulfilled at this precise moment! Tears welled up filling Emma's eyes with all the pain of rejection, the pit of her stomach ached with bitter damage caused by him, only those who had lost true love, could comprehend the feeling of desolation.

Emma had no hope in competing with a beauty queen, with the gyrating charms of a black widow spider. Stefan was caught firmly in her web. It was too much sorrow to bear, she would surly die of a broken heart.

Standing transfixed at the foot of the stairs, her tears flowed uncontrolled as she heard the sounds of the woman's rhythmic cries as her loud sexual progress increased until her orgasm. When her piercing witch like shrieks of pleasure echoing down the hallway. Oh Stefan what have you done! Emma had been deserted!

A tiny voice in her head beckoned Emma to walk away. Don't make things more painful, there was no point in wishing her gone. The mysterious blond was here to stay, Emma shuffled distraught into the kitchen, it was all she could do to stop herself from crying. The urge to raid the fridge and start comfort eating, then be sick, was so strong.

She was alone again, was this all there was for her! Emma had been happy at last, in the days she had been in Stefan's bed, she felt he had wanted her in all her plainness. He had said, that she was so refreshing and natural, he liked that! It felt like a delightful eternity, he had opened up to her, and she had trusted him like no other.

What a fool she was! To think that he might have desired her, Emma took a long look in the kitchen mirror above the alcove. She saw herself for the first time as she really was. Her pudgy face was pink and puffy from crying she was just ordinary, not pretty. Still a little overweight, being so busy, she had not bothered to put on any makeup, with her hands constantly in washing up water, it was pointless wearing nail varnish her nails had been completely ruined.

She had let herself go! Could he have just been using her for sex? In the last few days she had experienced a state of bliss with him, now she had hit rock bottom. Knowing she had just been played, like the other women in his life. He was so handsome and sought after by social climbers, wanting to bag the heir to a vast fortune. Emma liked to think she was different; but perhaps he was just not interested in her as a person after all.

The contrast between the two women in Stefan's life was stark. Emma was as ordinary and dull as dishwater, whilst the American blond bombshell was beautiful and glamorous in every way, even her walk was sexual. Emma thought, let's face it there was no comparison!

The worst thing was that every last penny she had in the world, had now been transferred to the business bank account, she was now completely broke.

Why has Stefan reacted this way? Emma thought, she could not understand it! He had assured her that his marriage was a sham, that his wife meant nothing to him. He told her he had filed for a divorce, that it was going through, just a matter of time! Saying they had never really lived together as man and wife.

Was he lying all along to get her to help him! Could he do that? Would he do that? She was no longer sure of anything her world had just been turned right around.

"Stefan could be the bastard of all time!" She muttered aloud to herself. "Could it get any worse?"

Was this what the wheel of fortune card foretold? Only time would tell.

CHAPTER 7

All the plans she had thought of in the business proposal could come to nothing! Emma knew that success was in the balance, the scales could tip either way let's face it, she was still a novice at best!

Clearing the clutter in the manor house had been tediously boring, and time consuming. With all her plans they required multiple sources of income quickly to keep hold of the Wychfield estate. Her master plans were ambitious and bold, needing both of their input and commitment to survive.

She had put all of her business talents and money behind the plans, Stefan could take all the credit for her ideas! She saw that clearly now, he had just used her. Emma had been stupid to trust him, her jealousy was surfacing he had betrayed her in the worst possible way.

Now she had no home, no partner and no money, could her life get any shoddier, she doubted everything. Yet she was not going to let him win, he would pay if that was his game!

She may be a flawed person, but stupidity was not

one of her flaws. Emma could learn to hate Stefan quite easily, but it was not in her nature to get knocked down and stay down. She would keep getting up, she would have her revenge and settle the scores. He had underestimated her, which was a bad move on his part. It would be his downfall she would make sure of that, she did not know how, or when. But it would happen, Emma would make it happen.

Waiting for the couple of love birds to emerge from Stefan's room. She tried pulling herself together by working in the dining room, re-checking the new business proposal, she was cross checking her figures to finish the nearly completed task.

Aware she had been living in a cocoon like a false bubble of reality, her task finished the business plan had been done. She was satisfied that she had produced her best work ever the plans were perfected, it was her masterpiece!

Emma had to focus and succeed on looking after herself, she must emerge from her shell and transition into what she desired herself to be. Aware she had nothing to lose it was in her own self interest to get the upper hand in the situation. Perhaps if she was crafty and acted as though she didn't care about them, it might work to her advantage.

Now she heard them getting up in the master bedroom, Emma heard them laughing as they descended the stairs, not knowing that she was working at the dining room table. As they passed the dining room door Emma heard them smugly discussing her by name, as they walked by the open doorway not knowing that she could clearly hear every word they said. Stefan made a nasty spiteful comment about her saying,

"Emma knew Lady Mary from years ago, but she was useful in drafting the business plan, she is a good typist, and useful as a cook! But that's all there is to it, she is as dull as dish water!"

The blond bombshell replied in her slow American accent.

"I thought when she opened the front door that she was the maid or cleaner. She looked so shabby! I knew that you would not be interested in someone so drab. Not really you're taste!"

"You're so right," he said laughing. As they stopped in the hall.

"She's not a distant relative is she?" the blond asked,

"Not really, as I'm adopted we are not blood relatives, we are not alike at all, Lady Mary is Emma's aunt." Pompously he added.

"I am the only heir to the estate! We did know each other when we were children, she stayed here sometimes."

"But I don't really know her at all! We move in different social circles, she would not fit in at all with my friends, who are mainly aristocrats."

"She is as they say in this country, one of the great unwashed!" Emma was listening closely, clearly distraught by their cutting comments.

They continued giggling at Emma's expense as they sauntered through the hallway to the back door. Stefan proceeded in showing his wife around the gardens outside, guiding her along the flower beds full of pink azaleas in bloom, up past the barn they walked to the Wychfield Way.

He was like the Lord of the manor taking immense

pleasure in showing off to her, pointing out the boundaries of the estate surveying all that he would one day own. Adding it was all going to be his property and land soon. He could be as pretentious as only the rich knew how, the bleached blond was lapping it up. He was thinking like the Sun King, presenting Versailles for the very first time to his mistress. Becky the blond wife was impressed with what she had seen so far, adding a question.

"I saw in the media that the manor and estate was on the verge of bankruptcy?"

"No way! Don't believe what you read in the papers. My business plan has been completed and is just being typed up by Emma. It's only a formality for the bank. As you can see I am asset rich, the wealthy always prosper." He believed in it, fake it until you make it, he was used to getting his own way. All he had to do was ask for whatever he wanted, and it would be received.

Meanwhile it could not have been a worst outcome for Emma, deeply hurt by what she had overheard. She was a complete idiot! Now she had heard it from his lips, he could no longer be trusted, her confidence was crushed, she expected him to be honourable and act responsibly towards her. He did not care about Emma at all he had shown her his true colours, she would not tell him she had heard what he had said about her. The main problem was that he was the trustee to the property, with the power of attorney. He was the rightful heir to the estate, unless there was a change to the will that Lady Mary had already suggested.

After an hour walking in the grounds they came back into the house Stefan wanted to find Emma, Stefan knew he had to talk to her alone, before he introduced her to his wife Becky properly. He wanted to clear the air before they met, and he was not sure how she would react to what he had to tell her.

While Becky went upstairs to change, he had his chance to speak to Emma, he found her in the dining room printing and binding her chunky business proposal. He peered around the door making her jump. "Sorry I didn't see you earlier, you look as though you have been busy," he said.

She wanted to give him the impression that she did not know what had been going on all afternoon. Smiling back at him as though there was nothing wrong, she said holding up her heavy impressive binder.

"At last it's finished, I had to go straight out to get a new printer cartridge when your visitor arrived," she lied.

"So I have been really busy getting this completed. Thank goodness it is done now, I can relax at last."

Emma wanted to ask him a killer question, but held back waiting to see what he had to say for himself. She had been completely humiliate beyond belief, but it was in her own interest to play along with him, she was going to give him enough rope to hang himself.

Stefan was relieved to think she had not seen them go straight upstairs to bed together, he wanted to give her a different version of the events that would suit him. Emma thought how devious a snake he was, he was interested in himself only. Not caring what happened to her, she must get the upper hand somehow.

"Well I must say I was surprised to see her," he said. Emma was intrigued to see how he was going to explain himself.

"She looked amazing, there's no denying it, as I hadn't seen her for two months it was a shock to see her again." He said trying to play it down.

"I now know what I had been missing, It came as a total surprise. I was not expecting her at all! I was going to get divorced as you know. But now we have decided to give our marriage another try!" Emma looked at him surprised.

"I thought you said to me that it was over between you! That she was your big mistake, you never wanted to see her again! You never even mentioned her name to me." He looked sheepish and submissive, he was such a liar.

"I know, it must sound ridiculous but there it is! We are going to try again, I owe her that. By the way her name is Becky, she has begged me to see how things go. I have agreed with her to give our marriage another chance to make it work. I hope you can understand that! She is still my wife after all, I could not say no." He looked straight at Emma's gaze, as he added.

"I'm sorry to say Emma, we cannot continue as we were, if you know what I mean."

Emma saw in his eyes, that he was scanning her face closely but would not lock onto her eyes, hoping she would understand. He could not look her straight in her eyes, it was a dead giveaway.

"Well that's all very well Stefan, but we have been sleeping together, so what about me and our relationship! Where do I stand?"

"Obviously she will be staying here. I don't want her to know about us! So I was hoping that you could keep it quiet, for my sake."

"Too late," replied Emma. "Some of my underwear

and clothing are in your room, she must have seen them."

Stefan had not thought of that, she was right Becky would have noticed the clothing. Panicking he added.

"It would be best for all of us, if my wife thinks we are just business partners, I will come up with an excuse to explain away your clothing. I need the chance to make this work out. Emma will you cover for me to help me out?" He pleaded.

Oh Hell! Emma could not complain, she was after all his wife.

"All right," she said hesitating. "I will agree for now. My money is tied up in this business venture, and I owe it to Lady Mary, and myself to get the business proposal approved by the bank. Because she is your wife I won't make a fuss." She answered, knowing he had completely breached her trust and broke her heart in the process.

Happy that an agreement had been made Stefan went to find Becky in the master bedroom, it was time for them all to make a fresh start. It was then as he heard Becky taking a shower in the en suite. He found Emma's clothing on the chair, and in the top draw. Gathered them up in his arms, he took the cloths into Emma's old room placing them in a pile on her bed.

He came back into his bedroom as Becky was coming out of the en-suite shower room. She had wet hair with a small towel covering her, it could hardly hide her ample bosom blossoming out from the side of the towel. Stefan found it easy to caress her shoulders as she sat on the edge of the bed drying her hair with another towel.

"Who's clothes were they on the chair?" She asked

in her American drawl, "has there been someone else staying in this room? He had hoped she hadn't noticed.

"When I first arrived this was Emma's room, Lady Mary asked me to swap with her, as this room was originally mine, larger with a shower." He answered innocently, expecting her to believe his version of events. He had stretched the truth to breaking point, but hoped she would be gullible enough to believe him.

"By the way," he said kissing and nuzzling her neck suggestively, she smelt delicious and was just as striking without make up.

"When you are ready I must introduce you properly to Emma, it's important that you get along."

"Well if we must, I hope she is not as boring as she looks." She said putting on her underwear.

"I will see you downstairs in a little while."

Later Becky had dressed in her casual combat jeans and red silk blouse, she had reapplied her makeup and curled her hair, she was ready to meet her. Emma and Stefan were in the living room sitting on the big sofa going over their bound paperwork one last time, making sure everything was ready.

Becky entered the room holding a chilled bottle of duty free champagne and glasses.

"I bring a peace offering for Emma," she said conscious of making an effort for Stefan's sake, she guessed it was important.

"I know when I arrived it was a surprise for you both, but I will try not to disrupt the household too much while I am here." Becky said holding out a glass for each of them like an olive branch.

Stefan stood up and gesturing to Becky to take his seat on the sofa next to Emma.

"Emma I wish you to meet Becky my wife from America, who you met earlier." Stefan popped open the bottle and poured the champagne.

"A toast to new beginnings, and lovely Wychfield manor," he said with an upbeat tone. There was an awkward silence as they sipped the champagne. The conversation was forced along by Stefan telling Becky about their options for the future, as he showed her their newly bound business plan.

It was obvious that Emma had applied a great deal of effort in getting the master plan ready for the bank. It seemed to Becky that Stefan tried to easily take the credit for all the hard work done by her. As the drinks flowed the atmosphere lightened, the two women warmed at last to each other. Emma asked Becky about her background in dancing, and what it was like to be involved in a glamorous show in Las Vegas, it was a fascinating different show business world.

The women continued talked for what seemed like hours, discussing Emma's college days, her catering and business degree. Stefan had never explained to Becky how clever she was, Becky could see that it was clear that there was much more to Emma than she had at first realised. She was not the stupid servant girl that Stefan had insinuated, but a clever well educated capable woman.

Another bottle of *Cristal champagne* from the wine cellar was opened, a readymade pizza was devoured as the night progressed. Stefan was pleased to see that any friction that had existed at first between the two women had vanished. They were all getting along fine on the surface, he had got away with his trick

During their conversation Stefan advised them both

that he was going to have to return to New York shortly. He had been away from work for far too long, his holiday allowance was coming to an end. He wanted to pack into wooden boxes the paintings that they had found in the attic, to take into the cargo hold of the plane. He would include them in the next catalogue for the next art auction in New York. Stefan was convinced that the original paintings would cause quite a stir in the affluent art collectors circle.

He was hoping to raise a good amount of money to pay for the next steps on their business plan. Leaving Becky with Emma at the manor for the time being. He felt confident that they were getting along well enough. Having obtained a promise from Emma, not to let on to Becky about their past relationship he was now secure to leave for New York.

CHAPTER 8

On the surface it looked as though the women were making an effort to get along with each other. However the toxic situation in their triangle was all that Emma could think of. She wanted to move forward but found that she had lost her appetite completely, feeling betrayed by Stefan, and his denial of their intimacy was having a bad effect on her emotions. After three days of not being able to eat she was beginning to come to terms with her situation, there was no way out, she would have to make the best of the circumstances.

She tolerated Becky being in the house but found that she expected to be waited on, as thought she was in a hotel which was of deep concern to Emma. She was hoping that when Stefan went back to New York and his wife stayed with her, that it would get better as they would have more time to have a girls talk alone together, without his interference.

It was time for Stefan to stand up and be a man, it was time for them to go to the bank to explain the business proposal in full. They both needed the approval to allow them to proceed with building work for the next phase of their plans. Stefan and Emma had already signed an equal financial partnership, to save the manor.

Emma had put her heart and soul into the campaign, she was going to make sure that it worked, there was no other choice. This was a different type of stressful situation, normally she would comfort eat under stress but now her appetite had diminished so much that she was hardly eating at all as her stress levels soared to new levels. Her clothing had started to get loose on her, her jeans were becoming baggy as she synched them in at the waist with her belt. This in her mind was a good thing as her eating had been so out of control in the past?

Stefan and Emma went to London again to see the bank manager. The manager took a long time reading through the details of the business plan, that Emma had put forward. He was surprised at how thorough it was, his initial thoughts were favourable. There seemed to be a sensible approach, and a realistic time line. As they both had paid a large initial payment to the creditors, with further funds coming from the sale of the paintings in the New York auction. The manager agreed the business plans, Emma had been so thorough she had been exacting in her checking everything needed, she had put forward a clear and precise plan to supply multiple streams of possible income, with a clear focus and time line for completion of each task. At last they could move forward to save the manor, Lady Mary would be relieved and pleased with their progress.

Stefan was so glad that the first stage of their plans were in order, he could now pack up the paintings and board a plane back to his job in New York. Knowing he had already stayed away from work far too long. Confident that Emma's very capable help would pull all the strands of the plans together. She had not let him down, he now owed her his full support. It was his task to get the best possible price for the paintings at auction.

Stefan was aware that Emma was hurting emotionally, but he could not help being the vile way he was. Women had never been of any importance to him, there was a side to him that was loathsome. His good looks always ensured he was a magnet to women, he used them whenever he wanted. He was like a hunter enjoying the dominance it gave him. But now it had become complicated, he had been skilled at averted a scene, and was glad to be going back to New York to get himself out of the difficult state of affairs.

He proceeded over the next couple of days in packing into wooden crates the watercolour paintings. The large pre Raphaelite oil painting was insured, ready to take to the cargo hold on the plane. Stefan was all set to go, happy that Becky was willing to stay at the manor with Emma. Excitedly he arranged to have professional photographs taken of the paintings as soon as he arrived back at the auction house. The large oil painting was to take pride of place as the cover shot on the next catalogue.

It caused quite a stir in the art world as the art collectors catalogue was emailed, and sent to all of their prospective customers worldwide. Stefan was hoping to set a record high price at auction the following week.

Meanwhile back at the manor the women tried at last to get along. After an awkward start when Becky used to snap her fingers at Emma, they now decided to try their hardest. Gradually they warmed to each other with Becky surprisingly helping Emma, by cooking and keeping the house tidy, when she was preoccupied working on the various building stages of the business plan.

There was still a lot to be done, It was important to Emma that the next stage of plans got going quickly there was no time to lose. They needed to make money sooner rather than later, slowly she was able to move forward to the next step. Confident that Stefan was doing his important part in New York, heavily promoting the paintings to the elite clients. Emma was feeling better now that the plan was on schedule, the volume dial had been turned up a notch.

The time frame was exceedingly tight having a Christmas deadline to meet, which meant being fully open for business by the next spring. Brandon the gardener was proving to be a great help, he explained that in years past the gardens had been of a higher standard and open to the public. He felt sure that given a little help he could get the grounds up to standard again.

They often all sat in the orangery when having a lunch break, Becky was enjoying giving her support and ideas, wanting to become part of the team. She had realised how important Emma was in planning the rescue at the manor. They became the musketeers, all for one and one for all, they laughed constantly as they divided tasks between them. It became fun to see who was making the most progress on their individual responsibilities.

Over the next few weeks Emma and Becky became much closer, as a former dancer Becky was agile and limber, which she claimed was mainly down to keeping fit with yoga and running. As Emma was keen to tone up they decided on a keep fit regime. In the morning they went for a run up the Wychfield way and looping back around the grounds gave them a good start to their day. Emma found it hard to keep up with Becky, but was spurred on as Becky ran faster ahead of her and then turned back frequently to find her, as Emma ran and walked in short intervals. As her weight reduced she found that her running was getting better and better. Emma was beginning to time her runs to get faster as she got fitter. They often chatted as they jogged back to enjoy the scenery, the manor estate was so beautiful in the summer.

Beautiful Becky was proving herself to be a fantastic site manager, organising the builders and materials to work closely with the architects plans for the barn. Making sure everything required was on site in the right order, she used her considerable feminine charms when leaning over them, to get the men eating out of her hand to work faster.

The workmen were eager to show her their skills in building, and took great pride as she inspected their work. She negotiated excellent prices on the telephone for building materials with her American accent. She was skilled at sticking closely to the architects drawings, she was becoming an essential part of the musketeer team. Emma and Becky were becoming firm friends at last.

Brandon for his part in the grand scheme, was directing a small team of local lads to dig out new wider boarders around the gardens. Building new screens, and paths to meander through to different themed planting beds. The walled garden was re designed to add additional coloured shrubs to bloom in all seasons. He was so proud to at last be able to bring the gardens back to their former glory, it was lovely to see how much he cared about the overall effect with his high standards.

It was Emma's job as boss to oversee the works, keeping every element of the work tight to the time frame on her work spread sheet. The funds were allotted in stages to pay builders and the young gardeners monthly, making sure to have the jobs completed on time, or Emma would give them penalties.

She was starting a business that she loved; it seemed natural for her, no matter how complex or what problems she faced it could be done. It had been a leap of faith to get to this stage of the plan, Emma was happy to have such good company at the manor.

There were numerous pieces of paperwork to complete licenses to apply for, including food and alcohol. She already had her food safety certificates in place but would need an inspection to be completed of the commercial kitchen, once the equipment was installed in the barn. As well as installing a coffee machine in the orangery, where they planned to have a café as well as selling plants already growing in the greenhouse. Her most ambitious plan was to have a wedding licence to hold marriage ceremonies and blessing in the grounds, or the church at the end of the Wychfield Way.

The local vicar was excited at the prospect of having his church used for wedding ceremonies, and blessings he was supportive of Emma's plans helping her by giving advice when asked. He was becoming a regular visitor at the house, he also visited Lady Mary in the hospital regularly, he was fond of her and had known her all his life as he had grown up in the village.

CHAPTER 9

Money was going out too fast, Emma was getting agitated that the payments for the builders would have to stop, if Stefan could not sell the paintings in New York. He was emailing and calling her on a regular basis with updates of his progress, his list of art collectors in the States was extensive and he assured her that the interest in the paintings was growing worldwide daily. The auction was scheduled for later in the week, the marketing was completed, so they were both keeping their fingers crossed that the art auction would be a real success. If not then they were in real financial trouble.

Emma and Becky were nervously waiting for news as the auction started, the band of builders would be laid off if no funds came forward. Money in the business account had dwindled down alarmingly, Emma was getting worried. Stefan had worked his hardest to get the paintings sold, he had to succeed or their dreams were dead in the water.

The bidding began for the watercolours by Blake each one was unique, causing a frenzy in the crowd of wealthy patrons. Seated clients sat in vast rows of chairs in the large auction room, full to overflowing, every person eager to see the bidding war commence. Each water colour was sold easily, some to the same bidder, some sold on the phone as the gavel went down. Each painting was popular and of a size easy to display, the crowd were astonished at how quickly the prices rose in the room. There had been some controversy about the paintings, as the collection had been split up in the auction. However the auction house was happy, as many of the paintings were sold to British buyers, galleries had viewed the paintings as individual, and not a complete set.

Already Stefan had made a killing on the paintings, he had made far more returns from the sale than he had expected. But the star of the show was the last painting on the agenda the large oil painting from the front cover of the brochure.

Silence was shushed across the room, a hushed pause began while they quietly waited. It was time for the largest painting, everyone eagerly held their breath, for the auctioneer to start proceedings all in the room was still. The large painting was wheeled into view at the front of the stage, to gasps of wonder as the crowd whispered patiently looking forward.

Describing the oil painting as the most important Pre Raphaelite English painting that had been in private ownership. Full provenance and authenticated as, he paused for effect; by William Holman Hunt. There were gasps of glee as the auctioneer fully depicting an English pastoral scene, with sheep in the foreground lit by an early dawn. Stating It was the best painting of its type and unique, it should be purchased by a prestigious gallery or an art investor of note.

Stefan was nervously listening to the description

knowing that Emma was following the proceedings on her lap top. The bidding war started, hands were raised high with their paddles in the audience as a swift battle commenced. Billionaires were bidding by phone, and on line there was no shortage of interest, while galleries around the world listened intently. One million, one and a half, two million, the price was escalating fast and furious as internet bidders pushed the price way beyond the reserve.

Emma and Becky were listening in awe as the price went higher and higher as two bidders went up against each other, pushing the price off the scale. The Tate gallery was one bidder that was trying to lay claim to the painting scrambling to increase its bid at the last minute. The gavel went down at last *"SOLD to the phone bidder,"* securing the painting for a mystery client in London.

Stefan was delighted that one of these bids was successful he wanted the painting to stay in the United Kingdom, as England was the paintings rightful home. The auction house had made a substantial profit by hosting the auction. The commission paid persuaded the directors of the auction house to give Stefan an offer of promotion he could not refuse, his career in the art world was escalating beyond his wildest dreams.

His reputation as a leading art historian was now undisputed, he was offered a place on the board of Directors which he gratefully accepted. He had profitably sold the paintings for a record sum, and the icing on the cake was the place on the board, which he had not expected, it was the best possible outcome for him.

Emma and Becky were waiting for Stefan to call them

with the final bulletin of the total of money made, less commission to the auction house. It was Emma who took his call on her mobile.

"Good news, Emma we made over two million pounds on the collection of Blake watercolours, and over five million pounds on the large Holman Hunt oil painting." He was so excited he could not believe their luck.

"Emma we can proceed with all the building plans now, so don't hold back, get going were cash rich!" It was such good news Emma wanted to celebrate their success.

"Fantastic well done!

"I'll get the builders to complete the old barn immediately. I'm so pleased! I will go and tell Lady Mary she was so much better last time I visited her. We will all celebrate properly when you get back, when can we expect you?"

There was a long pause as he considered how to tell her, there was no easy way to break his other good news.

"I have had some rather excellent news!" He said waiting for her response.

"Well do tell me! You do keep me in suspense," she answered sounding frustrated, he was such a complex character, she never knew what would happen next.

"It's going to affect us all," there was another pause as he gathered courage to tell her.

"I'm not going to be coming back!"

"What," she replied sounding rattled.

"The chairman of the auction house was so pleased with the sale, he has given me a promotion. I am now on the board of Directors. It is something I have always wanted, It's my dream come true."

"But what about our business! You can't just abandon it." She was furious that he was not coming back to help her get the business underway. She was aware he dumped women easily but not like this. He owed her, and Lady Mary and what about Becky his wife, not to mention the manor and the estate.

"Emma the business is really your baby, you are the brains behind it, you were destined to have your own business. I was only ever involved to save the house and estate. You'll do a much better job on your own, you can be your own boss! Which I know is what you always wanted!"

She knew he was right about that, she could do it on her own without interference, but it was a scary thought.

"But what about the partnership and the finances? We signed an agreement." She replied.

"The agreement can be revised to give you a majority share in the company. " He was going to add he was just the sleeping partner, but thought it would open old wounds so paused to re think. Before he continued.

"As for the finances I agreed with the bank to pay enough to get the business going. Talk again to Lady Mary she might have some views on the outcome, as the paintings were owned by her to start with!"

"OK fine I will do that, are you sure you will not make your home at Wychfield?" Emma continued, just to be certain of his intentions. Stefan was sure that he would not be moving back to England. He had made his home in New York and now as a director and leading art historian of the largest auction house, his future was set doing the one thing he really enjoyed. He didn't want to be tied to a lonely country estate.

Becky was becoming a real problem that he thought he had solved once, but she had come back into his life to entice him back, she was becoming a thorn in his side. Now he wanted to sever ties with her for good, she may be his wife, but she did not fit in with his new promotion or life in New York, he would have to tell her somehow.

He called her later that day when the dust had settled, he presumed that Emma would have told her the news that he was staying in New York.

It was a call she was expecting from Stefan, Becky answered her mobile, she had been forewarned by Emma that he was not coming back to Wychfield, she wanted to hear from him what was going on.

"Hi Becky I promised Emma I would call you, has she told you about my promotion at the auction house?"

"She certainly has! You had better tell me what is going on, I thought we were making a go of our marriage and that we were staying in England. Why are you doing this? And when should I join you in New York?"

Stefan had to be honest with her.

"You are extremely beautiful, but I have to change my life, to do what is right for me, to do what I should be doing here!" He said.

"Sorry, but you do not feature in my plans for the future to be honest! You would not fit in my social circle! I have been given an incredible promotion, this is the life I always wanted, and I am going to grab the opportunity with both hands." He was waiting for her response there was a deathly silence. As he added.

"We will be getting a divorce, I need my freedom."

She was in freefall freaking out, he was so cruel and unfeeling, she had given up everything to be with him; she had left her good job dancing at Caesars Palace. He had used her in the most horrible way, and been nasty about Emma who was supposed to be his friend.

"You bastard I have given up my dancing career for you. I should have known when you left before that you were a worthless player!"

He listened but was not responsive, Becky was right, but it made no difference, his directorship was too important. An ex bimbo, burlesque dancer would not fit in with his image and social status in New York, she was finished.

Stefan clicked off his phone.

It was then that Becky really understood what it was like to be dumped! No man had made her feel like shit before. She had always been able to use her feminine whiles to get ahead, she was irresistible to men. Her face and figure were her fortune, was it all a mirage! Was she just a body to be used by men for pleasure.

She went to find Emma the only person she could talk to, they had become good friends as the weeks had flown by. She would understand how she felt and re build her trust in men, and in herself. It was awkward for her to admit defeat, she had expected to stay married, and live a comfortable wealthy life with Stefan.

Emma was going through invoices in the dining room and working hard on the bank statements to see which invoice needed to be paid first. Seeing which deliveries of building materials could wait until the funds from the auction were transferred into the business account later in the week. She was glad of the distraction when Becky walked in.

"Thank goodness, I can have a break good timing," she said.

"He wants a divorce!" Was all Becky could say, her mind whirled like a spinning top, with all that had happened in the last twenty four hours. One minute she was elated at the success of the art auction, now her hopes of a future with her husband had been dashed.

Emma took her hand in a gesture of support for her new friend.

"I thought there was a good chance of you two making the marriage work." Although she had originally been interested in Stefan for herself, she had gladly stepped aside when Becky arrived on the scene, she would not want to interfere in their marriage, it would not be fair to another woman.

There was a girl code, Emma had fallen for him also, and crossed the red line in sleeping with Stefan. But would Becky understand what had happened to her. She decided to keep quiet about what went on in the past, as both women had no future with Stefan now!

"So what will you do now," Emma asked Becky gesturing her to sit beside her at the dining table.

"What can I do, it's such a mess my dancing career was everything I had ever dreamed of, but I gave it up to follow him." She answered.

"I'm so bewildered I didn't see it coming. He made me believe that he loved me, it was all an act. He's a snobby bastard who just cares about himself and what he wants!"

"I know, he's a player," said Emma with a strange knowing look on her face, that gave her inner feelings away.

Emma felt that everything Stefan had done to herself was just part of his haughty character, she was surprised she had not expected to hear it from beautiful Becky. Thinking that they were a married couple trying to make it work out together, that they were both looking forward to their new future at the manor.

What a mess, it couldn't get any worst or could it!

CHAPTER 10

Both women were aware Stefan enjoyed playing mind games, he looked like a Greek god but inside he was a nasty bully. He had stooped to a new level of cruelty. Now they had both experienced what he was capable of in the extreme, he had not practised any remorse for his actions, he was severing ties coldly without any consequences.

He was capable of dropping all of them, just like that without care, including Lady Mary who was not aware what had occurred.

"For what it's worth Becky I'm sorry that you are in this situation, he has surprised me too he can be so calculating. No one wants to be used!"

Emma and Becky went into the kitchen to make coffee, they sat at the kitchen table trying to work out what the hell to do. Emma suggested that they could stay together at the manor as Becky had no job to go to.

"I don't think that's a realistic arrangement my home is in the States," she answered.

"I could try and re ignite my dancing career, but I'm not sure that the casino in Vegas would take me back.
I would have to audition elsewhere, but there must be

possibilities in other places! I will have to try my luck and start again."

"As far as divorce is concerned, when I go back I will take legal advice." Becky said adding,

"I don't see any way out, what is annoying is I don't think Stefan ever acknowledged our marriage, he has always been single in his mind and on face book. He never invited me to meet any of his friends or work colleagues, it's as though I didn't exist in his mind at all."

They had another coffee and slice of chocolate cake as a reward, the last few days had been a whirlwind of emotions for both of them. Emma knew there was more to be said but hesitated in telling her, not wanting to hurt Becky further. It was then that Emma found her inner strength and decided to break the news to her about sleeping with Stefan. She didn't want to do it, but felt she owed it to her to know the truth.

"We do share something." Emma said looking at her directly.

"Stefan really hurt me, as well as you! Before you arrived we had been sleeping together." Hesitating trying to read her reactions.

"You know the clothing you found on the chair in his room, that was mine from the night before." Becky's mind was whirring back and forth with bits of information being pieced together like a jig saw puzzle.

"Before you judge me, listen to me." Emma didn't want to ruin what had become a close friendship.

"I was told your marriage was a sham, Stefan had said it was a mistake he said exactly the same to Lady Mary. He made me believe that you were not involved with him at all, you were separated and that was it. I'm sorry to say I was taken in by his smooth talk, in the same way you were."

"But why didn't you tell me before," Becky asked.

"I was asked not to! By Stefan he was embarrassed that you had found him, he had not expected to see you again. I'm sorry to say it, but I did cover for him, it hurt me beyond belief that I was in the wrong. I had to make out that there was nothing going on between Stefan and me. I'm sorry, but I did what he asked me to do."

It was an eye opener for Becky she wanted to hate Emma but couldn't, they had both been duped by Stefan for his own ends. The worst thing was that they were both under the same roof, and both in love with him.

"It's OK Emma I understand, it's not your fault! Emma had previously thought Becky was a gold digger however she could now see clearly her heartbreak.

They had developed a firm friendship and as they had both been used by Stefan. It was agreed that they could survive what he had done to them. A pact was made between them, that a new girl code would be started from now on. Both agreed that Stefan would not win!

The two women who had been getting on really well had now a real reason to distance themselves from Stefan. He was a toxic mix of male testosterone who prayed on vulnerable women. They both decided he had just used them for his own gain, one for an advantage in implementing the business plan, which he tried to take credit for as being his own, and the other to satisfy his carnal needs.

"I left Ceasar's Palace so suddenly, without giving

notice, they will not take me back." Becky said looking glum. It was then that Emma and Becky arranged that whatever happened to them in the future they would have a bond tying them together. They would support each other in the future, keeping in touch wherever life took them, it was time to move forward.

As Emma had been going to the hospital on a regular basis, Stefan always told her not to mention Becky. Lady Mary was making a steady recovery from her stroke, undergoing physiotherapy and had greatly improved. Emma decided it was only fair that she should meet Stefan's wife at last. It seemed that Stefan had kept her and his friends in the dark about his wife. It was as if she was a ghost, no one seemed aware of her existence, he had been in denial about Becky. So that afternoon they made plans to both go to the hospital at visiting time.

It cheered Lady Mary to see them both, Emma introduced Stefan's wife to her, which came as a total surprise. She had not been told that Becky was staying at Wychfield at all Stefan had kept it quiet. Her aunt looked well, and seemed much better she was now more talkative than usual, so pleased to have visitors. She expressed her hope of leaving hospital soon, waiting to go for a convalescence stay, at a new residential village near Hastings where they specialised in recovery from strokes.

There were issues Emma needed to discuss with Lady Mary, as Becky listened in to the conversation it became obvious to her that Stefan had neglected the mother who had adopted him. He had only come to the manor to save his inheritance, not to see Lady Mary. It was her niece Emma who had really tried to help her to save the house, and estate from financial ruin. During their chat, Becky could see that Stefan could be cold and calculating, she was rapidly seeing another side to his nature she did not like. He was one of life's users, the sole purpose in his life was gaining money and a position in society and to hell with anyone, or anything that stood in his way.

Lady Mary had many contacts in royal circles all over the world, and suggested to Emma that by using her connections she could find a way of using the land at the manor to full potential. Stating that she had nothing to lose and telling her about the manor's glorious past. The land and stables had been used to house polo ponies for the local club to train, ready for polo matches. Long-ago the manor had been a hub of activity with grand gala's and parties, that her wealthy contacts would remember.

She gave Emma her valuable book full of contacts to go through, telling her who could be interested in talking to her about the land. Lady Mary urged her to make contact with all on the list, as they would no doubt be interested in the update of her health, and to advise them on progress at the Wychfield estate.

The one good thing was that the paintings from the loft and the artefact's stored in the barn had fetched exceptional bids, enough to fund the business plans Emma had put forward. Lady Mary was relieved that she had arranged the sale of her possessions, knowing it was important to save the house at all costs, it also cleared the house of her hoarding problem, which came as a strange relief to her.

Becky had to tell her that the marriage to her son was over, and that she would be going back to the

United States soon. Lady Mary was not surprised that Stefan was staying in New York, he had made his home there, she could not see him coming back to Sussex at all. Adding he had never bothered to come back when she had needed him, so there was little chance of him staying now that he had been promoted by the auction house. Being a CEO was what he had always wanted, the manor house in England was only useful to sell to get at the money, not to live in for the future which saddened her.

Of all the people she knew her niece Emma was the only person who truly cared about her, she could see it now. Once Stefan had gone back to the United States Lady Mary guessed that he would not want to be bothered with her at all. As she had become older and more frail she had become a burden to him, which is not what he wanted. So perhaps things had worked out alright in the end, destiny had a funny way of making things happen.

Although he was Lady Mary's adopted son, his character was so manipulative, and cold she had now seen him truly for the first time, for who he really was. It pained her to feel alone when she needed him, but she knew she would have to get used to living alone again. When Becky and Emma had said their goodbyes and left her when visiting hour ended, Lady Mary decided at last to change her will, she had considered it long enough.

Stefan had cost her a small fortune so far with his college fees, and apartment in New York. She had always paid him a generous monthly allowance to keep up with his lifestyle to impress his prosperous friends.

She could no longer fund his lavish lifestyle, his

expensive holidays, and polo expenses had been going through the roof, it would come to an abrupt end. He now had a promotion and money from the art auction; she was going to make changes, before it was too late. He had never appreciated what she had done for him in the past, or what she had sacrificed in order for him to live an affluent life. It was now or never, he had deserted all three of them it was enough to push her over the edge.

Lady Mary was now much better and of sound mind and body, she was going to write him out of her will as soon as she could. The alteration to the will was now her priority.

Meanwhile when they were back at the manor, Emma and Becky's relationship flowered to a new level, they both were relieved to be away from vermin like Stefan the parasite.

The rain was torrential all day, blowing a gale right across the south downs. They stayed inside keeping dry, even Brandon the gardener was busy in his potting shed.

Becky was lightening Emma's hair setting it on huge rollers, to transform her from a dull blond, to give her a make-over, to reflect her new status as a business owner. She now looked amazing, it gave her a real boost to how she was feeling. In returning the favour Emma helped Becky in producing a stunning CV to bait the right dancing career for her. She did have choices for international work, Emma would help her find the right job. They considered work for her with a dance troop on a cruise liner, or in the theatre. Becky was beginning to see other options with Emma's help.

Stefan did have a good side, but it had become too

hard to find, it was buried too deep in his selfish lifestyle. He was never going to be a good companion for either of them, they had both acknowledged that. Emma was adamant that they would win in the end, saying.

"Karma had a funny way of smoothing out injustice!" She would do a tarot card reading for Becky to see what was in store for her in the coming months.

Becky was another typical Leo, she could always grab attention with her sleek American style and glamorous sultry smile. She would easily take centre stage, and steal the limelight. Emma had grown to really like her, they were so opposite, that they attracted each other's friendship.

Taking out her pack of Gilded tarot cards Emma proceeded shuffling the pack for Becky's reading.

"Wow it look's amazing, what a great spread for you!" She said laying the cards out quickly in a Celtic cross pattern from left to right. Turning each card over to show her, Emma said.

"Look here I am the Empress, and look here you are Becky, the Queen of Swords." Becky looked puzzled.

"Are we like Thelma And Louise?"

"Gosh, I hope not," laughed Emma I'm not ready to drive off a cliff any time soon." Becky laughed as she saw the funny side, wanting her to go on to say what was going to happen for her future. Emma laid more cards.

"This is the past, can you see the five of cups three have been knocked over, and spilt something has happened that has caused a loss, but two cups are still standing upright. There is a problem and I see a conflict, but there will be a better outcome not everything is lost." The overall reading was favourable for the future something exceptional, and unexpected for her career was clearly on the horizon for Becky!

Becky was happy to hear the surprising outcome, as the wheel of fortune and the ten of pentacles was laid down for her future.

"Remarkable luck is on the way." Emma smiled at her friend.

"See here it's not all doom and gloom." It was later in the week that Emma had a surprise of her own, which pleased her. She had started to contact the affluent people on Lady Mary's list. It became obvious that her royal and wealthy contacts were delighted to hear from Lady Mary's niece. There was a lot of catching up to do, Emma spent many hours on the telephone getting the back story on the former social life of Lady Mary, before her husband passed away.

In the past there had been grand gala's at the manor, as well as many royal events. They all wanted news of Lady Mary, glad to hear that she had made such a good recovery from her stroke. Emma knew some of the royal contacts from many years ago when she was a child. Some remembered her from royal weddings and social gatherings in the distant past that she could only just recall herself.

Invitations were made to Emma over the phone which was a surprise, she had been warmly welcomed by Lady Mary's circle of former acquaintances. It seemed they were all keen to keep in touch, to welcome Emma into their fold. Becky had agreed to stay as long as she could to help Emma to finalise her plans to save the manor. Her return to the United States could be delayed until her friend had firm control of the business.

The two women were enjoying their time together, holding their focus firmly on improving health and well being, supporting each other in keeping fit. Becky was having fun turning Emma's life around, she enjoyed styling her hair, and applying the latest cosmetics. As a dancer she was experienced at applying makeup, and knew which styles would suit her. Often they went out together shopping, Emma's stocky figure had slimmed down considerably, due to Becky teaching her yoga every afternoon, slowly and surely Emma's image was changing.

Emma was being turned from an ordinary duckling into a beautiful swan, she was starting to enjoy the attention she was getting from men. It had never occurred to her what a difference it could make if you looked good and felt good. She was spending longer on her grooming, enjoying the effect on her own image and self respect. Her casual shabby chic style was morphing her into a sophisticated lady of style. Becky had worked her magic Emma loved her new look, and took great pleasure in updating her wardrobe taking pride in her new appearance, the ladies were turning heads wherever they went.

An important invitation arrived by courier for Emma, it was in a large gold envelope, with an embossed card inside with the red, blue and gold coat of arms of the Duke of Norfolk. It was an invite to a Polo Ball in aid of charity at Arundel Castle. Situated up the south coast in the market town, not too far away from Wychfield Manor. It was a location Emma knew well, she used to visit the antique, and bric-a-brac shops in Arundel with Lady Mary many years ago. Her favourite record shop A

Ray Of Light, owned by her good friend Malcolm was there. She used to spend many happy nostalgic hours listening to vinyl records, taking her back in time to her cheerful past.

Emma was delighted to have been invited to such a prestigious event, she asked Becky to go with her as a way of showing her what British high society was all about. They giggled together surprised by their new inclusion and the significance of the invite to be part a of the lofty circles of the upper classes.

The day of the charity ball eventually arrived, Emma had been looking forward to getting dressed up. After all of the hard work cleaning, and arranging building work, she had been constantly in dungarees, this was her first time to really shine since arriving at the manor, they were both so energized and excited.

"Wow look at you! you look amazing," Becky said as Emma emerged from her bedroom, Emma was wearing a new off the shoulder black dress with her best silver stiletto sandals, the dress accentuated her new slimmed down figure and tiny waist.

"Are you sure it's not too tight!" Emma said turning to look at herself in the full length mirror on the landing, surprised at how skinny she now looked.

"No it's just right, I love the length of the dress just below the knee it makes you appear much taller." Becky added.

"Tonight we are going to knock them dead!" Becky was so thrilled to be going to the charity ball at the castle, she heard from Emma that all the members of the local polo club had been invited. She was sure that she could attract the most handsome men at the ball. With her blond Marilyn Monroe hairstyle and ample cleavage on display, she was going to cause quite a stir.

The contrast of her humble beginnings crossed her mind, when she grew up in Kentucky her family were extremely poor. She felt hungry all the time, her parents were poor farmers scratching out a living as best they could in the dirt, raising enough money for the family to eat was a constant problem. She remembered her mother spent many hours crying, trying to make ends meet. Selling and pawning whatever she could in the local pawn shops.

Her parents were good country folk, but only just surviving poverty. Becky wanted more out of life, so when she was old enough she waved goodbye to her parents as she boarded the coach going west to Los Angeles. Making a living in the seedy strip clubs along the Hollywood Boulevard, it was her break from hardship, but it had a profound effect on her. She swore she would never be poor again, as she drifted from club to club enhancing her skills. She took dancing classes whenever she could to help lift her out of scarcity.

Along the way Becky had some lucky breaks, a talent scout from the Las Vegas casinos took a chance on her. Taking her to Ceasar' Palace to audition for their dance group. Her stunningly good looks helped her career along, giving her the chance to head their Marilyn Monroe dance sketch, mirroring scenes from Some Like It Hot.

The best news was that she had the chance to sing whilst performing, taking her Marilyn doppelganger to a higher level. She caused a sensation in the dance act taking centre stage, which is where she felt she belonged. It was not long before her fans were queuing up for her autograph outside the stage door. She knew then that she had arrived in more ways than one!

Becky had explained in the past her own rise to fame to Emma who was astonished at her humble beginnings. However Becky understood that Emma had no idea of poverty herself. Emma had been born with a silver spoon in her mouth, and had not had to fend for herself. It was Becky's drive away from poverty, that had spurred her on to rise to new heights. In a strange way Stefan and Becky both had a grasping nature, and a need to attain wealth at all costs, Becky had the strength of a lion and would allow nothing to stand in her way.

Becky had already decided on wearing a full length red dress to the castle with a matching lace wrap, her blonde hair had been curled into an elegant chignon, with minimal jewellery she looked striking. They both took numerous photo's on their mobiles to show Lady Mary.

The girls sent a large bouquet of flowers to Hastings where Lady Mary was convalescing after her hospital stay. Thanking her and letting her know that they were attending a Polo Ball, at the castle thanks to her royal contacts. Promising to let he know later the outcome of the event. She had made good progress after her stoke and was almost back to normal, her speech was good, but her walking was slower, she was now using her walking stick again to steady herself. Emma had told her aunt that by having telephone conversations with her old circle of acquaintances, it had generated a mass of interest in what was happening at Wychfield.

Lady Mary had received so many get well cards, bouquets, and gifts for her at the convalescent home in Hastings. She was absolutely delighted that she had not been forgotten by her old affluent friends.

CHAPTER 11

Emma and Becky were arriving at the Castle to a fanfare of trumpet blasts at the entrance. They were escorted to the main hall by the organisers assistants, where they were to be announced formally at the grand door way, to the throng of gathering people.

A few well known celebrity's were spotted by Emma as she scanned the room, she was really glad to have Becky with her for company. The two great beauties made quite a stir when they were introduced entering the crowded room. All the men gathered were astonished at their elegance, and beauty wondering who the two ladies were? Not having seen them in royal circles before it was quite intriguing, as the two captivating ladies were obviously important guests.

Cathy the organiser of the Ball and charity secretary stepped forward to introduce Emma and Becky properly to the other guests. There was a great swarm of people all gathered talking to each other excitedly at the entrance to the main hall. They were delighted to be introduced to Emma, as Lady Mary's niece and to Stefan's American wife neither of whom they had met before.

Exchanges of information and titles of the aristocracy made Emma's head spin, she would not be able to remember all their titles and backgrounds, as she gave them a much needed progress report on Lady Mary's heath. Emma recalled having spoken to one or two on the telephone, while Becky was mesmerized by the atmosphere of the surroundings inside the castle.

It was such an eye opener for her to listen, enthralled to see how the other half lived, she enjoyed people watching as they talked with one another. Becky was elated to be in such prestigious company, they were equally amazed to meet her, as most of them knew Stefan well, but had not had the opportunity to meet his mystifying American wife.

Suddenly Emma was frozen in time, as she was approached by the most handsome man in the room. He was heading straight towards her, luckily Cathy the organizer was still on hand to introduce them.

"Alex, please meet Emma who is lady Mary's niece, staying at Wychfield Manor." Turning she introduced Emma.

"I am pleased to introduce you to Count Alexander, he is from an old aristocratic family in Russia, now living in London."

He had such dark and mysterious features, his thick black long hair framed his olive skin and aquiline nose. His eyes sparkled when he smiled, taking her hand and kissing it in an old fashioned way, as he bowed low. He was so striking his dark brown eyes bored straight into Emma's sole, he seemed to fix his gaze directly on her eyes. Emma was struck dumb by his presence, there was an uneasy silence before Becky returning to Emma's side with glasses of champagne, she was thrilled to also be introduced to Alex.

"Becky is Stefan's wife from the US." Cathy said, he bowed in response, his Russian accent was obvious but his English was perfect.

"I know your husband well, we used to play polo in the season a few years ago. I am delighted to meet the two most beautiful women in the room."

He meant what he said and was glad to meet them both, he appeared to be on his own at the party. Although he knew most of the guests and was comfortable in their company, he was obviously part of their inner circle. He kept his twinkling eyes firmly on Emma, which she found disconcerting expecting him to be more attracted to beautiful Becky.

It was a preoccupation of his to see what trinkets the women wore, he explained to them that he was a diamond merchant and maker of exquisite diamond jewellery, with his premises in Hatton Garden. Adding he favoured antique pieces that had been handing down through the generations as beautiful jewels had tales to tell of their owners. He seemed to be in no hurry to move on talk to other groups, happy having small talk to both ladies.

He noticed that Emma was bare of jewellery no rings or bangles, all she wore was a pair of gold and pearl drop earrings to enhance her black gown. Turning to her taking her hand in his he said.

"You are such a stunning creature, yet you wear no rings or adornments. Do you prefer simplicity?" He asked, giving her fingers a slight squeeze as he glanced into her hazel eyes for a response.

She was melting in his fixed gaze, but he needed a reply. Shyly she answered him.

"I own very little jewellery, I was a student until recently studying for my degree, so I only have costume jewels, not suitable for wearing today. Coming here I guessed I would be outshone, so I preferred the simple look, unadorned I'm surprised you noticed!"

He had noticed everything about her, the elegant way she carried herself, her serene smile and her gestures when she talked to others. He had noticed it all when he had watched her from across the room. He felt instinctively as though they were destined to meet.

"You have an understated elegance, as a diamond merchant I do notice these things, I see you have no wedding ring are you seeing anyone?" He asked with direct probing he was trying to figure her out, she intrigued him. Emma responded to his very direct question.

"I was in a short relationship which ended recently, since I have been living at Lady Mary's estate, I am far too busy to be seeing anyone as you put it!"

Becky was pleased and astonished by his obvious attraction to Emma, and how forward he was in pursuing her. She had never seen Emma look so coy and bashful, her cheeks were flushed red. She was attracted to him but embarrassed by him at the same time, he was still holding firmly on to her hand, he was attentive and reluctant to let go of her.

At this point Becky could see quite clearly their magnetism, she decided to let them have some time together. Smiling at them both she made her weak excuses to leave them alone for a while, allowing her time to mingle with the guests she had spoken to earlier.

It was then that Emma had a chance to be alone with

Alex, they took a seat on a chaise longue in a side corridor away from the crowds. Which gave them time to talk quietly together. He did not want to leave her side, and made a conscious effort to try to make the evening special he wanted her to feel comfortable in his company.

Emma found Alex fascinating his Russian accent was adorable, she would not forget this night. Here was the man of her dreams, she was surprised at how instantly they were attracted to each other, never in her life had she experienced such rapport with a man.

He was utterly charming, polite in an old fashioned way. Yet he was forthright, he made no effort to disguise how captivated he was by her charms. She was utterly surprised at the effect she had on him but loved the unexpected attention. He seemed to prefer talking to her rather than Becky which amazed her, as her friend was so stunningly beautiful.

They talked for a while about Stefan as he said he was a mutual acquaintance. Alex knew him well from when they had both been in the same polo team. Emma told him that Stefan had gone permanently back to New York. She advised him how delighted he had been with his recent promotion at the Auction House.

Alex mentioned to Emma that he knew Lady Mary and Wychfield Manor, from when he went to local polo matches with Stefan. Emma felt that it was a happy coincidence, they had a talking point of shared interest in common, to ease the conversation. Not wanting the discussion to centre around her, feeling that his background was much more exciting than her study's at University.

It was during their conversation Alex explained to Emma that his aristocrat family used to live in St Petersburg. His attractive family mansion was seized from the nobility after the 1917 revolution. His family suddenly fled Russia in disguise, travelling incognito under another name to Paris. His parents had set up their diamond merchant business in premises close to the Champs Elysee. His family upbringing seemed so remarkable to Emma, she had always been keen on history, but knew little of the radical Bolsheviks in Russia.

"I feel to a certain extent French and Russian, but I have now permanently made my home in London. My house is near the Royal Albert Hall in Kensington, I expect you know the area!"

It was a small world, Emma had the idea that she knew exactly which house he was talking about. As Alex described the grand façade of the building where he now lived. She explained to Alex that when she rented the flat in the mews house in Notting Hill. She had a friend who lived in a flat above the shops in Kensington High Street, very close to his house. She had always thought what a magnificent building it was, not knowing that Alex owned it, she knew the house must be worth a small fortune at today's prices.

They sat engrossed in conversation Emma was transfixed with the story about his ancestors, his family had lived through such a turbulent time, she wanted to know all about his life. There was so much to talk about as the music played in the ballroom, they were fortunate to have a quiet moment to themselves. Alex was interested to hear about Emma's family connections with Stefan and Lady Mary, it was an

extraordinary coincidence that their paths had crossed now, how strange! Emma thought .

Emma condensed as much as she could about what had happened to her life in the past few months, she detailed her obligation to her aunt Lady Mary. Telling Alex that because of her father's investment fraud during the cascade of bank failures. It was her duty to protect her aunt and right the wrongs done to her. She opened up honestly about her reason for staying on at the manor. Explaining It was a way to help her aunt to keep her home, as well as building a profitable business to secure the house and estate from the creditors.

Her dedication to her aunt was endearing to Alex, he took great delight in telling her that he had visited the manor many times over the years, so he knew all about the house and the adjoining land. He mentioned he had attended local polo matches when Stefan was part of his team. Saying Lady Mary had been very kind to him, and showed him fully around the grounds on the estate.

Alex was the captain of the polo team and owned a string of polo ponies, he then asked if the estate still had the stables. Mentioning he would like somewhere local to keep the ponies between future matches. Emma confirmed that the stables were there but no longer used, so the opportunity may be available in the future to keep the ponies liveried there. She knew of a local polo club in the area, so suggested that she would take advice from them and keep in touch when she had further information, as she had no experience of horses herself. Emma was delighted that an idea they shared had future possibilities. How odd things kept happening to her, seemed puzzling yet wonderful.

Becky was more than happy to have been given the

chance to circulate alone amongst the crowd. She was kept smiling by a deep and amusing conversation, with a famous dance talent agent and promoter, she had recognised him at the bar. He had been talking non-stop to her about her dancing career experience, as a show girl in Las Vegas. She was elated to have a dialogue with someone who had skill in putting on shows around the world. The agent discussed his work in Monte Carlo, Paris and New York although he now lived in London.

Becky had kept an eye on the time, and a watchful eye on Emma, aware she was not in the main room. Guessing she must still be talking to Count Alexander in the side room where she had last saw them together. What bewildering fun they were both having, she would need to thank Lady Mary for suggesting that Emma networked with her contacts. It was a special night to recollect for both of them, the champagne kept flowing as the dancing and conversations went on into the late evening.

Emma was thrilled when the Count asked her to dance, he held her close in his powerful arms. They stayed locked in each other's embrace dancing most of the evening to the rapture to the music. Alex was most attentive and danced very well, he made her night the most wonderful event she could ever think of.

Becky also had an amusing evening although she had been separated from Emma, she met so many useful influential contacts. She was kept busy and danced with most of the good-looking men who asked for her hand, it was a magical moment for her too.

The charity event was a great success the night finished with a select charity auction on the stage. This was no ordinary auction, there was an all expenses holiday on a yacht based in the Mediterranean. A custom made luxury sports car, then came the star attraction of the auction. There in an exquisite highlighted glass show case taking centre stage, was a stunning modern diamond cuff bracelet, by Count Alexander Visiliev. Donated from his exclusive collection at his Hatton Garden showroom,

Becky and Emma at last found one another, as they stood together in the middle of the ball room to watch the auction. Neither of them were in a financial situation to partake in the auction. However they enjoyed watching the frenzy of bids made by the wealthy patrons. Both women had been in a severe cash flow situation lately, but what fun to dream of what could be if prince charming ever came along. Emma after tonight, knew at least who he was!

A rich abundance was evident everywhere in the castle as Emma and Becky had a taste of another life, almost another dimension. Away from the everyday struggle of existence keeping their heads above water. Here all was possible, it truly was like another parallel world away from reality.

Emma knew her financial constraints were temporary at best, but longed to take a glance through the window of opportunity. Then it dawned on her that Alex was indeed the Count, who had donated the bracelet for the charity auction.

He was such a special man in so many ways, how fortunate she had been to have met him at the castle, how lucky was she! Yet Emma had an uneasy feeling creeping upon her, something was peculiar about tonight. Alex reminded her so much of Adam Ant, as

Prince Charming, nothing to be scared of!
How weird!... She couldn't get the song out of her head.

The evening eventually came to an end, as the music died down, it was time to leave. Count Alexander had exchanged telephone numbers with Emma, as she said her goodbyes to the organisers of the ball. They stood together at the entrance to the castle, waiting for her car. Both reluctant to say goodbye, wishing they could continue the evening. It was Becky who arrived by Emma's side to hurry her up, their car and driver had come around to the entrance, waiting to take them home.

The Count took hold of Emma's hand he bowed low, slowly kissing the back of her hand in a suitable and appropriate way, as the throng of guests passed them on the entrance steps. He was so endearing and courteously correct, he took her breath away she felt so special and valued by a man for the first time.

Too late to say more, she was ushered into the waiting car, as they were whisked speedily away by the driver. Like an ending to a wonderful dream the ladies night came to an end. Emma and Becky looked out through the darkened car window as they sped through the pitch-black countryside, back home to the manor.

CHAPTER 12

What happened next was totally unexpected and bizarre in the extreme, it pulled the rug from the floor right from under Emma's feet.

The bank called to say that the cheque paying her builders had bounced! This was embarrassing for her in the most heart wrenching way, her concerns were growing into a blind panic, what could she do she was now totally broke!

Where was the expected injection of funds from New York? She had no other funds to transfer into the account as her own bank account was a big fat zero.

"Oh Shit." In her state of alarm Emma called back the bank manager urgently.

"No it cannot be! It must be a mistake, my business partner Stefan, was due to put in over a million pounds to be transferred into the business account yesterday, to cover this payment." Emma was waiting anxiously for the managers reply, while he put her on hold again.

The cheque to pay the builders was for an unusually large amount this time, the sum was supposed to cover full and final expense for the oak beams, including plumbing materials. Ordered for the next phase of the building work, to complete the minstrels gallery and fit out the new kitchen in the old barn. Most importantly she was worried about the next cheque for the builders wages.

The manager came back to the phone.

"This payment cannot be honoured Miss Taylor, no funds have been received or transferred at all from the bank account in New York."

"I will have to get back to you!" Emma said from her mobile phone, her face had drained of colour as she rushed to her laptop to send an urgent email as quickly as she could to Stefan.

"Oh no!" As she was typing the email to Stefan, she remembered that earlier in the day she had ordered the steel industrial kitchen units on line. Payment was due on delivery, that sum could now not be paid and she could not stop it! Her gut feeling was that something was drastic wrong. She was out of fresh idea's what to do, she felt completely alone, thank goodness she still had Becky to turn to.

Tapping the email to Stefan in New York at break neck speed she then pressed send.

He had better have a good answer, or they were done for! Well at least she didn't have to wait long, his reply popped up there on the screen, she was almost too scared to open the email, but open it she must. There it was in black and white, the money had gone!...

He started the email with an apology. Sorry that the money was missing from the business account. He stated that he was unable to make good his promise to bolster the account, with money from the sale of the paintings at auction.

His reason for the non-payment staggered Emma.

He admitted being in Las Vegas, adding that he had a gambling addiction which had got the better of him. He had spent the last week in celebrating his new job and vast fortune from the auction sale. He was on a high! The champagne had flowed like water, he had become a high roller at the gaming tables. Everyone there was watching him win...win...win! It was incredible, the exhilaration had been intoxicating, and then he lost! Lost! Lost! Not just a little, but lost it all!

Stefan had crossed the red line, there was no going back he was a complete bloody fool with money, it had taken time for the facts to come to the surface. But now Emma knew where a great deal of Lady Mary's cash had gone, she had supported him for many years while he was squandering the money. Why would he let it happen, she emailed back to him. There was no answer, she knew there could be no answer! He was lost in a mess of his own making, the worst of it was she had trusted him, he was after all her business partner.

Emma called out loudly for Becky who was in the kitchen cooking chicken for dinner, she didn't want to bother her, but was hoping she could raise her deflated spirits. She had to talk it through with someone or go nuts, the strain was too much to bear alone.

"What's the matter?" Becky called out annoyed at having to stop prepping vegetables for their evening meal. She walked into the dining room drying her hands on a tea towel.

"What's up?" Knowing it had to be something to do with the business spread sheets, Emma had been busy working on all day.

"I don't know how to say this." Emma said getting her to take a seat at the dining room table.

"When you met Stefan in Vegas, were you aware he was a big gambler?"

"Well yes." She answered sheepishly.

"He gambled a lot of the time, he really enjoyed it! Why do you ask?" Becky replied concerned at the strange vacant look on Emma's face.

"The business account is empty, the auction money was never paid in, Stefan has been back to Vegas and gambled it all away. Nearly four million dollars went on the roulette tables." Emma's face was white with panic her voice faltered.

"Did you know he was addicted to gambling." Becky was looking vague, but disturbed by the idea, she had met a lot of gamblers in her time in Las Vegas, but never guessed that Stefan had a real problem.

"No! No idea at all, we just had fun at the tables, his gambling seemed normal to me." She said shrugging her shoulders, it was a shock to hear that he had gambled all the business funds away.

But if the money was not there, what was she going to do next! Emma's plans were now impossible her future was now in tatters. The building work was only half completed, there was still an awful lot to do to complete the barn. Emma needed the barn finished, as it was the heart of the operation, she wanted to host weddings with a huge marquee on the lawn, able to accommodate two hundred guests. The kitchen in the barn had to be finished or her ideas were a non starter. Emma had faith in herself, she had a belief that anything was possible, but now she was not so sure how. Her mantra had always been, there must be a way; she knew she had to manifest it for herself.

Talking to Becky helped a lot to re think her ideas, it

was a crisis point. But there had to be some financial possibilities, she hoped and prayed to find the way forward, time was ticking down at a grotesque speed.

At least Becky's life had taken a turn for the better, it looked as though her recent tarot reading was coming true. The celebrity agent she had met at the charity ball was a top talent, night club promoter. He had been true to his word and had sent Becky's details to his best contact in Paris, at the famous *Folies Begere* cabaret music hall. Becky had an audition scheduled in a couple of days. She had never seen Paris, so was very excited at the prospect of a possible new start, confident that she would be a suitable dancer for the show.

It had been the one thing that Emma admired in Becky, she never had any doubts or hang-ups about who she was, or where she was going, there was a determination in her to succeed, she was not afraid of hard work or taking action when required.

Emma would follow her example, she was also full of renewed dedication and hard work, with certain focus she would win!

Someone in the universe must have been listening to her thoughts, her mobile phone rang it was Count Alexander. His sexy Russian accent was still delectable.

"Hello Emma I'm so glad I caught you, is it convenient for you to talk? I know how busy you are at the Manor?"

Becky heard who it was on Emma's phone, so went back into the kitchen to check on their dinner, leaving Emma speak to him properly. Emma was so happy to hear from him it changed her mood immediately, after such a disastrous morning.

"Alex how lovely to hear from you, I had such a great

evening at Arundel castle I am so glad we met. I just wish we could have stayed a little longer."

"I know so do I," he replied in his charming accent.

"We should see each other again! Can you come up to London tomorrow? I would like to take you out to dinner."

Emma's nerves were bubbling away under the surface, she was longing to see him again. But was also desperate to solve her immediate business problems. Would he mind if she said no at this precise moment?

Knowing that Alex would be a welcome distraction she answered him.

"Look that would be so nice, I would like that, but tomorrow is very short notice I am in the middle of a crisis here. Can we leave it for now. " He wanted to see her, but did not want to distract her from her problems at the manor.

"Whatever crisis you have I am willing to help you out, It is very good of you to assist Lady Mary. I do understand , can we meet in a couple of days perhaps at the weekend? A problem shared is a problem halved you know."

" When exactly? What time do you suggest meeting, and where?" She wanted to see him more than anything in the world, it was just such bad timing.

"Could you be ready Saturday at six pm? I will send my car down to Wychfield to pick you up, we can go for a meal in London!"

"Yes that's fine, Saturday will be OK. I can be ready at six, I am excited to see you again." She answered surprised to be seeing him so soon.

"See you Saturday." With that said he was gone.

Wow, he was the most handsome man on the planet,

and he wanted to take her out. Think, believe and you shall receive, seemed strange to her, but she would not knock it, when it had worked so well.

Then she was scared, what to wear, she had no idea where they were going for the meal, she had forgotten to ask. Her Aquarius instinct for reassurance made her check again her horoscope. At the last tarot reading the cards had indicated there would be a stranger looking out for her, and there he was! You could not make it up, it was so thrilling, just what she needed to lift her mood.

However much her good fortune was as far as romance was concerned, she could not ignore the severe financial trouble she was in! But she could postpone it, the builders were still on site, Emma would talk to the foreman to try and avert trouble. The foreman was busy over at the barn, securing a new oak timber in place across the roof span, to strengthen the gable end of the old structure. Ready to secure the stairs up to the minstrels gallery, before finishing for the day. Emma could not let him go without tackling the looming problem head on, there was no point in putting off the inevitable predicament.

He was pleased to see Emma, he wanted to ask her a few questions regarding positioning of the electric sockets for the new kitchen units, arriving later in the afternoon. Emma was listening to his questions as they reviewed the plans pinned up on the far wall of the barn. Agreeing the exact placing for the ovens she wanted to faced her dilemma head on.

The foreman was understandably annoyed at her cash flow problem, but strangely not surprised, he said it often happened in large building projects. He suggested laying off the workers and taking them onto another job until she had money coming in again; Emma was reluctant to halt the work as the deadline was tight. However there was no other choice she had to agree for now. It would give her a little breathing time to re think the next step.

Stefan had landed her in this current predicament he had just been able to walk away, she hoped he would get help with his addictions, or it would ruin his life like it had for so many others. She decided to send him an email, explaining how let down she felt, she had also tried hard to understand his gambling but it seemed impossible to fathom, why did he lay another bet. He knew exactly the consequences of his actions. Emma found it hard to understand why he could gamble with money at this time, especially as the manor was at stake.

The business of saving the manor house as it stood was not working, she tried to explain in her email that she had found her calling, continuing with the business of saving the manor against the odds. Hoping he would comprehend, describing to Stefan that she was here every day, fighting to save the business and the manor. She added that she would get solicitors to change the business into her sole ownership. Releasing him from any obligation which would take the pressure off of his shoulders.

She could not risk him being involved in the day to day running of the business at Wychfield, he could be a silent partner in name only. His reply came swiftly back to her, he granted her wish to take charge of the business and apologised again for the situation she found herself in. Knowing what a humiliation she had been through when the cheques had bounced.

At least she could now get on with a plan B, changes to their business contract would be easy to achieve it would now give her sole control. Which was daunting as she was left with no money or income from the estate.

She did have something to look forward to in seeing Count Alexander on Saturday.

Becky's plans had changed, she advised Emma that she was flying to Paris in the morning from Gatwick Airport, and would let her know when she was settled into the hotel in the city centre. Becky told Emma not to worry about her, convinced there would be a silver lining for both of them. They needed to follow their dreams and be grateful for their blessings.

CHAPTER 13

The next day was charged with an electric excitement for Emma and Becky, they said there goodbye's as Becky left by taxi for the train journey from Brighton to Gatwick Airport, en route to Charles de Gaulle airport.

It had suddenly become extremely quiet at Wychfield Manor, the builders had taken their tools and gone from the old barn. They had been sent on to other smaller building sites in the area for the time being. Luckily Lady Mary had scraped up enough money for the builders wages up to date, so that they honoured their commitment so far. Later in the day the kitchen equipment order arrived, there was just enough money left to cover the invoice, thanks again to her aunt. Emma realised there would be no resources left now as even Lady Mary was now completely out of funds, she only had her pension left.

Emma was grateful her aunt had stepped in to help in her humiliating hour of need. She was surprised that Stefan had almost gambled away their future, saying it could be a wakeup call for him to straighten out his life.

The foreman agreed to resume building work at

Emma's request, when she was ready to resume completion of the barn. There was nothing else that could be done about it, so she resigned herself to get ready for her date with gorgeous Count Alexander.

She was a survivor, it was time to hold her head high to be proud of what she had accomplished so far. With a determined attitude to have fun, to lighten her recent struggles, she set out her clothes to wear for the evening. It had to be something suitable for wearing anywhere, she had no idea where they were going for the date. This was the only chance she had to escape the pressure she had been under. Smiling to herself in anticipation of the date, she took a shower and set her newly highlighted hair onto big heated rollers as Becky had instructed before she left. She tried relaxing by listening to soothing music as she got ready for her Prince Charming.

Count Alexander was so good-looking it was an astonishing dream date. It was so important to her that the evening be a success, she was looking forward to it and would make sure it was. Deciding on a smart royal blue trouser suit with a soft cream silk blouse it was feminine, and yet smart for any occasion, it was her favourite outfit. She felt confident that she looked good, yet under stated. Her blond hair was perfect, softly curled, and not too formal. She wore her gold and pearl drop earrings that she had worn when she met Alex at the castle, knowing that he would surely notice.

The Bentley arrived precisely on time passing through the ornate gates, up the private drive to the manor. Emma heard the car approaching tyres crunching along the gravel, it was time for her to leave for London.

Emma was delighted to be chauffeur driven to Kensington in the comfortable luxurious car, as she sunk into the sumptuous leather back seat. They cruised through the country roads of West Sussex then joined the motorway traffic, arriving into London in good time.

Turning the car into Kensington High Street, Emma recognised where she was, not far from the magnificent Georgian building where Alex lived. Now she was getting nervous for the first time, she was having butterflies in her stomach. Would he still find her as attractive as he had at Arundel castle? Would they still have the same chemistry?

Arriving at the distinguished building, it was too late to worry. Before she had a chance to ring the door bell, a butler suddenly appeared, as she stepped from the car, the chauffer held open the car door.

"Count Alexander is expecting you, please come this way Miss." The formal butler took her suit jacket over his arm then led her through the imposing black and white mirrored hallway, into the main sumptuous living room at the far end of the hall. Alex had called this his London house, yet it was a magnificent mansion inside. An impressive grand room, with high ceilings and white marble pillars, huge ornate gilt mirrors hung from floor to ceiling reflecting the light back from giant cut glass chandeliers.

The Count heard her approaching, as her stiletto court shoes clicked on the shiny black marble floors. Alex was standing in front of a Georgian fire place waiting for her, his dark eyes looked openly at her making an immediate connection. He smiled at her with his arms outstretched, welcoming Emma into his distinguished home.

Meeting his piercing gaze, Emma's face lit up with a coy expression, she had been waiting longingly for this moment. She felt a fluttering in her heart in anticipation of being with him again. He looked formal, yet striking wearing all black, his black shirt with turned back cuffs showed off his tanned forearms, with his long dark hair swept back over his collar. He stepped forward slipping his hand around her waist without uttering a word, he pulled her firmly toward him as she succumbed to his embrace then placed his first kiss firmly and securely on her lips. Melting her heart, instantly his kiss sent a tingly sensation throughout her body. She was unable to break away, she responded spontaneously placing her fingers through his hair, she became lost in the moment of sweet surrender as his lemon cologne encircled her.

There was a natural instinct at play, the laws of attraction had brought them together at the castle. He had wanted Emma from the first minute he had set eyes on her. Emma was equally fascinated by him, he intrigued her more than any man before, it was as though he had cast a spell on her. Her intuition was to suppose that he had been at the castle on purpose. Somehow it was no coincidence, as though they were meant to meet there at exactly the same time.

It felt as if she had unconsciously asked the universe for love to fill the gap in her life, like a magnet they were led to each other's side, now she had to believe anything was possible. Their first kiss was so tender his arms surrounded her in a comforting hug, it was a completely perfect moment. In her eyes he was flawlessly masculine, and unspoiled although obviously a cultured elite gentleman from the best of circles. He appeared so different from Stefan who was cunning and spoilt by his wealthy upbringing, Stefan was so messed up by comparison.

Count Alexander pulled back from the embrace, Emma opened her eyes to look at him, his striking black eyes sparkled a smile back at her. She noticed his clean rugged jaw and his long black lashes, he still held her fast not wanting to let her go.

"I hope you do not mind if we have dinner at home." He asked.

"My new chef has created a wonderful three course meal for us." He was eager to get her opinion on the cuisine, knowing she was a well qualified chef herself.

"Yes, I would find it interesting Alex. But I must warn you I am looking for new menu ideas for the manors choices. I might steal the ideas!" She laughed enjoying the taunting banter.

"I can see you are a devious woman, trying to steal my cook, and his menu's away from me at the first opportunity." There was a special rapport building between them, the regal yet modern atmosphere within the richly decorated house with opulent decor was superb. Emma was transfixed taking in her surroundings, which Alex enjoyed, he was proud of his Kensington home yet there was no sign of arrogance, or superiority in his manner.

They were at ease having fun as Alex opened a bottle of Crystal champagne to toast their first date together, while Emma relaxed on the deeply cushioned couch.

There was a moment when Emma thought she must be dreaming, the evening was perfection, Alex was attentive and yet gracious. He made her feel at home in his presence, they sat and sipped champagne chatting and laughing. She never felt that he over stepped the boundaries of propriety, he was always the perfect gentleman, she enjoyed his quiet cool charm.

Looking around the large room she was amazed at how superbly decorated the space was. There was a careful choice of different textures, silks, and satins in lush rich colours, with large Turkish rugs and velvet drapes against a neutral background. It was as though he had a woman's eye for furnishings, the room had a mixture of Georgian elegance with numerous expensive works of art, with modern sculptures.

It was then as her eyes scanned the room that she noticed an exact copy, of Lady Mary's pre Raphaelite oil painting. Filling the space from floor to ceiling It was carefully lit, hanging in pride of place on the main darkened wall behind her.

Now that was spooky! She had a sudden eureka moment, so many threads of their lives were joined together in her mind all at once.

"Is that a copy of Lady Mary's painting from Wychfield?" She asked intrigued.

"Or is it the real thing?" Her mind was racing ahead of her, he wouldn't have a copy surely!

"How did it get here? The gallery in New York sold it?" The Count smiled broadly back at her, as an inquisitive expression showed clearly on her face, in his Russian accent he replied.

"I know, you are right it is the real thing! I bought the painting at the auction over the phone."

"This painting is so exceptional, I remembered seeing it hanging in the stairwell of the hallway at Wychfield

Manor. This painting is so special, I knew it should stay in England. I am pleased to say that I am the mystery bidder, who won the painting! I just had to have it as the centre piece of my collection!"

Emma was completely perplexed how did he know about the painting being up for sale? Also the timing of the auction in New York? Alex saw her still puzzled expression adding.

"I collect Pre Raphaelite paintings it is my passion, William Holman Hunt is my favourite artist, Stefan had put me on the auction house's list of collectors. When the brochure arrived by email. I knew it was another painting for my collection, it is now in pride of place." He was aware from the start of the provenance having seen it on the wall at the manor house. Because it had been owned by Lady Mary, the painting was even more special to him.

Emma got up and walked over to the painting, it was a strange eerie feeling. In the darkened space seeing the large painting highlighted here in this house, she was having a deja vous experience. She would enjoy telling Lady Mary that she had seen her painting, in the best of homes, against all the odds. Knowing that it had found its way to Count Alexander's house in London, Lady Mary would be so pleased, and yet Emma was startled and strangely unnerved by seeing it here.

Alex looked closely at the painting standing right by her side, he made her look at it with new eyes. He explaining the details pointing to the wild flowers and brambles in the foreground, they were so realistic you could almost touch them. The colour was luminously transparent with the sunlight emanating from the sheep's woolly coats and reflecting light right out from the canvas.

"This painting is very similar to the painting Strayed Sheep, by Holman Hunt which is why I love it." He said with a wistful look in his eye. She was having an art class by his side, he was so knowledgeable about fine art, like Stefan he knew artistic genius when he saw it. He told her about the study of nature and myths, Emma was appreciating the painting in a whole new way.

He was such good company and so interesting to talk to, she knew her time was so short she wished that she lived nearer, so that she could be in his presence more often.

The butler announced that their dinner was served in the dining room! Alex took her hand leading the way, they passed a large Dutch display cabinet full with numerous polo trophies. It was obvious that his mainly Etonian players in the team were very capable, as the trophies covered two shelves, with many silver cups of various sizes. There were photographs covering the walls of his polo team in winning action.

"After dinner you must show me these photos in more detail. You're team look superb in the team colours," Emma said noticing that there was a large photo of Alex and Stefan together. Alex pulled out a chair for her to take a seat at the long dining table.

The chefs first course was served immediately by the butler, they were both hungry and enjoyed the delicious spread before them. When the meal was finished Alex took pride in showing Emma the photographs on the walls of the room in more detail, an elegant bureau was covered with smaller silver framed photographs of all the horses he had owned over the years. Emma was very impressed he was obviously a good rider, going horse riding was the one thing that she had always wanted to do, but had never had the opportunity she told him.

"We must make time to go riding." Alex said

"I would love to teach you how to ride you can be my pupil, it will be great fun you'll see, it will be my greatest pleasure to teach you."

"Really that would be amazing." Emma replied thinking that she must be the luckiest woman alive, he was so dashing and gallant in an traditional way. His Russian ancestry showed his regal upbringing he was kind and thoughtful. Her mind was whirring with wonderful thoughts of them galloping through parks together, she could not help herself she was falling for him, as any female would. He had a charming way with him she found mesmerizing.

"I noticed there is a lovely picture of you and Stefan, when was this photo taken?" She asked pointing it out.

"Oh yes that's a nice one, must be many years ago just before Stefan went to New York to attend college. It was the last polo match we played in together, we were good friends, he was a good player in more ways than one! If you know what I mean. He was always popular with the ladies. We haven't seen each other since then, this photo was taken when I came to the manor and met Lady Mary."

Emma could have kept quiet, when he mentioned that Stefan was a player, but felt she wanted to set the record straight about her own recent relationship with Stefan. She was fully aware it might burst the romantic bubble they were in, but she thought it was better he knew.

"I suppose I should come clean with you. When

Stefan came back to England, he told me that his marriage to Becky was over. I'm sorry to say that we did have a sexual fling, it was not until Becky his wife turned up unexpectedly that it ended. He had previously told me that they were separated, no longer a couple. But then suddenly they were going to try again to save their marriage, I was surprised but I knew I had been fooled by him, it just made me feel awful!"

Alex looked at her with an awkward grin.

"I know exactly how deviously well my friend played women. So I'm not going to blame you for getting involved with him. Even an angel could get her wings scorched with Stefan, he is such a performer there are a lot of skeletons in his cupboard!" He said with a grin.

"I understand why you wanted me to know. I'm glad you told me, we all have a past. I'm sure we have both done stupid things." Emma felt instant relief, that he was not annoyed at her, she was only human after all.

They eventually retired back into the living room, taking their champagne with them, they carried on talking well into the night there was so much to discuss as Emma told Alex about the missing bank transfer and the ensuing panic it had caused her. Stefan had let her down at a crucial time, Emma explained that Lady Mary had saved the day providing her last remaining savings. Adding she was also in the process of selling her jewel collection, to further increase her savings with her pension.

Alex decided to be direct with her and asked why there was a problem with the bank transfer from New York. Knowing that Stefan had secured a senior position now at the Auction House, he was surprised at Emma's answer about Stefan's gambling debts. The evening had flown past, Emma suddenly saw the time, it was past one o clock in the morning, she would be so late getting back to Sussex.

Alex wanted her to stay the night but did not want to give her the wrong impression, or act too forward. Especially as she had been honest with him about her dalliance with Stefan. He asked her if she would like to stay in one of the spare rooms.

"I would love to show you around my workshop tomorrow. If you do not have to rush back to Sussex." It was such a tempting idea, they were enjoying each other's company so much that Emma considered the offer, she had no pressing reason to go back to Sussex. The builders had been laid off for now, Becky had gone to Paris, and she would be all alone.

"Yes Alex, I would like to stay, if you're absolutely sure that I will not be in the way!"

It was out of character for her to make such a rash, on the spot decision, but as an Aquarian she had an impulsive side. Which was coming out in the most exciting way imaginable.

CHAPTER 14

The next day was a cloudy Sunday morning with a fine drizzle of rain as Emma awoke, pulling open the heavy drapes in the spare room. She watched the rivulets of water channelling down the window pane overlooking the main street. The traffic was heavy as usual, busy with people rushing around making their way about in the drizzling rain.

She was glad to be back right in the heart of London the steady pulse of cars was a reassuring beat, she had missed the buzzing haste of the city. After having been in the quiet countryside of the South Downs, for the past few weeks. It was a welcome break from the pressure of setting up the business, with the myriad of spread sheets. She needed to relax, it was time-out and came as such a relief.

It was a pleasant change for her and stimulating to be back in the centre of the city again. Alex had said last night he wanted to show her his showroom in Hatton Garden. She knew nothing about jewels but was fascinated to see his family's jewellery business. He was so passionate about the company it had become his main focus, he made it sound so interesting.

Emma had a shower in the en-suite bathroom dressed again in the blue trousers and blouse she had worn the evening before. She made her way downstairs to find Alex, she found him arranging breakfast in the kitchen.

"Hello Emma good morning, I usually just have cereal and fruit in the morning, with some coffee is that ok for you?"

"Yes that's fine, I don't want to put you to any trouble."

"I try to fend for myself in the mornings, as much as possible." He said, taking care to butter some toast before it burnt. Alex explained that the chef was employed only for special occasions, and was not part of the permanent staff. Adding that his trusted butler was in charge of his household maintenance, and also supervised the cleaners, who were employed in the afternoons.

After having breakfast they both left in the chauffeur driven Bentley for Alex's showroom, Hatton Garden was not far away. The premises was closed to the general public on Sunday's, but open for private appointments. Arriving at his exclusive showroom, Emma was dazzled by the halogen lights brilliantly highlighting the stunning Russian centre piece displayed in the front window.

There in pride of place was an ornate Russian crown, with antique religious triptych pictures on either side in heavy gold frames. The vivid colours shone out as bright lights shimmered their splendour, below the crown were golden domed boxes looking like Faberge eggs, containing diamond rings and bracelets in gold and red velvet boxes. The sumptuous display was so striking and different it caused a stir in the crowd of tourists jostling to get a view of the unique jewellery display.

Fine diamond shops, and select showrooms lined both sides of the street in Hatton Garden, but Alex's showroom shone out like a star on the street. It was a part of London Emma did not know well, there were fine jewellery shops, pawn shops, plus safety deposits where the workshops and the rich stored their exclusive small possessions.

Emma was enthralled with the unexpected pleasure of viewing Count Alexander's world. Alex took great pride in showing Emma around his showroom, his small workshops and office above the retail area.

Walking around the inside of the sales area he showed her the display cases, they were filled with exotic gold items for sale. Many of the items on display were original second hand Russian jewels, selling at a realistic price.

"These jewels are mainly sought after by our wealthy clients who want quality items, as well as unusual antique jewellery." He said.

"Most items are unique bespoke pieces, set with diamonds and semi precious stones." Emma was amazed at the wide variety of multi coloured gem stones of all sizes.

Emma was fascinated by the exhibits so elegantly displayed, she had never really appreciated the skills involved in creating such beauty. Later Alex lead Emma upstairs to see the tiny workshops, where an experienced lapidary graded and sifted the newly cut gem stones, carefully matching colours while a jeweller was setting these stones by hand into their mounts fixed onto wax posts. Each diamond ring was carefully expertly worked on, above their leather aprons on the wooden work benches.

She watched over them silently for a long time, their fine nosed tweezers delicately holding each diamond steady, inserting each one carefully into the open settings, cupping each diamond with precision. Placing diamonds carefully into platinum and gold, then closing and filing the claws.

Alex then lead Emma to his office, pulling out from his desk draw some fine detailed ink drawings, of the rings he had designed himself. Emma was astonished that the drawings were painted by him, he was obviously very talented at designing jewellery. Advising her that he had been taught mainly by his father, plus a stint at art school.

He told Emma that his father had set up the original jewellery shop in Hatton Garden many years ago. Revealing to Emma that his family moved to London from Paris after the dissolution of the Soviet Union. Alex had taken the shop over from him when he retired a few years later. Explaining he was proudly carrying on the family tradition. Emma then followed him into the back of his office, noticing a certificate above his desk, Alex was a Gemmologist as well as a designer. She now knew there were no ends to his talents, he was certainly clever.

She was so impressed by him, he had so many talents he had hidden from her until now, she understood clearly how focused he was about the business. Every facet of the jewellery trade was under his command.

Emma was truly inspired by him as she sat listening in awe at his skills in business. Alex explaining in detail how the manufacturing process gave him an edge in the trade, he could supply other jewellers with his unique online designs. He had contracts with many jewellery houses to supply them mainly diamond rings on an approval basis. It meant no up-front payments but after six months any returns not sold would be exchanged for brand new designs. It kept his work shop fully operational at all times not just seasonal, he had thought carefully how to have a unique selling point that had given his business enormous potential for growth.

"I have an idea." Said Alex. "If you find the jewellery interesting we should go to the Tower of London tomorrow, to look at the crown jewels, or to the V & A Museum." Alex was eager for Emma to stay a few more days, he enjoyed her company. He was hoping she was in no hurry to go back to Sussex.

"That sounds a good idea, but I will have to think more about it. Time is short at the moment, and I have no extra clothing. " She said.

Her mind was whirring with the opportunities he had grasped with both hands. His progress in expanding his family business had given her food for thought. The more she was with him the more inspired she was, hoping that some of his spark for business would help reignite her plans.

Emma was learning a great deal from her time spent with Alex, she was forming new ideas of how their business paths might cross with her own plans at Wychfield. One door had been firmly shut with another financial deadline looming. Yet as one window of opportunity closed, the imminent crisis just spurred her on, other possibilities were opening up in her mind.

Alex was keen to show Emma his most prized possession, something extra special that he had been working on with his jobbing jewellers. The piece was now finished making it the shining star of his collection.

While they were chatting he went to the large safe in the far corner of his office, carefully lifting out a diamond and ruby choker. Alex explained.

"The pigeons blood ruby and diamond necklace was made especially to be debuted at the Russian Summer Ball, held at the Whitehall Palace in London." The choker had been made on loan for Princess Dimitri of Russia who is guest of honour at the Ball. Alex allowed Emma to try it on, she stood transfixed looking at her reflection in the mirror and was instantly in awe of the collars beauty.

"Alex it is truly magnificent, I can see why it was made to be worn by a princess, have you designed it yourself?" She asked.

" Yes it is my design." Then he surprised her.

"I would be honoured if you could accompany me." Taking her hand gently in his, he continued to gaze into her eyes. Emma was instantly stuck dumb, by his suggestion.

"It will be a spectacular Ball I would like you to be with me, the Ball will be overflowing with old Russian charm, I'm sure you would enjoy."

Emma was elated hearing about the Ball, she had had such a good time at Arundel Castle. The invitation was something she was unable to resist, the offer to go with him next week was too good to say no.

"I would love to go with you it sounds magical, the only problem is, what am I going to wear? I have absolutely nothing suitable."

"Don't worry you can go shopping, I will see to it that you find something in the Kensington stores, I can arrange a personal shopper that I know to help you find something that is suitable." Alex had many Russian friends in his social circles in London who attended the Ball every year, they would advise her exactly what style of gown she should wear.

So it was agreed, Emma would stay in London until then, she could easily go shopping for extra clothes and find a suitable gown for the Ball.

Shopping for further clothes was easy, Alex arranged a shopping assistant from a leading department store to delivered to the house. All the items Emma had put on her list including a selection of clothes for day wear, evening outfits to mix and match. Emma felt privileged having space to try things on, giving Alex a fashion show to help choose suitable clothing. Her bohemian retro dress sense she had worn over the years was now firmly in the past. Becky had helped her to refine her style of clothing, and with the help of a very smart personal shopper she was now transformed completely.

Her evening gown for the ball was a different matter, now that she had a more sophisticated taste, she looked forward in going herself to choose a gown. After taking advice from Alex's Russian friends who were happy to be of assistance.

Emma's bank balance had taken a nose dive lately it had been at zero recently, however Lady Mary hearing of her plight with what had happened regarding Stefan's gambling habit, could not bear to see Emma penniless. She had increased extra funds to go into Emma's account, determined to help her out in the short term. Emma thanked her for stepping in to help her financially, knowing her aunt's finances were also in a precarious state Emma vowed to repay her in due time.

Resolute in getting back in control of the finances at the manor. Emma and Lady Mary had both given their last savings to be put into the business account to satisfy the bankers. They both knew the bank was ready to pounce if they defaulted on any payments.

There was no need for Emma to go back to the manor immediately, she had already contacted the bank to arrange the next payment which was due at the end of the month. To give her a breathing space she had re arranged the payment schedules until she had regained a firm plan of action. This was her first chance to have a break since she had arrived at Lady Mary's manor house. She would not feel guilty deciding to make the best of the opportunity, Alex was turning out to be a real friend and confidant.

The day at Hatton Garden was such an eye opener into a different kind of business. Emma had really seen how the wealthy shopped, she rarely wore jewellery as she had never had the right occasion to wear anything exclusive or expensive. During the visit to the showroom she had a chance to try on jewellery that she could not afford, it was exhilarating to see how the rich women had such opulent taste.

Alex took Emma out in the evening to The Ivy for a meal to make the day extra special for her. They had both enjoyed their day so much, they had not stopped talking. It was a genuine interest that they shared in each other's business, Emma was starting to be more open about her plans for the manor and estate, to help Lady Mary get back on her own feet. She felt at ease talking to Alex, he was so experienced at making a business work, he gave her good feedback on her plans. He was pleasantly surprised at her variety of ideas, she was putting her business degree to good use.

As the meal progressed to the dessert selection and while they were having coffee, Emma confided in Alex why Stefan was no longer part of her business future. He sensed that she had major problems at the manor with her new emerging business. Understanding why she felt that Stefan could no longer be connected to the business, or have any part in the loop, Alex was intrigued to know why. It was then that Emma told Alex about Stefan's bad gambling addiction, talking to him about how he was tackling his problem head on. She explained he had dropped the bombshell that the money raised for the painting which Alex now owned, had been lost at the gaming tables at Las Vegas.

At least Stefan was now seeking professional help, he was having counselling in New York. But knew it would take some time to overcome the addiction that had taken hold of him so easily, Emma said she could not blame him for what happened. But it had left her in a dire financial situation with no immediately way out, she was genuinely worried for her business plans. The bank and builders were expecting funds to be paid soon, admitting that she had been waiting on the money from the art auction which was now never going to materialise.

He could see through her mask at how distraught she really was, she had tried to hide her feelings from him, however he could sense there was something very wrong. Her pretend smile was saying "it is alright," was covering her true despair, she had come so far and had been so sure of success, Stefan had pulled the rug right from under her feet. It may have been a reaction to the alcohol they drank at dinner or her cosy chat with Alex.

As he watched her closely telling him, he saw large tears emerging on the lower rim of her pink eyes. He put out his hand to steady her.

"It will be OK let me help you." Alex said squeezing her hand in a reassuring gesture.

Emma looked back at him with eyes overflowing with tears of emotions.

"I'm sorry to cause such a scene, we have had such a lovely day now I have spoilt it." She said annoyed with herself.

"No don't worry," he replied softly.

"I could tell there was something that you were worried about, I'm glad you told me." There was no way Emma could lean on Alex, she had to stand on her own two feet. However he was adamant in wanting to help her.

"I have a suggestion, something that could help you in the short term." Alex said suddenly, remembering their conversation the night before regarding his polo trophies. It was something in the back of his mind regarding the Polo Club that he had mentioned briefly before.

Emma dried her moist eyes with the napkin embarrassed by her show of weakness, she would not forget his kindness to her when she had faltered. Her business meant everything to her it defined who she was as a strong person. She wanted to make good her promise to Lady Mary, to undo the financial damage her father had inflicted. During her conversations with Alex she had come clean about her reason for making the business at the manor work, and why it was so important to her not to fail.

He was steadfast in his reaction in wanting to help

her, he saw in Emma a strength not to give in, it was her resolve to make a success that had endeared him to her. Emma was no weakling, she had business skills that she desperately wanted to use, he was sure he could help her succeed. Taking her damp napkin hand again in his, he spoke softly to her.

"You said to me before that your idea was to have multiple streams of income at Wychfield manor." Alex explained slowly taking his time to outline his idea.

"What if my polo ponies could be based at the manor stables? I would be able to pay you upfront for their livery and move the horses soon if you agreed." He peered at her closely to gauge her expression.

"Exactly how many horses do you have?" She asked thinking ahead to see how it would work out.

"Nine horses at present but my polo club may also have horses that would appreciate additional land to exercise their horses."

Emma agreed that she could make use of the stables and grazing land that was available. She had a few stables, but not nearly enough to house all of the horses, however there was plenty of land suitable with extra fields to exercise the horses.

"It sounds like a good plan, but I will need additional stables built." She replied, hoping that they could come to some sort of arrangement knowing that his contacts at the local polo club, could help her with advice.

Alex responded positively.

"Don't worry Emma, I have many Russian oligarch contacts interested in polo who would be happy to assist both of us. I am willing to fund the next phase of building work for you, and to help install more stables on the estate. In return if you can look after my string of polo ponies we can call it a deal. Shall we say two million pounds up front."

She was relieved beyond words, it would solve her immediate problem and take the stress off her, as she was so scared of what could have been a total disaster. Alex had turned the problem around for her, she felt as though she could breathe again. He had been so supportive and kind, it seemed that their chance meeting at the castle was meant to be.

Try as she might her thoughts kept coming back to her childhood sweetheart Stefan, he had tormented her dreams day and night over many years. They had developed a deep sexual chemistry between them, his rampant masculinity had become totally intoxicating, yet her heart had been broken by him.

Count Alexander was so different he had a gentle and quiet gothic allure, he was an irresistible force she found exhilarating especially when he invaded her space. He only had to look at her with his black eyes to make her swoon. She had never met anyone quite like him before, her intuition told her he had a dark side! There was no real comparison, between a player and a charmer, or was there?

Now she was even more confused, sex had never been enough, not for Emma she wanted more, much more, a real relationship and companion. It dawned on her perhaps men needed something superficial, just sex with no strings. Sadly she had always required more than any man was willing to give. She was looking for a real love, a soul mate, someone to take away her feeling of loneliness.

CHAPTER 15

When they were back at Alex's house in Kensington, Emma felt more at ease with her situation, she was bursting with optimism. Alex was doing everything he could to make her happy, willing to help her to ease her immediate financial problems. It was her dream come true, she was so happy to have the weight of the world lifted temporarily from her shoulders.

They settled back in to the sumptuous living room, Emma had agreed to stay until after the Russian Ball, to give herself a much needed break. Having a nightcap before retiring for the evening, Emma could not stop herself falling for him. As they sat together, she became bolder reaching out her arms for him to be enclosed in her embrace, Alex was just as happy to be wanted by her. Now she was ready and able to take their relationship to the next level, if that was what he desired. It had come as a complete surprise that someone as handsome and impressive as Alex, with his noble heritage should be interested in her, all her romantic wishes seemed to be coming true at last.

Alex was surprised at her passionate embrace, he usually distanced himself as the perfect gentleman, but something had changed between them she was like an irresistible force of nature. This time he held her closer placing his kisses firmly, deeper more passionate than ever before on her moist lips, his tongue pushed longingly into her mouth. He had waited so long to taste her, waiting patiently for her to be ready for him. Emma was everything he wanted in a woman; to him she was flawless like a perfect diamond. Stefan had been an egotistic fool to ever let her go, she was a strong single-minded woman, he was attracted to her steadfast determination, with her spirited passion for life as well as business.

The time was right for Emma she was ready to surrender herself to him, after her previous heart break, it was time for her to trust again. Alex's previous reserve in holding back his strong feelings was an aphrodisiac for her, his tenderness had aroused an enthusiasm she could no longer suppress. He was a nobleman, and careful not to take advantage of her, which she found enchanting plus tempting.

Stefan had been his exact opposite, grasping and conniving he had used her in the most cruel way and laughed at her expense, she would never forget the humiliation. Feeling that she was partly to blame because he was after all married. Emma was now taking the lead, to let Alex know that he was the right man for her, there was no doubt in her mind, she had fallen for his gentle temperament. She had tried to move slowly in this new relationship, but now it was time for them both to let go of any fear before the night was over, there was nothing to be scared of.

Alex led reserved Emma up the marble staircase to his luxurious dimly lit bedroom, he slipped off her clothing until she was in her silk underwear. Laying her down on his bed her shyness apparent, he teased off her bra, and peeled down her black silky French knickers, until she was finally naked awaiting his attention.

He was eager to take her nervousness away, boldly taking her in his arms to sooth her worries. Alex then undressed himself eagerly, he could not take his eyes off her naked form, stripped of his trousers and shirt he took a long sultry look at her unadorned splendour.

Emma felt a little self-conscious as his dark eyes slowly scanned her body until he reached her hazel eyes, kissing her lashes as they closed. She was blushing pink with anticipation yet not afraid, her fair hair was softly fanned out across the bed cover, she felt beautiful and desired. He could sense her hunger for him as he nuzzled into her neck, kissing every inch of her shoulders down to her white breasts, teasing her with his lips sucking gently at her nipples. She was aroused as never before, his hands strayed over her breasts down to sooth her mound, cupping her with his hands letting his fingers stray, teasing with his gentle touch tenderly stirring her. Emma held him firmly caressing and stroking, pleasing him until he became erect ready to make love to her.

Then slowly with sexual stimulation he tenderly surrendered to the moment until they could hold out no longer, as their taut bodies could stand no more their desire became too intense to hold back. Several times they explored each other, searching out each inch of their bodies, savouring every silky touch. Alex was a magical sensual partner, caring for her every desire, not stopping until all her needs were satisfied, until the early hours of the morning.

When they awoke Emma was nestled inside his strong arms, she felt the warmth of their naked bodies as they spooned together in the cool silk sheets. She tried to move to get out of bed without waking him, but she could feel that he was already aroused there was no way he was going to let her go. He slowly awakened grasping her from behind, Emma was a willing subject, whilst he manipulating her with his fingers and tenderly kissed her back, stoking her gently between her legs. It was ecstasy Emma was in heaven waiting for him to slip inside her, his motion increased as his body tensed again. Alex was fully alive and hard in the vital moment as his penis fully extended reached her pleasure zone stiff with yearning.

Their day had started as it meant to go on, Emma adored him, his body was softer and more tender than Stefan's muscular toned physique. Yet her body was taut and aching, with their full-on gyrating night of pleasure. But she now knew she was fully prepared for the consequences of exhaustion later.

Her life had turned out better than she could ever have dreamt of; the man of her dreams was a reality. Alex was happier than he had ever been, he was finding it hard to suppress his feelings for Emma, she was a unique woman like no other. He found her fascinating fully aware she had tried everything to save Wychfield. He saw her resolute dedication, she had a clear focus on completing the task, it was a mirror of his own working life. She had a strength of character as fierce as a lion, she would not let anything stop her success, she was determined and would follow her vision until completion, he understood her self-discipline.

The day progressed at a slow pace, they were enjoying some time off together, walking to a local café for a leisurely breakfast. Emma was in no hurry to get back to the manor, Alex had made her feel so at home again in London, she was conscious of what she had missed about the bustling city.

In the afternoon she was able to go shopping properly on her own as Alex went back to his office in Hatton Garden. She was concerned about getting the right gown for the ball, she only had a few days to find the right dress for the special evening.

The personal shopper had suggested a few exclusive shops in the area, where she could find the correct gown. Emma had looked on line at photographs of the Summer Ball from previous years so knew the style of dress to wear for the event, knowing how significant the ball was for Alex.

He had told her it was the highlight of the summer calendar in London, all of his best friends would be there. She was told to expect Russian royalty mingling with ultra rich Russian oligarchs. It was important that she created the right impression for Alex, she would not want to let him down.

Her number one shop mentioned by the personal shopper proved to be the best, it was an exclusive couture showroom in Kensington. A selection of the most exquisite designer gowns were on show. She was thrilled to have the opportunity to try on the unique dresses which were displayed on slender manikins throughout the show room.

Emma was looking for something outstanding to show off her new shapely figure, she had worked so hard at getting fit, having spent so long working out in leotards. All of her hard work had now paid off giving her the chance to shine.

There was one gown that caught her eye instantly, it was a full length peacock blue gown, embellished with tiny shimmering white and pale blue crystals hand sewn onto a tight fitted bodice, the off the shoulder style was elegant. The full plain long skirt was blue satin with silk petticoats which swished when she walked out of the fitting room through to the store, looking at herself in the huge mirror wall. It was the most divine gown fit for royalty, Emma was told by the store proprietor that it was an exclusive dress from Paris. It was an exceptional gown, expensive but worth every penny, it fitted Emma's trim waist like a glove it was the most beautiful dress she had ever seen, it was meant for her.

Now she could look for the accessories with elegant silver high heeled court shoes to complete the look, the rest of the day was a absolute whirlwind of shopping in the fashionable stores in London. Alex had insisted she send him the bill, it was going to be his treat for her.

Emma booked an appointment at a beauty salon to have her hair and makeup professionally done on the day of the ball. Then she headed by taxi to meet Alex for dinner at the Ivy, she was exhausted but excited to tell him all about her wonderful but tiring day.

During their lengthy dinner date Alex and Emma came to a financial agreement, regarding the polo livery contract. Alex explained that she would be doing him an enormous favour, he trusted her to make it happen. She happily agreed as they shook hands on the deal, with a signed contract to follow.

The next day Emma was determined to get to grips with her new revised business plan, she had let things slide for too long. She began the day by phoning the builder, he was pleased to hear back from her saying that the building work at the manor could re commence whenever she wanted. He did stress sooner rather than later, as the small job his workers were on was coming to an end. He told her he would take charge of ordering the men back to work while she was still in London if she wanted. Emma was desperate to get the new kitchen completed in the barn, the builders foreman was very competent, she agreed he could take charge until she returned which was a great relief.

Emma had kept in close contact by phone to Lady Mary who was making good progress at her convalescent home. Emma kept her up to date with every step of the building progress, she explained how much more cheerful she had become, thanks to Alex. Telling her how he had stepped in to help fund the next stage of the project, advising she was ready to expand the stabling facilities for his ponies.

As they talked Emma could see Lady Mary was happy at last, she seemed in no hurry to get back to the manor. Lady Mary had formed a new circle of friends at the home, and was eager to tell Emma all about her new life there. They spent an hour discussing their future plans to save the manor; both agreed that things had turned out in their favour, things were looking up at last.

The main benefit was that Lady Mary was no longer alone, she had made some friends her own age. Life was looking up for her, the sadness of the past the hoarding, and loneliness she had experienced seemed like years ago. During their conversation it became obvious to Emma that Lady Mary had found a perfect solution to the problem of her depression, and emotional problems.

She seemed much brighter and happier in herself, she explained to Emma that a nurse had found a nice independent living care home nearby, where she could have the community that she needed. It was a fair trade off considering how much better Lady Mary felt about her future she was so happy when she viewed the care home. She had signed to move into the home permanently within the next month.

It was obvious to both of them that Stefan was busy fighting his demons, he was seeing the addiction councillor in New York. He would not be coming back to England. Emma then mentioned that Becky was going on a round of auditions in Paris and would let her know when she had found the right position.

Then the conversation again returned to the building progress, Lady Mary asked Emma if she could cope alone with the business, now that Stefan was back working permanently in New York. Emma had to admit that she was quite ok with being alone now, she had Count Alexander to lean on.

Telling Lady Mary of their plans to expand the equine facilities in the grounds behind the barn. Admitting how much he had helped her financially by offering to pay in advance for her livery yard. She had been in a tight spot, he had not held back or hesitated to assist her he had turned out to be a good friend.

Lady Mary then surprised Emma.

"I do appreciate your inner strength of character in setting up the business, I know it is an enormous task to save the estate from bankruptcy." She then shocked Emma.

"My will has been completely changed and updated, I move into the care home soon. You are now the main beneficiary of the Wychfield estate. Because of your enormous efforts to put right your father's wrongs."

She knew that her adopted son Stefan would be annoyed, however she would not change her mind. Because of to his gambling problems, she was reluctant to give him the reins. Knowing that It could further increase his gambling addiction, and in view of his senior job at the auction house. He now had a secure future, if he was careful with his considerable salary as a Director.

Emma appreciated what her aunt said about the inheritance, knowing that they both dearly loved the manor. To give the estate to Emma seemed like a natural choice for Lady Mary, setting up the business was a real challenge, but would be worth the effort in the long term. It was agreed that Stefan would need to know soon about the changes to the will, so that he could come to terms with the result of Lady Mary's decision. Emma just hoped he would not go off like a ballistic missile on her, she was immensely scared to talk to him, but it had to be done.

An email was sent from Emma to Stefan in New York asking him to call her urgently, Emma knew he must be told quickly, to be fair to him. She wanted to tell him herself over the phone, he could then confirm the news of the will with Lady Mary. If he wanted confirmation from her while she was in convalescence.

The next few hours were busy, Emma spent time catching up with suppliers, checking delivery dates, and going over her accounts, logging onto Alex's computer while he was at work.

The call she was dreading arrived, her mobile phone rang it was Stefan, she managed to calmly tell him of her conversation with Lady Mary. Explaining to him that her aunt's will had been changed, detailing exactly why it had been necessary. She was waiting for him to explode about the changes. But he understood the reasons why, and said.

"I have no problem with it!" Emma could not help letting out a sigh of relief.

"In fact I have no plans to come back to Sussex to live, so it was probably a blessing. I think if you had not arrived when you did we would have a bankruptcy on our hands!" Knowing the house and estate would have been on the verge of insolvency, if it had not been for Emma's timely intervention. They had both been broke for the first time in their lives, however they were not poor. Stefan had to admit that to Emma.

"You are the one person who can save the economic situation. You have done everything for the right reasons, I do trust your instincts and intuition."

"Thank you Stefan, I thought you might be angry with me, but honestly I had no hand in changing the will."

It was at this moment Emma thought he might change his mind, if he knew she read tarot cards regularly, or that astrology and reading her horoscope was an obsession. Hopefully he would never know her dark secret, she would keep it firmly under wraps.

This big moment for Emma's life was pivotal, she was now free to start the business without the fear of interference from afar. Stefan's life was settled in a different sphere, he was content to mould his own life in New York, doing what he loved. He was a flawed personality with his addiction to gambling. But Emma wanted him to find his own level of happiness, he had to work his own problems, having to rid himself of his demons.

His character was arrogant and disturbing, but she knew he just had human failings, just like everyone else. She still had a soft spot for him in spite of his flaws, he would always have a special place in her heart from when they were young.

He wanted Lady Mary to find her own peace of mind and was aware how loneliness had affected her. He hoped she would be able to live the rest of her life with company of her own age around her. If Stefan had inherited Wychfield the pressure and upkeep of the estate would have been too much for him and might tip his gambling over the edge.

Stefan knew with his gambling addiction it would make a strong temptation to sell the estate, and gamble with the proceeds, it would be his worst nightmare. He was glad that she was willing to sacrifice her future to save the manor. It seemed right for her to make a business work, which could set her up for life. He knew she had the ability and drive to complete the task started, he admired her courage and did not blame her for Lady Mary making the decision to change her will.

He was just beginning to realise just how truly extraordinary Emma was. Stefan began to wonder, if his wife hadn't turned up when she had. Would things have been different for them, could Emma be the right one for him? The seed had been sown in his mind! It would germinate, and grow to haunt his long nights, when he would dream passionately of Emma.

CHAPTER 16

When Emma and Alex awoke in his king size bed the next morning, it was obvious that she was on an unwavering mission to fulfil her wish to conclude the business at the manor. She was so excited and bubbly with renewed enthusiasm, they sat in bed talking eagerly about her additional plans, thanks to Alex. He was happy that he had played his own small part in her future. He felt confident in her abilities to turn the business into a roaring success.

Emma was aware she had not mentioned to Stefan that she had met his old friend Count Alexander. Careful not to mention their developing romance, or his help securing new finance for her plans. It did cross her mind that she should have told Stefan everything, but for some reason she was reluctant to tell him. Alex was her dark knight, her knight of swords in the tarot deck, he had been showing up with the lovers card constantly in her recent readings.

Determined to enjoy the city Emma said she would like to visit the Victoria and Albert Museum. Alex had sparked an interest in her for antique jewellery, he luckily had some spare time so agreed to show her around the museum, until he went to a business meeting later in the afternoon.

She was conscious that he had his own successful jewellers to run, aware she could not take up too much of his time. Alex was enjoying their time together so made an effort to be with her as much as his business allowed.

However he was in the process of getting ready for a trade fair later in the year, where he would show case his new collection of designs to the worldwide buyers. Manufacturing was a big part of his family's achievements. Alex later suggested using photographs of the manor house as a backdrop in his promotions.

Viewing the jewellery at the museum Emma realised the wealth of knowledge Alex had about Russian jewels. They spent many hours viewing the intricate items on display, she leant from him all about the history of the house of Faberge. Her interest in his business was spiked, Alex was making her aware of how he had found a real passion for jewels, and their history.

Later they met up for dinner at an exclusive restaurant overlooking the Thames. They were both looking forward to the Russian Ball the next evening, it would be the highlight of Emma's short stay in London.

The next morning was a glorious sunny day with light streaming in through the open bedroom curtains. Emma stretched out to place her arm around sleepy Alex holding him close. They were becoming inseparable as they cradled each other's bodies, nestling together in their warm silky nest. It was a haven from the troubles and stress in the world, they were content in each other's caress satisfied to just be together, lingering quietly for a few more minutes before waking as the day began.

"I know it will be a wonderful event tonight, I'm so looking forward to the ball." Emma said, as Alex lay in a comfortable slumber stretched out in bed beside her. She had not had an opportunity to go anywhere as splendid as the grand Russian Ball in London. It was an exciting prospect a chance to mingle with Russian aristocracy, she was well aware of the amount of wealthy Russian residing in London, although she had had not had an opportunity to meet them before.

"I'm looking forward to seeing the gown you bought for tonight." Alex replied.

"I bet you will look sensational."

He was proving to be so supportive of her, he could not hide his attraction to her, which was a real surprise to Emma. She was glad now that she had taken more care of herself recently, losing the extra weight and making an extra effort with her grooming had been a real bonus. The pounds of extra weight had been lost easily with her new fitness regime, it was thanks to Becky's determination and her strict healthy diet that she was seeing real results so quickly.

In the past her weight had held her back, Emma had felt so self conscious, not wanting to be seen naked or even in underwear. She was so different now, Alex had made her feel so special, he loved her figure the trim waist accentuating her curved breasts. He made sure she felt confident in his embrace. She had become a goddess for the first time in her life, determined her light would shine brightly tonight at the ball, she was determined not to disappoint him, she wanted to make him proud.

Alex was going to Hatton Garden to work in the

morning, giving Emma a chance to go to the highly recommended beauty salon in Knightsbridge. They were going to have a dinner at the Summer Ball, so we're meeting up at home in time for Alex to shower and change before leaving. As she kissed him goodbye at the front door her butterflies were building, it was the most exciting day she could ever remember.

Glad she had decided on having a total makeover at the salon a layered cut, colour and new style. She wanted to be totally transformed for the evening. Dashing to the salon, she grabbed a take away coffee at the local café, there was no time to stop for breakfast. It was her first formal date with Alex, where she would be introduced to his London friends. Daunted yet unafraid of the prospect of meeting them, she was ready to be pampered.

Her hair was layer cut and highlighted, ready to be put up in a French chignon style with some loose curls. Her facial had been done at home the day before, so when her hair was completed it was time for a makeup artist to apply the finishing touches. When Emma saw her hairstyle in the mirror she was so pleased it was chic and fresh.

With minimal make up her appearance was completed, finishing touches of a crystal and pearl clip that secured her French hairdo, allowing soft curls to fall around her jaw line. The total effect was understated elegance, which was exactly what Emma had hoped for.

Alex arrived home just in time as Emma was arriving back from the salon, her hair and makeup had taken most of the day, she was quite euphoric. Knowing she had no jewellery apart from her pearl earrings and watch, he had brought her something special to wear for the ball from his new collection, he took delight in was teasing her about his surprise.

"You will have to wait, to know what it was!"

Alex was taking a shower while Emma poured glasses of champagne. Emma showered carefully making sure not to disturb her professional make up, putting on a dressing gown sitting on his bed pausing to sip the cool champagne. Alex was so appealing in his dark mysterious way, he sat beside her in his boxer shorts. Stretching over her grabbing at his jacket hanging on the chair, he took a large expensive looking black velvet box out of his inside jacket pocket.

With the box firmly in his grasp he turned to Emma.

"I have been saving this for you to wear tonight, to complete your outfit." Handing her the box to open. It was embossed with Alex's Russian coat of arms, that she had seen before on a plaque above his showroom.

She knew immediately that whatever was inside would be expensive, and unique. Emma gasped with delight when she opened the lid. Inside was an intricate necklace set with diamonds, with small seed pearls in white gold. The diamonds were set in delicate clusters of stars dropping from a central chain. It looked new and yet it was a delicate Edwardian style, exquisite in its fine detail, which complemented the celestial diamond star droplets.

Alex took the box from her holding the necklace up high into the air to catch the light from the window, and then handed it back to Emma's hand, as she smiled back at him.

"Alex it is magnificent, thank you for letting me borrow it to wear tonight. I absolutely love it, and will take care not to lose it." He leant forward to kiss her.

"I look forward to you wearing it for this evening, the necklace will complete your attire. On loan from me, for an extra special evening." She was amazed, standing at the full length mirror as he place the necklace around her neck. He stepped further behind her slipping off her dressing gown and looked at her pale nakedness.

"I chose it especially for you, it will match your pearl earrings. You see I do notice the finishing touches." He would have liked to have made love to her there and then, as her state of undress was so enticing. But time was short, they had to dress quickly to be ready in time.

Normally Emma would have felt too self conscious to be naked in front of a man but there was something different about Alex. He made her feel so alive and special he appreciated her natural curves. She perfumed her body, ready to step into her matching French lingerie. Her full length dress was hanging high off the ground on a hanger in the separate dressing room. Taking the dress out she carefully shimmied her body slowly into the gown rustling the petticoats. The bodice snugly shaped her form perfectly; tightly accentuating her waist, for the final touch Emma put on her pearl earrings to complete the ensemble, stepping into her high court shoes, matching the blue colour of the gown and purse.

Peering at her reflection in the dressing room mirror, she was astonished at how elegant she looked, the effect was eye-catching. It had taken her all day to perfect, but now she knew it was worth it.

Alex was putting on a dark Armani suit and white dress shirt, he called Emma to help him with his tie and cufflinks. He walked into her dressing room as she was finalising her appearance. He was taken completely by surprise when he saw her, dressed in her peacock blue gown she looked so serene, appearing much taller in her high heels and full skirt.

"You will be the belle of the ball; you're a magnificent creature." He guessed that all men would desire her for good reason, she was like Venus a dazzling goddess.

"I am truly proud to be with you tonight as my partner." Alex said taking the time to scan slowly every part of her attire; sure there would be no one to rival her beauty at the ball. Emma had a modest genuine beauty that shone out.

Her eyes lit up when he said the words to her, it was the effect she was hoping for, she did not want to let him down knowing it was an important event. Emma replied to him.

"The diamond necklace is the perfect finishing touch; I can't thank you enough for letting me wear it tonight." Alex took her hand delicately in his.

"I told you before; it is yours for tonight, It is worth over a million pounds, so I will be pleased to be your bodyguard." She blushed back at him unable to fathom why he would let her wear such an expensive piece of jewellery. She was realising how truly blessed she was that he had come into her life, just at the right time. Emma helped Alex to straighten his bow tie, and fit his gold cufflinks neatly into his shirt cuff; he was even more handsome than ever.

The chauffeur brought the Bentley around to the front of the house at six o clock. They arrived on time at the venue, escorted to the main entrance room, waiting to be announced to the other guests. Emma was pleased to be introduced as Count Alexander Vasiliev's partner, it made her feel very special indeed when all eyes swivelled in her direction. He was a very sought after aristocratic bachelor, the ladies were watching Emma's every move in envy. Not sure who she was, or where she had come from, they knew she was not Russian or from their social circles.

The introductions came thick and fast Alex mentioned to his friends and acquaintances that Emma was Lady Mary's niece. Which seemed to go down well, his friends were either aristocrats or rich oligarchs who bought houses in London. Alex explained the introduction to them in English, he made a point of keeping his Russian to a minimum to help Emma feel included in the conversations. He was always so correct and polite, which was one of the reasons why she was so drawn to him, apart from her obvious attraction. Champagne was flowing freely as they talked to Alex's friends, while orchestral music played in the background. The group of guests mixed and mingled with each other, in a frenzied buzz of non-stop chatter.

Then there was a striking hushed silence as another introduction was made. Pray silence for our guest of honour; Princess Volkov, she slowly entered the room as all eyes watched her approach, the men bowed low, women curtseyed as she passed them by. The Princess was wearing Alex's distinctive ruby and diamond necklace. Which he had loaned to the Princess for the evening from his jewellery showroom collection. Her jet black dress, and silver silk wrap set off the choker to perfection, she certainly created a stately impression intending to steal the show, and be in the heart of crowd. Alex leaned to Emma and whispered quietly that the name Volkov meant wolf in Russian, and that she lived up to her name. Emma was not sure what he meant by that phrase, but she was about to find out.

The princess was tall and slender with long curled raven black hair, matching her jet black ball gown. It reminding all who watched her of a prowling panther, her slow gracious walk into the room was breathtaking to watch. She glided through the room with a serenity, as all eyes watched her every move. Like a cat she surveyed the crowd of onlookers, inwardly she looked down on them with her haughty gaze. Her persona was of the elite from Russia surveying the masses of commoners, she acknowledged only the titled few that were perhaps related to her from long ago.

Like the others gathered in the ball room she saw Emma standing next to Alex and was intrigued, as to who she was not recognising her at all. Wondering what stone she had scuttled out from, as Alex stepped forward to address her in Russian, he bowed low in her presence and took her gloved hand to kiss. Emma could see clearly the attraction in the Princesses eyes as her eyes lit up instantly, as he kissed her hand slowly, she was obviously expecting his adoration of her. Alex continued talking to the Princess in Russian and turning to Emma, he then changed back to English to introduce her to the Princess as Lady Mary's niece.

The Princess's facial expression dropped immediately it was a clear indication, Emma understood that Alex had introduced her as his partner, not a paid escort. Suddenly the Princess shunned her, as though she had seen a ghost she turned abruptly, and walked away without saying a word to her. Leaving her looking bewildered as Princess Volkov stepped quickly away in obvious disgust from her.

Emma could see undoubtedly that her claws were out, She had a target on her back for sure the Princess reminded her now of a cat about to pounce on her pathetic prey.

But Emma did not know what she had done wrong, or what could have caused the Princess to walk away so suddenly, just because she was there as his partner. Was it the necklace? Had he branded her with his collar, a mark of his possession. Then she realised that there must be a history between Alex and the Princess, there was something she was clearly not aware of.

Alex had never mentioned his past relationships to Emma, she knew he was single but there was something else! Some piece of the puzzle was missing. Her intuition told her there was a giant part of information not there, she had not been told the full story of his family background. When the Princess walked away, she noticed that Alex's gaze followed her like a puppy dog. Alex watched the Princess's every move, he could not help himself, Emma felt he was mesmerized by her.

During the dinner the Princess was seated at the head of the table. Alex was next to her with Emma on his other side, it proved to be awkward. They spoke in Russian together constantly laughing animatedly, during their long in depth conversation. Emma had no idea of what they were talking about, or if they were talking about her, which made her feel completely left out.

The chitchat around the long table made Emma feel alone and withdrawn, this was not what she was expecting. The Princess made a point of talking mainly to Alex, they seemed immersed with each other's company, with such a lot to talk about.

Later in the evening the usual charity auction took place, starting with some smaller items first to get the auction under way, then it was the turn of Alex's ruby necklace as worn by the Princess. It was the main item to be auctioned off which started with a frantic set of bids. Hands were quickly raised as the Princess stood on the stage displaying the piece which spurred on a large amount of interest in the room, the necklace would have great investment potential for the Russian audience. A hectic bidding war between two leading oligarchs ensued until the gavel went firmly down, sold to the highest bidder. Emma watched in awe to see the vast sums of money changing hands at such a pace, there seemed to be no limit to the amount of currency spent during the evening.

There had been no time to talk to Alex about the Princess, she would have to be patient to find out what the history was between them. There was definitely a bond connecting them, she would find out, she was sure to get to the truth.

The orchestra played on into the night as Emma enjoyed dancing with Alex, she could only just keep in step with him as he took the lead. She could not fail to notice that the Princess was keeping a close eye on Alex. Emma danced with other men too who were eager to have a dance with her; she was amused to see such abundant wealth on display in London. The Russian women wore the most exquisite jewellery; there were diamonds, emeralds and rubies in profusion. She now understand why Alex could not fail to notice such things.

It was all part of how they lived their lives in their

opulent wealthy circles in Europe, London was like a magnet to the rich and famous from Russia. The life they lived was a rich haven away from the ordinary, poor and working classes in the former Soviet Union.

But it crossed Emma's mind to wonder what they thought as they observed the poor, and homeless living on the streets of London. It seemed that Dickensian London was not far away, but could they ignore what was around them, as they went about their everyday lives in the rich parts of the capital.

Some of the individuals had riches past down from previous generations. Many had new wealth created in their own lifetime, they enjoyed spending their money and flaunting their obvious prosperity to each other. There was no place for poverty in their lives, having a charity auction was the nearest thing to compassion, a way to show that they were at least aware of others plight. Those who had risen from humble beginnings knew how lucky they were to enjoy such a lavish event. Emma made an effort to make friends with as many people as possible, but could not penetrate the clique surrounding the reserved and frosty Princess Volkov.

The spectacular Russian Summer Ball eventually came to an end, although it was a great success, Emma was bemused as they said their goodbye's to everyone leaving the ball. The Princess was standing at the main door as the special guest of honour, she was busy saying goodbye at the exit, as everyone filed their way out of the reception doorway. Royally courteous to them both, with no show of the earlier hostility to Emma, it was as though she had forgotten she had clearly snubbed her. The correct royal protocol took precedence over her hostile feelings for Emma, as Alex was nearby.

Although Emma had enjoyed most of the evening she was intrigued to know the back story, of the friendship between Alex and the haughty Princess. She had been kept in the dark but why? She had to know!

The chauffer drove them back to Alex's Kensington home. The time was right to find out, they had a nightcap together in the sumptuous lounge, before going to bed. Curiosity had got the better of her; what had caused the Princess to snub her in such a way?

"Alex, I loved this evening it was truly special, and I want to thank you for inviting me, and for giving me a chance to wear the diamond necklace. But there is one thing that is bugging me, when you introduced the Princess to me she blanked me!" Emma said fixing her gaze right on him.

"I know you noticed it too! But why did she do that?" He knew exactly what she meant, but he was embarrassed to give a full explanation to her. He hesitated in speaking.

"It's a long story, but I will try to put it in plain words. Many years ago when I lived in Russia with my family we had a grand manor house in St Petersburg on the river embankment, near the Winter Palace." Alex sipped his glass of wine, as she listened intently to his every word.

"Our families were allied in many ways, the young Princess became a regular visitor because of our family business connections. We became the best of friends, you see the links between our families had been built up over the generations. In royal circles it was quite normal to chaperone children, so we were never left alone. It was always expected by our family that we would marry when we were older; however history has a funny way of changing everything."

Emma was fascinated to hear of another life that was steeped in old Russian history, it was another world completely, she urged him to go on with his tale. After experiencing the Summer Ball she felt she had been immersed into another dimension. Since she had known Count Alex he had opened a fascinating door into the realm of Faberge, religious icons, and a way of life few had access to.

"I was a small child when it had been agreed by our families that the Princess and I would marry. Neither of us expected it to happen in the modern world that we live in now. Since the breakup of the Soviet Union, our family lives have altered beyond recognition." Alex was explaining things in a matter of fact way, easy for Emma to understand. However she could tell there were raw emotions well hidden under the surface, more than she could have ever guessed.

"My family had business connections with many Russian Jew's in Paris and London. My father procured graded cut diamonds from Amsterdam, for the majority of the jewellery companies in Hatton Garden. When the opportunity arose for him to open a retail jewellery showroom there, it seemed an obvious decision to take. The rest is history, Princess Volkov was in college and later went to work as a historian in Moscow where she still had family, so we drifted apart quite naturally."

Emma could see how this could happen as she too had drifted apart from Stefan, when they went their separate ways to University.

Alex explained to Emma that of course they had both tried to keep in touch, but circumstances made it difficult to see each other, after a few years they were no longer in touch. So the years rolled by and their new lives took over, Alex soon settled into the family business in London with his father, his mother had died when he was a young boy living in St Petersburg. Alex studied in London to become a gemmologist, taking over the Hatton Garden business himself when his father retired and later died.

The Princess became a leading historian writing in Moscow, her focus was on the Russian aristocracy as she had insider knowledge, her books were published worldwide to great acclaim. She found that most of her family and friends in royal circles like Count Alexander, had moved abroad to start new lives.

But she never forgot their parents expectation that she and Alex would eventually marry, and although she had many male admirers, her chances of finding a suitable royal partner were diminishing while she stayed in Russia.

It was only now that she was older, she felt the need to spread her wings by living abroad herself. She had turned thirty and her biological body clock was ticking, she wanted to re kindle old friendships. She had renewed contacts recently with Russian ex pats living in London, and had met Count Alexander again through mutual friends. She was instantly smitten by his good looks, he had grown more mature and sophisticated.

As soon as she laid eyes on him again it was love at first sight, he was much taller than she remembered, his masculine physique and old world charms delighted her. It had been ten years since they had met, the Princess was delighted to hear that he had not committed himself to anyone. Alex had been far too busy keeping the business buoyant in Hatton Garden to settle down into a serious relationship.

Alex was also pleasantly surprised at the Princess's beauty when they met. As he thought back to the past, perhaps the arranged marriage could have worked after all, If their circumstances had been different. He was trying to explain things to Emma, as much as he wanted her to know, but he was careful not to tell her everything.

Emma nodded in approval, she now understood the reasons for being snubbed by the Princess. Alex was indeed a prize catch, he was the most striking man Emma had ever seen, his dark mysterious allure was certainly Prince like. She could not blame the Princess for her jealous reaction, yet it was obvious he had not told her the full truth behind the story. Would she ever know the full details? She was not at all sure!

The Princess was jealous to her core, like Red Riding Hood, Emma would need to keep her distance from the wolf.

CHAPTER 17

It was Alex who then surprised Emma with a mystery trip, arranged with his Russian friends for the following week.

"We are taking a mystery flight on a private jet, far away for a special secret weekend."

"Really how exciting." Emma said completely taken by surprise.

"When we were at the ball, you heard me talking in Russian to my friends at the dinner table, for quite a long time. It was my intent to invite them to join me on the trip. I must apologise, for seeming to be rude. It was just that I wanted to make sure everyone could come, and keep to a strict code of secrecy."

"Are you sure I am invited too?"

"Of course, you are my guest of honour." He laughed, he enjoyed seeing the expression on her face.

"I won't leave you behind." Emma's broad smile shone out from her eyes. He was too good to be true, she was wondering what was the catch?

They both went up to bed excited by the prospect of their group weekend away. Emma felt better now that he had told her of his background with the Princess, and understood the reason for privacy when he had spoken in his own language. She could now sleep without worrying, after they made love again with more passion than ever. It was a night she would remember for several reasons.

The next week went by without incident, Emma was intent on getting the builders focused on completion of the kitchen at the barn. She had called Brandon the gardener many times, he was a great character always willing to help her, repeating don't worry he would not let her down agreeing to oversee the finishing touches in her absence. It he understood the immense pressures she had been under, and realised how important it was for her to have a break away from the estate. She was giddy with excitement, all set to go on a luxury jet for the first time, with the man of her dreams.

The chauffeur drove them in the Bentley from Kensington to small Biggin Hill Airport. The leisurely drive was such a delight for Emma, she had never experienced travelling on a private jet before her anticipation was building. She had no idea where they were going the destination had been kept a strict secret. She had packed minimal clothes in a soft canvas bag as instructed for the American challenger jet. Alex had been careful that none of his friends had been told their true destination, although many were guessing wrongly.

They were all assembled in the quiet airport lounge waiting for the Princess to arrive. Emma was not sure if it was a good thing, the Princess had been included in the weekend, but was determined to make an effort to talk to the her at some point to clear the air. As Alex had renewed his friendship with the Princess, Emma decided to be discreet not wanting to cause friction with his circle of friends. Alex said it would not have been correct to leave the Princess out of the weekend, when most of his friends in London were invited.

Right on time her Rolls Royce drove up to the front door of the terminal building, Princess Volkov stepped out looking suitably dressed in casual clothing for their flight. The soft overnight bags were loaded onto the aircraft as they boarded the plane. The Challenger jet held seventeen passengers comfortably. A plentiful stock of champagne with nibbles was onboard ready for them to help themselves to during their flight.

The two American pilots had completed their pre flight checks, ready for take-off as soon as they saw their passengers arrive at the airport. Alex as the organiser had taken charge making sure everyone was comfortably into their seats, as they were ready for imminent takeoff. There were so many giggles, excited wild guesses as to where they were headed, but no one was correct it was a true mystery journey.

Without delay the jet sped along the runway and soared through the thick clouds of gentle drizzle, up high into the open blue sky beyond. Emma helped to serve drinks from the chilled cabinet, everyone relaxed taking pleasure in their guessing game again. The plane flew quickly over the outskirts of London, heading north following the east coastline. The Princess was seated facing forward beside Emma at a small table with Alex seated opposite, both were observing the views of the Norfolk coastline from the window. The champagne flutes kept being topped up by Alex as they relaxed in the cream leather seats of the comfortable jet interior.

It was Emma's chance to talk to the Princess, she

struggled in finding the right topic of interest, it was daunting to start the conversation with Royalty. Her knowledge of Russian history was almost nonexistent. They discussed Lady Mary who the Princess had heard of, but had never met. Emma explained briefly her interest in Wychfield manor relieved to have a talking point of interest. It gave her the chance to explain about the importance of make a success of the business, in order to save the estate from creditors.

The Princess was at last warming to Emma who was making a real effort to talk to her, both women were glad of the stimulating company en route to their mystery location. Alex took great delight in keeping the secret guessing game alive, as the group of his friends were getting closer with their guesses, causing raucous laughter as the abundant alcohol started having an effect.

Alex knew that as the jet flew on up hugging the coastline into Scotland, that he would have to come clean as to their final destination.

"Look everyone we are now over the North Yorkshire coast." All guests craned their necks to look out of the windows as they flew further northwards, up past the moors, up past Aberdeen, then over the sea into the wild shore line of Scotland. He knew they would soon see where they were heading.

"Look again now, this is where we are going," said Alex excitedly pointing at the small window on the left hand side of the plane. They gathered looking out across the horizon, into view came a crenulated tower with cold high stone walls rising up from the listed building standing proud on the rugged Caithness shoreline. The tall stone walls looked hard and ominous almost ghostly. Yet it was a magnificent highland scene set amongst green gorse, and tufted grass fields of purple heather, the setting sun began breaking through the grey threatening clouds, casting mottled sun streaks in patterns on the ground below.

The jet circled the five story tower flying north to the remote Wick airfield, which came suddenly into view. As they flew down toward the secluded runway, as they noticed a line of land rover's waiting on the country road near to the run way for their arrival. They buckled their seat belts ready for touchdown, they were all set to land and enjoy the adventure, eager to see what was in store for them over the mystery weekend.

There was much excitement as they made the short trip by land rover to the exclusive tower. On arrival a loud Scottish piper escorted them into the tower on his bag pipes. Entering the old stone way in, through the panelled wood door, with large intricate wrought iron hinges.

Once inside the imposing tower, it was cosy and warm, greeted by the house staff, with huge trays filled with the finest Scotch whiskey in cut glass tumblers. As glasses clinked in appreciation for the warming elixir, the group surveyed their grand surroundings at the foot of the great staircase.

After they assembled in the large hallway, the Russian group were taken to the boot room to put on Wellington boots. Then proceeded to stroll across the rough grass in the surrounding fields. Stretching their legs clutching their coats closer, taking in the stiff Scottish breeze from the sea, while they still had some day light left. The guests squealed with delight as they squelched their way across the fields, their boots stuck knee deep in severe mud. As darkness fell the group enjoyed the views, the full moon reflected in the water on the far horizon over the dark ominous ocean.

When they returned to the tower their bags had been placed into each of the guests rooms by the staff. Everything was so well organised and welcoming, as they each found their own single rooms. It was such a homely, welcoming atmosphere at the tower, Emma noticed that each room had a special name, which was a nice unique touch.

Strangely none of the rooms had locks on the doors, it was a private Scottish country home not a hotel. However she was not bothered about it, she felt quite safe in the friendly surroundings. It was more like a cosy highland retreat, Alex and the others had their rooms just up the hallway from her own room.

The ladies in the group found tartan sashes waiting for them on their beds with a note saying, there was a banquet followed by Scottish dancing scheduled for the evening. What fun! She only had an hour to get ready, thankfully Alex had advised them all to bring one evening outfit. Taking out her court shoes and plain figure hugging long black dress from her bag, she hung it up on the back of the door whilst taking a shower.

Alex called for Emma when it was time to go downstairs to the banqueting hall. He had arranged the entertainment carefully hoping a change of culture would impress his Russian friends. Emma was surprised but pleased to see that Alex had worn the tartan kilt provided by the staff, his dark complexion and black hair tied back, made him look like a Scottish Laird in his black watch tartan. She was excited to have been invited on the weekend trip, Alex fitted the tartan sash over her plain black dress she was ready to be escorted into the great hall.

It was time, all the guest proceeded to go downstairs filing into the hall as pipers started to play, adding to the magical Scottish atmosphere. Seating them along both sides of the banqueting table, the staff proceeded to serve the sumptuous meal. Alex was seated at the head of the table in an enormous carved oak chair with Emma and the Princess next to him facing each other.

For some reason the Princess proceeded talking to Alex in Russian, and took great delight in keeping Alex amused as Emma just look on in dismay at being left out of the conversation. It was becoming awkward for her as the pair locked eyes on each other, oblivious to Emma's feelings. Thank goodness the evening came alive for Emma after the meal, everyone went into the main room to partake in Scottish dancing. At last she had the chance to take part in highland dancing in a group.

The Princess as part of was taking centre stage as usual, taking her full part in the dancing, enjoying the jigs and reels. As the night went on it became apparent that the Princess still had strong feelings for Alex, unable to conceal her fascination for him. There was definitely a hidden agenda, Emma sensed that she needed to be on her guard, all was not as it should be.

Pushy Princess Volkov was clearly used to getting her own way, she had always been the centre of attention nothing had changed. Perhaps the Princess was intrigued as to why Emma was invited at all, she could clearly not be good enough for a Russian Count.

At the end of the evening Alex whispered quietly to Emma, he wanted her to share his bed when they retired for the night. Emma was at last enjoying her own enchanted fairytale, hoping her story would have a happy ending, as they retired to Alex's bedroom!

In the middle of the night the Princess was on the prowl, true to her wolf name and nature, ready to stake her claim on her willing subject. She was searching the long corridor looking for Alex's room, to surprise him at last to claim her princely prize. Unaware that Emma had been invited to spend the night with him before her.

At last she found his room, quietly she prised the door open, his room was in complete darkness. But she could make out figures moving on the bed at the far side of the pitch-black room. The Princess adjusted her eyes to the gloom making out the shapes, as she stalked her way quietly on tip toes into the centre of the bedroom.

There on the bed cover was Alex, totally naked like a toned Adonis, raising his agile body effortlessly mounting her as rigid as a stallion, she lay ready with her exposed legs wide apart. He was grinding her, making love to her, caressing her body, pulling her closer, loving her, kissing her. The one hot blooded Count, she had set her heart on was having wild sex with Emma. Writhing on top of that common bitch. She couldn't un see it!

The image was etched onto her royal brain. She turned silently unseen, and closed the door quietly behind her, they did not hear her at all. But the appalling moment would not go away like a film reel, it kept replayed again, and again in the Princess's mind, it would take an act of sheer revenge to satisfy her anger.

She had secretly longed for the time when Count

Alexander would make love to her. However royal protocol had held her back from expressing her real feelings for him. Now she realised that was a mistake, time was short, she would have to stake her claim on him quickly. Alex would be hers; no other woman would be allowed to stand in her way.

The next day everyone was suffering with hangovers from the night before. The Princess could not get Alex and Emma's having sex out of her thoughts, she would never forget it.

Having her buffet breakfast early in the dining hall before the others woke, she needed time to think. In her mind a plot was hatching, she had to make Alex want her more than ever. She was going to be irresistible to him, forming a plot to enticing him into her trap, as quickly as she could. No cheap slut was going to have him, no matter how experienced an escort she was, this society hooker knew all the tricks of the trade.

Her plan had to be fool proof and daring; she would have to be deadly devious, knowing her titled status might not be enough to win him over. There was no way she would let Emma steal her man from under her nose.

Later in the day after their leisurely breakfasts to sooth their sore heads from the Scotch the night before. It was time for the group to try their skills at the shooting range. They were having individual rifle scores at targets set up in the indoor shooting gallery. Alex had tried to have a variety of events set up for the weekend to keep everyone amused.

The Russians had to lay down one by one with their rifles each taking aim at the bulls eye, each trying to become the best shot, in the shooting party. Scores were kept until the last shot was performed, Alex took the prize for the highest score with most shots into the centre of the target. He was always so competitive, never keen to be the loser.

It had crossed the Princess's mind while at the rifle range to accidentally shoot Emma dead. She also imagined enticing her up to the roof, pushing her off the crenulated tower, imagining her body hurtling down onto the concrete below. Her jealousy was building to new heights, she had to find the best way to get to Alex, and get rid of the bitch once and for all.

It was a fun start to the day for Emma, after the shooting range they had a picnic lunch. Then the group were moving on to a treasure hunt within, and around the high tower. They were separately looking for clues hidden in various rooms in the vast tower, starting with clues found in the small library.

It was here that the Princess cornered Emma who was straggling behind the others on her own, the Princess was adamant in staking her rightful claim to Count Alexander. This was her prime opportunity to get Emma on her own, determined to stop her in her tracks.

Sitting on a library chair ticking off the clues on her check sheet, Emma looked up to see the Princess hovering over her.

"Of course you must know that Alex and I were betrothed to each other in the past." The Princess commented casually waiting for a response from Emma.

"Oh yes, Alex did explain the connection with you, your highness. But I understand it was all so long ago, many years ago in fact." Emma was trying to deflect the unwanted attention, but knew exactly why she had raised the subject.

"Obviously, it was years ago when we were both living in St Petersburg, the bond and past connection between us has been fully re kindled. I do hope you understand." The Princess paused for effect, raising herself to her full height looking firmly down at Emma.

"The Count and I have unfinished business, we have a future together as man and wife. I don't want you to be disappointed, when you are discarded by Count Alexander. He has been so kind in taking you under his wing." She smirked, hating her rivals claim to his affections.

"But your friendship is undesirable, and unacceptable. I do hope you understand." Emma tried not to show her true emotions, or the hurt she felt inside, Alex was so special. Emma knew she was lucky he had shown an interest in her at all.

"You can see the Count, is completely out of your league. Of course he is too good for you, we have Royal connections. I am a relative of the Romanov's, our family's go way back our families had generations together."

"In our Royal circles it would be unacceptable for a commoner to be accepted as a partner, I do hope you can understand." She continued in her haughty Russian accent.

"Alexander is such a kind and handsome man, I must make sure he is not taken advantage off. She smiled down at Emma who sat there meekly wanting to disappear.

"There are so many gold diggers these days." Looking straight at Emma's startled gaze to emphasis exactly who she meant was taking advantage of him.

Emma had to defend her position.

"I can assure you that I have never asked for anything from Alex. He has kindly offered to help me to save the manor and estate, nothing more."

"Let me make it clear to you." The Princess stressed pointing her spiked finger straight at her.

"I will not tolerate another woman sucking up to my future husband, we are secretly engaged. Making Alex strictly off limits!" She then walked away abruptly storming off out of the room, knowing her point had struck home. Emma was shocked at her reactions, but knew how jealously she would be guarding Count Alexander.

The pleasant weekend was turning into another nightmare, she had one more night to endure the Princess's company. It would be impossible to avoid her, how was she going to explain what had happened with the Princess to Alex?

Emma had given up the trivial pursuit of the hunt game. Whilst in a daze she waited in the hallway to see if the group had completed the treasure hunt. Emma received an unexpected text on her mobile from Stefan, the message said. He was on his way over to England from JFK New York. The message read. See you at Wychfield tomorrow!

"Holy crap what now!" She could not take any more upset. Her stomach churned over at the thought of what could be wrong? Something had brought Stefan back urgently. Emma knew he must be in more trouble! She hoped he had purged his demons, and would not bring problems with him. It had been a while since she had seen him, she was looking forward to catching up with his news, although she was also scared to see him for too many reasons. Alex found her looking pensive reading messages on her mobile phone.

"You have a worried look on your face, what's up?" Looking up she said.

"Do you want the good news or the bad news!" She looked as though she was in a dilemma. He could not guess what had just happened to her. When they were in the shooting gallery, she was not anxious but happy, the last thing he wanted was for her to be worried this weekend. This was supposed to be her one chance to relax. His whole purpose in arranging the weekend retreat for them all was to include her in his life, and to give her a chance to mingle with his circle of friends. His concern grew when she told him what the Princess had said, it was clear the Princess had staked her claim on him in no uncertain terms.

"I'm sorry she gave you a hard time." He said. "Perhaps I should explain properly." Emma was ready to hear what he had to say, knowing there might be more to their background than he had admitted.

"The Princess and I did want to make love many years ago, but we were so closely chaperoned. When we left to go our separate ways it simply did not happen! So we were never lovers! We re-kindle our relationship when she came over on visits to Europe, we met in London and she attended some polo matches."

"We always kept our friendship on a platonic level it may be her royal protocol, which kept us from making any move of that kind, her body guard was usually in attendance, which made it awkward anyway." Emma had sensed all along that there was a sensual connection between the two of them. Princess Volkov always used her royal title, she wanted nothing less than adoration and utter devotion, whilst Emma would settle for love and romance.

"So you haven't made love to her, not yet anyway!" She said half jokingly to him.

"I think that the Princess wants you! She has warned me off you. I am not worthy to be with you in her opinion, she made that very clear. For some reason she is Royally pissed off with me!, she told me you two are secretly engaged!"

"Really" Alex replied perplexed.

"I was not aware of that." His face had an amazed reaction to the news, he seemed shocked at the new revelation. His tone changed to a brusque manner, as he tried to change the subject by adding.

"Is there something else wrong? You seem disturbed."

"The other thing strange is, I received an unexpected text message from Stefan, he is rushing back to Wychfield from New York, but he didn't say why!
When we land back at the airport tomorrow, I shall have to go straight back to the manor. I have really been away far too long already!" She said.

"Something must be very wrong."

CHAPTER 18

The last night at the tower in Scotland was strained to say the least. Emma could not sleep with Alex in his room, for fear of the Princess finding out. A scene on their last night was the last thing she wanted, Emma had always hated confrontation of any kind, it was just not in her nature. She left Alex to smooth things out with the Princess, fearing he had some explaining to do.

Alex and the Princess went up to the small library to discuss their future relationship. It was made abundantly clear to him, that she was calling in their former promise between the families. In no uncertain terms she told him to come to heel, as her fiancée. Alex was now hooked in an awkward situation, but felt obliged to agree. Leaving Emma out in the cold, he explained to the Princess that he would have some business dealings at the manor, as contracted. He agreed with her to keep his contact with Emma to a strict minimum.

Emma being timid by nature had not dared to sleep with Alex. She did not want to inflame the Princess any more, or face the repercussions. It was now the Princess's mission to make Alex her life partner. It was time to call in that obligation to make him her future husband, his commitment would be complete, and total he had a duty to her. Knowing she could pull his strings, making him her puppet, she had become the sinister skilful puppet master.

She had successfully scuppered any idea of Lady Mary's niece the upstart, making a claim on him. He was far too superior to make love to a commoner, the Princess made herself the priority. She now had her claws firmly into Alex, determined he would not get away for a second time. Securing her prize, he would become her trophy, his respect for her would be total!

When Princess Volkov and count Alexander met on their last night's stay at the tower. She made certain he would agree to a spring wedding, the following year. She had every confidence in her tempting abilities it was time to convince him of their positive union. She made sure Emma was going to be kept out of his life, he was never to mention her name again. Emma was being erased from his existence once and for all, the Princess had to be obeyed, or there would be hell to pay. He had a very weak side, a traditional sense of duty, which she fully exploited.

"Yes, of course a spring wedding." His agreement signed his defeat as the Princess smiled in triumph.

Alexander found she would not let him go! He felt the trap had been sprung, he could see no way out of the situation. The Princess made sure he had no way to back out of their long standing marriage commitment. Why would he prefer plain, ordinary Emma to a royal Princess, who could offer him so much more!

As soon as they were back from the mystery weekend, the Princess announced their forthcoming wedding on social media. A glossy full page spread in the press, spilling their secret hush-hush engagement, was organised. She was flying straight back to Nice airport from Gatwick, while Alex travelled on to London.

She had already told him the style and carat weight of diamond engagement ring, she wanted him to make especially for her. She had full control over him, Alex was far too polite and well-mannered to turn down a Princess. He was royally trapped by his Princess and their close circle of mutual friends. Somehow he had come around to thinking it was for the best, it worked out in a way almost pre ordained. His Russian friends were keen to hear about the wedding arrangements, it was going to be the highlight of their social calendar for the coming year. The Princess had made sure the Russians in London had saved the date, for their grand wedding on the Riviera.

The one thing the Princess was curious about was why Alex had invited Emma to Arundel Castle in the first place. Was he deliberately trying to make her jealous? If he was his actions had worked to perfection.

Alex had explained to the Princess that he would be going to the manor soon, to settle in two of his polo ponies in the stables. He had decided there was no point in dragging out his decision to agree his engagement. He would have to let Emma down gently, and tell her before pictures emerged in style Magazines, scheduled for the following week.

The contrast between the Princess and Emma was so stark, they were as different as night and day. His attachment to the dark Princess was tied like a knot, he just hoped it would not be a noose around his neck. He did not want to end up like the hanged man.

Emma had told Alex when they left the airport that Stefan was due at the manor, she decided under the circumstances that he did not need to know exactly why, she didn't actually know herself at the time. Alex said he would be delivering the ponies to the stables in a few days. Time for Emma to find out exactly what was going on in the background, before they met up again at the manor.

***

In the meantime the three hundred and fifty foot yacht Labyrinth was anchored out at sea in the Mediterranean near Nice. Princess Volkov was standing on board the top deck waiting for the tender to take her to shore, her luxurious dark hair was blowing in the breeze she was wearing a soft white kaftan and gold sandals. A Russian diplomat Dimitri and his wife who was her guests for the weekend were patiently waiting to go ashore with her for lunch. The Princess divided her time between her writing den, which was her Dacha near Moscow located in the grounds of her country house, and her elegant two floor apartment in Paris.

She was very rarely alone when in France, as a historian her alone time was precious. When she was writing her Russian history books in her Dacha, she would immerse herself in her research not wanting to be disturbed. However her time in France was different it was her time to enjoy the pleasures of shopping in Paris and invited numerous friends into her hectic social life. She was immensely wealthy, her celebrity was sought after by the rich and famous in Europe, however unusual for a Princess her age, now thirty to be single.

Now she was on a mission to choose her perfect

wedding dress in Nice, the date had been set. Dimitri's wife was delighted to accompany the Princess to choose the special wedding dress suitable for royalty. It was going to be the highlight of the social season, with a honeymoon touring the Greek Islands on her yacht, all expenses were scheduled for the following spring.

Arrangements were going ahead at a fast pace, the future was looking bright for them both, their joint wealth would ensure a lavish, comfortable lifestyle. Complementing their already wealthy existence, the wedding would be the central strand uniting their two families. Hello Magazine had been contracted for the exclusive shots of the wedding on the Riviera, her glam squad would ensure she was the most beautiful royal bride of the year. However Alex was concerned that they had still not consummated the union. The royal protocol of waiting for the wedding night was being strictly observed by the Princess. There was never the right opportunity to go further than they wanted sexually.

In the past Alex had a sneaky suspicion that Stefan might have bedded the Princess before him. Knowing how much he would have enjoyed the thrill of taking a virgin Princess to bed. When he broached the subject to Stefan he had a strange and guilty look on his face, but would not admit to any indiscretion. Alex found a real seed of doubt had been planted deep in his mind, the rivalry turned into a resentment at his friends possible betrayal. His friend was such a well known player, it was exactly what he would do, given the chance!

There was now a festering friction between them, Alex had his suspicions yet could not be sure, it had peaked his resentment. As a competitor Stefan was a fierce team player at polo, yet he would take advantage of any titled woman who strayed innocently across his path at matches. He was a star player and star performer, Alex was often left in awe of his womanising skills. He could persuade any woman he wanted to sleep with him, he became the English Casanova, adding willing ladies to his harem.

Finding Emma to be so beautiful, charming and an astute business woman, had struck an unlikely chord within Alex. He sought after everything Stefan possessed, as a way of getting his own back on him. Owning the painting had just been a start on his journey, his clear distrust of Stefan had grown to new proportions. It was payback time, unfortunately Emma was caught right in the middle of their competition. But all was fair in love and war, he guessed, that the challenge was about to get awfully messy.

On the flight back to Biggin Hill the next morning there was a weird atmosphere, as they sat apart from one another. After landing at the small airport, Emma said her goodbyes to Alex, and his friends she felt she had guessed right about the Princess and Alex. Emma's knew her relationship with him was over she could tell. During the drive down in her taxi to the Sussex Downs she had time to reflect on events at the Tower.

Alex had seemed distant when they parted, he had been talking to the Princess alone on the last night. Now everything was different, Emma was not sure of the outcome, but his mood had rapidly changed he was more remote with her. With no chance to talk to him before she rushed off to the manor, she said she would call him later. Things had not turned out so well in the end, a firm wedge had been pressed in between them.

Suddenly there was another text from Stefan to say he would meet her at the manor later in the day, for a progress report on the building work. It struck Emma as being weird, he could have checked with her progress by email, or skyp any time from New York, but he obviously wanted to see her in person.

Emma sent a message back saying she had been away for the weekend, but would be back at the manor by mid day today. She was hoping to be there before he arrived, having spent so long away, it was time to get back in harness with the building work, and to reality.

She sent urgent text messages to Brandon the gardener and to the builders, saying to expect her back shortly. Adding she would need a quick progress report when she arrived. Her mind was in a whirl there was so much to discuss with Stefan, she wanted to find out why he was coming back so unexpectedly.

CHAPTER 19

The wrought iron gates at the manor had been propped opened wide for her arrival, she noticed delivery vans arriving full of kitchen equipment. It looked as though good steps forward had been made while she had been away, she could not wait to see the results in the barn.

Brandon was waiting for her at the front door with his wheelbarrow. It was filled with an array of bedding plants to put into the newly dug borders at the front of the house.

"Wow, what a difference you have made it looks wonderful." She said smiling widely at the old gardener, he was delighted to see her reaction.

"It has been a labour of love Miss, thank you for providing the funds to do a good job."

"The mauve wisteria will look lovely growing up over the door arch." Emma added.

"It's such a good colour to go with the pinks and purples of the rhododendrons, the manor house is well known for." Emma pushed her soft overnight bag into the stone entrance porch, then returned to Brandon's side as they walked to the barn for the great reveal.

Turning the corner to the side of the stone manor

she could see the full effect of the magnificent gardens, stretching out down to the verdant green, south downs in the distance. The fully stocked borders, and neat clipped hedges were a colourful revelation. Quite different from when she had left to go to London to see Alex. Brandon and his band of young part timers, had transformed the walled gardens with manicured lawns, into a picturesque garden worthy of being opened to the public.

Emma was delighted with the gardens, the smell of freshly cut grass filled the air, as sea gulls soared in the bright blue sky above. Brandon had excelled himself in redesigning the borders, she noticed a new path with fragrant rose covered arches, installed as a canopy ready for future weddings. As they continued to the great barn at the back of the house, they spotted feverish activity. The industrial kitchen units were being lifted into place with electrics installed.

Walking in through the large open door, the old barn exuded a rustic charm, which is just the effect she had wanted. There was a vast area for dining parties and wedding receptions, with an inside bar complete with an awning erected outside for drinks on the terrace, overlooking the fountain. The builders had moved suits of armour from the house, positioning them around the interior edge of the oak structure. Colourful pennants hung down from the cross beams, leading to a minstrels gallery with stairway above. They had successfully turned the barn into a magnificent banqueting hall, fit for Knights of the round table.

It reminded Emma of the Knight of Swords in the tarot deck, the meaning of the card was a mirror of how she felt at this precise moment. She was so single minded with her goal clearly in her mind, nothing could stand in her way. Her excitement at the progress was astonishing the transformation was almost complete.

The day had started well, she hoped that it would continue to do so. Emma was expecting Stefan to arrive by taxi from Brighton Station soon, following his flight.

She went back to the manor to unpack picking up her overnight bag from beneath the stone porch. Her bedroom was as she had left it, with her lap top and tarot cards on her dressing room table. Opening her lap top to check recent emails, she noticed several attachments from the council, permitting the change of use of the barn, with the alcohol licence she had been waiting for. It was now all systems go, time for her new beginning at last!

Knowing Stefan would appear soon, she checked the livery contract then transferred the funds Alex had forwarded to her for the agreement. The next stage of the business plan, would be the finishing touches at the end of the week. She smiled when she checked the new healthy bank account Alex had kept to his word, as she knew he would, the livery for the polo ponies had been paid in full.

It was a god send for her, allowing funds to go forward to provide additional stables to be erected in the furthest field. Experienced part time staff had been employed by an agency to manage the stables. Everything was coming together nicely, it had cost a small fortune but was worth it. She had a strange sense that there was something not right, niggling at her back of her mind, things were going too well what could possibly go wrong.

Emma was alone in the manor house, she loaded the

washing machine then heard someone at the front door, Stefan had arrived. Switching on the machine she went to the door to greet him. She could see instantly see that his face was ashen, he looked so haggard his face was drained of colour, as though he had been through hell. Stefan mumbled something, dropping down his heavy suitcase as he walked head bent low slowly towards her.

"I'm sorry to say I have some bad news; I had to come back to see you!" Emma looked concerned at him.

"My god. You look awful what has happened?" Stefan was clearly distraught as he approached her.

"I haven't slept for two days, thank god you're here. I wanted to come back to the manor to be with you. I hope you don't mind? I didn't know where else to go."

Emma was clearly surprised by his demeanour, he had changed completely from the person she knew. The upper class snobbish behaviour had gone, here was a person obviously needy. He was unshaved, his curly blond hair was tousled his clothes crumpled, he looked dreadful as though he was ill; she could not turn him away.

Whatever bad karma had happened between them in the past, had instantly dissolved when she looked at him. She could tell he had hit another crisis in his life, it was ironic that he had turned to her for help. Emma's caring and capable nature, had brought him back to his old home. It was times like these when she recognised he still needed her, he was at a cross road, returning to her side with a yearning to be cared for.

Not knowing what was wrong, Emma led Stefan into the kitchen it was time at last to talk; to find out what had happened over coffee. He knew Emma would not judge him, she would never let him down he had every confidence in her. He had treated her badly in the past, he had hurt her, the one person who was always ready to be there for him, no matter what!

He could not change what he had done to people in the past, he had been constantly manipulating. But he now recognised his appalling behaviour to them all. He was truly ashamed of who he had become. Stefan wanted at last open up to Emma like never before. His life was at an all time low, he had hit rock bottom!

About to embark on the truth he slumped down at the kitchen table and spoke quietly, wanting to tell her everything, why suddenly he had come back to her side. She sat in silence riveted to the spot as she listened intently to him without interruption.

"Look, there is no easy way to tell you this, it's Becky my ex wife she's dead!" It was not something Emma had expected to hear, the shock of what he said showed instantly in her expression of horror, stupidly Emma replied.

"You're joking, right?"

Shaking his head with tears welling up in his eyes. "No I'm not! She was found dead in her room at the small hotel in Paris. I'm waiting for a toxicology report from the coroner, I think she took her own life; committed suicide." Emma stood up taking his hunched head in her hands, stroking his blond tangled hair, as he sat rigid with tears streaming, beginning to fall. It was the first time the realisation had hit him, Emma had never seen him cry before. The flood gates opened as his tears flowed freely down his anguished face, as he sobbed uncontrollably.

Meeting his tear filled gaze she asked for a breakdown of events, to take the facts slowly into her mind. As though it was too much information to take in, too fast for her thoughts to catch up and process. Emma's mind was whirling from what she had just heard. She sat down again patiently waiting to hear more.

"Perhaps it was meant to be Becky my ex wife was never a free spirit like you, she had deep concerns and emotional issues, that no one except I knew about." Emma broke in looking perplexed.

"What happened to her? The last time I spoke to her she was on top of the world, working nights at the *Folies Berger*, it was the new start she wanted."

"Apparently the contact she originally had, some agent in Paris let her down, there was no job after all! Becky had been devastated and was completely broke. She began working at a seedy strip club in the red light district to make ends meet. I can't imagine what she went through. You were not to know, she would have been far too humiliated to tell you." Stefan said with tears rolling steadily down his cheeks.

"I let her down by turning her away." He looked distraught and empty drained of all emotion. Exhausted by events he was an empty shell of his former self, he had learned a hard lesson that sapped all his strength.

He continued his eyes red rimmed with sorrow.

"Her male contact had used her; she had not left a suicide note at the scene just bottles of pills, and an empty vodka bottle. The police investigated and interviewed a female friend from the strip club, who knew all about it, and gave them a full account of what had happened to her."

He held Emma's hand to stop it from shaking.

"Don't feel bad, you could not have known; she would have been too embarrassed to say."

It was not what she wanted to hear it came as a total shock, she had no idea. She felt Becky's past life must have been so different from the life she had portrayed.

"Please tell me the truth Stefan, don't hold back." She had to know everything, before she could understand exactly what had gone on in Becky's past.

"She was not as strong as her image, aware one day she might end up like her idol Marilyn." Stefan took Emma's hand again, standing at her side hugging her gently to his chest. They both cried with sorrow at the enormity of Becky's shattered life. Guilt was going to haunt him forever, how could he possibly make amends for his actions. He was like a small child once more, unable to come to terms with the circumstances, he had spiralled down to a new level of pain.

Emma had to tell him a close secret, that Becky had confided to her, Becky had truly loved Stefan. That her love for him was not just an act, to get money from him. He thought she was just after his inheritance or whatever wealth he had, but that was not the case! When Emma told him, it was a huge blow to his feelings, his gilded life had a false facade. It concealed his many faults, he still had much to learn about life and relationships with women, Becky made her own sacrifices. Emma continued.

"But she left Ceasar's Palace to be with you! She told me it was the best job she had ever had, she was the big star of the show. The Marilyn Monroe musical was the heart of the cabaret, she was at the height of her career."

"I know." He replied. "But at the same time It just didn't register with me, the forfeit Becky had made."

"You look shattered, take your suitcase upstairs and have a lay down, it's pointless to blame yourself, you're OK now. You're home at last!"

"I will unpack the food shopping that has just been dumped in the front porch, then make us an evening meal." Emma would speak to him later, he looked exhausted she could see he needed to sleep.

Later that evening after Stefan had slept, he felt a lot better, he had little appetite but was relieved to be back in his former home. After Emma made a makeshift dinner, they took time to relax in the lounge, Emma opened a bottle of red wine to help Stefan to unwind. There was a great deal to discuss, she wanted to know the full details no matter how painful.

He was grateful to have Emma to talk it through, she had always been so strong he was glad she was there to lean on. He felt guilty about the way he had treated her in the past, he resolved to try to make it up to her in some way. His American wife had been beautiful and fascinating, but she was nothing like Emma, who had many qualities other women lacked. He was now pleased to be home again, glad he had turned to her in his time of need.

Emma would be forever grateful to her friend Becky for helping to change her hippy looks. Turning her appearance into a more sophisticated persona. In keeping with her new image, as she emerged into a business woman in her own right, ready to run the new events business at the manor.

Becky's unexpected death was an immensely sad episode, yet it had brought Stefan back to her again.

Emma felt that Stefan could not have prevented it, perhaps he could use this tragic event as a gateway for a new beginning. There was no way he could have foreseen that Becky would take her own life, the fault could not be his alone. Circumstances had a way of intervening in life for good or bad. Becky just did not have the inner strength alone to survive what happened to her.

"Do tell me as much as you know about Becky's past, she told me so little about her upbringing." Emma reassured him that it was OK to be open, it would be good to talk about it.

"I don't know where to start, perhaps I should start at the beginning. " Stefan seemed relaxed as he sipped more wine, when his glass was empty Emma topped up the glass again.

"Becky was brought up in the deep South in an orphanage, both her parents had died in a car accident. Being an only child with no other family she survived by dancing and singing. When she turned eighteen it all changed, she moved to Los Angeles, and joined a dance company." Emma listened hearing for the first time the story of Becky's tragic beginnings.

"Life was extremely hard for her as she moonlighted her way through the seedy nightclubs in Atlanta and Los Angeles. She resorted to lap dancing sometimes to make ends meet financially. Her idol was as always Marilyn Monroe, so she styled herself to look exactly like her. Following her gestures and mannerisms until perfected, she was being noticed, turning heads wherever she went. Always keeping in character as though she was the real Marilyn, she caused quite a stir and a following of ardent admirers." He felt better, more at ease being able to talk to Emma at last openly.

"At one point she even joined a look alike agency in L.A. She was paid to attend parties and grand store openings. The rest was like a dream for her, she auditioned for an agent with contacts in Las Vegas. Joining the troop of cabaret dancers, quickly gaining her own central show playing her idol Marilyn. She became HOT property quickly in Vegas and the new rising star of Ceasar's Palace."

"So what happened next?" Emma was spellbound wanting to hear more.

"I guess she was lucky in Vegas, so many try to make a life there, but not many could find the enormous popularity she had found. She became obsessed with her celebrity." Stefan was fired up and spellbound when meeting Becky for the first time.

"She was truly beautiful and knew it; she was hard to resist. I was in a fantastic mood! Having won big on the roulette tables, her gaze found mine as I reached across the green baize to scoop up the thousands of dollars worth of chips from the table. Her heavy breasts swung into view as she bent down to congratulate me from the far side of the table." Emma had previously heard this version of their meeting from Becky, and nodded to him in accord.

"Inviting her to join me, was such a buzz as all eyes followed her curves as she sat beside me. Men pushed forward gathering around us, to watch us play the house and win with obvious jealousy. She stayed in her Marilyn character; it was hard to fathom out where Becky began or ended. She had become Marilyn in every way, her voice, her body and her Chanel no. 5 perfume. It was a heady mix of hormones and sexual chemistry, there was no escape for me I was completely hooked on her."

"Becky was riding high and so was I, we had an instant rapport we clicked naturally, we both could not miss out on the opportunity as the champagne flowed." Emma saw the wonder in his eyes as he described her.

"What seems strange now, was that I never saw her without full make up on. It was like a mask she hid behind, so that no one knew who she really was. It was as though she had been born again into a masquerade the pretence was perfect."

"That night when we went to my hotel room, I made love to Marilyn Monroe not Becky, how was I suppose to really know her. She was more than willing! Also very able to please me sexually, as only a professional could. I thought at one point that she might charge by the hour! Believe me I would have happily paid for the privilege, but instead she asked for nothing, just my company."

"We stayed locked together in my room for several days with the do not disturb sign firmly placed on the door. We were in a sexual bliss, one I have never experienced before. It was extraordinary she had the flexibility of a dancer, and the stamina of a tiger."

"What about Becky was she happy with her life? Did she tell you anything else about her background?" Emma asked.

"Only that she had missed the opportunity to find love, she was passionate about her quest finding the perfect man. It was like judgement day, I had passed the test, her duty became the desire and fulfilment of pleasing me. Between her search for love, and our sexual desire, somewhere along the way she confused the two." Emma was then passed an envelope with a letter inside addressed to Stefan in New York.

"Although she did not leave a suicide note she had sent a letter to me. By the time it was received it was too late, she had died; you had better read it." With her hand trembling she opened the letter from Becky.

Dear Stefan, Sorry to tell you this but I have come to a decision, which has been shaped by my colourful past. When you read this, I will be gone, I am going away where I cannot be contacted.

I just wanted you to know, as you may have guessed, that on my way up the show biz career ladder, I sold sex and my body to survive. I never told you this, it is not something I am proud of. I was abused by my father when I was a child, it had caused me so much confusion in my mind between love and sex. Nothing worked out for me in Paris, I could not go back to the sad life I endured before.

You were willing to be my partner when we married, but I realise now it was never true love for you, only lust on your part. I wanted so much to be a good wife, and to have your children, to have a normal life full of love that I have never experienced.

Take good care of Emma for me, we became good friends in the end. Your loving wife Becky xxx

Stefan was watching Emma's expression to gauge her thoughts. As she quietly closed the letter and folded it back into the envelope, unable to speak a desolate pain covered her face. She wished she had known, she would not have judged her, or thought it was wrong. Something so sad could not have been easily swept away; it would have been so deep in Becky's consciousness.

Emma could never have guessed what a sad life Becky lead in the past, she never let it slip. Could she have helped her, or stopped her from killing herself? Now it was too late, she would never know.

CHAPTER 20

Changing their mood the conversation altered to the frantic business progress at Wychfield. Emma was keen to update him on what had happened since he had been in New York, when Becky stayed on to help her.

She emphasised how her friendship between herself and Becky had slowly blossomed, considering how difficult it was when they first met.

"Becky used to click her fingers." Emma said.

"At first she expecting me to wait on her like a personal maid. But after a while things changed as we got to know one another better."

Her own figure was being transformed by Becky from being a dumpling, into a healthy and lean string bean. Emma had re invented herself with Becky's help, she explaining how punishing the new keep fit regime was that her new best friend had insisted on. The extreme diet of low carbohydrate, low fat they suffered came as a total shock to Emma. She realised quite quickly that Becky had a severe eating disorder of her own. She told Emma how she had endured anorexia for years, whilst working in the dancing profession in California. Emma explained to him.

"The social media frenzy hadn't helped as she gained followers on line, eagerly waiting for the next pictures of her in the skimpiest of clothing. She had to maintain an unrealistic perfection at all times, with two hours of pounding out reps in the gym, along with running on the tread mill. Becky had become a walking talking Marilyn doll, never allowing herself, or the mask to slip."

It was not unusual for Becky to skip meals entirely for days, it had become her habit. They both had eating disorders of different kinds. Becky could not eat at all, whereas Emma could not stop eating; it was something they were both battling. The pressure to look good was becoming an obsession for both of them, especially as Becky was constantly taking pictures for her many on line fans.

Emma had noticed straight away when Stefan had arrived, that major character changes in him had occurred; his old arrogant ways had disappeared totally since Becky had died. He had grown up overnight from the self centred, Chelsea snob of the past.

Now a humble empty person stood before her; she could sense a growing unease in his posture, as though he could no longer cope with what life had thrown at him. His lessons had been harsh and immediate urging him to look closely at his past behaviour.

Mourning was not going to get them far, Emma had to pull him together, before he broke. Seeing the emptiness in his stunned blank stare, she gripped him tightly, pulling him towards her in a hard bear hug. Holding him as close as she could, trying to squeeze out any further pain while his tears flowed.

"It is what you do now, that matters!" She said in a low whisper.

"We have both made mistakes, let's not waste a moment more in regret, we cannot bring her back." A peaceful contentment was pulling him back into the world, he knew she was right; everyone had free will to end their life. He was just sorry he had not seen it coming, Becky had hidden her true feelings so well. Tragically he had no idea that he was really loved by her. Surprising Emma, Stefan suddenly broke away.

"Can we start again," he said hurriedly, taking the opportunity to throw them both a lifeline.

"What do you mean? Start again!"

"I have learnt not to be so selfish to appreciate what you have done for me, we were good together. We owe it to each other to try and make our relationship work. We have always had a spark between us! Let's get that feeling back." He held her hand looking at her carefully, trying to gauge her facial appearance.

Emma shifted back quickly, this was not what she had expected, it was becoming an awkward moment. Wishing she had not held him so close, perhaps she had given him the wrong idea. There had always been a chemistry between them, but this was not the time to rekindle old firestorms of passion.

Emma realised she was now in a mad conflict of interests, not wanting to hurt him further. She felt he had suffered so much turmoil since Becky had died, but there was no way she could go on taunting him. She always tried to hold herself to a higher standard, as a workaholic there had been little time for pleasure. It was the occasion to come clean with him, and nip any leftover feelings in the bud.

"Stefan look, you are right we have always had an attraction to each other; but you must know that I have been seeing someone else, someone you know."

"Who is it?" He said awake suddenly with the bolt from the blue.

"Your friend Alexander, from the polo team. We have been spending time together at his home in Kensington." He was in no mood now for her to spoil the moment.

"For heaven's sake; he didn't waste any time. Did he! Emma you are so gullible, it didn't cross your mind that I asked him to look after you while I was away!"

"Not to shag you! It's obvious he didn't tell you."
His anger was building, as Emma was left open mouthed in disbelief. Stefan's rage was evident and vicious, any nice spell, was clearly broken as he turned to her in his spite.

"That's a real kick in the teeth, while my back is turned you're fucking with Alexander the Great."
Emma regained her composure to face him head on.

"Don't tell me what to do! You are so manipulative." she said.

"How was I supposed to know you had someone spying on me. Why should you care who I sleep with anyway. Let's face it you were the married one! Trying to make your sham of a marriage work."

She was on a roll now, remembering everything so clearly, all the nasty things he had done to her in the past. It was all coming flooding back into her mind fast, blurting out of her at great speed. Her face grew redder with anger.

"I remember when you and Becky on the first day went upstairs to the bedroom at Wychfield, I could clearly hear you two having sex together. Then to top it all, you both came downstairs and talked about me as though I was just a servant. I heard you telling Becky all about me, you treating me like shit. I was in the dining room as you both passed by the door, laughing at me. I was totally humiliated. Not once did you care about how I felt!" She was incandescent with rage, now that she was on a roll.

"I can tell you exactly what you said; word for word, I will never forget it! You were a complete bastard, you are so arrogant. Just this afternoon I thought how much you had changed, how much better you were behaving now. How wrong was I, it was just an act."

"At least Alex looked after me, you just left me to it, with no money to push forward the plans for the estate. You make me sick!" She was targeting him hard with her words, pushing him away with her arms to get a reaction.

"With your stuck up ways, why don't you let me see who I want to see. You don't own me." Emma was getting mad and even, determined he would not pierce her armour again. She could twist the knife in, just as easily as he could, it stuck in her mind that both men had used her, using her body pure and simple. But she was the stupid, enthusiastic idiot to let it happen!

Alex had always been a perfect gentleman with her, he had an old school vibe, she had slept with him willingly. Now she was unsure of where she stood, totally confused. It hurt her deeply that he had not told her, Stefan had instructed him to watch over her, it was totally infuriating.

She was determined not to feel bad about the late nights, and time spent with Alex, he had made her feel alive again and wanted. Emma had been falling like crazy for Alex, but if it was not meant to be, could she walk away, she was not sure? At least she was convinced the business deal she had signed with Alex to was sound and watertight. She was relieved to have it in writing, pleased now, she had taken the time to make it a legal contract.

Amazingly she felt strong, if the past few months had taught her anything, it had taught her to be even more self reliant. No man would be able to match her for perseverance against the odds. The opportunity to set up her own business at the manor had sparked a lifelong desire, lighting a flame of enterprise so strong, she could not resist the challenge.

Stefan butted in again to diffuse the situation.

"Look if it upsets you to know that Alex has over stepped his role in looking out for you. I can assure you that I will call him, and have it out with him. He took advantage of you, for sure. He won't get away with it, I can guarantee that. " Emma needed now to set the record straight.

"You don't understand my new business connection with him, I now have a signed contract for his polo ponies to be liveried in the stable yard." Emma continued.

"He paid up front, for the livery thank god! Good job he did, or I would be in a serious financial crisis again."

"Alex is coming down to the manor soon, to help install the first two polo ponies into the stables." Emma guessed that this visit, could go horribly wrong, she had naively become a sitting duck, a target between the two friends rivalry.

She tried to disperse the situation.

"Look I don't want you both to fall out with each other over me. This is ridiculous, let's agree to be civilised. I have been told by Princess Volkov that she is secretly engaged to Alexander. So now I don't know where I stand, Alex has not really denied it, this is turning out to be such a mess. He was very distant when we parted at the airport, I think our short relationship is over!"

Stefan appeared to calm down, his pride was dented, he felt his friend had over stepped the mark; Emma hoped he would be an adult and get over it. He was becoming jealously possessive, he felt Emma was being manipulated on purpose by Alex. Convinced he would be able to put a stop to it. He was now curious as to what had occurred at the weekend.

"Were you with Alex at the weekend? He asked.

"Yes but not alone, we flew by private jet to Scotland, with his Russian friends, we stayed in a luxury tower retreat. That's when the Princess warned me off him, saying they were secretly still engaged. I had no idea, it came as a total shock! I feel such a fool for being taken in like that, but what could I do, it's an awful situation." Tears started to form, welling up in her eyes.

"I know the Princess well, she is a real predator." He said gently dabbing tears away from her eyes.

"She tried to bewitch me, when we met at polo matches. It was difficult to get away from her, she used her title to lure men into her net, I was the lucky one that got away. It sounds as though she has her talons securely fixed into Count Alexander, he won't be so lucky."

Stefan felt a strong urge to be protective and

passionate, he leant forward roughly grabbing Emma in his arms, squeezing her tightly around the waist so she could not get away. Emma felt his hot breath on her neck, smothering her moist cheeks with kisses. His aromatic lemon cologne filled the air, her senses heightened as his wandering cold fingers wandered longingly under her blouse, loosening her bra cupping her silky smooth breasts in his large hands. She became unintentionally aroused, when she felt his erect ardour pressing his groin firmly against hers, pinning her firmly to the wall, sliding his fingers tantalisingly across her stiff nipples. Stefan's wet lips pushing ever closer to her open mouth, she let out a sigh of disbelief as his tongue found hers probing her hard forcing her forgiveness.

Her longing for him was reignited, her passion burned into the old familiar flames of desire. Emma tried in vain to stop her feelings for him, she hated his arrogant carnal nature, he was like the devil yearning for lust, he ached to ravish her body. Still she could not stop her feelings of longing, he had mesmerised her, she wanted him inside her again, to make passionate love to her hotly like he had before.

Their past love making seemed like a hazy recollection, a strong flash back to a reflection of her innocent love for him, when she was a just a child. The sensations heightened as he stroked her legs beneath her skirt, finding her moist with anticipation, he growled in appreciation as her legs parted.

Stefan was beyond controlling himself with a mad craving for Emma, he had waited so long for this moment. There was no turning back now, he would take her unexpectedly once more. As their bodies writhed with shuddering vibrations he lifted her easily onto the fireside rug, the atmosphere was electrified. She was purring with pleasure in his arms as he entered her, both pulsing in slow motion rhythmically with renewed satisfaction as he grasped her buttocks firmly.

The torture of being apart was becoming apparent, their bodies were a perfect fit for one another, could the flaws each possessed be over looked, if they concentrated on looking after each other? Would the mistakes of the past be wiped clean in a new beginning, it was a tantalising possibility.

Alex had been forgotten as though he was just a past distraction, Stefan had staked his claim sealing his devotion. He had found the woman he loved more than anything in the world. She was steadfast and true, he resolved that no other man would possess her. Stefan's enthusiasm was total Emma's passion for him was clearly apparent. She had loved him most of her life. Now he would show his dedication to her in the best way possible. He decided at that moment to make her his bride.

CHAPTER 21

Aware it was the final countdown for her business plans at the manor, Emma's anticipation was building. Her grand opening was scheduled for one month's time, printed invitations were being hand delivered to the villagers. By Christmas she was hosting a wedding fair ready to take bookings for the new year. She was in her element, laying out the advert for the local paper. A top photographer and web designer were scheduled for later in the week, it was all systems go. Her dreams of creating her own business were coming true at last.

She found that Stefan was paying special attention, he marvelled at the progress when surveying everything she had done so superbly at the manor. Her skills were immense she had left no stone unturned in her professional endeavours, he was truly amazed at what a difference he found at his old home. The orangery had large opulent blue and gold screens, with an old traditional cash register as a centre piece. The room had been transformed into an elegant coffee shop, with wicker tables and chairs surrounded by tropical plants, her creative flair shined bright.

The tour of the grounds continued as Stefan looked

on completely stunned at the progress. Emma was elated and proud at his reaction to the vast improvements.

"I do wish I had a camera to photograph your bewildered face." She said taking his arm as they strolled outside under the tunnel of rose arches.

"The look on my face must be quite a puzzling sight, I can't believe the advances you have made in a just a few months. You have transformed yourself into a stunning business woman, and changed the manor at the same time. The house and striking grounds are amazing, well done!" He squeezed her arm in appreciation as they sauntered along the path then stopping her in her tracks when he added.

"I just want to say thanks for all your efforts, I'm sorry, I let you down badly in your hour of need. It was unforgivable, I was in a very dark place, with a deep sinister depression."

"Are you ok now?" She asked knowing Becky's suicide had knocked him back again severely.

"I have learnt such a lot recently about my life and where I was headed, it is reassuring to be back at the manor with you. Talking it through has helped a lot; I have had counselling for my gambling addiction. I can assure you now, that I will never gamble again." Stefan felt as though he was on the road to recovery at last, but it made him look at other aspects of his life. It had taken a tragedy to make him look closer at his greed, and addictions in a new light.

Pulling Emma towards him in a reassuring hug, his strong arms held her captive as he planted a gentle kiss on her lips. She was shyly responsive to his soft touch in a new way, she had been infatuated with him as a child. Now he had reverted to his childlike youth again, it was a significant change and endearing.

"My Mother paid fully for all my years of education at University, my privileged easy background left me no real value of the people, in my life. My experience of an advantaged life, had a long term toxic effect on me! I now see it clearly, and regret how much I hurt the people I love."

It was the first time he had ever really mentioned love, did he mean just a love for his mother? Or a love for her? Looking up at his tanned face, she brushed her hand through his tousled blond locks. It was time to tell him how she really felt at last, her eyes were misting up with pent up emotion.

"Look I don't know where we go from here, but I do know one thing. I have always loved you!" There she had said it once and for all. Unable to hide her feelings for him she looked straight at him, her love was like a locked safe waiting to be opened, only Stefan had the key.

He was not surprised that she loved him, he had felt her unconditional love forever. Only he had been too selfish to acknowledge that he felt it too. It was a momentous admission on Emma's part, he responded in the only way he knew. He took her hand under the rose canopy and knelt down on one knee.

"I love you, Emma will you marry me!"

He stood up waiting for her answer, the tears flowed as she answered.

"Yes I will marry you." Her eyes sparkled at the full impact of what had happened so unexpectedly.

"I came back for you!" He said looking at her lovingly.

"You are very special to me in so many ways. I seem

to have been in love with you all my life, but tried not to admit it to myself. Please forgive me for being such a stupid fool." She could forgive her old friend almost anything as long as they were together, Stefan spoke again softly.

"We have both been rash and foolish, no one is perfect we all come with our own faults. But I believe we have a chance to make a new start here together." He was hoping she agreed, with him, Emma was perplexed at how they could be together in Sussex, when he lived in New York. He could see the shadow of doubt crossing her mind, as she tried to make sense of their possible future.

"I said I came back for you, it's true I have come to claim you as my own. When I left the auction office in the New York, the board agreed with me, that I would be responsible for opening a new London auction house. So we can live here together at last! My childhood home is now where I want to start my new life with you."

"Oh I see, well that puts a new light on things." She said looking relieved. He was not expecting her to uproot and live in New York, her home was firmly now at the manor in the South Downs.

"Now look at me," he said pulling her closer.

"I have to clear up a few details! How do you feel about Count Alexander?" She was glad to set the record straight.

"I must admit that I was falling for him, as any woman would! He was just the most cultured and polite man I had ever met, his manners are impeccable. His royal Russian breeding is so resilient." She held fast to Stefan's gaze shielding herself from his possible anger.

"But I don't love him! He's simply not the man for me!"

"Are you sure?"

"Yes I'm sure, it became clearer when the Princess warned me off Alex, let's face it he is from a completely different world. Alex lives in billionaire central in London, it's not my playground to be honest." It was nice for Emma to get an update on how the ultra rich lived their lives, but she had lost everything at one point, and now held entirely different values, trying to explain her feelings she said.

"I have had a taste of the paparazzi chasing me. The Princess loves using her ludicrous title, being the centre of attention so let her have it! I prefer the quiet life I can have right here, in the country running the business. I know I can make a successful income, I'm truly at home in the manor house." Stefan was glad to hear her views, she certainly showed no signs of envy. He was tired of playing the field, thankful he could spend the rest of his life with her.

"You sound so sure." He said taking her in his arms.

"Do you have any doubts about us?" Emma then responded.

"No doubts, I know you have changed as much as I have recently. Are you truly ready to settle down to the next phase of your life?"

He answered her truthfully.

"Sometimes you have to lose everything you have, to notice what you are missing. I'm ready for love and commitment at last. I now want to feel something real, to have a companion and soul mate to share my life for better or worse. I wasn't even looking for love, but you're love found me." For once in his life he wanted to make someone else happy, to give her all the support he should have given her before.

Stefan had been given the chance to change the roulette wheel for the wheel of fortune, he would take his last gamble on Emma. She had seen her tarot cards recently, the magician was crossing the wheel of fortune, clarified by the lovers. She would love and look after Stefan forever securing their future, that she had so carefully prepared for. They had both learned valuable lessons along the way, the time was right for their dreams to be fulfilled.

Warmly holding each other as the scent of honeysuckle wafted in the afternoon breeze, they strolled slowly arm in arm up the path to the barn. The evening sun was beginning to hang low in the sky casting an amber haze on the horizon, as they reminisced about their past childhood at the manor together. Stopping taking her face in his hands, smoothing her fair hair away from her rich lips he sealed their love one more time as he whispered softly.

"Just think our children will have an idyllic life here, like we did all those years ago. My womanising days are long gone; my hedonistic lifestyle is a dim and dark shadow of the past. We have a bright future, built on strong foundations I'm sure we will create a good life together."

Emma realised the loneliness she had felt most of her life had been replaced by what mattered. To be with Stefan was all she had ever wanted, but she had to wait for the lessons life would teach them both. The fates allowed their paths to cross at the right time again, in the right way.

Entering the barn which was the pinnacle of her success, the finishing touches were perfect. Stefan was mesmerised at how she had taken the barn back into an age of chivalry, it was so impressive he chuckled at her daring sense of style. She was so exceptional the manor reflected her distinctive style in every way.

"Wonderful," he said, I love the minstrel's gallery you've created, what a great scene it would be for our wedding breakfast." He was fully immersed in getting her to see his vision of their special day.

"Let's hold our wedding here at Christmas to start off the wedding season!"

"Not so fast" Emma said, her mind was quick, but he had put her thoughts in a tail spin.

"Show me don't just tell me that you love me, I need to really feel loved. So much has happened to me recently, this is all too quick."

"I promise to show you how much I love you very day for the rest of my life!" With that said, he held her so tightly not wanting to ever let her go. Her breath escaped her as he kissed her passionately in his strong embrace. Stefan had no doubts about her being his bride, but knew he had to show her his true feelings.

The whirlwind of emotions continued back at the manor as they spent the rest of the day under covers. Not wanting to break the spell of love that had brought them together at last. It was a wonderful experience for both to take time to reconnect in an intense way.

Alex was expected to arrive the following day, Emma was not sure what reaction there would be to the news they had to tell him. He had not call her at all since he left to go home to London, so it would be a peculiar reunion. Emma was hoping that Stefan would be civilised and cool with Alex, her having sex with him was not something she was proud of, but she could not turn back the clock. Perhaps it was the tarot cards that had led her astray after all. Yet she had free will, and he was undeniably the best looking man she had ever seen. He had a fairytale charisma in bucket loads, wouldn't any woman be swayed by his charm.

The tarot cards had been an obsession with her for so long, it was hard to break the habit. But she had decided the symbolism of the tarot cards packed with meaning, would be best placed in the past. Her new life with Stefan would have a special meaning of its own to her; Emma would discard divination for her faith in a higher power.

All her secret wishes and desires had been granted, in the most surprising way. She would let go of her demons and fears at last, putting away forever, her tarot cards.

Astonishingly when Alex appeared the next day with his horsebox. Driving up the private gravel road, Emma greeted him like an old friend not a lover. Overnight they had turned into mere acquaintances not friends with benefits.

Emma surprised herself with her restrained attitude, it was an Oscar winning performance, as she welcomed him shyly onto the manor estate ready to greet Stefan. She was not sure what response Alex was going to get from his old friend.

"Alex how lovely to see you." She said approaching him from the porch, as Alex stepped down from the horse box. He was as good-looking as ever in his casual jeans and cowboy boots. Emma stepped forward awkwardly dodging him, not wanting him to greet her with a kiss. It was time to set the record straight before he met Stefan again.

"I'm so glad to see you." Alex said extending his arm into the cab pulling out a bunch of yellow roses from the seat.

"A peace offering for you! I think we need to talk straight away." It was a good idea, Emma was ready to explain what had changed at the manor recently.

"Let's take a walk in the grounds; It's necessary to talk through what happened at the mystery weekend with the Princess." She said, while walking along the path towards the walled garden, as Alex followed on behind.

"I guess things have altered since we came back from the tower." Emma said going straight ahead with the subject of concern.

Biting his lip in anticipation, knowing he had to come clean with what had altered between them, Alex told Emma the obvious.

"As you know there had been an engagement promise, made many years ago by my family with the Princess. She now insists on me honouring that old pledge. In principle and with respect to her, I have to recognise the obligation. We are now officially engaged! This has come as a complete surprise to you I'm sure, but it is a long standing arrangement. I'm sorry if I lead you astray, but I must show consideration for the prior commitment."

Emma was not really surprised, she had already guessed that he would fall in line with the Princess. Plus she had her own news to tell him, which would come as a complete surprise.

"I think we can say our relationship was a mistake in

that case." She said. Alex then surprised her by saying what she had not expected.

"The engagement promise with the Princess was a big mistake! But it will prove to be very difficult to back down out of the commitment. However I do have something important to say to you. If you would agree to be my wife, then I will gladly turn down the Princess." He took her hand, looking closely for her response as he said.

"I realise that I love you Emma! Not her, I want to be with you!" Emma was reeling with this proposal completely shocked by the turn of events."

"I have a high opinion of you Alex, especially for helping me out financially when I really needed it. But Stefan has made me fully aware that you were told to look after me, while he was away." They stopped to sit on a bench as she continued to talk, Alex realising how he had been caught out.

"I was unaware of this fact, Stefan was furious with me when I told him that we have been seeing each other, obviously sleeping together. You have some explaining to do! We are both responsible I know, but Stefan wants answers."

"There could be some friction between you two that I'm not aware of, I don't want to be caught in the middle of some vendetta. Can you explain what happened, so that I can understand?"

Alex knew he would have to come clean, he had taken an unfair advantage of Emma, to get his own back on Stefan. He was not proud of what he had done, but in hind sight he was not sorry. Emma was special he could see why Stefan was defensive, in his accent he tried to explain his actions.

"I think I owe you a big apology for my behaviour, however the time we had together was fantastic I can't regret it. Or take it back, I do love you, and hope you can forgive me for my conduct. Why I slept with you was just plainly unwise, firstly I found you to be irresistible. Secondly I was infuriated with Stefan, I was quite sure he had taken sexual advantage of the Princess. He slept with her before I had a chance to. He denied it, but I have had my suspicions all along." Emma had to put him straight, she knew he was mistaken.

"I know Stefan was a player, but you are wrong about him and the Princess, he told me truthfully he has not had sex with her. She did approach him at a polo match she had a clear line of attack, but he wanted nothing to do with her, he thought she was predatory, she had become his stalker at matches. But he was aware of your old connection with her, he told me he did not want to upset you, so he retreated from her advances."

Alex looked as though he was on the verge of a revelation. He had wrongly judged his old friend, he was aware how manipulating Princess Volkov was, but had not realised that Stefan had rebuked her advances. Emma tried to make things right between the two men, it was time to explain also what had occurred in Paris to Stefan's wife.

"The reason Stefan came back to Wychfield so suddenly, was that Becky his wife committed suicide in Paris, he wanted to tell me himself. He was in a terrible state of panic." Alex responded shocked at the eye opening news.

"Oh god no! No wonder he returned so quickly to the manor. How is he now?"

"Much better than he was when he arrived," she replied.

"He is getting over the shock slowly, at least Becky is at peace now! It is not easy to deal with death it has really changed him, he is like a kid again. He is a typical Leo, wanting to be the centre of attention, now the womaniser and gambler of the past has long gone. It was as though he needed a great shock to bring him back to his senses." Emma felt Alex's eyes boring into her , he wanted an answer to his proposal.

"Alex I would have to say no your proposal, because I have been in love with Stefan most of my life."

Emma decided to keep the news of their forthcoming wedding a secret for now, wanting to give Alex time to digest what she has told him so far.

CHAPTER 22

It was the ending of their last chapter, but not the end of their story, life had taken them all on a long journey. Their actions had turned out to be under their own free will after all. Emma's possible fairytale life with Count Alexander had been a non starter however appealing, but the continuing circles of life kept going around, just as it should.

What had happened to the friends was as it was meant to be, the wheel of fortune kept turning. The tragedies that had brought them together, swung slowly in their favour like a great pendulum. They had each leant a great deal along the way, but their friendship now had a chance to move closer.

Alex and Emma walked back to the manor house in complete silence, aware a new beginning was taking place for all of them. Their lives were taking different paths changing their futures forever.

"Go in," she said opening the front door under the porch. We can settle the horses into the stables later."

"I will make us all a cup of tea; you must be parched after your journey. Thanks again for the roses, I'll put them in a vase. Go through to the lounge Stefan is waiting to see you." It was Alex's turn to be hesitant, as he tried to act relaxed, walking through the stone porch into the hallway in front of her. Aware he could be walking into the lion's den, not sure what kind of reception he would get from Stefan, it had been months since they had last met.

As he approached the lounge the door was open, Stefan was sitting on the sofa looking through a dense pile of paperwork. Alex made sure he heard him enter the room not wanting him to be startled.

"Hi Stefan, I have been talking to Emma she has just told me about Becky. I'm so sorry for your loss! It can't be easy to come to terms with someone ending their life like that." Stefan looked up, but continued sitting.

"It wasn't something I expected at all," he replied.

"I'm glad I came back to tell Emma, however I hear you have been taking advantage of her! Nice of you to let me know what was going on." He looked at Alex with a serious expression on his face, as he waited for his lame excuse.

"Look I know I owe you an apology for my actions! However it was partly because of my suspicion that you had slept with the Princess. I was convinced you had! Emma has explained to me that you never had sex with Princess Volkov at all." He looked sorry for what he had done, sheepishly looking at Stefan.

"I just took advantage of Emma to spite you. I'm sorry, it's all my fault I didn't understand. As awful as it sounds Emma was single, she is so lovely I had the chance and took it. Let's face it you messed things up with her too." Stefan had to admit he was correct, he did have a point he had treated Emma appallingly.

"You're absolutely right of course." Stefan admitted.

"I was a fool to let her go!" Then he told Alex.

"I have asked her to marry me, as soon as we can! There were so many mistakes made, I wish I could turn back the clock." Alex was surprised to hear he wanted to get married again, so soon after his estranged wife had died. Stefan stood up, ready to shake Alex's hand at last, in a gesture of renewed friendship. There seemed no point in being angry.

"I'm a very lucky man." Stefan said,

"She loves me and has said yes, we are hoping to get married by Christmas at the manor!"

"Congratulations Stefan, she's a very special lady, I expect you have guessed, that I am now formerly engaged to the Princess. However I must admit Emma would have been the perfect partner for me!" Stefan was pleased for his old friend, but not surprised the Princes had persuaded him to fall in line. But he knew she could never get him to fall in love with her."

Stefan just hoped that Alex would not regret it, but also glad he had not been able to steal Emma away from him. Stefan extended his best wishes, not wanting to sound too smug.

"We both have good reason to celebrate, I know you had a long standing arrangement with Princess Volkov. Are you sure she is the one for you?" Alex had to think hard, he had a soft spot for Emma now, but it was no good changing course.

"Too late to change my mind! The wedding has been booked for next year in the South of France." He answered knowing full well he had been trapped by his re union with the Princess, as Emma had turned him down by saying no to him, he had to re think the whole scenario.

As they were discussing the forthcoming weddings, Emma entered the room with a selection of sandwiches, biscuits, and tea for the afternoon.

"I'm glad you two are friends again! It's a new start for all of us, we have a real connection to Wychfield there must be some form of magic at work here.

There seemed to be no lasting animosity between the two men, slowly the atmosphere had cleared. It was strange that both lovers Emma had slept with were here in the manor together, being very civilised.

Emma's marriage decision had been complicated, she had to chose between Prince charming or the bastard of all time. But love was burning a light through her soul, she could forgive the man who had hurt her. The unconditional love she felt was so strong, Stefan was her soul mate and always had been.

"Alex has just told me he is getting married to the Princess next year in France." Stefan said to Emma as she looked on, taking her plate of snacks. Her face gave nothing away, she was going to act as though Alex had never asked for her hand in marriage.

Later the horses were settled into the stables and Alex left the manor for London. It had ended as a good meeting between the friends, both had new futures ahead. Emma and Stefan went back to the barn to discuss the wedding arrangements, looking forward to their new opening.

"Of course you realise that my wishes have already been fulfilled. A Christmas wedding is my ultimate dream." Emma said taking the stairs up to the minstrels gallery with Stefan following up behind her. They surveyed the grand hall below as she selected the ideal spot for the Christmas tree as the central feature.

The ceremony would be conducted inside the barn right next to the nativity scene. Emma looked down to where they would be standing on the day, she felt as though her desires had all been granted Wychfield was indeed a unique place. As a wedding gift to Stefan, Emma arranged with Brandon to turn the potting shed into his own writing retreat. Stefan had his first art book about *Victorian Symbolism* to complete, the manor was the perfect place to set up his writing den.

The wedding invitations embossed in gold with the family griffin crest, were sent out. Lady Mary was guest of honour delighted to see the manor back to the old days. Most of all she was enjoying the true love, Emma and Stefan had found at last, in the place of their childhood.

As for Count Alexander he was absent from the wedding party, not wanting to intrude on their special day. His own wedding was scheduled for the following spring but he realised that Emma had stolen his heart he would never forget their special time together.

By marrying Stefan, Emma was fulfilling a longing she had held inside all her life, it was a secret wish which she could reveal at last. Her absolute love for him had surfaced once more, it was time to treasure the moment and appreciate their many blessings.

Emma put away her tarot cards for the last time, the future events would unfold naturally from now on. She no longer had a desire to look into the future, her focus was now on a higher power. Divine and perfect timing had played a big part in her plans, her extraordinary experiences had flipped her life onto a unique path with a partner she loved.

The shift had changed her forever, love had a new

meaning for her now, it was an uplifting feeling taking away her loneliness. She now had a real faith with no doubts about the future, she would always cherish Wychfield manor, it was such a special magical place.

Leading her back in time, yet forward into the future with a renewed belief in a higher power. Gifts are sometimes overvalued, the couple had learned to be grateful for love, to use their talents and resources wisely.

On many evenings she walked alone to the barn, taking the stairs up to her favourite spot on the minstrel's gallery. Emma noticed through the skylight in the barn the dark night sky, glowing with a big full moon in Scorpio. Shining down brightly on her, such a good omen for a new beginning, how wonderful.

The End

Also by the author

THE LURE OF GOLD

By S.P.Hurst

The story is about a stubborn young woman in a man's world. A historical romance set in the gold fields of Northern California and the wilderness beyond.

Emily Porter, a pretty English virgin, arrives alone in Sacramento in the hot summer of **1850**. The sheriff is instantly attracted to her, but another rival for her affections is on the horizon. An exciting romantic adventure full of conflict and tension unfolds, as a mystery propels Emily into the dangerous wilderness.

A word from the author.
This first book was the launch of my career as a writer. The Lure of Gold was started on Valentine's day 2018, so it is very special to me.
I hope you love it, as much as I do!

Sheila P. Hurst

Coming Soon

By

S.P.Hurst

THE BILLIONAIRES REQUEST

A modern day romance set in the rolling hills of Herefordshire.

Petra Wyatt has a complex defiant spirit, with a moral streak to her personality. Dark haired and strikingly attractive, she has an inner charisma. Known as a brilliant yet headstrong interior designer. She is propelled into a world of extravagant luxury only billionaires can experience. A rich story full of conflict and tension, with multi faceted characters.

A reclusive and powerful billionaire hero emerges, Marcus Aubrey is strong willed but full of inner turmoil. Yet a softer side emerges winning her heart. During tragic divine timing a disaster strikes, as Petra vanishes without a trace. As the mystery unfolds and deepens, Marcus has to find her before it is too late, knowing her life is in danger. Will he Find her in time? He is on a determined mission to protect her, handsome Marcus wants to give her one final request.

ABOUT THE AUTHOR

Sheila Hurst writes as S.P.Hurst this is the second romance book published by the author. She is a contemporary and historical romance writer. What interests her most is fascinating characters and their relationships with a strong tale. The settings and characters are closely entwined, in a compelling turbulent and intriguing story.

Sheila is married and has one grown up daughter, and several rescue cats. In her previous life before becoming a writer she had worked in aviation and the travel industry, travelling the world extensively.

Becoming a published author was a long held dream and desire since childhood. Interests include history and reading.

46851017R00160

Printed in Poland
by Amazon Fulfillment
Poland Sp. z o.o., Wrocław

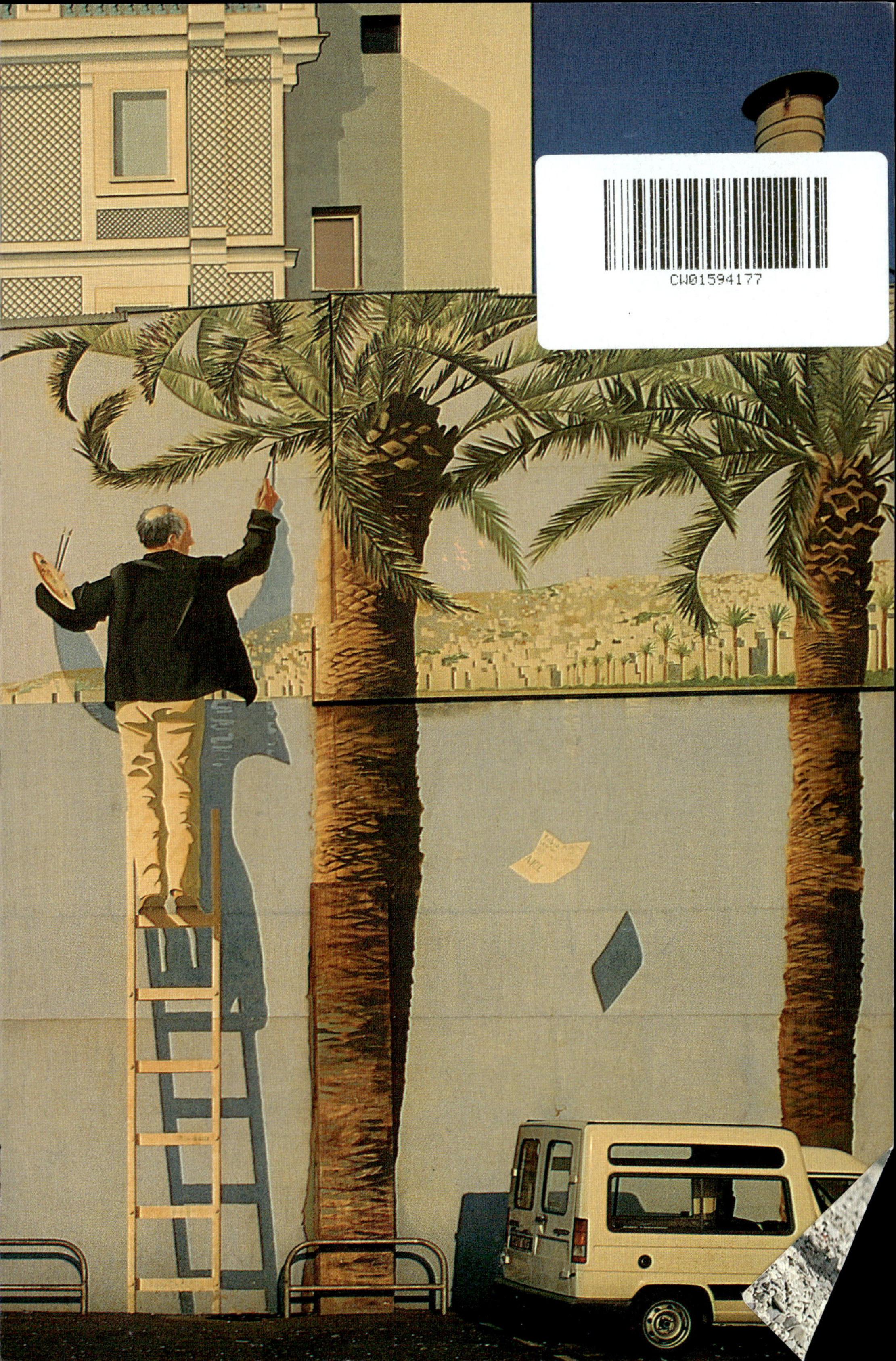

INSIGHT GUIDES

Series Created by Hans Höfer

The French Riviera

Edited by Rosemary Bailey
Principal photography by Catherine Karnow
and Douglas Corrance

Editorial Director: Brian Bell

APA PUBLICATIONS
Part of the Langenscheidt Publishing Group

Bailey

A travel guide to the French Riviera inevitably presents problems: how do you say something fresh about a region which has been for centuries a holiday destination favoured by royalty and some of the worlds most famous writers, and how do you give an honest appraisal of a place which is frequently cited by critics as a chastening example of how untramelled tourism can turn beauty into beastliness?

The Côte d'Azur presents a lesson for the travel industry everywhere, especially since it is now beginning to tackle some of the problems which threaten to undermine its considerable charms. Celebratory and critical where appropriate, this guide takes a fresh and clear-eyed view of this wonderful region.

This new edition of *Insight Guide: The French Riviera* has been lovingly and painstakingly updated by its original editor, **Rosemary Bailey**, whose love of the South of France has led her to live there most of the year. She fell in love with the Côte d'Azur at the end of the 1970s, when she stayed on a rose farm near Vence.

An author and journalist, Bailey contributes travel articles to the London *Sunday Times* and many other publications. Here she has written about the regions she knows best: Cagnes and St-Paul, Grasse and Cap Ferrat. She has also explored the famous perched villages of the Alpes Maritimes, and has contributed features on history and contemporary life.

A distinguishing characteristic of the Insight series, of course, is its superb photography, and this guide combines the work of two of its most talented photographers: **Catherine Karnow**, an American whose sensual appreciation of France combines with a particular skill for revealing portraiture, and **Douglas Corrance**, a Scot whose photojournalist's eye produces an exciting immediacy.

Karnow

Corrance

Miles

Bailey was assisted by **Barry Miles**, whose books include acclaimed biographies of Allen Ginsberg, Sir Paul McCartney and William Burroughs. He has been a frequent visitor to the Riviera since 1968 and a devoted fan of Brigitte Bardot for even longer. Here he writes about the BB phenomenon, and about Picasso and the many other writers and artists inspired by the region. He particularly enjoys the combination of ancient history and modern living that typifies life on the Côte d'Azur – "satellite dishes on 13th-century houses," as he puts it.

A formidable team of contributors, both Riviera residents and devoted visitors, explored the myriad aspects which make the region such a rich subject. **Lisa Gerard-Sharp**, a London-based writer and broadcaster, and a regular contributor to Insight Guides, here applies her fearsome research skills and trenchant perceptions to the impact of the British and other expatriates, as well as contributing chapters on Monaco, Menton and the Border Country of the mountains. She has been coming to the Côte d'Azur since she was a child, when, she says, "our caravan holiday in St-Tropez was enlivened by the proximity of a nudist colony."

Gerard-Sharp

Tony Rocca, who has spent many

Rocca

years living on the Côte d'Azur is a British writer based in Le Cannet, he offers an enticing insider's guide to Nice and Cannes. After spending 20 years working for Britain's national newspapers, mainly the *Sunday Times* and the *Daily Mail*, Rocca escaped in the early 1980s to Cannes, from where he contributes to a variety of UK and US publications.

Peter Graham, another frequent contributor to Insight Guides, here writes about food, his favourite subject, and the contretemps between Graham Greene and Nice's headline-making mayor, Jacques Médecin. Graham lives in a small village in the Auvergne, writing regularly for London's *Guardian*, *Times* and *Sunday Times*. His book *Classic Cheese Cookery*, was the winner of the André Simon Memorial prize. Appropriately, he was responsible for translating Jacques Médecin's very own Niçois cookbook into English.

Sweeney

Philip Sweeney, another Insight regular, writes frequently about travel and music and has published a guide to world music. For someone addicted to people-watching, St-Tropez proved a honey-pot.

Chris Peachment, a film writer and former arts editor of London's *Times*, has contributed a wry and amusing behind-the-scenes look at the Cannes Film Festival.

Stratte-McClure

Joel Stratte-McClure, an American-born Côte d'Azur resident, is based in Valbonne. He has written a number of guidebooks and is a regular contributor to *Time, People,* the *International Herald Tribune* and a host of other publications. In this book, he explains the wheeling and dealing involved in the business life of the area.

Radice

Sophie Radice, who has explored Hyères and the surrounding region, was *Vogue*'s Young Writer of the Year in 1988 and now contributes articles on France to a variety of publications from the rambling mill-house in the forests of Compiègne.

Rowlinson Carter, whose many Insight contributions have proved that historical narratives need never contain a dull moment, provides a dramatic description of the wartime Riviera.

Mike Meade, the Canadian editor of the *Riviera Reporter* and a devoted yachtee, explains the niceties of yachting culture to the uninitiated.

Adam

Jill Adam, who has put together fact-packed Travel Tips sections for several of Insight's France titles and has also edited the *French Farm and Village Holiday Guide* for some years, has compiled the comprehensive information listings at the end of this guide. She welcomes any opportunity to spend more time in her house in southwest France.

Nicky Burton made an invaluable contribution to picture research and information on hotels and restaurants. She is based in Tourrettes-sur-Loup, from where she writes for *New Riviera Côte d'Azur* magazine, and travels throughout the region as sales representative for Penguin Books.

Special thanks are due to **Hertz Cars** for supplying photographers' transport and to Apa managing editor **Martha Ellen Zenfell** for her inspiration during the gruelling picture-editing process. The original book was proofread and indexed by **Carole Mansur**.

CONTENTS

Preceding pages: ***trompe l'oeil*** **in Nice; on the beach at Menton.**

Maps

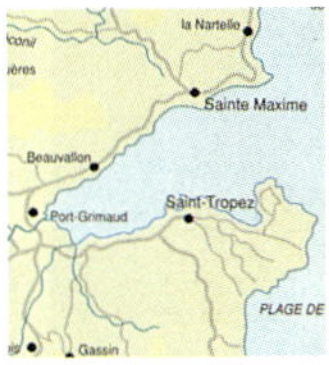
la Nartelle
Sainte Maxime
Beauvallon
Port Grimaud
Saint-Tropez
PLAGE DE
Gassin

TRAVEL TIPS

Harley

BRASSERIE DES

CAFE DES ARTS
BILLARD
BOULES

DES ARTS

THE BUSINESS OF GAIETY

The Côte d'Azur, the French Riviera: the names alone retain an enduring allure. Strung along the Mediterranean coast of France is a glittering necklace of exotic towns redolent of glamour and luxury: Cannes, Nice, Monte-Carlo, Antibes, St-Tropez.

The coast's plentiful pleasures include not only sun and sea but magnificent art and architecture, glorious perfumes and flowers, world-class yachts, casinos, film and jazz festivals, food, wine and spectacular scenery. As one of the world's most glamorous holiday destinations, the French Riviera has attracted visitors for over two centuries, from Queen Victoria to Madonna, Picasso to Brigitte Bardot.

The actual geographical limits of the region are a matter of debate. Traditionally the Côte extends from Menton to Cannes. The French Riviera usually designates the coast, despite its infinite variety, all the way to Marseille. Certainly property developers like to think so.

This guide takes a middle path, starting from Hyères and its islands in the west, one of the destinations first favoured by early visitors such as Queen Victoria. It extends as far as Menton and also includes the Haut-Pays in the east, where the villages close to the border are more Italian than French – appropriate since the Italian influence is a significant aspect of the region.

The Côte d'Azur for most people is the classic image of a summer holiday. Its clichés persist: glorious blue sea, virtually guaranteed sunshine, waving palm trees and serious sun-tans. For most of its visitors the Côte d'Azur continues to supply all in liberal quantity; satisfaction guaranteed. Today, however, tourism is no longer the sole *raison d'être* of the region, which is now also aspiring to become a "technological Eden", the high-tech capital of the Southern European sun-belt.

We have tried in this guidebook to present an accurate picture of the contemporary Côte d'Azur, from its yacht culture to Grimaldi gossip; from the best restaurants to the crime figures; from where the financial investment is coming from to the best museums and the most perfect gardens, views and beaches. We have also delved into its history to put it all in context: its early beginnings; the influence of the British; the hedonistic jazz age of the Americans; the sun cult of Bardot and St-Tropez. We describe the many writers and artists who have been inspired by the region, and those, like Graham Greene, who have sometimes been enraged by it.

We have tried to be honest, to acknowledge the problems as well as exploring the pleasures, because it is these issues as much as its traditional diversions that make the Côte d'Azur today such a fascinating place to explore.

Preceding pages: St-Tropez sun-lover; the Carlton Hotel, Cannes; Harley-Davidsons, the quintessential accessory in St-Tropez; a game of *boules*; artist in the Café des Arts, St-Tropez. Left, a fête at Biot.

"It is to be tranquilly overwhelmed to see the Mediterranean just before dawn, stretching out beneath your windows. There will be the grey satin of the sea, the mountains behind, the absolutely convincing outline of Reinach's Greek villa at the end of Beaulieu Point. And the memory of Greek gods...

"It is one of the greatest pleasures of my life that a legend avers that Ulysses once sheltered in the sea cave below my garden. If I close my eyes I can see Pallas Athene with shield and spear stand in the sky and brood above her sea. Or if you quote to me, *Saepe te in somnis vidi...* or merely mention to me the name of Catullus you will have me in such a state that I must leave my writing and walk from end to end of the terrace for some minutes."

– Ford Madox Ford: *It Was The Nightingale* (1933)

A first glance at the stretch of Mediterranean coast which we now call the Côte d'Azur suggests that little evidence of the past can possibly remain amongst the super-highways and shopping centres. While it is true that this region of France is not as rich in antiquity as some, it does have a past and the clues are there for those who wish to imagine the lives of earlier inhabitants. The region has numerous museums of archaeology and early human habitation as well as many delightful local museums devoted to Provençal daily life and traditional crafts.

The history of travel to the region is a story in itself; antiquarian travel books abound from the days when 18th-century visitors like Tobias Smollett were more concerned with discovering antiquities or restoring their health than with suntans and casinos.

The writers of these books, rattling about in their horse-drawn carriages along dusty roads lit only by fireflies or moonlight, or clambering over headlands still rich with fragrant *maquis* in search of Roman inscriptions and rare butterflies and plants, supply us with a wealth of classical learning and acute observation about the region, both as it used to be in ancient times and as it appeared to them in their own time.

Some of the most fascinating include the Rev. Hugh Macmillan's scriptural reflections in his 1885 *The Riviera,* Edward Strasburger's *Rambles on the Riviera*, with its loving detail of the long-lost flora of the region, Sir Frederick Treves's highly-coloured historical anecdotes in *The Riviera of the Corniche Roads* (1923), or the altogether racier picture painted by Charles Graves in *The Riviera Revisited*, written just after World War II, and rather more concerned with the price of a good *coq-au-vin* than with anything else. Their tales of hoary peasants, newly discovered ruins or 1946 menus provide us with an excellent reference point for linking the rich history of the region with its all too present reality.

Some of the very first signs of human habitation have been discovered here; in the Vallée des Merveilles are Bronze Age rock carvings, and evidence of Cro-Magnon man has been found in caves around Grasse.

The earliest known settlers along the coast were the Bronze Age Ligurians but little

Preceding pages: tuna-fishing in the Mediterranean. Left, Roman legionnaires in stone basrelief. Right, 19th-century travel guide.

survives of their passing except the faint remains of their forts, built of unworked stone, and some fragments of pottery and beads. Anyway, according to Norman Douglas: "Their reputation was none of the best; they were more prompt, says Crinagoras, in devising evil than good."

Roman occupation: It is not until the Greeks and Romans that we have much knowledge of everyday life. The Greeks traded throughout the Mediterranean and were responsible for founding both the city of Nice, which they called Nikea after Nike, the goddess of Victory, and subsequently, Antibes, called Antipolis, meaning "the city opposite" (to Nice). Traditionally all trading was done

outside the city walls and today the Antibes covered market is still located in almost the same place on the Cours Masséna.

The Roman occupation began in 125 BC and there is considerable evidence to be seen today; although their primary intentions were military, the Romans can in a sense be regarded as the first visitors to appreciate the pleasures of the coast, building themselves luxurious villas on the shore of St-Raphaël, near to their headquarters at Fréjus.

One of the most magnificent sights in the entire region is the gargantuan monument at La Turbie, which still towers over the landscape today, dwarfing the little village of the same name, and providing an enduring emblem of the power and self-confidence of the Romans. On the base of the monument, a long inscription lists all the subjugated tribes of the region.

The Via Aurelia, the main Roman road from Rome to Arles, passed through Menton, La Turbie and Cimiez, part of the route following what is now the Grande Corniche. La Turbie was the highest point of the road and a landmark which was visible for miles; and what is today a charming backwater of a village was then an important staging-post, bustling with merchants, centurions, slaves and gossip from Rome.

The Romans set up their capital in Narbonne and founded substantial towns throughout Provence including Arles, Nîmes and Fréjus. Everywhere they built arenas, baths and temples of which substantial ruins still remain today; in some cases entire towns like Cimiez have been excavated, and everywhere there are stones with Latin inscriptions which have been re-used in much later buildings.

In Fréjus the amphitheatre and arena is one of the largest built in Gaul by the Romans. The cathedral in Vence was built on the site of a Roman temple and throughout the town are scattered fragments of blocks with Roman inscriptions. Vallauris was founded by the Romans and was famous for its pottery even then, thanks to the quality of the red clay of the surrounding mountains.

Roman rule brought peace to the region for a time and the hill tribesmen ventured down from their fortified hill settlements to establish themselves in towns along the coast. However, with the fall of the Roman Empire chaos reigned once again, and Goths, Vandals and Lombards ravaged the area, leaving little in their savage wake.

Saracen invaders: Marauders also came from the sea; the Saracens were to devastate great swathes of the Mediterranean coastline from Rhodes to Spain and foray inland as far as the Loire river. They were Arabs originating from North Africa and the Eastern Mediterranean coast, and appear to have been exceptionally violent and terrifying. By about the year 800 they had taken power in Èze, La Turbie and Ste-Agnès and by the 10th century occupied nearly all the coast.

Finally in 980 a concerted effort was made to drive them out by the Count of Provence, who numbered amongst his soldiers a Genoese named Gibellino Grimaldi, the first mention in the region of a Grimaldi, the name of Monaco's name ruling house today.

It was a period of internal strife in which everybody fought with everybody else for dominance. As Sir Frederick Treves succinctly puts it: "They fought in a vague, confused, spasmodic way, with infinite vicissitudes and in every available place, for over 500 years." The history of almost every small village records the constant turmoil suffered by the people as they were attacked by invader after invader.

The history of Èze in particular is an astonishing summary of violent attack and subjugation, with generations of inhabitants being murdered and pillaged, the village itself continually burnt and razed to the ground. What is remarkable is the tenacity with which the village has always risen from its ashes – and today continues to flourish on the lucrative proceeds of tourism.

Neither France nor Italy was a united nation in the way that we know them today. Instead, both were divided into warring little fiefdoms, with towns constantly at war with each other, Pisa at war with Genoa, and Genoa at war with Nice, even tiny Gorbio at war with neighbouring Roquebrune.

Siege of Nice: The famous long-running conflict between the Guelphs and Ghibellines, defenders and enemies of the Pope, also engulfed the towns and villages of the region. Nice itself has been a constantly shifting pawn on the Mediterranean chessboard, and was frequently besieged, often by the French. On one memorable occasion, usually referred to as *the* siege of Nice in 1543, the town was saved by the heroic action of a stout laundrywoman who beat back the Turkish invaders scaling the walls, with her washing stick. From the 14th century, Nice and the surrounding region was under the protection of Savoy and did not elect to become part of France until 1860. The Italian influence is everywhere apparent, both in architecture, place names and the Niçois dialect.

Left, 19th-century Cagnes. Above, Nice in its nautical heyday, as seen in the Naval Museum.

Monks and pirates: Religion, of course, played a great part in the area's early history and a wealth of religious art survives. It sometimes seems as if almost every village has a religious festival or procession to celebrate, often revived for the benefit of tourists, but authentic nonetheless. One curious example is "*La procession aux escargots*" which takes place in Gorbio. It is not in fact a promenade of snails, but a festival celebrated by the White Penitents when all the streets and houses are illuminated by oil flames lit in a multitude of snail shells.

There are Penitents' chapels in Nice, Cannes and Sospel near the Italian border; these were lay brotherhoods that appeared in the 14th century and proliferated throughout the Midi. They were denoted by the colours of their hoods, the most important being Penitents Gris, Blancs and Noirs, and were devoted to charitable and sacred duties.

All over the Côte d'Azur are sanctuaries and pilgrimage centres, often in high mountain reaches, and heavily festooned with votive offerings. The Knights Templar also had a presence here and there are vestiges of their castles near Vence and La Gaude.

Among the most interesting ecclesiastical locations are the Îles de Lérins; the monastery on the Île de St-Honorat was for hundreds of years after it was founded in the 5th century the centre of Christianity in Southern Europe, described by the Rev. Hugh Macmillan as "the Iona of the South".

St Honorat was, like St Columba, a man of noble birth, born in Belgic Gaul in the 4th century. He renounced his worldly life and and went off on a pilgrimage to the East with his brother. Here he was inspired to return to one of the Lérins islands to found a monastery. The island was inhospitably swarming with serpents, crawling in and out of the Roman ruins that remained. Undeterred, Honorat established himself, and his holy life attracted many followers. A well was rediscovered, a church built and a garden planted. Honorat's sister, Marguerite, also started a convent on the next island, now named after her.

St-Honorat rapidly became a centre of religious learning and was in the thick of the great religious controversies of the Middle Ages. It was a centre for missionaries and supplied bishops to Arles, Avignon, Lyon, Vienne, Fréjus, Nice. Many ecclesiastical names are associated with Lérins, including that of St Patrick, who according to tradition was educated at the monastery.

Lérins became very wealthy, and owned land right along the coast from Grasse as far as Barcelona, including the village of Cannes itself. At one time nearly 4,000 monks lived on the island. But such riches were a great temptation and attacks by pirates and quarrels between the monks and Pope-appointed abbots undermined the monastery. By the 17th century it had finally collapsed, and eventually the island was bought by the Cistercians, who built a new monastery, and today supply visitors with their home-made liqueurs and cultivate the land using traditional medieval methods.

Damsels and pirates: Romantic stories also abound; the history of the region is awash with pirates, troubadours, distressed damsels, grand feats of bravery, dramatic betrayals, and princesses both pure and poisonous. Even today, among the high-rises and pink villas, the remains of a staircase, a curiously carved door lintel or a Renaissance window can evoke a past both humble and heroic.

As Sir Frederick Treves observed in 1923, it was a time of "general and brilliant disorder... a time to read about rather than to live in; a period that owes its chief charm to a safe distance and to the distortion of an artificial mirage. In any case one cannot fail to realise that these scenes took place in spots where tramcars are now running, where the char-à-banc rumbles along, and where the anaemic youth and the brazen damosel dance to the jazz music of an American band." And little did he know what was yet to come.

Left, Brea's painting, *La Brigue*, is a reminder of the region's ecclesiastical traditions. Right, a fountain at Mougins.

NICE 1903
COUPE ROTHSCHILD

SERPOLLET

THE BRITISH INVASION

"Cannes is for living, Monte-Carlo for gambling and Menton for dying." Such was the Victorian popular wisdom on the Riviera. During the days of the Grand Tour, France was considered a mere antechamber to classical Rome. But in the 1850s the South of France replaced Italy as the British home from home. Previously, the British invasion had been entirely bellicose: the Duke of Berwick, serving Louis XIV, razed Nice fortress to the ground in 1706.

The peaceful colonisation was led by Tobias Smollett, the Scots doctor and writer who pioneered sea-bathing as a cure for consumption. During his stay in Nice from 1763 to 1765, Smollett enjoyed the climate but deplored the uncultured locals, especially the "pot-bellied" women. He also found fault with the garlicky Niçoise cuisine but his ill-humour melted on contact with fruit sorbets. These "sorbettes, which are sold in coffee houses and places of public resort... are very agreeable to the palate."

In Smollett's day, medical fashion favoured spas such as Bath and Cheltenham but the prescription in the following century was for Riviera resorts. The avowed travel motive was health but, as William Chambers noted in 1870, "Fashion, *ennui* and love of gaiety seem to send quite as many abroad as absolutely bad health." At any rate, visitors in search of health were followed by social-climbers and pleasure-seekers. According to David Cecil, the British merely wanted to escape from "the chatter and clatter and hustle and guzzle of literary and fashionable London." One hidden impulse was the Victorian restlessness Alfred de Musset called "*la maladie du siècle*", the desire to flee.

The British followed the flock, migrating south in autumn and north in spring. As the American novelist W. D. Howells commented: "October was the month of the sunsets and the English." From May to September the Riviera villas were shuttered and the resorts deserted by all but unfashionable merchants, gamblers, prostitutes and, horror of horrors, the locals. But the British stranded on the Riviera out of season were vocal. Christopher Home Douglas, in Nice in May, was distressed by "a toilet table festooned with spiders' webs; decayed boots and chicken bones are also objectionable in a bedroom, even though under the bed and supposed to be out of sight."

By the 1830s, the days of corsairs and Barbary pirates were over and the civilised world could travel freely once more. For the British upper classes this meant travelling by private carriage to the Riviera, stopping at inns along the way. In 1832, the wealthy Boyle family travelled south in a drawing-room on wheels and, at a maximum speed of 35 miles (56 km) a day, there was time to admire the view. Money bought only comfort and convenience, not speed. The journey to the Riviera took up to three weeks, as long as in the time of the Roman Empire.

Alternatively, visitors could hire a *voiturin*, a French contractor, who provided coaches and horses all the way to the Côte. As late as 1875, Dr Bennet described this as "the most comfortable, pleasant and hygienic of any for

Preceding pages: early steam-powered car from series of tile pictures, Michelin Building, London. Left, Lord Brougham who first "discovered" Cannes in 1834. Right, a stroll in the Nice public gardens, 19th century.

tourists not much pressed for time or very particular about expense." Passengers who could not afford private transport were not so fortunate. Their fate was the diligence, a contraption built like an overgrown haywagon. Weighing up to five tons, the diligence carried 15 to 30 passengers and travelled at little more than walking pace.

In 1829 one disgruntled passenger, Dr James Johnson, likened French diligences to "locomotive prisons... in which one is pressed, pounded, and, what is worse than all, poisoned with mephitic gasses and noxious exhalations evolved from above, below and around." Passengers faced the unpleasant choice between the outside *banquette*, the in light seas the ships swayed dangerously. British voyagers cried discrimination at every turn. In the 1880s the Rev. John Aiton complained that "the passengers are actually starved; English passengers are insulted by Frenchmen... and as to a Frenchman lending an English voyager a spyglass or telling him the name of an island, he would rather spit in his face."

The arrival of the railway in the 1850s dramatically reduced the hardships of travel to the Riviera. Yet horse-power was not rendered obsolete overnight since key stretches of railway were not complete before 1870. Until then, carriages bridged the gaps. Diligences would be placed on a rolling platform

cold, hard seat beside the driver, or the cowshed odours of the seats in the *intérieur* and the *coupé*. For the middle stretch of the journey south, travellers usually switched to a river steamer from Chalon to Avignon. The Austrian-built river steamers found favour with the British but nothing but scorn was poured on the French steamships.

From the 1830s, steamships linked the Riviera ports and, to avoid the stultifying diligence, the British often opted for this sea voyage. Despite the *fin-de-siècle* opulence of the later steamers, there were justified complaints about vibration and noise. In calm conditions the French steamers were fine, but and hitched to a train: a forerunner of the modern Motorail service south. Dr Bennet enthused about the new service: "Railways have all but annihilated space... A traveller may leave the London Bridge station at 7.40 on a Monday morning, by mail train for Paris, and be at Nice or Menton for supper the following day." The most luxurious trains included private saloon carriages, each containing a bedroom, sitting-room, smoking-room and study.

Queen Victoria, travelling incognito as the Comtesse de Balmoral, arrived in such style that her identity was no secret. The royal train was hung with silk and was partly decorated with Louis XVI furnishings. Naturally, the Queen travelled with supplies of familiar foods, including Irish stew, kept lukewarm in red flannel cushions. In the mornings, the train was halted to allow the Queen an hour to dress and her male staff to shave. From 1882 onwards she was a regular winter visitor and her presence did much to soothe troubled Anglo-French relations.

Health was the Queen's motive for visiting the Riviera since her son, Prince Leopold, suffered from consumption. Until the 1870s, consumption was the killer disease in Victorian Britain. The only remedy was believed to be a warm climate. Climates were labelled as "tonic and exciting" or "sedative and relaxing". As tonic climates, Hyères, Menton and Cannes were considered ideal for invalids suffering from such esoteric illnesses as consumption, delicacy, gout and clergyman's sore throat. In no time, the Paris-Riviera Express became known as an ambulance train to death's waiting-room.

Queen Victoria wintered in Hyères before finding a more desirable address in Nice. Hyères was the first Riviera resort to be patronised by the British. Although later upstaged by Nice and Cannes, Hyères had a solid British clientèle from the 18th century onwards. Robert Louis Stevenson came in search of a southern cure and settled in the romantic retreat of La Solitude. Luxuries were cheap but essentials were dear. By this token, the British freely purchased carriages, villas, wine and entertainment but stinted on fuel, food, servants and travel. By the 1890s, Hyères' date palms incongruously sheltered an Anglican church, English estate agencies and public tennis courts.

Compared with the privacy of Hyères, Nice was a more ostentatious resort, with British residents living in grand hotels in the public eye. By the 1820s Nice had a flourishing British community who sketched and botanised their way through the mild Mediterranean winters. Visitors indulged in literary readings, *soirées musicales*, "quantities of gossip and a great deal of dressiness."

Left, the 19th-century Nice shoreline. Above, verandah view of Monte-Carlo.

The Victorian obsession with standards and public works soon had an impact on Nice. Winter residents insisted on better roads, English plumbing, new bandstands and public parks. The British imported nurses and ladies' maids, gardeners and grocers, lawyers and estate agents, but the local labour force had to conform to quirky British requirements. Hotels advertised "drainage executed by English engineers." French hoteliers grumbled about the demands of English hygiene, the frostiness of English manners and the sibilance of English speech.

Yet British philanthropy was also grudgingly acknowledged. After the failure of the olive and citrus crops in 1821, the impoverished locals were offered employment by the Rev. Lewis Way and Charles Whitby. Funded by British families, the scheme subsidised the building of Camin des Angès, the coastal road now known as the Promenade des Anglais. Only the uncharitable questioned British motives: the Promenade provided better access to the shore and effectively shielded Victorian strollers from the hordes of beggars. In 1931, British interests were again served by an enlarged Promenade des Anglais.

of Wales and his yacht *Britannia* were regular fixtures from 1878. He used to say: "I go to the Riviera as I would a club. It's a place with good company where everyone mingles, just like a garden party."

However, it was an earlier and more endearing Englishman who put Cannes on the map. In 1834, Lord Brougham "discovered" this charming fishing village while looking for a suitable home for his invalid daughter. Brougham built several villas in Cannes and wintered there for almost 35 years. Under his patronage, the village became one of the Riviera's most British resorts and was home to over 1,000 English residents shortly after the arrival of the railway in 1862. The atmos-

The development of a British quarter known as Newborough attracted a new wave of Victorian visitors, as did the arrival of the railway link in 1864. Queen Victoria set the tone, wintering in the palatial Hotel Regina in the Cimiez district of Nice from 1895 onwards. There she entertained the Emperor Franz Josef, other European royals and heads of state.

Regal Nice was eventually eclipsed by stylish Cannes – in British eyes, at least. Queen Victoria's son, the future Edward VII, was not alone in thinking Cannes Cercle Nautique the most exciting club on the Côte. Still, in his inimitable way, Edward did as much to keep the *Entente Cordiale* as his mother. The Prince

phere, heavy with Victorian divinity and charitable works, changed with the Prince of Wales. By the Naughty Nineties, Cannes was a cosmopolitan resort with a reputation for vice second only to Monaco's.

Baptist ministers, such as Charles Spurgeon, condemned Monaco as "the serpent in paradise". Queen Victoria was not alone in refusing to stay in this "moral cesspool". Dr Bennet also feared "the proximity of a gaming table" in this warm and wicked resort. Before the turn of the century, Monaco was labelled "a sunny place for shady people," the haunt of arms dealers, courtesans and gold-diggers. But the glamour drew British gamblers such as Charles Wells, the fortune-hunter who became famous as "The Man Who Broke the Bank at Monte-Carlo". Cora Pearl, the Duke of Hamilton's extravagant mistress, was an *habituée* at the casino in the 1860s.

The archetypal British resort was Menton. In its heyday, in the 1890s, it boasted the largest British colony on the Continent. As the main Riviera sanatorium, the resort had at least 50 British doctors and several rest homes. It was quieter and cheaper than Cannes and combined a dowager-like atmosphere with a seductive setting. Yet the heady, Italianate exoticism could not be openly acknowledged in a resort favoured by Anglican clergymen and consumptive ladies. Instead, "Everyone indulged in *à la mode* church-going excess, with all its formality and display."

Menton's dullness could be attributed to Dr James Henry Bennet, an eminent Victorian doctor who came "to die in a quiet corner". Instead, his consumption was cured by "the bracing, stimulating climate." From 1859 to 1891, he promoted Menton as the ideal health resort and his book, *Winter and Spring on the Shores of the Mediterranean*, became a European best-seller.

Consumptives were told to wrap up warmly but to have as much fresh air and exercise as possible. Invalids followed the strict regime prescribed by local British doctors. Flannel underwear and woollen clothes were obligatory, as were shoes with india-rubber soles, designed to insulate one against cold stone floors. For the invalids there was little light relief: "Bath chairs monopolised the Promenade du Midi by day, and by night their premature retirement imparted a hospital hush to the atmosphere." Despite John Pemble's sombre comments, Menton, like Brighton, had British appeal.

Anglo-Saxon names flattered the insular vanity of the British and stores stocked British delicacies such as Guinness and port, York ham and smoked goose breast, as well as "strange red, green or blue sauces in boxes marked 'by royal appointment'."

In between shopping and prayer-meetings, there were sketching trips and rides in donkey-drawn buggies. The British introduced donkey rides to Menton. Even in cold weather, the "*Miss Anglaises*" took part in donkey races on the beach or went on picnic trips to perched villages. Much to the astonishment of the locals, the young ladies still had enough energy to ride all the way down to the Italian frontier before returning to Menton. From her Chalet des Rosiers overlooking the Bay of Menton, Queen Victoria also found time for

Left, Queen Victoria on one of her visits. Above, high society in a Monte Carlo restaurant, 1907.

donkey rides. In the event of a chill in the *Entente Cordiale*, the Queen had a carriage ready to whisk her to safety in Bordighera, just over the Italian border.

In Victorian times, Britannia literally ruled the waves. Such was British chauvinism that the Franco-German War of 1870 was interpreted in Britain as a capitulation of the south to the north. On the Riviera, belief in British supremacy was widespread, and British values reigned: deference was expected and granted. In 1879 Dr Edward Sparkes wrote: "English tastes are well understood and carefully consulted in all the hotels." English was often used as a generic term for all foreigners. As such, the *"Miss Anglaises"* were sometimes Russian or German.

The British rarely ventured into "foreign" shops and relied on safe English staples. English eating habits and appetites were notorious. Queen Victoria's typical Riviera lunch included risotto and mutton chops, chicken with noodles, followed by tapioca, meringue and strawberries. Dr Bennet wrote that "the dinners we positively require every day" were considered "festive dinners" by the natives. To supply the daily British intake "the country had to be ransacked for a hundred and fifty miles around." The Prince of Wales also had an enormous appetite and, as the unwitting inventor of *crêpes suzettes*, probably lost no time in polishing off both the *crêpes* and Suzette herself.

Victorian life on the Riviera was deeply institutionalised. The British day followed a pattern: breakfast, early stroll, correspondence in the hotel, lunch, afternoon stroll and 5 o'clock tea. In Nice, there were English signs for "5 o'clock tea – any time". Afternoon variants included gentle shopping or a concert at the bandstand. The British community organised regattas and whist drives while the big hotels held weekly tea dances and balls.

Depending on taste and morals, residents spent their evenings in the casino, cabaret or at home, reading. Victorian music hall was popular as were theatrical performances by Sarah Bernhardt. By Edwardian times, Folies Bergères and Moulin Rouge troupes were often in residence in casinos along the Côte. Yet after Menton opened a casino, it incurred the wrath of the moral minority. The Rev. Eustace Reynolds Ball found Menton guilty of *fin-de-siècle* decadence, "infected by the Monte-Carlo contingent".

But Victorian puritanism was often outdone by patriotism. Well before the turn of the century, British competitive sports played a major role in life on the Riviera. The British upper classes were serious about sport but defensive about games in a sunny climate. Author Charles Kingsley scorned "the English hedge-gnats who only take their sport when the sun shines." Still, there were enough hedge-gnats to indulge in horse-racing at Cannes, skating in Menton and Nice as well as golf in Monte-Carlo and Sospel.

Sea-bathing was not in vogue on the Riviera until the 1930s. Although the Italians had been swimming just down the coast in San Remo since the 1850s, the British regarded this as Italian perversity. The British swam at home, of course, but believed that the Riviera's hot climate was suitable only for seaweed and anemone hunting.

The Menton Lawn Tennis and Croquet Club was founded in 1901 and held international tournaments. The dominance of British cultural values ensured a copycat reaction: King Gustav V of Sweden and the Queen of Siam were dedicated yet hopeless players.

The British drawn to the Riviera included sportsmen and statesmen, royals and writers, artists and intellectuals: in short, the missing apex of the British social pyramid. British politicians were part of Riviera life from Victorian times onwards. When Lord Salisbury was in his villa at Beaulieu and Victoria in residence at Cimiez, state business moved from London to Nice. The Queen bombarded the Prime Minister with her views on heads of state, foreign affairs, church and army appointments. A monument on Avenue George V in Nice pays tribute to the warmth of royal Franco-British relations on the Riviera: "*À la mémoire des membres augustes de la maison royale de Windsor qui depuis deux siècles furent nos hôtes.*"

British eccentrics were not thin on the ground. Trahorne Moggridge, the Victorian entomologist, published a book on indigenous spiders. James Bruyn Andrews translated local legends and wrote works on the Mentonnais language. Edward VII's presence assured the Riviera of style. In more recent times, Amy Paget, an elderly Riviera resident, flew the Union Jack from her villa throughout World War II. Nora, Lady Docker, flew in the face of postwar austerity by flaunting zebra-skin upholstery on her Daimler (she found mink was just too hot to sit on). The latest candidate for eccentricity is the British academic John Cairncross, widely alleged to be the "Fifth Man" in the Cambridge spy-ring of the 1930s.

However, if one had to select the quintessential Briton abroad, it would be Dr Bennet. As well as pioneering the Riviera as a sanatorium, James Bennet was a linguist, writer, botanist, environmentalist and man of action. He represented the best face of the eminent Victorian abroad: duty led him to set up a medical association which monitored public health and instigated street-cleaning services, sewers and abattoirs. It was largely thanks to his efforts that in 1892 the Association for the Advancement of Science declared Menton to be the cleanest, most efficient town in France.

Bennet also personified the British love of gardens. He pressured Menton council into creating public parks and funding nature campaigns to protect plants and wildlife. Queen Victoria and Princess Beatrice often sketched and strolled in Bennet's exotic garden, created with the help of "an intelligent peasant... raised to the dignity of head-gardener." Wherever the British settled in the area, they cultivated magnificent gardens.

In Menton's Jardin Botanique, Lord Redcliffe, the Governor of Malta, favoured a didactic approach, with thematic gardens illustrating the range of Mediterranean flora. Miss Campbell, a later owner, introduced exotic plants from Asia and Central America. Just around the corner, Major Lawrence Johnston changed the Riviera landscape by

Left, the new fashion for sea-bathing. Above, a more cautions approach.

introducing rare trees from China, Japan, Asia and Africa. Sir Thomas Hanbury, a Victoran spice trader, made his fortune in China and retired to the hills on the French-Italian border. There he introduced Norfolk pines and exotic plants from all corners of the British Empire. In Cannes, an early Victorian, Thomas Woolfield, introduced the gooseberry and the sweet potato, eucalyptus and acacia.

The British landscaped large sections of Nice, Cannes, Menton and Cap Ferrat. To some locals, Somerset Maugham is merely the person who introduced the avocado to the Riviera. When it comes to garden snobbery on the Riviera, it is hard to know whether it is a British import or a French anomaly.

killjoys and the women as philistines or prudes. Henry James commented on the British "insular faculty to gush".

Katherine Mansfield confined herself to mocking English insularity, with liking for Dundee cake and familiar nursery foods. Mansfield, living in Menton in the 1920s, avoided the most anglicised spots, such as Monaco. Even so, she couldn't fail to notice the pervasive British influence. The Riviera was home to British charities, lending libraries, boarding schools and Scottish tea houses. Local British animal protection societies made sure bull-fighting did not spread to the Riviera. By 1928, Menton competed with Monaco in welcoming Girl Guides and Brownies.

But the British visitors offered more than blue blood and green fingers. For British writers and artists, the Riviera became a place to express smothered sensibilities. Enchanted by the soft light and dramatic scenery, these hot-house plants hoped to stretch out in the sun. Yet, once transplanted, they remained rooted to a British social code. Even for D. H. Lawrence and Somerset Maugham, the lotus-eating south was a miasma. Outsiders viewed the British on the Riviera more critically. Locals on the Côte d'Azur disliked patronising references to "our Gallic friends". Berlioz rued the day he married an Englishwoman on the Riviera. Stendhal saw the men as morose

Despite the virtuous Girl Guides, pleasure not duty was the keynote of the 1920s. A poster in Menton contrasts an ailing Victorian gentleman with an elegant 1920s flapper: "In the old days visitors apparently came here for their health. Today, it is a town of luxury and gaiety." If the Edwardian visitors were dutiful, the Americans embodied the pleasure principle. Riviera residents were now judged on the size of their pools and yachts, not their consciences. The British played only supporting roles in a glittering American show.

Although the Americans wrote the script, the British occasionally upstaged them. Glamorous stars such as the Duke of Westminster regularly sailed the Côte d'Azur. "Whose yacht is that?" Amanda asks in *Private Lives*. Elyot replies: "The Duke of Westminster's, I expect. It always is." Noël Coward and Gertrude Lawrence rehearsed the play in Edward Molyneux's villa on Cap d'Ail in 1930.

In 1934 the Prince of Wales stayed in Cannes with Wallis Simpson's party and presented her with a diamond charm as a sign of his infatuation. It was to Cannes that Mrs Simpson retreated when it became clear that the King would abdicate rather than give her up. The couple even contemplated marriage on the Riviera but bowed to George VI's wishes for a more discreet ceremony, far from the Riviera playground. The couple later spent their early years of exile in a luxurious villa on the Cap d'Antibes.

In 1945 the Windsors' villa proved a major embarrassment to Winston Churchill. After her fraternisation with German officers, Coco Chanel was arrested as a collaborator but was quickly released after threatening to expose Churchill. He had made secret payments to the Germans to secure the protection of the Duke of Windsor's villa during the war.

Even so, Churchill was the best-loved British star of the period. Towards the end of his life he was an honoured guest on the Onassis yacht. Patrick Howarth in *When the Riviera was Ours* describes how Aristotle Onassis could be seen feeding the enfeebled Churchill caviare, a symbolic tribute from "the new power on the Riviera to the most famous representative of the grandeurs of the past".

From the 1950s, a new wave of expatriates settled in Haut-de-Cagnes, Vence and Grasse, attracted to the arts and crafts traditions in the foothills. In the 1970s, the British built Isola 2000, the skiing resort, and invested heavily in Cannes and St-Tropez. The current boom town is Sophia-Antipolis, the Riviera's Silicon Valley. Here, there is little sign of the tweed-suited matron, the elderly naval captain, the Anglican clergyman or other British Riviera stereotypes. Mike Meade, editor of *Riviera Reporter*, claims never to have met "the retired colonel who doesn't speak a word of French, scowls continually at the natives, and thinks that the Queen's Birthday should be a national holiday here."

If this Riviera stereotype is extinct, *tant mieux*. In today's Riviera, the emphasis is on integration, aided by bilingual psychiatrists and dual-language colleges. There are Anglo-American schools in Mougins, Nice and Sophia-Antipolis. Monte-Carlo's Riviera Radio can be heard from St-Tropez to the

Left, Aristotle Onassis (left) and Sir Winston Churchill boarding the millionaire's yacht, 1959. Above, the Duke and Duchess of Windsor.

Italian border and the station claims that four out of five English speakers regularly tune in.

Socially, expatriates can choose from the Riviera Singles Group, the Conservatives Abroad, the Oxbridge Set or the Dog Exchange Club. The Anglo-American Group of Provence indulges in Scottish dancing and Marseille cuisine. The Franco-Irish Friendship Group competes fiercely with the Association Franco-Irlande. The British Association has branches in Cannes, Nice, Menton and Monaco.

The Riviera Establishment survives, nonetheless. One English agency supplies British nannies, housekeepers and butlers. British antique dealers regularly advertise for "1920s

cocktail watches, Fabergé enamels and Edwardian gem set jewellery'".

English lending libraries exist in Menton and Vence, as do English bookshops in Cannes, Antibes, Monaco and Sophia-Antipolis. Anglican churches are active in most large resorts, including Nice, Menton and Monaco. Elsewhere, there are British banks, pubs and the long-established John Taylor & Son estate agency. The British distrust of French plumbing remains as a relic of a bygone age. Still, one sign of the times is the existence of an Anglo-American hospital for alcoholism and drug dependency.

For some Britons, the Côte d'Azur was the place to die – D. H. Lawrence in Vence, Aubrey Beardsley in Menton. But today it is a place for the living, a second home to countless British celebrities, though Joan Collins, Ringo Starr, Michael Caine, George Michael or Elton John are hardly typical of British expatriates. Nor is the image of the retired English colonel, playing golf and downing snifters at sundown, very accurate either.

Mike Meade describes the difference between the Old Riviera Establishment and today's expatriates. A well-meaning English gentleman suggested that a Tuesday afternoon whist drive would attract young members to his club. But, as Meade points out, "The typical 25 to 55 Riviera anglophone is an executive at Sophia-Antipolis or a business whizz-kid. He could be an independent professional or part of a yacht crew. On weekends he's probably playing squash or tennis, sailing or skiing, or on a Hash House run… There's a 51 percent chance that 'he' is a 'she'. Whoever he is, it's quite likely that, at 4pm on a Tuesday afternoon, he's working. And whist isn't his thing."

The Riviera is arguably a British creation. Here they recreated decorous anglophile enclaves in balmy, lemon-scented surroundings. The British simplified the south yet were deeply affected by it. Nor was this aesthetic sensibilty a fey whim of the consumptive artist or the cultural élite. It was a creative urge to leave a lasting mark, whether a gallery or garden, a civic statue or a treatise on spiders. Even retired Empire-builders, spice traders and clergymen succumbed, becoming art collectors, landscape gardeners or benefactors.

The Noël Coward song *I went to a Marvellous Party* was inspired by his visit to a high society gathering on the Riviera. Yet the British legacy encompasses more than glamour. Frederic Harrison, a Victorian visitor, defined the British contribution more prosaically: "tea, tubs, sanitary appliances, lawn tennis and churches." Rather like a grand jumble sale, the British gift was a magnificent white elephant. Glorious gardens vied with eccentric institutions, alien churches and curious new games. British names and niceties, philanthropy and prejudice are part of the job lot. In the words of Edward VII, that notorious Riviera adventurer, *"Vive l'Entente Cordiale"*.

Left, a languid moment under the pines, Juan-les-Pins. Right, the winter season, Nice.

LORENZI
NICE

HOTEL
SITUATION
RESTAURANT

GRESCO
E EN FACE LA MER
REMIER ORDRE
V. H. LORANT 1912

ROGER BRODERS
ANTIBES
SA PLAGE DE JUAN-LES-PINS
SON CAP.
STATION D'ÉTÉ ET D'HIVER

"The resplendent names – Cannes, Nice, Monte-Carlo – began to glow through their torpid camouflage, whispering of old Kings come here to dine or die, of rajahs tossing Buddha's eyes to English ballerinas, of Russian princes turning the weeks into Baltic twilights in the lost Caviare days."

Tender is the Night is a champagne toast to an end of an era. Published in 1934, Scott Fitzgerald's novel is infused with the American glamour that flooded the Riviera from the 1920s. This seductive vision of the "hot sweet south" is not a true mirror but a montage of magical moments. Strictly speaking, the kings, princes and rajahs ruled an earlier age and a moral climate conditioned by Victorian values. Even then, the balmy Mediterranean climate wrought its own magic: these were Victorian values on vacation.

The post-war Americans may have invented the summer season but the Victorians and Edwardians were pale winter migrants. Renoir called this winter sanatorium "a hothouse into which fragile people take refuge". During the *belle époque*, from 1862 until World War I, the Riviera became the royals' winter retreat. The arrival of the railway link to Cannes in 1863 stamped the Riviera with the public's seal of approval. Invalids were the pioneers of the Côte d'Azur, a trend started by the British in the 1850s. Within 10 years, Hyères, Cannes and Nice had large foreign colonies in the winter. A few years later, Beaulieu, Menton and San Remo competed for the aristocratic clientèle while Monte-Carlo catered exclusively to the rich and pleasure-loving.

It was a short step from royal retreat to winter playground. "Princes, princes, nothing but princes. If you like them, you're in the right place," complained Guy de Maupassant of Cannes in 1884. The royals were headed by Queen Victoria, the Empress of Russia and Emperor Frederick of Germany. At the turn of the century, Menton alone received the Kings of Italy, Sweden, Saxe, Belgium and Bulgaria, as well as visits by Count Pushkin and Russian Grand Dukes. The Shah of Persia and President Kruger of South Africa stayed in Menton at the same time. They narrowly missed Emperor Franz Josef of Austria and his wife. Sometimes the royals literally crossed paths: while on a carriage drive near Villefranche, Queen Victoria passed King Leopold, out on his regular daily stroll.

In the same year, the young Aga Khan III arrived on a steamer from India and found Queen Victoria in Nice and the Emperor Franz Josef at Cap Martin. In addition, there were "a score or so Russian Grand Dukes and Austrian Archdukes in their villas and palaces, half the English peerage with a generous sprinkling of millionaires from industry and finance; and most of the Almanac de Gotha from Germany, the Austro-Hungarian Empire, the Balkan countries lately emancipated from Ottoman rule, and Tsarist Russia." As the Aga Khan modestly put it: "The young man from Bombay was dazzled and awed."

The royals visited not as Grand Tourists of the 18th century, explorers on a unique adventure, but as *habitués*, comfortable in their

Preceding pages: Hôtel Negresco, Nice. Left, 1920s Juan-les-Pins poster. Right, a fashionable cocktail, by Edmond Lahaye.

second homes. Second palaces would be a more accurate description. Queen Victoria had a huge residence in the Cimiez quarter of Nice. Menton's magnificent 18th-century Palais de Carnolès was owned by the Queen of Prussia in the 1860s and by Prince Metternich shortly afterwards. But given the difficulties of finding suitable French servants, royal visitors often preferred to spend the whole winter season in hotels.

Unsurprisingly, such hotels were known as *les palaces de la Côte d'Azur.* Amongst the grandest were L'Hermitage in Monte-Carlo and the Victoria Hotel on the Promenade des Anglais in Nice. Charles of Prussia stayed in the Victoria in the 1860s while Tsarevitch Alexander made it his home until his accession to the Russian throne in 1881. Menton boasted two *belle-époque* hotels on the Avenue Riviera: the Winter Palace was favoured by Oriental royals while Grand Duchess Anastasia, Tsar Nicholas II's aunt, occupied the Riviera Palace in the 1880s. In the lovely *salon de musique*, a Parisian orchestra played Gregorian chants or gypsy music before Anastasia's afternoon nap.

When the Riviera was Ours, Patrick Howarth's wonderful but unashamedly chauvinistic account, argues that even foreign royals followed an English lifestyle on the Riviera. Prince Albert of Prussia regularly attended Anglican services at Christ Church in Cannes where he made it known that he hoped the hymns would include "The Son of God goes forth to war." Tea and tennis were immovable fixtures; Russian Grand Dukes wore starched white linen; Belgian and Swedish aristocrats challenged one another to jolly polo matches.

Chauvinism aside, the royal way of life on the Riviera was not so much English as regal. Crested dice were thrown in the Monte-Carlo Casino; coroneted carriages paraded the Promenade des Anglais in Nice; the aristocratic *jeunesse dorée* dined on caviare, blinis and pink champagne in the Hôtel de l'Hermitage. Leopold I of Belgium was Queen Victoria's domineering uncle but it was his son who made an indelible mark on the Riviera. As an ageing playboy, Leopold II wintered in the Riviera from the 1890s to his death in 1909. Leopold resided in Les Cèdres villa on Cap Martin and filled the grounds with lush vegetation he had transplanted from the Belgian Congo.

Princess Daisy of Pless described Leopold peeling grapes with "a look of cruelty on his face as if he were skinning alive all the members of the Aborigines Protection Society." Apart from rare orchids and palms, Leopold's only hobby was young girls. Princess Daisy describes how his lecherous pursuits were hampered by a dangling white beard and grotesquely long fingernails.

Empress Eugénie of France, often described as the *doyenne* of the Riviera royalty, also held court on Cap Martin in the 1890s. Although Spanish-born and married to a French Emperor, Eugénie was an anglophile who had been educated in England. After the Empire collapsed in 1870, she left Deauville for Kent. By the 1890s her husband and son had died and Eugénie relished her role of *grande dame* in exile, even managing to charm Queen Victoria. Eugénie had long been a diplomat behind the scenes and, after a dull period of suburban exile in Chislehurst in England, found the Riviera a more satisfying stage. From her rococo-style Villa Cyrnos, Eugénie quietly advised a variety of foreign sovereigns and ministers on world politics.

Eugénie's neighbour and contemporary was Elizabeth, Empress of Austria, married to Franz Josef I. Known as Sissi, Elizabeth was a daughter of a Bavarian duke and married her cousin at the age of 15. Sissi led a troubled life and, as Queen of Hungary, had a high political profile which was her downfall: she was assassinated by an Italian anarchist in Geneva. Sissi's restlessness and spontaneity offended Viennese society so she was delighted to find that the Riviera was not etiquette-bound. Considered the most beautiful Princess in Europe, she nonetheless had an unhappy marriage and was labelled neurotic. Her secluded villa, the Grand Hôtel du Cap Martin, represented comfort and privacy, and she found solace walking the long coastal path around the Cape. Having no wish to meet her husband in Monaco, she usually walked the other way, towards Menton.

Teutonic aristocrats regularly wintered in the Riviera, particularly after a German edition of Dr Bennet's *Winter and Spring on the Shores of the Mediterranean* appeared in 1863. In the same year, Maximilian II of Bavaria bought a huge Niçois villa that had previously belonged to the Russian Empress Alexandra Feodrovna.

Cap Martin became a Germanic haunt by the turn of the century. The Grand Duke of Saxe-Weimar bought a villa there in 1894 and was soon joined by an exceedingly minor royal, Jean II, Prince of Lichtenstein. Frederick William, the last Crown Prince of Germany, wintered on the Cap and was known as "Little Willie" long before he retired to England in 1918. However, the German aristocrats were generally more discreet than their British and Russian counter-

Left, Juan-les-Pins Casino by Edmond Lahaye, 1927. Above, the Grand Hotel, Juan-les-Pins.

parts. When a German claimed to be on the Riviera for health, not high jinks, he was generally believed.

The same could not be said for the Russians. Before World War I, the Russian community was second only to the British in size and influence. In 1856 Alexandra Feodorovna, the widow of Tsar Nicholas I, bought Villa Acquaviva in the Promenade des Anglais and forged the early Russian links with Nice. Not that the Russians needed much encouragement. French was the language of the Russian court and the Riviera made a restful second home, a welcome change from Russian winters and rebellious serfs. Alexandra's son, the Grand Duke Con-

stantine, followed in his mother's footsteps and bought Villa Lavit in the Promenade des Anglais. The seafront and the Boulevard Tzarewitch soon became distinct Russian colonies, set at a safe distance from the English camp at Cimiez. The Russians congregated in the Ferme Russe, Russian tea rooms run by the formidable Madame Chirikov. The pastries provided stiff competition to the cream cakes in Perrimond-Rumpelmayer, the German haunt. Below the domed winter garden of La Ferme Russe, imported Russian servants worked the samovars while their mistresses discussed charity balls or rheumatic gout.

The opening of the railway to Nice in 1864 had an immediate impact: Tsar Alexander II arrived a week later and was soon enthralled enough to consider building a Russian Orthodox church in Nice. The flamboyant green-and-gold domes remain a testament to the importance of the Russian community in the 19th century. In 1880 Grand Duchess Anastasia, Tsar Nicholas II's aunt, founded the Association Orthodoxe Russe which looked after consumptive soldiers and students. After the Revolution, the home became known as the Maison Russe and, linked to the Russian Red Cross, still welcomes Russian émigrés.

The Russian women had a particularly high social profile on the Riviera. One *grande dame* was the Princess Kotschouby whose ochre *belle-époque* villa is now the Chéret Museum in Nice. The Princess Caramachimay abandoned her troublesome Russian estates and emigrated to Cap Martin at the turn of the century. Princess Anna Chervachidzé settled in a grand estate nearby; it later sheltered a skulking Greta Garbo and is now owned by a Lebanese millionaire.

Unlike the Germans, the Russians were enthusiastic gamblers. Armed with boxes of gold and silver pieces, they whiled away the afternoons in the Monte-Carlo Casino. Princess Souvorov arrived in Monaco in 1869 with an "infallible" method. After visiting all the casinos in Europe, she had made copious notes of every winning number in all the games she had witnessed. But despite thousands of files, she lost 300,000 francs in a couple of hours. Suddenly her luck changed and she won eight nights in succession, breaking the bank twice.

To celebrate the win, she scandalised high society by holding a party for complete strangers. The only entry requirement was that guests should be amusing. The Monégasques closed ranks and refused to let her rent a room so she bought a villa and gave it away the next day. To encourage guests to perform party tricks, the Princess broke open thousands of cases of champagne and celebrated with a gypsy band and a Romanian dance troupe, the latest craze at the time on the Riviera.

Non-European royals were also drawn to the Riviera, including the Princess of Siam and the Bey of Algeria. One of the most eccentric visitors was the Maharajah of

Kaputhala. In 1897 he arrived at Monte Carlo's Hotel de Paris with a vast retinue. One servant, dressed in national costume and bedecked with gold and jewels, would stand behind the Maharajah's chair at dinner. When signalled, he sprinkled flakes of real silver on the royal curries. A later maharajah was instrumental in opening the Martinez Hotel in Cannes in 1926: he insisted on Louis XVI bedrooms for all the guests.

Sir Mohammed Shah, the Aga Khan III, was one of the few hereditary rulers whose affection for the Riviera has been echoed by his descendants. In 1908, the Aga Khan married an Italian dancer and installed her in a Middle Eastern-style villa above Monaco.

Their son, Major Aly Khan, was a member of the Free French forces that helped liberate the Riviera. Aly then went on to marry Rita Hayworth while his father competed by marrying Yvette, a "Miss France" bathing belle. The current Aga Khan lives in an art deco mansion in Antibes where "the only unguarded exit is the chute from the swimming pool to the sea".

Foreigners maintained a frontier mentality. The only local people they met were shopkeepers and servants; even this problem could be circumvented by importing staff or by choosing to live in hotels. Expatriates further down the social scale often ignored all other foreign residents.

"You may see English, German and French families pass many weeks together in the same house, eat twice a day at the same table, and sit for hours in the same salon without even exchanging a word." Such was Frederic Harrison's view of sour-faced Victorian visitors in 1887.

The Riviera was only relatively free from social restraints; even in Menton cemetery, each nationality and religion was accorded a separate burial tier. Nor were the pleasures of the South egalitarian; the Riviera was the preserve of the rich until the Edwardian era. In the 1840s, a house in Nice could be rented for £300 a year while in the 1880s it cost £1,200 for the winter season. In 1896, the writer Augustus Hare commented approvingly: "Nice is a home for the millionaire and the working man. The intermediate class is not wanted. Visitors are expected to have money, and if they have to look at pounds, shillings and pence, had much better remain at home."

Victorian and Edwardian visitors were not exclusively aristocratic. "Money increases quickly," wrote Trollope in 1866, "and distances decrease." Bourgeois visitors were,

Left, Tsarina Maria Alexandrovna, a frequent visitor, in 1865. Above, Nice Casino.

however, in the minority until the 1920s.

While the flow of royal visitors continued during the inter-war years, a new élite emerged: the American dollar kings. Dr Bennet's *Winter and Spring in the Mediterranean* was published in New York in 1870 and provoked a new wave of wealthy visitors. The simple yet sophisticated pleasures of the Mediterranean appealed to jaded American tycoons. In 1898 Dr Allis, the art collector, was attracted to the unspoilt site of the Palais de Carnolès in Menton. After adding two new wings and replanting the gardens, Allis installed his priceless paintings. The watchword may have been simplicity but it was expensive simplicity.

James Gordon Bennett, the proprietor of the *New York Herald*, started a European edition of the paper as a pretext for living on the Riviera. As well as running the *International Herald Tribune*, Bennett found time to indulge fellow-Americans at his Beaulieu villa. As for his yacht, *Lysistrata*, even Vanderbilt was impressed. Manned by a 100-strong crew, the yacht had three decks, Turkish baths and a resident Alderney cow. The millionaire once invited Drexel, Biddle and Vanderbilt to dine at the Café Riche, his favourite restaurant in Monte-Carlo. The Americans were turned away from the restaurant terrace when the management decided that only cocktails should be served there. An outraged Bennett immediately bought the restaurant for $40,000 and sacked the manager. In appreciation for well-cooked lamb chops, Bennett promptly handed over the restaurant to Ciro, his favourite waiter, by way of a tip. The fortunate Ciro then went on to open successful restaurants all over Europe.

Bennett was only one of the profligate Americans who stayed on the Riviera. J. Pierpont Morgan, the steel magnate, was a notorious gambler at the Monte-Carlo Casino. Morgan asked if the individual limit for bets could be virtually doubled to 20,000 francs. When Blanc, the director, refused, Morgan left on the spot, complaining that he wouldn't waste his time gambling for such paltry amounts. Morgan, of course, went on to form the United States Steel Corporation with Andrew Carnegie. Charles M. Schwab, the President of the Corporation, was also an inveterate gambler. After tales of Schwab's profligacy reached the American press, Morgan somewhat hypocritically took him to task. Schwab's defence – "But I sin openly, not behind closed doors" – was countered with, "But that's exactly what doors are for."

Closed doors were needed with such colourful courtesans as Mata Hari and "La Belle Otéro" working their way through the foreign ranks. Although Mata Hari's spying was beyond the pale, until 1914 courtesans had an accepted status in Riviera society. As Mata Hari, the Dutch show-girl Gertrud Zelle came to Monte-Carlo to perform "exotic dances". Her stage name, meaning "sunrise" in Malay, was matched by exotic looks that captivated the French and German Ministers of Information. One night in the Casino, an agent accused her of secreting stolen documents in her bodice. Mata Hari promptly shot him and was excused on the grounds of self-defence.

By contrast, La Belle Otéro was apolitical. At the age of 14, Caroline Otéro, a Spanish gypsy, married an Italian baron and spent her honeymoon in Monaco. After her husband had lost in the Casino, she removed all the gold buttons from her dress and, as well as causing a stir, amassed a fortune on the tables. Caroline quickly abandoned her husband and began a new career as a *grande*

Left, The Riviera Express.

THE BLUE TRAIN

Along with the Santa Fe Superchief, the Orient Express and the Trans-Siberian Express, the Blue Train was never just a train; to travel on it from London to the Côte d'Azur in the 1920s and '30s represented the epitome of style and fashion. It was said that, for a woman to have made it in the world, she should have dined at the Ritz and Colony Restaurants in New York, the Everglades Club in Palm Beach, the Ritz in Paris, Claridge's in London and the Hôtel du Cap in Antibes, sailed on the *Berengaria* and the *Aquitania*, and, of course, travelled on the Blue Train. It was the *only* way to travel to the Côte d'Azur.

From the 1850s onwards the South of France was opened up to foreign visitors as trains reduced travelling times from about three weeks by carriage to just a couple of days by train. All that was then needed was sleeping accommodation, of the type pioneered by Pullman in the United States.

The first manufacturers of sleeping cars in Europe was the Compagnie Internationale des Wagons-Lits, founded by an enterprising Belgian, Georges Nagelmackers, in 1872. Its sleeping cars became famous, and the Calais-Nice-Rome Express, the first train to the south to be equipped with sleeping accommodation, began operating in 1883, about six months after the Orient Express. The Italian section was little used and the train eventually became known as the Calais-Mediterranean Express. It was popularly known as the Blue Train after 1922 when blue and gold painted sleeping cars first appeared. The words *"Train bleu"* were painted on the carriages only after 1949.

This luxurious palace on wheels, whose carriages catered to only 10 passengers, would leave Calais at 1pm, arriving in Monte-Carlo at 9.30 the next morning. For early British visitors travelling south for the winter, nothing could beat the pleasurable contrast of boarding under the grey skies and smog of London and waking the next morning to the blue skies, terracotta roofs and orange-trees of the Mediterranean.

It became known as the "millionaires' train" with some justification. The American James Gordon Bennett, owner of the *New York Herald* and famous for his profligacy, once, to the horror of his valet, tipped the conductor 20,000 francs. The conductor used the money to open a restaurant in Boulogne. When Charlie Chaplin came to stay with Frank Jay Gould, he arrived on the Blue Train. The Duke of Windsor had a carriage with a specially designed bathroom. When the casinos brought girls down from Maxim's in Paris they were guaranteed return tickets on the Blue Train (to be used if they failed to snare a rich husband). The fame of the Blue Train has been enshrined by the arts; Agatha Christie set a Hercule Poirot story on it, *The Mystery of the Blue Train*. Diaghilev directed a musical called *Le Train Bleu*, which was written by Jean Cocteau, with bathing costumes by Chanel and curtain by Picasso.

For Charles Graves in *The Riviera Revisited,* his account of the Côte d'Azur just after World War II, being able to board the Blue Train again meant the war was truly over. He even records the menu: "Off to the Gare de Lyons, where the Blue Train itself is waiting with a six-course dinner of clear soup, red mullet, pâté with truffles, chouxfleur au gratin, cheese, fruit and coffee. Then bed in the same speckless sleeping compartment which has miraculously survived all bombing by the British and American aircraft."

Today the Blue Train is no more, though its name endures. Monte-Carlo Casino has a restaurant called Le Train Bleu, using its traditional decor. However, it is possible to travel in considerable comfort overnight through France, still a romantic journey; half-waking at dim-lit stations in the dead of night and rising to the golden sunlight glinting off the southern roofs and the blue waters of the Mediterranean. Plans for the new TGV line have been shelved and, for the time being at least, the train track still hugs the shore, providing tantalising glimpses of villas, pools and rocky coves – all the pleasures to come. ■

Right, a poster by Cassandre.

horizontale. Her voluptuous figure was appreciated by Edward VII and Kaiser Wilhelm II. One of her lovers was a hideous German millionaire but, as La Belle Otéro pointed out, "Such a rich man can never be ugly." Caroline retired to Monaco in 1922 but her legendary figure lives on in Cannes' Carlton Hotel: the twin domes are said to have been inspired by La Belle Otéro's perfect breasts.

There was a distinct change of climate after World War I. The courtesans were no more; the Russians were dead or in exile; the Kings of Italy, Spain, Albania and Yugoslavia clung to their thrones; most royals were in financial straits.

Only the Americans had the means to live

out their fantasies. With the glamorous new arrivals, winter was banished and the summer season launched. Writer E. Phillips Oppenheim slept aboard a yacht which was known as the floating double bed; the women were expected to stay awake at night to deal with the mosquitoes.

There was no shortage of eccentrics on the new summer stage. Mr Neal, an American millionaire guest at the Hôtel de l'Hermitage, installed an artificial moon in his window to remind him that it was night and therefore time to go to the Casino. One of his milder whims was to invite 80 guests to a free dinner, provided that they laughed at his jokes. His peremptory method of summoning staff consisted of firing one pistol shot for room service and two shots if he required a chambermaid for personal services.

Henry Clews, the wealthy American sculptor, was also a noted eccentric. In La Napoule, his Saracen castle, Clews recreated a medieval setting, complete with minstrel gallery and staff dressed in Provençal costume. His wife's pet peacocks were notorious, frequently straying onto the railway line where they often brought the Blue Train to a halt. As Patrick Howarth remarks, "It happened so frequently that the SNCF felt obliged to make a formal demand that the peacocks shouldn't be allowed on the line."

Not for nothing were the 1920s known as *les années folles*. Even if the bodies of bankrupt gamblers were no longer immured in the Casino walls, fortunes could still be won or lost on a dropped gold button. But, amidst the wanton partying, creativity seemed to flourish. Colette, Scott Fitzgerald, Somerset Maugham, Katherine Mansfield and Blasco Ibañez were writing themselves into different patches of the Riviera.

In Monte-Carlo, the impresario Raoul Gunsbourg was the first to stage Wagner outside Bayreuth and, as Director of the Monte Carlo Opera, also introduced the public to works by Berlioz, Massenet and Tchaikovsky. Ravel was invited to compose for the orchestra and created the *Ballet Pour Ma Fille*, based on Colette's work. But Gunsbourg's greatest coup was to convince Sergei Diaghilev and his Ballets Russes to settle in Monaco. In turn, Diaghilev persuaded the greatest composers of the age, including Debussy and Stravinsky, to write for the Ballets Russes. The company, starring Pavlova and Nijinsky, danced to such modern classics as *L'Après-midi d'un Faune* and *The Firebird*.

As if this were not enough, the costumes and sets were designed by Picasso and Matisse, Utrillo and De Chirico, Georges Braque and André Derain. Unsurprisingly, the ballets ran at a financial loss but Diaghilev was not deterred: "I don't spend a sou on myself. I have very simple tastes: only the best is good enough." Diaghilev praised Isadora Duncan for breaking with classical tradition but she spurned an invitation to see the Ballets Russes: "I don't care much for acrobats." Instead, she ran up huge hotel bills at the Negresco in Nice and, before her tragic entanglement with a silk scarf, indulged her penchant for chasing young men, including Zelda Fitzgerald's husband.

In the 1920s and '30s, the Riviera was in glamorous American hands. Scott Fitzgerald enthused about "the soft-pawed night and the ghostly wash of the Mediterranean far below." Gerald and Sara Murphy, the originals for Dick and Nicole Diver in *Tender is the Night*, had discovered it some years before. After being introduced to the Riviera by Cole Porter, the couple bought Villa America on the Cap d'Antibes and there entertained the Lost Generation. Dorothy Parker, Hemingway and the Fitzgeralds needed little encouragement to sample swimming and sunbathing.

The Goulds, along with the Murphys, entertained *le beau monde*, welcoming André Gide and Giraudoux as well as American high society. Frank Jay Gould, heir to a railway empire, virtually created Juan-les-Pins. For Florence, his Californian wife, the Riviera was also a *coup de foudre*: she quickly opened a casino and hotel and created a neo-Gothic villa for herself. Although long treated as arrivistes, the couple exerted great influence over the Riviera for 50 years. The tasteless splendour of Juan-les-Pins is their lasting imprint.

World War II drew the curtains on old American glamour but the Riviera has proved irresistible to Hollywood stars. The Hôtel du Cap-Eden Roc provides the sumptuous link. Situated on the tip of the Cap d'Antibes, this gilded white palace has long been the mecca for the American set, from the Murphys onwards.

A new wave brought such stars as Clark Gable, Humphrey Bogart and Rita Hayworth. At different times, John Wayne and Charlie Chaplin were entertained by the hotel's private funicular to the beach. While indulging in cocktails and caviare, John F. Kennedy admired the exotic gardens from the gigantic stone terrace.

The star-spangled tradition continues. The Cote d'Azur has not lost its glamour, and continues to attract the rich and famous who rent or own villas hidden away on Cap Ferrat or Cap d'Antibes. Rock stars and supermodels still flock to St-Tropez, to dine at the beach clubs or sip cocktails on quayside yachts. The grand hotels retain their legendary status and helicopters, private planes and limousines still provide luxury transport for the privileged percentage to keep the dream of Caviare days alive for everyone else.

Left, Frank Jay Gould and his wife, Florence. Above, Grand Hôtel du Cap-Eden Roc, 1929.

The 1939 summer season on the Riviera attracted the customary cosmopolitan crowd and, enlivened by the novelties of water-skiing and skin-diving, was said to have been the best yet. Colonel Josef Beck, the Polish Foreign Minister, rubbed shoulders with Sir Robert Vansittart of the British Foreign Office and Crown Prince Umberto of Italy. The Duke of Windsor, licking the wounds of the abdication which had ended his brief reign as Edward VIII of England, took a 10-year lease on a villa near Cannes, then preparing for its first film festival in September.

There were, however, intimations of the sinister clouds gathering over Europe. The shadowy face within a large car which cruised around San Remo – and was once seen parked advantageously above the annual military parade in Nice – belonged to Hermann Goering. In the Hôtel Beaulieu in Cannes, Dr E. Wightman Ginner gave a series of lectures on what to do in an air raid. Rumour spoke of secret landings at Cap Ferrat and Cap Martin – spies! Hitler occupied Austria, the Czech Sudeten, and then invaded Poland. World War II was on.

In the uneasy calm of the "Phoney War" while Hitler gathered strength for his attack on Western Europe, the Riviera prepared for the inevitable. Two British colliers arrived in Cannes to evacuate British subjects but some, such as the septuagenarian Miss Amy Paget, chose to stay put and ran up the British flag over her Cannes villa.

The Windsors, who also remained, invited Maurice Chevalier to their villa "in the perhaps forlorn hope," the controversial duchess wrote later, "that he might be inspired to supply a last flash of lightheartedness in that dismal atmosphere." The local labour force on which the expatriate colony depended was swallowed up by France's mobilisation. Waiters and tradesmen were transplanted to the concrete bunkers of the Maginot Line, facing Nazi Germany across the Rhine, the Moselle, the Saar and the Meuse. Yet still no shots were fired.

On 10 May 1940, Hitler's army simply side-stepped the Maginot Line by marching through the Low Countries and attacking France from the north. The Nazis marched into Paris, which had been declared an open city, on 14 June. From there they pushed south to Nantes, Vichy, Dijon and Lyon and west to Bordeaux and the Spanish frontier. More than 250,000 British and French troops cut off by the speed of the advance were evacuated from Dunkirk by the famous flotilla of small boats, but there were many who could not reach the coast.

Left, Resistance fighters in Hyéres. Right, American troops rounding up Germans.

Most of the stranded troops joined the exodus south. For a while, however, the supposed sanctuary of the south looked threatened by Mussolini who, feeling that he had been rather left out of things, declared war on Britain and France and occupied Menton and a few villages just across the Italian border.

The Axis advance was suspended when the French government resigned and Marshal Pétain asked for, and was granted, an armistice. France was divided into two zones. Germany occupied the Atlantic coastline from Spain to the Low Countries and the industrial north above a line drawn roughly between Tours and Dijon. The unoccupied zone consisted of the relatively barren mountain areas, the Rhône valley, the Mediterranean coast and a puppet government named after its "capital", Vichy.

There was, of course, no certainty that Germany would not renege on the armistice and take over "Free France" as well, but in the circumstances it was very much more congenial than the north for stranded soldiers, downed Allied air crews and persecuted minorities like Jews, gypsies and Communists. For the following four years, the war in the South of France was mostly about providing a safe passage for these fugitives. Many of the civilians were helped across the Mediterranean to French North Africa. The escape route for Allied military personnel, including those arriving from Central Europe via Switzerland, was along the Riviera to neutral Spain.

Once the evaders had crossed the demarcation line into Vichy France they were still liable to arrest by the police but were not normally in danger of being handed back to the Germans. There were plenty of Vichy officials ready to give them a nod and a wink, but if caught they were assembled in Fort St-Jean in Marseille or, later on, at St-Hippolyte du Fort at Nîmes or La Turbie, outside Monte-Carlo. They were then neither quite prisoners nor free. In Marseille, for example, Allied officers reported on Monday mornings for a roll call, collected their rations, sold them on the black market, and applied the proceeds to renting lodgings in the city. Their ambition was somehow to slip away to Spain, and British Intelligence created a branch known as MI9 to help them realise that objective.

With a long history of underhand survival, the Marseille Mafia was fitter than most. To make contact with these dubious characters, British Intelligence turned to Nubar Gulbenkian, the son of the legendary Iranian oil dealer. Young Gulbenkian tackled the undertaking with the help of Bailey, his English valet, and it nearly came to grief at

the outset in the Hôtel des Ambassadeurs in Vichy. Bailey, having borrowed an iron to press his employer's clothes, bumped into a delegation of German officers and dropped the iron on the foot of Field Marshal von Brauchitsch, Commander-in-Chief of the German Army. Brauchitsch stared at Bailey, assumed he must be American, and chose not to pursue the matter.

The pair were instructed by London to go to Perpignan and look out for a garage proprietor named "Parker". In time-honoured fashion, he would be reading the newspaper *L'Indépendant* upside-down. In case he was not alone in this curious habit, a test question was provided: "Have you got a Parker pen? A Parker Duo-fold?" The reader in question passed with flying colours. Within 20 minutes Gulbenkian had negotiated a price for guides to smuggle men across the frontier: £40 for an officer, £20 for other ranks. Payment was by results and the money would be deposited in England for collection after the war. "Parker" was clearly willing to bank on the ultimate outcome.

Several British officers who had recently escaped from France were sent back under the auspices of the Special Operations Executive, a unit established by Churchill to keep the enemy on its toes by organising and supplying national resistance movements. They arrived by parachute, by submarine and from Gibraltar either in an armed British trawler flying false colours or in feluccas manned by Polish crews so exuberant that even the Polish Navy preferred to manage without them.

The Poles did not deign to conceal their activities. "The reception mob is there every night and... carry on like a Bank Holiday crowd on Derby Day," reported Peter Churchill, one of the British agents. Like many of the SOE operatives, he was in his early 20s and the whole affair was treated like a game. Churchill (no relation to Sir Winston) affected Damon Runyon prose in his official reports, the dubious theory being that any Germans intercepting his messages would be completely baffled.

"It is a lucky thing that the Chief Constable of the Department where this comic opera takes place is a great friend of England. He knows all about this particular performance and last night in a friend's house he is seen beating his hands against the wall and crying, 'I close my peepers to what the Albions do right under my nose, but in the name of the Holy Virgin why do they not help me and themselves by picking any one or all of the 17 to 20 nights in the month when there is no moon whatever'."

When not pretending to be Damon Runyon, Churchill was "Pierre Chauvet", estate agent. Flush with British War Office money, he moved into a comfortable flat in Cannes and had a regular table at Chez Robert. The British government seems unknowingly to have treated every secret agent passing through town – all the more so if they were female, young and pretty – to M. Robert's excellent fare. Churchill's memoirs are a litany of *pièces de résistance* and the search for a complementary wine. A bottle of 1911 Château Chambord was just the ticket to

Left, the American landings. Above, beach at Juan-les-Pins in 1944.

wash down a herb omelette and M. Robert's miraculous chicken on the occasion of Churchill's lunch with a charming "Madame Rondet". At their next meeting – at Chez Robert again, of course – they are joined by "an aristocratic Frenchman with a monocle". Churchill divides his attention between "an excellent *loup de mer*... with a dry white wine", Madame Rondet's beautiful face, and "the vast expanse of the blue Mediterranean, calm and untroubled below a cloudless sky". He has to tear himself away from the cheese, coffee and brandy – "all as delicious as the rest of the meal" – to mount his bicycle and race off to the station to attend to some urgent undercover business.

Churchill soon made the acquaintance of Lise, an agent who arrived by felucca and was, if possible, even lovelier than Madame Rondet. "This girl's dynamite," he noted in his journal and, as things turned out, he later married her. But it was about then, November 1942, that the Allies invaded North Africa. Hitler immediately terminated the French "free" zone, the occupation of which was entrusted to the Italians.

SOE and its guerrilla bands had worked out plans to blow up roads, tunnels and bridges in such an eventuality, but these were countermanded by superiors in London who were pleased at the prospect of troops being absorbed by garrison duties away from the active battleground. The disappointed saboteurs took up positions on the Rue du Canada to witness the arrival of the Italians. "Below the feathers of the Bersaglieri hats," Churchill observed, "their faces seemed ready enough to break into an answering smile." He subsequently conceded that under the Italian occupation forces, "if anything a greater atmosphere of peace prevailed in the district and all persecution of the Jews came to an end."

When Italy surrendered in September 1943, the Germans themselves took over the occupation. By then the fate of the Dunkirk stragglers had long been settled, and the combined efforts of SOE and the French Resistance were devoted to the repatriation of downed air crews and escaped prisoners-of-war and to longer-term planning of an uprising in support of an Allied invasion, whenever that happened. The most famous of the escape routes was the so-called "Pat Line" run by a "Lieutenant-Commander Patrick O'Leary" who was in reality the Belgian Count Albert-Marie Guerisse. Hacksaws and other useful implements were smuggled to interned air crews at La Turbie to facilitate, in one instance, a mass escape down a coal-chute and through the sewers. About 90 percent of the 3,000 Allied airmen shot down in northwest Europe before the Normandy landings (the majority Americans) managed to avoid capture and were smuggled back to base via the Riviera.

Joint operations with the Resistance were complicated by the exiled General de Gaulle's notorious prickliness about foreigners, even friendly ones, giving orders to Frenchmen on French soil. The artist André Girard, who as "Carte" ran a section of the Riviera Resistance, shared these feelings and claimed to have no fewer than 300,000 Frenchmen under his independent command and ready to take up arms when the word was given. In the event, the word was cloaked in confusion as it rested on the misconception, which in the end may have been deliberately left uncorrected, that the Allies would crush the German forces in France between simultaneous and equal operations from north and south, "Hammer" against "Anvil".

The change in plans, Winston Churchill declared later, was "the first important divergence on high strategy between ourselves and our American friends." A simultaneous invasion of the Côte d'Azur would have drawn Allied troops from Italy, and he was keen to push through Italy and into the Balkans before the Russians got there. Nor were there sufficient invasion craft to mount two assaults.

Invasion plans: The Normandy operation was renamed "Overlord". "Anvil" was put back a few months and became "Dragoon". Even so, says Patrick Howarth in *When The Riviera was Ours*, the plans for the invasion of the south "were among the less well kept secrets of the Second World War, not least because of the frequency with which officers who were to take part in the operations themselves, or in their planning, asked for guidebooks to southern France in the bookshops of Rome."

The German defence strategy in the south was to concentrate forces around Marseille and Toulon while at the same time making an Allied landing anywhere along the coast as difficult as possible. Villas, hotels and restaurants overlooking the shore were bricked up and turned into strong-points.

Any spot that looked suitable for a landing was sown with "Rommel's asparagus", underwater posts tipped with explosive charges set to detonate on contact. The beaches were lined with trenches, tank traps and emplacements for flame-throwers; secondary defences ran 20 miles (32 km) inland and included sharp stakes to impale paratroopers and wires to impede glider landings.

Of the German 19th Army in the south, three divisions were withdrawn to fight in Normandy, leaving about 250,000 men made up largely of battle-weary veterans of the eastern front and non-Germans pressed into Hitler's service. German Intelligence estimates put the number of Allied troops available for Dragoon at 500,000. The Allies enjoyed enormous superiority in aircraft: 5,000 based in Corsica and Italy against 186 German aircraft.

Dragoon was preceded by naval and air bombardment which began towards the end of May. On the 26th, bombers hit marshalling yards and the St-Roch freight depot in Nice in a raid which killed 283 civilians and destroyed 500 houses. St-Tropez suffered too, and the Carlton Hotel in Cannes was only spared, so the story goes, by Herbert Matthews of the *New York Times* telling American naval gunners that in his opinion it was the best hotel in the world and they ought to take special care not to hit it.

Taking the bombardment as a signal for insurrection, the Resistance swung into action by blowing up bridges which isolated St-Laurent, Cagnes-sur-Mer, Antibes and Cannes, cutting power lines, and attacking factories and German installations. German reprisals were swift and unselective; 99 hostages were hanged at Tulle, for example, after the shooting of an SS officer. Even schoolboys were rounded up in Vence and deported to concentration camps, many of them never to return. For their part, the Resistance fighters, who were soon uncomfortably aware that they had rather jumped the gun, were not slow to execute suspected collaborators.

German commanders were inclined to think that one of the most likely places for the seaborne invasion which had to follow was below La Croisette and they accordingly reinforced their positions with heavy gun emplacements disguised as bathing huts and beach cafés. Some officers were convinced they were facing a double-pronged assault on Marseille and Genoa, a deception encour-

Above, Churchill watches St-Tropez landings from the destroyer *Kimberley*.

aged by the pattern of pre-invasion bombing and, as time went by, thousands of rubber mannequins dropped by parachute over the mouth of the Rhône.

For weeks on end, however, the action remained stubbornly in the air, although the targets changed. "In the blue August sky," wrote an eye-witness subsequently, "formation after formation of silver planes no longer contented themselves flying overhead with that majestic indifference which until now had only drawn the glances of the curious: now the whole coast was itself attacked, point by point.

"Little by little, the fires caused by the explosions coalesced and huge eruptions of black smoke rose menacingly behind the rocky scarps… Thunderbolts and Liberators staged a veritable rodeo over Cap St-Pierre, near St-Tropez, and above the tiered vine terraces of Ste-Maxime. Allied aircraft making the most fantastic manoeuvres seemed to be playing cat-and-mouse with the coastal batteries, shooting up minefields and blockhouses, showering the corniches with explosions of water and flame, brewing up colours that even our skies had never known until that day." Between 28 April and 10 August, the Allies flew more than 10,000 sorties over the Côte d'Azur and dropped 12,500 tons of bombs on it.

On 14 August the cryptic "personal messages" which followed the BBC news bulletin provided what the Resistance had been waiting for. "Gaby is sleeping on the grass" and "Nancy has a stiff neck" were among those which signalled an Allied invasion the next day. The American 7th Army under General Patch and the French 1st Army led by General de Lattre de Tassigny landed along a 35-mile (55-km) stretch of coast east of Toulon while an airborne division dropped inland near Le Muy. The invasion force was carried in 500 troop transport ships and 1,200 smaller craft backed up by six battleships, four carriers, 21 cruisers and more than 100 destroyers.

Sir Winston Churchill, a regular pre-war visitor to the Riviera, watched the landings on Pampelonne Beach near St-Tropez from the destroyer *Kimberley*. He was frustrated to learn that his ship would remain 10,000 yards off St-Tropez for fear of mines. Had he been told in time, he said, he would have arranged a launch to take him ashore. "As far as I could see or hear," he wrote, "not a shot was fired either at the approaching flotillas or on the beaches."

He consoled himself in the captain's cabin with the novel *Grand Hotel*. It kept him, he said, "in good temper", his mood improving even more when he heard that in their cabin the Supreme Commander and the Naval Commander-in-Chief had spent "an equally dull day".

It was not so quiet nearer Cannes, where Germans and Americans fought for possession of the beaches at Agay and Dramont. The unluckiest unit in the invasion force were French commandos who landed in the early hours of the morning on the Pointe d'Esquillon. Their mission was to climb the rocky Estérel and blow up roads to prevent German reinforcements from moving west. They had been led to believe that the area was free of mines, but only hours before their arrival German sappers had laid a field across their course. Eleven out of a unit of 67 were killed, 17 badly wounded and the rest captured. Ten were rescued by the daring intervention of the Resistance.

German sappers had actually wired up charges to blow up every hotel, public building and monument in Cannes in the event of their withdrawal. The Carlton Hotel alone was sitting on 50 canisters of explosive, but it seems that a senior German officer relented at the last moment and revealed the whereabouts of the central detonator to the Resistance. It was in the wine cellar of the Hôtel Splendide.

Grenoble was retaken by elements of the US 6th Corps on 23 August, while the Germans put up a fighting retreat along the coast. Marseille and Toulon were liberated after two weeks' fighting, and on 1 September Nice, to which many of the German forces had withdrawn, was regained after stiff street fighting between the Germans and the Resistance fighters. On 12 September a Free French patrol moving north near Châtillon-sur-Seine ran into scouts from General Leclerc's French 2nd Armoured Division coming south. That emotional encounter meant the respective invasions of Normandy and Provence had linked up. Operation Dragoon was sewn up 77 days ahead of schedule.

Right, local children greet their liberators.

THE SUN CULT

For over a century British, American and European visitors flocked to the Côte d'Azur in search of status, health and pleasure, not to mention rare spiders and Roman antiquities. But after World War II the spotlight shifted to the French. Picasso moved to Antibes in 1946 and spent the rest of his life on the Côte d'Azur. The artists Arman, Klein and Raysse, all born in Nice, created the School of Nice, diametrically opposed to what was happening in the Paris galleries. Parisian bohemian stars like Juliette Greco began to visit St-Tropez in the footsteps of Colette, Poiret and Anaïs Nin.

The first Cannes Film Festival in 1946 attracted world-wide attention, publicising the Riviera as the land of the bikini. This was reinforced by Brigitte Bardot's 1956 film *And God Created Woman*, in which her unabashed sensuality and particularly her penchant for nude sunbathing scandalised the world. It popularised the sun worship which had started in the 1920s, as people began to associate health with a golden tan.

Even now the dangers attributed to sunbathing appear to have made little impact and sun-worshippers continue to baste themselves slowly on the sand, as if, in Françoise Sagan's words, they are "nailed to the beach by the forces of summer".

Sagan's highly successful novel *Bonjour Tristesse* also helped to popularise the region. With the advent of the post-war youth culture, and paid vacations for French workers, the Côte d'Azur entered the late 20th century. It was opened up to everyone, beyond the wealthy aristocracy that had frequented its glamorous hot spots for more than 100 years, and the show business people and shipping tycoons who dominated the scene immediately after World War II.

The Côte d'Azur was the quintessence of glamour: sun, sea, sand and sex with the added frisson of famous film stars who just might be, but never quite were, sunbathing

Preceding pages: 1953 Cannes Film Festival: Dany Robin, Kirk Douglas, Olivia de Havilland, Edward G. Robinson, and members of the festival's jury. Left, Brigitte Bardot arriving at Victorine Film Studios in Nice, 1959.

on the next *matelas.* But with a sun tan, a bikini and a pair of sun-glasses, who was to know the difference anyway. Here was a whole new swinging lifestyle that was emulated by millions, all hoping that two weeks on the French Riviera would somehow rub off, making them richer, more beautiful or at least more sun-tanned.

As Roger Vadim described St-Tropez: "It was the happy mixture of old and young, wealth and class. A person with no money could live like a millionaire and a millionaire could have fun living like a bohemian."

In her autobiography *With Fondest Regards*, Françoise Sagan captures the rapid change that took place in the formerly quiet fishing port in the late '50s, "a village that triggers off a daydream." When she arrived in 1954 with a crowd of young, wild Parisians, they were the only young, wild people there; they found a scene of timeless calm with village women knitting and fishermen bringing home their catch.

But the very next year she describes "wild and disorderly groups of urban bathing beauties as they rush from street stall to street stall in search of a swimsuit, speed-boats and the rowdy screaming and shouting of young people who roar off in unruly disarray – all for the feeble purpose of lying on the sand five hundred metres farther down the beach." Suddenly St-Tropez was the "metropolis of illicit pleasures": "Germans, Americans, Italians and others think they're buying themselves enchantment as they pour marks, dollars and lire onto the blue carpet of the Mediterranean, a Mediterranean in which fish die from all the petrol, where the beaches are filthy by the first day of spring." She concludes nonetheless that St-Tropez has an indestructible beauty with its tonic winds, its peaceful yellow sun, and "the red-hued coastline with its intricate inlets".

An incident in Roger Vadim's autobiography typifies the period. "It was 1958. Tahiti beach in St-Tropez. One evening the sound of a Ferrari drowned out the crickets. The roar of a Mercedes 300 SL replied to the Ferrari. It was a duel." Roger Vadim and Gunther Sachs started up their cars positioned either side of a bend in the road with a huge parasol pine in the middle. Neither driver could see the other car and had to guess which way the other would turn at the tree. If they both found themselves on the same side of the tree there would be a head-on collision unless one of the drivers yielded. "It was a sort of Russian roulette with wheels," writes Vadim. He was driving the Ferrari, and the judges included Françoise Sagan, Christian and Serge Marquand and Marlon Brando.

In the second round the two cars came face to face and a split second before they crashed Sachs lost his nerve and plunged his Mercedes into the ditch. He wasn't hurt and the next day a crane hauled the car out; Gunther, who later became Brigitte Bardot's third husband, was very wealthy and could afford the damage. That evening he gave a celebration dinner at the Restaurant Tahiti; an enormous dish was served which turned out to be Serge Marquand decorated with mayonnaise and gherkins.

Just a typical day in St-Tropez when the world was young and not just anybody came to the Côte d'Azur in the summer. Vadim was an old hand, having spent previous visits there with Brigitte Bardot, his former wife. It was here that they shot *And God Created Woman,* the film that made her a star. Bardot is still held largely responsible for starting the sun cult on the Côte d'Azur, and her signature pony tail, short gathered skirt, low-cut peasant blouse and flat shoes established a look imitated by young girls everywhere.

The Côte d'Azur, and St-Tropez in particular, remained immensely fashionable throughout the 1960s. It was here that Mick Jagger married Bianca at the luxurious Byblos hotel, pursued by the world's paparazzi who made sure the region stayed in the headlines.

Being the world's favourite holiday destination naturally took its toll; millions flocked every summer, renting anything from exclusive *pied dans l'eau* villas to caravans, from sailing yachts to surfboards, and from motocyclettes to Mercedes. The property market boomed. What began as merely good investment was rapidly exploited by developers and by the 1970s property prices were sky-rocketing, with luxury villas in areas like Californie and Super-Cannes commanding record prices from Arab oil sheiks and wealthy Europeans.

Left, aspiring starlet, Cannes. Above, Robert Mitchum, 1954.

What the French termed "caviarisation" began, as every rich globule on the coast began to connect up. Soon there was barely an inch of coastline left that was not built on. Vast marinas were constructed, and the coast became a mecca for boat owners everywhere. Every fat cat from Aristotle Onassis to Donald Trump had to have a yacht as big as a ferry moored in Antibes or Monte-Carlo.

Instead of mere luxury villas, huge apartment blocks rose everywhere. For a while it was a free-for-all, with ugly results. By 1980 the development had reached its zenith and the government began to crack down. B.B. also put her foot down, threatening to leave

BRIGITTE BARDOT

When the film *And God Created Woman* appeared in 1956 it made the young Brigitte Bardot a world-famous star and a sexual icon. "You are going to be the respectable married man's unattainable dream," her director-husband Roger Vadim told her.

It also put St-Tropez on the map and sun worship on every budding starlet's agenda. Today the film seems tame, but in 1956, when sexual union was represented by fireworks or waves crashing on to rocks, its nudity and love scenes caused a furore, particularly in the US. In 1957 it earned over $8 million, more than France's biggest export, the Renault Dauphine.

It was Bardot's 17th film, and hers was by no means a rags-to-riches story. Her parents were well-to-do: her father was an industrialist and her mother ran a clothes boutique in Paris. At 14, Brigitte, having done some modelling, was recruited as a cover girl for *Jardin des Modes* and *Elle*. Her parents insisted she could only be identified by her initials, "B.B."

Film-director Marc Allegret was developing a film-script written by a 19-year-old White Russian, Roger Vladimir Plemiannikov (known as Vadim). He asked Vadim to investigate the new *Elle* cover girl. While they made a formal visit to Brigitte's parents, the 15-year-old Brigitte and Vadim sneaked out onto the balcony together. Although the resulting screen test was a flop, Vadim and Brigitte soon became lovers, though Vadim had to change his religion and wait until Brigitte was 18 before they could marry.

Enthusiastically promoted by Vadim, Brigitte was given a number of small parts in a series of mediocre films. Her fifth film, Anatole Litvak's *Act of Love*, starring Kirk Douglas, in which Bardot had a minuscule part, was promoted at the 1953 Cannes Film Festival. It was the opportunity Vadim had been waiting for. The United States aircraft carrier *Midway* was in Cannes to show the flag, entertaining the best known film-stars on deck: Edward G. Robinson, Gary Cooper, Lana Turner, Olivia de Havilland and Leslie Caron all paraded for the cameras, smiling and waving in time-honoured tradition. But the cameramen began to slip away, turning their backs on the stars and focusing instead on a slender girl in a raincoat who had not been invited on board. Brigitte let slip her coat to reveal a tiny little-girl outfit, tossed her pony-tail and smiled. The next day her face and figure were on the front pages of newspapers around the world.

She became an international star with a British film, *Doctor At Sea*, starring Dirk Bogarde, and caused a sensation with the press. When they asked her what wardrobe she had brought with her she replied, "Several nightdresses because I hope someone will take me out." Although the film was terrible, Brigitte's role received rave notices, and young girls everywhere copied her pony-tail and affected her famous pout.

Her movies became more and more daring, until *And God Created Woman*, which was such a *succès de scandale*. It was after this that Brigitte bought La Madrague, a large villa near St-Tropez. She has lived there ever since.

The presence of the most famous woman in France drew the tourists and an enterprising American tourist agency offered Riviera tours with the "possibility" of seeing B.B. bathing in the nude. Her fame attracted other celebrities and jet-setters whose presence transformed the tiny fishing port. St-Tropez has never been quite the same again.

Neither, indeed, has Brigitte Bardot. After three marriages and numerous love affairs she declared that she preferred animals to men. She began to devote her life to various animal causes, from saving the whales to rescuing her neighbour's donkey, and established her own animal sanctuary at nearby La Garrigue.

Since then, however, she has shocked the world again, first by marrying Bernard d'Ormale, a leading member of the Front Nationale. Then she published her controversial autobiography, which caused so much furore that her ex-husband and son tried to have it suppressed. ■

Left, the young Bardot.

St-Tropez if the mayor went ahead with a new development scheme. She insisted that the town must decide who was the greater tourist attraction. The mayor backed down.

From 1980 new building was forbidden within 100 metres of the sea; high-rise apartment buildings were banned, and new ones limited to seven floors; nothing was to be built in designated "natural zones" of virgin woods and fields. In many areas new houses can only be built using traditional materials and methods.

The permanent exception to this rule is Monaco where skyscrapers cram the tiny principality like Hong Kong or Manhattan, the most recent of them built on landfill, often blocking light and views from older properties. Since many of Monaco's residents are domiciled there for tax purposes, nobody seems to complain.

Today, within the Alpes-Maritimes *département*, 94 percent of the housing stock is still located along the coast, although villages further and further inland are being enthusiastically restored. Of more than 300,000 residences, over a third are second homes. But, despite such unbridled development and the inevitable problems generated, in many essential respects this charmed coastline offers to the visitor the same interest and pleasures as ever. It has a near-perfect climate resulting from its blessed geographical position nestling between snow-crowned mountains and palm-fringed sea. The scenery remains sensational, eclipsing even the most grotesque architectural mistakes. The same bare red porphyry rocks and glittering turquoise sea, silvery olive trees and fragrant broom greet new arrivals as they have always done. Matisse's "glaring festive light" still bathes everything in a luminescent glow that Matisse felt was so strong that no one would believe such intense colours were possible.

Inland the mountains are covered in lavender and broom, high mountain plateaus remain silent and windswept, and if the medieval villages are less desolate than they were, so much the better. The current wave of restoration has preserved many buildings which would otherwise be reduced to rubble. The more hedonistic latterday attractions still hold good; Scott Fitzgerald's "lost caviare days" endure for some. In Monte-Carlo the casinos still draw the gullible rich; the nightclubs of Juan-les-Pins continue to attract swarms of young people for whom a day on the beach, a good sun-tan, the latest fashion in beachwear (or even no beachwear at all), followed by a night of dancing, con-

Above, Monaco's high-rise prosperity.

stitutes a perfect holiday. For the gourmet francophile, the area abounds in fine restaurants and top-flight chefs, and those of cultural aspirations cannot fail to be stimulated by a huge number of museums and art galleries. Sporting opportunities are endless, from water sports of every conceivable variety to skiing, golf or mountain-climbing. Even at the height of the summer season, it is perfectly possible to enjoy the Côte d'Azur, though you may need to be a little offbeat if you want to be alone.

The glamorous image of the Côte d'Azur undoubtedly remains. Perhaps what is most remarkable about the region is that it has, somehow, tenaciously hung on to its image and not gone slithering downmarket, the almost invariable fate of other popular holiday destinations.

Image, after all, is what it is all about, and it is the image of the Côte d'Azur that attracts not only 8 million tourists a year but swarms of business visitors, and entices companies to relocate here. Increasingly the Côte d'Azur is becoming the centre of the European sunbelt and a high-tech paradise along the lines of California's Silicon Valley. (Now the Provence-Alpes-Côte d'Azur region is formally twinned with California and the Var aims to become, somewhat dubiously, the "Florida of Europe".)

In fact business receipts now actually outweigh receipts from tourism. Traditional tourist attractions have been repackaged. Business tourism is very successful and there is a huge year-round conference trade. The region is second only to Paris in the number of new companies created. They relocate here, attracted by the climate, lifestyle and image of the Riviera, and take advantage of improved transport and communications systems – the second largest airport after Paris, and the densest telephone and telex system in regional France.

In particular, the high-tech sector has boomed with the development of the Sophia-Antipolis technology park and related projects. The attractions are not hard to understand; the so-called "beach boffins" enjoy all the advantages of a high-tech working environment with in-house swimming-pools, good weather, pink, palm-fronded villas and frequent trips to the sea, not to mention reflective jogs round the Provençal countryside, newly landscaped for their convenience. Such developments result in strange anomalies; next to the 14th-century Chapelle Notre-Dame-de-la-Protection in Haut-de-Cagnes is the world's first fully computerised car-park; your car is shunted by computer 14 floors down into the bowels of the earth and automatically parked. It is a typical

Côte d'Azur conjunction of modern technology and ancient history.

But a "technological Eden" it is not. Despite such visionary developments, the Côte d'Azur can sometimes look as if it is approaching its zenith. Although the tourist authorities continue to talk in traditional terms about increasing the number of visitors, anticipating an increase from 8 million to 10 million a year, they do concede that it is important now to focus on "quality rather than quantity" and stimulate interest in art and culture as well as sun and sea.

There is now some recognition that to carry on regardless would be to risk killing the golden goose. The besetting problems of the downfall of Jacques Médecin, the infamous mayor of Nice who was eventually brought to trial for corruption, has been considerable.

Nor was Médecin alone; throughout the region mayors and public officials have been indicted, and even imprisoned for corruption and underworld dealings. Hyères became known as the "Chicago of the Côte" after a series of bomb attacks and the mysterious assassination of a local official campaigning against corruption. The mayor of Cannes was brought to trial over a casino scandal and the mayor of Frèjus was investigated for financial irregularities. Politically the region is leaning further to the right with the Front

overcrowding and increasing pollution will eventually put off even the most weathered sun-worshipper. The early 1990s saw several disastrous seasons, with the Gulf War, fear of recession and a particularly ill-timed oil slick resulting in deserted beaches and empty restaurants. In 1994 major floods throughout the region caused severe devastation washing away bridges, roads, houses and several miles of railway track. The strength of the franc has discouraged many visitors, and the political fall-out following

Left, welcome heat on a St-Tropez beach. Above, unwelcome heat: forest fires are a constant threat.

National leader Jean-Marie Le Pen increasing his influence.

Pollution continues to be a volatile issue, and beaches now do have flags to warn bathers of excess contamination. Even so, there is a general tendency to try and minimise the problem rather than tackle it fundamentally. Toxic algae in the sea has become an increasing problem, due in part to yacht anchors damaging the sea bed, and new jetties and marinas affecting currents. According to the experts, the only real way to tackle it is to put an embargo on any further development and demolish nearly half of all the current developments.

Forest fires are another growing problem, with more financial resources being required every year to combat them; fire destroys between 30,000 and 50,000 hectares of land in the French Mediterranean every year.

While fire has always been a threat, the scale of the disasters has grown because incendiary material in the forests is no longer cleared by local inhabitants. Owners of forest land are now required to clear their own grounds and from 1 July to 15 October, the *période rouge*, no fire kindling is permitted in high-risk zones. Air surveillance is used to spot fires and fire-fighting technology has become increasingly sophisticated with water-filled planes, vaporised water hoses and motorbikes equipped with hydraulic pumps.

Appalling traffic means the coast roads are frequently choked, and car parking is always a nightmare. Transport remains the key to the development of the region, both for enhancing tourism and developing new business. A new airport is being built and a new métro system planned for Nice. An extension of the TGV is planned, though there has been controversy over the environmental effects of its routing. A relief autoroute further inland from the A8 is also planned to improve communications along the crucial Barcelona-Genoa Mediterranean axis and to connect the new technology parks like Sophia-Antipolis to the autoroute system.

But this plan, too, has run into local difficulties. While new companies are welcomed for their revenues and promise of employment, there is still some reluctance to provide facilities essential for their survival.

It remains to be seen whether the Côte d'Azur can juggle all its golden eggs successfully and retain its allure while exploiting it enough to survive. There are many contradictions in this richly endowed and over-exploited region of France. When a proud new villa-owner happily pays 2,000 francs for an ancient olive tree to be planted in his designer-landscaped garden, while centuries-old olive groves are ripped up to make way for new building, it is time to invoke the spirit of Renoir, who bought his land at Les Collettes with the express intention of preserving the grove of olive trees that had been growing there for centuries.

Right, crowded beach at Cannes.

CARLTON
INTER·CONTINENTAL

WHEELING AND DEALING

Wheeling and dealing on the French Riviera doesn't mean just bicycle riding and blackjack. It is also the euphemism for a Mediterranean style of life that prompted Somerset Maugham to call Monaco "a sunny place for shady people".

It is endemic in both legitimate and illegitimate business sectors and evident in everything from cocktail party bravado and taxi-driver stings to corrupt commercial practices and crude political machinations.

If Maugham considered Monaco shady he must have thought Nice, not to mention Marseille, were pitch black. The fact is, everyone on the Côte d'Azur, from much-maligned Marseille to not-so-nice Nice and spick-and-span Monaco, wheels and deals to some extent.

Some people even get caught. Former Nice Mayor Jacques Médecin, who ran the town known as the Riviera's Big Olive like a personal fiefdom with just a little help from his friends, was fingered for financial shenanigans. He fled to Uruguay and was eventually extradited to serve a short prison sentence. Customs agents at the Nice-Côte d'Azur International Airport, who regularly pilfered from passengers' baggage, were themselves searched, confiscated and sent from the Big Olive to the Big Prison. A crop of croupiers at the Cannes casinos were nailed red-handed for helping selected "customers" to cheat.

A number of villas near Mougins lack patriarchs, including one formerly prominent Dutchman, because they are serving time for running dope. Drug-busts are so common that a haul of 120 illegal immigrants pushing heroin barely merited a line on the front page of *Nice-Matin*, the Riviera's monopolistic daily paper. Even a Monaco bank was shut down, with its bosses earning interest in the slammer, when it was discovered laundering drug money. Creating fraudulent bills, which has landed other members of the Nice political and business community in jail, and accepting bribes, are all a part of doing business in many Riviera communities. Try to work a deal with some local municipalities and you may find yourself allocating part of your budget to a local youth project, or some equally undefined cultural scheme, in order to get the contract. Try to pay your plumber with a cheque and you get a look that would block any respectable drain.

This type of activity occurs throughout the world, of course. But, like many other endeavours, it is much more prevalent on the French Riviera. The good climate, the glare from the morning sun or perhaps a plethora of *pastis* at sundown make everyone feel they can get away with absolutely anything. Something on the Riviera seems to encourage an abundance of excesses. A plumber in Valbonne was imprisoned because he tried to collect his bill in sexual favours rather than French francs.

Not everyone gets nailed, of course. A number of restaurants in St-Laurent-du-Var were burned down mysteriously and no one claimed responsibility or even explained why. The apprehension of a purse-snatcher or an arsonist would merit a front-page story because it happens so infrequently.

Typically, the wheelers and dealers will swear they don't cheat any more or less than the local priest and most are pretty straight (except when it comes to taxes, where the people on the Riviera perhaps play a little more with their returns than their northern brethren). But legitimate businesses complain on a regular basis that they pay hefty local taxes to support the Riviera's unceasing growth.

Naturally not all business is illicit. The Cannes Film Festival is just good-natured "stick a cigar in your mouth and sit on the Carlton terrace" business. Not all the yachts sold in Antibes go to drug-runners and some agents selling those 140 million franc upmarket homes on the Cap Ferrat are making an honest buck. The paparazzi in Monaco waiting to get a compromising photograph of the royal family are just doing a hard day's work. And people operating in seasonal businesses *need* that seasonal profit.

Tourism and high-tech: There is also legitimate big business on the French Riviera

Preceding pages: Monaco harbour. Left, Carlton Hotel, Cannes.

which generates more than $30 billion worth of economic activity. Tourism and high technology were two highly visible money-spinners and each sector brought in over $4.2 billion. But other traditional areas, from public works to perfume, remain important. The perfume business, for example, employs almost 3,000 people and exports over 50 percent of its sales. Tourism brings about 8 million visitors to the region each year and provides plenty of seasonal employment. But the down side has been the string of shoddy buildings and unattractive developments which line the coast.

The problem with tourism is that it remains concentrated between May and October, when events like the Cannes Film Festival and the Monaco Grand Prix set the pace. During the silly summer season it is rare to find a hotel, restaurant or service business which does not jack up the price a bit. This is the period when people like Ivana Trump will happily pay 250,000 francs a month to rent on Cap Ferrat.

There is a transformation in more than prices. The normally sensible people on the coast go crazy with the summer influx of Americans (who talk too loud), Brits (who are too polite), Italians (who wear their furs in July) and Scandinavians (who crowd like lemmings on the beaches). Riviera automobile drivers, who tailgate throughout the year and take it very personally when a light turns red, get remarkably aggressive in the summer with visitors who do not know who has right of way.

Foreigners on vacation are, by nature, dumber than locals. They are prime targets for stings – usually unsophisticated purse-snatchings but also elaborate burglaries that bring back the delightful era of Cary Grant and Grace Kelly in *To Catch a Thief*. Thievery (check your purse – *now*!) is very much alive and well.

Yet nothing is more nonchalant than a local policeman's shrug when a foreigner comes in to report a crime. There is some improvement in the crime area, though – the forestry department have begun cleaning the carcasses of stolen cars out of the Esterel valleys, the traditional graveyard of many heisted vehicles.

What's worse is that much of the infrastructure, especially the road and sanitation systems, simply cannot cope with the surge of visitors during summer. By September, the Riviera can, and often does, look like a garbage dump.

The authorities are trying to spread some of the tourism to the hills and planning events throughout the year but they face a summer seaside tradition which has been alive and well since the 1920s. And most locals tolerate three months of heated hell and the invasion of the body-watchers because it has led to a proliferation of services and income they can enjoy all year round.

Indeed, about the only good tradition that has withstood the test of money and tourism is that most shops still close between noon and 2 or 3pm for lunch. Restaurants like Barale or La Mérenda in Nice still coolly close their doors during the high-flyer month of August.

Conventions and conferences: Business tourism continues to boom: the Acropolis in Nice and the festival hall in Cannes attract a huge variety of conventions and congresses. These include not just the Cannes film, television and music festivals but more "strategic" events like the International Duty Free Conference in Cannes and the annual insurance convention that takes place every September in Monte-Carlo.

There is growth everywhere. There is a new domestic airport in Nice and the international terminal has been renovated and extended. Combined traffic is almost 6 million passengers a year. The Arénas business complex ("Off the plane and into the office" is the promotional slogan) was created across from the airport almost overnight and is now one of the leading business sites in the South of France.

Drive along the coast and there is a commercial complex rising in Antibes-Golfe Juan and a cultural, convention and exposition centre under construction in Monaco, as well as a complex in Fontvieille that houses a host of new museums and even a subterranean railway station. There are now plans for further developments.

Property development, of course, is one area that remains ripe for exploitation. A foreign stooge will get taken not only by the real estate agent (there are more pages of real estate agents than restaurants in the telephone book) but also by everyone down the line – plumber, gardener, maid and electrician. They will pay exorbitant prices which can wreck the market for locals – who must then, of course, wheel and deal with even greater dexterity.

"The demands from clients are the same as always – an address with a cachet like Cannes or the Cap d'Antibes, a sea view, isolation from neighbours and enough rooms and salons to invite guests during the season without getting in the way of each other," explained José Tauzia, a typical architect, interior decorator and landscape artist, based in Cannes.

Foreign business: Foreigners still like the place because of the sun. The Japanese bought the golf course in Valbonne and instantly made the green fees the coast's most expensive. Setting up business here is an attractive proposition. For one thing, there is an eager and wealthy local market that has not only attracted more banks and financial services than elsewhere in France; the Côte d'Azur now has the greatest concentration of French and foreign banks after Paris, but also many entrepreneurs.

For example, Lebanese businessman Nabil Boustany spent $300 million completely rebuilding the Metropole Palace Hotel in Monte-Carlo. "Every whim – from chocolates to diamonds, from a brasserie to royal cuisine, from a junior suite to your own apartment – can be satisfied under one roof," he boasted, claiming that despite the price the development is still considered a great investment.

Former Formula One race driver Fulvio

Left, apartments for sale in Cannes. Above, Jacques Médecin and friends.

Maria Balladio chose tiny Monaco as the place to build his "Centenaire" cars – only 100 of them, selling for $500,000 each.

And in the land that helped form Picasso, Chagall, Matisse and Monet, art continues to be a lucrative commodity, with a proliferation of galleries and art dealers, many of them foreign, often situated in the smallest villages.

Technology transfer: The high-tech boom has produced an even more prosperous, budding business community. The Riviera has undergone a transformation, making technology a foundation of its economy. Today 40 percent of the high-tech revenue is generated by electronics and data processing with an additional 20 percent of high-tech business coming from the chemicals and pharmaceuticals sectors.

The high-tech bandwagon began in the early 1960s when IBM created a telecommunications research laboratory in La Gaude and Texas Instruments located important research and production facilities in Villeneuve-Loubet. "The French Riviera is Europe's closest equivalent to California," said an IBM executive. It has progressed in the 1990s and numerous studies have been undertaken, by companies such as Coopers & Lybrand, to illustrate why the Mediterranean is *the* European place to invest.

But the Riviera is still perhaps best for self-employed professionals – like journalists, writers and consultants who choose to live and work there. While they generally refuse to acknowledge that they too are wheelers and dealers, they do create a diversity of nationalities.

However, all this business activity has taken its toll on the Riviera's infrastructure, one of the reasons that the current business thrust is to expand by pushing pan-regional projects in the Provence-Alpes Côte d'Azur region of France. One important project is "The High-tech Route of Southern Europe" aimed at improving communications, promoting technical cross-fertilisation and prompting a variety of cooperative projects at the regional and European level. The Riviera's high-tech sites have joined a strong and competitive technological network that stretches from Valencia in Spain to Liguria in Italy – around a sea becoming as renowned for science as sun.

People are, however, starting to question the direction of growth. There is debate about the wisdom of creating new autoroutes when many municipalities cannot even keep potholes filled. In fact, local uprisings have finally begun to limit the scope of many projects. In Valbonne, the mayor was told to "stop the massacre" when he proposed a vast building scheme.

There are also objections to a new ring road around the Sophia-Antipolis technology park and locals are questioning the wisdom of the new 25 km (16 mile) metro line planned to link it to Nice airport. A new TGV track has been planned to extend along the coast from Marseilles to Nice but this has met enormous opposition from local environment and resident groups and the project is now on hold. The new autoroute intended to relieve the A8 between Frèjus and Monaco and a new expressway to link Cannes and Grasse with the A8 has also met local opposition.

Even in the perched village of Peillon, back from the coastal frenzy, there is a poster reading "The back country must not be a victim of the coast's frenetic development." The big question remains: how long can the Riviera keep its goose alive and its golden eggs forthcoming?

Left, the Cannes Casino.

Beach Boffins

There has been nothing more prominently touted in the evolution of the French Riviera during the past decade than Sophia-Antipolis, the high-technology park developed just off the autoroute between Nice and Cannes, that derives its name from the Greek words for wisdom and Antibes. "Sun, silicon and software" and "Silicon Valley South" are typical descriptions of the 6,200-acre (2,500-hectare) park with its constantly expanding mix of buildings, from high-tech pyramids to banal low-tech monstrosities, its natural forests and brand new road networks.

Brain power, the argument goes, works better in a good climate and since Sophia was founded by Pierre Laffitte (who became a senator) in the early 1970s, there has been a flood of companies, from Allergan to Zamboni, and self-employed individuals, from architects to zoologists, proving the premise that only fools or Eskimos prefer London or Stockholm.

Laffitte was inspired to build Sophia after a visit to Stanford University in California in the late 1960s. He wanted to duplicate the ingredients of Silicon Valley and create a technopole with a university, a strong infrastructure, good communications, established companies and high-tech start-ups in a pleasant environment.

Sophia grew quickly, not least because it became the focal point of the local government's efforts to diversify away from tourism and attract educational institutions, scientific ventures and high-tech industry. Aided by the national and regional governments (every politician is now claiming to have been behind the impetus of Sophia-Antipolis), Laffitte's vision became a combination of dream-come-true and nightmare.

In 1975, Sophia-Antipolis contained only five companies over an area which involved the communes of Antibes, Biot, Mougins, Vallauris and Valbonne. Rolling hills and greenery were more prominent than concrete. Of the 30 largest companies 70 percent are French-owned, 17 percent are American and the remainder are European with only one small Japanese research outfit.

Digital Equipment Corp. is the largest foreign firm on the site with a work force of over 1,000 people. The company bought and built on 50 acres (20 hectares) of land and its presence includes its world centre for telecommunications. Telecommunication is of major importance at Sophia since the European Telecommunications Standards Institute arrived. There are companies manufacturing fibre optic cable; France Telecom has installed its most advanced digital networks and software programmers are creating new services for the Minitel. A new university has been established, the Nice Sophia-Antipolis University, with students specialising in industrial economy, pharmacology, immunology and a variety of other disciplines.

But the infrastructure has not kept up with the advertisements and many locals feel the park is a development nightmare. Authorities, for example, did not always respect the edict to maintain a certain percentage of natural greenery and forests. And Sophia has stretched many local resources to the limit. Despite advances (such as the computerised touch-screen directional finders at the entrances to the park which were finally introduced in 1991), there are still numerous complaints about parking, roads, housing costs and schools.

Right, the Sophia-Antipolis technology park.

Relief looks unlikely to come from local government and development agencies whose internal politics have delayed simple improvements and inhibited the creation of a long-term plan. A new ring road around the park has met local opposition as have plans for a new 16-mile (25-km) metro line to link Sophia-Antipolis with Nice Airport. Companies, including Wellcome, Dow France, Allergan, France Telecom and Cordis, have banded together to form a "Club des Dirigeants" to resolve the problems. If the target working population of 25,000 by the year 2000 becomes a reality, then a future problem may well be the buses bringing tourists to stare at the latest manifestation of the changing Riviera. ■

Our vision of the Riviera was first shaped by a handful of writers, most of all by Scott Fitzgerald and his portrait of life on Cap d'Antibes in the glittering 1920s. The French themselves have a different vision; the Riviera for them is not glamorised and mythologised as it is for the British or Americans. In 1927 the writer Colette moved into a villa in St-Tropez where she wrote *La Naissance du Tour*, set in the then unspoiled fishing village.

It wasn't until the 1950s, however, that a double impact did wonders for local tourism. In 1955 the 18-year-old Françoise Sagan had an enormous success with *Bonjour Tristesse*, in which Cécile, the spoiled teenage narrator, manipulates her father's love-triangle in a villa somewhere between Fréjus and Cannes. A year later, Brigitte Bardot's film *And God Created Woman* did the rest.

But British and American artists has long made the Côte d'Azur a port of call. The Americans arrived in France in the 1920s, in the aftermath of the Great War. A combination of reasons prompted their arrival: Prohibition, puritanism and the cultural wasteland that was then America. This, combined with the buying power of a strong dollar against a weak franc, meant that a poverty-stricken young writer could live very well on very few dollars and in luxury on a moderate income.

Scott Fitzgerald and Zelda first arrived in France in 1924, on the *Aquitania*, docking at St-Raphaël where they stayed at the Villa Marie in Valescure, the wealthy annex where villas and hotels are scattered over wooded hillsides overlooking the sea. They had found themselves with $7,000 in the bank and realised that, given their expensive lifestyle, it would not go far in Great Neck, Long Island, but they could live very reasonably in Europe for some time. "We were going to the Old World to find a new rhythm for our lives," Fitzgerald wrote, "with a true conviction that we had left our old selves behind forever." Initially, all went well and that June Fitzgerald wrote: "We are living here in a sort of idyllic state among everything lovely imaginable in the way of Mediterranean delights... I am content to work and become excruciatingly healthy under Byron's and Shelley's and Dickens's sky."

They saw their wealthy American friends Gerald and Sara Murphy, who were living at the Eden Roc Hotel while their Villa America was being built. They had invited Gilbert Seldes and his new bride to spend a few days of their honeymoon at the Villa Marie. Seldes recorded the experience: "The road from their villa had been built for carriage traffic and there was one point at which it dangerously narrowed and curved. Every time, just at this point, Zelda would turn to Scott, who was driving, and say, 'Give me a cigarette, Goofo'." In the terrified silence that followed, Fitzgerald was always able to give Zelda her cigarette, and manoeuvre the Renault around the narrow turn to safety. Clearly, not all of their old selves had been left behind forever.

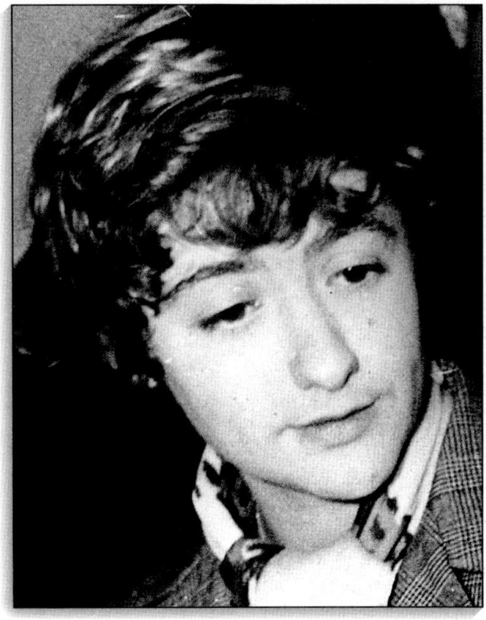

Left, Colette. Right, Françoise Sagan.

The climate and relaxed lifestyle proved beneficial to Fitzgerald, who was able to unwind and concentrate on getting some work done on *The Great Gatsby*. Zelda, however, was not so happy. With Fitzgerald writing every day, she became bored and began a casual affair with a handsome young French aviator named Edouard Josanne. Everyone could see what was happening, it seemed, except Fitzgerald, and it was only when the Frenchman proposed marriage and Zelda asked Fitzgerald for a divorce that something was done. Fitzgerald asserted himself. Zelda acquiesced and Josanne departed, but the affair soured their marriage. Long after the event, Fitzgerald wrote in his notebook, "That September 1924, I knew something had happened that could never be repaired." The Fitzgeralds spent the winter in Italy and in April went to Paris.

In August 1925, they returned to the Riviera, staying with the Murphys at the now completed Villa America just below the lighthouse on Cap d'Antibes. The terrace of the

villa was the model for the Divers' in *Tender is the Night* (and incidentally was also used as the setting for the play *Hotel Universe* by Philip Barry). Gerald Murphy himself became the unwitting model for Dick Diver, the book's hero. The opening scene of the first edition of *Tender is the Night* (later moved to the second chapter) takes place on Garoupe Beach on Cap d'Antibes: the "bright tan prayer rug of a beach" which Murphy discovered and cleaned of its thick encrustation of seaweed.

Fitzgerald brought the Jazz Age to the Riviera; and gave a name to the frivolity, hedonism and arrogance of the rich young people who arrived daily on the Blue Train – people like Dick Diver in *Tender is the Night*: "'I want to give a really bad party. I mean it. I want to give a party where there's a brawl and seductions and people going home with their feelings hurt and women passed out in the *cabinet de toilette*. You wait and see'." Fitzgerald was essentially writing about people like himself and Zelda, when he wrote: "One could get away with more on the summer Riviera, and whatever happened seemed to have something to do with art."

On their first sojourn on the Riviera Fitzgerald and Zelda dined with Sara and Gerald Murphy at La Colombe d'Or. There is a sheer drop away from the walls of the restaurant terrace and Murphy sat with his back to the parapet from which 10 stone steps led to a path. Isadora Duncan sat at another table and Fitzgerald went over to introduce himself. Seeing him kneel at the dancer's feet, and knowing by the way that Duncan ran her fingers through his hair that she had selected him as her partner for the night, Zelda, without warning, stood on her chair and threw herself into the darkness of the stairwell. She reappeared, with blood all over her dress.

In 1926 they settled into the Villa Paquita in Juan-les-Pins, but it was not large or comfortable enough for the Fitzgeralds so they moved to the Villa St-Louis, which was nearer to the casino and had a private beach.

They passed the Villa Paquita on to Ernest Hemingway and his wife Hadley who had to leave the Villa America because their son, Bumby, had contracted whooping cough and had to be quarantined. Everything was going well for Fitzgerald, but Hemingway and Hadley were less tranquil. They had been living in a *ménage à trois* with the rich American heiress Pauline Pfeiffer in Schruns, Austria. With Bumby in quarantine, the Hemingways were stuck in the Villa Paquita, but Pauline Pfeiffer, who was writing to Hemingway every day, suggested that, having had whooping cough as a child, she was not afraid of catching it again and proposed that she join them. Hemingway was enthusiastic and Hadley soon found herself again living in a threesome.

When the lease ran out, they all moved to the nearby Hôtel de Pinède. Hadley wrote: "Here it was that the three breakfast trays, three wet bathing suits on the line, three bicycles were to be found. Pauline tried to teach me to dive, but I was not a success.

Ernest wanted us to play bridge but I found it hard to concentrate. We spent all morning on the beach sunning or swimming, lunched in our little garden. After siesta time there were long bicycle rides along the Golfe de Juan." Hemingway set much of *The Garden of Eden* at La Napoule, which they visited on an automobile drive with the Murphys.

By June the Hemingways and Murphys had moved on to Pamplona and the Fitzgeralds were back in Paris. In August the Hemingways returned to the Villa America, all pretence of being happily married gone. Their return trip to Paris was their last together, divorce from Hadley followed and Pauline Pfeiffer soon became the second Mrs Hemingway. The Fitzgeralds returned to the States, lured by Hollywood.

Left, Ernest Hemingway. Above, Scott and Zelda Fitzgerald in 1932.

The New Zealand writer Katherine Mansfield moved to the Riviera to find relief from the tuberculosis which eventually killed her, going first to San Remo, on the Italian Riviera, in September 1919 with her husband Middleton Murry and her close friend Ida Baker. Murry returned to London where he edited the *Athenaeum*, leaving the two women to spend the winter alone. Katherine Mansfield's father had a cousin, Connie Beauchamp, who spent her winters in Menton with an elderly friend, Jinnie Fullerton. Touched by Katherine's plight, and hoping to convert her to Roman Catholicism, Connie Beauchamp invited her to move to Menton where the weather was warmer and installed her in a nursing home. The home was noisy and far too expensive and it was not long before she and Ida were being fussed over in Connie and Jinnie's Villa Flora on the outskirts of Menton.

Mansfield spent the four summer months in England with Murry, then in September 1920, she and Ida returned to Menton where they had arranged to rent the Villa Isola Bella, another of Connie and Jinnie's places which was built at the other end of their garden. Here Katherine relaxed and wrote many of her best short stories: *The Young Girl, The Stranger, Miss Bull, Passion, The Lady's Maid.*

Two days after Christmas 1920 she wrote in her journal: "I went out into the garden just now. It is starry and mild. The leaves of the palm are like down-drooping feathers; the grass looks soft, unreal like moss. The sea sounded, and a little bell was ringing, and one fancied – was it real, was it imaginary? – one heard a body of sound, one heard all the preparations for night within the houses. Someone brings in food from the dark, lamp-stained yard. The evening meal is prepared. The charcoal is broken, the dishes are clattered; there is a soft movement on the stairs and in the passages and doorways. In dusky rooms where the shutters are closed the women, grave and quiet, turn down the beds and see that there is water in the water jugs. Little children are sleeping."

Having failed to convert her to Catholicism, Connie Beauchamp was rather hoping to have the villa for someone else, and since Katherine had grown dissatisfied with Menton, it was mutually convenient when on 4 May 1921 Katherine and Ida departed for a Swiss chalet, high in the mountains. Katherine Mansfield never again saw the Mediterranean. She died in January 1923.

One of the most prominent English writers

to settle in the South of France after the Great War was Ford Madox Ford who arrived with his wife Stella at St-Jean-Cap-Ferrat in the winter of 1922. After three days of freezing rain in Paris and sitting up all night in a second-class railway carriage they were astonished by the light and warmth of the south. Their villa had been lent to them by Harold Munro, the owner of the Poetry Bookshop in London, and they delighted in its simplicity and charm. Stella Bowen described it in her autobiography *Drawn From Life*: "You climbed to it by a rough mule track, or alternatively by long flights of stone steps of a giddy and exhausting steepness... The garden terraces which overhung Villefranche harbour appeared to have been levelled and stoned up since the dawn of history. The villa only had three microscopic rooms in front and two behind. The only provision for cooking was the usual peasants' charcoal contraption, but there was electric light and the water was laid on... The front windows opened wide on to a great luminous sky with a Saracen fortress on the skyline opposite... Behind the villa you looked over Beaulieu towards Monte Carlo and Italy."

It was on a still winter night while walking among the ancient olive trees in Munro's garden, watching the lights of Villefranche reflected across the motionless water of the bay and surrounded by a great chorus of frogs, that Ford conceived and began work on his masterpiece, the war tetrology *Parade's End*. Ford was very afraid that his memory of the war and his creative powers "might have deteriorated" and wrote, "There remained then for me, under Munro's olive-trees, a final struggle with my courage... one day I sat down at Munro's grandfather's campaign-secrétaire – it had been on the field at Waterloo – I took up my pen: saluted St Anthony who looked down on me, in sheer gratitude for his letting me find my pen at all, and I wrote my first sentence." *Parade's End* is both Ford's most highly acclaimed work and – at four volumes – his largest. It is the basis for his reputation as one of the greatest novelists of World War I.

Aldous Huxley lived in the South of France from 1930 until 1937, when he moved to California believing that the climate would help his eyesight; his near-blindness had been a constant burden. Though he lived in the writers' colony of Sanary, near Bandol, he often visited friends in the Riviera or accompanied his wife Maria to Nice to get her red Bugatti fixed. It was in Sanary that he wrote *Brave New World*, and *Eyeless in Gaza* is set there: "The eye was drawn first towards the west, where the pines slanted down to the sea – a blue Mediterranean bay fringed with pale bone-like rocks and cupped between high hills, green on their lower slopes with vines, grey with olive trees, then pine-dark, earth red, rock-white or rosy-brown with parched heath..."

Huxley's neighbours included Thomas Mann who, together with other German intellectuals and writers, moved there in 1933 to escape the Nazis, and also Cyril Connolly who was writing his first and only novel, *The Rock Pool,* set further along the coast in Cagnes-sur-Mer and Juan-les-Pins. Connolly and his American wife Jean adored the South of France and spent the years before the war living an idyllic bohemian life, supported by Jean's small income and whatever Cyril made as a book reviewer for the *New Statesman.* They lived simply, surrounded by their ferrets and lemurs, drinking brandy before lunch (to Huxley's horror) and eating dinner with their fingers while reading beside the fire.

Connolly had lived in Cagnes in the 1920s after coming down from Balliol College, Oxford and *The Rock Pool* is in many ways a

roman-à-clef about his experiences among the English and American community there. In the book Cagnes becomes Trou-sur-Mer, but Juan-les-Pins, Antibes and the other settings all retain their proper names including the beach at La Garoupe: "This time he bathed at La Garoupe, floating on the waters of the wooded cove and looking across at the remote and snowy Alps beyond. It was his favourite beach: for him the white sand, the pale translucent water, the cicadas' jigging away at their perpetual rumba, the smell of rosemary and cistus, the corrugations of sunshine on the bright Aleppo pines, held the whole classic essence of the Mediterranean." It is very much a 1920s book, as Connolly says: "It was a period when art was concerned with futility, when heroes were called Denis and Nigel and Stephen and had a tortured look... I think I may claim to have created a young man as futile as any."

Connolly's love of the Riviera is nowhere more evident than in his wistful memories in *The Unquiet Grave*: "Early morning on the Mediterranean: bright air resinous with Aleppo pine, water spraying over the gleaming tarmac of the Route Nationale and darkly reflecting the spring-summer green of the planes; swifts wheeling round the oleander... armfuls of carnations on the flower-stall... Now cooks from many yachts step ashore with their market-baskets, one-eyed cats scrounge among the fish-heads, while the hot sun refracts the dancing sea-glitter on the café awning, until the sea becomes a green gin-fizz of stillness in whose depths a quiver of sprats charges and counter-charges in the pleasures of fishes."

Somerset Maugham bought a house on Cap Ferrat from King Leopold II of Belgium for $48,500 in 1926. He called it the Villa Mauresque, after its Moorish architecture and lived there for at least six months each year until his death in 1965. Here, served by a cook, a butler,

Left, Katherine Mansfield. Above, Thomas Mann and his wife, who moved here to flee the Nazis.

a footman, a chauffeur, two maids and seven gardeners, he created the Maugham legend. His hand of Fatima trademark was painted on the gatepost and above the door through which passed many of the most famous people in the arts, letters and society of the time; his neighbour and friend Winston Churchill, Jean Cocteau, Noël Coward, Harold Nicolson, Ian Fleming, the Aga Khan and even a few famous women: Edna St Vincent Millay looked out over the Bay of Villefranche from the terrace and exclaimed, "Oh, Mr Maugham, but this is fairyland!" She was not intending to pun, but the fact was, Maugham was able to live with his lover on Cap Ferrat without the scandal this would have attracted in England.

However, political events were transforming Europe and by1939 there was an anti-aircraft battery on Cap Ferrat and Nice golf course was covered with soldiers' tents. By the time the war ended, the Villa Mauresque had been badly damaged by a combination of German and Italian occupation, shelling by the British fleet and looting by the French. The Germans had drunk the contents of the wine cellar, stolen Maugham's cars and mined the garden, part of which had been destroyed by an incendiary bomb. After the American Seventh Army landing of 15 August 1944 the villa was used as a rest house for officers on leave. Undaunted, Maugham started again from scratch, restoring the villa to its former glory so that the gardens once again were filled with the chatter of rent boys, reprobates and royalty.

Among the most celebrated expatriate writers in recent times was Graham Greene, who moved to France to "escape the braying voices of the English middle-class." Greene lived quietly in Antibes, where it was his habit each day to leave his modest flat at the Résidence des Fleurs and walk to the gates of the Old Town. There, at Bernard Patriarch's café, he would buy *Nice-Matin* and a copy of *The Times* and then make his way to Chez Félix for lunch. He once wrote: "Since 1959, Chez Félix was my home-from-home. I found short stories served to me with my meal."

One of these was "Chagrin in Three Parts" which is to be found in his collection, *May We Borrow Your Husband?*: "It was February in Antibes. Gusts of rain blew along the ramparts, and the emaciated statues on the terrace of the Château Grimaldi dripped with wet, and there was a sound absent during the flat blue days of summer, the continual rustle below the ramparts of the small surf. All along the Côte the summer restaurants were closed, but lights shone in Félix au Port and one Peugeot of the latest model stood in the parking-rank. The bare masts of the abandoned yachts stuck up like tooth-picks and the last plane in the winter-service dropped, in a flicker of green, red and yellow lights, like Christmas-tree baubles, towards the airport of Nice. This was the Antibes I always enjoyed; and I was disappointed to find I was not alone in the restaurant as I was most nights of the week."

The short story which follows reads as if he simply transcribed the conversation of the two women in the restaurant. In the dialogue, he found a way to introduce the proprietor: "But before Madame Dejoie could reply, Monsieur Félix had arrived to perform his neat surgical operation upon the fish for the bouillabaisse..." Shortly before his death in April 1991 at the age of 86, Greene travelled to Switzerland for his health. In a letter to the Mayor of Antibes, Pierre Merli, he said: "I have always been very happy in Antibes. It is the only town on the Côte d'Azur where it was possible for me to live... I am going to keep on my apartment there in the vain hope of returning to it one day."

Left, the legendary Somerset Maugham.

Graham Greene's War

In 1982, the novelist Graham Greene caused a minor sensation when he took up the cudgels for Martine Guy, a friend's daughter who was living in Nice. In a booklet entitled *J'Accuse – The Dark Side of Nice*, he bitterly attacked Martine's husband, Daniel, for his behaviour in a long-drawn-out dispute over the custody of their children; he threw doubt on the way Daniel had got rich quick; and he accused local police and magistrates of corruption.

Nice, he said, was "the preserve of some of the most criminal organisations in the south of France." He concluded, sarcastically: "Of course Nice has its sunny side also, but I can leave it to the Mayor of Nice, Monsieur Jacques Médecin, to talk about that side of the city."

Médecin dismissed Greene's booklet as an "extraordinary hotch-potch of fiction and rumour" and made the absurd claim that the illustrious 77-year-old author was trying to "get some free publicity for himself". He called a meeting of Nice city council to decide whether to sue Greene. But in the end it was Daniel Guy who took Greene to court – and won damages from him and his publishers. Subsequent events showed that Greene's half-voiced suspicions about the mayor of Nice were well-founded: in September 1990, with the judicial authorities breathing down his neck and the taxman demanding arrears of £900,000, Médecin did a bunk to Uruguay.

The story of the rise and fall of Jacques Médecin is the stuff that novels are made of. His father, Jean, became mayor of Nice in 1928, the year Jacques was born; and he held the post until he died in 1966, when his son took over. The citizens had loved "*le Roi Jean*", and did their best to regard Jacques with equal fondness.

Like his father, he ran the city as though it were his own preserve and built up a large network of faithful, and often grateful, supporters. Questions began to be asked about his use of public money. Between 1983 and 1989 seven paramunicipal associations headed by Médecin himself (such as Nice-Opéra) together received some £100 million from the city of Nice, which they spent more or less as they wished. Médecin, nicknamed "Monsieur 10 Percent", set up a nexus of letter-box companies both in France and in the United States, where he passed himself off as "le Comte de Médicis" (*sic*). He even succeeded in spending up to six months a year away from Nice without the Niçois noticing or caring, mostly in his second wife's native California, where he owned considerable commercial and property interests.

Right, Graham Greene: a brave campaign.

By the mid-1980s, the storm clouds were gathering. Claudette Berke, who had fallen out with Médecin after representing his interests in the US, denounced Médecin's business practices. Médecin began lengthy libel proceedings. Berke told friends she was determined to reveal all. Early in 1989, just before the case was due to be heard, Médecin withdrew his suit. A few months later, Berke was found dead in her California jacuzzi. Cause of death: unknown.

Médecin also alienated Nice's large Jewish community. He made no secret of his far-right views, but an anti-Semitic outburst in 1990 proved too much for three Jewish members of his city council and they resigned.

After finally being forced to flee in 1990, Médecin wrote, in a letter to a friend which was read out before the city council: "I am now in a

position which few people, I suppose, have experienced before me. I am a dead man, yet I have the enormous privilege of being present at the kill and of observing from a distant planet what men and women who owe me everything are doing with my effects and my legacy." If by that time Graham Greene's animosity had turned to *Schadenfreude*, he could surely be forgiven.

Greene's campaign was finally vindicated when Médecin was extradited in 1994 and brought to trial in France, where he served a short prison sentence. There was a lot of political fall-out after his downfall, as Nice began to discover the extent of the corruption. Indeed, several more of the region's mayors have since been exposed for corruption and financial irregularities, further vindicating Greene's brave battle. ■

Picasso's nymphs and sea urchins; the Promenade des Anglais seen from Matisse's balcony; Dufy's triangles of white sails on a blue sea; golden light through the olive trees of a Renoir landscape; Bonnard's red tiled roofs and palm trees from an open window; Léger's doves – the visual image of the Côte d'Azur has undoubtedly been created by the many painters who have been inspired by the intense light and colour of the region.

It is the Impressionists who first come to mind, because it was their business to paint light itself. Although best known for his waterlilies and studies of Rouen cathedral, Claude Monet also painted in the South of France which he visited for the first time with Renoir in 1883.

The "glaring festive light" was so strong that he feared the critics, who had not seen it for themselves, would be angered by his bright palette, even though he pitched his tones somewhat below the intensity of the real thing. He compared the light to the colours on a pigeon's throat or that of a flaming bowl of punch – shimmering, evanescent films of coloured light.

In 1888 he returned, staying in Antibes and Juan-les-Pins, where he relied upon tourist guides to show him picturesque spots as he did not know the region. By painting local beauty spots he also made his work more saleable as collectors liked to buy paintings of familiar places, rather like buying upmarket postcards. He spent the winter and early spring in the south, as was the custom in those days. He only worked when the weather was good, believing that this was a landscape which demanded the sun. He exhibited his Antibes paintings at Theo van Gogh's gallery in the early summer of 1888, causing his friend, the poet Stéphane Mallarmé, to write to him in admiration, saying: "This is your finest hour."

It was not until old age that Auguste Renoir moved to Cagnes-sur-Mer. He was born in 1841 in Limoges and moved to Paris four years later. Claude Monet, Alfred Sisley and Renoir were all students together at the École des Beaux-Arts. Under the influence of Courbet, they tried to paint only what could be seen with the eyes as accurately as possible. They painted outdoors, and soon realised that the colour of objects changed with the lighting conditions. It was their attempt to capture this light that gave rise to Impressionism.

In 1889 Renoir suffered an attack of rheumatoid arthritis which forced him to spend the winter months in the south. He first settled in Magagnosc, near Grasse, in 1899, then moved to Le Cannet in 1902. Hearing that a venerable old olive grove overlooking Cagnes was to be pulled up and built over, Renoir saved it from the developers to use as an outdoor studio. Finally in 1905 he decided to live there and had a modern house built for himself and his large family. He lived here for the rest of his life but not without some disturbance as hotel porters suggested his house as one of the sights to tourists and he was often disturbed by businessmen wanting him to paint their wives and children. Sometimes he did.

Illness and old age took their toll. By 1904

<u>Preceding pages</u>: *Night Fishing at Antibes*, 1939, Picasso. <u>Left</u>, Renoir's studio, Cagnes. <u>Above</u>, *Little Road in Le Cannet*, 1924, Pierre Bonnard.

he weighed only 7½ stone (48 kg) and found it difficult to sit. He used crutches to get about but by 1910 onwards even this was too painful and he became a prisoner of his wheelchair, his hands deformed and bandaged. His paintbrush had to be wedged in between rigid fingers and yet, day after day, he continued to paint. In his lifetime, he painted more than 6,000 pictures, making him almost as prolific as Picasso. Even in the last two painful decades he still painted an Arcadian wonderland of light and colour, naked girls bathing in shallow ponds, washed by the Mediterranean light. "I'm still making progress," he said a few days before his death. On 3 December 1919 as an assistant arranged a still life for him, he uttered his last word: "Flowers."

Born in 1867 in Fontenay-aux-Roses, Pierre Bonnard's early career included furniture design, theatre posters and book illustration but from 1905 onwards he concentrated principally on painting, working in the Post-Impressionist manner which he quickly made his own. He studied at the Paris École des Beaux-Arts and came under the influence of Gauguin and Monet. But it was from Degas and his paintings of women at their toilet that Bonnard created his own "intimist" style of interiors.

Bonnard first discovered the Midi in June 1909 when he took a villa in St-Tropez. From then on he returned practically every year, staying in St-Tropez, Grasse, Antibes, Cannes or Le Cannet, where he rented the Villa Le Rêve. In 1925, shortly after marrying his model, Maria Boursin, with whom he had lived for the previous 30 years, he moved to Le Cannet permanently.

Garden inspiration: Le Cannet is a small village on a hill, which has now been engulfed by Cannes. There Bonnard bought a small pink house nestling high among the trees called Le Bosquet on the Avenue Victoria. The mountainside climbed above it, covered with olive trees where herdsmen tended their flocks of goats. He delighted in his garden which was filled with plants and birds; mimosa in January, the flowering almond tree in spring and the fig tree in October. He made more than 200 paintings, his subjects including every inch of the interior of the house and the views from its window out across the red tiled roofs and palm trees of Le Cannet to the bay and surrounding mountains.

After the Impressionists, painters began to arrive in the south in droves. First came the Post-Impressionists such as Paul Signac, who painted a number of important works in the Riviera using the divisionist colour theory, or Pointillism, in which the picture is literally made up of coloured dots using the rainbow palette - colours that are found only in nature.

Then came the Fauves ("Wild Beasts"), known for their unnaturally bright and wild colours and deliberately unrefined painting technique: Henri Matisse, André Derain, Georges Braque and Raoul Dufy.

In 1908, Raoul Dufy spent the summer in close collaboration with Braque at L'Estaque, which caused him to abandon Fauvism for the Cézannesque palette from which he developed his mature style – his *Bâteaux à L'Estaque* can be seen in the Musée des Beaux-Arts in Nice. It is the work produced between 1926 and 1929 that makes us associate him with the Riviera. During this time he worked first in Nice and Golf-Juan, painting panoramic beach scenes and his characteristic views through windows. In 1927, he also made ceramics in the pottery town of Vallauris.

Between 1928 and 1929, he executed mural decorations for a semi-circular room in Arthur Weisweiller's Villa L'Altana at Antibes and did a number of paintings of Nice and Cannes. At the same time, he continued to design fabrics and make lithographs. The archtypical Dufy view remains a patch of pure blue sea, dotted with triangular white sails, as seen from a hotel window with a few palms neatly framing the picture. A deceptively simple and attractive picture, perhaps, but as Gertrude Stein said in 1946: "One must meditate about pleasure. Raoul Dufy is pleasure."

Greatest painters: Two giants of 20th-century painting are Picasso and Matisse, both of whom settled in the Riviera. (For details of Picasso's work, *see* pages 200–201.)

Henri Matisse was born in 1869 and studied law in Paris. Strangely, he showed no interest in art and during his two years of law studies did not visit a single gallery. He took a job as a clerk in a law office in St-Quentin where his family lived. It was not until he was 20 years old, and convalescing from an appendix operation, that he started to paint. The man in the bed next to him spent his time copying popular colour prints and Matisse asked his mother to buy him a paintbox. He began by copying prints and on leaving the hospital began taking lessons. Even after such a late start, Matisse clearly felt that painting was his vocation. Against his father's wishes he gave up his secure job and moved to Paris where he enrolled in the Académie Julian. He failed the entrance examination for the École des Beaux-Arts and went to study with Gustave Moreau.

At the end of 1898 he and his new wife, Amélie, visited Corsica. He marvelled at the light and the climate of the Mediterranean. He wrote: "It was in Ajaccio that I became enchanted with the south." The paintings made in Corsica were his first attempts to escape the realist tradition; his colours and shapes are simplified and more evenly distributed. His compositions became bolder

and, most important, his range of colours was widened. Matisse, the great colourist, was beginning to emerge.

For Matisse, 1904 was a key year. He spent the summer in St-Tropez, where he was again exposed to the Mediterreanan light and there he met Paul Signac and Henri-Edmond Gross, both strict practitioners of Seurat's Pointillist technique. Matisse tried it, and though he did not respond well to such a systematic approach to painting, he produced some important work, particularly *Luxe, calme, et volupté* (now at the Pompidou Centre).

The use of the rainbow palette finally set

Left, *Antibes*, 1888, Claude Monet. Above, *La Baie de Nice*, 1918, Henri Matisse.

him free from the formal constraints of outline and into a realm of pure colour. Matisse could not abide the use of small even brushstrokes and soon gave up Pointillism, which only Seurat himself was able to use expressively. His paintings were now filled with luminous colours, often clashing. His *Portrait of a Woman*, done in 1905, was subtitled *The Green Line* because the line ran from the top of her forehead to the tip of her nose.

Colourful wild animals: Matisse and his friends Derain, Vlaminck, Manguin and Louis Valtat all exhibited together in Room VII of the Salon d'Automne in 1905. The critics were aghast and dubbed them "Fauves"; wild animals, and proclaimed Matisse their leader. Fauvism lasted only three years in France, after which the artists went their own ways but traces of Fauvism always remained in Matisse's work even at its most decorative.

By now Matisse was well known and collectors such as Sergei Shchukin and Leo and Gertrude Stein were buying his work. It was shown in London, Stockholm, Moscow and at Stieglitz's famous 291 gallery in New York. Matisse was well off and able to concentrate entirely upon painting. His work consisted of colourful portraits, often of his daughter or wife, nudes, bathers and groups of nudes. The human figure was always an essential starting-point for him, though he did sometimes paint a few landscapes. Cubism also made its impact on his work, and many of his figures have the "African mask" face of pre-Cubist Picassos.

Matisse's move to Nice at the age of 48 was to precipitate a change in his work because at no previous time in his career did his physical environment play so powerful a role in his art, or contribute so much to the appearance of the resulting paintings. The proximity of North Africa enhanced his interest in the exotic and resulted in the wonderful odalisque series.

But most of all it was the light. He had experienced the Mediterranean light many times before, most notably in L'Estaque where he and his old friend Albert Marquet spent December 1915 sketching and painting. He returned again in December 1917 and later wrote: "I left L'Estaque because of the wind, and I had caught bronchitis there. I came to Nice to cure it, and it rained for a month. Finally I decided to leave. The next day the *mistral* chased the clouds away and it was beautiful. I decided not to leave Nice, and have stayed there practically the rest of my life."

He first stayed at the Hôtel Beau-Rivage, 107 Quai des États-Unis, an extension of the Promenade des Anglais past the market and the old town. Here he had an uninterrupted view of the sea, the beach and the full trajectory of the sun. At least nine paintings made in this hotel room survive. "Most people came here for the light and the picturesque quality. As for me, I come from the north. What made me stay are the great coloured reflections of January, the luminosity of daylight." He rented a studio in the building next door and began painting.

When his hotel was requisitioned for soldiers, he moved his family to the Villa des Alliés in the hills which rise steeply above the old port of Nice, on the pass over to Villefranche. Here he took to painting landscapes and watching the dawn arrive. He wrote, "Ah! Nice is a beautiful place! What a gentle and soft light in spite of its brightness!" For the next three years he spent the summer travelling, then returned to Nice where he always stayed at the Hôtel Méditerranée at 25 Promenade des Anglais – now demolished. During the winter of 1918–19 he employed the 18-year-old model

Antoinette Arnoux, who was to figure in many nude and costume paintings made at the hotel, often posing in front of the huge windows with their decorative iron grilles, a palm tree silhouetted against the blue sea. A model, posed against a room interior, became one of his favourite themes and there are literally dozens from this period

The year 1920 saw the arrival of Henriette Darricarrère, who became Matisse's primary model for the next seven years. It was Henriette who entered most fully into Matisse's exotic odalisque fantasy and he painted her dozens of times in this role. Having painted and repainted his Niçoise model, and explored the limits of hotel interiors, Matisse now felt ready to become a resident, and took a large flat on Place Charles-Félix, in the old town, overlooking the old market and with an uninterrupted view of the sea, the Promenade des Anglais curving round to the west with its elegant rows of palms and the roof-tops of old Nice.

He remained in this building until 1938, posing his models against the window or using the spacious interiors. He loved the densely patterned wallpaper and introduced it into many of his paintings. To it, he added his own collection of masks, fabric hangings and mirrors, so the studio had the lush atmosphere of an oriental bazaar. The period 1927–1931 was characterised by decorative odalisques in highly stylised settings

After a year-long visit to the United States in 1930, his style changed and he used more and more areas of flat tone. After a variety of models, in 1935 he settled upon Lydia Delectorskaya who remained his model and assistant for the rest of his life. In 1938 he moved to the Hôtel Regina in Cimiez, and it was here, being too disabled by arthritis to paint, that he began to work seriously at the paper cut-outs. "Cutting straight into colour reminds me of the direct carving of the sculptor," he wrote. He began his cut-outs at the age of 70 and was 84 when he did the last one. He made the medium his own, creating several important works: the famous "Jazz" series, which he executed betwen 1943 and 1944 at the Villa Le Rêve in Vence and his wonderful monochrome *Blue Nude* of 1952, which showed that all the subtlety of painting could be brought to this simple medium. Matisse died on 3 November 1954 at Cimiez.

Though the work of Fernand Léger appears throughout the region, particularly in the impressive museum devoted to his work in Biot, Léger always worked from the studio on Rue Notre-Dame-des-Champs in Paris

Left, *The Green Line* and above, *Femme au Divan*, 1920, both by Henri Matisse.

that he first took in 1913 and retained until his death. He first visited Biot in 1949 with his former pupil Roland Brice to design their first ceramics together and the next year set up a small factory-workshop there which he visited until the end of his life on 7 August 1955. His intention was to find a way of using ceramics for monuments. Together with Brice, he found a method of accentuating the figures or abstract forms he was using by underlining them with black rings, a technique which enabled him "to house sun in my ceramic works and simultaneously to give a light, airy quality to the relief".

The large ceramic panel set in the terrace wall at La Colombe d'Or restaurant in Vence is a very good example of his success. The museum in Biot exhibits his monumental work to good effect, beginning with the 150-ft (45-metre) long ceramic originally designed for the Olympic Stadium in Hanover. But in his case there is no reason to believe that living in the South of France would have appreciably altered his work since, as he observed in 1942: "My work continues to develop and is in no way dependent on where I am situated geographically."

Inhumane solitude: On the corner of Rue de Revély in Antibes, close to the city wall next to the Grimaldi Museum, is a small 19th-century house that the road encircles. It is the only flat-roofed house on this part of the wall and in the 1930s a loggia was built on the roof with a terrace, to make an artist's studio. It was here that artist Nicolas de Staël spent the last six months of his life.

He arrived in September 1954 and began getting to know the town, making sketches and painting small-scale landscapes. He felt lonely, an "inhumane solitude"; he was 40 years old, cut off from his family and devoted every hour of the day to working on his outdoor terrace, from sunrise – which is the only time of day that Corsica is just visible, shimmering on the horizon, to sunset – when the Garoupe lighthouse on Cap d'Antibes begins its regular sweep across the seascape.

With de Stäel's work less is more: "I paint as I can and each time I try to add something by removing what encumbers me." He made 354 paintings in six months: "One has to get used to finishing more, without finishing," he wrote.

On 5 March 1955, he made a short trip to Paris where he saw a Webern concert. In the programme from the Théâtre Marigny he noted, "red, red/ochre violins." Upon his return to Antibes, he began work on a huge canvas, 20 by 9 ft (6 by 3 metres), designed to fit a wall in the Picasso Museum next door, in the room which nine years before had been Picasso's studio.

After preparing the canvas, and making preparatory sketches, de Stäel worked feverishly for three days on *The Grand Concert*, which was to be his *chef-d'oeuvre*. It is composed of two elements: a horizontal black piano to the left and a vertical cello to the right painted in ochre, but it is the background that causes astonishment. Behind the stage is a backdrop composed of 130 sq. ft (12 sq. metres) of bright transparent red paint, spread across the canvas in one bold gesture.

The day after completion, de Stäel wrote three letters, including one to his daughter, then, on 16 March 1955, "as a spiritual act, inoffensive, as it were, and undertaken in a spirit of total goodness towards humanity", he threw himself to his death from the terrace which had been his studio for the past six months. *The Grand Concert* now hangs on the wall he intended it for, among a collection of his other works from the same period.

Chagall's return: After escaping to the United States for the duration of the war, Marc Chagall returned to France in 1948 together with his companion Virginia Haggard and their son David. They lived in Orgeval, near Paris, then in the early spring of 1949 settled in a *pension en famille* in St-Jean-Cap-Ferrat where the light and the sight of the Mediterranean released an explosion of new ideas in Chagall. They began looking for a house, something grand, as Chagall was always deeply jealous of Picasso and Matisse and in moving to their territory he obviously wanted to show the world he was their equal. "Chagall can't live in a house that has cow dung on the driveway," he said, despite the fact that, even then, there was very little cow dung to be found in Cap Ferrat.

They decided on a large furnished house called Le Studio, outside Vence, while they searched for a permanent place. Then in the spring of 1950 they moved into Les Collins. Unfortunately for Chagall, Henri Matisse lived further down the same road and not long after Chagall moved in the road was renamed Avenue Henri Matisse.

Left, *Intérieuré à la fenêtre ouverte*, 1928, Raoul Dufy. Above, *Women Running on the Beach*, 1922, Picasso.

A long driveway lined with cypresses climbed up to the house, the terrace was shaded by vines and roses and there was a stand of eucalyptus in the grounds. From this studio, Chagall had views of the ancient walls of Vence, which later inspired a number of paintings, along with the Mediterranean Sea itself.

The influence of the Riviera is less obvious in Chagall's work than in that of other artists; he continued to paint fish climbing ladders and trees upside-down and his greatest inspiration remained the Old Testament. After seeing Matisse's chapel, he went to some lengths to find and decorate one of his own, but it was not until 1973, when he completed his Message Biblique Museum in Nice, that he achieved this aim, though many churches and chapels in the region contain examples of his mosaics.

Aimé Maeght, the art dealer, and his wife Marguerite lived nearby, though they had not yet opened their foundation, and it was not long before Maeght was Chagall's sole dealer. Chagall married Vava Brodsky and moved to St-Paul which remained his home

until 28 March 1985, when he died at the great age of 97.

New style: In the 1950s Nice produced its own school of artists: the Nouveaux Réalistes: Yves Klein, Arman and Martial Raysse, all from Nice; César, born in Marseille but settled in Nice, plus Ben Vautier from Naples and a group of associated artists: Tinguely, Niki de Saint-Phalle, Daniel Spoerri, Chubac, Rotella, Sosno and others. The Nouveaux Réalistes came as a reaction to American Abstract Expressionism and the more refined Parisian Lyrical Abstraction.

Born of Neo-Dadaism and experiments with Minimalism, the Nouveaux Réalistes are united by a common appropriation of the material surfaces of contemporary life: paint tubes, trash, packaging, the contents of the industrial junk heap. Arman packed trash into transparent containers, freezing them in acrylic so they seemed set in aspic. He created a flock of birds, made from identical heavy-duty pliers, and exploded and deconstructed violins in every possible way including a violin and its case, neatly sliced like an onion and set in concrete.

César presented automobiles, compacted into neat cubes by a scrapyard. What the Nouveaux Réalistes also had in common was a light-hearted, easy-going approach to art: "Although we of the school of Nice are always on vacation, we are not tourists. That's the essential point. Tourists come here for vacations; we live in a land of vacations, which gives us the spirit of nonsense. We amuse ourselves without thinking of religon, art or science," wrote Yves Klein.

Yves Klein is the acknowledged leader of the movement. In 1955, when abstract painting ruled the world, Klein set up an easel on the Promenade des Anglais; gazing out to sea, he covered the canvas with blue pigment - one of his famous monochrome paintings - it was not abstract, it was real, literally just a canvas covered in blue paint. His *International Klein Blue*, or IKB as it is known, became his symbol, used over and over in different contexts. During his brief life, from 1928 to 1962, Klein astonished and irritated critics and the public with his radical inventiveness, particularly with his Anthropometries, in which he coated the bodies of nude models with paint, usually IKB, and either pressed them against the canvas or gave them directions to move their limbs or crawl. Some paintings were made before a live audience, with a 20-piece orchestra.

He worked on Cosmogonies in which the painting was shaped by the wind, rain and other natural phenomena, and made portraits by casting his subject in plaster. He worked with fire, sometimes combining the effect of fire with his Anthropometries. His stated aim was to sensitise the whole planet, to return to the state of nature in a technological Eden – as good an aim as any in an artist's paradise.

Above, Picasso Museum, Antibes. Right, Picasso and Françoise Gilot, Golfe Juan, 1948.

There still persists in the public's mind the notion that the Cannes Film Festival is a sedate affair, where the very best of world cinema is screened to the film critics so that they may report back on the state of the art, prizes are awarded by a jury composed of international alumni of the film world, judgements made, followed perhaps by a little lunch on the beach.

Nothing could be further from the truth. Of the 50,000 foreigners who descend on this small seaside resort every May, only 2,500 are journalists. Of the rest, there are the usual chancers, liggers, young hopefuls and fading starlets, but the greater majority are businessmen. They don't look like the businessmen you might expect to see in the City of London or on Wall Street, however.

Everywhere there are men in sharkskin suits, crocodile shoes, pony-tails and Hawaiian shirts that look like a nose-bleed on a road map. They lie around the hotel pool, sipping from Perrier bottles and murmur at each other, hoping that their dark glasses will mask the fact that they are watching the topless bathers.

Every so often, one of them will break off to do a quick calculation on a pocket computer. He will then say something like "But I get the satellite rights on this one," or something to do with a "four walls deal". They then shake hands on a movie deal, and say, "I'm sure we can get into bed on this one." But each party knows that the handshake will not be binding once they return to the real world and the balance sheets look a bit different away from the glare of noonday sun.

The origins of the festival lie in the French distrust of the Venice Film Festival. Mussolini had begun the Venice festival in the mid-1930s, and it soon became clear that it was simply an exercise in propaganda, with all the major prizes being awarded to the Fascist films. France proposed retaliation, with an international festival at Cannes set to begin in September 1939. However, the timing was not right. Mae West and Norma Shearer arrived on the steamship *Normandie* to be greeted with the outbreak of war. They re-embarked almost immediately and sailed home again.

After this false start, the festival had its première in 1946, and was consciously designed to be part of the general optimism in a New Europe. In those days Cannes was still part of the playground favoured by the Riviera set. It was common to see the Aga Khan strolling into the screenings. One British critic records that as late as 1955 he was invited into a small private screening of *The Cranes are Flying*, only to discover that he shared the auditorium alone with Picasso and Jean Cocteau.

Preceding pages: spectacular Cannes. Left, Elizabeth Taylor, a veteran visitor. Above, guests arriving at Cannes party.

Throughout the 1950s it was possible to fit everyone involved with the festival onto a small motor-boat and all go for an outdoor lunch on the nearby Île Ste-Marguerite. It was also common for the jury to include illustrious members of the Académie Française; one particular member gave an opening speech in which he said he was delighted to return to watching cinema since the last film he had seen had been in 1913.

The festival may have been small in those

days, but it still attracted its share of publicity and scandal. An English starlet, Simone Silva, made history by ripping off the top of her bikini and thrusting her talents into the surprised arms of Robert Mitchum, who just happened to be strolling nearby. There also happened to be a corps of press photographers present, and the pictures were duly printed world-wide, leading to the horror of the American leagues of decency and to general increase in interest in the festival. And Brigitte Bardot made such an impact on the festivals of 1955 and 1956 that there were complaints about her hogging the limelight, much as there were in 1991 over the appearance of Madonna.

it seemed more of a gesture of solidarity with the revolutionaries and a demand for more publicity for their own films, than any serious political gesture. Nonetheless the mayhem caused the festival to be cancelled that year. The following year, Robert Favre Le Bret, the president of the festival, exercised his usual diplomatic skills and began the Director's Fortnight, a sidebar event for new and off-beat films which were not eligible for the main competition. It continues to this day, along with other extra sidebar events which have subsequently developed.

The best film in competition each year is awarded the Palme d'Or. Outside Hollywood, it is the highest award a film can gain.

It was in 1959 that the festival began to take on its modern crowded aspect. There was a large American presence for the first time. They had realised that Cannes was a perfect opportunity to set up a European shop window for American products, and very soon the *marché* was established, showing films to the world's distributors and journalists outside the official festival.

In 1968, moved by the spirit of *les évènements* in Paris, the stage at Cannes was invaded by Jean-Luc Godard, Claude Chabrol, François Truffaut and many other of the younger talents of the French New Wave. Their demands were unclear, indeed

It confers upon the film considerable prestige, but this is usually the limit of its effect. Only an Oscar can have a noticeable effect upon the box-office take. In recent years, a quality film such as *The Mission* is a good example of a movie which gained the Palme d'Or but did not live up to the makers' hopes at the box-office.

Like the Oscar ceremonies, the awarding of the Palme d'Or is also prone to vested interests, in-fighting, and the general muddle and compromise which always attends the workings of any jury. In 1984, the competition included both Robert Bresson's *L'Argent* and Tarkovsky's *Nostalgia*, two films of unquestionable excellence. The Palme d'Or went to a lesser work, Imamura's *The Ballad of Narayama*, with the other two films being forced to share a specially created prize, the Grand Prix de Création.

Cannes today is all about excess – excessive posing, excessive indulgence and excessive spending. Cannes has never been a real town at all. The Croisette, or main promenade along the shore, with its rows of *grande luxe* hotels, was created largely to please the English taste for the Riviera in a more gracious age. Even the beaches are false; sand is imported to cover the pebbles and is duly raked over each morning by minions from the hotel opposite. Each section of the beach is privately owned by its nearby hotel and the visitor will pay heavily for lunch in the restaurant at the back of the beach, or for the mattresses and parasols invitingly laid out near the water. Few complain since everyone is on expenses.

Even the harbour, the oldest part of the town, has a suspect air about it. No-one ever sees a *bona fide* fishing vessel land its catch there. This may not be surprising since during the festival it becomes jammed with every kind of non-fishing boat from small pleasure-cruisers to the sort of yacht that Clint Eastwood must be seen in. The harbour becomes a forest of masts and silver rigging. There is very little serious nautical activity from these yachts other than a good deal of posing in Armani, designed scuba gear by their owners.

Recently there has been an imposing three-masted galleon of antique design moored near the harbour mouth. Even this is a fake. It was brought here to publicise Roman Polanski's *Pirates*. When the film failed to find favour, the film's main prop was left where it was. Perhaps it was intended as a warning to all. But its presence is simply one more instance of the artificiality which predominates everywhere.

Left, star line-up. Above, paparazzi opportunity.

The main films in competition used to be screened at the Grand Palais, a magnificent old cinema with a marble foyer and one of the best projection systems in the world. Since each film was usually a brand new print, and the projection was pin-sharp, the viewing often took on an almost hallucinatory quality. It was like watching a moving, three-dimensional piece of sculpture.

Alas, the numbers of people clamouring to get into the relatively small cinema meant that a larger venue had to be built. Some years ago, a hideous piece of neo-brutal architecture emerged down near the harbour, designed by a British architect whose name is now mercifully lost to history. It was immediately nicknamed "*Le Bunker*". And while it contained many screening rooms of various sizes, nothing, sadly, quite matched the quality of the old Palais.

Finding the way around inside takes years of practice, since much of the interior resembles a glass maze. The deep stage between the front row and the screen betrays the true nature of the building. It was not designed as a cinema at all, but as a conference centre. Cannes has become a conference town.

Entering the screenings, however, takes many years of assiduous reporting for quality newspapers before the lucky journalist is allotted the coveted *pastille d'or* (gold spot) on his press card. This, when waved at the doormen, will allow entry into most, if not quite all, the screenings, many of which begin at 8.30 in the morning.

For the novice hack with a lesser entrance card, life can be tiresome. As always with French officialdom, the golden rule is: Yes, it might be possible... but first there must be drama. A stout "*Non*" from a doorman barring your way is often the opening round in a vicious battle. Protestations that you do indeed have the right card, and the auditorium is half-empty, usually produce a shrug. A little barging often produces the desired result, although this has to be done carefully. The doormen at Cannes seem to be recruited from the lower ranks of the French riot police. A frustrated critic was once spotted trying to take a flying leap over the phalanx at the door. He failed and was led away in disgrace.

The year that the bunker was built saw a riot outside its portals. It was not, in fact, the local citizenry protesting at the hideousness of the building, but merely some medical students protesting at a cut in grants. Huge squads of riot police were deployed, outnumbering the students by three to one. They duly let off some CS riot gas, which has the effect upon innocent bystanders of feeling as if they have inhaled a mouthful of wood splinters. The sight of several indignant film critics being held down on the ground by the determined *flics* will long be cherished by film directors who believe that this is their proper fate.

The debarred critic can always take refuge on the Rue d'Antibes, the main shopping street, inland from the Croisette, and running parallel to it. Apart from the inordinate number of expensive lingerie shops, there are also half a dozen multi-screen cinemas, and film companies from all over the world hire them to show their films around the clock in the hope of attracting distributors and exhibitors. Hopping from screen to screen, without checking what is on, can often yield surprise catches. Many critics hope to increase their reputations by spotting unsung masterpieces and recommending them to a distributor; Bob Swaim's *La Balance* was discovered in this fashion.

There also used to be unlimited screenings of hard-core pornography, although these have been banned in recent years. They could always be counted on to keep the most jaded hack awake. It was even reported one year that a whole row of Chinese, identically clad in blue denim, were discovered at one of these screenings, politely laughing into the palms of their hands. This was in the days of Chairman Mao, and there was much speculation about what their official report would look like once they returned to Peking.

Then there are the parties. It is possible for the poorer journalists to survive at Cannes simply by party-hopping, if they do not mind existing on a diet of canapés. The parties are thrown by distributors, exhibitors, public relations companies, producers, national film bodies – in fact, everyone who wants to make sure that everyone else knows they can afford it. No-one enjoys them. The same faces turn up at each one.

The jaded gossip does the circuit, as does the warm white wine. The Japanese party is noted for the lavishness of the gift given to each invitee. The Australian party usually involves debauchery at a barbecue on the beach. A New Zealand party one year was notable for a girl who turned up in an official capacity wearing nothing but a carefully applied coat of green paint. Since the evening was far advanced, everyone thought she was wearing a leotard and so the effect went for nought. But there is always the feeling that, somewhere else, there is another party going on, to which one has not been invited, and which is much, much better than this one. It is not so.

<u>Left</u>, Roman Polanski's abandoned pirate ship. <u>Above</u>, behind the scenes.

Every year, there will come a point at three in the morning when some over-indulged producer will raise his head from the pool of liquor on the café table, and announce that he had just had the brainwave of making a film set at the Cannes Film Festival. It would be about a struggling young film company with a hot starlet, touting a brilliant script around town to all the money men. And it would capture the intensity, the sheer white heat of this creative chaos.

Most years, the idea will lie there on the table where it belongs. For the chaos of Cannes is not to be captured. It is pure, formless anarchy.

HUILE D'OLIVE
VIERGE DE MIRABEL
LE VIEUX MOULIN
Huile d'Olive
de Nyons
Vierge Extra
Pression à Froid
COOPERATIVE OLEICOLE
de NYONS
1/2 litre
HUILE AUX HERBES
LE VIEUX MOULIN

L'Etat de droit contre la justice

"My accent has a touch of garlic," says the film actor Charles Blavette in his book of memoirs, *Ma Provence en Cuisine*. The remark is not surprising coming from a native of the Midi. In no other part of France are the characteristics of a regional culture so closely bound up with food.

Characters in the films of Marcel Pagnol, for example, not only put down their cultural markers by using quaint Provençal expressions and speaking with thick southern accents, but often refer to local dishes and the ritual of making them. Indeed, the lilting words for many such specialities – *bourride, bouillabaisse, ratatouille, rouille* and *ailloli*, for example – might almost have been designed so that Pagnol's favourite actors could wrap their tongues around them.

The cuisine of the Côte d'Azur does not differ much from that of Provence, except that it is a little more fish-orientated and offers the added attraction of Nice's idiosyncratic specialities. It was forged centuries before the Côte d'Azur became a string of seaside resorts, at a time when transport was difficult and people needed to rely essentially on local ingredients. Its most famous – and most often traduced – dish, the fish stew *bouillabaisse*, often used to be cooked on the beach or the boat after the catch. Many different kinds of Mediterranean fish both great and small – whose kaleidoscopic hues before cooking have inspired more than one painter – should go into *bouillabaisse*, each providing its distinctive flavour.

There are no hard and fast rules about which fish are mandatory, though there seems to be a consensus that no *bouillabaisse* worthy of the name can do without *rascasse* or conger eel. Other ingredients include olive oil, onions, garlic, tomatoes, fennel and saffron. *Bouillabaisse* usually comes in two courses (first the broth, poured over croûtons, then the fish) and is served with *rouille*, a fiery chilli-laced version of the garlic mayonnaise *ailloli* (or *aioli*). Spiny lobster in *bouillabaisse* is regarded by purists as historically unsound and the grated cheese that is often served with the dish is a naff and relatively recent innovation; above all, it makes little or no contribution to the flavour. Be warned: a good *bouillabaisse* makes an ample meal on its own (and so it should, given the price it commands).

Preceding pages: market olive display. Left, Café des Arts, St-Tropez. Above, Cours Saleya café, Nice.

Fish soup, which when properly prepared consists of more or less the same ingredients as *bouillabaisse*, but sieved to remove the bones, is equally filling; once again, the grated cheese can be dispensed with. In

bourride, another delicious fish stew, *ailloli* is used to thicken the cooking liquid at the last moment, producing a creamy and perfumed sauce to go with the fish (which is sometimes filleted). An ubiquitous dish on Côte d'Azur menus is fennel-flavoured grilled *loup* (sea bass), which is often overcooked and dry. Grilled fresh sardines with a squeeze of lemon are a better bet. On no account miss sampling that most delicately flavoured of Mediterranean fish, red mullet (*rouget*), best cooked very simply.

In the old days, it was difficult for people living in the hinterland to get hold of fresh fish, so on Fridays they tended to make dishes using salt cod (*morue*). If salt cod sounds dreary, you will probably change your mind after tasting *brandade*, a rich, aromatic blend of that ingredient, olive oil, garlic and (usually) potato. Poached salt cod is often the centrepiece of a *grand ailloli* or *ailloli garni* (sometimes it is called just *ailloli*), a cold dish that is marvellous on a hot summer's day.

Ailloli is just a sauce, of course, but like *pistou* (of which more in a moment) it has also come to denote a whole dish. In addition to the salt cod and garlic mayonnaise, it consists of cooked vegetables (potatoes, French beans, carrots, small local artichokes), hard-boiled eggs and, sometimes, cold

poached snails. Curnonsky, self-styled "Prince of Gastronomes", rightly urged his readers not to eat *ailloli* at midday unless they were able to "doze off after lunch, for those who partake of it generally have an irresistible urge to take a nap."

A word here about garlic. Gone, fortunately, are the days when most British regarded garlic with distaste and a Pelican book on herbs written in 1949 could write: "Anyone who travels in Italian buses might be forgiven for deciding never to grow this evil-smelling plant." But there are lingering reservations even today: a pocket guidebook recently published in Britain notes that in the south of France garlic "is used so carefully that it rarely leaves its usual unpleasant mark."

The exact meaning of "its usual unpleasant mark" eludes the present writer. But if the classier restaurants on the Côte d'Azur are careful in their use of garlic, that is not the way it is eaten by the locals: they rub it enthusiastically into croûtons, pound it into *ailloli*, pile it into meat stews, strew it chopped on baked *tomates provençales* – indeed, in restaurants all over the world the term "*à la provençale*" or "*provençale*" tells customers to expect lashings of garlic. Garlic also goes into *ratatouille*, that resonant mixture of tomatoes, onions, courgettes, peppers and aubergines which can range in quality from the practically inedible to the sublime.

A dish that combines so many vegetables is symptomatic of the way the cuisine of the Côte d'Azur revels in the ingredients which the region produces best, whether they be vegetables, fruit or herbs. Local sun-gorged tomatoes taste of the sweet fruit they really are (surprisingly, in view of the important role they now play in the cuisine of the Côte d'Azur, tomatoes were initially viewed with suspicion and became widely used there only from the 19th century on).

The luscious, almost caramelly flavour of melons from Cavaillon is unrivalled. The taste of fresh figs belies their dull appearance; startlingly complex and not too sweet, the fig is sometimes exploited in meat dishes. Most households boast several pots of lovingly watered basil. Aromatic rosemary, savory, fennel and thyme grow wild on the parched hillsides. The herbs and other vegetation of the *maquis* are ideal food for the sheep that graze there: the lamb of the Côte d'Azur is justly celebrated.

But, on the whole, meat does not feature prominently in local cuisine – until recent times there was little available - though *daube*, a wonderfully rich-flavoured beef stew, is a great favourite. In his book, Blavette gives a recipe for it: a large quantity of shin is put for 24 hours in a marinade of red wine, bay leaf, thyme, pepper, zest of an orange, cloves and grated nutmeg, then cooked gently for five or six hours with salt pork, a calf's foot, garlic, onions, tomatoes and pork rind. He recommends using even a very good burgundy like a Pommard in the dish, remarking that "what you put into the casserole you'll find in your plate."

In the Niçois version of *daube*, dried *cèpes* (mushrooms) add a further distinctive flavour. All wild mushrooms, and especially *cèpes* and *sanguins* (the aptly named *Lactarius deliciosus*, or saffron milk cap), are highly prized on the Côte d'Azur. Thrushes and blackbirds are regarded as very tasty by locals, who still hunt them. But under French law they can no longer be served in restaurants. Tinier birds that Blavette recalls eating with relish, such as the robin and the cirl bunting, are now, fortunately, protected even from hunters.

This taste for our smaller feathered friends is an Italian trait. Italian culinary influences are strong on the Côte d'Azur, partly as a result of considerable immigration from Italy in the early part of the 20th century. They are particularly noticeable in Nice – though the proudly individualistic Niçois would deny it.

The Comté de Nice (Nice and its surrounding area) has been French only since 1860. Before that it was part of the Kingdom of Sardinia, which also included Savoy, Sardinia and Piedmont. From a culinary point of view, Nice straddles several cultures but has retained its own special character.

The best way to get an idea of what Niçois food is all about is to stroll through the old quarter of the city, which is packed with small food stores. Cheese shops are stacked high with Parmesan and mature Gouda (both are used grated in cooked dishes) as well as local cheeses like fresh *brousse* (often made from ewe's-milk) and the rare *tome de Rouré*.

Left, Nice *marchand*; the makings of bouillabaisse. Above, Côtes-de-Provence vineyard.

Tubs of capers and salted anchovies serve as a reminder that it is in Nice that the finest version of *anchoãade*, a sauce served with vegetables in the same way as *ailloli*, can be sampled (it contains not only anchovies, olive oil and garlic but capers, unlike its cousin found along the Côte to the west).

Alongside slabs of salt cod you may see large, curiously emaciated fish that seem to be screaming (their open "jaws" are in fact the gill-bones of the beheaded fish): this is stockfish, the wind-dried cod that goes into *estocaficada*, a pungent fish stew that is Nice's proudest speciality. Shops displaying fresh pasta and gnocchi often also sell the strange cuttlebone-shaped *panisses*, made from chickpea flour, deep-fried and served with salt and pepper. Chickpea flour, a peculiarity of Niçois cooking, also goes into *socca*, a very thick, tasty pancake sold in chunks by street vendors.

Other snacks that can be eaten on the move in Nice and in many resorts along the coast are *pissaladière* (a cousin of pizza consisting of black olives, cooked onions and anchovy spread on a bread dough base) and *pan bagnat* (a small round loaf cut in half and stuffed with the ingredients of *salade niçoise* - tomato, hard-boiled egg, anchovy, tunny, spring onion, cucumber and green peppers).

There is a wide range of Niçoise *charcuterie* that can only excite admiration - your gaze may even be returned by the spectacular *porchetta*, a boned, stuffed and reconstituted roast piglet which is cut into huge slices from the back end. Greengrocers always have a good stock of fresh basil, handfuls of which go into that truly wonderful Niçois soup, *pistou* (though *pistou* strictly refers to the paste of pounded basil, garlic and Parmesan that is usually added to the minestrone-like soup at the last moment).

Baby courgettes, with their orange-yellow flowers still attached to one end, form the basis of a subtle gratin called *tian*. The flowers alone are also sometimes stuffed with a rice-based, Parmesan-flavoured mixture.

Also on sale in markets and at greengrocers all along the Côte d'Azur is *mesclun* (or *mesclum*), a mixture of baby salad plants which includes all or some of the following: rocket, dandelion, lettuce (Cos, oak-leaf), watercress, chicory, radicchio and chervil. *Mesclun* has been something of a success story: it is now common, if not *de rigueur*, on the menus of restaurants all over France.

With its wealth of top-quality ingredients the Côte d'Azur should be renowned for its restaurants. So it is, up to a point. If you want to splurge, you cannot go wrong. The Louis XV, in the Hotel de Paris in Monte-Carlo, combines the peak of luxury with sublime food and towering prices. Roger Vergé's Le Moulin de Mougins and Jacques Maximin's eponymous restaurant in Nice offer similar fare in more relaxed surroundings.

All three establishments offer some dishes which reflect or reinterpret local culinary traditions, as is the fashion nowadays. Problems begin to arise when it a question of choosing restaurants in the middle or lower price ranges. Chancing one's arm with a village bistro or tiny restaurant tucked away in some Cannes or Nice backstreet may not be too hazardous. But as soon as you decide to eat on or near the beach, or in some otherwise fashionable location, an apparently honest establishment can turn out to be a tourist trap. Our advice is to consult one of the specialised food guides like the Michelin or the Gault-Millau (many hotels have them at reception). Otherwise, you may find yourself paying through the nose for watery, overcooked ratatouille, thin tasteless fish soup, *bouillabaisse* that is little more than a fish soup – at five or six times the price - with a few flakes of fish and a couple of fish bones in it, and a bottle of Côtes-de-Provence rosé that produces instant heartburn.

To ensure that your stay leaves a pleasant taste in your mouth, it is a good idea before leaving to browse round a street market or food store and stock up with the kind of preserved or dried staples which any good kitchen requires and which are more expensive and/or of inferior quality at home. There is a wide range of olives available, the best being the tiny black Niçois olives marinated for six months in thyme and bay leaf. These are available in jars from Alziari in Nice, a firm celebrated for its smooth and subtly flavoured olive oil, unquestionably the best on the Côte d'Azur.

Other possibles for your shopping-bag include fragrant local honey, crystallised flowers from Grasse, dried cèpes, Parmesan cheese, anchovies in glass jars (better than in tins), and maybe a bottle or two of good Côtes-de-Provence (Ott, Jas-d'Esclans and Château Minuty are reliable growers), or that rare and surprisingly strong port-like Niçois wine, Bellet.

But there is one widely available product which, once you are back home, can conjure up memories of those lazy holiday meals more powerfully than any other, when for example spread on warm toast or used as a stuffing for hard-boiled eggs: *tapenade*, a smooth purée of capers, black olives and anchovies with olive oil, plenty of pepper and a little thyme.

Left, a tempting stall on St-Tropez waterfront. Above, dining *al fresco*, St-Tropez.

PLACES

From the world-famous beaches of the Côte d'Azur to its Provençal heart, here we explore the region in depth. From the ancient stones of Roman ruins to the villas of present-day inhabitants fully equipped with swimming pools and satellite dishes, we look at every aspect of this rich and complex area – its past, present and future.

The contrasts are legion: the cool clear waters of the Golfe de Giens, the ultra-chic beach clubs of St-Tropez, the glitzy heights of Cannes and the medieval charms of its old town, Le Suquet, the millionaire yachts of Antibes' Port Vauban and the fabulous Grimaldi Picasso collection. Other facets include the perfumes of Grasse, the high-tech industry of Sophia-Antipolis, the pulsating beaches of Juan-les-Pins, the exclusive luxury of Cap d'Antibes, the art galleries of St-Paul-de-Vence, the street markets of Nice and its stunning modern architecture. Here too are the exotic gardens of Cap Ferrat, the fishermen of Menton, the sophisticated hotels of Beaulieu, the winding streets of ancient fortified towns, the rococo facades of Monaco, the celebrated perched villages of Éze and Roquebrune and the remote secret places of the mountains.

Play *boules* in the village square or roulette in the Casino; eat three-star *nouvelle cuisine* or a *pan bagnat* on the beach; windsurf for recumbent admirers or wander a lonely hillside; investigate medieval villages or watch dolphins at play, sunbathe by the pool in isolated splendour or head for the shore.

Whatever your inclination, the Côte d'Azur encompasses such a variety of landscapes, culture and facilities that every whim can be satisfied. And if all you want to do is spend your entire time sea-gazing, no beaches are better designed for the purpose. You can rent a parasol-shaded *matelas* for the day and only rise for an ice bucket of Provençal rosé and *moules marinière* in the beach restaurant. Should your activities stretch to the need for a good book, this Insight Guide will certainly assure you of plenty to read.

Preceding pages: jardin exotique, Èze; yachts in Antibes; the terrace of a mansion in Nice. Left, Menton harbour.

HYÈRES

One of the longest established and most southerly of the Côte d'Azur resorts is **Hyères**, although it is often viewed as an unfashionable and slightly shabby cousin of the "real" Riveria towns of Cannes or Nice. This unfair reputation has its seeds in Queen Victoria's flippant patronage of Hyères in 1892, for no sooner had hotels and palm-lined avenues been built in honour of Her Majesty and her entourage than she decided to move on to Cimiez, rendering the town *passé* almost overnight.

However, the French never ceased visiting Hyères-les-Palmiers, and it has long been a centre for the seriously *sportif*, who take advantage of the subtropical climate to sail, scuba-dive, windsurf and water-ski. There are now three vast leisure ports and 22 miles (35 km) of beaches to be sampled. The town is not wholly reliant upon tourism and is surrounded by vast greenhouses cultivating early fruits such as strawberries, peaches and kiwis as well as ornamental plants, rare flowers (orchids in particular) and potted palms. Close by are many good vineyards which thrive in excellent growing conditions. The busy atmosphere of the modern town combines charmingly with its backdrop of faded *belle-époque* grandeur, the setting for Joseph Conrad's atmospheric last novel *The Rover*.

The distinctive colonial feel of Hyères has meant that it has also been popular as a location with French film-makers. Man Ray's *The Mystery of the Château of Dice* was filmed in 1929 in the villa of the modernist architect Mallet-Stevens. In 1930 Charles de Noailles produced the first film of Jean Cocteau, *The Blood of the Poet*, here and the same year risked excommunication for financing Luis Buñuel's *L'Age d'Or*.

Preceding pages: diving in the Golfe de Giens. Left, Île de Porquerolles. Right, Church of St-Paul, Hyères.

More recently, in 1982, François Truffaut made *Finally Sunday!* in Hyères using black and white film and the eclectic mix of seaside town architecture to create a mood of tension and claustrophobia. The town continues to link itself to experimental cinema and has held an International Festival for young cinema for 20 years.

Pause for coffee under the plane trees of the **Place de la République**, before setting off on the steep climb through the twisting medieval streets of the old town built on the Castéou hill, and up to the ruins of the 14th-century **château**.

Close by is the **Church of St-Louis**, who recuperated here in the 13th century when the now disused port of L'Syguade was a base for returning crusaders. This calm, elegant church is an example of a successful marriage between Italian Romanesque style and Provençal Gothic.

Entering the **Vieille Ville** through the 13th-century gate, you will find yourself in the Rue Massillon, named after the great preacher of the court of Louis XIV who was born in the nearby Rue Rabaton. On the left is the **Collegiate Church of St-Paul**, with an interesting Gothic nave and Romanesque bell-tower. In the **Place Massillon**, a food market is held each morning, and Arab

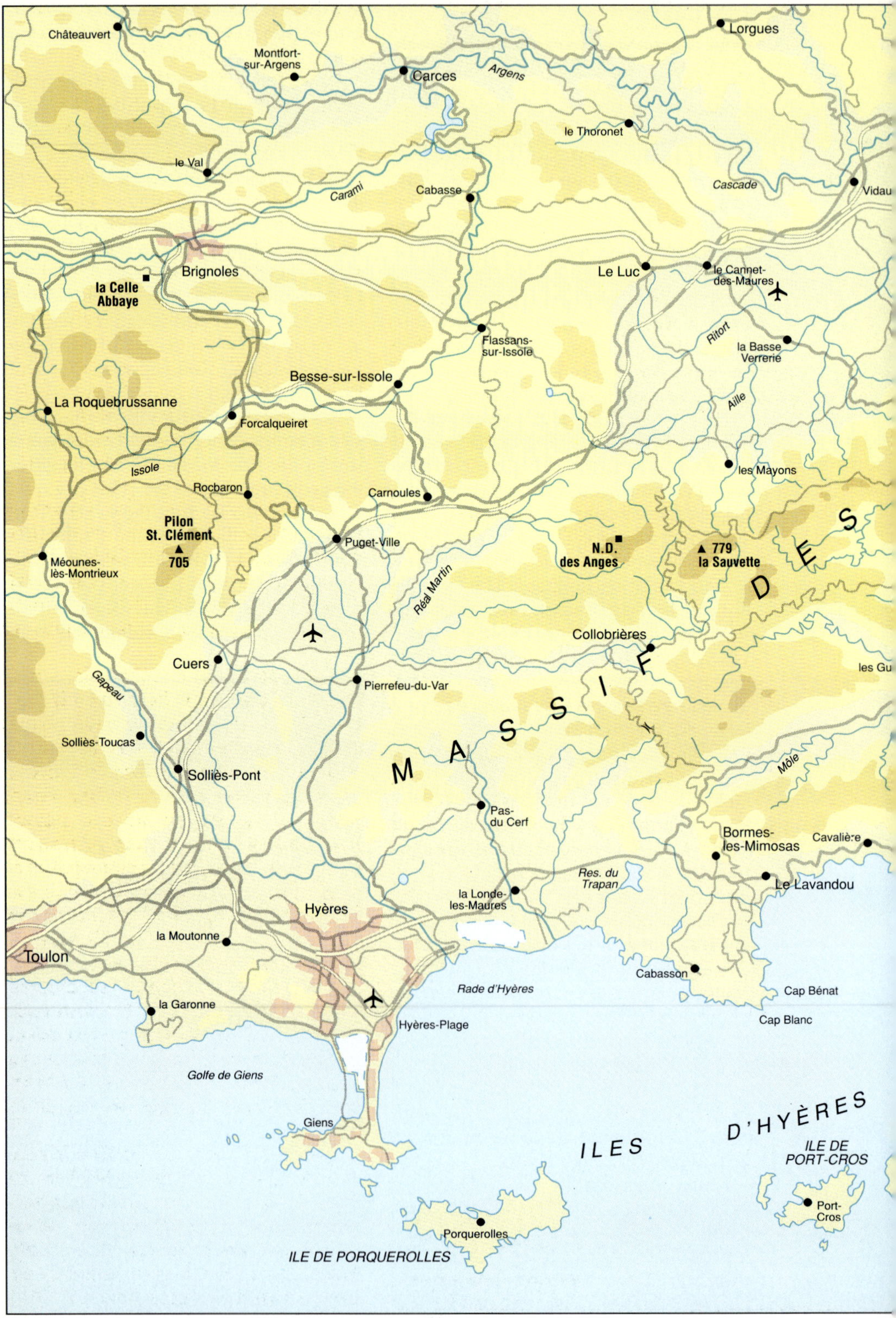
Châteauvert
Montfort-sur-Argens
Carces
Argens
Lorgues
le Thoronet
le Val
Carami
Cabasse
Cascade
Vidau
Brignoles
la Celle Abbaye
Le Luc
le Cannet-des-Maures
Flassans-sur-Issole
Ritort
la Basse Verrerie
Besse-sur-Issole
La Roquebrussanne
Forcalqueiret
Aille
Issole
Rocbaron
Carnoules
les Mayons
Pilon St. Clément
705
Puget-Ville
N.D. des Anges
779 la Sauvette
Méounes-lès-Montrieux
Réal Martin
Cuers
Collobrières
les Gu
Gapeau
Pierrefeu-du-Var
MASSIF DES
Solliès-Toucas
Solliès-Pont
Môle
Pas-du Cerf
Bormes-les-Mimosas
Cavalière
Res. du Trapan
Le Lavandou
la Londe-les-Maures
Hyères
la Moutonne
Toulon
Cabasson
Rade d'Hyères
Cap Bénat
la Garonne
Hyères-Plage
Cap Blanc
Golfe de Giens
Giens
ILES D'HYÈRES
ILE DE PORT-CROS
Port-Cros
Porquerolles
ILE DE PORQUEROLLES

and Provençal delicacies can be bought. The square is overlooked by the 12th-century **Tower of St-Blaise**, last remnant of a Knights Templar command post, set up in Hyères after the town gained royal status with the blessing of Charles I of Anjou.

Continue up the pretty Rue Barbacane and walk through an arch and Romanesque house to Rue Paradis, where a calf-achingly steep track snakes past the **Parc St-Bernard**, a garden of Mediterranean flowers and plants, to the castle.

The panoramic view from the castle's turrets provides a strong sense of the geography and history of the town. Over to the east are the dark curves of the Massif des Maures, while in the south you can see over Les Oiseaux peak and the Costebelle hill to the Giens peninsula and the islands of Hyères.

The American novelist Edith Wharton fell in love with the view when she first visited Hyères with André Gide in 1915. She returned after World War I and wrote that she was ravished by "views of land and sea such as were never seen before".

The château has its foundations on a Greek defence wall from the 4th century BC when a Greek trading-post called Olbia was founded on the coast at Almanarre which was later to become the Roman town of Pomponiana. Fragments of pottery, spears and statues have been excavated from Almanarre and can be seen at the municipal museum. The castle was established by the Lords of Fos and passed to Charles I in 1257. In the 16th century Charles IX was brought here by his mother Catherine de Medicis and was enchanted by the profusion of orange blossom trees. In 1662 the castle was pulled down during the wars of religion. Without its stronghold the importance of the town was drastically reduced in favour of Toulon.

Round the castle is the **Rue Victor Basch**, a road cut through layers of slate. Here is the unremarkable house where Robert Louis Stevenson convalesced and whose words, "I was only happy once - that was at Hyères," are immortalised on a blue plaque.

The street curves down to the **Rue Edith Wharton**, named in honour of her efforts to restore the ruined castle of St-Clair and its garden. Bernard Berenson pronounced the old Clarisses convent and its views to be "sheer paradise... with the incense-like fragrance of the pines and cypresses and the artistic beauty of the rocks." Other literary figures to visit St-Clair were William Gerhardie, Robert Norton, Sinclair Lewis, Kenneth and Jane Clark, H. G. Wells and Aldous Huxley.

Another famous inhabitant of old Hyères, with a tomb in the grounds of St-Clair, is Olivier Voitier, the 19th-century naval officer who discovered the statue of the *Venus de Milo*, now in the Louvre, when on a maritime campaign in Greece.

The road back into modern Hyères passes a pink house with a bridge across to the upper road which would look perfectly at home in Lisbon, and then down a delightful spiral rampart. The large number of clinics and convalescent homes are evidence of the continued belief in the health-giving properties of the town's situation and the local *Source de la Vierge* whose waters were enjoyed by Tolstoy who took a winter "cure" in Hyères in 1860.

The modern town has its own attractions with many Moorish-style buildings, such as **La Tunisienne** in the Avenue de Beauregard, **La Mauresque** in the Avenue Jean Natte, and the seaside neo-baroque rotunda tourist office in the Avenue de Belgique-Hyères. You can see just-married couples jostling to pose for the wedding photographer against the tropical plants and flowers, the peacocks and the ornamental lakes of the **Olbius Riquier Gardens**. For beaches, head for Hyères Plage or the isthmus of Presqu'île de Giens and the long sandy expanse of La Capte. Safe shallow waters make it very popular in summer.

The approach to **La Tour Fondue**, where ferries and glass-bottomed boats leave regularly for the Hyères islands, is by the tow roads on the peninsula of Giens either side of the Marais Salins

Moorish influence in Hyères.

des Pesquiers, the coast's only working salt marsh. In Roman times this strange narrow strip was probably still an island and briefly became one again in the great storms of 1811.

At the foot of the tower, which the young Napoleon re-established as a stronghold when he was an artillery officer at Toulon, happy day-trippers with hampers and gaggles of divers congregate. It is a half-hour trip to the beautiful and densely vegetated **Îles d'Or**, also known as Iles d'Hyères, so called because of the Mica or "Fool's Gold" which sparkles in the sand and rocks of the islands.

François I granted the right of asylum to convicts provided they would live on the islands and protect them against corsairs and pirates. However, the criminal underclass flooded the islands and turned to piracy themselves, rewarding the king's generosity by trying to capture one of his ships.

The three small islands have been unable to escape the troubles of the mainland for in 1793 the British landed on Porquerolles and blew up the fort, and in August 1944 American troops landed on the islands of Port-Cros and Le Levant to fight off German batteries.

Porquerolles, so called because of the wild boar that once roamed here, is the largest and most popular of the islands. It offers the most amenities for families, pleasure-craft owners and the less intrepid while its white sandy beaches and woods of pine heather, eucalyptus and myrtle remain remarkably unspoilt. Porquerolles has been protected from developers by State ownership, with a large conservation area established in 1972.

The island's village, also called Porquerolles, has a strong colonial flavour in the simple style of its houses, built by the military in the mid-19th century. The small village church has a wooden Stations of the Cross carved by a soldier with his penknife. Inexpensive lunches can be enjoyed at one of the many restaurants around the main square. Alternatively, hire mountain bikes (beware of uncomprising seats) or

Ferry ride to Porquerolles.

the gearless *classique* and set off with a picnic to the lighthouse or beaches on the north or south coast.

Climb the **lighthouse** to enjoy dramatic views of the hills of Le Grand Langoustier to the west, St-Agatha's fort to the south as well as the cliffs of the south coast, the Hyères roadstead and the Maures Massif.

Port-Cros is more rugged and quiet and is worth a whole day's visit. The island is named after the hollowed-out *(creux)* shape of its harbour. Explore the island by walking through the Valley of Solitude to the only hotel in the National Park of Port-Cros. The Manoir d'Hélène is named after the heroine in Melchoir de Vogue's novel *Jean d'Agrève* which is set on the island. It was here that D. H. Lawrence is supposed to have met the Englishwoman whose confessional post-coital conversation inspired *Lady Chatterley's Lover*. Continue to **l'Estissac Fort**; the botanical path is overgrown with wild flowers whose scent accompanies you down to the sheltered beach and turquoise waters of La Palud.

Île de Levant is a strip of barren rock only 5 miles (8 km) long and 1,300 yards (1,200 metres) wide. Bare all at the nudist village and beach of Héliopolis which used to be the "Mecca of Naturism". The nudist colony was founded on the island (once inhabited by Lérins monks) in 1931 by the doctors Gaston and André Durville who urged their patients to enjoy the physical and psychological benefits of "the childlike liberation of nakedness". Since it has become acceptable to take off your swimsuit on many beaches around the Mediterranean, the island has lost some of its *risqué* reputation, but is still popular with dedicated nudists. There is not much of the island to explore as most of Levant is owned by the navy, but there is the strange sight of shopkeepers, estate agents and waiters going about their daily routine in a G-string or less.

Exploring the Massif des Maures: The oldest range of mountains in Provence is the **Massif des Maures**, separated from the Estérel range by the valley created by the Argens river; the mainly

Golfe de Giens.

Schistous rock was originally part of the huge Tyrrhenian massif which once included Corsica and Sardinia. The name of *Maures* is not an allusion to the Moors (Saracens), who occupied the area for more than a century and who were finally driven out in AD 973, but to the Provençal word *Maouro* which describes the dark density of the cork oak, chestnut and pine forest.

The glorious views and abundance of flowers and plants such as yellow gorse, flowering lavender and wild roses are enjoyed by drivers, walkers and cyclists who use the Massif's towns and points of interest to shape their route through the mountainous forest, stopping en route for a meal, a coffee or a night.

La Garde-Freinet is the capital of the Maures and full of left-overs from the 1960s, as you will notice drinking in the bar of Claire Fontaine, watched by a large signed photo of John Wayne, or hanging out in the *Brasserie le lézard.*

In the 19th century the town produced more than three-quarters of France's bottle corks and the oaks are still farmed every 8 to 12 years with a yielding life of 150 years. The light, impermeable and elastic outer bark is cut in strips by a knife from the cork oaks, leaving a clean red-brown trunk. The cork is then broken up, steam-cleaned and pressed into moulds of the desired shape. As well as being made into tiles and stoppers many cork craft ornaments are on sale at the Rue St-Jacques or on display at the disused St-Eloi chapel at the entrance to the village.

The Rue St-Jacques caters for the tourists from the coast with local antiques, pottery and ornamental flower shops. There is also some exquisite but expensive jewellery made from the local blue and green serpentine stone.

The Saracens are credited with building the castle on a high point to the northeast of the village, but it is now thought that it may be of a slightly later period. Some have attributed it to Count William who spared many Saracen prisoners and who, in return, taught his farmers how to roof their houses with flat tiles, how to make use of the oak

Street in Collobrières.

trees for cork and resin and, probably, the secret of *marrons glacés*, chestnuts crystallised and preserved in a sugary syrup, now the main local industry.

The road to **Collobrières** is dedicated to fire-fighters who died in 1971, and the large areas of blackened and twisted trees are evidence of the constant forest fires, sparked spontaneously by thoughtless visitors, or, as some locals think, by arsonists. Throughout the forest fire-fighters can be seen carrying out their daily duties of strimming down the undergrowth and creating fire-blocks. There are points all along the route for cars to stop and admire the breathtaking views of the Maures or simply to let an impatient hill-farmer overtake in his van. Tracks and paths are clearly marked for groups of hearty walkers in plus-fours and heavy boots.

Before reaching the village one can take a detour to the eccentric Merovingian priory of the **Notre-Dame-des-Anges**, which shares its high point with a large communications tower and transmitter mast. The 19th-century chapel is filled with offerings made by pilgrims who have climbed to the spot where a statue of the Virgin Mary was found by a shepherd in the 11th century. Babies' bonnets and pictures of the sick being cured cram the dark chapel and, more mysteriously, two stuffed alligators hang from the ceiling.

Café in La Garde-Freinet.

Much more aesthetically pleasing is the **Chartreuse de la Verne** which is southeast of Collobrières. The Carthusian Charterhouse stands by a spring on a plateau overlooking the holm oak and chestnut forest. Most of the structure was built in the 17th and 18th centuries, after which it was abandoned by revolution-fearing monks, but the blue-green serpentine cloisters and four restored monks' cells reveal medieval origins.

While tourists are welcome to walk through the beautiful semi-ruin, remember that the Charterhouse has been occupied by nuns from the order of Bethlehem since 1984.

The centre of **Collobrières** is not the attractive main square with its Spanish feel, or the main boulevard with its grand mercantile houses, but the extensive bouledrome by the river. Nearby is the **Confiserie Azuréenne**, attached to the delicious-smelling factory famous for its chestnut sweets and purées. There are often long queues here, so it is worthwhile taking advantage of the less expensive chestnut delicacy stalls on the way out on the D14 road.

The Maures corniche: White, sandy and relatively uncrowded beaches can be found just a short walk down from the scenic coastal road of the D559. The main resort of this corniche is **Le Lavandou**, whose name recalls the lavender fields on the banks of the Batailler. It is now a resort catering mainly for the teenage holiday market and the owners of pleasure-craft although it does still function as a fishing port. It is a mixture of nightclubs, bars, cheap hotels and leather jacketed *mecs* on motorbikes.

The main square next to the marina is named after the composer Ernest Reyer who lived in the town in the 19th century. From here ferries leave regularly for the Hyères islands. The town's best point is its sandy beach with a long, tree-lined promenade; quieter beaches can be found at the less built-up and much smaller resorts of **St-Clair**, **Aquebelle**, **Cavalière** and **Pramousquier**.

To the west of Le Lavandou is **Cap Benat**, France's equivalent of Camp David, with most of the beaches inaccessible by car but possible on foot. The rocky promontory with its two ruined castles is a military training ground leading to the official summer residence of the President.

Visit the delightful **Bormes-les-Mimosas** for a tantalising flavour of Provence. Take the road from Le Lavandou through an avenue of eucalyptus and mimosa. The coral-coloured houses nestle on the steeply sloping roads, one of which is aptly called *rompi-cuou* - the neck-breaker. The beach at L'Estagnol is a wide bay fringed by parasol pines.

In the **Place St-François** is a statue of Francesco di Paola whose visit to the town was said to have miraculously ended an outbreak of plague. In the chapel of St-François there is a monument to the landscape painter Jean-Charles Cazin whose works are on display both in the town hall and in the small Museum of Bormes. At the top of the town there are excellent cafés and magnificent views of the coast and the forest of Dom spread out below. Nearby is a marina, with a capacity for 800 yachts, and three attractive beaches.

It is worth stopping at the beach of **Rayol-Canadel-sur-Mer** at the base of the Pradels range, flanked by two pinewoods sheltering it from the *mistral* winds. The village sits in a natural amphitheatre in the wooded hillside.

Cavalaire-sur-Mer is a town built for the convenience of yacht- and boat-owners. It has mooring for 1,200 yachts, good shops, a post office, doctors and a long sandy beach. You can catch a ferry from the new port for the Hyères islands or for the market on Wednesday in the Place Jean Moulin. Here you can savour an abundance of regional produce: honey from the forest, olives, olive oil, *saucisson* and the essential local rosé.

Rooftops of Bormes-les-Mimosas.

PHÉNIX
HOUBLON
Le Var

ST-TROPEZ

Like Hollywood, **St-Tropez** ranks among an élite handful of place-names to have achieved practically mythical status. To large numbers of French, the myth is still one of the *ne plus ultra* of summer chic. To others, St-Tropez typifies over-commercialism and vulgarity. Needless to say, the reality is somewhere between the two, and varies in any case according to the season.

Crammed with between 60,000 and 100,000 visitors in July and August, in winter St-Tropez's population returns to a placid and neighbourly 6,000. Though obviously not for those in search of rustic serenity, at least in summer, a visit to St-Tropez can be considerable fun, taken in the right spirit, and preferably equipped with a generous budget. Perhaps the best approach is to that of the town as a sort of Mediterranean extension of the Left Bank of Paris, with all that this implies in terms of parking problems and expense.

St-Tropez's original attraction was based on the beauty of the dusky pink and ochre houses of the old town, its position on the southern curve of its large, sheltered gulf, and the climatic conditions which contribute to its beautiful, clear light. Uniquely on the French Riviera, St-Tropez faces north, so that the quayside cafés receive the famous golden evening light, as well as the bay's stunning sunsets.

As neither railway nor major trunk roads passed through the town due to its peninsular position, it escaped the late 19th-century development of earlier resorts such as Juan-les-Pins and Cannes. Its restricted road access is now a mixed blessing, since the advent of the famous summer traffic jams the length of the D98 to the blocked roundabout at Le Foux, and, sometimes, the whole way round the bay to Ste-Maxime. (The times absolutely to be avoided on this road are late morning until early afternoon, and between 6 o'clock and 10 o'clock in the evening.)

St-Tropez is named after Torpes, a Christian Roman centurion, steward of the Emperor Nero's palace at Pisa who, according to legend, was beheaded for his faith and cast adrift with a dog and a cock in a boat which eventually drifted to the site of the present port. The early town was sacked and its population killed or dispersed by Saracen raiders who occupied the region in the 7th and 9th centuries. In the 15th, St-Tropez was ceded to a Genoese nobleman, Raphaël de Garezzio, with rights tantamount to those of a republic, and was populated by a number of Genoese families, some of whose descendants remain today.

The citadel overlooking the town dates from the ensuing period of well-organized security, provided by an elected "town captain" and defence force; the current *bravade* ceremony which takes place in June every year, involving musket firing and 16th-century uniform, commemorates the successful repulse by Tropeziens in 1637 of a raiding force of Spanish galleys.

By the late 19th-century St-Tropez was primarily involved in tuna fishing,

Preceding pages: Café des Arts, St-Tropez. **Left**, first encounters. **Right**, St-Tropez, view of the old town.

shipping wines from the region to Marseille and Toulon, and making corks from the bark of the local oaks, while a handful of large houses outside the town had been restored or constructed by prominent individuals such as Napoleon III's minister Émile Ollivier, who retired to the château of La Moutte, in whose grounds his tomb stands, "seeking only peace, but finding delight".

In 1887 the writer Guy de Maupassant arrived in St-Tropez aboard his boat *Bel Ami* and found it "a charming, simple daughter of the sea" with "sardine scales glistening like pearls on the cobblestones." It was the painter Paul Signac, however, who, sailing into the port on his yacht in 1892 and falling in love with the light, acquired a small house overlooking the beach of Les Graniers and began to attract friends and painter acquaintances: Matisse, Bonnard, Camoin, Dunoyer de Segonzac. In 1927 the novelist Colette moved to her villa La Treille Muscate. She was followed by 1930s *beau monde* such as the couturier Paul Poiret, the writer Anaïs Nin, and after the interruption of World War II, when the long Pampelonne beach was used for the Allied liberation landings, by the first of the St-Germain bohemian stars, Juliette Greco.

In 1959 Roger Vadim shot *And God Created Woman* in St-Tropez, with the sex-kitten Brigitte Bardot wreaking havoc around the old port, and the floodgates of the town's modern show-business invasion were opened. The *yé yé* industry – pop stars led by Johnny Hallyday and record magnate Eddie Barclay – followed the film world, and in 1969 the opening of the luxurious Hotel Byblos marked a turning point in the transformation of the hitherto simple fishing village into a fully paid-up jet-set destination. It only remained for the masses to follow, and the seriously rich to move out of town to luxurious and secluded villas, or the staterooms of their substantial yachts.

The St-Tropez season starts around the beginning of April, peaks in the frenzy of the national holiday month of August and continues until the end of

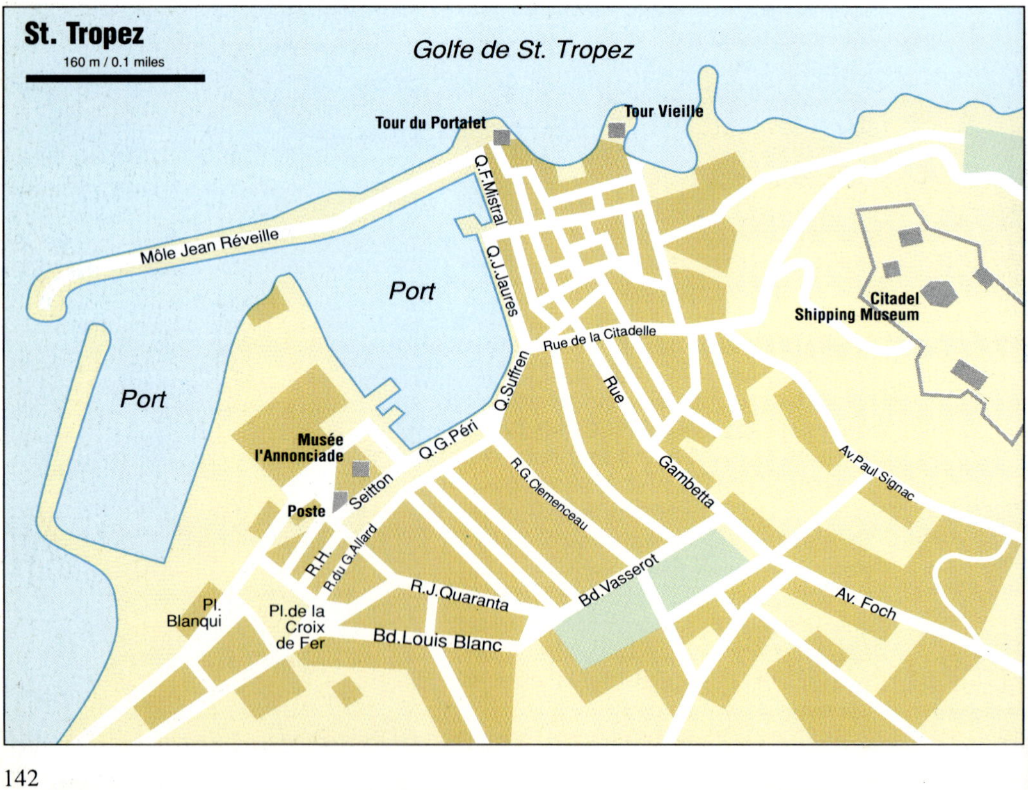

the fashionable Nioulargue yacht-racing week in early October. The quiet winter months are interrupted by a substantial mini-season around Christmas; many shops and restaurants close during the off-peak period.

The centre of St-Tropez is the old port (which has been undergoing restoration), enclosed by the long stone **Jean Reveille jetty** extending outwards from the squat, round 15th-century **Portalet Tower**. Along the **Quais Frédéric Mistral** and **Jean Jaurès** are the fashionable cafés, notably the all-red Sennequier, formerly a pâtisserie and still famed for its nougat, and, stern to the quay, the great yachts – futuristic white plastic gin palaces or gleaming teak classics – with uniformed crews and, increasingly, non-sailing corporate charterers. Distributed throughout the old, and adjacent new, ports is a wide range of craft, from vintage sailing yachts to the long, spearhead-shaped, V8-engined, offshore "cigarettes" that drone across the bay at 60 miles an hour (100kph). Between the new port and the small sea-front heliport is a huge, continually packed car-park, with a small shaded area for dogs with bowls of water and an attendant, financed by the Brigitte Bardot Foundation.

On the west side of the old port is the **Museum of the Annonciade**, a 16th-century former chapel attractively converted to house a large and excellent collection of paintings and sculptures, donated by the Tropezien philanthropist Georges Grammont, by artists who have lived or worked in the town. The Annonciade's collection constitutes one of the most important assemblages of early and mid 20th-century French art outside Paris. Signac is represented by a rotating collection of 10 watercolours and five oils, and other high points include works by Van Dongen, Matisse, Seurat, Bonnard, Rouault, Utrillo, Dufy, and Charles Camoin, whose 1925 game of *boules* in the Place de Lices is one of the most atmospheric of the scenes of St-Tropez itself.

A little way beyond the Annonciade is the **Quai Suffren**, with its bronze

View of Golfe de St-Tropez.

statue of one of St-Tropez's most illustrious adopted citizens, the Bailli de Suffren, whose late-flourishing nautical career ended with a famously successful Indian campaign in the 1780s and the command of the French navy. De Suffren's name was retrospectively applied to the 10th-century square tower just behind the Quai Mistral, used along with a similar building in Ste-Maxime by the Knights Templar to protect the gulf's settlements from the North African Barbary pirates whose raids plagued the region until the 15th century.

The so-called "**Corsairs' House**" behind the church dates from 100 years later; it is unclear whether its fine Renaissance doorway and carved stone balustrade were ever actually used by pirates. In the centre of the old town, St-Tropez's 19th-century Italian baroque parish church, with its typical Provençal wrought-iron campanile, contains statues of the town's patron saint both headless and recumbent, plus menagerie, in his boat, invariably festooned with votive offerings of flowers and hearts.

A block away is the attractive town hall and all around the lovely narrow stone streets, those nearer the port lined with smart shops and restaurants, those further back residential and surprisingly quiet and unspoilt even in August. In the old *quartier* of **La Ponche**, reached through the 15th-century stone Revelen gate-tower, the small remaining corps of Tropezien fishermen keep their boats and in a few cases sell their catch fresh from small garage/stalls. Nearby is the charming medium-priced Hôtel La Ponche with its popular terrace restaurant, and around the corner the similarly elegant Yaca Hotel with a lovely ivy-surrounded central pool and patio. La Ponche and Le Yaca (then known as L'Aioli) were the first hotels, in the pre-Byblos 1950s and '60s, to accommodate the Sagans and the Vadims, and both have managed to update their facilities and decor (and prices) with great taste, retaining the charm of the lovely old buildings.

Other points of interest in the centre of St-Tropez include the 15th-century

Repairing a fishing boat in the old quarter of La Ponche.

semi-ruined **Jarlier tower**, the 16th-century **Chapelle de la Miséricorde** with its blue, green and gold tiled belfry, and the pretty old **Place des Herbes** with its morning vegetable and fish market. Best of all, though, is the general effect of the little streets, warm pastel walls enlivened by pots of geraniums (once put on the window ledge to keep out mosquitoes) and glimpses of oleander or bougainvillaea peeking from walled gardens.

Ten minutes from the centre, overlooking the whole bay from its grassy, pine-dotted hillock, is the triangular **Citadel**, surrounded by an extensive wall and dry moat, and patrolled by peacocks. Apart from the superb view from the ramparts, the maritime museum within the Citadel offers displays of torpedoes (the town still possesses a torpedo factory, moved from Toulon after World War II) and of maps, uniforms and guns relating to the 1943–45 Resistance and Liberation. Below the Citadel, on the opposite slope of the hill from the town centre, is the cemetery, its rows of white headstones outlined strikingly against the blue of the sea it overlooks. Another excellent view is available from the 16th-century **St Anne's Chapel**, 15 minutes' walk via the road which also passes the St-Tropez wine cooperative.

St-Tropez itself has very limited beach areas, being centred around the port: the famous golden beaches are on either side of the town, and, in the case of the biggest, Pampelonne beach, 2 miles away in the commune of Ramatuelle. Most of them are occupied by a series of beach "clubs" which are usually not clubs at all, but concessions rented by their proprietors from the local council and offering their bars, restaurants, parasols, loungers, and some cases shops, hairdressers, and tenders to pick up customers from their offshore yachts, to anyone who is willing to pay for these services.

This is not to deny they can seem as cliquey and exclusive as clubs, with different social sets patronising different establishments. Beach life tends to

The fashionable Sennequier café.

ST-TROPEZ STYLE

St-Tropez is a barometer of style, a sort of summer alternative to Paris, just as ski resorts such as Mégève are winter ones. Fashion professionals have always patronised it, combining holidays with studying the market. Daniel Hechter showed his first collection in town in the early 1960s, and more than 30 years later top names such as designer Jean-Paul Gaultier or London-based retailer Joseph Ettedgui still make a point of visiting regularly to hang out at the fashionable Sennequier café by the port and see who's wearing what.

Getting the measure of the St-Tropez look is deceptively complex. Informality has always been the keyword – but *studied* informality; St-Tropez is certainly not a place to go if you don't want to bother about what you look like. On the other hand, one should never underestimate the democracy of French public life: just when it seems a certain restaurant must be reserved exclusively for golden-limbed 22-year-olds in leather jackets and white lace shorts (and that's just the men), along comes a couple of elderly hippies in bulging denim and pony-tails to take the best table. And since everyone stares at everyone else all the time anyway, it doesn't seem to matter whether it's out of contempt or admiration.

Retro fashion means the Bardots and Vadims still represent the height of chic. And, though there are convertibles and buggies by the dozen, it's hard to think of a modern vehicle – Porsches being as 10-a-centime as they are – that would outclass a 1960 MGA or Citroën DS *décapotable* in the traffic jam along the D98 today. Harley-Davidsons have hardly changed since then anyway, and if there's one quintessentially Tropezien accessory, it's a Harley.

Some long-established boutiques, such as Vachon on the Quai Suffren, are still doing good business with silk shirts, stretch dresses, T-shirts – all the things the Parisians need. "Lots of people come here immediately they arrive to get their holiday outfits," Vachon's manager will tell you, "they look ridiculous in their Paris clothes, they've brought all the wrong stuff..."

These days, of course, shops such as Vachon face plenty of competition. All around the old port, in chic little shopping streets, and in the increasing number of mini-malls, the cream of European *prêt-à-porter* is available in season – many shops close in winter. Hermès has long been established with its own shop; the Hotel Byblos shop sells Yves St-Laurent; Joanna sells John Galliano, Dolce & Gabbano and Sybilla, while Uomo deals in Gianni Versace, Thierry Mugler and Claude Montana for men.

Perhaps the most surprising thing is how fashionable St-Tropez remains. Like much of the Côte d'Azur, it tends to be dismissed as overcrowded and over-rated, but for a lot of people (usually the ones with the yachts and the private villas) it has remained as chic as ever. They still want to be seen in St-Tropez. Supermodels such as Naomi Campbell and Elle Macpherson stroll barefoot and casual, but never unrecognisable, through the Place des Lices. Roger Moore is glimpsed canoodling on a yacht. Elton John flies in for a day by helicopter to buy a property like his friend, George Michael.

Major villa properties sell for anything between £2 and £5 million (US$5–8 million), fully equipped with pools, helipads, mature olive trees and serious security. Luxury yachts are chartered at around £13,000 ($20,000) a day – then, if the beach scene palls, you can take off for a really expensive lunch offshore.

■ **Night life.**

begin late morning, proceed to a leisurely lunch at the restaurant and peak during the post-prandial mid to late afternoon lazing time.

The beaches actually forming part of St-Tropez are: to the west of the town centre the **Bouillabaisse**, showing signs of a return to fashion after a decade of decline, with its new Golfe Azur establishment; the simple little local beach, a favourite of native Tropeziens, **Les Graniers**, just below the Citadel; the slightly larger **Plage des Canebiers**, overlooked by Bardot's villa, La Madrague; and on the eastern edge of the peninsula and now rather crowded, **Les Salins**.

Along the great golden sweep of the **Plage de Pampelonne**, the concessions, from north to south are: Tropezina; Tabou-Plage; Tahiti-Plage, a big long-established showbiz favourite including a hotel and shops; Bora Bora and the very chic Moorea; La Voile Rouge, home of topless nymphettes and a rock-star/Hollywood ambiance; the new Sun 77 with its teenage offshoot Hysteria; the quieter Force 7 and Le Club du Planteur; the naturist Le Blouch; Club 55, the oldest (founded in 1955 by the de Colmont family) and classiest of the concessions; Nioulargo, with its traditional and Indo-Chinese restaurants; La Plage des Jumeaux, noted for excellent Provençal cuisine; fashionable L'Epi-Plage; La Cabane Bambou; Tropicana, another showbiz favourite with excellent local cooking; and La Bastide Blanche, which is accessible only by boat and therefore relatively quiet and exclusive.

At anchor off the shore of Pampelonne are the dozens of major yachts and the smaller craft used for the very Tropezien custom of sailing out for lunch to yet another exclusive restaurant - the Mas du Langoustier on the island of Porquerolles, for example.

If the duo of Sennequier and Le Gorille (named after its proprietor's hirsute torso), and the other lesser quayside cafés are St-Tropez's supreme breakfast and coffee haunts, they are rivalled in the evening by the cafés on the **Place des**

Handy water transport.

Lices five minutes' walk away. Under the five rows of big plane trees, illuminated by long strips of light bulbs, hundreds of people play *boules*, still occasionally in the traditional celebrity teams hosted by the Eddie Barclay set, stroll, sit on benches, or in the case of younger holidaymakers, on motorbikes and scooters.

This is the night-time centre of the Harley-Davidson cult still led by Johnny Hallyday (you can rent Harleys complete with fringed leather mudflaps by the day for a couple of thousand francs in St-Tropez). The terraces of the Brasserie de la Renaissance, successfully relaunched by the Colmont family of Club 55, and of the old favourite Café des Arts, with its crammed, jolly bistro interior, are excellent places to dine well at a medium price with a view over the fascinating bustle.

Elsewhere around town, a thoroughly Parisian range of restaurants buzz with diners till midnight. At the foot of the slope housing the Byblos Hotel, Michel Rochedy's smart Le Chabichou offers specialities such as pig's trotter stuffed with lobster and peach soup with an excellent Beaumes de Venise wine; Le Chabichou's cooking is generally regarded as the most refined in town, along with that of the restaurants of the elegant, exclusive beach-front Résidence de la Pinède (specialities include pigeon with green lentils, truffles and bacon) and the wildly flashy new hilltop Château de la Messardière (iced potato soup with truffles).

All of these restaurants, incidentally, operate also as de luxe take-aways, with a catering service for opulent dinner parties in the villas in the hills outside town. Around midnight, queues start to form outside St-Tropez nightclubs, which range from the exclusive and glamorous Caves du Roy at the Hôtel Byblos, with its Ancient Egyptian theme decor, and the classic 1960s favourite Papagayo, to the Pirate's Studio, a sort of VIP French karaoke joint, and Le Bal, a favourite on the gay and supermodel circuit.

After a heavy night at one of these

The golden stretch of Pampelonne beach.

establishments, it is worth remembering that the most revivifying of hangover cures, a gentle sea excursion, is not only available to boat-owners. The regular ferries that leave the old port for Port Grimaud, Ste-Maxime and St-Raphaël offer a delightful and relaxing run across the bay.

To arrive at St-Tropez in this manner not only entitles you to the classic and most enchanting view of the old town, but can also be two or three times as quick, from Ste-Maxime for example, as a similar journey spent sweating in a semi-stationary car.

Inland from St-Tropez, the gently rising terrain is dominated by vineyards. Viticulture accounts for 40 percent of the agriculture of the region, and the St-Tropez peninsula is an important part of the Côtes-de-Provence *appellation contrôlée* area. Running through this region, the "Route des Côtes-de-Provence" (maps and details available from all local tourist offices) is a signposted itinerary passing by some of the most important individual *domaines*, all of them open for visits and sales, such as the elegant Napoleon III **Château de Minuty** with its family chapel, surrounded by cypress, mulberry and eucalyptus, and the **Château de Barbeyrolles**, its neighbour just outside the village of Gassin.

The interior of the peninsula is dominated by the three beautiful hilltop villages of **Gassin**, **Ramatuelle** and **La Croix-Valmer**, their old stone centres rising above the surrounding oak and beech woods to command superb views of the sea, and on a good day, far back to the north, glimpses of snow on the peaks of the lower Alps. In and around them are opulent holiday homes and, in their centres, pretty, chic, tree-shaded restaurants offering a slightly more secluded alternative to those of St-Tropez.

Gassin, the most elevated of the peninsular trio, is an exquisite little town with a 16th-century church and town hall, a pretty central square planted with African lotus trees and surrounded by a warren of tiny roads and alleys, and a circular boulevard with magnificent

views over the entire gulf. Gassin's position was its early *raison d'être*; as a look-out post, from the 10th century manned by Knights Templar, who did not, however, prevent a Saracen raiding party in 1394 carrying off 33 of the village's inhabitants.

The Saracens are said to be responsible for the name (from *Rahmatu 'llah*, Arabic for "God's Gift") of Gassin's neighbour, **Ramatuelle**, which also retains two 10th-century doors in the remains of its fortifications from its Saracen occupation. Other significant episodes in the village's martial history include the unusual and apparently effective use of hives of bees hurled from the ramparts to repel a Royalist siege in 1592, and during World War II, its role as a point of contact for the Resistance with Allied submarines, attested to by a monument near the cemetery.

Another pretty, tile-roofed, flower-bedecked village of narrow, winding streets, Ramatuelle is also noted for its annual summer jazz festival and, especially, for its theatre festival, both held in an open-air auditorium on the southern slope of Ramatuelle's hill. The theatre festival, named from its inception in 1985 after the famous actor Gérard Philippe who is buried there, was disassociated from his name on the request of his daughter due to what she regarded as "over-commercialisation". Just outside Ramatuelle, a further magnificent view is available from the road running past three ruined oil mills known as the **Moulins de Paillas**.

On the southern slope of the peninsula, looking down across vineyards, reed-beds and pine groves towards Cavalaire Bay, the village of **La Croix-Valmer** contains few vestiges of its Roman past. Its name, however, is believed to derive from the legend whereby the Emperor Constantine, while passing en route to Italy, was persuaded by the vision of a cross in the sky to convert to Christianity.

For the most part dating from the late 19th century, La Croix-Valmer also contains some striking modern buildings, including the parish church. In addition to its role as a centre for vacation homes, it is an important wine-producing centre. It is a good place to spend a day following a wine tour; as a winter resort in the 19th century, it used to claim the benefits of its healthy climate – and maintains the tradition these days by specialising in a "grape" cure.

West of St-Tropez, just before the coastal plain begins its long mutation into the hills of the Massif des Maures, sits the larger town, equal to St-Tropez in population, of **Cogolin**, General de Lattre de Tassigny's headquarters during the 1944 battle to liberate Provence. Although possessed of a pretty old centre with 16th-century church, numerous green marble doorways and vaulted passageways, Cogolin is also a working town; in addition to wine, it produces furniture, naval armaments, hand-woven fine wool carpets, fishing rods and clarinet mouthpieces from the surrounding reed beds and pipes carved from the roots of local mountain heather.

Its seaside extension, 3 miles (5 km) from the town, comprises a good, sandy beach and a large marina, with 1,800

St-Tropez golden boy.

berths, which attempts perfunctorily to echo the style of Port Grimaud, its near neighbour.

Across the gulf from St-Tropez, **Ste-Maxime** is a prosperous and pleasant resort of 8,000 inhabitants with a modern 750-berth leisure port and a pretty seafront marred only by the traffic passing along its main coast road. The centre is occupied by the massed red, blue and green striped sun-shades of the main beach, the pastel bulk of the casino, with an art deco bas-relief of swimming girls, and well-kept gardens of palm trees, mimosa and oleander.

Just behind the centre, the old town is pedestrianised, if busy in the summer; on its edge is the cool, immaculately kept 19th-century parish church and a square 16th-century defensive tower, now a museum. The town contains a number of modest hotels retaining a distinct and non-conformist character: the pleasant, old-fashioned Les Palmiers, with its promenade terrace and old leather armchairs and also the idiosyncratic 1920s mini-palace of La Résidence Brutus. Cherry Beach is the chic choice and further on Plage des Eléphants is a bit more affordable.

Six miles (10 km) behind Ste-Maxime, in the foothills of the Massif des Maures, by the small **St-Donat park**, a privately-run **Phonographe Museum** houses a curious collection, displayed in an amiable jumble as in a bric-a-brac store, of 350 assorted antique record players, barrel organs, and other mechanical music-makers, including an 1860s clockwork songbird.

Just as the Massif de l'Estérel, to the north, acts as a buffer against the urbanisation of the coast between Cannes and St-Raphaël, so the great wild bulk of the **Massif des Maures** counterbalances the St-Tropez build-up. Indeed, until the seaside boom at the beginning of the century, the presence of the Maures kept the coastline isolated and undeveloped for centuries.

The Maures are among the areas of the Riviera worst afflicted by brush fires, however, and long stretches of the roads which wind north through the low hills

One of St-Tropez's famous sunsets.

above Ste-Maxime pass acres of sinister, fire-blackened, dead trunks, protruding from the thistle, thyme and broom scrub. Patrolling fire engines and look-out points are a common sight in summer and occasionally the big yellow Canadair flying boats which alight on lakes and scoop up tons of water to deposit on the burning forest.

Inland from the Gulf of St-Tropez, the massif rises gently - its highest peak, La Saurette, is a modest 2,500 ft (780 metres) – dotted with the familiar fortified villages. **Grimaud**, 10 minutes' drive from its scene-stealing new offshore **Port Grimaud**, is a typical and beautiful example, flower-decorated and immaculately maintained by what appears to be a population containing an inordinate proportion of Range-Rover-owning architects. The name of the village derives from that of Gibelin de Grimaldi, a knight who was given lordship of the area in the 10th century as a reward for his part in the expulsion of the Saracen occupiers; the name is also that of the Monégasque royal family.

Modern-day Grimaud, clustering around the ruins of its medieval castle, contains an impressive small Romanesque church, St-Michel, once used by the Templars, after whom the lovely arcaded street nearby is named, an old square with *boules* pitch and huge micocoulier tree, and no shortage of chic and pretty hotels, one of the prettiest being the small, traditional Coteau Fleuri, with its flower-packed garden and wonderful terrace view.

At the northern perimeter of the Massif des Maures, the land levels off, vine-covered, peaceful and still dotted with medieval-centred villages, until it reaches the first slopes of the Lower Alps. This is the heart of the Côtes-de-Provence wine appellation, whose capital, if such a thing existed, would be the small town of **Les Arcs**. Here, the **Maison des Vins**, down on the main road, provides copious information and sampling facilities for the many *crus* of the region, while its restaurant offers hundreds of bottles, often at good prices, to accompany a traditionally-based but still very imaginative cuisine.

Les Arcs' medieval village, known as the **Parage**, is as lovely as any in the region, winding down the slopes of the hill on which stand the remains of the Château de Villeneuve.

The former château complex, with its watch-tower and flat stone assembly-point, is now occupied partly by exquisitely pretty little houses, tiny olive-shaded squares, and partly by the very beautiful hotel/restaurant the Logis du Guetteur, with its vine-draped terrace and shuttered bedroom windows looking out over the vineyards beyond the town. Diners tired of exquisite views may opt to eat inside the Logis restaurant, which is the stone vaulted former dungeon of the castle, now made unmedievally comfortable.

Among the vineyards to the north of Les Arcs is the **Chapel of Ste-Roseline**, a former abbey of which chapel and cloisters remain. The recently restored chapel contains two Giacometti sculptures and modern stained-glass windows, and the relics of Ste Roseline still attract pilgrimages, six centuries later.

A game of *boules*.

PORT GRIMAUD

Inhabitants of Port Grimaud like to ask visitors jokingly if they have ever visited St-Tropez –"you know, that little village across the bay." The implication of the newer resort's fame is by no means all hyperbole: it now rates as one of the most popular tourist attraction in France, averaging over a million visitors a year – not bad-going for a town which 25 years earlier did not exist.

Port Grimaud, furthermore, is the creation essentially of one man, the Alsace-born architect François Spoerry, whose world reputation was made by this little Provençal Venice, and who went on to consult on similar schemes in New York, Louisiana, Mexico and Japan. Spoerry's idea for Port Grimaud was nurtured in the 1950s at his parents' holiday home along the coast in Cavalaire. "I found it dreary to have to get up in the middle of the night, if there was a storm, and go to the port to secure our boat's mooring." He determined to design a leisure port, with yacht-owners primarily in mind, on the model of Venice, where the "ground floor" of the buildings serves as a reception area and mooring for the owners' boats and those of traders and delivery men.

In 1962 Spoerry obtained a stretch of marshy land by the mouth of the little river Giscle at the end of the Gulf of St-Tropez in the commune of Grimaud. The area was a mosquito-infested sand-pit, and it took Spoerry four years to obtain building permission for a project widely regarded as crazy. The earliest houses went for as little as 150,000 francs; 25 years later they were fetching between 10 and 20 times that.

Spoerry's guiding principles were those of what he describes as *architecture douce* (soft architecture). Buildings, he believes, should be unassuming, human in scale, and functional, and should avail themselves of local traditional materials and techniques. He therefore designed Port Grimaud in the traditional local style with terracotta tiled roofs, and facades painted in the wonderful shades of ochre and cream that characterise so many Provençal villages.

Every house has a waterfront and boat mooring – later "streets" have small front gardens with lawns and trees – and access roads at the rear permit vehicle access for deliveries, but not in theory for parking. Movement between the 2,500 houses, two squares, 30-odd bars and restaurants and several dozen shops is on foot, via the little wood or stone-clad bridges connecting the little islands, or by the small electric powered boats used as runabouts.

It's meant to remind you of Venice.

Port Grimaud is an impressive achievement and in many places extremely pretty, but ultimately it is a stage-set. The French, German, Italian and British owners of the huge yachts moored outside the houses are absent for a large part of the year, consigning their properties to resident caretakers.

If the development lacks the soul of a true Provençal village, however, its manifest convenience attracts buyers, including François Spoerry himself. The buildings are acquiring a patina of age, and cigales have begun to chirrup in the main square, adding that quintessential Midi sound-tract to the pastiche.

The town council of Grimaud, meanwhile, has been planning a major extension to the site, to be designed jointly by François Spoerry and the equally famous modern urbanist Ricardo Bofill, with an eye on the year 2020. By that time, they confidently assert, the Var will have become "the Florida of Europe". ■

ST-RAPHAËL/FRÉJUS

If the Fréjus/St-Raphaël region is rather overshadowed by world-famous neighbours such as St-Tropez to the west and Cannes to the east, it is by no means totally eclipsed. Economically and demographically, the area is booming - the local population, rate of employment and small business sector all grew substantially in the 1980s and 1990s.

In Fréjus, it possesses a visible Roman architectural heritage of national importance as well as a medieval centre the equal of any on the Riviera. And the wild forested hills of the Massif de l'Estérel, by ensuring that a large tract of the interior remains undeveloped, has assisted this easternmost part of the department of the Var (which surrounds the Alpes-Maritimes just south of Cannes) to retain its reputation as the green *département.* Even the coast, while built-up and crowded in summer, is relatively lightly so.

The Fréjus/St-Raphaël conurbation may be reached inland from Cannes via a sprint down the A8 autoroute (*la provençale*), a slightly longer but still brisk drive along the pretty winding Route Nationale 7 just south, or via the Corniche de l'Esterel road (N98) which twists along a narrow strip between the sea and the steep red rock edges of the massif. The corniche road, and the railway line it approximately accompanies, pass beside a succession of coves, small beaches and villages surrounded by a scarcely interrupted fringe of villas, hotels, restaurants and campsites: in July and August the traffic is heavy, if not as bad as in the Ste-Maxime–St-Tropez stretch further to the west. To one side rear the red porphyry peaks of the **Pic de l'Ours** and the **Pic du Cap Roux**. To the other, the sea is dotted with little islets, forming part of the same ancient rock mass.

At the eastern edge of the Massif de l'Estérel, just beyond Cannes, is **La Napoule**, in effect a sea-front extension of the mimosa centre and Cannes-satellite, Mandelieu. La Napoule possesses three sandy beaches, a leisure port, a magnificent view across the Golfe de Napoule to Antibes from the top of St-Peyré hill (a half-hour climb from the centre) and the **Château de la Napoule**, an arts foundation set in a (visitable) converted medieval castle filled with the idiosyncratic sculptures of the American artist/philanthropist Henry Clews, whose grandson Christopher now runs the château.

The series of increases of building density which follow along the coast – for this is what the formerly separate villages have become – are distinguishable from each other by features such as a 19th-century soap factory turned château at **Théoule**, or a deeper than average natural harbour in the former Roman port of **Agay**, where there is a lovely bay shaded by pines and red cliffs. Just beyond Agay, covering the long slope of the hillside above the wide beach of **Dramont** (a key landing-point of the American 7th Army in August 1944), is a development which symbolises the nadir of the rampant over-build-

Preceding pages: St-Raphaël carousel. **Left**, St-Raphaël fisherman mending his net. **Right**, another traditional occupation.

ing of the 1970s and '80s, but which may also represent its belated check. **Cap Estérel**, a vast, self-contained concrete "Provençal village" of holiday apartments, centred around a pair of stadium-sized, screamingly blue swimming-pools, was obliged to stop construction in July 1991 when the Nice regional tribunal revoked building permission, a landmark decision in an area long milked with impunity by French hotel and property companies.

As in even the most densely touristed places, however, oases of calm subsist, surprisingly near to the beaten track. At **Boulouris**, a resort of pine-shaded villas just outside St-Raphaël, the **Plage D'Arène Grosse**, tucked behind the garish hotel complex of Le Toukan, is a pleasant spot to sip an evening apéritif and watch the pin-prick shimmer of lights on the far-off dark bulk of the St-Tropez promontory. A sea-front walk here, similar to the Chemin des Douaniers (Customs Officers' Path) across the bay at St-Aygulf, is also pretty and (relatively) quiet. The gardens of a series of large, elegant villas stretch down to the edge of the path, with their umbrella pine and yuccas. On the benches against the walls, elderly couples sit looking out to sea, and the occasional dog races in and out of the gentle waves lapping on the flat rocks and little stretches of sand.

Even the earliest citizens of **St-Raphaël** came looking for sea air and relaxation. They were wealthy Romans from the important naval and military settlement of Fréjus, and they built terraced villas decorated with mosaics close enough to enjoy the restorative properties of the sea; the same motive is as strong as ever today. One of the first buildings you encounter on entering the town along the coast road is the big white Centre de Thalassotherapie (sea-water cures). Next to it is a modern Palais de Congrès (conference centre) and the serried ranks (1,800 berths) of the new yacht harbour, observed from a couple of hundred metres offshore by the two distinctive rocks, the **Lion de Mer** and the **Lion de Terre**, which

St. Raphaël, Fréjus and Massif de L'Esterel

explain St-Raphaël's occasional description as the "Town of the Lions".

A little further on, along the **Boulevard du Général de Gaulle** and the **Promenade de Lattre de Tassigny**, are the luxury shops and the handful of turn-of-the-century hotels and apartment blocks which lend the town its air of a little Cannes. Curlicued art nouveau balconies, the moulding painted pistachio and cream, look out over the tall palms which line the raised promenade.

At the end of this sweep of passable Riviera elegance stands the **Casino**, in front of the dome of the late 19th-century church of **Notre-Dame-de-Victoire**, the two main features (with a large pink block of flats characteristically obscuring both) which mark out the town if approached from the sea. The Casino shares its evening roulette and *chemin de fer* rooms with a new all-day *bandits manchot* (one-armed bandit) salon, where paisley bow-tied attendants supervise the 98 machines recently authorised for installation. It represents St-Raphaël's most recent mass tourism phase, as well as the town's heyday of bourgeois gentility, and its earliest origins, too, as the Casino site was occupied by the first Roman settlement.

In the Middle Ages, the settlement was sacked by the Saracens; it was re-inhabited by monks from Marseille, placed under the protection of the Knights Templar and subsequently attracted a small fishing and agricultural community. In 1799, Napoleon entitled St-Raphaël to one of its rare entries in the history books by disembarking there on his return from Egypt.

In the 1860s the celebrated Parisian journalist Alphonse Karr moved along the coast from already-crowded Nice and began to invite down the advance guard of metropolitan intellectual trend-setters (including writers Alexandre Dumas and Maupassant, and composers Berlioz and Gounod) who, rapidly augmented by rich English, made St-Raphaël a fashionable resort. In 1864, the arrival of the railway provided a major boost (the modern station with its

Notre-Dame-de-Victoire and the Casino, St-Raphaël.

abstract stained-glass roof panels is still a magnet for the younger end of the summer clientèle over a century later).

The so-called "old port" in front of the Casino is another construction of the late 1800s. It is now home to a small fishing fleet, a number of pleasure-craft, the occasional visiting naval vessel, also small, and the regular ferry service to Ste-Maxime and St-Tropez. (The 50-minute journey to the latter is the pleasantest, and in August the fastest, way of getting there.) The fishing boats' daily catch is on sale between 7.30am and midday at the wood-beamed fish market on the **Place Ortolan**. Close beside, the simple traditional restaurant La Bouillabaisse, with its check table-cloths and ivy-covered terrace, is an excellent place to consume good value bouillabaisse and langoustes.

Running along two sides of the square port basin, the **Cours Jean-Bart** with its stone benches and double row of big plane trees is the night-time centre for strolling and sitting at café terraces consuming beers, lurid ice-cream confections and cocktails. Entertainment is provided in the high season by the usual panoply of itinerant pavement artistes, street performers, Senegalese fake Louis Vuitton pedlars, and, in some of the cafés, resident entertainers on Yamaha keyboards. At its western end, marked in summer by a plastic reproduction 18th-century Venetian fairground carousel, the bustle of activity merges with that of Fréjus Plage, which is much the same minus any trace of the architectural grace of the Cours Jean-Bart.

St-Raphaël is not a town of monuments. Traces of its Roman past are restricted to a substantial collection of amphora in the **Musée Archéologique**, most of which have been obtained by local diving teams from the sea. The museum also contains prehistoric material as well as documents and photos of the 19th century, Alphonse Karr memorabilia, and so on.

In the pretty, but minuscule, old town, nestled five minutes' walk behind the old port, the 12th-century **Église St-Raphaël**, from which the town took its

St-Raphaël beach.

name, provides a link with the period of the Knights Templar. The small, plain, single-nave church was used as a fortified refuge in case of attack by pirates, as its military-looking watchtower may suggest.

In the leafy hillside suburbs to the north and east of the town centre are the Edwardian-Provençal villas surrounded by gardens built for the early moneyed English visitors. These are concentrated particularly around the suburb of **Valescure**, with its large golf course whose perimeters feature an increasingly common Riviera combination – golf facilities and holiday flats – in developments such as Valescure's Résidence Le Birdie.

If present-day signs of St-Raphaël's medieval past are limited, and of its Roman past virtually non-existent, the reverse is true of **Fréjus**. The larger town (40,000 inhabitants as opposed to St-Raphaël's 30,000) retains extensive remains from the period during which it was second only to Marseille in size and importance as a Roman military port. Its medieval centre bears even more visible and impressive testimony to its status in the early Christian world; Fréjus was a bishopric as early as AD 374 and remained one until 1957 when the diocese was merged with that of Toulon. Though Fréjus lost its maritime functions in the 10th century as the sea receded, it has responded to the demands of 20th-century tourism by acquiring two offshoots radically different in style from the old town, and both closer to St-Raphaël.

Fréjus Plage is a 1960s and '70s development of apartment blocks and hotels running the length of a fine flat sandy beach bordered to the east by the old port of St-Raphaël and to the west by the new yacht basin of Port Fréjus. Its attractions are by day quite simply the beach, which is separated from the accommodation by the quadruple line of parked cars along a beach-level promenade, and by night the numerous cafés, shops and stalls which stay open, and thronged, until 1 or 2am, along with two discotheques. Fréjus Plage thus constitutes the newer, brasher end of a con-

The land of the disposable bikini.

tinuum which reaches its "classiest" point a mile east on St-Raphaël's Promenade de Lattre de Tassigny.

Port Fréjus, whose new harbour was inaugurated in 1989, is a mixed-investment development designed to provide accommodation for 10,000 people and mooring for 700 yachts of up to 100 ft (30 metres). Its first constructions, rather hopefully described as "neo-Palladian", are six- and seven-storey apartment blocks set on wide, concrete quays with restaurants and shops at ground level. If Port Fréjus is symptomatic of the dynamic and expansionist future, it also aims to relate to the conurbation's ancient past. Port Fréjus is at the mouth of the original Roman port, which was connected to a second basin inland beside the settlement of Forum Julii by a broad, half-mile long canal. The aim is to re-excavate this channel as the final stage of Port Fréjus and thus to return to Fréjus town the sea access it lost to Saracen depredations and silt.

Fréjus was founded by Julius Caesar as a stopping place on the route (the Aurelian Way) heading ultimately to Spain. It was rapidly expanded into an important military port by Augustus Octavius, and at its Roman zenith had as large a population – around 40,000 – as it has today. Its Roman remains are no less interesting for being dispersed throughout the town. Just beyond the enclosed remains of the **theatre**, for example, a sizeable chunk of Roman wall sits incongruously in the middle of a council housing estate. The 2,500-capacity theatre is largely destroyed, but the low remaining section is used, with scaffolding benches, for concerts.

Major Roman remains include the base of the western citadel, known as the **Butte St-Antoine**, which connects via a partly-ruined wall to the stump of a tower, the "**Lanterne d'Auguste**". This structure once held a flame marking the entrance to the port, and at night was the anchor point for an iron chain across the canal which denied access from the sea. Other important remains are the **Porte d'Orée**, a decorative arched entrance, probably once to the baths, the **aqueduct**, which once supplied the whole city with running water from the river Siagnale 25 miles (40 km) away, and of which a large and impressive section straddles the road at the junction between the N7 and the autoroute *péage* link, and the **arena**, just outside the centre of the town.

The Fréjus arena, half resting against a grass knoll, has suffered from centuries of stone looting, and is neither as large nor as sumptuous as those at Nîmes or Arles, being designed for a simpler, lower-class audience, primarily soldiers and townspeople rather than the rich or elevated. Its huge sandstone arches loom out of the bushes and lawns of a small park just outside the old town centre, as though they have survived years of mortar attack unbowed. The arena is in regular use for rock concerts and, several times a year, corridas. Fréjus is, in effect, the most easterly outpost of bullfighting in France, although its taurine life is not booming, like that of Nîmes, but rather in the same state of decline – diminishing audiences, poor quality *corridas* – as its fellow seaside bull-

Fréjus fountain.

fighting town, Les-Stes-Maries-de-la-Mer further down the coast. The final substantial Roman remains, the large, level area of miscellaneous masonry known as the **Plateforme**, of which the only intact item is a vaulted subterranean water reservoir, are scheduled for excavation and fuller display.

The old central area of Fréjus has considerable charm, particularly by contrast with the brashness and the crowds of summertime St-Raphaël and Fréjus Plage. This is due partly to its handsome architecture and partly to its slightly elevated position, looking out over the flower and fruit smallholdings of the flat Plaine area to its west. At the centre of the old town is the **Quartier Episcopal**, a medieval complex comprising the 12th-century, double-naved **Cathedral**, the small stone **baptistry**, one of the oldest in France dating originally to the 5th century, and the lovely two-storey **cloister** with its ceiling composed of 1,200 little square painted wooden tiles. Visits to the baptistry and cloister must be conducted, and are worth waiting for, as both are fascinating, particularly the tall, narrow, sombre octagonal baptistry with its separate entry and exit doors, octagonal baptismal pool and dolium for liturgical oil. The cloister, by contrast, with its white marble columns, central tile-roofed well and laurel bushes, is pretty and sunny. The collection of Roman and early Ligurian tiles, mosaics and sculptures in the archaeological museum off the cloister includes the fine double-faced head of Hermès, discovered in 1970, which Fréjus has made its symbol. In front of the carved door to the baptistry and the facade of the **Hôtel de Ville**, formerly the Bishop's Palace, which adjoins it, the **Place Formigé** is used for public entertainment in the summer – a military brass band plays on a tree-shaded podium there on Sunday mornings.

Round the corner, the larger triangular **Place Paul Albert Février** contains the prettiest open-air restaurants, though not necessarily those with the best cuisine; nonetheless, tables can be hard to obtain by 9pm in summer. The Saturday

12th-century cloisters, Fréjus.

market (local peaches and roses a Fréjus speciality) takes place on the square. The other main centre of café life, the **Place de la Liberté**, with its fountain and four big plane trees, is the best place for coffees, mid-afternoon beers, apéritifs and midnight café-cognacs. Much later Fréjus closes down, and you have to head down to the sea-front.

The streets and alleys surrounding the pedestrianised medieval centre and the Rue Jean Jaurès, which circles downhill through town bearing a constant stream of traffic, are extremely pretty, with numerous ornate doorways, cats peering through lace curtains and geranium-clad windowsills. A brief pause at the Tourist Office at the beginning of the Rue Jean Jaurès to pick up a free copy of the leaflet *Fréjus, Ville d'Art et d'Histoire* is recommended: the publication contains good, concise photographic details of the best facades and doorways to look at in the old town.

An enjoyable stroll just outside the town centre might also take in the lovely 1906 **Villa Marie**, now the public library, in its garden, and the slightly older Palladian style **Villa Aurélienne**, set in an even finer small park. Ten minutes' drive outside town on the N7, the small circular chapel of **Notre-Dame-de-Jerusalem** was designed by Jean Cocteau in 1961 and the beautiful cool, blue and pastel murals inside are among the poet's last work.

Two other architectural curiosities just outside Fréjus are connected with the town's continuing military tradition – it is home to 3,000 men of the Fourth and Twenty-First Marine Regiments, who formed the core of the Daguet Battalion sent to the Iraqi border in 1990–91. Both buildings acknowledge the role of troops from France's former colonies. The **Missiri mosque** is a replica of the Soudan style of Northwest Africa, while a **Buddhist pagoda** commemorates France's Vietnamese operations.

The interior of the Massif de l'Estérel is easily explored by car, with walks of between half an hour and an hour and a half on scrub-surrounded paths to reach the panoramas available from the tops

Roman remains, Fréjus.

of the main peaks: the **Pic de l'Ours**, **Pic d'Aurelle** and **Pic du Cap Roux** via the D37 out of St-Raphaël; further inland **Mont Vinaigre**, with its old watch tower, via the RN7. Both roads wind prettily through a landscape of low but massive hills, with open stretches of scented thyme, thistle broom and eucalyptus interrupting the wooded expanses of cork oak and chestnut.

By the side of the RN7, in the lee of the forested Mont Vinaigre and a couple of miles from the simple and attractive village of **Les Adrets**, is the **Auberge des Adrets**, an 18th-century former coaching inn once patronised by the local highwayman Gaspard de Besse.

Further inland, the D837 road through Les Adrets crosses the autoroute and shortly afterwards arrives at the **Lac de St-Cassien**, an extensive stretch of water, still relatively wild in aspect but heavily patronised by fishermen, picnickers and dinghy sailors in summer. Northwest of Fréjus, the N7 main road follows the valley of the River Argens through flat, flower and vegetable cultivated fields, gradually climbing through vineyards – this is the eastern extremity of the region of the Côtes-de-Provence appellation and rockier olive, pine and oak groves.

The most substantial villages on the way to **Draguignan**, the former departmental capital 20 miles (30 km) inland from Fréjus, are **le Muy**, with its medieval centre and 16th-century parish church, and **Trans**, with its unusual little 18th-century town hall, perched on the edge of the deep boulder-strewn bed of the small River Nartuby, and its dubious distinction of possessing the only McDonald's in the region. **Draguignan** itself is the biggest army base in France. It is a solid, pleasant country town with several attractive hotels (including the extraordinarily preserved Grand Hôtel Berton, with its dowdy but intact 1930s to 1950s interior decor) and a beautiful old centre around the market place with a 17th-century Tour d'Horloge. Just beyond Draguignan is the Pierre de la Fée (the Fairy Stone), a huge dolmen.

Massif des Maures.

LE
CALIFORNIE
PROPRIÉTÉ PRIVÉE

LE CALIFORNIE

CANNES

"Cannes: Côte d'Azur. Some gleaming town of rose and white, there where the Alps like elephants come down to kneel beside the calm and azure sea. On the sky and the water lies a hard glaring glaze of gold. The Mediterranean, level and smooth, lips the shore with a slow rise and fall of sound like the breath of a sleeper – a gentle insistent rhythm – brushing the beach with sound. The cactus clumps (aloes) like spiky octopi. The palms that stud the Croisette at Cannes with tignasse tufts and thick pineapple stems. At night the pale dark peppered with stars like the finest of silver tinsel. The last soft red streamers of the sunset faded behind the gray silhouette of the Estérel, and from the jetty I saw the green trees and the red roofs of the houses that mount the little hill to the square Saracen town grown somber and black above the silver blue-gray water of the harbor, where the little boats were neatly moored in a fringe about the shore: above the boats was the low avenue of lindens and along between their trunks were the lights of the shops."

– Edmund Wilson, *The Twenties. From Notebooks and Diaries of the Period.* Cannes, 1921.

Cannes has undoubtedly developed since Edmund Wilson recorded its charms, but the surprising news is that in a changing world where the character and soul of lesser oases have been swept away in a tide of mass tourism, Cannes sparkles miraculously as a jewelled survivor of a bygone age.

Skirting the skies above Cannes, sumptuous summer palaces still glitter like golden eggs. Here there is a hidden lane – the road to Heaven on Earth – which hardly figures on some maps; a bumpy corniche endowed with hundreds of what the French call chicken-nests, and we know mundanely as potholes. Here is the best view of the city of stars, along the **Corniche du Paradis Terrestre** or, one level higher, on the **Chemin des Collines**. But it is precisely to deter *hoi polloi* that the road has been left unpaved. Much of the wealth up here is Arabian and royal, and you might think their owners would be satisfied with such residences worthy of *A Thousand and One Nights*, but no. If you can afford to live in neighbourhoods with names like **Super-Cannes** and **Californie** you have to think big. Twin marble palaces built in the early 1980s for two brother princelings who never spent a night in them were demolished and resurrected as apartments in classic Palladian style for sale at over £3 million each, including individual swimming-pools. Disgracefully, there was but one, shared, helipad.

Keeping up with the high-rollers takes on new meaning here, where you may find yourself rubbing shoulders with the likes of the Gulf sheikh who frittered away a world-record £8.8 million in one binge at roulette. Certainly, the extent of Cannes' dependence on Arab money has its place in history. When King Fahad ordered a total exodus of holi-

Preceding pages: La Californie, wealthy enclave of Cannes. Left, the busy beach. Right, gracing the Carlton Terrace.

daying Saudis from the Riviera there was such a scramble they only just squeezed aboard two chartered Airbuses. Cannes may seem Elysium to those fleeing the crushing heat of the desert, but neither have its attractions gone unnoticed by the world's hedonists, who have been beating a path to its beaches and casinos since the 1920s. Long before that, even, British royalty and nobility were drawn here like iron filings to a magnet.

Nothing has devalued Cannes' aura of glamour, sophistication or exclusivity. The pristine **Croisette**, with its haughty palms and flower-beds manicured 12 months of the year by 130 full-time gardeners, is the most internationally-recognised of all seafront promenades, yet not one advert for fast food or tanning cream has been allowed to sully its Edwardian elegance.

True, a new Hilton now stands in place of the old Palais des Festivals, where Vadim launched Bardot. But the wedding-cake facade of the **Carlton Hotel** only a few yards away has barely changed in over 80 years, complete with its twin pepper-pot cupolas modelled on the breasts of La Belle Otero, a famous courtesan of the period. It symbolises Cannes just as much as Big Ben does London, its name a synonym for comfort and grace.

A minor breach of these tasteful standards was noted when the city twinned itself with Beverly Hills to celebrate its links with the film industry. But nobody was really scandalised and life quickly reverted to what passes for normal out on the Carlton Terrace, where even pet poodles have their own Hollywood-style Doggies' Bar. Sighs of relief were heard when another twinning operation took place, this time with London's Royal Borough of Kensington and Chelsea. Cannes is most definitely not Tinseltown-on-Sea. At heart it is a sweetly modest provincial resort, more like a sub-tropical Hastings if anything, with about the same number of inhabitants (around 75,000). The difference is that it is as cosmopolitan as Paris and almost as rich in terms of personal

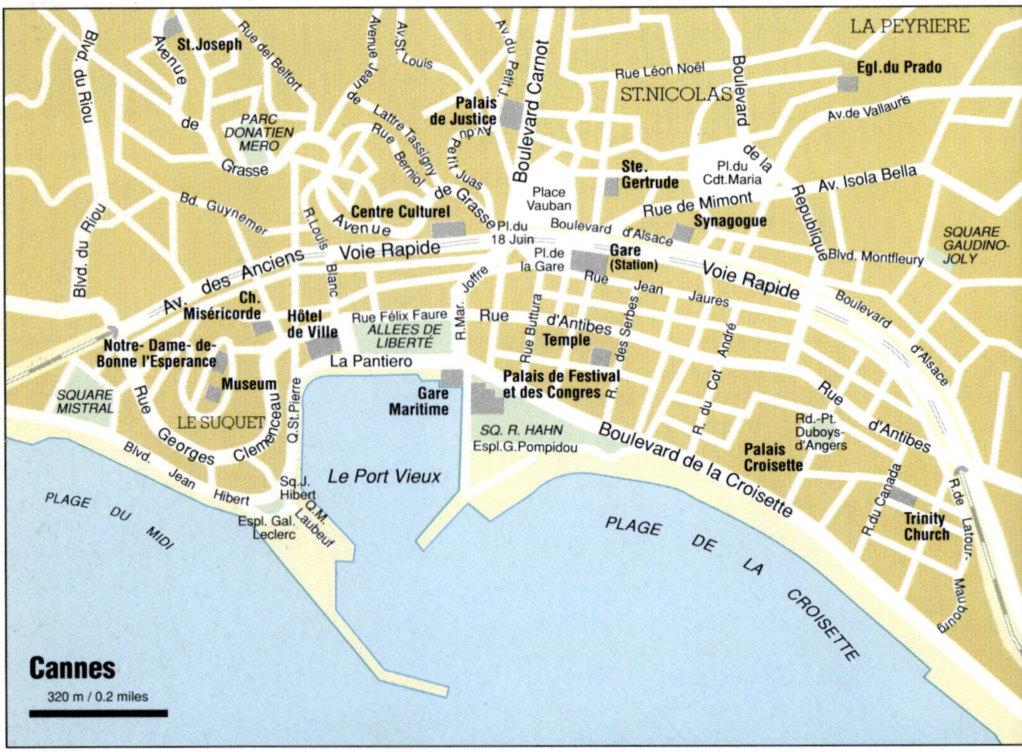

wealth, for many of these residents are Parisians with second homes.

It guards some delightfully down-to-earth secrets nevertheless. Take, for instance, the fishing boats, or *pointus*, with their nets piled up in the **Old Port** within hailing distance of the vast concrete bunker of the **Palais des Festivals**. The dazzling white hulls, shining brass and polished teak of greater vessels sharing this little basin dwarf them, and the fishermen themselves are becoming fewer and fewer each year like an endangered species, now that 7,000 registered craft are based in these waters.

These status symbols belong to some of the world's richest individuals, or corporations. Yet the *manja pei* (literally, "fish-eaters") still chug past them to bring in their catch in the early dawn. Strange Mediterranenan fish with names like *rascasse, rouquier* or *blavier*, some of which have poisonous, spiny fins and are best enjoyed in a bouillabaisse on the quay, flip and flop as they have always done.

The last vestiges of the fishing village of pre-Victorian days can still be seen from the **Quai St-Jacques**, and in a little lane no wider than an ox cart only a minute's walk away you can still find *coquillages* spilling from the fishmongers' open-air displays.

Time has not changed these salty scents, nor can it the smell of chickens roasting in a coating of Provençal herbs that wafts down the lane. **Rue Meynadier**, always a boisterous pedestrian thoroughfare, is where Le Tout Cannes shops for the best home-made pasta, the freshest cheese, and the most mouth-watering delicacies its master *traiteurs* can produce.

Around the corner in the **Marché Forville** smallholders from the back country bring their produce to market proudly marked with the name of the village of origin instead of some new-fangled notion of a "sell-by" date. Nobody has to ask. It is always dew-fresh. Their clamorous cries and good-natured banter fill a pitch half the size of a football field with their twanging Provençal accents.

The rose-tinted night.

This festival predates the film festival by 100 years. Long before the stars lived in Beverly Hills its French twin's roots were firmly established in the dark red earth of the Midi. Here they run a continuous performance – a free spectacle for the eyes, ears and nose.

They say the Duke of Windsor, when he was Prince of Wales, deliberately gave his bodyguards the slip on one of his many visits to Cannes in the 1930s. There was panic, of course, and for hours they scoured all his favourite haunts: the casinos, the *boules* pitch on the **Allées de la Liberté**, the restaurants of the **Rue Félix Faure** and the flower stalls facing them, all in vain. Friends and courtiers combed the best hotels, the beaches and boutiques of the fashionable **Rue d'Antibes**.

Finally, someone had the wit to eschew the ritzy side of life and investigate the market and the Old Port. There, in the back lanes, he found the future King of England sitting in the sun outside a tiny *auberge*, eating sea urchins in garlic sauce. Pleased with himself for his few hours' freedom as a commoner, the Prince looked up and said (according to local history, which must have had a reporter present): "Cannes is like a beautiful woman. Charming, but full of secrets." How much *aïoli* he had consumed by that stage is certainly not recorded.

This is the oldest part of town, **Le Suquet,** still with secret alleys, passages and half-hidden *auberges* and bistros. Its hill and its moorings date from Roman times (they named the site Canoïs Castrum because of the reeds and canes growing there). The landmark **Tower** at its summit dates from the 11th century, however, and was built by the monks of Lérins to guard against Saracen attack. From the **Place de la Castre** you can appreciate its commanding view all along the shore and back to the hill of La Californie, but to get this far is an achievement. These cobbled lanes are steep and narrow and the temptation to emulate the Prince has spelled the ruin of many a latter-day photo expedition.

Another secret Edward must have

The pristine Croisette.

remarked upon lies in the city's residential streets away from the front. Mrs Simpson took sanctuary in a villa here when the King was preparing to abdicate, and they planned to move into one of their own which they rented on a 10-year lease but never took up because of the outbreak of war.

Now, these same bourgeois houses built at the turn of the 19th century are nervously lying in wait for the century to turn once again. They do well to veil their charms behind sentinel palms and wisteria-entwined pergolas, for like the fishermen they too are a dying species. They are the last bastions of the *belle époque*, under siege in a less-mannered age when site values are appreciating faster than the properties standing upon them. The approach of the third millennium has brought soaring land prices in these desirable neighbourhoods and no matter how sweetly they evoke a lost chapter of history, it counts for little with unsentimental property developers who are changing the face of Cannes remorselessly.

How it has changed. Three roads with fishermen's houses, the tower of La Castre and an inn serving bouillabaisse were all there was to Cannes before a chance incident altered its destiny late in 1834. Fatigued after six years as Lord Chancellor of Great Britain (where among other achievements he championed the abolition of slavery), Henry, Lord Brougham, resigned and set off from London with his sickly daughter Eleonore in search of a mild climate on the Riviera, where the British were already making their presence felt in increasing numbers.

He intended to go to Nice, travelling in a six-horse berlin as far as the River Var which then formed a formidable frontier between Provence (France) and the Kingdom of Sardinia (Italy) - though this stretches the imagination today, looking at the unremarkable trickle that skirts Nice airport. However, he found more than a raging torrent barring his way. Soldiers refused to let him through as cholera had broken out in Provence. They forced him to turn back, first to

Closing a deal?

Antibes which displeased him, then to Cannes where an inn which had previously accommodated Victor Hugo and Pope Pius VII proved more to his liking. Brougham was so captivated by the countryside that within a week he had bought a plot of land and built the **Villa Eleonore** to the west of Le Suquet along the Fréjus road. It still stands, tastefully converted into flats, on Avenue Docteur Picaud.

So began the Anglicisation of Cannes. Other rich and influential British visitors soon followed, encouraged to find an alternative winter retreat to Nice where an "inferior class" was establishing itself, and a highly cultivated society took root. Quite literally, it seems: they even had their new villas' lawns relaid annually with turf brought from England by boat. Brougham extracted one million francs out of King Louis-Philippe – 33 times the town's municipal budget – to fund a new harbour where it could dock.

Royalty was not far behind. Though Queen Victoria did not disdain Nice, it was here, 18 miles down the coast, that her sons Leopold, Duke of Albany, and Edward, Prince of Wales, discovered the more entertaining aspects of Riviera life. Poor Leopold, who was a haemophiliac, vaguely remembered for having introduced croquet to the coast, died after falling down stairs at Cannes' Cercle Nautique. Edward (later King Edward VII) on the other hand is hugely famed for having indulged his appetite for gambling, tobacco, food and sex.

Cannes today still has streets that bear the names of Sir Walter Scott, Lord Byron, Shakespeare and Milton. A much-praised hospital called Sunnybank administers to resident English-speakers' medical needs. La Côte d'Or, in the Rue d'Antibes, purveys everything from bacon and kippers to kedgeree and curry paste. The Cannes English Bookshop, in the same street, takes care of more cerebral requirements.

Brougham died in 1868, two years before the railway came to town and spelled the end of an idyll. A statue of him stands in the **Allées de la Liberté,**

Read all about it.

not far from another, of Edward VII, as if emphasising the diverse roles which the British have played in the city's history. Today the whole area turns into a flea market every Saturday morning.

What of Cannes today: its conventions and congresses, its beaches, its shopping, its "Season"? Everyone knows "the Festival": two star-spangled weeks in May when the movie world turns this dowager resort into a painted lady, starlets cavort topless on the sands and big deals are clinched by moguls clenching big cigars in their even bigger teeth. The images are the same every year and their ritualism would be dismissed as quaintly amusing but for the revenue – around £3 million – the event generates.

Casual it may seem, but behind the scenes a huge effort goes into ensuring that those 50,000 people visiting this affair, with all its hype and hoopla, are not disappointed. Those golden sands, for instance, are raked and disinfected fastidiously every day, and on the private beaches are groomed to perfection before the *beau monde* gathers for cocktails beneath pastel-coloured parasols.

Likewise the floral arrangements. The municipality grows 400,000 bedding-out plants a year and out on the Croisette they are replanted every spring, summer, autumn and winter. Notice, too, how the streets are mercifully free of parking meters – scrapped years ago in favour of "pay and display" ticket dispensers powered by solar energy. Cleaning crews on motorbikes with high-pressure vacuum pipes are meanwhile supposed to eliminate that other pavement peril left behind by dogs, not always successfully.

Nature also deserves an Oscar in Cannes' success story. In February and early March mimosa spreads yellow fire across its hills. Boughs of mauve wisteria snake around its old ochre facades in April. Gardens burst with oleander pinks in summer and for much of the year splashes of purple and red bougainvillaea everywhere are taken almost for granted.

Lord Brougham's mild climate has

Cannes street chic.

not changed much despite global warming. October to January is usually dry and rewardingly sunny and when it does rain it rarely sets in for days. Even in the off-season it is possible to sit outdoors to sample the mountains of seafood available along the Rue Félix Faure, where the restaurants tuck in together like pearls on a string.

The city has more than its share of sophisticated Riviera socialites who will shop only in the designer boutiques of the Rue d'Antibes – Rodeo Drive, if you must – or at the exclusive haute couturiers of the Croisette, which serve as clubs for the fashion-conscious 12 months of the year. Entrance is free, but please bring your traveller's cheques. This city does not nurture its image for the faint of heart or light of pocket.

Even out on the street everyday citizens seem dressed to kill, from mini-skirted *Cannoises* who carry pet Yorkies like fashion accessories to traffic wardens in periwinkle blue uniforms stalking anyone failing to appreciate the nuances of high-tech parking.

Dining out in Le Suquet, the oldest part of town.

The Season, of course, puts a great strain on the city from mid-July until the end of August and many find the crush intolerable, though thousands of other masochists love it here then. The sand disappears under the press of near-naked bodies. "Full" signs go up in restaurants and hotels. The thermometer soars and the hot *mistral* wind can blow to disastrous incendiary effect.

Yet there are three dates which should be marked in everyone's diary as moments of light relief: Bastille Day (14 July), Assumption (15 August) and Liberation Day (24 August). At night, crescendoes of fireworks and classical music burst around the Croisette in a spectacular summer celebration lasting half an hour, provided free by the city council. Each show is different, involving tons of explosives launched from barges, and if you don't have your own personal yacht as a vantage point (some coming into the bay are the size of cross-Channel ferries) there are alternatives. Exceptionally, the beach restaurants which normally close at night offer superb dinners and a front-row seat under a sky that suddenly erupts in a storm of light. Or for a dress circle view you could retreat inland to a hill and watch the pyrotechnics while listening to the music on local radio.

One admirable viewpoint is **Place Bellevue** in the old village of **Le Cannet**, worth a visit for its good-value restaurants and intriguing little lanes where several musical evenings are a big draw in summer. It's a short ride by No. 5 bus. Originally Cannes formed part of the commune of Le Cannet, and the little village still insists on the definite article prefixed to its name.

Across the bay lie the pretty **Îles de Lérins**, noted more for daytime than nocturnal delights though a summer *son et lumière* show on **Ste-Marguerite** is a rewarding excursion and a glass-bottomed boat, *Nautilus*, skulks around its waters at night with its giant underwater searchlights illuminating the seabed. The mysterious Man in the Iron Mask was held prisoner here in Fort Royal from 1687 to 1698. Every day, boats leave regularly for Ste-Marguerite and the smaller island of St-Honorat from the Gare Maritime alongside the Palais des Festivals. Most holidaymakers head for Ste Marguerite where they roam around trying to find a place to picnic in the peace and quiet denied them on the mainland. They are more likely to find it on **St-Honorat**, 437 yards (400 metres) wide and mainly covered by parasol pines, eucalyptus trees and cypresses. St-Honorat has an impressive ecclesiastical history commencing with the monastery originally founded by St Honorat in the 5th century. Ste-Marguerite is named after St-Honorat's sister, who founded a nunnery there.

For hundreds of years St-Honorat was the centre of religious life for the whole of Southern Europe, and was so powerful that it owned much of the land along the Mediterranean coast, including Cannes itself. At one time 3,700 monks lived on the island, and the monastery was responsible for the training of many important bishops, including Ireland's St Patrick. But its wealth meant it was subject to constant raids from pirates, as well as papal corruption, and its decline was inevitable.

The 11th-century tower of the fortified monastery remains, with a chapel and cloisters, and of the seven chapels originally scattered across the island, the Chapel of the Trinity at the eastern end of the island still celebrates mass. In 1869 it was bought by the Cistercians, who built a new monastery on the site of the old one. The museum and church are open to visitors but mainly it is the private domain of the monks who grow lavender, grapes and oranges and are pleased to sell their own honey and Lérina liqueur to visitors.

This is the last secret. Out here on a fine summer's day only the distant jetwash of planes making their final approach to Nice airport reminds you that the centuries have marched on. It is a negligible price to pay, because a sound as old as time, the *kriii-kriii-kriii* of the cicadas, quickly reasserts itself to convince you that here you have indeed found that elusive prize: a true little corner of Heaven on Earth.

Île St-Honorat, remains of 11th-century monastery.

DOMIE
TOULON

ALMA

PLANETE

ANTIBES AND PLATEAU DE VALBONNE

Cap d'Antibes has secured its legendary status through the work of Scott Fitzgerald and its popularity with American expatriates in the 1920s and '30s. Although it is sometimes hard to imagine the original attraction of the quiet beaches and clear sea as one sits in a traffic jam in the middle of Juan-les-Pins with disco music blaring and beach shanty towns rising on all sides, it is still possible to discover and understand its special charms and sample its undoubted luxuries.

It must be said, however, that its real pleasures remain reserved for the rich with their *pied dans l'eau* villas, hotels and private beaches, from which they can contemplate the sea in the same exclusive calm enjoyed by Scott and Zelda, forgetting the milling crowds outside. The coast itself is nearly always crowded, and venturing on to a public beach should be done with people-watching firmly a priority; inland the popular towns of Vallauris and Biot also draw crowds of visitors to their craft workshops and glass factories. But even here within a very few miles of the coast the roads are quieter and one can seek respite in charming towns such as Valbonne, Mougins and Mouans-Sartoux. The region is famous for its flower production, in particular roses, carnations and anemones.

Antibes itself is surprisingly untouristy; its venerable history gives it a gravitas which is undeterred by waves of tourism, and the old town offers many instructive sights. Ultimately Antibes is a yachting town, with **Port Vauban** the true centre of Mediterranean yachting. Its inner harbour is home to several hundred vessels and the outer port shelters some of the world's most prestigious yachts on a wide *quai* known as "millionaires' row". The presence of these yachts, and the considerable crew and services required to support them, means that Antibes functions all year round, and is not as limited to seasonal visitors as are other parts of the coast. Graham Greene, who was a longtime resident, always preferred the winter. In *May We Borrow Your Husband?* he wrote: "Then Antibes comes into its own as a small country town with the Auberge de Provence full of local people and old men sit indoors drinking beer or pastis at the *glacier* in the Place de Gaulle. The small garden, which forms a roundabout on the ramparts, looks a little sad with the short stout palms blowing their brown fronds; the sun in the morning shines without any glare, and the few white sails move gently on the unblinding sea."

The area of interest in Antibes is really quite small so you would be well advised to park in one of the multi-storey car parks as soon as you enter the town (do not forget to keep your ticket with you as you need it to pay before reclaiming the car). A good free map is available from the Maison du Tourisme on the **Place Général de Gaulle**. This used to be the Place Macé and the Maison de Tourism is in what was once the

Preceding pages: a nautical *tricolor*. **Left**, Juan-les-Pins. **Right**, reflecting status.

Grand Hotel and home of the Municipal Casino which opened in 1911.

Antibes, now the third largest town on the Côte d'Azur, began life as the Greek city of Antipolis, "the town opposite", facing the earlier settlement of Nice. The Greeks held only a narrow stretch between the sea and the present **Cours Masséna**; it was a narrow enclosure filled with warehouses and only one gate, entered opposite the present **Hôtel de Ville** on the Cours Masséna at the Rue Pardisse.

The settlement traded with the Ligurian tribes along the coast but did not allow them to enter the city so all dealing took place outside the city walls; the covered market is still located on the Cours Masséna at roughly the same spot. But nothing more, save the name and a few objects in the museum, remains of this distant period.

The Romans, in their turn, built an important city at Antibes and the ruins of the baths, the aqueduct, the circus and the theatre stood until 1691 when Vauban used the stones to construct his massive fortifications. Vauban's ramparts were demolished in 1898 except those which constituted the sea wall; today the **Promenade Amiral de Grasse** runs along the ramparts, beginning at the **Bastian St-André** in the south. This now houses the excellent archaeological museum; two huge barrel-vaulted rooms with a well organised display of Greek, Etruscan and Roman pottery and exquisite examples of Roman glass. The remains include a large collection of amphora, stacked as if in the hold of a Roman galley.

The original Roman camp was built on the ruins of the Greek acropolis, on a terrace overlooking the sea; in the 12th century the **Grimaldi Château** was built on the same site. Many of the Romanesque features remain, including arched windows and the square tower which dominates the old town, though the building was reconstructed in the 16th century. Some of the tiny inner doorways have very attractive carving. The château is now the home of the Picasso Museum and contains a remarkable,

Cap d'Antibes and Valbonne Plateau

unified collection of more than 50 works Picasso executed there in 1946, when he was offered the keys to the château to use as a studio.

He painted solidly for five months, revitalised after spending the war years restricted to his Paris studio. The light and intense colour of the south were immediately incorporated into his work in a series of drawings and paintings of fish, sea urchins, goats, stars and the sea shore. He was captivated by the antiquity of the Mediterranean. Standing on the terrace of the ancient castle the site of a Greek acropolis, a Roman castrum, the residence of the Bishops of Antiboul and the16th-century Grimaldi, he invented a mythological cast of characters to inhabit his drawings and paintings: a faun, often playing the double flute of antiquity, a bearded centaur (undoubtedly himself) and a beautiful nymph, sometimes dancing with a tambourine (Françoise Gilot).

The paintings and drawings of these figures eventually resulted in a major work, *La Joie de Vivre*, which symbolised his entire stay in the château. The fishermen provided another source of inspiration, as they had done before the war in his huge painting *Night Fishing at Antibes*. Some of these, such as *Man Gulping Sea Urchins* are on canvas and later x-ray photographs revealed that Picasso, holding the keys of the château, had raided the storerooms and painted over what he regarded as mediocre 19th-century paintings. It was also here that Picasso painted the *Antipolis Suite*, a series depicting highly stylised, pared-down nudes, often reclining.

In an unusual act of generosity, Picasso left virtually everything to the museum in which they were created. Now on display are 27 paintings, 44 drawings, two sculptures, 50 engravings (mostly from the Vollard Suite) and 75 original ceramics – a major collection and in fact the first permanent collection devoted to the work of a living artist. It is supported by works of tribute by other artists, photographs and documentation.

The museum also has one of the larg-

Port Vauban and Fort Carré.

est collections of the work of Nicolas de Staël, who lived in Antibes and also painted in the château. There is an important collection of the modern Nice School of César, Arman, Spoerri, Klein and others. Provision is made for the blind with paintings reproduced in a form of braille (with braille explanations alongside).

The château was bought by the city of Antibes in 1925, and founded as the **Museum of Art, History and Archaeology**. Among its numerous Roman artefacts is one which gives an evocative glimpse of Antibes' past – the charming 3rd-century Roman stela to the slave child, a dancer named Septentrion, whose Latin funerary inscription reads: "To the Manes of the Child Septentrion aged twelve who at the theatre at Antibes on two days danced and gave pleasure." On the terrace overlooking the ramparts is a series of sculptures by Germaine Richier, César and Miró, in a fragrant Mediterranean garden with the sea providing a dramatic backdrop.

To the north of the château is the old cathedral, the **Church of the Immaculate Conception.** The square Romanesque bell tower is a converted 12th-century watchtower but only the east end remains of the original 12th-century building, the west end being 17th-century rebuilding. The 1710 doors are worth noting. The old town gate with its two round towers on the Cours Masséna survives. The Orme Tower now houses the **Musée de la Tour**, a museum of popular arts and traditions, concentrating on 18th- and 19th-century costumes, furniture and objects.

The ramparts continue past the cathedral to the Vieux Port. Below is the small **Plage de la Gravette**, a sheltered sandy beach, separated from the Vieux Port by the Quai H. Rambaud. From the ramparts there is a gateway to the **Rue Aubernon** where there is a regular flea market. Just around the corner, opposite the gate to the old fishing port, at 50 Boulevard d'Aguillon, is Restaurant Chez Félix, the old-fashioned bistro where Graham Greene took his lunch and often found inspiration. The restau-

The ubiquitous baguette, lunch on the sea wall.

rant remains unchanged, its decor determinedly unpretentious, with flowery tablecloths and a motorcycle parked at the bar. And there is the same proprietor, who will always show you the fish you have ordered before it is cooked.

On the other side of the old port is the massive yacht harbour of Port Vauban, and the imposing mass of the 16th-century **Fort Carré**, where Napoleon was imprisoned for a time. The old town of Antibes quickly outgrew its medieval walls and expanded inland. The grid of old lanes between Rue James Close and the bus station are worth exploring; here life continues much as it has always done, with washing hanging from windows, pots full of geraniums, and children playing games between the ancient stone walls of the narrow streets.

The **Place Nationale** is the home of the Musée Peynet, whose delightful, somewhat coy drawings have made him a cult figure. In the Place Nationale and many of the narrow streets leading to the cathedral there are lots of restaurants, so this is a popular place to stop for lunch after the morning market (arrive not long after midday to be sure of a table).

Cap d'Antibes is still very much the preserve of those fortunate enough to have villas there, but as a result it has retained much of its charm, and rewards exploration. There is a public beach with golden sand stretching from the **Pointe de l'Ilet** down to the **Port de la Salis**; although not large, it is the only sandy beach this side of the Cap apart from the tiny Plage de la Garoupe. Most of the beach clubs here suffice with wooden decks built out over the rocks, the lack of sand compensated somewhat by the clear waters this far out.

The famous **Plage de la Garoupe** is more of a reference to a beach than anything else. Scott Fitzgerald's description of the "bright tan prayer rug of a beach" is most accurate in calling it a rug, and a fairly moth-eaten one at that. Had Gerald Murphy, the original for Fitzgerald's hero in *Tender is the Night*, known the fate of his quiet little cove he may have been more inclined to cover it

Antibes, the old town.

Riviera Yacht-Watching

Luxury yachting has always been part of the Riviera legend but in recent years it has become a fully-fledged industry, vital to the region's economy. Nowhere else on earth is there so much extravagant floating real estate in one place. While some harbours – like Cannes or St-Tropez – see the traditional *pointu* fishing boats go happily about their business alongside sleek luxury vessels, the many new ports designed exclusively for private yachts have made the Riviera the uncontested world centre for a new type of craft, dubbed the "megayacht" – fully crewed private vessels over 120 ft (36 metres) long.

Riviera harbours are open to anyone wishing for a closer look at the lifestyles of the rich and famous. Between the Italian border at Menton and the port of Marseille 127 nautical miles (235 km) to the west there are 130 of these harbours, totalling over 52,000 moorings. French Riviera ports shelter a third of the world megayacht fleet of about 3,500 yachts. Yachting occupies 1,500 local businesses, including many small craftsmen and tradesmen, and provides 6,000 jobs, not including crew.

Monaco was Aristotle Onassis's favourite harbour, and remains the permanent home-port of his compatriot Stavros Niarcos's *Atlantis*, a vessel of cruise-ship proportions. But Antibes' Port Vauban is the true centre of Mediterranean yachting. The inner harbour is home to several hundred smallish vessels (under 120 ft) but the IYCA (International Yacht Club of Antibes) outer port, built to shelter Adnan Kashoggi's Italian-built 270 ft (80 metres) *Nabila* is now the home of 20 of the world's most prestigious megayachts, berthed with their sterns to the wide quay known as "millionaires' row".

Famous names still frequent Riviera ports but, except in a few cases (terrorism and taxman *oblige*), with cautious discretion. Some of the more flamboyant owners, however, make no secret of their possession and the name of a yacht is often a clue to who her owner could be.

The costs of running one of these boats often means that an entire offshore company is set up to own and manage the vessel, which partly explains the majority of British-flag yachts on the Côte d'Azur. Some of the owners are indeed British, but many are not and are only attracted by British tax law which, given the nation's maritime tradition, is more favourable than in other European countries.

If a taste of the seafaring life sounds tempting, a used 60-ft (18-metre) displacement model can be had for about £1 million. If you want something with a bit more speed or cabin space you should be thinking in the neighbourhood of £3 million. Today, yachts worth more than £20 million are not at all uncommon and you should count on 10 percent of the boat's value as the cost of annual upkeep.

Chartering offers a cheaper solution for those on a budget and the American dollar is the trading currency. For about $4,000 a day you can hire a modest yacht, but if you plan on sailing farther afield or throwing large parties on board you'll need a bigger model at up to $20,000 a day. Prices include yacht and crew but not berthing fees, fuel, food or drink. Sailing is perhaps an overstated term for the activities of many of these yachts, since they seem to spend more time quay-side than they ever do at sea. Sometimes it seems as if their sole purpose is to host ostentatious cocktails on deck for the entertainment of spectators on shore. On the Côte d'Azur more than anywhere else, a yacht truly is a hole in the water you throw money into. ■

A yacht's name often gives a clue to the owner.

up with rocks than painstakingly remove all the seaweed, as he did in the 1920s. Today wooden sundecks on stilts extend the tiny beach out over the rocks with beachclubs charging for the use of a mattress.

In 1923, Gerald and Sara Murphy stayed with Cole Porter in a rented villa on the Cap, then moved to the Hôtel du Cap. "Right out on the end of the Cap there was a tiny beach," wrote Murphy, "the Garoupe – only about forty yards long and covered with a bed of seaweed that must have been four feet thick. We dug out a corner of the beach and bathed there and sat in the sun." The Murphys' constant companions that summer were Picasso and his wife Olga, who liked the area so much that they decided to take a villa in Antibes.

The Murphys decided to settle there and bought a villa with a huge garden just below the lighthouse, naming it the Villa America. While the villa was being remodelled, Gerald was clearing the beach of seaweed at the rate of eight square feet a day. One of the first visitors from the Hôtel du Cap to use it was Rudolph Valentino.

Between the beach at La Sallis and Garoupe, is the rocky outcrop of **Pointe Bacon.** From Garoupe you can walk out to the rocks at Cap Gros, following the cliff path. The **Pointe de l'Ilette** is the southernmost point of the Cap with spectacular rocks and another lighthouse sweeping the night sea.

The coast between here and the **Musée Naval et Napoléonien** is the preserve of the **Hôtel du Cap-Eden Roc**, the most glamorous hotel on the Riviera, popular today with Cannes superstars, including Madonna. It is expensive, of course, but can be visited for drinks or a day at the pool. You can drive in, use the free undercover parking, and stroll through the parasol pines to the restaurant and terrace bar.

It was originally built by the founder of *Le Figaro* newspaper, supposedly as a home for impoverished artists and musicians, but in 1863 was taken over by Russian princes who transformed it into a hotel. It was one of the first luxury

Villa entrance, Cap d'Antibes.

hotels on the Riviera and has always attracted shoals of celebrities, but it remains most famous for being the setting of Fitzgerald's *Tender is the Night*. The Murphys stayed here in 1923 and persuaded the owner to open during the summer, thus launching the Riviera summer season.

Sipping an Americano cocktail on the 1930s-style terrace with its elegant white railings and yellow cushions, watching the colour-coordinated yellow buoys bobbing about in the sea below, is the essence of luxury, as is swimming in the organic, shaped pool cut into the rocks (where mad Zelda used to dive). It is as good a way as any to appreciate the enduring allure of the Côte d'Azur.

Dominating the skyline of the Cap is the **Phare de la Garoupe.** The lighthouse itself is of recent date, since the retreating Germans dynamited the old one in 1944. The chapel next to it, **La Chapelle Notre-Dame-du-Bon-Port**, however, is old, with two naves, one 13th and one 16th-century. Despite its setting amid luxury villas, it is still used by the local people and feels like a small village church.

For centuries seafarers have left votive offerings in the church which now resembles a Portobello Road junkshop of naïf paintings, drawings and medals. To the right of the entrance, low on the wall is an extraordinary drawing of a wrecked car, smoking in a ditch. Its owners pray to God for their survival but unfortunately for their future prospects they are kneeling right in the middle of the road. In front of the chapel is a viewing platform; looking east you can see as far as Cap St Erasmo in Italy and to St-Tropez to the west.

Not far from the chapel and lighthouse, on the Boulevard du Cap, and a fairly easy walk from the public beaches of Antibes or the Casino end of the Plage de Juan-les-Pins, is the **Jardin Thuret**, with its collection of exotic trees and plants, many of which have been successfully introduced to the region. Right next door is the Villa Thenard, where the Grand-Duke Nicholas of Russia died in 1929.

Plage de la Garoupe. Only the beach is missing.

Back up the D2559 to Juan-les-Pins, there is a marina at **Port Gallice** and the tiniest of sandy beaches reaching out to the **Port du Croûton**. The sheltered sandy beaches of **Juan-les-Pins** reach almost this far down the Cap and stretch the full length of the town, providing plenty of space for a frenetic beach life of intensive sunbathing and shoreline promenading; the palpable pleasures which for many visitors fulfil their expectations of the Côte d'Azur. This is also the place for nightlife with its casino and throbbing discos, and lots of people-watching pavement cafés. In July an annual jazz festival is held under the famous pines.

Between Juan-les-Pins and Cannes is **Golfe Juan**. The bay is famous for Napoleon's ill-fated return from exile on Elba in 1815. He apparently met the Prince of Monaco on his way to reclaim his own throne after the Revolution and said to him, "Monsieur, we are in the same business." Napoleon headed north with his troops through the rough terrain of the Alps to Paris. The path he took, via Grasse, Sisteron, Castellane and Digne is now commemorated as the **Route Napoleon**.

On the way into Golfe Juan there was once a strip of 1930s villas, jammed in between the railway and the coast road to Antibes, facing the beach; now predatory tower cranes menace the buildings, and the old villas near the port are being torn down, their gardens uprooted, and in their place is a row of high-rise apartment blocks which will eventually stretch all the way to Juan-les-Pins. The kilometre-long beach, however, remains the same with its elegant line of palms, golden sand banned to dogs, and with a seductive Cap d'Antibes shimmering across the bay.

The part of the old fishermen's port at Golfe Juan which faces the enclosed harbour has not changed much; the traffic on the coast road has always been busy and the fact that the old port is cut off from the main town by the railway tracks has preserved it. After the war Picasso and Françoise Gilot had an apartment overlooking the boats. It was on

The essentials.

the beach at Golfe Juan that Picasso met Susanne and Georges Ramié, owners of the Madoura pottery in Vallauris, an event which was to transform the fortunes of the inland town.

Vallauris is less than three built-up kilometres from Golfe Juan and the coast, and resembles a seaside town with rest homes, private hospitals, and a tourist strip, except in this case, the souvenirs are pots. Vallauris has always been a potters' town, a tradition begun by the Romans and continued by Italian potters fom Grasse, but its fortunes declined drastically and did not improve until Picasso began patronising the Madoura pottery workshop. His output was prodigious, 2,000 pieces in the first year which required a whole team of people to prepare and fire. The pottery was permitted to make limited edition copies of his plates and vases, which they still do, and his presence attracted other artists, including Chagall.

Today Vallauris is one of France's largest pottery centres and virtually the whole of the Rue Clemenceau from the museum to the edge of town is lined with pottery shops. Behind them are the kilns and workshops that produce the pottery, open to the public when in operation (though not at weekends).

A wide variety of pottery is for sale, some of it good value, although sadly much of it is dull and occasionally ghastly. Basic terracotta cooking-pots are worth buying, and the Galerie Madoura is still the best place to shop for high-quality, though expensive pots. There are other crafts available including wickerwork, glass and woodwork, the most interesting is a shop specialising in perfume flasks made from rare woods. There is a small private pottery museum, with a kiln, and a variety of presses and mixes for treating the clay. The "Picasso experience" is fully exploited with photographs and even a wax model of the master at work.

The Vallauris Museum is housed in the château, originally a 13th-century Lérins priory. It is entered through a courtyard shaded by a huge lime tree, with a 1985 Riopelle mosaic on the

Potter at work in Vallauris.

wall. The château was rebuilt in the 16th century and has a round pepperpot tower at each end in the Renaissance style, unusual in Provence. There is also a splendid Renaissance staircase. Of the priory, only the Romanesque chapel survived intact. It is a fine example with barrel vaulted ceiling and round arches.

In 1952, at the request of the town, Picasso decorated it with a huge composition called *War and Peace* painted in his studio on hardboard panels which would bend to follow the curve of the roof. It is by no means Picasso's best work and is not improved by the fact that he neglected to prime his surface so the dull brown of the hardboard shows through the large fields of white paint and scrubbed brushwork. The colours seem to have sunk into the boards, sapping the painting of its vitality. It is worth seeing but *Guernica* it is not.

The museum also contains other work by Picasso: a collection of lithographs on the ground floor and a display of ceramic work, mostly glazed plates and dishes with a few larger painted jugs, produced in a limited edition by the craftsmen of the Madoura pottery to Picasso's designs. Although they carry the usual themes of the bullring, owls and faces, these, too, lack a certain vitality, the touch of the master perhaps. But there are some very good photographs by André Villers of Picasso in Vallauris.

The museum also has six rooms containing the work of Alberto Magnelli (Florence 1888–1971), including some of his important early abstract works from 1914.

Because Picasso saved the town's principal industry, he was made an honorary citizen. In 1950 Picasso in turn presented Vallauris with a life-size bronze statue, *Man Holding A Sheep*, which stands outside the church in the Place Paul Isnard.

Picasso regarded it as an important work: "I did this statue in a single afternoon, but not until after months of reflection and I don't know how many sketches… It was much too weak; it wouldn't hold. The statue began to stagger under the weight of the clay. It was

Picasso's *l'Homme à l'Agneau* in Vallauris.

dreadful! It was threatening to collapse at any moment. I had to do something quickly… We took lengths of cord and lashed *l'Homme à l'Agneau* to the beams. I decided to cast it in plaster immediately. And it was done that same afternoon. What a job! I'll never forget it… I had intended to go back to it, to work on it again. You see those long thin legs, and the feet, just indicated, scarcely separate from the ground? I would have liked to model them, in keeping with the rest. I didn't have the time…"

Picasso connections in the area abound. If you head inland from Vallauris, picking up the D35 to Mougins, you should visit the small chapel of **Notre-Dame-de-Vie** on the way, taking an easily missed turning east on the D3. The one-way lane winds up the hillside and the chapel is reached when the car-park appears on the left, immediately after the sign to the chapel. The 17th-century chapel has an outdoor porch and is on a beautiful site overlooking Mougins. The area is popular for walking and to the south on the same lane, is an entrance with parking to the Parcs de Mougins which border the Parc Départemental de la Valmasque. It is beautiful forest land and very popular for weekend picnics.

Picasso spent the last 12 years of his life in the neighbouring Villa Notre-Dam-de-Vie; it remains extremely well protected, not open to the public or visible from the road, much like most of the expensive villas in this area. The house was a former *mas*, converted before the war into a luxurious villa by Benjamin Guinness, who also paid for the restoration of the chapel.

Mougins itself was also "discovered" by Picasso, along with Francis Picabia in 1936 and they were followed shortly after by Paul Eluard, Man Ray and Jean Cocteau. It is a pretty hill town, surprisingly small, with wonderful views of the Mediterranean, surrounded now by a rash of more recent housing, including some discreet but sumptuous villas. Today Mougins is best known for its restaurants, in particular Roger Vergé's

17th-century chapel of Notre-Dame-de-Vie, near Mougins.

Moulin de Mougins and his famous "*cuisine du soleil*".

Even if you forswear more serious gourmandising, Mougins is a pleasant place for a stroll and a drink. The site has been occupied since Roman times, and during the Middle Ages was owned by the Abbey of Lérins. All that remains today of the original ramparts is a 15th-century fortified gate, called the Saracen Gate, which originally had a portcullis. The church, L'Eglise St-Jacques-le-Majeur, was begun in the 11th century but has been heavily restored. The bell tower is open to the public; the key is available from the Museum of Photography round the corner. Here there is a good collection of photographs of Picasso by Lartigue, Villiers, Doisneau and others.

Between Mougins and Grasse on the N85 is **Mouans-Sartoux.** The village was reconstructed in the 15th century on a grid plan like nearby Valbonne, with five streets in each direction and space for a pretty square outside the church and facing the castle. The chapel has huge buttresses on its northern side facing the Château Mouans-Sartoux, which has round towers on each corner. There is also a small formal garden and an old well in the middle of a lawn.

It was from this castle that Suzanne de Villeneuve offered obstinate resistance to the Duke of Savoy in 1592 during the War of the League. He destroyed her castle and sacked the village despite the convention signed by the Duke who was in retreat. Enraged, she pursued him, overtaking him at Cagnes. Seizing the bridle of his horse, she reproached him in front of his whole army. Embarrassed, the Duke had 4000 écus indemnity counted out to her on the spot and she returned to rebuild her ruined town.

The Château is now a centre for modern and contemporary art, **L'Espace de l'Art Conoret**, one of the regional venues selected by Jack Lang, the former socialist minister for culture. Next to the car-park is a small chapel with a naïf carved typanum over the door featuring a nativity scene with church, shepherds and dozens of sheep.

The Provençal pastiche of Sophia-Antipolis.

Sophia-Antipolis – or, to give its full name, Parc International d'Activités de Valbonne Sophia-Antipolis – covers an enormous area of the Valbonne plain; miles and miles of new roads have been laid, sympathetically following the gentle contours of the wooded hills.

The development, which accommodates scores of high-tech companies, is much more than just a green-site technical park; it also includes housing, shopping, schools and research institutes, many of them in futuristic modern buildings – horizontal cylinders, mirror pyramids and more.

The Parc is continuing to expand, and a metro link to Nice airport is planned. The success of Sophia-Antipolis reflects the region's determination to become the Silicon Valley of Southern Europe, though the site of eager young American executives jogging along the landscaped roads has an inescapably bizarre quality.

As a result of the Sophia-Antipolis development, nearby **Valbonne** has seen its population increase dramatically. It was laid out in the 16th century by the Lérins monks, on a strict grid four blocks wide and 10 blocks long.

In the centre is a beautifully proportioned arcaded square shaded by old elm trees. The church, built on the river bank just outside the grid, began life as part of an abbey founded by the Chalais order who built it on the shape of a Latin cross. The abbey was taken over by the Lérins and the present building finally became the parish church. Sadly, the building has been very badly restored. The adjoining convent is also being restored by the commune.

The road between Valbonne and Opio passes through pleasant green and shady woodland, shielding an abundance of luxury villas and hotels. **Opio** is a bijou little village, well maintained with painstakingly restored houses and neatly trimmed hedges. Here you can visit the Roger Michel olive oil mill, where you can see the olive-crushing in operation, and buy a variety of olive oil-based products.

Returning to the coast from Valbonne along the D4 is the ancient town of **Biot.** Although tourists are encouraged to visit its potteries and glass making ateliers, parking provision is poor, and you would be well advised to park instead at the foot of the hill near La Verrerie de Tines, one of the glass factories for which Biot is famous, and walk up the hill to the Port des Tines.

The climb, in any case, is a more authentically medieval way to enter the town; a rather run-down cobblestone ramp takes you through the 16th-century Port des Tines and into the old walled village. Here the narrow lanes and *ruelles* house the citizens of Biot in quiet retreat from the tourist-oriented main streets and shops; truly the very best part of Biot.

The Rue de Mitan has a number of untouched examples of medieval shops and the entire quarter has a charm which is missing from some of the more popular hill towns. The Rue Plus Basse, the Rue Basse, the Rue du Mitan and Rue des Orfèvres all run parallel, connected by steep steps that climb the hillside. The closer you get to the church, the

Poodle power.

older the streets and houses become. The Rue de la Vieille Boucherie still has its old butcher's shop with ceramic tiles and metal meat racks hanging in the street outside.

The village centre is the Place aux Arcades, originally the Roman forum, for this was a Roman town. It has two long 13th- and 14th-century arcades either side of an oblong plaza; one later doorway is dated 1579. The 15th-century church leads off the east end of the Place aux Arcades and has one very unusual feature: because of the slope of the ground, the visitor is immediately faced with a flight of 20 steps, leading down into the nave. It is built upon the foundations of an earlier Romanesque church, and rebuilding continued from 1470 until 1655, when the lateral chapels were completed. The old cemetery, just a few streets to the north, is also well worth a visit.

In the Rue St-Sébastien are all the potteries and glass shops, along with cafés, tourist information and a small local history museum; it is often the only part of Biot visitors ever see, which is a pity.

At the foot of the town, on a small hill, is the National Fernand Léger Museum, conceived by Madame Nadia Léger and the present director George Bauquier and purpose-built to hold Léger's work and archives. It contains a complete cross-section of over 300 works executed between 1905 and 1955. It suffers from the usual problems of "estate museums" in that Leger's greatest works are scattered among the major museums of the world. Though he kept examples of all periods of his work few of them were among the very best.

It would take a retrospective exhibition to show the full range of his achievement and this museum is of the most interest to those who already know his work. Still, there are enough of his early post-Cubist paintings to show his importance, and his gigantic ceramic panels and mosaics exhibited on the exterior walls of the building are a spectacularly colourful sight burnished by the strong sun of the Midi.

A fête at Biot.

PICASSO COUNTRY

Pablo Picasso was the greatest artist of the 20th century: he broke new ground in painting, sculpture, lithography, engraving, pottery and book illustration. He is an all-pervading presence, a bench-mark against which all 20th-century work is measured.

Every phase of his work has been tremendously influential; indeed it has been said that anything painted since the war can be traced back to Marcel Duchamp or Picasso. His sad Blue Period portraiture and wistful Rose Period style have both been widely copied, ultimately by sentimental chocolate-box artists. His Cubism and collages began a line of development from

Schwitters, Miró, Léger, Ernst, Dubuffet, Motherwell, Nevelson, Rauschenberg and the Pop artists to Arman and the School of Nice. De Kooning's women, early Pollock, the work of Henry Moore, Victor Pasmore, Hans Arp, Elizabeth Frink, all show the influence of Picasso.

From day one his life attracted legends. On 25 October 1881, the midwife attending his birth gave him up for dead and turned her attentions to his mother. But his uncle, Don Salvador, blew cigar smoke in his face, thus making the baby cry and saving him from suffocation. It is a classic story of Picasso triumphing over all odds.

His first 10 years were spent in Málaga, where his painter father taught art. His father encouraged his talent until the decisive moment when, in Picasso's words, his father was so impressed with the work of his 13-year-old son that "he handed me his paint and his brush and never painted again." Picasso entered the La Longa school of art in Barcelona where he skipped the beginner's course. To take an advanced course in classical art, he had to submit a project file within a month. The other students earnestly began their month-long preparations but Picasso handed in his file of far superior work the very next day. A child prodigy, he graduated at the age of 14.

By 1896 he had his own studio and was exhibiting regularly – but the world centre of art was Paris. He took his first studio in Montmartre in 1900, painting life in Paris: old age, loneliness, poverty, and using mostly blues and greens – his "Blue Period". In 1905 he began painting circus acrobats and jugglers – the "Rose Period". By 1907 he made a major breakthrough with *Les Demoiselles d'Avignon* which was essentially the first Cubist painting with the picture plane distorted into flat slabs and the faces simplified into African masks. He and Georges Braque took Cubism to the limit, painting the subject-matter from all angles simultaneously, then went their separate ways. Picasso developed many sides of the technique, from collage to the distortion and abstraction, which irritated so many early critics.

Picasso's love affair with the Riviera first began in 1920 when he spent the summer at Juan-les-Pins; the beach there inspired him to create a series of monumental neoclassical nudes. But it was not until after the war that he moved there permanently. In the pre-war years, he often spent his summers there, returning to Paris for the winter season. In 1923 he painted harlequins in Cap d'Antibes. In the summer of 1924, he painted a series of large still-lifes at Juan-les-Pins and spent most of 1926 and 1927 at Juan-les-Pins and Cannes, working chiefly on etchings, and he continued to visit until 1939 when he made a hurried retreat to Paris as war broke out.

He had been living in Antibes working on a major painting, *Night Fishing at Antibes*, a very large work, 6 ft high and over 10 ft wide (2 by 3 metres), a format he used only for important subjects. This painting summed up many of his feelings about the Riviera, a luminous nocturnal seascape with the fishermen and their boats illuminated by white acetylene lamps – a common sight in the Mediterranean. It turned out to be more of a leave-taking than a summing-up for he was not to see the Riviera again for six years. Picasso openly refused to collaborate with the Nazis during the Occupation of France.

In 1946 he left Paris to settle in the Riviera for good, going first to Antibes. Here was the same intense light and warm Mediterranean lifestyle as his native Spain, to which he could not return while Franco remained in power. He responded to the clear silhouettes of the mountains, the hard shadows and bright luminous colours. Though he rarely painted a traditional landscape – his paintings are almost always populated – he responded to the familiar. At Vallauris in 1953, for instance, he painted 13 variations of a view of the elecricity transformer near his house. These post-war paintings have a freedom he could not find in his Paris studio. He felt at home and remained in the region for the rest of his life, leaving only for short visits.

Picasso country is a very small area, a few square miles between Antibes and Cannes, though he moved constantly within this area. He and Françoise Gilot, whom he met in 1943, spent the summer of 1945 at the Villa Pour Toi, facing the fishermen's harbour at Golfe Juan, but it was not until the following year that he acquired his first property in the south. He exchanged a still-life for a house in the village of Menerbes, which he gave to Dora Maar, his companion of many years.

In the early summer of 1946, Picasso and Françoise Gilot returned and Picasso was given the keys to the Grimaldi Palace to use as a studio. He donated most of the work to the museum, including the delightful *La Joie de Vivre.*

He and Gilot moved to Vallauris, to La Galloise, a "small rather ugly house", as she called it, and Picasso began his experiments with ceramics, evolving new techniques of glazing to suit his unusual needs, and single-handedly reviving the town's fortunes. It was there between April and June 1954 that Picasso painted his famous series of more than 30 drawings and paintings of Sylvette David, a young English girl who worked next door to his studio on the Rue de Fournas. Sylvette herself posed for the paintings, causing him to paint her in every conceivable style from naturalistic to highly abstract Cubist variations (his portraits were usually done from memory). Her long neck, thick blonde hair held high in a pony-tail, straight nose and sloping shoulders created a fashionable, much copied style *à la Picasso*. The pony-tail, introduced the year before by Bardot, became all the rage.

After Picasso's relationship with Gilot broke up, he lived alone for a time at La Galloise, painting interiors. The break-up, however, released a flood of energy; the 80-odd drawings made between 1953 and 1954 of the artist and his model; the old artist always in the act of creation, painting the young model. It was to be a recurring theme.

Picasso began living with Jacqueline Roque, whom he married in 1958. In 1955 he moved from Vallauris to La Californie, a large, ornate turn-of-the-century mansion overlooking Cannes. The space caused him to invent the term *paysages d'intérieur* for the series of interiors he painted, driven by an urge to fill the echoing empty rooms.

In 1958 he was again on the move and bought the huge Château Vauvenargues near Aix-en-Provence but this move from the Riviera did not last long and in 1961 he returned, to Mas Notre-Dame-de-Vie, on a hill overlooking Mougins surrounded by terraces of cypresses and olives and named after a nearby chapel.

He remained prolific to the end. During his last five years, he created over 1,000 works of art: drawings, paintings and graphics. His Riviera period was perhaps his most obsessional; he would take a theme or a new medium and work at it until it was exhausted. The astonishing productivity continued until, on 8 April 1973, Picasso died at Mas Notre-Dame-de-Vie, at the age of 92.

Two aspects of Picasso: left, *The Doves* (1957) and, right, *Jacqueline with Flowers* (1954).

Today Picasso is a constant theme on the Côte d'Azur. Antibes has a major museum in the Château Grimaldi, with a superb collection of work painted there and donated by Picasso. Mougins has an exhibition of photographs of the artist, including works by Lartigue and Doisneau. Vallauris has his *War and Peace* in the château museum and the sculpture of *L'Homme à l'Angeau* in the centre of town. Sometimes it seems as if every town or village is anxious to claim some connection with the master. ■

8533 XC 78

GRASSE AND THE LOUP VALLEY

The ancient town of Grasse is an excellent place to appreciate the acute contrast between the Côte d'Azur and its bucolic hinterland. The town is set on a fabulous site, cradled by sheltering hills and surrounded by flowers, and with splendid views all the way to the sea. Beneath its palm-fronded terraces, elegant pink villas decorate the hillside, sloping gently down to the highly populated valley below, thick with executive housing and high-technology parks. Here the desired synthesis of modern technology with the peace and beauty of the countryside seems entirely possible.

Beyond Grasse are craggy mountains terraced with lavender, meandering river gorges, and the medieval villages of Provence. Within only a few miles spectacular drives and walks are possible. The Gorge du Loup, in particular, makes a wonderful excursion, leading you rapidly into an altogether more elevated universe of alpine pastures and mountain mists.

It is the centre of the perfume industry, and at almost any time of year the air is laden with fragrance; golden mimosa flowers in March; in early summer there are acres of roses waiting to be picked and lavender to be processed; in the autumn the tiny white stars and heavy perfume of jasmine appear.

As well as being a base for the major fragrance manufacturers, Grasse is the hub of an idyllic industry of small flower farms and perfumeries. These days, Grasse concentrates more on processing raw materials from other countries, but it is still possible to see vast mountains of rose petals, vats of jonquils and spadefuls of violets and orange blossom waiting to be processed each morning.

Preceding pages: shuttered lives. Left, negotiating the medieval streets of Grasse. Right, nose at work.

The flowers must be picked early, when the oil is most concentrated and delivered immediately. It takes enormous quantities of blooms to produce even the tiniest amounts of perfume; about 1,650 lb (750 kg) of roses for just 2 lb (1 kg) of rose "absolute", about 8,820 lb (4,000 kg) for 2 lb (1 kg) of essential oil.

Of the basic methods of extracting the scent, two of the oldest are still in use today. They are described in exquisite detail in Patrick Süskind's sinister and compelling novel, *Perfume*. Steam distillation is now mainly used for orange blossom; flowers and water are boiled in a still and the essential oils extracted by steam. A more expensive method, mainly used for jasmine and tuberose, is *enfleurage*; the flowers are layered with lard which becomes impregnated with the scent and is then washed out with alcohol. More modern methods include extraction by volatile solvents.

The highly-trained perfumers of Grasse have been world-famous for centuries. Each "nose" can identify and classify hundreds of fragrances, and working rather like a musician, blends together different "chords" of scent to create a harmonious combination that will radiate around the body in a slow process of diffusion that the French know as *sillage*.

Grasse has a venerable past; between 1138 and 1227 it was a free city, allied to Pisa and Genoa, and governed by a consulate, like the Italian republics. It became a bishopric in 1243 and remained so until 1791, thus becoming a focal point for local power. Its most famous cleric was the 15th-century Bishop Isnard de Grasse who was head of the monastery of the Lérins Islands.

The town was annexed by the counts of Provence until 1482, when Provence was united with France. Grasse continued to trade with Italy, importing animal skins and selling linen and leather goods. Grasse leather was of very high quality, characterised by its greenish hue, caused by treating it with myrtle leaves. In the 16th century, the fashion for perfumed gloves (masking, along with pomanders and handkerchiefs, the undesirable smell of the populace) was introduced by Catherine de Medici. This encouraged the perfume industry in Grasse, but it was not until the 18th century that tanning and perfumery began to develop as separate trades.

Grasse is a very satisfying town to visit; there is much of historic interest to see and perfumeries abound, but it does not feel like a touristy town. It has a working feel to it, the main square full of real shops, selling cheese, buckets and brushes and washing machines instead of Provençal lavender bags, though these are to be had if you want them.

In the architecture of Grasse the influence of the Italian Renaissance is clear; as the city guide points out, "It is to Genoa that the city is indebted for its austere medieval facades, for its Renaissance staircases, for its houses furnished with arcades..."

The town walls were not demolished until the mid-19th century and so, as in Edinburgh, the buildings crammed within the walls were extended vertically; the majority are six storeys high, even in the narrowest of alleys, many of which are dark medieval tunnels reeking of garbage and poverty (a side of Riviera life rarely encountered by the tourist). The southern part of the old town houses many Algerians, bringing

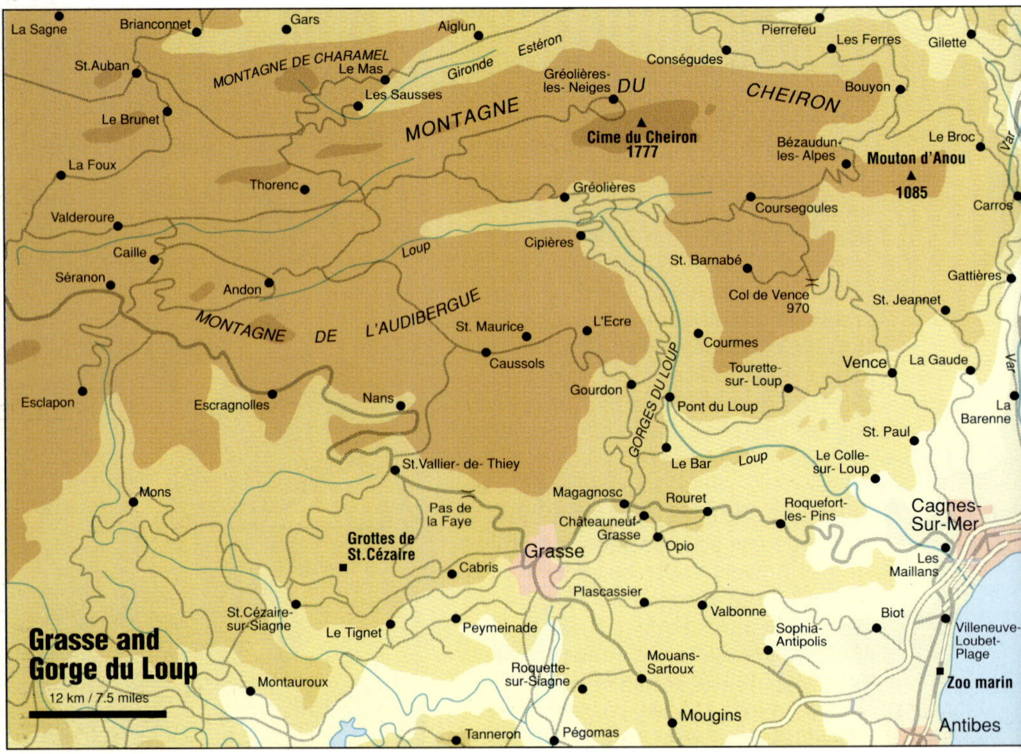

Grasse and Gorge du Loup

a lively street life and Arab music to the lanes and squares.

The **Place Cours** is a good place to begin a tour of Grasse; a number of museums flank a charming terraced garden full of fountains and waterfalls. Here is the **Musée International de la Parfumerie**, housed in an elegant 18th-century mansion, where you can witness the entire history and manufacture of perfume, see a beautiful collection of related items from exquisite perfume bottles to Marie-Antoinette's travelling case. Best of all is the greenhouse garden of Mediterranean and sub-tropical perfumed plants.

A little further down is the **Fragonard perfume museum** and, opposite, the **Villa-Musée Fragonard**, the 18th-century villa where Fragonard, who was born in Grasse, lived with his family for some years before the Revolution. The museum contains drawings and etchings, and two self-portraits by Fragonard as well as copies of the famous panels made for the Comtesse du Barry which are now in the Frick Collection, New York. There are works by other members of his family and other documentation. The building is surrounded by a charming formal garden.

On the corner of the Boulevard du Jeu de Ballon is the **Musée de la Marine**, the beautiful 18th-century former town house of the Pontèves family. The museum commemorates the life and career of Amiral de Grasse (1722–88) who was born locally in Le Bar and played a decisive role in the American War of Independence at the Battle of Yorktown, Virginia, the final battle of the campaign against the British. The museum contains flags and memorabilia, and has a delightful garden with neatly trimmed hedges surrounding roses and small lemon trees, and a pair of cannon captured from the British.

The **Place aux Aires** is long and narrow, with shady trees and an 18th-century fountain facing the 1781 six-storey Hôtel de Ville, with its slightly incongruous portico of pillars supporting a balcony. The square dates from the 14th century but the row of arcaded buildings which are its pride and joy are wealthy family town houses from the 16th and 17th centuries, mostly six storeys with shutters and washing hanging from the windows, giving a rather Italian feel to the scene. A market is held in the square every morning.

Turning south, down the narrow steps of the Rue des Fabreries, you encounter the remains of a 14th-century mansion on the corner of the Rue de l'Oratoire. The first two floors are rusticated in the Italian Renaissance manner and there is a very fine two-arched window on the third floor, below which runs the line of corbels for a missing balcony. You could be in Lucca or Florence.

As you continue along the Rue de l'Oratoire, you reach the 14th-century **Église de l'Oratoire** with its 14th-century doorway and window, though the bright yellow ochre paintwork on the walls makes the building look much more recent. Everywhere you walk, there is evidence of great age in the buildings, with blocks of stone and fragments of arches peeking through the now flaking rendering.

Street games in Grasse.

Return to the Place Jean Jaurès and make a right down the very narrow and rather creepy Rue Répitrel to the **Rue Mougins-Roquefort** where a 14th-century double round-arched window survives. It has Italian Renaissance corbels and, like many of these buildings, was obviously originally arched on the ground floor. Further down, close to the cathedral and contemporary in date is a 13th-century house.

The **Place du Petit Puy** is the centre of the medieval town. Facing the square is the **Cathedral of Notre-Dame-du-Puy**. It has a very high nave with a ribbed vault supported by four enormous 12th-century pillars, scarred and worn, evidence of the burning of the building in 1795 when it was transformed into a forage store. View the nave from the west door looking straight down to the altar. It was altered considerably in the 13th century and remodelled in the 17th century.

The classic Italian Romanesque facade now has a double staircase by Vauban, architect of the ramparts of Antibes, in a failed attempt to give this crude and powerful building a touch of 17th-century elegance. The ground-floor side windows were restored this century; they had been previously cut into by insensitive "modern" windows at a higher level.

The high vaulted nave of the Cathedral of Notre-Dame-de-Puy.

The interior features some interesting works: a rare religious painting by Fragonard; *The Washing of the Feet* (1754), in the south transept, and three works by Rubens on the south wall of the nave: *The Crown of Thorns, the Crucifixion* and *St Helen in Exaltation of the Holy Cross,* painted in Rome in 1601. There is a triptych attributed to Louis Bréa, and some interesting reliquaries and church treasure.

Outside there is a good view of the south transept from the Place St-Martin, and through a tunnel to the Place Godeau the Bishop's Palace forms the other side of a small square. Arrow slits in the palace are aimed straight at the north doorway of the church. The Palace once had an elegant three-arched loggia in the Italian manner but this was mostly infilled in later years, leaving only the passage through from the Place Godeau. The group of buildings is completed by a good tall 12th-century square tower in red tufa.

To the east of the Bishop's Palace, on the Place du 24 Août, is a solitary clock tower, the remains of the 13th-century consulate (law courts).

Rue J. Ossola has another former townhouse of the Villeneuve family, with parts dating to the 14th century, below which is a 14th-century passage leading to the ramparts, and on the Rue Mirabeau are the two townhouses of the Clapiers de Cabris family, one 17th-century and the other, now the **Musée d'Art et d'Histoire de Provence**, built in 1771. The museum has a good collection of regional crafts including ironwork, ceramics and furniture, and a library of Provençal documents.

Gorge du Loup: The area around Grasse is traditionally dependent on the flower industry, and a good way to take in a number of interesting villages is to follow the Gorge du Loup north. At **Le Bar**, a pair of cannon, captured by

Amiral François de Grasse from the British, stand either side of the door to l'Amiral restaurant on the Place F. Pault. De Grasse (1722–88) was born in the 16th-century castle of Le Bar and played an important role in the Battle of Yorktown, the final battle in the American War of Independence, after which Rue Yorktown is named. Le Bar is a centre for walking and itineraries are available in English from the Syndicat d'Initiatif located in the strange *donjon* in the middle of the village. The Gothic church has been extensively remodelled but has fine door panels by Jacotin Bellot, who carved the choir stalls in Grasse. There is an extraordinary 15th-century painting of *La Danse Macabre* (The Dance of Death) in the nave.

Pont de Loup, at the south end of the Gorge du Loup, is like an Alpine village with palm trees. The village is framed by mountains on either side with spectacular views, making it a good place for walking tours. It is dominated by the remains of a railway viaduct, blown up by the Germans in 1944 and never repaired; great ruined monoliths rise hundreds of feet over the houses and trees.

Gourdon, one of the most dramatic *villages perchés* of them all, is still relatively inaccessible, though the new road to it is an easy ride in comparison with the steep mountain track the peasant with his mule used in centuries past. The approach gives a stunning view of the village with its sheer drop of several thousand feet below the castle walls.

Today only the castle's living quarters have survived and where the tower once was, is now laid out a formal French garden, providing an almost surreal contrast between the neatly trimmed low hedges and topiary and the wild backdrop of the surrounding mountains. The castle has a museum containing some very interesting (and valuable) armour: suits of plate armour, chain mail, broad swords, rifles and various types of ordnance. All of the rooms have huge fireplaces, even the private chapel, certainly necessary because Gourdon is a cold and rugged place for much of the year. On the upper floor is a large and

The perched village of Gourdon.

exceptionally good collection of naive painting, including a Henri Rousseau portrait with an excellent Proustian moustache.

The Gorge du Loup itself is glorious and terrifying by turns, tunnelling through the rock, past magnificent waterfalls and over bridges from which you can peer down to the river rushing far below. The footpaths along the gorge are very well maintained with steps cut in the steeper parts.

Beyond are the Clues (gorges) de Haute Provence, a barren remoter region which comes into its own in the winter skiing season. **Gréolières** to the west is on an alpine slope, remote and quiet, the hillsides dotted with violets and spring flowers. Eleven miles (18 km) beyond is **Gréolières-le-Neige**, the nearest ski resort to the Mediterranean. Turning east you will come to **Coursegoules**, a pretty town of muted terracotta stone nestling protectively against the bare rock of the mountain side, surrounded by sheep pastures and tinkling bells. Surprisingly it is not tumbledown and deserted as you might expect; indeed, there is a considerable amount of new building – basic apartments, not tourist villas – and a lively school housed in a beautifully-restored old building. Remote as it may seem, Coursegoules is only 10 miles (16 km) from Vence and the excellence of the roads means local people can commute to the coast. The next village is **Bézaudun-les-Alpes** which has a fabulous view of the Montagne du Chiers and is equally well-maintained and prosperous.

Beyond Bézaudun, the road becomes more exciting; the rusting hulks of cars halfway down the mountainside and skidmarks burned into the road at every blind turning add a frisson to an already discomfiting mountain drive. Here the D8 meets the D1 which leads back to the coast. An alternative route from Grasse follows the D2210 to **Tourette-sur-Loup**, clinging to the rock between two deep ravines. To the west of the village are great expanses of sheer rock, and at the cliff edge are troglodyte houses carved from the living rock. Today

Tourette-sur-Loup.

Tourette is an important centre for violet production, supplying Grasse perfumeries and the factories manufacturing candied violets in Toulouse.

The village is in an ideal defensive position, and began life occupied by Ligurian tribes. In 262 BC, the Romans established an observation post there: "Turres Altae", which became corrupted to "Tourette".

The Romans left in AD 476, after which the village suffered the same series of invasions and massacres that befell its neighbours. The Saracens were responsible for fortifying the site. In 1387, Tourette came into the hands of the Villeneuve family, where it remained until the French Revolution when the Villeneuves fled, never to return. The Black Death, the Wars of Religion and the Revolution all took their toll and by 1944 the population had shrunk to 850. Today the revitalisation of the area has resulted in a population of over 3,000.

The old village is quite amazingly crooked, with no two windows alike or a straight line anywhere, and the twisting streets feel completely enclosed until a cool, dim little alley unexpectedly emerges on to a windblown mountain panorama. The horse-shoe-shaped Grand Rue is lined with art galleries and craft shops but is not over-commercialised, and there are medieval shops, now private houses, and numerous interesting doorways still visible.

In the centre of the village a very formal Hôtel de Ville looks rather out of place. It incorporates an 11th-century watchtower, and has a pleasant courtyard with a tinkling fountain. The 11th-century church has been rebuilt on and off from the mid-16th until the 18th century and has a simple stylised Virgin and Child over the front door. To the north of the village is the chapel of St John with recent naive wall paintings.

A little further along the D2210 is **Notre-Dame-des-Fleurs**, a perfume museum and restaurant, "Château des Aromes", offering a delightful way to appreciate the pleasures of perfume. The 19th-century **château** was built by a Grasse perfumer on the remains of an 11th-century Benedictine monastery, and behind the facade on the ground floor are the monks' cells and private chapels, all beautifully restored. The large chapel has a high vaulted ceiling, a 16th-century Provençal font, and stunning modern stained-glass windows high in the walls. Through the massive oak-studded door at the back is a recently discovered sarcophagus with the skeletons of 9th-century monks. The small chapel is a charming odd little niche with an 11th-century stone virgin and vestigial Romanesque columns.

The restaurant in the magnificent old chapter house, hung with tapestries and huge iron candlebra, specialises in perfumed dishes. The museum exhibits include a history of perfume, and a collection of copper vats, presses and bottles. Most beguiling of all is the garden, a terrace with a great variety of aromatic plants and herbs, gloriously fragrant in the sun, overlooking cool fountains, orange trees, figs and roses, and an impressive park full of modern sculptures. The coastline of Cap Ferrat is visible beyond.

The deep ravine of the Gorge du Loup.

CAGNES, VENCE AND THE VAR VALLEY

The coastline between Antibes and Nice is perhaps the most exploited on the Riviera, although the beaches themselves are often unappealingly pebbly. Inland the property development from Cagnes to Vence is almost equally unbridled, and St-Paul-de-Vence is claimed to be the most visited village in France after Mont St-Michel.

Popularity should not dissuade anyone from visiting this area, however – it is entirely justified. Both St-Paul and Vence are of enormous historical interest and the area has long been a thriving artistic centre; St-Paul, for example, is home to the Fondation Maeght, one of the world's great art museums.

Try and avoid visiting at peak times, but otherwise grit your teeth and anticipate the pleasures to be had once you have found a parking space. And only a few more miles inland to St-Jeannet and the Var Valley, the roads are much quieter, and you can find yourself in relatively sleepy Provençal villages which seem light-years away from the coastal cacophony.

Still on the coast, the N7 highway closely resembles a Hollywood-style strip of neon lights, hoardings, gas stations and huge drive-in supermarkets (well worth checking out, nonetheless, by anyone with serious shopping to do). The view is dominated from all directions by the **Marina-Baie des Anges**, at **Villeneuve-Loubet Plage**, a much reviled piece of modern architecture, built in the 1970s.

Actually it is by no means out of place, its curving terraces echoing the sea waves and the mountains behind. Easiest access to the marina, sardine-packed with hundreds of magnificent yachts, is from the N98 coast road. Next to it is the Hippodrome race-track, and on the other side is Marineland, a big marine zoo with dolphins, sea-lions and whales to be seen.

The original medieval village of **Villeneuve-Loubet** is just off the N7, east of the river Loup. Surprisingly it still has an authentic feel to its steep narrow lanes and lived-in ancient buildings which resist gentrification with layers of cement and pebbledash. They huddle at the foot of the château, restored in the19th century and now private property. The path round the château walls gives a good view out to the Baie des Anges.

There are two museums. The **Musée Militaire** specialises in the two world wars, as well as the colonial wars in French Indo-China (Vietnam) and Algeria. Particularly recommended is the **Fondation Auguste Escoffier** (Museum of Culinary Art), housed in the great chef's birthplace, a few steps up the hill from the main square. Exhibits include an old Provençal kitchen; gleaming copperware and kitchen utensils; Escoffier's own inventions, like his device for making breadcrumbs; a roomful of mouthwateringly beautiful old menus; some wildly imaginative examples of sugarwork, including a haywain and a model of a Loire château; Escoffier's

Preceding pages: La Colombe d'Or, St-Paul-de-Vence. **Left**, market in Vence. **Right**, Grimaldi Château, Haut-de-Cagnes.

own hand-written recipe book and, touchingly, the master's last *toque*. There is also an excellent selection of old photographs, including a number of Dame Nelly Melba, for whom Escoffier invented the Peach Melba while he was chef at the London Carlton Hotel. And there are a couple of gratifyingly good pâtisseries in the square below.

Surrounded by a tangle of freeway intersections is **Cagnes-sur-Mer**, which divides into three very distinct parts: the modern seaside resort of Cros-de-Cagnes, the modern town of Cagnes-sur-Mer with its shops, supermarket, public park and a good covered market (mornings only), nestling at the foot of the hill, and the celebrated old town of **Haut-de-Cagnes**, crowned by its 14th-century château.

The history of the town begins with the monks of Lérins, who founded an abbey at Saint-Véran in the 5th century, now the site of the Hippodrome. By the 14th century Cagnes became a Grimaldi possession and subject to the constant turmoil of the Middle Ages. It has always depended on agriculture for its economic survival, notably olives, vines and flowers. By the 19th century Mentonnais fishermen had settled on the coast, and the town thus developed between coast and castle. Today it is an important artistic centre, a popular tourist destination, and particularly noted for its flower production. Every spring the Exposition Internationale de Fleur takes over the town, château and the Hippodrome.

The world's first fully computerised car-park marks the entry to the old town; a typical Côte d'Azur conjunction of modern technology and ancient history. Nearby is one of the oldest buildings, the **Chapelle Notre-Dame-de-la-Protection**, a bijou 14th-century structure erected as protection against plague and pestilence and containing some beautiful 1530 frescoes. There is a large open-sided porch with a wide view south over Cagnes-sur-Mer to the Mediterranean and Nice airport. A narrow, hidden path curves round the outside of the apse and down the hillside.

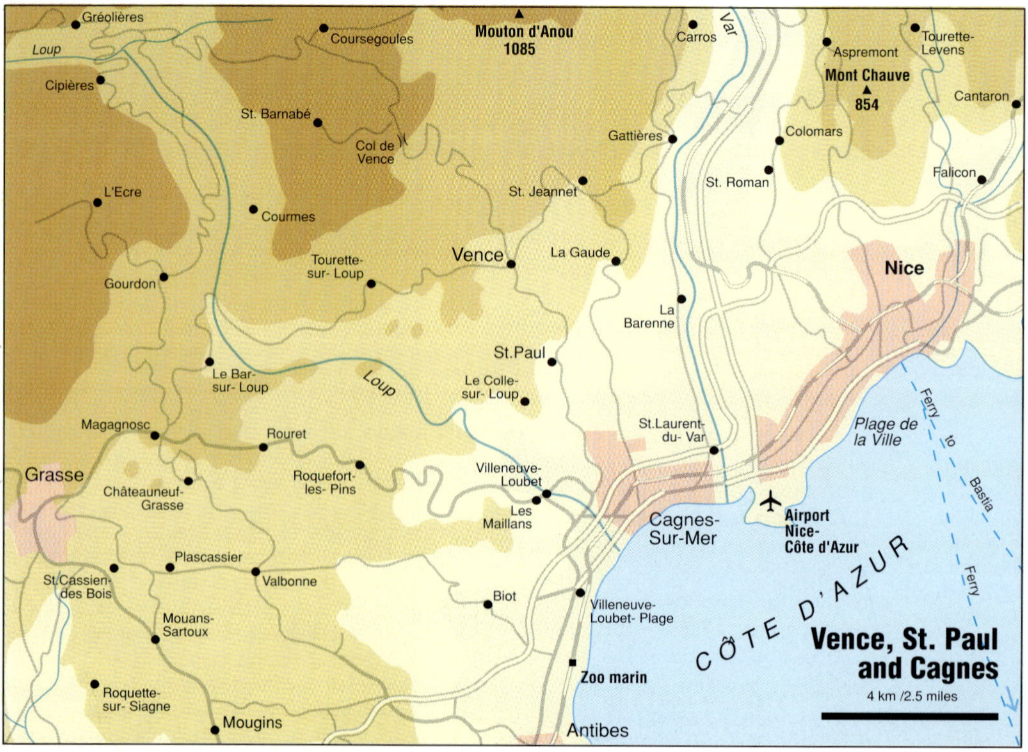

If all you see of Haut-de-Cagnes is the château and main square it would be easy to dismiss it as irredeemably touristy, but in fact, like so many of these over-visited villages, most of the populace continue their lives as they have always done. The steep, winding streets and tiny squares are as carefully tended as their own living-rooms, decorated with terracotta pots of flowering jasmine and geraniums. Fig trees and wisteria overhang tantalisingly from roof gardens and the traditional garden *potagers* serried beneath the ramparts are still zealously cultivated.

The restaurant row of Haut-de-Cagnes is Montée de la Bourgade. Steps to the left lead to the Rue du Portis Long, a lane following the inside of the ramparts through a continuous barrel vault past the ground floors and basements of the buildings – pleasantly cool and medieval in the heat of summer. You can also follow the outside of the ramparts by leaving through one of the many medieval gateways. Cagnes has many 15th- and 16th-century houses and there are some Renaissance houses with arcades near the castle.

L'Église St-Pierre is worth a visit to see the Grimaldi tombs and Gothic nave. Place de l'Église features a number of jettied, or overhanging buildings, most unusual for this area. There are squares on either side of the **Grimaldi Château**; the Place du Château is filled with cafés and nightclubs, and to the north looks out over distant and frequently snow-covered mountains. A medieval archway will take you through to the Place Grimaldi and the entrance to the **Musée Grimaldi**.

Within is an unexpectedly cool and pleasant open courtyard shaded by tall trees, with flags flapping three floors above; fortified outside walls meant this was the only source of light and air. The Musée Grimaldi is the very best sort of provincial museum: local history and artefacts, bad local paintings housed in wonderful rooms and, amidst the clutter, one or two absolute gems. A detailed history of the olive and its importance to the region includes a collection

The curving terraces of Marina-Baie des Anges.

of old olive presses and implements. There is an excellent fireplace, an old well, a magnificent ceiling, and red brick floors polished to a glassy patina by centuries of feet.

You can ignore all the paintings except for those in the Suzy Solidor collection. In the 1930s singer Suzy Solidor had a famous nightclub, the Vie Parisienne, in Paris. She was a modern young woman with bobbed hair who moved in artistic circles and had the brilliant idea of having her many artistic friends paint her. In the end, she had 224 portraits of which 47 are on display here. It is fascinating to see so many artists approaching the same subject: an excellent Van Dongen of Suzy in a sailor suit; Foujita's gold-leaf panels surrounding an oriental-looking Suzy with adoring dog; a colour wash Marie Laurencin; a Lydis treating her as a Vargas pin-up; a naïf Kisling; an odd, rapidly executed Francis Picabia; drawings by Raoul Dufy and Jean Cocteau; and the jewel of the collection, a Tamara de Lempicka nude of her with a Cubist cityscape background. The Lempicka alone is worth the admission charge. On the top floor is the **Musée d'Art Moderne Méditerranéen**, dedicated to artists who have worked on the Côte d'Azur.

The building itself, a solid square keep built as a prison in about 1300, has been disgracefully treated and takes some sorting out architecturally. It has been described as the finest specimen of a medieval stronghold in this part of France but at some point large modern windows have been cut through its great walls, some even cutting away the machicolations which are the castle's finest feature.

The main hall has a 17th-century ceiling by Carlone representing the fall of Phaeton, but this has been heavily restored. This is because in 1815 the castle was occupied by Piedmontese soldiers who, lolling on divans, amused themselves by successfully firing at the head of Phaeton.

In the 1920s, Cagnes became a popular bohemian haunt for artists, and was the setting for Cyril Connolly's only

Roof-top technology, Cagnes today.

novel, *The Rock Pool*, in which the town becomes Trou-sur-Mer. He describes the louche doings of "the doomed tribe" of failed artists, "the mysterious jungle atmosphere... intense nocturnal life... where the hopelessness of the struggle was admitted with fatalism, yet where all fought on."

A rather more celebrated local artist is Auguste Renoir, and his house in the suburb of **Les Collettes** is a wonderful place to visit. It is surrounded by a magnificent olive grove: five and half acres of 300-year-old olive trees, spread out across the hillside with superb views of the old village of Haut-de-Cagnes, the Mediterranean and Cap d'Antibes – a view which has, of course, changed dramatically since Renoir's day. There is no admission charge to the grounds which provide a welcome haven of shade on a hot summer's day. The house itself is now the Renoir Museum; Renoir spent the last 12 years of his life there and the building still feels like a private home. Nine of the rooms are open, including his two studios, still filled with memorabilia: his easel, his wheelchair. In the small studio is his palette, a square of white ceramic, wiped clean after use, so that he could see the pure colour as it would look on a white canvas. Not for Renoir the heavily encrusted kidney-shaped wooden palette of the stereotype artist. Even the bathroom is on view, with a wonderful tub and, low on the wall next to the bidet, a small ceramic tile of a nude, probably by his son Claude.

There are 10 original paintings by Renoir in the museum, including a large sketch for *Les Grandes Baigneuses* in which he roughs in the form with cross-hatch pencil work over the paint. There are also drawings, busts and other work. They are interspersed with reproductions, often quite crude ones, which give the museum a homely feel.

On the way between Cagnes and Vence is the small but perfectly fortified town of **St-Paul-de-Vence,** now one of the region's main tourist spots, besieged today by coach parties which invade its tiny streets and buy St-Paul embossed T-shirts and Provençal lav-

***Terrasse à Cagnes*, as Renoir saw it in 1905.**

ender bags. If you drive straight to Vence in the high season you will have ample opportunity to examine St-Paul's fortifications from the traffic jam which extends all the way down the D36.

Parking is always a problem here so expect to leave your car outside the town if you drive at all; the Café de la Place just outside the main (north) gate is a good place to stop for coffee and watch a *boules* game.

The circle of ramparts, built in 1536, remains unbroken. A walk round them gives a good view of the surrounding countryside studded with dark cypresses and azure swimming-pools, as well as a better sense of life in St-Paul than a walk down the Grand Rue provides; glimpses of bougainvillaea-filled gardens and treasured terraces hint at an insider's life beyond the stout wooden doors visible from the street.

A cannon captured at the Battle of Cérisoles in 1544 defends the north gate, la Porte Royale, where a machicolated 13th-century tower houses the tourist centre. The gate opens straight on to the Grand Rue, a narrow crooked street which runs the full length of the village passing Place de la Grande-Fontaine with its pretty urn-shaped fountain. Many of the the 16th- and 17th-century houses bear coats of arms and are now "artists'" ateliers. Some of the medieval shops survive, usually as private homes; look out for a wide arch, beneath which is a doorway and an adjoining window. The window has a large marble sill which used to be the shop counter, a direct descendant from the Roman shop.

The church (La Collégiale de la Conversion de Saint Paul) was begun in the 12th century and has an 18th-century bell tower. Among its treasures is a painting attributed to Tintoretto of Ste Catherine of Alexandria, at the end of the north aisle. Also displayed is a 13th-century enamel virgin and child and the shoulder blade of St George enclosed in a curious silver reliquary (visible upon payment of 1 franc).

Across from the church is the donjon, a tower which completes a pleasing group of buildings; it now contains a

La Colombe d'Or restaurant, St-Paul-de-Vence.

museum of local history in tableaux of wax figures – more endearing than it sounds. Much more interesting, however, is an exhibition of photographs of celebrities taken in St-Paul: Garbo, Mitchner, Brynner, Loren, Lancaster, Cocteau, Sartre and de Beauvoir, Baldwin and Belafonte all on vacation. Many are caught off guard, Catherine Deneuve in a girlish Provençal dress, Gene Wilder and Gilda Radnor getting married, Minister of Culture Jack Lang in designer suit. The rich and famous really do come to St-Paul, most often to eat at the still celebrated **La Colombe d'Or** restaurant.

In the 19th century, the village of St-Paul declined and it was not until the 1920s that it was "discovered" by a group of artists which included Bonnard, Modigliani, Soutine, Signac and others who used to gather in a café which has now become La Colombe d'Or; they paid for meals and rooms with paintings and sculptures and the Roux family proprietors assembled an enviable and now priceless collection of art. The dining-room walls are adorned with works by Picasso, Braque, Miró and Matisse, the garden wall features a huge brilliantly-coloured Léger mosaic, there is a Calder mobile and a Braque mosaic dove by the cypress-sheltered green swimming-pool and works by Dufy, Chagall, César and more at every turn. The hotel itself is charming, cosy even, a feast of warm terracotta, bright ceramic tiles, painted wooden ceilings and burnished wood. Dining outside on the terrace is one of the pleasures of Provence; sampling the 15 famous hors d'oeuvres and the Grand Marnier soufflé an essential – if expensive – experience.

There are further riches close by; within easy walking distance of the village, on La Gardette Hill, is the **Fondation Maeght**, a world-class museum of modern art, with a sculpture garden full of works by Miró, Giacometti, Calder and many others.

A short drive up the D2 is **Vence**, a delightfully civilised town, perched high on a rock promontory, surrounded by rose farms and orange groves which are

St-Paul-de-Vence, small but perfectly fortified.

THE FONDATION MAEGHT

Visiting the Fondation Maeght outside St-Paul-de-Vence is a bit like finding London's Tate Gallery set in steep pine woods. It is a world-class museum of modern art, housing not only exhibition galleries but a library, residences and artists' workshops, as well as an entrancing sculpture garden. The foundation itself has an ever changing exhibition, but the permanent collection is very strong in Miró, Braque and Giacometti, and examples of their work are always on display. Giacometti's attenuated club-footed bronze figures stride across the central sculpture court and are the most photographed pieces in the collection. There is art everywhere; even the door handles were designed by Miró.

Behind the gallery is the Joan Miró labyrinth: a series of connecting spaces designed by Catalan architect Josep Luis Sert, who also built the main galleries. Each of the big humorous sculptures has its own special setting, in water or silhouetted against the sky. Miró made the ceramics at the foundation workshop and the large concrete pieces were built *in situ*.

Outdoor sculpture at the Fondation.

Children adore the Pol Bury, which is easily missed, tucked in a little space between the café and the chapel. The chapel itself was also built by Sert; it contains Georges Braque's beautiful *White Bird on a Mauve Background* (1962), a delicate stained-glass panel set high above the altar. Below it is a large 15th-century Spanish Christ strongly carved from an ochre wood which contrasts well with the Braque panel. There is a Léger ceramic on the outside wall.

The tiny chapel building was actually the first building on the site, erected in memory of the child of the founders of the museum, Aimé and Marguerite Maeght. Aimé came from Nîmes, where he had shown some aptitude for engraving, and he met Marguerite in Cannes. They married and set up in business together with an electrical goods shop which was very successful. Marguerite indeed had such an instinct for business that she once said of herself, "If I were cast up naked on a desert island, I'd make money."

During World War II many Jews fled to the relative safety of the South of France, bringing with them art works to sell. The Maeghts seized the opportunity and replaced the electrical appliances with paintings. The supply of work was increased when Pierre Bonnard, who lived in Le Cannet, noticed Aimé's engravings and asked for his assistance. Because Marguerite's father ran a grocery business, they were able to make judicious swaps of scarce wartime provisions for art works. Bonnard then introduced his new friends to Henri Matisse in Vence, another artist in need of groceries.

Within 10 years the Maeghts, famous for their wheeling and dealing, had risen to extraordinary prominence in the art world. Their Paris gallery represented, amongst others, Matisse, Miró, Giacometti, Kandinsky, Braque, Chagall and Calder.

Following the tragic early death of their child, the Maeghts decided to build a chapel in his memory, which evolved into the foundation. Maeght was an art dealer who did something no art dealer had ever done before: he created a museum in his own name, paid for entirely by himself and filled with art from his own extensive stock.

At the inauguration in 1964, André Malraux, the Minister of Cultural Affairs, said: "Here something has been attempted which has never been attempted before: to create, instinctively and lovingly, the universe in which modern art might find both its place and the other world once called supernatural." ■

sheltered by the mountains to the north. Its gentle climate has made it popular, especially with invalids – D. H. Lawrence died here in 1930 – and has resulted in property development scarring the surrounding hillsides.

Such popularity has its advantages; today Vence provides excellent food shopping for fresh fish, vegetables and pâtisserie, as well as a market twice a week, and it is always pleasant to stroll round its leafy squares and ancient streets. It has a chequered history. It was occupied by the Phoenicians and the Gauls, savaged and ruined by the Saracens and the Lombards before the Romans named it Ventium and made it an important religious centre. Vence converted to Christianity early, a change usually attributed to St Trophime. The first Bishopric was founded in Vence in AD 374 and the town quickly grew to become an important regional centre. Bishops remained until the outbreak of the French Revolution when Bishop Pisani fled the country; the see was never restored.

Below, Place du Peyra, Vence. Right, Chagall mosaic in Vence's Old Cathedral.

Much of the history of Vence has been the conflict between the power of the bishops and that of the Villeneuves, because the lords of Villeneuve-Loubet shared seignorial rights over the town with the church. Vence won a great victory in the Wars of Religion against the Huguenots, but it suffered horribly from the Black Death in 1572.

Vence drifted into steady decline so that by the beginning of the 20th century it was half-deserted with many houses in ruins and a population of a mere few thousand, mostly in the new parts of town. Tourism and sun-belt industries have transformed it into a bustling centre of more than 15,000 people.

Before you reach the old town, you pass through the Place du Grand-Jardin, and Place du Frêne with its huge ash tree planted in 1538. The medieval centre of Vence is very picturesque and once you get away from the souvenir sellers, the lanes and alleyways are little changed from previous centuries – except that many of the lanes in the northeast side of the old town now have light and air

where they end at the town ramparts; the walls have been cut down to waist height so that now there is a mountain view instead of a prison-like wall.

The ramparts were built in the 13th and 14th centuries and used to have a broad walk running along the top. In the northern section, this promenade still exists where it has become Boulevard Paul André. The south section of the ramparts has been repeatedly pierced to make shops along Avenue Marcellin Maurel. Vence has retained its town gates: the 13th-century Signadour Gate incorporated into a defensive tower; the round arched Porte d'Orient pierced through in the 18th century (the date of 1592 refers to a battle during the Wars of Religion); the 14th-century Portail Levis which once possessed a portcullis and opens on to Rue de la Coste, one of the oldest lanes in the town; Le Pontis, built in 1863 by literally driving through the medieval houses. Most impressive of all is the Portail du Peyra built by Good King René who died in 1480. It is much restored and in the 17th century an imposing square tower was added to its side.

Portail du Peyra, one of the ancient gateways of Vence.

The entrance through Portail du Peyra leads past a small fountain to the Place du Peyra which has a grand and ancient chestnut tree shading the cafés. Place Godeau, named after the famous poet Bishop, is outside the cathedral and was once the cemetery. Today it is a pleasant place to stop for a drink. There is a granite Roman column in the centre of the square and some fine old houses: a 13th-century house with a two-arch Romanesque window, and another dated 1524. Many of the windows and doors in Vence have suffered from modernisation though some old iron-nail studded doors and a few medieval shop fronts have survived.

The 15th-century watchtower rises next to the church, which is entered from Place Clemenceau, the old Roman forum, where there is a flea market held every Wednesday. The cathedral has plenty of interest to see even though its outline is virtually hidden by later buildings. Buried in its outside walls on the Passage Cahours are reused Roman stones bearing inscriptions, mostly of a commemorative nature, one to the goddess Cybele and the ceremony of the Taurobolium, in which a bull was sacrificed to the gods, and another to Lucius Veludius Valerianus, decurian of Vence and his wife Vibia.

The church is 10th-century, though what you see was built between the 12th and 15th centuries. It was the site of the Temple of Mars in Roman times but the first Christian building was the Merovingian church of the 5th century. The first Bishop of Vence, St Eusebius, was in office in the year 374 and he must have adapted the Roman temple for Christian worship. It is a building of great antiquity.

It consists of a nave with four aisles. The roof is carried on immense square pillars, lacking in ornament. The two side aisles were roofed over in the 15th century by a wide gallery which looks down into the nave through a row of arches, built to accommodate an enlarged congregation. Either side are two more aisles, which contain the chapels:

one, which is said to contain the body of St Veran who died in 492, uses a carved Roman sarcophagus as both tomb and altar. Other Roman figures can be found in the walls, one in the pillar before the chapel of St Veran.

In 1499, at the same time as the roofing of the aisles, a tribune was added at the west end, housing the choir on a gallery high above the door. This contains the 51 famous wooden choir stalls imaginatively carved by Jacotin Bellot of Grasse who began work on them in 1455 and finished them 25 years later. He carved animals and plants and recorded the everyday life of the people and clergy, sometimes not at all reverently. The church also has a wonderfully carved wooden door taken from the destroyed prévôté or chapter house. It is from an earlier date than Bellot's work but may be by the same master who carved the lectern housed in the choir. In the baptistry there is a mosaic design by Marc Chagall of Moses in the bulrushes.

Throughout the church there are exquisite examples of Carolingian carving incorporated in the wall and columns, taken from the previous church. Outside the city walls is the **Château de Villeneuve**, which has been renovated as an exhibition space for modern art.

The other church of interest in Vence is quite different: **the Rosaire,** designed by Henri Matisse between 1947 and 1951. The architecture now clearly shows its origin in the 1950s, indicating perhaps that Matisse was more at home with the fine arts, though its most original element, the chapel's ultramarine and white tile roof still looks superb. The yellow-and-blue stained glass, based on a leaf motif, works very well with the simple wall decorations chosen by Matisse: instead of frescoes he painted his designs for the walls on uniform white tiles, specially made for the building. Unfortunately quite a few on his Stations of the Cross wall cracked when the building settled.

The drawing itself is confident and strong, remarkably so considering Matisse's advanced age and terrible ar-

One of Vence's tree-shaded squares.

thritis during its creation. Many of the original drawings for the project are on display and well worth examination. Of the greatest interest are the details: the candlesticks on the altar and the confessional door – an assemblage of wooden shapes painted white echoing the traditional perforated doors in medieval churches. The road was renamed Blvd Henri Matisse in his honour.

From Vence the road climbs to **St-Jeannet**, towered over by the great **Baou de St-Jeannet** like a huge headland (*baou* is the Provençal for rock). In fact it is an ancient coral crag that did once look down upon the Mediterranean, many aeons ago. It has inspired many painters, among them Poussin, Fragonard, Renoir and Chagall. The village of St-Jeannet nestles on a terrace at the foot of the Baou. In some lights the village looks no more than a natural outcrop of the rock; at other times the rock itself looks like a craggy château.

At one time St-Jeannet was famous for its grapes and wine but today production is concentrated on flowers. However, locally-produced wines and jams are sometimes available for sale in the village – and if the shop is shut you may find them left outside with a little box for payment.

St-Jeannet is a town of quiet courtyards, arched doorways and sloping lanes of stone steps. On a pleasant square with a four spout fountain, is the Chapelle St-Bernadin, built in 1666 and lit by only three recent stained-glass windows. Behind the church is a wonderful panorama from a small platform partly covered by an old archway with thick beams. It is amazing to see how the narrow terraces below accommodate carefully tended *potagers*, parked cars and even swimming pools,

St-Jeannet has a number of good restaurants making it a good place to stop for lunch – before or probably after, a climb. There is a path to the top of Baou St-Jeannet which starts from the Auberge St-Jeannet and takes about an hour each way. There is a spectacular view of the French and Italian Alps from the viewing platform at the top.

The craggy outcrop of Baou de St-Jeannet.

Gattières, further along the D2210, is a working perched village with steep streets filled with washing lines and barking dogs. The ancient buildings are there but covered in pebbledash or rendering, making it an interesting contrast to many other self-consciously picturesque villages with virtually identical housing stock.

South of St-Jeannet, on the D18, is **La Gaude**, a small lively village built high above the River Cagne; it is the nearest village to the massive IBM Research and Study Centre on the D118 to St-Laurent. When Breuer's IBM centre was built it was highly praised for harmonising with the landscape – as well as two giant Y-shaped blocks supported by concrete pillars can. Now the area has become heavily built up and the IBM architecture no longer looks so modern or interesting.

Le Broc is another classic perched village, this time high on a rock overlooking the River Var. The view is extraordinary because the scale of human intervention on the landscape comes as a shock; the Var has been straightened out like a canal in a gigantic feat of engineering, taming it and binding it with freeways and industrial zones on either side.

Nearby is **Carros**, perched on a rock, commanding a bend in the river. A new town has been built down on the flood plane called **Carros-le-Neuf** which is also worth a visit. The city centre is familiar enough, with high-rise flats and shopping malls, but the scale is miniature and the streets curve and wind. Part of the residential area hugs a ridge like a hill town and the houses imitate a higgledy-piggledy medieval hill town with funny dead end lanes and squares making parking almost as difficult as in the medieval originals.

Returning to the coast, take the D118 to St-Laurent-du-Var, the higher of the two corniche roads following the Var. There are spectacular views over the Var Valley and and a chance to see the phenomenal industrial development that has taken place beside the river and all the way to Nice.

Human intervention on the landscape: the view of the Var valley from Le Broc.

NICE

Rain or shine (and there is much of the latter), the man up the ladder on the seafront at Nice has been standing immobile on the top rung for years now. Precariously poised, with an artist's palette in his left hand and a brush in his right, he is attempting to paint a palm tree while feathery shadows of a real one creep across his canvas.

You may think this odd – even more so when you realise the artist's work will never be completed. For the twist is he himself is the focal point of a painting within a painting, an artistic joke which never fails to cause merriment among Nice's visitors.

Whoever painted the man up the ladder has done more than transform the outside wall of an Indian restaurant from a banal stretch of white plaster into a witty set-piece tableau of life along the Baie des Anges. Nothing better serves to symbolise the *savoir vivre* of the Niçois, their very un-French ability to laugh at themselves and their delight in taking the visitor by surprise.

Welcome, then, to a carnival town where not everything that meets the eye is as it seems, from painted pigeons that are surely the only ones in the world not to leave droppings, to *trompe l'oeil* doorways and windows that don't need oiling or cleaning.

Un-French? Certainly. Nice has officially been part of the French Republic only since 1860; before then it was part of Italy. Local jokers, however, like to dispute even this, saying that for 62 years up to 1990 Nice was the personal fief of the Médecin men – first Jean, then his son Jacques – both of whom ruled as mayor and left indelible marks.

Jacques was a man up a ladder if ever there was one, and no mean political artist either. When he tumbled and fled in 1990 his downfall closed just another chapter in the city's see-saw history of changing management which began in 350 BC with the Greeks, who named it after the goddess, Nikea ("she who brings victory"), and variously saw in power Romans, counts of Provence, dukes of Savoy and kings of Sardinia. As a tug-of-love baby, the "Maid of Provence" certainly had a turbulent upbringing, and was a ward of the Italian court for most of 500 years.

Today Nice is essentially French but its character and temperament remain Italian, with constant reminders that the frontier is still just 25 miles away. However, it is rightly proud of its own language, Nissard, its own surrounding "county" of the Alpes-Maritimes and its cuisine, which goes much further than just a famous salad.

It is now a unique city of western, medieval and oriental influences, a provincial metropolis that is the richest, most attractive tourist centre outside Paris. Nice is France's fifth-largest city with the second-busiest airport (after Paris), and is rapidly becoming a business and cultural centre to be reckoned with as well.

It was the British who invented the name "Riviera". They laid the foundations for its present-day capital and were

Preceding pages: Nice *trompe l'oeil*. **Left**, golden glamour. **Right**, Italianate Nice facade.

certainly in no doubt about its being the brightest jewel in the river of towns sparkling all the way from Cannes to Monte-Carlo.

A thriving English colony subsequently developed. Well-heeled British *fainéants* and aristocrats and retired army officers zealously set about turning Nice into a kind of sanitised Bournemouth, with hotels called Westminster and West End in a sector they named Newborough.

Indeed it is an English clergyman, the Rev. Lewis Way, whom we must thank for the Promenade des Anglais, which remains the main thoroughfare of the city. He was a skilled missionary with remarkable powers of persuasion who talked his flock into providing construction work for men thrown out of work by a severe frost which killed the area's orange trees in 1821.

By 1887 when poet Stephen Liégeard first named the coastline the Côte d'Azur, Nice had already expanded to the size of Cannes today, and was regularly attracting over 25,000 winter visitors, mainly by train. There were shops selling trinkets made of olive wood inscribed with the words "Nice", and "*Je reviendrai*" – forerunners of today's "Nice is Nice" T-shirts and "*J'aime la Côte d'Azur*" bumper stickers.

There was an air of prosperity, electric lighting in the streets and, naturally, guidebooks. "Nice is a home for the millionaire and the working man," one proclaimed. "The intermediate class is not wanted. Visitors are expected to have money, and if they have to look at pounds, shillings and pence had much better remain at home."

The Promenade des Anglais, the little coastal road that was then used by about 100 English families and their carriages, has today become one of the most clogged thoroughfares in France. It is an eight-lane highway, 3 miles (5 km) long, on which only the aggressive survive, and you need to be alert. Watch your window, too, if you stop at the lights in summer. Resplendent with marching palms and flowerbeds, the Prom (even the French call it that) has a concealed automatic watering system

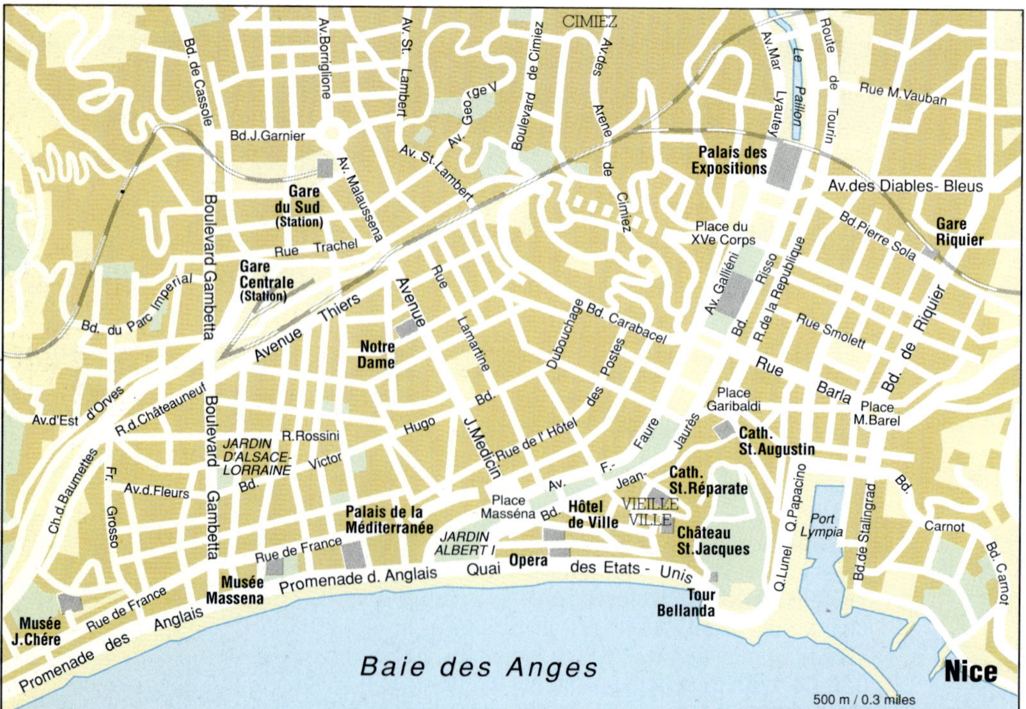

and the sprinklers are liable to turn your car into a jacuzzi if your reflexes aren't sharp enough.

Today's scene on the Promenade des Anglais is very different from its 19th-century counterparts. When Henri Negresco's palace first opened its doors in 1913 they pointed north: 150 years after Tobias Smollett introduced sea-bathing here it still had not dawned on anyone that the future of tourism lay in hotels with their resplendent fronts, not their backs, to the sea.

The famed **Negresco** remains the crown of the Promenade; it is a national monument where visiting heads of state still occupy entire floors, and the flamboyance of the exterior is only eclipsed by the jewels within. This was where Scott Fitzgerald stayed and although you won't find a Diamond as Big as the Ritz there is a crystal chandelier by Baccarat with 16,309 stones and weighing more than a tonne, designed originally for the Tsar.

There are a number of fine museums clustered around the Promenade des Anglais. These include the **International Museum of Naïf Art** in the Château Ste-Helène on the Avenue Val Marie with its collection of 600 works from 27 countries, and the **Musée des Beaux-Arts**, a *belle-époque* villa built for Russian royalty at 33 Avenue des Baumettes, mainly devoted to 19th-century painting. Here too is the **Musée Masséna** at Rue de France 65 , a mixed bag including École de Nice tableaux and regional artefacts.

Also worth noting on the Promenade itself is the active **Ruhl Casino** and the very passive former **Palais de la Méditerranée**, now undergoing much needed restoration.

The seafront: The locals' sunny disposition derives from an ability to use the **beaches** every day in summer, in the grinding halt between noon and 3pm. The 3 miles (5 km) of curving seafront may be disappointingly pebbly, but they are clean, like the sea, and run right through the heart of town. For a quick dip, there is nothing wrong with the public beaches (there are 80 free show-

The Negresco Hotel.

ers), but 15 private establishments offer excellent facilities at half the price charged down the coast at Cannes. One favourite is **Opéra Plage**, which claims to be the oldest in France, run by the same family since 1906, just a towel's shake from the old Opera House and the man up the ladder.

Where the English Prom crosses the Atlantic is known as the **Quai des États-Unis;** here is the small but delightful Dufy museum. Traffic barrelling down the Prom vanishes into a tunnel in front of the old Opera House and emerges in the port area, a long-neglected side of Nice which, with its disciplined quays lined with terracotta and ochre buildings, bobbing yachts and excellent restaurants, is the epitome of the Mediterranean harbour.

For a city whose history depends so much on the sea **Lympia** is disappointingly bereft of tourist attractions, its main attribute being the bathing rocks on its eastern edge from which you can see the Corsican ferry glide by. However, all this may rapidly change as a new jetty is planned which is expected to attract cruise ships, and a revival of fortunes is anticipated in their wake.

An overview: For the best overview of what is not really a very complicated city you should have a car and drive up to the ruined fort of **Mont Alban**, approached through 140 acres (345 hectares) of municipal forest on **Mont Boron,** a good place for picnics. It is easy to see how the city has evolved in three different parts, with the **Paillon River** in the middle. Don't bother searching for that on a map: it is only a trickle and the entire river-bed has been covered over with the new promenade, roads, parks, and hanging gardens hiding a bus terminus and car-park. Here is the new **Acropolis** convention centre decorated inside and out with the work of contemporary artists, the **Musée d'Art Moderne et Contemporain** and the **"Promenade des Arts"**. It is a masterpiece of municipal planning, and whatever they say about Jacques Médecin this city is his living monument. Look for Avenue Félix Faure and Boulevard Jean Jaurès.

Nice's beachfront.

To the west is **Place Masséna**, the modern heart of the city, with its neo-classical red colonnades. This is the new town, with shops, hotels, and an extensive pedestrian zone housing smart boutiques with all the big designer names. **Avenue Jean Médecin**, a wide thoroughfare lined with plane trees to the north of Place Masséna, is the main business and shopping street. The **Jardin Albert I** is a refreshing oasis of fountains and from here you can take a mini-train for sightseeing.

To the east of the Paillon is the old town, signposted either as **Vieille Ville** or Vieux Nice. This has to be the *pièce de résistance*: a cracked basin of russet, yellow, pink and beige earth tones. You are now entering the Painted City, where the municipality is breathing new life into the 13th century.

The renaissance seems to be working all right, though the task may seem equivalent to the cleansing of the Augean stables in this warren of pedestrian alleys. There is always a remarkable busyness about the place. For all its medieval seductions, scaffolding is a perpetual hazard and ladders and buckets of paint are being winched away with bewildering urgency in a society more at ease with the Midi spirit of *farniente*. Look up and admire facades adorned with *trompe l'oeil* and frescoes, especially at the so-called Adam and Eve house in **Rue de la Poissonnerie**; the "Pistone" building in **Rue du Marché**; No. 20, **Rue de Malouat**; No.27, **Rue Benoît Bunico**; and in **Rue Pairolière**, where the "Maison de la Treille" (the house with a climbing vine) inspired one of Raoul Dufy's pictures. The showpiece is the **Palais Lascaris** (No.15 Rue Droite), a 17th-century mansion now completely restored as an elegant museum, complete with pharmacy and a splendid open staircase in the Genoese style.

The streets become darker and narrower the further in you go, with intriguing scents and smells coming from the doorways. As you advance through the labyrinth look at the lintels, some of which are inscribed with dates and in-

Well-entrenched, the Promenade des Anglais.

cantations; INTERNA MELIORA – "Inside it's Better" – hangs over a former brothel, now a crowded used-book store on **Rue Place Vieille.**

The 18th-century **Place Garibaldi** echoes the style of Place Masséna; nearby is the church of St-Martin-St-Augustin, where Garibaldi was baptised and Luther celebrated mass.

Place St-François is the morning fish market. **Rue Miralheti** is the place to sample classic street food such as *socca*, a delicious chickpea pancake not found anywhere else in France. **Place Rossetti** across from the painted facade (1650) of the **Cathédrale Ste-Reparate**, the city's patron, is the spot for ice-cream or coffee; admire the cathedral's bell tower and beautiful roof of coloured tiles. After years of neglect, it is all coming back to life again as the city's magnificent homogenous heart.

The markets: The promenade between the old city and the sea is known as **Cours Saleya**; famous residents like Matisse, who lived at the end of the Cours in a big yellow house (No. 1: it has snarling faces of plaster lions protruding from it), and Chagall loved the city and their work fills the museums.

It was from his third-floor window in the Vieille Ville that Matisse painted those cheerful little pictures of the blue sea, the palm trees and the houses with green shutters. He surely painted the market that is still held in the Cours, 655 yards (600 metres) long, separated from sea by the **Ponchettes** on one side and from the older part of town by the palace of the Sardinian kings, now the **Préfecture**, to the north. Don't miss the famous flower market open all day, or the fruit and vegetable market which vanishes at noon. On Mondays there is a large flea market; although bargains are unlikely there is bountiful variety of antique furniture, china and linen.

Artistic heritage: Nice has made an impressive contribution to the history of art; it first produced a school of primitive painters in the 15th and 16th centuries; it was home to the Van Loos in the 17th; Rodin worked here in the 19th and it has given its name to the modern

Shopping in the Place Masséna.

École de Nice centred around Yves Klein, Arman and César. This was born in the Vieille Ville and some of the best young artists of modern France now have their ateliers on **Rue Droite**, so named not because it is straight but for the fact that it directly connected the two main gates of the old city. As long ago as 1764, Tobias Smollett observed high society taking its *passeggiatas* along the Cours; one wonders what he would have made of the new lift shafts for the underground car-park, cunningly tricked out with paintings of market stalls with striped awnings, reflecting the bustling morning scene. It is so hard to distinguish fact from fiction, disguise from decoration.

Don't go looking for the **château,** by the way; it is just a trick of the tongue to match all this *trompe l'oeil.* One has not existed since the illegitimate son of James II razed it in 1706 on the orders of Louis XIV, thus sealing the fate of a citadel that was more than 2,000 years old. In its place on the 300-ft (90-metre) high hill are gardens, playgrounds, an artificial waterfall and a couple of discreet snack-bars – all very welcome on a hot day, but it's the panoramic views that attract people.There is a lift from the end of Quai des États-Unis.

Cimiez is most easily reached from the Boulevard de Cimiez. Here the Romans built their Cemenelum to compete with rival Greek Nikaïa down the road. It is noted for its recently excavated Roman ruins, including baths and the amphitheatre which is often used for festivals; the Archaeological Museum; the Chagall Museum (Avenue Dr Ménard), specially designed to house Chagall's masterpiece, *Messages Bibliques,* and the biggest single collection of his work. Most popular is the recently restored **Musée Matisse**, a 17th-century Genoese villa which cunningly conceals a new gallery wing beneath. It houses Matisse's personal collection, with works from every period, as well as the vases, shell furniture and Moroccan wall-hangings – even the giant cheese plant, which he so often included in his paintings.

Sculpture on the roof of the new art museum.

Once-fashionable Cimiez still has intimations of empire. The crowned heads of Europe – Britain, Sweden, Denmark, Portugal, Belgium and the entire Russian Imperial Family – once wintered up here in nine "palais-hotels" modelled on the ghastly Regina Palace, opened by Queen Victoria in 1897. In the western suburbs, on boulevard du Tzarewitch, you can find evidence of a once-thriving Russian colony, the finest **Russian Orthodox Cathedral** outside Russia. Its five green-and-gold onion domes pleased Tsar Nicholas II himself. Services are held in Russian.

Nice is nice: Nice might miss its castle but not much else. Despite being top dog in the holiday league with 8 million summer visitors and a comparatively small resident population of not much more than 400,000 it hasn't allowed its character and unique ambiance to be subsumed into soul-less skyscraper blocks. The newly-expanded airport still has orange trees in its car-park. Coconut-icing villas hide among the olives and parasol pines on the hills overlooking the Baie. Tunnels of plane trees on the main streets, Boulevard Victor Hugo and Avenue Jean Médecin, lead to shaded squares and fountained gardens. Downtown, the *fin-de-siècle* glory of the buildings, all of uniform height and rococo charm, sings to you in friezes, frescoes and domed arpeggios. The city has a human scale. Nice really is nice.

It is a real gutsy town with its own gutsy wine (Bellet, whose vines were planted by the Phoenicians who founded Marseille), a commercial life based on more than just its flower industry and a cultural richness second only to Paris. It is also surprisingly efficient and clean, equipped with automatic loos with piped muzak, spotless bus shelters and public phones which actually work. There are 40 wardens employed to prevent vandalism in its 750 acres (300 hectares) of public greenery, and 280 gardeners who start work at 5am daily.

Nice also has all the Identikit street furniture common to other big conurbations of the Fifth Republic, plus bendy buses to negotiate the corners, the

Three miles of pebbly beaches.

Galeries Lafayette (a kind of French John Lewis), C & A, Habitat, and yes, even a couple of McDonald's.

And for all its Mediterranean *laissez-faire*, Nice is developing into a highly modern city: the Acropolis conference centre, in the middle of town, with a 2,500-seat auditorium – the biggest in France; the Arénas business centre opposite the airport; the expensive and carefully landscaped Haliotis sewage plant; and, on the way to the airport, the Parc Floral, the world's largest conservatory with seven different climatic zones.

There should be more to come. Other major projects include an ambitious métro system linking the northeastern edge of the city with the airport in the southwest, eventually branching inland and on to the Sophia-Antipolis science park 12 miles (19 km) away. There is plenty of action too. Its opera, concert-orchestra and international jazz festival are famous. Carnival has become a safer event now that the confetti is made of small bits of coloured paper rather than lumps of hard plaster (confetti once meant anything from small sugar-coated sweets to rotten eggs, flour, plaster, chickpeas, to egg-shells filled with soot and sand). The practice of throwing flowers became separated from the main event, and the Battle of Flowers is now an established attraction in its own right.

The Cours market in the Vieille Ville is perhaps the best place to take the pulse of Nice, a complete antidote to the pace of life on the other side of the Paillon. The performance is never-ending, though it is transformed dramatically with the firing of a mid-day gun, which is the time to discover that the pigeon you thought was painted was not. To the sound of clattering wings, the scenery changes miraculously as gangs of sweepers armed with brooms and high-pressure hoses march in and the market is cleaned up. Chairs and tables come out. Hardly a piece of ground is left unoccupied as the stage is set for a bravura performance of Niçois life. The whole place is turned into a sea of happy people absorbing the scene unfolding before them.

Cours Saleya flea market.

CAP FERRAT AND THE GOLDEN TRIANGLE

The area known as the **Corne d'Or** – Golden Horn or Golden Triangle – which includes Cap Ferrat, Beaulieu and Villefranche is very different from the Côte d'Azur to the west. The terrain changes dramatically beyond Nice, from wide bays to dramatic towering cliffs. Every view is dominated by the mountains, giving it a grandeur that would be impossible to spoil – though thankfully, apart from in Monaco, no one has really tried.

The famous corniche roads are spectacular, snaking one above the other round the mountain side. Along the cliff top, the **Grande Corniche** follows the old Roman road, the Via Aurelia, to Italy, and was built by Napoleon for military purposes. After passing through La Turbie it descends at Roquebrune and ends at Menton. The Lower Corniche road, **la Basse Corniche**, built in the 18th century, emerges from Nice at the old Port Douanges, then winds its way around the Cap de Nice, offering spectacular views across Villefranche Bay to the high ridge of Cap Ferrat.

The traffic is worse on the Basse Corniche than the higher roads, but it is well worth it for the views. The Moyenne Corniche is the most recently built of the roads. All the corniche levels are connected by roads, and there is also a railway running along the coast.

Villefranche-sur-Mer is a surprisingly unspoiled little town, given its proximity to Nice and the fact that the American 6th fleet used it as a base until the French left NATO. Villefranche was founded in the 14th century as a customs-free port by Charles II of Anjou and British and American ships still use its wonderful harbour, which is one of the deepest in the world.

The town itself is well restored but not bijou; there is plenty of authentic laundry hanging from the balconies and inquisitive matrons leaning from their windows to gossip across the narrow streets. The entire town of citadel, port and old streets has retained an homogenous, medieval character.

The huge 16th-century stone **Citadel of St-Elme** dominates the bay and looks impregnable enough to still fulfil its original function, though the deep dry moat is now used, intelligently, as a car-park. It is like an enormous quarry, with sheer walls set at an angle for greater stability and tiny watchtowers and viaducts crossing on slender pylons.

There is a bridge over the moat entrance to the citadel, marked by what used to be a drawbridge in a portal dated 1557. Now the giant iron-studded doors to the fortress have an incongruous modern letterbox. Within the walls are housed the town **Mairie**, the chapel of St-Elme, and several museums.

The Henri Goetz-Christine Baoumeester Museum is a collection of about 100 minor works by Picasso, Han Hartung, Picabia and Miró, all of which were gifts to the couple. Volti was a resident of Villefranche and the Volti Museum has a good collection of his monumental smooth figurative sculp-

Preceding pages: the bay of Villefranche from St-Jean-Cap-Ferrat. **Left**, terracotta hues of Villefranche harbour. **Right**, Villa Kerylos, Beaulieu.

tures, most of them female, some of which are displayed outside in the main courtyard of the citadel. The citadel also contains the museum of the 24th Batallion of the Alpine Light Infantry.

The old town of Villefranche nestles in the protection of the citadel, very Italian in its architecture and atmosphere; along the front of the old Port de la Santé the houses have a cheerful, faded air, each facade a different colour ranging from terracotta and ochre to rose and magnolia with the shutters painted half a dozen different shades of green. There are lots of attractive little bars and restaurants along the quay and in the alleyways leading to it. On the Quai Courbet is the tiny 14th-century **Chapelle St-Pierre**, with a candy-coloured facade and interior decorated by Jean Cocteau, who spent his childhood in Villefranche.

Many of the houses in the old town are built on the Italian model with large arched loggias on the ground floor, most of which have subsequently been filled in. The area around the church features the steepest, most winding streets and twisted houses. The church itself is 18th-century Italian baroque, with an early 14th-century origin of which little can be seen. It features many religious statues, including one of Jesus and another of Mary, both with electric halos.

The town seems to specialise in *trompe l'oeil* wall painting: usually windows, often with cats in them. There is a good window with cat on the **Place de la République**, a charming little square with a large shady pine tree in the centre and houses dating from the 17th and 18th centuries. In one instance the eye is deceived by a chapel with an entire *faux* Pisan Romanesque facade, which has what appears to be a genuine Pisan-style doorway dated 1590, right next door to the American Navy judo school on the Rue de l'Église.

The main street of the old town is the **Rue du Poilu**, which leads to the tiny Place du Conseil, from which there is a good view of the harbour and Cap Ferrat. Starting from the Place du Conseil is the celebrated 13th-century **Rue Obscure**.

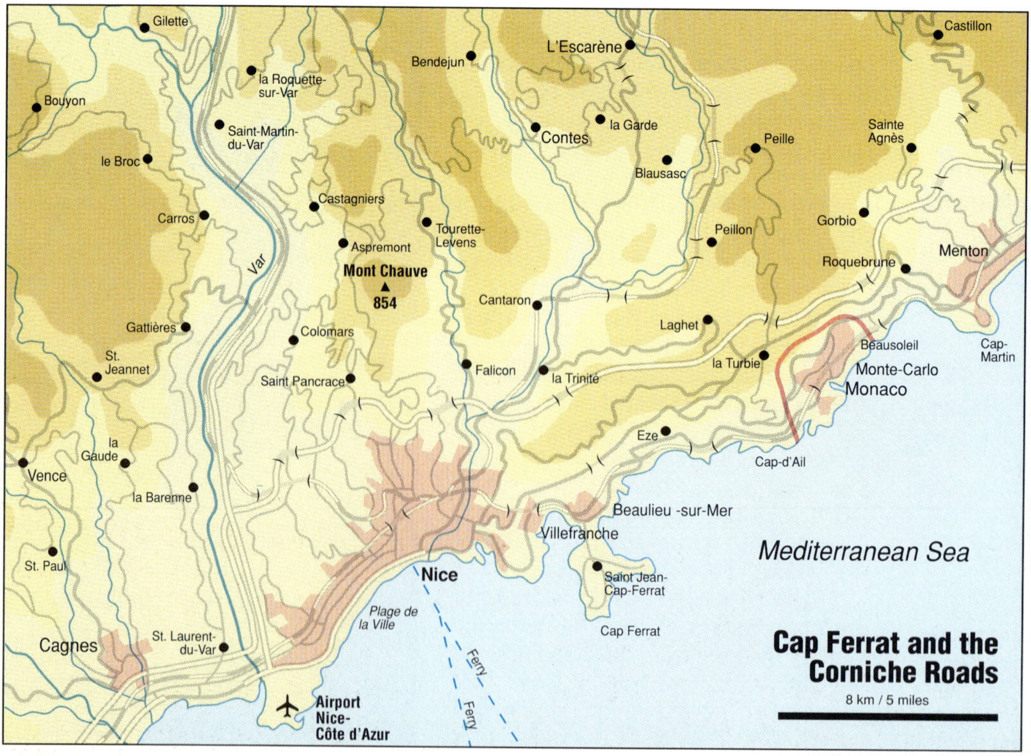

Cap Ferrat and the Corniche Roads

Steps lead down to an arched passage which has changed little since it was built; the street is almost entirely composed of covered passageways which the inhabitants could reach from back doors or intersecting streets and squares. Here the inhabitants would shelter whenever the town was bombarded, which, given its strategic position and excellent harbour, was often.

Where the Rue Obscure crosses the **Rue de l'Église** is perhaps the most picturesque spot in the town. The blue waters of the harbour glint through an arch at the end of the street.

The turning off La Petite Corniche for **Cap Ferrat** is marked, significantly, by a shop offering electronic surveillance systems and 24-hour personal security. This is a very expensive, very private place but well worth a visit, if only to see how the other 3 percent live. A 6-mile (10-km) road right round the Cap offers glimpses of luxurious villas and magnificent gardens, all secreted behind high hedges and serious gates.

The **Musée Ephrussi de Rothschild** is a good example of how they used to live. Seventeen acres (7 hectares) of gardens spread right along the crest of the Cap with wonderful panoramic views on all sides. The pink-and-white *belle-époque* villa was built to house the personal art collection of the Baroness Ephrussi de Rothschild and includes a magnificent variety of mainly 18th-century furniture, porcelain, carpets and paintings. The ceilings were specifically designed around her Tiepolos.

The grand salon leads out on to a marble terrace with views to each side of the Cap and down to the gardens. They are perfect for gentle strolling, through the cactus grove, the Japanese garden, the Italian sunken garden with grotto, even a temple of Diana; all, it must be said, looking somewhat neglected. But sitting under the deep green shade of the umbrella pines, cooled by gentle breezes, looking out to an aquamarine sea, it is easy to understand the appeal of such a perfect place. It is an appeal felt more strongly perhaps by latter-day visitors than the Baroness

Musée Ephrussi de Rothschild, St-Jean-Cap-Ferrat.

herself, who didn't get around to visiting the mansion between World War I and her death in 1934.

Cap Ferrat has the reputation of having the most pleasant climate on the Riviera and it was for this reason that Leopold II, King of Belgium, bought it. (He also bought the Congo, making Belgium one of the world's major colonial powers.) On the peninsula he created a large park, Les Cèdres, with a palace for himself and three houses, one for each of his mistresses, one of which, La Radiana, was recently up for sale for £9.5 million. With so many mistresses at hand, Leopold was concerned that he might die without absolution, so in 1906 he built a house near his palace for his confessor Monseigneur Charmeton.

It was this house, set in 8 acres (3.2 hectares) of terraced land, that Somerset Maugham bought in 1926. He called it the Villa Mauresque because Charmeton had it designed in the Moorish style. It is possible to visit the gardens of **Les Cèdres**, which has more than 15,000 rare plants set in 35 acres of woodland overlooking Villefranche Bay. There is a zoo in what used to be a lake on the estate, which is very popular for its daily chimpanzees' tea-party.

In 1938, the Duke and Duchess of Windsor arrived on the Riviera, adding even more cachet to the already exclusive Cap Ferrat scene. They rented Sir Pomeroy Burton's villa where the duke dug the garden and the duchess kept house. The Duke insisted that his guests refer to the duchess as Her Royal Highness, despite a strict edict from Buckingham Palace that she was not permitted to use such a title.

Soon the Cap was home to industrialists such as Singer, the sewing machine magnate, and show-business glitterati like Charlie Chaplin. Later residents included Edith Piaf, David Niven and Otto Preminger. More recent residents have included the Rolling Stones, who lived there as tax exiles, and Tina Turner. Despite the predominance of private estates, a great deal of the natural beauty of the peninsula, which includes some of the oldest olive trees in France, can

Interior, La Radiana, a villa built for Leopold II's mistress.

still be seen. There is a 6-mile (10-km) footpath all around the headland, most of it following the cliff edge or at sea level itself. It is clearly marked: approaching from Villefranche, it begins at Passable Beach and continues to St-Jean-Cap-Ferrat. Another promenade extends from the harbour at St-Jean-Cap-Ferrat around the Fourmis Bay to Beaulieu-sur-Mer.

The village of **St-Jean-Cap-Ferrat** consists of little more than a beautiful yacht harbour, once home to fishing boats, lined with a few old houses and cafés, with a small residential area extending up the hillside. There is a one-way system in and out of the village and parking is often difficult. On the very tip of the Cap is the exclusive and fashionable **Grand Hôtel du Cap Ferrat**, which is set in wonderful gardens at the water's edge.

Just the other side of the isthmus is **Beaulieu-sur-Mer**, a town with a slightly more refined air to it - the Cheltenham of the Côte d'Azur. Here beach clothes anywhere other than the beach are still rather frowned on, though all that is changing rapidly.

It always seems to be warm in Beaulieu, which claims to have the best climate on the coast, protected from the north wind by a great rock face. It is thus a popular retirement town, with many elegant rest homes and genteel hotels surrounded by softly waving palm trees, neatly clipped hedges and carefully weeded gardens. It is quietly stylish if a little old-fashioned, with shops offering goods of the highest quality.

It also boasts some of the best hotels on the Riviera; the Russian and British gentry spent their winters in Beaulieu, which used to be one of the most fashionable of the Riviera resorts. The elegant turn-of-the-century luxury hotels known as the Riviera Palaces, in which they stayed are still there, surrounded by beautiful, well-tended gardens.

The **Promenade Maurice Rouvier** extends along the sea front and follows the coast of Cap Ferrat all the way to St-Jean-Cap-Ferrat, past villas and hotels with beautiful gardens. In the town the

High society.

walk goes through formal flower gardens flanked by park seats looking out to Fourmis Bay.

One of the few remaining indications that Beaulieu-sur-Mer is an old town is the 11th-century Romanesque chapel near the old fishing port. It has a fine round apse and round arches and was sympathetically restored in 1960. Also worth a visit is the **Villa Kerylos**, a complete reconstruction of a Greek villa with marble columns and cool courtyards open to the sky and sea, housing a large collection of mosaics, frescoes and antique furniture.

Further along the Basse Corniche, the Commune of Èze has built a resort on the seafront of its land called Èze-Bord-de-Mer with its own private beach and Club Nautique. Just before Monaco is the secluded Cap d'Ail, a luxury retreat of private villas and hotels.

Èze itself is accessible from the Moyenne Corniche. It is possibly the most *perché* of all the perched villages, with steep lanes, tiny twisting alleys and crooked steps. The rock upon which Èze is built is so sheer that very little fortification was ever needed and there are only two gates to the town.

The **Rue du Barri** climbs up steps, tunnels under houses and meanders over them. There are wonderful features to be seen at every turn; here a cluster of medieval chimneys, there a Romanesque window or tiny rooftop garden. Some of the houses are still ruinous but on the whole the standard of the restoration has been very zealous; indeed, with very few residents remaining, the entire place is like a bijou museum, most of it given over to small shops, galleries and restaurants. From the terraces there are superb views of the surrounding cliffs and out to the Mediterranean.

Èze has almost ceased to exist many times, and its beleaguered past reflects the history of the region very well. For some of its history Èze has been nothing but a charred, empty ruin, at other times it has risen to become a great power. It was a Ligurian settlement later fortified by the Phoenicians and developed by the Romans, who established a harbour in the bay below. After the Romans came the Lombards, who in AD 578 murdered the inhabitants and burned the town to the ground. The Lombards held Èze until AD 740, when the Saracens appeared, enslaving any inhabitants they could capture and murdering the rest. It was they who built the first castle in Èze.

Èze was one of the last strongholds of the Saracens; they were not driven from Provence until 980. Naturally they razed the town when they left. After the Saracens things could only get worse; it was taken and retaken over and over, first by the Guelphs, then by the Ghibellines, then by the House of Anjou and the Counts of Provence. Èze was continually burned to the ground, its inhabitants tortured and starved into submission. It suffered from the plague and was devastated by fever, burned by lightning and toppled by an earthquake. In the 14th century it was finally bought by Amadeus of Savoy, whose family retained control until the entire area was ceded to France in 1860.

During the Middle Ages, Èze became

Wedding in Èze.

a centre of piracy, and vaulted passages and storerooms were built to hide the booty. A particularly nasty massacre took place when the French army of Francis I, aided by the Turkish fleet, launched an attack in 1543. The Turks were under the command of the corsair Barbarossa, known as Redbeard. Accompanying him was Gaspard de Caïs, a native of the area who, for a price, had agreed to turn traitor to his friends and kinfolk.

Yet again Èze was put to the sword. Street by street, the inhabitants were sytematically slaughtered. Such fortifications that could be destroyed were levelled and the castle was blown to pieces with its own store of powder. The town was looted and then burned. A new Èze slowly grew from the ruins. The castle, however, was dismantled in 1606 on orders of King Louis XIV. The earthquake of 1887 did more damage to the town and the lightning of the terrible storm of May 1887 split what remained of the town walls. The village was abandoned and by the 1920s was almost completely depopulated.

A 1921 guidebook to the area (*The Riviera of the Corniche Road* by Sir Frederick Treves) reported: "It is a silent town and desolate. On the occasion of a certain visit the only occupant I came upon was a half-demented beggar who gibbered in an unknown tongue."

Today there is little left of the castle, which is now surrounded by the **Jardin Exotique**, a fine collection of cacti and succulents. The church was rebuilt in 1765, though a 16th-century font remains. The 14th-century White Penitents' chapel on the **Place du Planet** should not be missed; it has an unusual 1258 Catalan crucifix with Christ smiling. Other features of the village include the narrow path to the coast favoured by Frederich Nietzche as he conceived *Thus Spake Zarathustra*.

The only pirates encountered today in Èze are those selling furry animals, handmade pottery, and Provençal fabric as wave after wave of tourists invade the village in centuries-old tradition. The views of the sea from the summit of Èze are spectacular.

The steep, twisting streets of Èze.

MONACO

Monaco's fiercest critic was Katherine Mansfield, who labelled it "*Real Hell*, the cleanest, most polished place I've ever seen". She preferred her home in sleepy Menton to this "procession of pimps, governesses in thread gloves - Jews – old, old hags, ancient men, stiff and greyish, panting on the climb, rich fat capitalists, little girls tricked out to look like babies".

Today Mansfield might be charged with ageism, racism and snobbery or just plain unfairness."Rich fat capitalists", for example, are now quite sleek through working out in Monte-Carlo Golf Club. And Monaco boasts an idyllic natural setting, glamorous residents, Americanised culture and international cuisine. Yet Mansfield's repugnance does strike a chord, at least with ordinary visitors. Society runs like clockwork: toy-town guards seem to be everywhere; and multilingual signs tell visitors not to walk around "bare-chested or barefoot".

"To live in Monaco, all you need is good taste and a lot of money," proclaims the principality's *Society* magazine. Money is essential but good taste is optional, even a liability. In short, everything – except perhaps Monégasque citizenship – is available at a price. The writer Anthony Burgess, who was a long-term resident, once called Monaco "the most uncultivated community I've ever come across."

Mere creativity cannot compete with financial talk. Residents have the highest per capita income in the world. Given its size, Monaco arguably has the greatest ratio of banks in the world. Its status as a tax haven has led to Monaco's claim to hold $25 billion in deposits, 60 percent belonging to non-residents. In fact, out of a population of 30,000, only 6,000 residents are Monégasques. Of the rest, 40 percent are French, 17 percent are Italian and 5 percent are British.

This pocket handkerchief of a country could fit neatly into New York's Central Park. Monaco's critics call it a princely theme park where fairy-tale lifestyles are shrewdly sold. The principality's tourist board boasts of "*Monaco – un rêve, une réalité*". Writer Jeffrey Robinson pokes gentle fun at the nonchalant vulgarity of the Monaco jet set. "On a grand yacht, a Chinese waitress lays a buffet for 20 guests who will shortly be leaving on a two-hour cruise to nowhere, burning 40,000 francs worth of gasoline in the process."

The current ruler, Prince Rainier III, rules like a Medici who has been on a marketing course. Monaco's independence is guaranteed by France but Rainier is nonetheless worried that Monaco will be dragged into the European Community. With the advent of the single market, Monaco's future is in jeopardy. The harmonisation of value-added tax would mean the end to Monaco's most lucrative source of revenue as would the possibility that European Union citizens might lose their tax-exempt status.

Still, Rainier is optimistic that Monaco can become "a financial outpost", the Hong Kong of the Mediterranean,

Preceding pages: Monaco Casino. **Left**, Monégasque chic. **Right**, a princely theme park.

with its own tax system and political status. The Grimaldi are survivors.

Sea, skyscrapers and mountains form concentric circles around the headland that is Monaco. A looming crag, the Tête de Chien, is the backdrop to Monaco-Ville, the medieval quarter built on Le Rocher. The Rock is flanked by two harbours, the artificial Port de Fontvieille to the west and the original Port de Monaco to the east. From here to Monte-Carlo stretches the dull Condamine quarter, an area in which *belle-époque* villas are fast giving way to high-rise sprawl. Monte-Carlo, perched on a skyscraper-studded hill, has been dubbed "Manhattan-sur-Mer" or "Las Vegas-Plage".

Princely sights: From the Place d'Armes it is a short but steep walk up to the **Palais des Princes**, Rainier's official winter residence. The walk, linking the port and the palace, leads through medieval gateways. Until 1863 the gates to the old town were closed at night, much to the annoyance of sociable Monégasques. The final arch, La Rampe Major, opens on to Palace Square, known as *Placa d'u Palaci* in Monégasque, an obscure Provençal-Genovese dialect. The square is dotted with old cannons, some presented by Louis XIV to the Grimaldi Dynasty.

The salmon-pink palace was pale yellow until it was redesigned by Princess Grace. When Prince Rainier's red and white diamond-spangled banner is flying, the Prince is in residence and the Palace is closed to the public. Rainier claims that people feel more secure when he is "at home" rather than on his Mont Agel farm in the French foothills behind Monaco. Visitors who arrive at 11.55 will see the changing of the guard, a daily ceremony performed by the Prince's French *carabinieri*. The Constitution forbids the use of Monégasque guards, a precaution designed to prevent a coup d'état. Depending upon the season, the *carabinieri* are dressed in winter blue and red-striped uniforms or in dazzling white.

The State Apartments are sumptuous recreations of palatial 17th- and 18th-

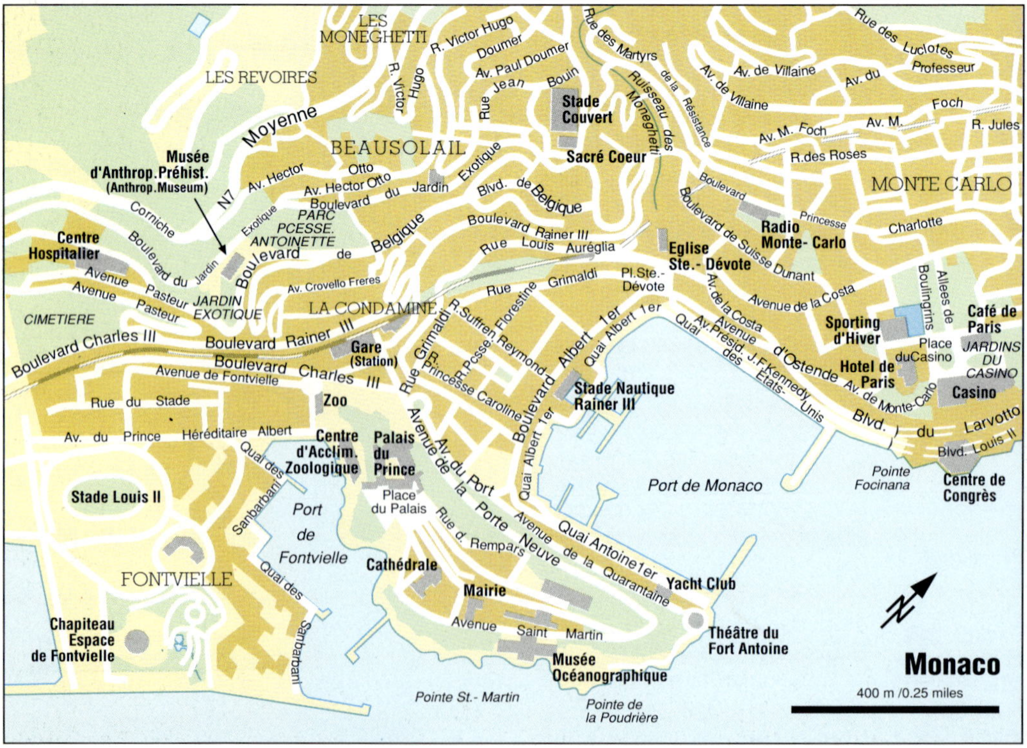

century decor. The Cour d'Honneur, an Italianate quadrangle, forms the backdrop for concerts. However, the most appealing room is the Chambre d'York, where the Duke of York, George III's brother, died. He was on his way to visit a mistress in Genoa when he was taken ill off Monaco. Here, reported Horace Walpole, "the poor Duke of York has ended his silly, good-humoured, troublesome career in a piteous manner." Still, he chose a bedchamber with a frescoed ceiling, Venetian furniture and a gilt-encrusted, canopied bed.

From outside the palace, there are fine views over the **Port de Fontvieille**, a hugely successful development. Built on 30 acres (74 hectares) of reclaimed land, it half-heartedly combines high-rises with Provençal colours. Also down below is the Parc de Fontvieille, the Princess Grace Rose Garden and the Terasses de Fontvieille, a new complex including several museums; the Prince's collection of vintage cars, a **Musée Naval**, and a **Musée des Timbres et des Monnaies** (Stamps and Coins).

In the 1970s Prince Rainier realised that he had to expand Monaco's economic base so created this quarter as a home to non-pollutant light industry, especially perfumes and electronics. These industries now produce 30 percent of state revenue while value-added tax provides 50 percent and, contrary to popular belief, gambling brings in less than 5 percent. As Rainier says: "Nowadays we probably have as many gardeners as croupiers." In fact, the proliferation of gardeners and gendarmes is proof that Monaco is a civil servants' paradise.

Monaco-Ville: From the Palace, a stroll through the old quarter leads to the cathedral and exotic gardens. This area is a labyrinth of covered passageways, tiny squares, fountains and tangerine-coloured facades. Rue Basse has old porticoed houses with carved lintels and vaulted cellars. But in the height of summer it is hard to appreciate the architecture since the quarter is given over to tawdry tourist trinkets, including Princess Caroline T-shirts, Prince Rainier

Monaco from the Corniche road.

mugs and Princess Stephanie's albums. The **Cathedral** dominates a rocky spur, like the figurehead of a boat. The clinical white building was built in 1884 on the site of a medieval church. Designed in neo-Romanesque style with Byzantine flourishes, it is at once majestic and oppressive. The greatest treasures lie in the Chapelle des Princes, the Grimaldi burial chamber. Princess Grace's tomb is nearby, adorned with fresh pink roses. Above is a series of lovely paintings, including the St Nicolas altarpiece by Louis Bréa, the great Niçois artist.

Just outside the cathedral are the lush **Jardins St-Martin**, descending to the sea. Tiers of Aleppo pines and yellow agaves wind around the headland. The gardens are dotted with 18th-century turrets and medieval fortifications. In these manicuredand neatly-labelled gardens, bossy signs forbid the feeding of goldfish and cats. In fact, the goldfish are fat enough already and the teams of watchful, uniformed gardeners are a definite cat-deterrent. Visitors who stop too often are virtually taken in for questioning. From here the Avenue St-Martin leads to Prince Albert's grandiose **Oceanographic Museum**. In summer, a tourist submarine plies the waters down below.

Known as the Navigator Prince, Albert is the best-loved of previous sovereigns. He dedicated his life to the oceans and this "temple of the sea" is his memorial. The undoubted star is the aquarium, a surreal home to weird species: secretive crabs called *dromies* hide in sponges clutched in their back legs; *Bernard l'Hermite* travels with a sea anemone permanently lodged on his back; the noble female octopus waits weeks for her eggs to hatch on her tentacles; as soon as her offspring are born, she dies, exhausted.

One of the most startling sights is not a fish at all but a model of a live coral reef taken from the waters off Djibouti. Children are drawn to the huge tank of *catsharks* and *black-tip reef shark,* which constantly circle a wrecked boat alive with yellow and blue surgeon fish. It is a sobering thought that every morning

The love of money.

the aquarium occupants devour over 8,800 lbs (4,000 kg) of mussels, sardines, seafood cocktail and spinach.

From Monaco-Ville a short bus journey or steep walk leads to the equally surreal environment of the **Jardin Exotique**. These tropical gardens are set just below the Moyenne Corniche. The former mayor of Monaco likens the scene to the Hanging Gardens of Babylon, exotic praise for gardens on the same line of latitude as Vladivostok. Naturally, it is Monaco's balmy climate that fosters plants normally found in Madagascar or Southern California.

Landscaping the cliffs was a mammoth feat of engineering, taking 20 years to complete. The result is breathtaking: tiered gardens are interlinked by high footbridges and canopies of vegetation; secluded spots are formed by pergolas and arbours; an ornamental pond is enclosed by jungle-like greenery. To weed the gardens specialists have to be suspended in parachute harnesses over the cliff. The stars are the fierce-looking cacti and succulents, in particular those on the path known as the Valley of the Candles.

Amongst the 8,000 species of plants are Mexican yuccas, Peruvian monster candles and Moroccan euphorbia that grow up to 49 ft (15 metres) high. Prickly pears, red aloes and downy-eared elephant ears climb up the rocky vaults. The most striking plant is the Mexican echinocactus: it resembles a spiky hedgehog and is better known as "mother-in-law's pillows".

At the foot of the Jardin Exotique is a series of strange caves known as the **Grottes de l'Observatoire**. A precarious descent through the garden is followed by slippery steps leading down to the bottom of the caves. All around are stalagmites and stalagtites, ice-blue pools and natural sculptures. The majestic Grande Salle resembles the inside of a cathedral, with Romanesque pillars and baptismal fonts. The galleries are impressive for their silence, broken only by the faint dripping of water.

Builder prince: Between Monaco-Ville and Monte-Carlo is the portside busi-

The Hong Kong of the Mediterranean.

ness area known as **La Condamine**. The railway brought prosperity but lemon groves were supplanted by villas and now skyscrapers. Not for nothing is Rainier known as the Builder Prince. A minuscule studio can cost in the region of 1.5 million francs. Rainier defends his record: "If I build, then I'm a spendthrift. If I don't, then what's to become of the working classes?" Princess Grace complained that one couldn't sunbathe on the beach after 3pm because of long shadows cast by the skyscrapers. In short, no one claims responsibility for Californian-style patios, hexagonal skyscrapers and a disfigured skyline.

However, the **Port de Monaco** is striking enough, particularly if filled with magnificent cruise liners. From the golden years of the 1950s onwards, Aristotle Onassis's boat *Christina* was moored here and often welcomed Princess Grace aboard. The 1960s and '70s saw the jet set take to water, with or without Greek shipping tycoons.

Here, Charles Revson, the cosmetics tycoon, dreamed up new products on his opulent *Ultima II*. Times have indeed changed: Donald Trump had his boat impounded for failing to settle debts. Current visitors are more likely to be bored Italian industrialists or South American gamblers.

In the right company, and with the right income, **Monte-Carlo** is still a name to conjure with. However, the only magical area is the Place du Casino and the Square Beaumarchais. As well as the Casino and the Salle Garnier, this golden square boasts the Hôtel de Paris, the Café de Paris and the Hôtel Hermitage, haunts worth visiting for their architecture as well as their atmosphere. Until the building of the Place du Casino, the steep-sided Mont Charles hill was known as a "desert riddled with insalubrious caves". In 1886 the new railway brought aristocratic visitors to gamble in a *belle-époque* setting – and the rest is history.

The **Hôtel de Paris** has a delightful setting, overlooking the lush Casino gardens, the Café de Paris and the sea. Built in 1864, this inspirational hotel set

Monaco Grand Prix.

the tone for the rest. It was designed with unbridled extravagance and borrows from an earlier rococo style. Exquisite details include the gracious rotunda with its fan-shaped portico, the curvaceous cupolas and the facades decorated with bare-breasted figureheads. The interior is equally captivating, with caryatids adorning the reception rooms and restaurants.

Alain Ducasse, one of the world's top chefs, presides over the Louis XV restaurant, following in the footsteps of the great Escoffier. The Louis XV is a neobaroque concoction with cream and gold decor surpassed by a frescoed ceiling. Here, Ducasse pampers the privileged with Italo-Provençal cuisine. Guests include Sophia Loren, Ringo Starr and Roger Moore, all of whom have apartments in Monaco. The Salle Empire restaurant is equally luxurious, decorated with frescoes of bathing nymphs. On its opening night in 1866, the restaurant served caviare and pink champagne, and little has changed since then. Le Grill rooftop restaurant appeals to the informal, younger set, including Boris Becker, Bjorn Borg and Princess Stephanie. Still, this motley crew of sportsmen and stars pales in comparison with the procession of grand dukes, royals and statesman who once peopled the hotel. After losing her last 100,000 francs in the Casino, Sarah Bernhardt made a failed suicide bid in her suite here. In more recent times, Onassis retained a suite for his special house guests, including Winston Churchill and his pet parrot. Here, Churchill and Lord Beaverbrook once polished off a bottle of 1815 cognac before breakfast.

In 1943 the Hôtel de Paris was occupied by the Gestapo. In theory Monaco was neutral but Rainier's grandfather supported the Vichy régime. Goering and Himmler used the principality as a place for laundering war spoils. The hotel manager feared for the loss of his finest wines and cognacs so concealed them in a crypt at the bottom of the cellar. The other bottles were drunk but his cache remained intact. It is still the deepest hotel wine cellar in the world

Palais des Princes.

GRIMALDI INC.

If Monaco is now referred to as Grimaldi Inc, it is thanks to the business acumen of the present ruler, Rainier III. The Grimaldi are Europe's oldest reigning family and the last constitutional autocrats. The male line has twice died out but then sovereignty has passed through the female line. Yet the throne is never totally secure.

This old Ligurian family from Genoa were exiled during the medieval political struggle between Guelphs and Ghibellines. The Grimaldi clan found a new power base in Monaco in 1297 and have ruled there ever since. Legend has it a woman wronged by Rainier I put a curse on the Grimaldi line, denying them lasting happiness.

Until the French Revolution, the princes lived on taxes levied on wine, lemons, tobacco, shipping and playing cards. Menton and Roquebrune formed part of Monaco until 1848 and their loss reduced Monaco's territory by 94 percent. However, the creation of Monte-Carlo by Charles III delivered Monaco to grand tourism, which flourished until the reign of Louis II, Prince Rainier III's grandfather. Rainier's mother, Princess Charlotte, was the fruit of Louis' liaison with a washerwoman he met in North Africa. Rainier, educated in England and Switzerland, is the first prince to have been born in Monaco and is also the first full-time sovereign. After acceding to the throne in 1949, Rainier set about running Monaco as a business empire, reducing its dependence on gambling.

Rainier's marriage in 1956 to the Hollywood star Grace Kelly brought a new glamour to Monaco, and her tragic death in a car accident in 1982 was a great blow. Grace's legacy lies in the Americanisation of Monaco, from the business ethos to the sophisticated social life, from the street names to the shopping malls. The Gallerie du Sporting is typical Monaco franglais, in keeping with Rainier's mixed marriage. The greatest crisis of his reign was in 1962, when President de Gaulle, trying to stop French citizens settling in Monaco to avoid paying French taxes, sealed off Monaco's borders until Rainier conceded the issue. Still, except for unlucky French citizens, Monaco remains a tax haven.

In 1997 Monaco celebrated 700 years of independence with great celebrations: musical concerts, sports events, boat races and an historic Grand Prix with classic cars, one of Prince Rainier's passions. Plans for further developments include an extension of the Fontvieille complex to include a new conference centre, a new deep-sea jetty and further offshore developments.

However, the fortunes of the principality are far from secure. The possibility that Monaco may be dragged into the European Union presents a major threat, especially if EU nationals lose their tax-exempt status. The 1990s saw a significant drop in tourism and disastrous losses for the casino business. Like the rest of the Côte d'Azur, financial scandals began to emerge.

Nor did the Grimaldi family escape disaster. Princess Stephanie's sad trail of broken romances (and failed careers) finally resulted in a particularly unsuitable liaison with her bodyguard. Princess Caroline, the eldest, has not escaped the Grimaldi curse. In 1990 her second husband, Stefano Casiraghi, was killed while competing in the World Offshore Boat Race, leaving Caroline with three children and huge debts. After Grace's death, Caroline assumed most of her mother's cultural duties but is tired of being Monaco's First Lady – but Prince Albert, Rainier's heir apparent, shows no sign of marrying. Despite his playboy tastes, Albert has been perfectly groomed to inherit a £200-million fortune. ■

Rainer III: victim of a woman's curse?

and boasts a "champagne alley" with bottles dating back to 1805.

Outside the hotel is a bronze statue of Louis XV on horseback. The gleaming fetlock has long been stroked by gamblers in search of luck. At the end of the facade is a secret bronze door adorned with a mirror. It conceals a lift which leads to the Casino via a secret passageway. During his time as owner of the Casino, Onassis installed the system so that no one would witness the jubilation or despair on the faces of gamblers returning to their suites.

The **Café de Paris** was once an equally glamorous location. It was built in 1865 but acquired an art deco interior in the 1920s. The overall effect is seaside Edwardian, with a delicious peaches and cream facade adorned with a fan-shaped portico. Floral mosaics and stained-glass designs lend sophistication to the interior. However, the Café's claim to fame is linked to the womaniser, Edward VII. Legend has it that Escoffier was preparing a special dessert which accidentally caught fire. Edward's companion was Suzette and the *flambé* was christened *crêpe suzette* in her honour.

Just around the corner on Square Beaumarchais is the **Hotel Hermitage**, the loveliest of the *belle-époque* hotels. It also lays claim to being the most discreet, not that anywhere with gold-encrusted cupids and rococo guests should be so bold. It has a dramatic setting above the port and opposite the Rock. Built in 1890, the hotel indulges in soft lines and sensual sculptures. With its understated elegance, the glass-domed Jardin d'Hiver is the ideal winter garden. Light is filtered through a stained-glass sunflower, a cool scene complemented by lush ferns and wrought-iron balconies.

The Casino: Terraced gardens and fountains lead down to the green-domed Casino and the sea. Amongst the lushness are pineapple-shaped palms, ferns and figs, jacaranda and magnolia. The Casino was created by Prince Florestan, the founder of Monte-Carlo. The Prince wanted a world stage for Monaco arts and, having lost Monégasque territory

The Grimaldis at the Monte-Carlo opera.

to France, also needed to generate new revenue. Inspired by the success of aristocratic tourism in Baden Baden, he realised that good health and gambling were a winning combination.

The early attempts were unsuccessful but the Casino's luck changed when François Blanc, a talented fraudster, bought the concession. He was helped by the arrival of the railway and by his European gambling monopoly. Business boomed in the *belle époque*.

If the Casino was losing heavily, a black cloth was placed over a table as a sign of mourning. Occasionally, lucky gamblers would "break the bank". If so, the coffers were ostentatiously refilled since Blanc shrewdly realised, "One winner always attracts a crowd of losers." One lucky loser was a bankrupt Pole who tried to commit suicide. With admirable sense of public relations, the Casino gave him a room in the Hotel de Paris and presented him with a ticket home. Cunning not charity was the name of the game.

But Lord Salisbury, Queen Victoria's long-serving prime minister, was refused admission to the Casino, having come to the Riviera without his passport. "You see, I'm the man who issues them," was not considered a good enough excuse.

World War I brought the end to grand tourism and Monte-Carlo faced competition from casinos in Cannes, Menton and Nice. In 1951, soon after Prince Rainier came to power, Aristotle Onassis took over the Casino. While Onassis wanted to maintain the Casino as a glamorous preserve, Rainier wanted to open up Monaco to bourgeois tourism. After a showdown in 1962, Rainier wrested control and made the state the principal shareholder.

Today, the Casino retains much of its old glamour as well as its strict rules. A sign by the Casino forbids ministers of religion or Monégasques to enter the *salles de jeux*. If the Grimaldi attend an opera in the Casino's Salle Garnier, they have to enter through a side door.

The Casino is decorated in exuberant *belle-époque* style. Daylight filters

Residents have the highest per capita income in the world.

through stained-glass domes and windows; bronze lamps are held aloft by sculpted nymphs.

To admire the architecture, one should come in the late afternoon but for atmosphere only the late evening will do. In the *salons privés*, serious bets are laid by cigar-smoking gamblers with glazed expressions. Games include roulette, craps, blackjack, baccarat and *chemin de fer*. Spectators eddy from table to table and sound is reduced to low murmurs and sliding chips. No one drinks; gambling is the only addiction.

The entrance staircase boasts a sculpted palm, welcoming one to the Salon des Palmiers and the summery feel of the Casino. Yet the *salons ordinaires* are disappointing. The slot machines seem out of place beside gilded mirrors, chandeliers, cut flowers and Fragonard paintings. In the plush Salon Rose bar, gamblers play on space invaders; on the ceiling, sculpted nudes puff cigars, a reminder that this was once the smoking-room. Just off these public rooms is Le Train Bleu, a chic restaurant modelled on the famous train that brought high society to the Riviera.

The *salons privés* are only private insofar as there is a second admission charge. That said, stakes are much higher and non-gamblers are discouraged by the door manager's penetrating gaze. This is no mere doorman but someone with a photographic memory for matching faces to gambling history. The most famous of these "physiognomists" was Monsieur le Broq, who claimed to have memorised over 60,000 faces. The Casino's main "bank" can also be made to vanish down a trap-door in the event of a hold-up.

In the *salons privés* there is a high ratio of croupiers to clients. The croupiers are Las Vegas-trained and form the most powerful lobby in Monaco. When workers went on strike in 1968, the croupiers were the only ones who picketed in Cadillacs. John Addington Symonds had little good to say of the breed in 1866: "The croupiers are either fat, sensual cormorants or sallow, lean-cheeked vultures, or suspicious foxes."

High rollers at the casino.

In the 1970s many of the major players were Arabs. Adnan Khashoggi and Prince Fahd played for $2 milion bets and insisted on playing alone. The Casino encourages the maximum number of players to spread the risk so was not pleased by the Arabs' dramatic winnings. To save its skin, the Casino made a deal: the Arabs could play in private at any time of day or night but had to stay until 6am and stop then, whatever the outcome. The Arabs tired and the Casino won.

Nowadays, the big gamblers tend to be Italian or South American. According to Raoul Bianchieri, the head of SBM: "There are big fortunes in South America, and they are gamesters by temperament." Because of his power in Monaco, Bianchieri is known as "the other prince". Gianni Agnelli used to be an *habitué* here but confessed to Rainier: "I can't allow myself to do it any more." If the Fiat workforce knew of their boss's gambling habit, Agnelli would have been in a weak position in calling for union wage restraints.

From the Casino, a period lift leads to Le Cabaret, a kitsch restaurant and floor show. Couples are tucked into pink velvet alcoves. The main lighting is provided by bare-breasted Amazons, lamps swathed in gold lamé below the waist. Between courses, artistes perform compulsory card tricks at one's table. After the cabaret, diners are photographed, presented with a plate of chocolates, then expected to dance. For less exhibitionist diners there is Les Privés, a discreet restaurant-bar overlooking the sea.

The **Salle Garnier**, situated in the Casino complex, is the prestigious setting for opera, ballet and concerts. It was here that Diaghilev's *Ballets Russes* once performed to great acclaim. Monte-Carlo has a noted orchestra which stages summer concerts in the medieval Fort Antoine. Monaco has the most sophisticated nightlife on the Riviera. The Red Cross Gala is the society event of the year, an occasion for the richest society ladies to flaunt their jewels. It is held at the Monte-Carlo Sporting Club, not a sports club at all. According to Prince

Princess Stephanie in happier times.

Albert, a bobsleigh champion, "to be a good Monégasque, you have to be sporty." The major event is, of course, the Grand Prix. This dangerous circuit involves 78 laps around the port, the Hermitage Hotel and the Place du Casino. The timing is perfect: it takes place immediately after the Cannes Film Festival so there are still plenty of stars around.

Stirling Moss, who won three times, loved the atmosphere. "When I was racing, I'll never forget looking at a beautiful young girl with pale lipstick who was always sitting in front of Oscar's bar. Every time I passed, I blew her a kiss. This sort of thing is only possible in Monaco."

During the Monte-Carlo season, evening is the time for dazzling displays of wealth. Stretch limousines ferry bronzed and bejewelled celebrities between the Hôtel de Paris, the Casino and Jimmy'z, Monte-Carlo's fashionable night spot. Boris Becker and Princess Stephanie dance under the stars at Parady'z nightclub. This is what the Monaco public relations department would have one believe. But these are troubled times for the Principality, which celebrated its 700th year in 1997. The Grimalidi family seems beset by tragedy and scandal, there has been a significant drop in tourism, and gaming scandals erode the carefully polished image.

Private snapshots of Monaco differ too. The ultra-discreet set do not stir from security-conscious apartments. In the Salle Garnier, a world-weary tycoon feigns an interest in the latest cultural offering and wonders why Princess Caroline always selects such obscure operas. Next door, in Le Train Bleu, a *grande dame* toys with her caviare, briefly leaving the table to place a losing bet on number 22, her lover's age.

Visitors listen to a Mozart recital in Fort Antoine, the open-air theatre. Monégasque bank clerks and shopkeepers watch their football team play Marseille. A bored croupier polishes his buttons. An Italian tourist wonders how a slice of Parma ham and melon can cost 300 francs. "*Monaco – un rêve, une réalité.*"

The glittering Port of Monaco.

MENTON

"Nowhere else have I felt such complete happiness," declared Franz Liszt of Menton. Sheltered by mountains, **Menton** basks in an enchanted setting with 300 days of sun a year. In this tropical greenhouse, Mexican and North African vegetation flourishes in a climate at least 2°C warmer than in Nice. *Belle-époque* villas aside, one could easily be in Sicily. But in the 19th century Menton's charm was as a winter sanatorium rather than as a hot-house. Royal visitors such as Queen Victoria and Edward VII helped Menton acquire a reputation as the most aristocratic and anglophile of all the Riviera resorts.

Nowadays the dowager-like image has softened: Menton is cosy rather than genteel, anglophile rather than aristocratic. But even this image is *passé*, since Menton has more young people than any other Riviera town. Certainly, the presence of Italian executives and trippers has revived the town, especially since the joining of Menton with Ventimiglia in 1993, as the European Union's first joint urban community, when frontier posts, municipal and business activities were combined.

Foreign history: Originally Genovese, Menton became part of the Principality of Monaco in 1346 and by and large remained a Grimaldi possession until 1860. However, the Grimaldi astutely placed Menton under the protection of the rising political powers, a form of opportunism still practised by the present Monégasque rulers. In succession, Menton became a Spanish, French and Sardinian protectorate. Given such a cosmopolitan past, it is hardly surprising that Menton can feel so deliciously foreign.

In 1848 Menton rebelled against high Monégasque taxes on oil and fruit. Along with Roquebrune, the town declared itself a republic but this was shortlived and in 1861 Monaco sold both towns to France. This coincided with the beginning of grand tourism and Menton was one of the first health resorts to benefit, thanks to the favourable publicity generated by Dr Bennet. The English doctor promoted Menton's mild climate as perfect for invalids so British and Germans flocked to winter there.

Sights: Set just behind the seafront, the sweetly-scented **Jardin Biovès** is a natural introduction to flowery Menton. Facing inland, one's eye is drawn to the gentle gradations of colour and height: lush pink borders and serried ranks of palms and citrus trees that fade to distant mauve hills. The lemon trees are carefully decorated with fairy lights. In the evening glow, the park's cosy prettiness envelops passers-by in a cloying embrace.

A voluptuous tone is set by a reclining nude statue and by a fountain dedicated to the "goddess of the golden fruits". Nearby, boughs of sharp Seville oranges and sweet Genovese mandarins intermingle with the Mentonnais lemon, the town's trademark. This oval-shaped lemon, introduced in the 14th century, is noted for its gorgeous scent and unacidic flavour. The Mentonnais boast

Preceding pages: the tropical greenhouse of Menton. **Left**, a local fisherman. **Right**, the Catholic influence is still strong.

that it keeps for months longer than its common Portuguese rival.

During the spring *Fête du Citron* the park looks good enough to eat. The fruit, moulded into such shapes as boats and cathedrals, attracts 300,000 visitors every year. When not pressed into promoting the tourist industry, the Menton lemon can be sampled as a refreshing *citron pressé* – at Parisian prices, of course. Menton's sweet aftertaste conceals very sharp marketing.

Overlooking the park is the splendour of the Palais de l'Europe, once the city's grand casino and now home to the helpful tourist office. The present Casino, facing out on to the seafront, is a staid affair, reduced to seaside cabaret, sedate *thés dansants* and low-key gambling. As if in disapproval, St John's Anglican church turns its back on the Casino. The church provides retired British expatriates with spiritual counselling, fêtes and free library books. In the afternoon, elderly visitors congregate on the **Promenade du Soleil** to enjoy the sea views. Along the seafront are vestiges of *belle-époque* villas, epitomised by the charmingly dilapidated Le Pin Doré and similar pastel-coloured hotels. Many of the finest villas have been converted into chic flats or homes for retired French civil servants. Below the Promenade du Soleil sun-seekers stretch out on boulders or on pocket handkerchiefs of sand.

Nearby, genteel dowagers sip afternoon tea in the George V's *salon de thé*. The solicitous service is reminiscent of an expensive nursing home. Here, life is meted out not in coffee spoons but in ice-cream scoops. Yet in keeping with the changing times, the cafés cater to both ends of the social scale, serving anything from chilled Chablis and bouillabaisse to hot dogs and Coke. In general, however, Menton's sea views are more memorable than the cuisine.

At the eastern end of the Promenade, the *belle-époque* quarter merges into Vieux Menton, the pedestrianised old town. The **Marché Couvert** provides the quirky link between the two quarters. The market, topped by a decorative

Menton's Lemon Festival.

clocktower, is adorned with comical sculpted faces. The profusion of lemons, figs and artichokes is a match for the market's green, yellow and brown ceramics.

Fishing: Rue des Marins, beside the market, is still the centre of Menton's small but thriving fish trade. As the only medieval guild to have survived on the Riviera, it retains a symbolic importance in local eyes. The trade, still passed from father to son, is based on small fry such as sardines and anchovies. In spring, anchovies are attracted to Menton's warm water and by May the season is underway. May is also the traditional time for salting and storing. Sardines, still fished from February to April, are eaten fried with lemon or in a spicy *omelette de poutines*.

Restaurants around the market are a good place to sample the local fish dishes, including *stockfisch*, spiced with garlic and white wine before being flambéed in cognac. A typical accompaniment to fish is *fleurs farcies*, courgette flowers stuffed with cheese, tomatoes and garlic. Aromatic *Côtes-de-Provence Blanc* is a good wine choice.

Beside the Marché Couvert is the Place du Marché, with its flower stalls doing a brisk trade in young lemon trees and cacti. Next door is the **Place aux Herbes**, a charming arcaded square. Ignore the antique shop, lavender stalls and North African trinket-sellers. Instead, focus on the chestnut trees, fountain and statue, best appreciated from an outdoor café. Place du Marché leads to the bustling **Rue St-Michel**, Menton at its most commercial. Avenue Félix Faure and Rue St-Michel provide ample opportunity to stock up on designer luggage, Provençal herbs and lemon-scented soap.

Seen from the old fishing harbour, Vieux Menton is stacked on the hillside, framed by rugged mountains and shimmering reflections. The finest coastal views are from the Empress Eugénie jetty: Cap Martin, the millionaires' enclave, lies to the west, with Bordighera, the Italian resort, to the east.

Viewed from the port, the clustered

Vieux Menton stacked on the hillside.

towers of the **Cathedral** and two chapels appear inseparable. From Quai Bonaparte, steep steps lead to a pebble-mosaic courtyard of striking Italianate design. Just above is the pink and ochre cathedral, flanked by two steeples. It was begun in 1619 by Honoré II of Monaco but its facade and atmosphere are essentially baroque. Inside are several heavily-restored chapels which were damaged in the 1887 earthquake. Just outside is the Place de l'Église, the setting for Menton's celebrated *Juillet Musicale* and August Festival of Chamber Music. This sunken square has excellent acoustics, framed by the cathedral and chapel yet open to the sea on one side. The unexpected blend of intimacy and sea views has also made it a sought-after film location.

Next door, the apricot-tinged **Chapelle de l'Immaculée Conception** is a much creamier affair. It was built in 1687 for the White Penitents, a lay confraternity who sought to return to a simpler faith. The 1887 earthquake damaged the church but after a restoration in 1987 it is now the city's pride and joy. Depending on taste, the baroque interior is garish or exuberant. It is lit by old coaching lamps but locals gaze up at the *lanteron* to appreciate the natural light. The *pièce de résistance* is the ceiling representing Heaven, a Mediterranean paradise with golden figures and blue skies. In the Hôtel de Ville, Cocteau's pastiche of a Mediterranean marriage shows the same *joie de vivre*.

The cathedral quarter, dating from the 16th century, is the oldest part of town. It is also the poorest, populated by Algerian and Moroccan immigrants as well as Mentonnais craftsmen. Renovation has yet to make an impact on this warren of vaulted brick and cobbled streets. Ramparts from the old fortress have been incorporated into existing buildings. Blind alleys end with tiny stone houses decorated with drying peppers. Inside one, a family sorts through a sack of pungent olives; a canary sings out of tune.

After running the gauntlet of the lavender sellers on Rue St-Michel, reach

Mentonnais fishermen, the only medieval guild to have survived on the Riviera.

the Bastion on the seafront. This fort was built in 1636, when Menton's Spanish rulers feared a French attack. The orange-brick bastion now houses the **Jean Cocteau Museum**, in homage to the painter and poet who once lived locally. Cocteau himself oversaw the restoration of the fort, designing the mosaic flooring and the bright tiling on the four turrets. He donated numerous works to the museum but sadly did not live to see the opening in 1967.

The ground floor, formerly the arms store, contains brilliantly-coloured abstractions, powerful self-portraits and *Judith and Holopherne*, Cocteau's first tapestry. Matisse loved it, praising this depiction of seduction, murder and flight as *"la seule vraie tapisserie contemporaine."* As an artist, the eclectic Cocteau dabbled in tapestry, ceramics, photography and scuplture as well as painting. Throughout the museum are examples of his beautifully crafted jars influenced by Greek, Hellenic and Etruscan designs. The upper floor, once the guards' room, still contains its original vaulted ceiling and brick oven. The highlight is the *Innamorati* collection, a series of love paintings inspired by the lives of Provençal fisher folk. With the sea beating against the bastion walls, the atmospheric setting is reminiscent of the Cap Ferrat tower where Cocteau worked.

Cocteau fans will head inland to the Hôtel de Ville to see the **Salle des Mariages**, designed by the artist in the 1950s. Cocteau's touch is evident in the Spanish chairs, the mock panther-skin carpet and the lamps shaped like prickly-pears. As for the murals, Cocteau's inspiration was the Riviera style at the turn of the century, "a mood redolent of art nouveau villas decorated with swirling seaweed, irises and flowing hair".

On the wall above the official's desk, Cocteau depicts the engaged couple trying to read the future in each other's eyes. The mural is full of Provençal symbols, from the sun and swirling sea to the woman's Mentonnais straw hat and her fiancé's fisherman's cap. Cocteau humorously gives the fisher-

View of Menton and the sea.

man a fish instead of an eye. The mural on the right features an exotic Saracen wedding, a reference to earlier Riviera settlers but also a pretext for a colourful ceremony and extravagant emotions. The bride and groom set off on a white horse amidst rejoicing, sorrow and mystery. Three wise friends bear gifts; a slave girl dances; a jilted girlfriend is comforted by her vengeful brother; a mother-in-law glowers; a gypsy guides the newlyweds towards the future.

Cocteau's aim was to "create a theatrical setting… to offset the officialdom of a civil ceremony". In this he succeeds, bringing wonder and an epic dimension to a dreary register office. Cocteau watched his adopted son get married in this very room. Since then, Menton has become a recherché wedding location, not just a joke to *"épater les bourgeois"*.

From Menton it is a pleasant stroll to **Garavan**, a chic garden suburb with the most exotic vegetation in France. At the turn of the century Garavan was in its heyday, a haunt for high society. Glamorous villas with matching landscaped gardens were *de rigueur*. Today, despite encroaching high-rise developments, *belle-époque* villas and art deco follies still survive. Sadly, many luxuriant gardens can only be glimpsed through *chien méchant* signs.

Menton Casino, a staid affair of *thés dansants* and cabaret.

The high inland road to Garavan is more appealing than the route along the seafront. From the cathedral, climb the winding Rue du Vieux Château to the **Cemetery** on the hill. The Italianate cemetery, built over the ancient citadel, spans four terraces, each devoted to a different faith. The tone is set by a smiling marble angel which looks set to soar over the *vieille ville*. The cemetery is noted for its foreign graves, a cosmopolitan cast-list of 19th-century celebrities who stayed longer than intended. Aubrey Beardsley, the illustrator, is joined by Webb Ellis, the founder of rugby. Nearby are graves of consumptive English girls who made a vocation of dying poetically. Cats sun themselves on Prince Youssoupov's tomb, unafraid of Rasputin's murderer.

The **Place du Cimetière**, just outside the cemetery walls, is a popular place for expatriate picnics and gossip. Count on sharing views of the **Vieux Port** and Garavan's modern marina. In the distance are signs for "*Frontière*", proof that the wooded headland beyond is, indeed, Italy.

From the square, **Le Boulevard de Garavan** leads past terraced gardens and villas hugging the coast. Rooftop villas are draped with mimosa, bougainvillaea, lentisks and giant cacti. Number 13, a *belle-époque* mansion built into the old city walls, is surrounded by olive and lemon groves. Next-door is an art deco villa with magnificent views of the old port. *"Attention aux chats gentils,"* a sign on the Villa Rayons et Ombres, is presumably a cover for pit bull terriers.

Several public paths lead down through lemon groves to the Garavan seafront. One such path, Sentier Villa Noël, leads to the **Jardin Botanique Exotique**, Menton's most successful park. This lush botanical garden was laid out by Lord Redcliffe, the Governor of Malta, in 1905. The last owner, the retiring Miss Campbell, continued to introduce plants from Asia, Africa and America, making this the most tropical garden in France. It now resembles a cultural melting pot.

Japanese cane bamboos and African succulents compete with Australian eucalyptus and Brazilian bougainvillaea; Arabian date trees and Canary palms dwarf Mexican yucca and Iranian pistachios. The fruit trees smell quite delicious: as well as *citrus amara* and *citrus blanco* lemons, there are also mandarins, bananas, oranges, figs and dates. Even succulents like the deep red aloes look distinctly edible.

Yet Menton's Jardin Botanique does not neglect quieter, more Provençal charms. Sweet-smelling myrtle, rosemary and thyme flourish, as do evergreen lentisks, drooping lilies and a riot of roses. One intimate patch contains an ordinary rockery, except that no rockery is ordinary in Menton. A balmy climate helps but these plants seem to have been raised on anabolic steroids.

Virtually next door is the **Olivaie du Pian**, Garavan's public park. It was once part of a Spanish estate but is now a wild olive grove. This variety of olive, *le cailletier*, has been grown here for over 2,000 years and stands out for its stocky trunk and succulent black olives. Some of the gnarled specimens are hundreds of years old. By day, the olive grove is a ball park but on summer nights it is an open-air stage.

On the far side of the park is Rue Blasco Ibañez, named after the Spanish novelist who lived in exile here. Shunning the military dictatorship in Spain, Blasco Ibañez settled in the Riviera in 1923. His villa, **Fontana Rosa**, is a piece of self-indulgence, heralded by ceramic portraits of Balzac, Cervantes and Dickens on the gateway. Surrounding the villa is the Spaniard's **Jardin des romanciers**, a further tribute to his favourite novelists. The grounds, planted with cypress and Mediterranean shrubs, reflect a pastiche of classical and art deco styles. A couple of follies take centre stage, adorned by sculpted *putti*,

Salles des Mariages, designed by Cocteau, now a recherché wedding location.

kneeling angels and busts of novelists. Mosaics represent Mediterranean fruit and flowers. It may be kitsch but it is fun. The ceramics have just been restored to their former splendour.

A short but steep walk along Avenue Ferdinand Bac leads to **Les Colombières**, arguably the most romantic gardens on the Riviera. The writer and artist Ferdinand Bac longed for an authentic Mediterrranean garden, planted with Provençal herbs, box borders and clumps of yews. The shaded terraces are punctuated by ornamental pools, fountains, classical urns and baroque statues. In fact, the hill-top location and the giant black cypresses closely resemble a French Tuscany.

But if the gardens are Italianate, the exuberant villa defies description. Decorated by Bac in 1926, it borrows freely from Hellenic, Roman and Oriental traditions. A colonnaded atrium contains frescoes of the Ulysses myth while the art deco music room is covered with murals of the nine Muses. In the grounds, a Moorish-style pavilion contains Bac's tomb. Although the villa and grounds are untended, the neglect adds romance to this lush wilderness.

From Les Colombières, steps cut down to the the Boulevard de Garavan and a turning right leads to **Avenue Katherine Mansfield**, the writer's retreat. The street boasts *belle-époque* villas, from the stuccoed *La Favorite* to *Chrisoleina*, a turreted folly. Before Garavan station, a sign indicates Mansfield's **Isola Bella**, a disappointingly small, lemon-coloured villa with a disfigured view. Despite suffering from tuberculosis, Katherine wrote some of her best work here, including *The Daughters of the Late Colonel*, an essay on genteel frustation. By contrast, she found Menton liberating, "a heavenly place" with "no division between one's work and one's external existence". Life was centred on "my pale yellow house with its mimosa in a slightly deeper hue." Soon after moving in to the villa, Katherine wrote: "When I die you will find Isola Bella in poker work on my heart."

Menton, popular for health benefits.

Mansfield would not have approved of the ugly high-rise sprawl on Garavan seafront, just around the corner. Nor would she have liked the tacky seafood restaurants lining the quayside. (She admired her maid's knack of turning any dish into an artistic still life, "the fish with its huge, tragic mouth stuffed with parsley.") For more stylish cuisine, follow the *Italie 1,000 metres* sign.

On Promenade Reine Astrid, just before the border, is **Villa Serena**, Menton's last major garden. Menton is famous for its gardens, many of them planted by English residents. Others worth visiting include nearby **Serres de la Madone**, which was designed and planted by Lawrence Johnston, and has a magnificent collection of palms and tropical plants; and the botancial gardens at **Val Rahmeh**, the Mediterranean outpost of the Paris Natural History Museum.

And the mildest climate on the Mediterranean.

From Menton, a brisk walk west along the seafront leads to Carnolès. This dull suburb is worth visiting for one site alone: the **Palais Carnolès**, once the Grimaldi summer home is now Menton's major art museum. This pink and white palace is encircled by parasol pines and 50 different varieties of citrus trees. In 1640 Prince Honoré II built a summer house in the olive groves but Antoine I remodelled it on the Grand Trianon. The well-restored palace mostly displays works bequeathed by Wakefield Mori, an eclectic English collector.

The museum's strengths lie in the Italian *Quattrocento* works, 16th-century portraits and modern Riviera landscapes. Amongst the ancient art, the Italian and French madonnas take pride of place. Louis Bréa, often called "Provence's Fra Angelico", is the only home-grown star of this period. The soft and spiritual *Virgin and Child* shows his delicate touch. The rest of the Niçois school cannot compete with the expressive *École de Leonardo* madonna presented here. The ground floor displays a rotating collection of modern art, including Kisling's *Paysage à St-Tropez* and Sutherland's *La Fontaine*, a glowing composition of fountain and leaves.

From Carnolès or Menton, a short drive north leads to the **Monastère de L'Annonciade** and arguably the loveliest views from Menton. By car, take the Avenue de Sospel and turn left into the Route de l'Annonciade. Alternatively, walk along the Chemin du Rosaire, a steep but delightful walk which, until 1936, was the only way of reaching the monastery. The path winds uphill through pine trees and spiky yellow agaves; small shrines represent the stations of the cross.

The path and the monastery were created by Isabelle de Monaco after her miraculous cure from leprosy. Apart from an interruption during the Revolution, a Franciscan community has lived here ever since. Inside the chapel is a bizarre collection of votive offerings, from boats and crutches to a Zeppelin fragment and a strip of parachute from the 1991 Gulf War. The monastery is perched among cypress and olive groves. From its terrace of swaying eucalyptus trees there are coastal views towards Italy, Corsica and Cap Martin.

A few miles west of Carnolès lies **Roquebrune-Cap Martin**, an historic commune sandwiched between Menton and Monaco. In the 1840s, the medieval village of Roquebrune was practically deserted and the wooded headland of Cap Martin was the preserve of sheep and cows. Before the turn of the century, however, Cap Martin was discovered by richer flocks, from Queen Victoria to Empress Eugénie. *Belle-époque* villas sprang up among the olive groves and Cap Martin remains the preserve of the rich today.

From Roquebrune station on the coast it is a short drive or an arduous climb to the medieval village. Steep staircases with vertiginous views lead up the reddish-brown cliff to **Roquebrune**. The distinction between castle and village only evolved in the 15th century. Before then, the whole of Roquebrune was a *castellum*, a fortified 10th-century settlement which remains unique in France.

The path finally emerges in Rue de l'Église, beside the parish church. Ste-Marguerite, originally Romanesque, was

The rooftops of Roquebrune, a unique fortified settlement.

heavily restored in the 18th century and looks classical. The facade is apricot-coloured, like much of Roquebrune, and overlooks a sweet Marian shrine. The welcoming interior is bathed in a soft pink glow.

But the village's vocation is for tourism, not for the priesthood. Lavender, honey and carved wood sculptures are Roquebrune's icons, in summer at least. Yet despite being overpriced, overcrowded and over-restored, Roquebrune remains a magical place. The apricot houses, chiselled out of the rock, overhang tiny squares and blind alleys. Narrow passageways burrow through a labyrinth of vaulted archways.

The geranium-covered walls present a misleadingly decorative picture. This ancient *castellum* was supremely functional. The château battlements commanded views of Mont Agel, Monaco and the coast; there were only two entrances, both heavily guarded. If invaders broke through the defences, they were quickly backed into cul-de-sacs and bombarded with boulders. As the oldest castle in France, Roquebrune was the prototype feudal château for centuries to come.

Roquebrune was built by the Count of Ventimiglia as a means of keeping the "Saracens" at bay. After a long struggle between the Genovese and the Counts of Provence, Roquebrune became a Grimaldi possession and remained so for five centuries. The grim **château**, situated on Place Ingram, is largely 13th century, although it was heavily restored this century by Sir William Ingram. The locals were outraged when the Englishman added a mock medieval *tour anglaise*. From the battlements there are magnificent views of the coast.

Rue Grimaldi, the main street, is marred by cute gentrification and craft shops. But even here, the eccentricity and friendliness of the traders sets Roquebrune apart. An artist with an *atelier* readily discusses local history or produces photos of himself dressed as a Roman centurion. Ever since 1467, when the Virgin saved the town from the plague, 500 Roquebrunois have re-en-

Paintings for sale at Roquebrune.

acted scenes from the Passion every August. A sculptor carves angels and virgins out of olive wood, boasting about his discovery of "*le plus vieil homme de l'Europe*" in a local cave. Certainly, Roquebrune is riddled with prehistoric remains. Although the most famous caves, the Grottes du Vallonet, are still being excavated, major finds are predicted.

Before leaving, stroll down Rue Grimaldi to **Place des Deux Frères**, named after the square's twin crags. In 1890 the square came into being when a huge outcrop was split to create an access road. The result is a success, a release from the slightly claustrophobic feeling of Roquebrune. La Grotta bistrot enjoys views of the château above and the Côte below. Be prepared to share a table with an American bee-keeper, Swiss banker or French artisan, all Roquebrune residents.

From Roquebrune, it is a pleasant, leisurely downhill stroll to **Cap Martin** and the coast. The prettiest route leads along Rue Souta Riba, a narrow, vaulted path edging round the outside of the village. Views through firs and pines reveal privatised Roman statuary in discreet villas. Soon after Souta Riba joins the Chemin de Menton there is a huge gnarled olive tree, reputedly over 1,000 years old. Further on are a couple of chapels, the dilapidated St Roch and the rural de la Pausa, which was built in 1462 as a plague offering. Faded frescoes of olive groves and angels cover the walls.

By the time the path reaches Avenue du Danemark, suburbia is underway. On Avenue Paul Doumer the Roman **Monument de Lumone** is a redeeming feature. These arches and mosaics are all that remain of the Roman settlement on the cape. Although its olive and lemon groves have receded, Cap Martin is still lusher and less spoilt than Cap Ferrat. However, none of Cap Martin's *belle-époque* villas are open to the public and most bask in smug, celebrity cool. Name-droppers have a field day on Cap Martin but it is unwise to label all its grand residents as slavish followers of fashion. Designer Karl Lagerfeld lives on the Cap both to service Monte-Carlo fashion victims and to be close to the Grimaldi family. Fragrant Coco Chanel wafted in to entertain German officers during the war. Empress Eugénie liked to play the *grande dame* here but presumably Greta Garbo didn't come for the company. Churchill and Le Corbusier came for the painter's light. Empress Sissy of Austria wintered here after a bad case of *fin-de-siècle* blues. W. B. Yeats came, and died, for reasons of ill-health.

The highlight of the cape is the **Promenade le Corbusier**, a lovely coastal path running west to Monaco and south-east around Cap Martin. The path crosses an olive grove and then hugs the shore. Willows, sea pines and white rocks typify this stretch of coast. The walk towards Monaco passes Le Corbusier's beach house, just before the Pointe de Cabbé. The architect drowned here in 1965 but had the foresight to design a splendid memorial to himself in Roquebrune cemetery. Cynics label this a supremely Cap Martin gesture.

Left, the coast from Roquebrune. Right, religion – the British prefer Anglican protection.

Perched Villages

For the adventurous prepared to explore further than the coast, a whole new world awaits: high mountain plateaux, plunging gorges, clear sparkling rivers and, crowning the most inaccessible craggy peaks, the justly famous *villages perchés.*

A number of these perched villages, such as Ste-Agnes, Gorbio and Peillon, are only a few miles inland, and yet provide a stark and welcome contrast to the urbanised coast. Even villages further into the mountains, such as Utelle, Lantosque or Luceram, can easily be visited in a day, since the roads are good, if often steep, and rarely busy.

However, it can be particularly pleasant to find a hotel and stay overnight in these beautiful mountains, to fully appreciate the pristine air and star-studded night skies, and to wake up to a deep silence broken only by cow bells. Spring, when the flowers are at their most beautiful, is perhaps the best time to enjoy these unspoilt regions, but during the summer they can provide a cool, refreshing break from the coast.

The perched village of **Falicon** is close to Nice and well worth a visit. It was the setting for Jules Romains's novel *La Douceur de la Vie,* and was also where Queen Victoria liked to stroll and take her afternoon tea whilst staying in Nice; an event commemorated by a restaurant called Au Thé de la Reine. The old village is very small, filled with covered passages and twisting lanes and is characterised by a series of picturesque little *placettes*, one of which has a rare perpendicular staircase leading to a raised front door. There is a baroque church dating from 1624.

Preceding pages: village women enjoy a joke. **Left**, typical Alpes-Maritimes hilltown. **Right**, remains of massive Roman trophy visible through the streets of La Turbie.

Peille and Peillon, in the valley of the Paillon river, are both superb examples of *villages perchés*, all the more so for their proximity to Nice. One has barely escaped the tangle of the city's industrial suburbs when these ancient craggy places rise up impossibly elevated above the valley floor.

It is surprising that **Peille** is not better known. It is a large, almost completely medieval village, with a wonderful variety of features and views. There is parking either end of the town, which is traversed by the Rue Centrale. There are two very old quarters, both of which were founded in the 11th century.

Don't miss the Place André Laugier, where there is a pair of 13th-century doors, one Romanesque, one Gothic, and a pair of matched Gothic windows. Behind this is the Place du Mont Agel, surrounded by very old houses, with a Gothic fountain in the centre. The Rue Lascaris leaves the square through the loggia of the ancient palais, and out to a viewing platform. From here, a short path leads to the cemetery and the war memorial. The view extends all the way to Cap d'Antibes.

All the roads leading from Place du Mont Agel are worth exploring: Rue du Moulins has double round-arched windows, probably 15th-century, Rue de la Turbie leads down stone steps under an arch to a charming square housing a small museum of local history.

Baus de la Frema
2250
Lac du B
Sauveur-sur-Tinée
Saint Martin-Vésubie
Cime de la Valette
2496
Lac Le Supe
2685
Cime du Diable
Lauvet d'Ilonse
1991
Valdeblore
Ilonse
Pierlas
le Mont
1789
Marie
Oglione
Pierlas
Tinée
Clans
Roquebillière
Pointe des 4 Cantons
1774
Lieuche
Clans
la Bollène-Vésubie
Figaret
Bairols
Lantosque
Col de Turini
1607
Thiéry
Vésubie
FRANCE
Bévera
Tournefort
Villars-sur-Var
le Suquet
Peïra-Cava
Saint Jean-la-Rivière
Cime de Rocca Seira
1504
Ascros
Malaussène
Utelle
Mont Vial
1549
Col de Brau
1002
Gorges de la Vesubie
Cuébris
Lucéram
Bonson
Levens
Roquesteron
Coaraze
Plan-du-Var
Estéron
Var
les Ferres
la Roquette-sur-Var
L'Escarène
MONTAGNE DU CHEIRON
Bouyon
Saint-Martin-du-Var
Contes
Peille
Coursegoules
Castagniers
Tourette-Levens
Peillon
Var
Col de Vence
970
Cantaron
Gattières
Colomars
Falicon
la Turbie
Saint Pancrace
Courmes
Eze
Vence
Beaulieu -sur-Mer
Villefranche
St. Paul
Loup
Nice
Saint Jean-Cap-Ferrat
Rouret
Roquefort-les-Pins
Cagnes
St. Laurent-du-Var

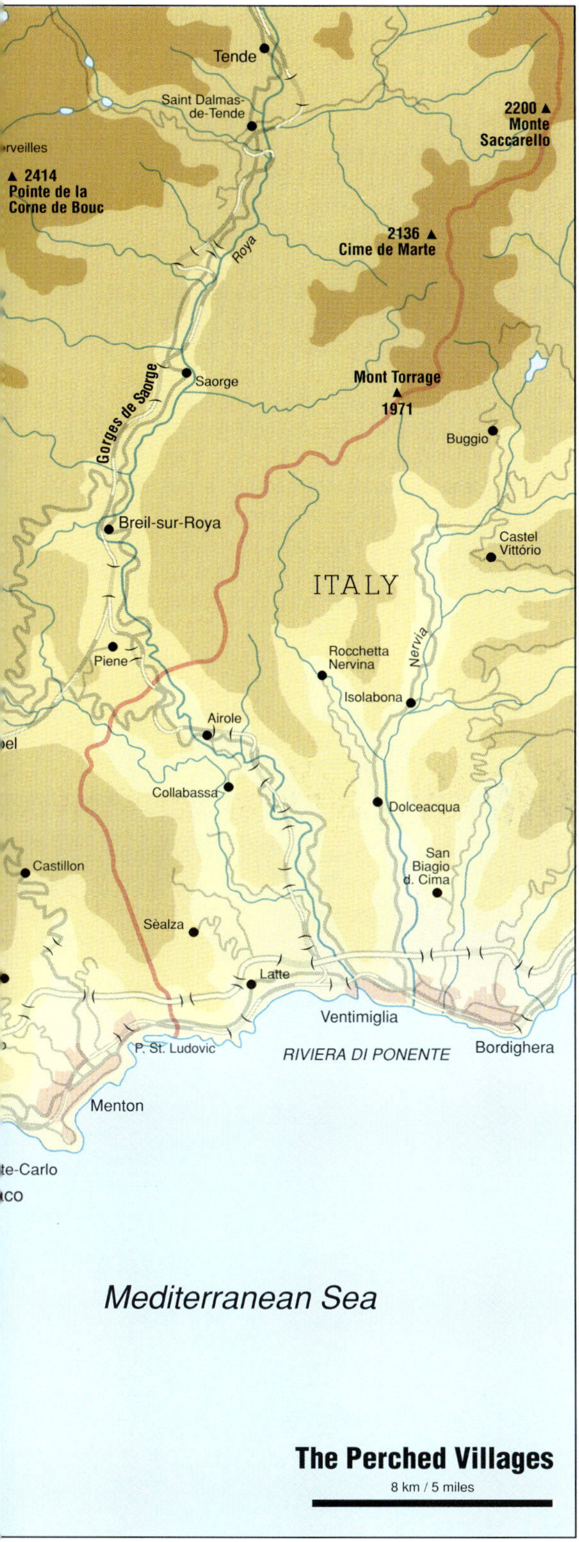

The Perched Villages

The finest feature is the large Église Ste-Marie, set at the head of the village and created from two adjoining chapels, the oldest being 12th-century. Two buttresses span the road, and a slender Romanesque bell tower dominates the village. A picture to the right of the altar shows Peille in the 16th century.

On the side of Montée St-Bernard next to the church are the ruins of a 14th-century castle, part of the original fortifications of the town which were mostly pulled down during the revolution. A very old part of the town lies directly below the castle, across the main road, consisting of very steep stone stairs and covered alleys. The Hôtel de Ville on Rue Centrale is housed in an 18th-century chapel, which has an interesting domed roof.

Nearby **Peillon** is regarded as one of the most beautiful of all the perched villages. Approaching from the main road it seems impossible to believe that 2 miles (3 km) will be enough to reach its dizzy heights amongst the olives and pines. As the French memorably put it, "*Peillon marque l'extrémité du monde habité*." Its charm is in the entire ensemble, the fantastic position, the winding main "street", which would be better described as a staircase, and the superb views from the square at the top. As you enter the village from the small square shaded by plane trees, there is a fragment of an old archway to the left, part of the springing is still visible. There is also a tower of white stone, very clean and well restored.

A number of houses have open top floors in the Renaissance manner. Its narrow streets have very steep stone steps through vaulted tunnels and sometimes as many as four front doors leading from someone else's basement. Footpaths start at the end of the village leading to Peille and La Turbie through the wonderful wooded mountainside.

La Turbie, high above Monte-Carlo, is one of the most magnificent sights of the Côte d'Azur but more easily accessible from the Provençale autoroute, leaving at the La Turbie-Monaco interchange. The autoroute is spectacular on this stretch, spanning great ravines and tunnelling through mountains. The name La Turbie comes from the Latin, *tropaea*, trophy, and it is named after the Trophy of Augustus, a huge Roman monument erected to commemorate the conquest of the 45 Alpine tribes who had been attacking Romanised Gaul. Augustus himself, the first of the Roman emperors, led the campaigns in 15 and 14 BC. The trophy was built between 13 and 5 BC, probably using the enslaved Alpine tribesmen as labour.

The structure was originally 165 ft (50 metres) high, and even now, 115 ft (35 metres) are still standing after 2,000 years. It consists of a large rectangular base supporting a cylindrical core of 24 huge Doric columns, some of which remain, their load bearing supports now visible. The columns once supported a masonry tower, surmounted by a stepped cone roof, topped with a giant statue of Emperor Augustus as the conquering general.

A nine-line inscription framed by two winged victories exists on the front face, the longest intact Roman inscription to come down to us from antiquity. From the 7th to 10th centuries its upper parts were used as a watchtower during the period of barbarian raids, and parts of its masonry were reused in ramparts to stave off the Saracens.

In the Middle Ages, the Lérins monks destroyed its statues because they were pagan. In the wars between the Guelphs and the Ghibellines, during the 12th and 13th centuries, the villagers took refuge in its passages and stairways. In 1706 it was partially destroyed because of its strategic location and later Louis XIV ordered the destruction of the "castle", not wishing any fortification to fall into the hands of the Dukes of Savoie. The ruins became a quarry and most of the town of La Turbie is built from the very stones which gave it its name. Only one other similar trophy is known, that of Trajan at Adam Klissi in Rumania, making this of particular interest.

It is set in a lovely clifftop park, ideal for picnics. There is a fine museum, displaying the many bits which have been unearthed from the monument,

A hill village at the turn of the century.

with a large scale model of how it originally looked, very useful for understanding the present remains. From the cliff is a spectacular view over the Mediterranean and to Monte-Carlo below. Yachts and speedboats go about their business and tiny cars crawl along the winding roads, but on the days when formula-one racing cars are in Monte-Carlo for the Grand Prix, the throaty roar is deafening, even 1,500 ft (450 metres) up.

The town is small, built in a quarter circle with two surviving town gates, one of which is best seen from the gardens of the Trophy, and many old buildings from the 11th and 13th centuries, particularly lining what used to be the Roman Via Julia which led to the Trophy. The baroque 18th-century church is built from stones taken from the Trophy and has attractive bands of coloured tiles on its cupola. The village is utterly charming with a wealth of odd little architectural details embedded in its ochre walls and vaulted arcades, large terracotta pots of geraniums and bougainvillaea, its narrow cobbled streets dominated by the vast monument, so large in scale as to be almost surreal in its presence.

Just north of Roquebrune and Menton are a group of hill villages which are just far enough from the bustling coast to have escaped the crowds. It helps that the villages lie at the end of tortuous roads and are literally hidden in mists. Not for nothing are residents of Ste-Agnès and Gorbio known as *les nébuleux*, the mist-dwellers.

Gorbio sits high on its hill looking out to the Mediterranean, amongst the olives which provided its livelihood until the 19th century, when its inhabitants turned to tourism, catering to the growing-numbers of visitors from Menton. It is famous for its narrow arched streets, and for its snail procession, *la procession aux escargots*, which, disappointingly, is not actually a promenade of snails, but a festival celebrated by the White Penitents when the streets are illuminated by oil flames lit in a multitude of snail shells.

Medieval walls and doorways of La Turbie.

Although close to Menton, **Ste-Agnès** belongs to medieval Provence, a landscape at once Mediterranean and mountainous. As a quaint *village perché*, Ste-Agnès is the most attractive in the area. Its eagerness to send visitors away with souvenirs rather than memories is the only jarring note.

En route to Ste-Agnès, the familiar olive and lemon groves merge into Provençal *maquis*. As the land climbs to 2,296 ft (700 metres), the olives disappear; sturdy juniper, pine and fir trees jut over the crags. By Ste-Agnès the mists and the temperatures fall, particularly in the early morning. "*Je vais me noyer dans la brume*," ("I'm off to drown myself in the fog,") is almost a cheery greeting in the village.

It is not clear how Ste Agnès acquired her sainthood. One legend has it that she was a Roman empress who sought refuge from a storm in a local grotto and, in thanks, built a chapel on the spot. The more colourful version is that Haroun, a Saracen chief, raided the village and selected a Provençale for his harem. The chaste Agnès resisted her kidnapper until he converted to Christianity.

From the 12th century the village was fought over by the counts of Ventimiglia and Provence. In the 16th century the ancient château was dismantled and its stones incorporated into existing houses. The ruined **château** overlooks an Italianate cemetery and pine forest. The walk up is especially pungent in spring: woodsmoke wafts through the cherry blossom, herbs and damp pine trees. At the top, if the fog has lifted, there are views towards the Alps, the coast and even Corsica.

Just below the château ruins is the village, clustered around the foot of a cliff. Place de la Mairie is a compact square lined with medieval buildings, including **Notre-Dame-des-Neiges**, the 17th-century parish church. The honey and herb shops outside are a prelude to the main assault on Rue Longue. With its neat stone steps and flower-hung archways, well-restored houses and well-trained dogs, Ste-Agnès is almost too perfect. On a summer's day, however, **Rue Longue** mills with enamelists and herbalists, soap-sellers and crystal-engravers, jewellers and dried flower designers.

Rue Longue leads to **Square Ste-Agnès**, perched on the edge of a ravine. This is where the original chapel was carved into the rock. All that now remains is a small shrine and a cute statue of the saint. The chapel was destroyed during the construction of a wartime fortification system along the border. From 1930 the Italian threat was ever-present so an extension to the Maginot line was created from the coast to the mountains beyond Sospel. Designed as an updated model of a Vauban fortress, Fort Ste-Agnès remains an impressive defensive system, only accessible via a narrow drawbridge.

Villagers whimsically attribute their wartime escape to the spirit of Ste Agnès, still lurking in her grotto within the military fort. On 21 January, her saint's day, a dawn concert and carnival are followed by a procession to Notre-Dame-des-Neiges.

Rue des Comtes Leotardi leads out of the village, past covered passageways and medieval ramparts. Along here is the Vieille Auberge, with its promise of *raviolis maison, tarte agnèsoise* and panoramic views. If not leaving Ste-Agnès over-fed or laden with pine-scented cologne and Saracen jewels, then consider a walk along mule tracks to Gorbio. The Chemin du Pierre Rochard is named after the wartime parish priest who regularly walked to Menton to bring back rations.

Castellar, just east of Ste-Agnès, is perched on a hillside covered with orchards and olives. The village is an acquired taste, historically richer than Ste-Agnès yet somewhat neglected. Entirely lacking in arts and crafts, Castellar is guileless, a traditional hill-top village. To Niçois, its sole function is to serve Sunday lunch in a rural setting. The rectangular village was laid out with military precision by the Lascaris Seigneurs. It remained in their hands until the Revolution, with peasants continuing to pay such feudal dues as a shoulder of pork for a day's grazing rights. Not until 1792 did Castellar become part of France, an event celebrated by *l'arbre de la liberté* in the **Place de la Mairie**.

From here, the formal grid-pattern is clear: three parallel streets, linked by covered passageways, lead to the church at the end of the village. Two encircling paths trace the outline of the former city walls. **Rue de la République** is lined with sober medieval houses with roughly-hewn stone staircases. An old-fashioned bakery produces *fougasse*, biscuits made from almonds and pine kernels.

Equally pleasant aromas waft from La Tour Lascaris, a rustic restaurant housed in the **Palais Lascaris**, the counts' former residence. Although the *salle d'armes* has lost its frescoes, it retains an austere charm in keeping with the cuisine. Apart from *tourte de courge*, a courgette and aubergine pie, there is *Barba Juan, crêpes* stuffed with mushrooms, cheese and rice. Food is simple and vegetable-based, a reflection of Castellar's peasant roots.

At the end of Rue de la République is **St-Pierre**, a baroque church with an onion-domed bell tower and pinkish facade. From here, Rue Général Sarrail leads back to the Mairie. The first house on the left was a medieval prison but is being converted into a crafts workshop. Opposite is the **Chapelle des Pénitents Blancs**, a restored baroque chapel hemmed in by medieval houses. Further along is the **Chapelle des Pénitents Noirs**, sadly in need of restoration.

Covered passageways on the right lead to **Rue Arson**, the prettiest part of the village, bordering the countryside. A circular medieval tower backs on to the ramparts and, close to the church, is an olive-processing mill and an old wash house. Jean-Paul Albin, president of the *comité des fêtes*, is keen to attract visitors to his village but not at the expense of peace and quiet. In short, scruffy Castellar will not succumb to the prettified Ste-Agnès effect.

Heading for the mountains: The route to St-Martin-Vésubie from Nice takes in more perched villages as well as the spectacular Gorge de la Vésubie. Es-

A floral retreat.

caping Nice on the N202 going north, take the D414 to Colomars, where it becomes the ridge road to **Aspremont**, a charming village of concentric picturesque lanes with lots of little winding alleys leading from them. At the foot of the village stands the chapel of St-Claude, built in 1632 to guard the inhabitants against the plague. The church of St-Jacques has an unusual 13th-century Gothic nave, contrasting in style with the other village buildings. Like the rest of the village, the church has been recently restored. A castle once stood at the top of the village, but now only the ramparts remain.

Follow the Rue des Remparts around the top of the village to reach the Place Leandre Astraudo, a small square with a fountain; on one side is the highest remaining section of castle wall with corbels and blocked-up windows. There is a stairway to a little children's playground with a superb view of the mountains and a grove of trees marking the position of the castle keep.

Nearby **Castagniers** is a tiny village, largely rebuilt in the 19th century. There is a wonderful view of the Var Valley from the small square in front of the 1817 church.

If you continue up the Var Valley, you will find **St-Martin-du-Var** just off the main highway; the old village is a small tangle of lanes tucked behind the huge main square. **La Roquette-sur-Var**, high on its hill, was built at a strategic position on the old international frontier with Italy and at the summit of the village there are the vestiges of a castle. The church of St-Pierre was completed in 1682.

Continuing north on the N202, you comte to Plan-du-Var, the last stop for pizza and cold drinks before the **Gorges de la Vésubie**, which lacks any kind of roadside refreshment. The gorge is stunning, its steep sides plummeting to the river far below, the road winding and tunnelling through the rock. In a car it can be difficult to stop safely to admire the view; cycling or rambling is a much better way to appreciate it all.

At **St-Jean-la-Rivière** the deep gorge is spanned by a dramatic bridge and the houses are built on top of each other either side of the river. Here the Vésubie canal, much of which is underground, begins. From here you can take the steep, winding road to Utelle, one of the villages on the original *route du sel* from the salt flats of Hyères to the Southern Alps, a route which was abandoned at the end of the 18th century.

This is real mountain country where you are more likely to meet a logging truck on a hairpin bend than a tourist coach. **Utelle** is a very pleasant little town, dependent mainly on olive cultivation. It is built like a star on a rocky outcrop, originally the crossroads of a number of mule paths over the mountains which surround it. The hillsides, covered in wild lavender and fragrant herbs, are perfect for walking and picnics. The 16th-century church of St-Véran replaced an earlier one destroyed by the earthquake of 1452. It is a curious mixture of architectural styles, with Romanesque columns and capitals, 18th-century baroque decoration, a Gothic loggia and 16th-century high altar. Don't

Ready for a stroll around La Turbie.

miss the 16th-century primitive painted altarpiece of the Annunciation in the north aisle or the doors with their 12 panels carved with dragons.

The village has some intriguing door lintels; near the post office there is one at knee level, carved with esoteric alchemical symbols.

The mountain road continues beyond the village, climbing higher and higher with hair-raising views to the valleys below, until you reach a magnificent wind-blown plateau and the sanctuary of Madone d'Utelle. According to legend, it was founded by sailors who were guided to safety during a tempest by a mysterious light on the mountain, and founded the sanctuary in gratitude. The chapel which is usually open, was restored in the mid-1970s, and the building next to it is used as a retreat.

There is a viewing platform with a spectacular 360-degree panorama of mountain peaks and valleys and beyond to the distant sea; on a clear day you can see as far as Cap d'Antibes and even Corsica.

The main road, D 2565, continues to Lantosque, climbing all the way. The gorge widens to meadows and pastures; this is an area of pony rides, horses, camping and caravaning.

There can be few things more pleasurable than sitting beneath a parasol at one of the cafés in the lively little square at **Lantosque**, with a distant view of the village of La Bollène Vésubie clinging to its hill-top further up the valley.

Lantosque itself is built on the rocky spine of the hill up which the streets climb in a series of staircases. There is a distinct Italianate influence in the architecture with open loggias on the top floors of many of the older houses.

A little further on is **La Bollène Vésubie**, a charming town with big, shady lime trees lining the wider streets. At the top of the village is a pretty baroque church dated 1525. There are no architectural highlights in the village; it is the total ensemble that makes it so delightful. Like many of these villages, it was badly flooded in 1993 and has taken some time to recover.

St-Martin-Vésubie, a popular summer retreat.

The D2565 leads on through trout fishing country to **Roquebillière Vieux**, an equestrian centre. A bridge leads over the river to new Roquebillière, attractively built with uniform red tiled roofs. High on the mountain, overlooking them both is **Belvédère**, a hill town with a rather good clock and sun dial on the bell tower and a large barn-like church. The houses are many-storeyed with balconies and top-floor loggias in the mountain tradition. Lavender and jasmine grows everywhere and the views are wonderful.

Once beyond Roquebillière, the architecture becomes noticeably alpine, with large overhanging roofs and balconies in the Swiss chalet style. Not for nothing is this area known as the "Suisse niçoise".

Located in the centre of it is **St-Martin-Vésubie**, the gateway to the Mercantour national park. It is a mountaineering centre and summer retreat, popular with the people of Nice. Even in high season it's a sleepy kind of place, certainly for the cat dozing in the window of the *boulangerie* along with loaves shaped like tortoises and crocodiles. The main shopping and restaurant street is the Rue du Dr-Cagnoli which runs the full length of the town. It has a fast-flowing gutter running down the middle and is lined with Gothic houses with corbels and balconies, the oldest of which are at the bottom, near the church. There is quite a mix of architectural styles, blending Swiss-style chalet roofs and wooden balconies with Italian loggias, Gothic doors and jettied roofs.

At No. 25 is the *maison Gothique* of the counts of Gubernatis, a national monument. It has a jettied first floor, ornamental frieze and arched ground floor. On one side of the street the buildings lean out over the river and the restaurants have tree-shaded dining terraces in the back. Near the 18th-century Chapelle-des-Pénitents-Blancs with its interesting bulb cupola, there is a tiny market place. The baroque church is 17th-century, but possesses a 13th-century virgin which is carried in procession on 2 July to the sanctuary of the

The total ensemble of La Bollène Vésubie.

Madone de la Fenestre, where she remains until the end of September.

From the terrace in front of the church door there is a view looking south to the perched village of Venanson and the surrounding mountains and forest. Behind the east end of the church, to the right, is the Place de la Frairie, a terrace looking out over the Madone de la Fenestre river, which has its origins in the Lac de la Fenestre in the mountains to the east on the Italian border. The steep river valley can be followed for 8 miles (13 km) along the D94, ending at the high mountain sanctuary of Madone de la Fenestre.

A variety of return routes to the coast are possible. You might go via **Peïra Cava**, which was originally a military camp but has developed into a winter sports and holiday resort. The view from the Pierre Plate, which is a half-mile walk or drive up the small road opposite the Hotel Truchi, is superb. There is parking near the top.

Lucéram is probably of Roman origin, situated at the crossroads of ancient paths, in particular the salt route from the coast. Until recently it depended on mountain farming for survival, mainly olive cultivation and also distilling wild lavender. Today the still fortified village, with its tall stacked houses in pastel colours of yellow, rose and almond green, and its sombre vaulted alleys, depends almost entirely on tourism. It is noted particularly for the church treasures in the 15th-century l'Église Ste-Marguerite, which include a silver reliquary and retables attributed to Niçois artist Louis Bréa.

Finally, **Coaraze** is worth a detour; a restored medieval perched village with concentric lanes, arches and covered passages and public gardens with cypress trees. The church is 17th-century in the *baroque-rustique* style and there are sundials in the square outside. Visit the graveyard which uses cement boxes for burials because the rock is so hard that graves are impossible to dig. At the summit of the village is the Place du Château, site of the now demolished castle.

Alpine view from Utelle.

BORDER COUNTRY

The **Haut-Pays** resembles Piedmont rather than Provence and, in accent, sounds Italian rather than French. The Italian influence colours the architecture: loggias, arcaded squares and onion-topped bell towers abound. A love of decoration is present in such flourishes as carved lintels, elegant balconies and madonnas in niches. The dreamy Italianate villages strive after colour, with painted facades, *trompe l'oeil* decoration and glinting fish-scale roofs. Sospel and the **Bévéra Valley** mark the transition from the outward-looking Mediterranean world to the inward-looking mountain world. Here olives, lavender and lemons give way to pine, oak, mountain laurel and vivid blue gentians.

The **Haute Roya Valley** begins just north of Sospel and from Breil-Sur-Roya the mountain atmosphere becomes more pronounced. The rural architecture acquires an alpine sturdiness, with dry stone barns and *cazouns*, the shepherds' primitive shelters.

Sleepy town: The natural gateway to the mountainous hinterland is **Sospel**, sprawling along the Bévéra Valley. As a great advocate of green tourism, Sospel offers a wide range of walks through classic hill country. Tourism is low-key and has not changed the character of this sleepy medieval town.

Sospel was an independent commune by the 11th century and an important trading post on the old salt route linking Piedmont with France. Medieval Sospel depended, in turn, on the counts of Ventimiglia, Provence and Savoy but retained a degree of autonomy. This was partly due to the presence of charitable confraternities which played a major role in city life. By the 17th century Sospel was a noted artistic and intellectual centre but fell into a gradual decline, not reversed by the town's return to France in 1860.

The town did, however, experience a brief period of glory, and much suffering, during World War II. In 1944–45 there were fierce battles in the area and occupying German forces only withdrew in April 1945. By then, many Resistance workers had been executed and other Sospellois had been deported to Italy. In recognition of Sospel's sacrifices, the town was awarded the *Croix de Guerre*.

The focal point of the town is the **Pont Vieux**, the 11th-century tollgate and bridge spanning the river Bévéra. It is the oldest tollgate in the Alpes-Maritimes and was still in use in the 18th century. Carriages from Nice transported salt, fish, citrus fruits, porcelain and silk towards Piedmont. In the opposite direction came rice, flax, muslin, lace and dry white wine.

Although the bridge was partly blown up in 1944, the stones were fished out of the river and the Pont Vieux was restored in 1953. The left bank of the river, originally outside the city walls, is lined with attractive pastel-coloured buildings.

Beside the old bridge is a small square with an arcaded medieval building and

Preceding pages: Sospel, cathedral and clocktower. **Left**, viewing the mountains. **Right**, the latest thing at Sospel.

fountain. This faded apricot-coloured building was the **Palais Communal** until 1810, housing both the town council and religious tribunals. Place Garibaldi, the adjoining square, has a series of medieval arcades incorporated into later buildings.

The riverside quarter, stretching from Place Garibaldi to Place Ste-Croix, consists of austere 14th-century houses, once home to Sospel's prosperous merchant class. The houses in Rue de la République contain vast interconnecting wine cellars. In the same street is the Maison de Toia, a sculpted Romanesque *hôtel particulier*.

Chapelle Ste-Croix, dating from 1518, is the oldest confraternity building and as the headquarters of the Pénitents Blancs still serves a charitable purpose. Medieval Sospel had five confraternities which offered hospitality to pilgrims and made loans to impoverished peasants. While most Franciscan confraternities were egalitarian, Sospel's were hierarchical: the Pénitents Noirs served the nobility while the Rouges only welcomed local dignitaries; the Blancs were for the bourgeoisie; the Bleus for the young; and the Gris for the poor.

From Place Ste-Croix it is a short stroll across the river to the main street, Avenue Jean-Médecin and Place St-Pierre, a market-place overlooking plantain trees. Rue St-Pierre, a medieval street leading to the **Cathedral**, is lined with dilapidated houses, including the Romanesque Maison Domérégo. This dingy passage astonishingly opens on to Place St-Michel, the most theatrical square in the region. Tucked into a graceful Romanesque clocktower is the cathedral's peaches-and-cream facade: frothy stucco and kitsch gladiatorial figures adorn the exterior.

Opposite the chapel is the Foyer Rural, also subject to the *trompe l'oeil* effect. This cultural centre used to be the Town Hall until an earthquake shattered the building in 1887. Next door is the Palais Ricci, an arcaded Romanesque mansion which in 1809 welcomed Pope Pius VII on his journey to Tuscany. Curiously, this baroque square echoes Pienza, the Tuscan Renaissance town built by Pius II.

Sospel's cathedral is in its element during a sudden summer thunderstorm. It is also magical in the late evening, when the bells chime and a sliver of moon is visible between the Lombard Tower and the baroque facade. The majestic interior is well-preserved and full of light. A touching invitation to prayer says, *"Cette lumière symbolise ma prière que je continue, tout en m'allant."*

The highlight is a 15th-century *Madonna* by Bréa, the renowned Niçois artist. The Virgin, dressed in a gold embroidered dress, stands in front of a Mediterranean coastal scene. Facing Bréa's work is a 15th-century depiction of the Virgin and Christ. The composition features the Pénitents Blancs, who commissioned the work. The painting, awkward and less idealised than Bréa's work, is also more moving.

Walks: From Place St-Michel, the Montée de Louis Saramito leads up to the ruined castle and abbey. From Sospel,

Mountain goatherd.

a signposted walk leads all the way through Provençal countryside to Olivetta in Italy. Longer hikes lead south to Castellar, or north to Moulinet and L'Authion, mountainous terrain where the Germans made their last stand at the Battle of Sospel.

War memorials are on every hill but the **Fort St-Roch** is the most impressive. Just south of Sospel, St-Roch was built in 1930 against the threat of an Italian invasion. It is virtually an underground village, protected by anti-tank defences where 250 soldiers, with artillery and equipment, could survive for at least three months. Local fears of an invasion were well-founded and although Sospel held out against superior Italian forces, occupation was inevitable, by the Italians in 1940 and the Germans in 1943. By September 1944 the Germans had lost Nice and Menton but hung on to Sospel, despite an Allied advance northwards.

Just 3 miles (5 km) south of Menton, the Allies were told to stay put and wait until the advance across northern Europe was established. As a result, Sospel suffered even longer in German hands and was exposed to American artillery attacks. In October the Germans retreated northwards and Hawaiians were the first Allies to enter Sospel. Cries of *"Vive Sospel! Vive La IV République!"* were shortlived, however, and the battle continued until April 1945.

Good *cuisine bourgeoise* is available at the *Hotel de France* but, for a foretaste of the Italianate Roya Valley, try the *tortellini* in *La Taverne Toscane*. Peaceful Sospel may lose some of its charm when the Menton-Sospel road is finally completed. So now is the time to sample the riverside walks and alpine liqueurs.

The Roya Valley: Compared with the Vallée de la Bévéra, the **Roya Valley** is wilder, poorer and more rugged. In the past, routes didn't follow the valley floor because of fears of flooding or landfalls in narrow gorges. Instead, paths were carved along the side of the mountains and through high mountain passes. The Roya's medieval villages, often

Heading down the Roya valley.

perched beside fearsome gorges, were linked only by the old salt route.

Until the 19th century this route was the only way through the region; the Roya Valley did not open up until 1860 when Napoléon III, newly in control of the Comté de Nice, wished to increase trade with Piedmont. The Italian influence, a troubled history, and terrible communications have all helped preserve the Roya in its splendid isolation.

Breil-sur-Roya makes an arresting first impression, particularly if reached by rail or via the precarious Col de Brouis. The train from Sospel emerges from a long mountain tunnel and suddenly there is a fish-shaped pattern of pastel houses clinging to a bend in the River Roya. The mountains bank steeply behind the red-tiled houses. A golden angel blows a trumpet from a chapel rooftop.

Breil likes to call itself the "French gateway to the Roya" since until 50 years ago the Italian border ran just north of the village. However, France is only skin deep. *Ciao* is a normal greeting; the *cuisine provençale* tastes of Piedmont; and Italy lies only a few miles east.

Breil was ruled by the counts of Provence, Ventimiglia and Genoa before becoming part of the House of Savoy until 1860. Unlike Sospel, Breil depended almost entirely upon olive growing and farming. The lower slopes are still given over to olives and 500 tonnes are harvested each year. As for farming, the village still operates traditional grazing rights: from October to April more than 2,000 Breil sheep and goats graze on communal land. It was a dispute about this issue that led to an 18th-century revolt against the feudal lords. The event is re-enacted every four years in *Staccada*, complete with mock battles and a show trial.

A gentle walk along the river leads to Place Brançion in the heart of the medieval village. Open to the river on one side, the square is dominated by an apricot-coloured church, **Sancta Maria in Albis**. This 17th-century baroque facade is echoed by a flamboyant Italianate

Serious mountain terrain.

interior, with a vivid Bréa panel-painting and a fine organ. The church, like many others in the Roya Valley, has a glittering multi-coloured onion dome.

Breil is well-worn hiking country; signed walks lead to medieval watchtowers like La Cruella or to isolated chapels to the west of the village. Longer hikes lead to Sospel or Vesubie.

Although many Breillois are civil servants or coastal commuters, the village is enough of a retirement haven to radiate relaxation. Residents include poets, local historians and the food-writer Mademoiselle Sassi whose book, *Recettes Breilloises*, provides a guide to Breil cuisine.

In April 1945 when General de Gaulle led the liberating French forces into Breil, he may have been tempted to stay behind. In its unspectacular way, Breil offers peace of mind.

Breil is, in many ways, untypical of the Roya Valley. The vegetation is lushly Mediterranean and blurs the impact of the brooding mountains. Relative prosperity and an influx of outsiders have diluted its Italian atmosphere. In the **Haute Roya**, however, the transition to mountainous terrain is complete. The dramatic Gorges de Saorge, immediately after Breil, announce serious terrain, with high waterfalls, deep forests, wind-blown alpine pastures and mauve-grey canyons.

Nor are Italian sentiments muted in the Upper Roya. From medieval times, the effects of epidemics and wars forced local *seigneurs* to recruit labour from further afield, particularly from Piedmont, Lombardy and Liguria. This influx of Italians continued until the 1950s and has left its mark on the language, culture and architecture.

In 1860, unlike the rest of the Comté de Nice, the Upper Roya remained with the House of Savoy, rulers since medieval times. La Brigue, Tende and the other villages in the Upper Roya were in an anomalous position. In the 1860 plebiscite they voted to rejoin France rather than remain with Piedmont but were refused permission by Cavour, Victor Emmanuel's astute Prime Minister. Cavour's subterfuge was to claim that the region, bordering the game-rich Mercantour, formed part of the King's *terrains de chasse*. The reality had nothing to do with retaining hunting grounds and everything to do with controlling the vital mountain passes.

It was not until the 1947 plebiscite that the Haute Roya was incorporated into France. The head rather than the heart determined this political allegiance: trading links were with the French coast and the French standard of living was far higher. So, while Niçois rightly claim that they were never Italian but merely Piedmontese, the same cannot be said of the distinctly Italian Roya Valley. Since becoming French, there have been no great social changes to this self-sufficient mountain community. The dialects still remain resolutely *Piémontais*, as do the local crafts and traditions.

Shimmering tiles: The most spectacularly sited of all Roya villages is **Saorge**. At first sight it appears suspended between a hazy mountain sky and the lush valley floor. The village forms a vast

Saorge, perfect example of a "stacked village".

amphitheatre around a sheer cliff. Down below flows the Roya and on the other side of the canyon lie olive groves rising to terraced alpine pastures.

Saorge looks like a traditional *village perché*: it is perched on high for defensive reasons and favours a south-facing slope, both as winter shelter and summer sun-trap. The painted Venetian facades and the bell towers covered in a mosaic of shimmering tiles are also typical of Roya hill-top villages. But the height of the narrow medieval houses, the disparity of street levels and the complexity of the interlinking passages mark Saorge out as a perfect example of a *village empilé*, a "stacked village".

Saorge is set at right-angles to the slope so that the equivalent to a 30-storey tower separates the foundations of the lowest house from the roof of the highest one. Each house can be up to ten storeys high, with entrances at five different street levels. The heights are so varied that some streets are merely corridors linking individual apartments rather than houses. This is a medieval version of the complex walkways found in modern shopping malls.

As a fortified village controlling the Col de Tende, Saorge seemed impregnable but was finally captured by French forces in 1793. Even though it later returned to Piedmont, this former capital of the Roya never regained its prestige. The building of a valley road in the 19th century turned the village into a backwater; only valleys prospered. In 1806 the chief tax-collector visited Saorge and complained of "a road riddled with wolves and bandits, crossed in peril of one's life". The dangers may have gone but the isolation remains.

Saorge is a remarkable composition, making it difficult to single out individual attractions. The rough slate roofs, a feature of the Roya Valley, add a severe touch to the 15th-century houses below. The facades are tinted pink, ochre and russet, bathing the village in a warm Ligurian glow at odds with the stark setting. The deepest alleys never see any sunlight.

In the 1960s, at the height of the rural exodus, houses in Saorge sold for 2,000 francs; now the average price is 300,000 francs, a sign that many have been snapped up as *résidences secondaires*. The population, a mere 200 in winter, swells to 2,500 in summer. In winter, the shutters are closed and the village only stirs on market day.

At the entrance to the village is a panoramic view of the valley below. On the square itself is a group of peach-coloured buildings, including a chapel and a Mairie crushed against the cliff. From here, Rue Ste-Jeanne d'Arc winds upwards through covered passageways. (The names of streets are usually meaningless in Saorge since most have three names, usually after rival Resistance leaders.)

At the top is **St-Sauveur**, the 15th-century parish church. The forbidding exterior is not misleading; inside is a damp, mauve-tinged interior and a chilly atmosphere not redeemed by a fine Italian organ. Virtually next door is a cheerful cafe, *Lou Pountain*, a chance to sample *quiques*, a local variant on spinach *fettuccini*.

Cobbled streets lead up to a **Franciscan monastery** set amongst cypresses and olives. The sunny terrace is a place for contemplation, with telescopic views of Saorge below and of barren mountains beyond. Although the monastery is built around a Romanesque church, it is essentially baroque.

A former mule track leads from the monastery to **Madone del Poggio**, an isolated Romanesque church topped by an octagonal tower. This graceful sliver of a tower is supported by a honeycomb apse, all that remains of the original abbey. The church and surrounding estate have been in the Davio family for years so the vivid frescoes in the crypt cannot be visited. One consolation is the view of Saorge at sunset. The light shifts across the terraced crescent, colouring the facades sienna and casting deep shadows over the onion-domed towers.

Despite the wonderful scenery, the inhabitants are a disparate, warring group. The core of the winter community consists of doddering *vieux du pays*, hippies and young professionals. The *vieux* are happy to let run-down shepherds' shacks and outlying farms to the *marginaux*. The profit from these latter-day hippies is frittered away in Chez Gilon bar. The hippies lead a pioneer lifestyle, bee-keeping, weaving and tilling the soil. It is subsistence farming; the pastures are known locally as "Siberia" because they receive no sun for four months of the year.

The yuppies are shocked to see mules laden with olives and ill-dressed children. The young schoolteacher's wife complains that the hippies and the retired railway workers are lowering the tone. "What do we want with *boules*, hunting and silly festivals?" Born and bred in Saorge, she loves the quality of life, the landscape and the dialect, an old Ligurian language that pre-dates Latin. Still, she has nothing but scorn for the left-wing mayor who lives in Nice and visits the village only at weekends. "Along with China, we're the last place in the world to remain Communist."

Gorges: Between Saorge and La Brigue the landscape is ravaged by a series of gorges. The building of the Nice-Turin railway brought much-needed work to the Roya villages. Although the line was begun in 1910, work stopped in 1914 and the track was destroyed during World War II. Finally finished in 1972, the result is a spectacular feat of engineering. The 39 viaducts alone make it the most acrobatic line in Europe. The track often does a loop in mountain tunnels so that a train emerges from a tunnel just above its entry point.

Just before La Brigue is **St-Dalmas** station, an overbearing piece of Fascist architecture which served as a major communications centre in Mussolini's time. Despite its baroque church and sturdy architecture, St-Dalmas-de-Tende is an unremarkable village. It is best-known as a touring base for excursions into the **Vallée des Merveilles**. This remote valley lies in the heart of the protected zone known as the **Parc National du Mercantour**.

Alpine pastures: La Brigue is at once the richest and simplest of Roya villages. Set amidst alpine pastures, La Brigue has always been a remote place,

Breil, French gateway to the Roya.

VALLE DES MERVEILLES

Cradled in a majestic circle of the Alps, the Vallée des Merveilles is aptly named and no mere marketing ploy. The valley is a vast open-air museum of prehistory. It is also a Wagnerian landscape of rock-strewn valleys, jagged peaks and eerie lakes. Thanks to the presence of minerals, the lakes are green, turquoise, slate-grey and even black.

Just west of the Lac des Mèsches is the Minière de la Vallaure, an abandoned mine quarried from pre-Roman times to the 1930s. Early prospectors came in search of gold and silver but had to settle for copper, zinc, iron and lead instead. The Romans were beaten to the valley by Bronze Age settlers who carved mysterious symbols on the polished rock, ice-smoothed by glaciation. These carvings were first recorded in the 17th century but investigated only from 1879 by Clarence Bicknell, an English naturalist. He made it his life's work to chart the carvings and died in a valley refuge in 1918.

The rock carvings are similar to ones found in northern Italy, notably those in the Camerino Valley near Bergamo. However, the French carvings are exceptional in that they depict a race of shepherds rather than hunters. The scarcity of wild game in the region forced the Bronze Age tribes to turn to agriculture and cattle-raising. Carvings of yokes, harnesses and tools depict a pastoral civilisation and these primitive inscriptions served as territorial markers for the tribes in the area.

However, the drawings are also open to less earth-bound interpretations. Anthropomorphic figures represent domestic animals and chief tribesmen but also dancers, devils, sorcerers and gods. Such magical totems are in keeping with Mont Bégo's reputation as a sacred spot. Given the bleakness of the terrain, it is hardly surprising that the early shepherds looked heavenwards for help. Now, as then, flocks of cows, sheep and goats graze by the lower lakes, especially at Fontanalbe. However, the abandoned stone farms and shepherds' bothies attest to the unprofitability of mountain farming.

The Vallée des Merveilles is accessible only by jeep or on foot, and now, due to increasing vandalism – even to the carvings themselves – you can visit the Vallée only if accompanied by an official guide. Given the mountain conditions, the drawings are only visible between the end of June and October. It is a 5-mile (8-km) drive west from St Dalmas to the information centre by the Lac des Mèsches. Then follows a 6-mile (10-km) trek through the woods to Lac Long and the start of the rock carving zone. To protect the engravings, the authorities now insist that visitors are accompanied by an approved guide. A range of different trips can be organised through Tende tourist office.

The Vallée des Merveilles is part of the Parc National du Mercantour, a vast conservation area worth visiting in its own right. Roughly 56 by 19 miles (90 by 30 km), Mercantour is a wilderness of pine forests, gorges and pastures. There are no permanent residents, just a few hamlets occupied by summer visitors. It is ideal rambling country with an amazing variety of flora and fauna. Wild geraniums, gentian violets and forest fruits are common on the lower slopes while orchids, edelweiss and rare saxifrage grow higher up.

The park is also a game reserve with huge ibex, wild boar and shaggy mountain goats. The only problem is illegal hunting on the edge of the Mercantour. The park is regularly raided to satisfy the Niçois penchant for venison or *marcassin*. ■

Animals inspire many of the rock carvings.

wholly dependent on the wool trade. Until the late 19th century, three-quarters of the population reared the sure-footed breed of sheep known as the Brigasque. After spending the summer in La Brigue, local shepherds took their flocks to winter pastures in Breil, Èze and Menton. The itinerant La Brigue shepherd, dressed in red velvet cap and green corduroy, has entered French folklore as a born storyteller.

The wealth created by the wool trade attracted Jewish merchants, money-lenders and goldsmiths to set up shop in the quarter known as Rû Ghetto. By the 15th century, wool merchants and notables could afford to indulge in artistic patronage. Italian craftsmen were commissioned to build new chapels and to adorn bourgeois homes with engraved lintels. The village was deeply influenced by the Italian Renaissance: the local architecture was enriched by arcaded streets and sculpted columns. Italian frescoes replaced traditional Niçois murals.

As late as the 19th century there was a flourishing crafts tradition in the village. However, La Brigue's return to France in 1947 divided the commune with scant regard for history. The "low" village of La Brigue became French while the "high" village, Briga Alta, remained Italian, along with virtually all the neighbouring hamlets. The population of La Brigue dropped from a peak of 4,000 to a mere 500, making it the same size as it was in the 12th century.

Still, there are compensations for such depopulation. With the exception of one ugly square, there has been little recent development. The remoteness of the location has deterred potential buyers of second homes, as has the impenetrable local dialect and the sense of a closed community. After the War, the villagers may have diversified into cattle-rearing but agriculture is the mainstay. Today's farmers are horse-breeders, cheese-makers and bee-keepers, not to mention amateur fishermen. The river Levenza is rich in rainbow trout and the speckled local variety.

La Brigue, lying along the Levenza

Lac Basto, Mercantour National Park.

river, is dwarfed by snow-capped mountains, including the majestic Mont Bégo. The oldest quarter fans out from Rio Secco, a dry river bed but the natural introduction to the village is Place St-Martin, an Italianate square. A cluster of trout restaurants border the square and the fast-flowing river. Apart from *truites vivantes* in their tanks, the rustic restaurants offer *gnocchi, lasagne* and *tantifauluza*, a leek tart.

A 17th-century chapel with a leaning *campanile* looms against mauve canyon walls. This is **L'Assuntà,** once the home of the *Pénitents Blancs*, a chapel which answered to Rome. Decorative Tuscan pillars adorn the facade, creating a purity of line which is not reflected in the interior.

Next door, bordering a more intimate square, is **St-Martin**, the village church. The Romanesque bell tower surmounts a mellow, stone structure. St Martin is said to have preached here before settling in the Loire Valley as bishop of Tours. The interior is the richest in the region, boasting Tuscan decor and striking 16th-century paintings. The ceiling, with its starry blue sky, is reminiscent of Siena Cathedral. Equally Italianate are the frescoes of angels in flight, the vaulted arches and the altar screen.

The works of art, including two attributed to Louis Bréa, are individualistic and memorable. Bréa's *Nativité* portrays a luminous Virgin and Child against a dark, craggy background resembling La Brigue. Like Bréa's *Assomption*, also in the church, the painting is a sober yet knowing work. The expressive faces and the delicate handling of drapery are typical of Bréa's artistic gifts.

Music: In summer, concert-lovers wallow in baroque waves of emotion as the church echoes to the sound of Boccherini and Respighi. The organs in La Brigue have been made by such masters as the Lingiardi brothers. Standard church organs weren't able to play baroque music and opera, still less Piedmontese airs and ballets. However, the church organs in the Roya were all adapted to respond to the 19th-century vogue for *Bel Canto*. On informal occasions the organs play shepherds' folk songs about love and war.

On the far side of the church is another fine Pénitents Blancs chapel, **L'Annonciade**. It has a lovely carved baroque facade, also built of the warm local stone. The interior is being transformed into a museum of religious art. From here, all alleys lead inwards, towards the medieval heart of the village. The cobbled streets are confusingly named in local dialect with Frenchified equivalents, so Rio Secco is also Rû Sec, a reference to the dry river bed that traces the arcaded street.

La Brigue has the greatest variety of decorative slate lintels in the Roya Valley. Made of green and black stone, these lintels are the work of 15th- and 16th-century Italian stonemasons. The lintels usually link a Biblical saying or a wise saw to a pictorial motif, such as a Renaissance dragon, cherubs, shepherds and lambs. Rue Filippi, Rue de la République and Rue Rusca are all good lintel-hunting grounds. The village is

The closed community of La Brigue.

completely unrestored and, depending on taste, either ripe for conversion or perfect as it is.

Gods and ghouls: Two miles (4 km) from La Brigue is **Notre-Dames-des-Fontaines**, arguably the most remarkable chapel in the Riviera hinterland. This simple medieval chapel, overlooking a mountain stream, has been a pilgrimage centre since the 14th century. The chapel is supposedly built over a Temple to Diana. Legend has it that after a serious drought, the region was saved by a miraculous outpouring of water from this spot. *Jean de Florette* legends aside, the chapel is celebrated for its 15th-century frescoes, painted by Jean Baleison and Jean Canavesio, Ligurian artists.

Baleison's frescoes, decorating the choir, are faded Marian images, painted as refined courtly figures. Jean Canavesio's frescoes, however, are more satisfying compositions, painted around a central figure. What sets his work apart is the drama and intensity of the moral message, designed to provoke pilgrims into repentance. A grotesque *Judas Iscariot* shows the traitor's disembowelment, performed by a demonic monkey. There is a Hieronymous Bosch quality to the most tormented work.

Elsewhere there are quieter scenes reflecting medieval daily life and landscapes. The *Garden of Gethsemane*, for instance, is full of lush Provençal plants. The artist's palette comes from the region too: the green is crushed slate; the white is limestone; and the black is burnt oak twigs.

Wooded walks: From Notre-Dame-des-Fontaines, walkers can hunt for mushrooms, strawberries and blackcurrants in wooded glades. The enchanting walk back to La Brigue is via a medieval bridge and small orchards owned by Filippi Frères, fruit farmers and beekeepers. A more strenuous hike leads to **Briga Alta**, the Italian village that once belonged to La Brigue. The villagers still meet during hunting and fishing competitions, a time to celebrate their common heritage: trout, *gnocchi* and *salumeria*, Italian salami.

Italian influence in La Brigue.

Tende is as strange as anywhere in the Roya Valley. Despite being a frontier post, it remains a musty, medieval town with its heavy wooden doors closed to the world. But what it lacks in charm, it certainly makes up for in atmosphere.

Tende guards the **Col de Tende**, the old mountain pass connecting Piedmont and Provence. Now bypassed by a road tunnel, the pass was once a fearsome experience. Smollett, crossing it in 1765, was "speechless in front of this celebrated and perilous mountain". His awe was not unjustified. Fears of bandits and smugglers aside, the crossing was undoubtedly beset with difficulties: it took six manservants to cut the ice with pick-axes before Smollett could get through.

Approached from La Brigue, Tende is still an impressive sight. The newer part of town hugs the river; behind is stacked the medieval town, rising in tiers to an Italianate cemetery and a stunted tower. The 14th-century tower is all that remains of the feudal château built by the Lascaris dynasty. The town's fortunes are a familiar story of a powerful church and the oppressed, poverty-stricken peasants.

At the beginning of the century, Tende's farmers and miners were still impoverished: travel was on foot or by mule; bread was a luxury and dried so that it lasted longer. Under Fascism, Tende became a garrison town with over 3,000 Italian soldiers throughout the war years. In 1947 Tende, newly French, was deserted by the military, as well as by Italian civil servants and manual workers.

The economic decline was only checked in the 1980s, with the opening of a new rail link and the creation of ski resorts. The Mercantour Park and the Vallée des Merveilles have also helped to attract visitors to the region. But Tende still remains oblivious to tourism; on the city map the *vieille ville*, the most interesting part of town, is paradoxically left blank.

The *vieille ville* is made of greyish-green schist, a type of slate still quarried nearby. Blackened by time and traffic

The vast amphitheatre of Saorge.

fumes, these sombre houses set the tone. The overhanging roofs are not decorative, as a glance at the snowy peaks will confirm. Nor is Tende ever hot: "*En été il y a toujours de l'air*," as the hardy locals say. Only the orange and pink belfries, decorated in Ligurian colours, generate any warmth.

The late Gothic **Cathedral**, tucked away down a dark alley, is made of blackened green stone and is badly in need of restoration. The sculpted Renaissance facade is framed by pillars propped on stone lions, an unusual feature in church architecture.

Ancient walnut doors lead to a majestic interior, adorned with a starry Tuscan ceiling and a nave emblazoned with the Lascaris arms, a two-headed eagle. Medieval houses and confraternity chapels are clustered around the cathedral.

The gloomy, claustrophobic atmosphere is intensified by a walk through the *vieille ville*. Thick oak doors are adorned with medieval lintels representing the medieval guilds. **Rue Béatrice Lascaris** climbs through the medieval quarter to the Lascaris tower, ruined ramparts and Italianate cemetery. At the end of covered passageways are blind alleys with views of terraced allotments beside a tinkling mountain stream.

Mountain huntsman.

Out of season *vieille* Tende feels medieval. *Les gens du pays* collect firewood and mule dung in hand-drawn carts; old men strip olive wood; chestnuts are roasted over open fires;dogs tear each other apart in dark corners. The air is rent with sounds of sawing, chopping and howling. Even the smells are unchanged since medieval times: sawdust and woodsmoke, dung and dog's piss, incense and roast chestnuts.

To dispel this oppressive atmosphere one can stroll down to the new town, centred on Place de la République. Here the aromas vary from *lasagne* and pizza to trout *soufflé* and Piedmontes *polenta*. The stodgy *polenta* dishes are a reminder of Tende's humble origins. Until recently, the poorest people lived on chestnut and cabbage soup or on a pasta made from flour, oil and potatoes. On Sundays, this was supplemented by *une bonne sauce*, generally rabbit.

Wild game, such as boar and deer, was caught in the woods then sold to wealthier citizens. Nowadays, the local cuisine is on a par with Sospel's but Tende still harbours hunters who stray into the Mercantour and wild boar are still caught in significant numbers. Certainly, it is best not to question the provenance of game in local restaurants.

Unusually for a frontier town, Tende is still a closed world, moulded by poverty and self-sufficiency. Until tourism makes a mark, Tende will continue to have few *résidences secondaires* or outsiders. Still tourism is beginning to make its mark slowly, and now a new museum is to open, the **Musée des Merveilles**.

But *les enfants du pays* have often kept a *pied à terre* here, wishing to return to their roots one day. In Tende, as in the rest of the Haut-Pays, there is a desire to perpetuate peasant traditions. It's a place to rear a few chickens and tend a garden in retirement. Underneath the glamour of the Côte d'Azur, the French provincial heart beats strongly.

INSIGHT GUIDES

Travel Tips

Getting Acquainted

The Place

The Côte d'Azur has a particularly varied landscape. In just 2 hours one can travel from the palm-fringed coast up to the high peaks of the Alps. In the east, the Mercantour National Park covers 265 sq. miles (686 sq. km) of forests, lakes, waterfalls and mountains. Its abundant flora is protected – as many as 30 different species are particular to this area.

While the popular resorts are fairly built up with hotels and apartments, the mountains and inland areas are mostly dotted with small villages and hamlets. The region was probably one of the first to be settled by humans, and even earlier evidence of Cro-Magnon man has been found in the caves around Grasse.

Along the coast the westernmost stretch is the least developed, dotted with fishing villages and behind them the maquis and cork-woods, which suffer so often from summer fires. This scenery is changing as more exotic trees are planted in an effort to save the woodland as the cork oaks are destroyed. Further inland are the olive groves, for which the region is famous, and the lavender-covered moorland.

Time Zones

For most of the year, France is one hour ahead of Greenwich Mean Time, so if it is noon in Nice, it is 11am in London, 5am in New York and Toronto and 8pm in Melbourne.

Climate

An extremely privileged region, both in its natural landscape and its climate, the Côte d'Azur is a popular resort all year round. It enjoys around 2,700 hours of sunshine a year, but the heat is never unbearable because of the sea breezes (nights can be cool). The highest temperatures are in July and August – around 24°C (75°F). Winter is mild and sunny – frost is a rarity.

There is snow on the mountains, but the heat of the sun means that it is quite possible to ski in a T-shirt. The wettest period is the autumn, but then the area is favoured with short, heavy downpours followed by bright sunshine. Spring, too, can have some wet spells when the sky becomes quite heavy and overcast. The worst aspect of the weather is that which only really affects the hinterland, the famous Mistral. This fearsome wind, said to be able to "blow the ears off a donkey", causes considerable damage and can have an extremely depressing effect.

Temperatures

Temperatures are always given in celsius (centigrade). For conversion to fahrenheit, see below:

0°C	=	32°F
5°C	=	40°F
10°C	=	50°F
16°C	=	60°F
21°C	=	70°F
27°C	=	80°F

The People

Culture & Customs

The history of the region is ancient with evidence of early human and even Cro-Magnon settlements. Up in the mountains, in the archaeological sites of the Vallée des Merveilles and the Vallon de Fontanelbe, an extraordinary number of stone engravings (over 100,000) bear witness to man's early habitation. Its later history was inextricably linked with the Greeks, and then the Romans. With the coming of Christianity, Latin became the lingua franca of the area. The Italian influence on architecture, culture and cuisine has been considerable.

Religion, of course, plays a great part in the development of any culture and this region is no exception, with much of the religious art here dating back to the 15th and 16th centuries. To this day, pilgrimages and other processions and festivals add to the folklore of the region.

Recent culture has benefited much from the contribution of artists drawn to the region. Since the arrival of Picasso, Chagall, Matisse *et al*, museums and art galleries have been established and become a magnet for other artists and art lovers from around the world. Indigenous arts and crafts, particularly the distinctive pottery and fabrics known as provençal can be seen all around the region.

Government

For much of its history, the Côte d'Azur, with Nice at its centre, was a disputed area. Its proximity to the Italian border meant that it was mostly controlled by the Italians under the House of Savoy and it did not become finally French until 1860.

For years the French were ruled by a very centralised form of government, but under the socialists (1981–86) the Paris-appointed *préfets* lost much of their power as the individual *départements* (or counties) gained their own directly elected assemblies for the first time, giving them far more financial and administrative autonomy. Each *département* still has a *préfet*, but the role is now much more advisory. The *préfecture* is based in the county town of each *département*: Digne in Alpes-de-Haute-Provence, Gap in Hautes-Alpes, Nice in Alpes-Maritimes, and Toulon in Var. These offices handle most matters concerned with the social welfare of their citizens.

Each French *département* has a number which is used as a handy reference for administrative purposes. For example, it forms the first two digits of the postcode in any address and the last two figures on vehicle licence plates. The *département* numbers for the Riviera are as follows: Alpes-de-Haute-Provence is 04, Hautes-Alpes is 05, Alpes-Maritimes is 06, Var is 83.

Each *département* is divided into a number of disparately-sized communes whose district councils control a town, village or group of villages under the direction of the local mayor. Communes are now responsible for most local planning and environmental matters. Decisions relating to tourism and culture are dealt with at regional level, while the state still controls education, the health service and security.

The Principality of Monaco is generally included as part of the region, but it is largely autonomous. It is still ruled by the Grimaldi family, who acquired it from the Genoese as far back as 1308. In the early 20th century, the then Prince of Monaco signed a treaty with the French to retain its autonomy provided its citizens conformed to French law. This had the perhaps unforeseen effect of attracting tax exiles to the principality (where no income tax was levied).

Economy

The Côte d'Azur is, as one would expect, heavily dependent on tourism, but efforts have been made to lessen that reliance. One of the major industries now, which is almost an extension of tourism, is the conference trade. The area is probably the most popular in France for conventions, with the Cannes Film Festival and the international music publishing fairs being the best known.

The area also has another glamorous industry: perfumes. Grasse is the acknowledged world perfume capital and it has benefited touristically from this as well by developing, among other attractions, an international museum of perfumery.

There is hardly any heavy industry in the region; however, the Var valley in the west is continuing to attract electronics and related businesses – Texas Instruments and IBM, for example. There is also an emphasis on scientific research, with centres set up for the study of astronomy, oceanography and health care. An off-shoot of the interest in health can be seen in the growth of treatment centres for thalassotherapy and balneotherapy.

Planning The Trip

What to Bring

Maps

A first essential in touring any part of France is a good map. The Institute Géographique National is the French equivalent of the British Ordnance Survey and their maps are excellent; those covering the Riveria are listed below:

Red Series (1:250,000, 1 cm to 2.5 km) sheet 115 covers the whole region at a good scale for touring.

Green Series (1:100,000 (1 cm to 1 km) are more detailed, corresponding roughly to individual départements – sheet nos. 67 and 68 cover most of the region, for the far north, sheets 60 and 61 are necessary.

Also available is the IGN tourist map *Alpes Maritimes* and highly detailed 1:50,000 and 1:25,000 scales, which are ideal for walkers (*see also the Ramblers section*). For planning your route IGN 901 covers the whole of France at a scale of 1 cm to 10 km and is regularly updated.

The Michelin regional maps are published at a scale of 1:200,000 (1 cm to 2 km). The whole region is covered on sheet No. 245 or at the same scale on two separate sheets: south No. 84, north, No. 81. Michelin also publishes town plans, as does Blay, but local tourist offices often give away their own town plans free of charge. Michelin's Route Planning Map 911 shows motorways and alternative routes and other travel advice.

Good mountain maps for walkers and winter sports are produced by Didier Richard, mostly at a scale of 1:50,000, but a few at the more detailed 1:25,000 scale.

Stockists in London are: Stanfords International Map Centre, 12–14 Long Acre, Covent Garden WC2, tel: (0171) 836 1321; The Travel Bookshop, 13 Blenheim Crescent, London W11 2EE, tel: (0171) 229 5260; and The European Bookshop, 4 Regent Place, London W1R 6BH, tel: (0171) 734 5259.

Compass Books, Freepost, Dereham, Norfolk NR19 1TE, tel: (01362) 691623 offer a mail order service (7-day money-back guarantee) and carry a wide range of maps and guides for the region and the whole of France. IGN Maps are also available by mail order from the IGN sole agent in the UK, World Leisure Marketing, 9 Downing Road, West Meadows Industrial Estate, Derby, tel: 01322 343332. In France, most good bookshops should have a range of maps, but they can often be bought more cheaply in hypermarkets or service stations.

Electricity

Electric current is generally 220/230 volts, but still 110 in a few areas. Current alternates at 50 cycles, not 60 as in the US, so take a transformer for shavers, travel irons, hairdryers etc., which also takes care of the fact that outlet prongs are different.

Entry Regulations

All visitors to France require a valid passport and a visa except for citizens of EU countries, Andorra, Monaco, and Switzerland. If in any doubt check with the French consulate in your country, as the situation may change from time to time. If you intend to stay in France for more than 90 days, then a *carte de séjour* must be obtained (again from the French consulate) – this also applies to EU citizens until restrictions are relaxed.

Animal Quarantine

No animal under three months of age may be taken into France. It is not advisable to take animals to France from the UK because of the six-months' quarantine required by the British authorities on the animal's return. However, if you do wish to take a pet you need to have either a vaccination certificate for rabies or a certificate to show that your country has been free of the disease for three years. For further information contact the French consulate in your country.

Customs

All personal effects may be imported into France without formality (including bicycles and sports equipment). It is forbidden to bring into the country any narcotics, pirated books, weapons and alcoholic liquors that do not conform to French legislation. Certain items (e.g. alcoholic drinks, tobacco, perfume) are limited as to the amounts you can take in or out duty free, and these amounts differ depending on whether you are coming from another EU country, a non-EU European country, or outside Europe. From 1 January 1993, customs barriers within Europe for alcoholic drinks and tobacco (bought and duty paid in France) practically ceased to exist, but the old regulations still apply for goods bought at duty-free shops on the ferry or aeroplane. The current allowances are shown below (with on-board duty-free shop allowances in brackets, although these can be exceeded if you prove the goods are for personal consumption (e.g. a family wedding) and not for resale. For information contact HM Customs and Excise, Dorset House, Stamford Street, London SE1 9NG, tel: (0171) 928 3344 or any Excise office.

Allowances for each person over 18 years old:

- 10 litres (1 litre) of spirits or liqueurs over 22 percent alcohol by volume
- 20 litres (2 litres) fortified wine
- 90 litres (2 litres) wine (no more than 60 litres of it may be sparkling wine)
- 200 cigars (50 cigars) or 400 cigarillos (100 cigarillos) or 800 cigarettes (200 cigarettes).

Health Care

The International Association for Medical Assistance to Travellers (IAMAT) is a non-profit-making organization which anyone can join free of charge (a donation is requested). Benefits include a membership card (entitling the bearer to services at fixed IAMAT rates by participating physicians) and a traveller clinical record (a passport-sized record completed by the member's own doctor prior to travel). A directory of English speaking IAMAT doctors on call 24-hours a day is published for members.

EU nationals should check before leaving that they qualify for subsidised treatment in France under EU rules. Most British nationals do – check with the Department of Health and ask for the form E111. The E111 does not cover the full cost of treatment, so you may find it worthwhile to take out private insurance as well.

IAMAT Offices

Canada: 1287 St Claire Ave., W. Toronto, M6E 1B9, tel: (416) 652 0137 or 40 Regal Road, Guelph, Ontario, N1K 1B5, tel: (519) 836 0102.

New Zealand: PO Box 5049, Christchurch 5.

US: 417 Center Street, Lewiston, NY 14092, tel: (716) 754 4883.

Money

The French Franc is divided into l00 centimes. A 5-centime piece is the smallest coin and the F500 note the highest denomination bill.

Banks displaying the Change sign will change foreign currency and in general, at the best rates (you will need to produce your passport in any transaction). If possible avoid hotel or other independent bureaux which may charge a high commission. Credit cards are widely accepted, but Visa is by far the most common and can now be used in hypermarkets and many supermarkets. Access (MasterCard/EuroCard) and American Express are also accepted in many places.

Credit cards and cash cards from many European banks can now be used in French cashpoint machines (ATMs) located outside banks. Check the validity of your cashcard with your home bank before departure.

Eurocheques, used in conjunction with a cheque card, drawn directly on your own bank account, can be used just like a cheque in the UK, though some French banks do not accept them. Apply for these, or if you prefer, travellers' cheques, from your own bank, allowing a couple of weeks before your departure.

Public Holidays

A list of major public holidays is given below. It is common practice, if a public holiday falls on a Thursday or Tuesday for French business to *faire le pont* (bridge the gap) and have the Friday or Monday as a holiday too. Details of closures should be posted outside banks etc. a few days before the event but it is easy to be caught out, especially on Assumption day in August, which is not a holiday in the UK.

New Year's Day: 1 January
Easter Monday: (but not Good Friday)
Labour Day: Monday closest to 1 May
Ascension Day
8 May: (to commemorate the end of WWI)
Whit Monday: (Pentecost)
Bastille Day: 14 July
Assumption Day: 15 August
All Saints' Day – Toussaint: 1 November
Armistice Day: 11 November
National holiday in Monaco: 19 November
Christmas Day: 25 December, but not Boxing Day 26 December.

Getting There

By Air

Best options from Britain are British Midland (0345 554554), British Airways (0345) 222111, or via Paris with Air Inter Europe (0181 742 6600). The budget option is Easyjet from Luton. **Note:** the 20 minute taxi ride from the airport is not value for money – so take the bus instead.

Helicopter transfer services operate from Nice to Cannes and Monaco (transfers can be included in ticket prices).

Although there are some scheduled flights from the US, travellers from America and other countries outside Europe may find it cheaper to travel by charter via Paris or London. Numerous companies offer flights to these two cities; Nouvelles Frontières offers some of the most competitive fares on both scheduled and charter flights to Paris from the US and Canada. It also flies charters direct from London Gatwick to Nice. Availability of charter flights is variable; for more details contact the company at:

Canada: 800 Boulevard de Maisonneuve Est., Montreal, Quebec H2L 4M7, tel: (5l4) 288 4800.

UK: 11 Blenheim Street, London W1, tel: (0171) 629 7772.

US: 125 West 55th Street, New York NY, tel: (212) 247 0100.

By Sea

There are several ferry services operating from the UK, the Republic of Ireland and the Channel Islands to the northern ports of France. All of them carry cars as well as foot passengers. Hovercraft crossings are fast, but more dependent on good weather than the ferries. The new Seacat catamaran service offers the quickest crossing but, like the hovercraft, can only carry a limited number of cars. The ports of Boulogne, Calais and Le Havre offer direct access by motorway to Paris; there is almost direct motorway access also via Dunkerque and Caen.

Brittany Ferries sails from Portsmouth to Saint-Malo and Caen, Plymouth to Roscoff, Cork (Eire) to St Malo and Roscoff, and a cheaper Les Routiers service from Poole to Cherbourg (summer only). Contact Wharf Road, Portsmouth P02 8RU, tel: (01705) 827 70l; or Millbay Docks, Plymouth PLl 3EW, tel: (01752) 22l 32l.

Hoverspeed operates hovercraft from Dover to Calais and Boulogne (crossing time approx. 30 minutes). The Seacat catamaran runs between Boulogne and Folkestone. Details of all services from Hoverspeed Ltd, Marine Parade, Dover CT17 9TG, tel: (01304) 240241.

North Sea Ferries connects travellers from the north of England and Scotland to France, via their Hull-Zeebrugge route. Situated 56 km (35 miles) from the French border, Zeebrugge gives good motorway access to Paris region. The overnight services offer entertainment; a five-course dinner and breakfast are included in the fare. Contact the company at King George Dock, Hedon Road, Hull HU9 5QA, tel: (01482) 795141.

P & O European Ferries operates the short sea routes from Dover to Calais, as well as Portsmouth to Le Havre and Cherbourg. Fares and schedules from P & O, Channel House, Channel View Road, Dover CT16 3BR, tel: (01304) 203388.

Sally Line ferries uses the smaller ports of Ramsgate and Dunkerque. Details from 81 Piccadilly, London W1V 9HF, tel: (0171) 409 2240; for reservations: Argyle Centre, York Street, Ramsgate, Kent CT11 9DS, tel: (01843) 595522.

Sealink Stena Line ferries operates from Dover to Calais (the fastest shipping route at 90 minutes), Southampton to Cherbourg, and Newhaven to Dieppe. Details and reservations for all services are available from Charter House, PO Box 121, Park Street, Ashford, Kent TN24 8EX, tel: (01233) 647047.

Irish Ferries offers a service from Rosslare to Le Havre and Cherbourg, with ferries leaving daily from 1 April to mid-September to one of the two ports. It currently runs a service once weekly from Cork to Le Havre and Cherbourg from June–August. Contact them at 2-4 Merrion Row, Dublin 2, tel: 661 511.

By Train

For visitors travelling from Paris, the train is a fast, efficient way to reach the region, especially with the high-speed express trains (TGV). All services leave from Paris-Gare de Lyon; the principal destinations in the region are Nice, Toulon, Fréjus/St-Raphaël and Cagnes-sur-Mer. Travel around the region by train is pretty good, although trains can be infrequent on some lines. Car and bicycle hire is available at most main stations – as a package with your rail ticket if you prefer (details from French Railways, below).

France has a fast efficient rail network operated by the SNCF (Société Nationale des Chemins de Fer de France). Its much praised TGV programme is developing all the time, offering comfortable express services from Paris to Lyon and the southeast and to Le Mans, Rennes and Bordeaux in the west and southwest.

For visitors travelling from Paris, the train is a comfortable way to reach any major destination in France with most express services offering refreshments (and even play areas for young children). There are five main stations serving the provinces from Paris, so check which one you need before setting off. Getting across country by rail is less easy. Car and bicycle hire is available at most main stations – as a package with your rail ticket if you prefer (details from French Railways).

Tickets may be booked for through journeys from outside France. In the UK, tickets can be booked from any British Rail Station, including ferry travel. British Rail travel centres can supply details of continental services or contact British Rail International Enquiries, International Rail Centre, Victoria Station, London SW1, tel: (0171) 834 2345. Students and young people under 26 years of age can get a discount. Eurotrain, tel: (0171) 730 3402, offers 30 percent off standard two-month return tickets for those under 26.

French Railways has opened a new telephone service, Rail Shop, in London to provide an instant booking service. The lines, however, are usually very busy and a little patience is required. A second Rail Shop is due to open in Manchester. The service includes ferry bookings, discounted tickets for young people, a *Carte Vermeil* for senior citizens, which gives a generous discount on tickets and Eurodomino rail passes (*see below*). Lines are open Monday to Friday and Saturday morning, tel: (0891) 515 477 (information only) or (0171) 495 4433 (reservations only).

Any rail ticket bought in France must be validated by using the orange automatic date-stamping machine at the entrance to the platform. Failure to do so incurs a surcharge.

Rail Passes

There are several rail-only and rail-combination passes available to foreign visitors. These must always be bought before departing for France. In the UK, a Eurodomino Pass offers unlimited rail travel on any 3, 5, or 10 days within a month. This can also be purchased in conjunction with an Air France Rail Ticket.

Visitors from North America have a wider choice of passes, starting with the basic France Railpass which offers four or nine days of unlimited travel within a month. Then there are various types of Eurail Pass which offer varying periods of first-class travel throughout Europe; the Eurail Youthpass offers a similar deal for young people under 26. The France Rail 'n' Drive pass offers a flexible rail and car-rental package, while the Fly Rail and Drive Pass combines internal flights on Air Inter with train travel and car hire.

Similar passes are available to travellers from other countries, although the names of the tickets and conditions may vary slightly.

SNCF has a central reservation office in Paris, tel: (1) 45 65 60 60 and information services in English, tel: (1) 45 82 08 41, and in French, (1) 45 82 50 50. The SNCF office in Paris is at 10 place de Budapest, 75436 Paris Cedex 09, tel: (1) 42 85 60 00.

Most French railway stations accept Visa and American Express.

Channel Tunnel

The Channel Tunnel offers fast, frequent rail services between London (Waterloo), Lille (2 hours) and Paris (Gare du Nord – 3 hours). Connections to other destinations are available. Rail passenger services are run by Eurostar a consortium of the French, British and Belgian railway companies, and tickets are bookable through French or British railway companies.

Le Shuttle is the name of the service that takes cars and their passengers from Folkestone to Calais on a simple drive-on-drive-off system. The journey time through the tunnel is about 35 minutes. No tickets are needed – you just turn up and take the next service. Le Shuttle runs 24 hours a day, all year round, with a service at least once an hour through the night. Enquiries in UK, tel: 0990-353535.

Motorail is another, if somewhat pricey alternative, solution for travellers wishing to have the freedom of their own car on holiday but hoping to avoid the long haul from the northern coast. The following routes are available: Boulogne or Dieppe to Fréjus/St-Raphaël (summer only) and Calais to Nice. There is also a service from Paris to Fréjus/St-Raphaël.

By Coach

Eurolines European coach services operate regular services from London (Victoria) to Nice, Cannes and Grasse. The ticket includes the ferry crossing (via Dover) and National Express coaches have connections with the London departures from most major towns in the UK. For details contact Eurolines UK, 52 Grosvenor Gardens, Victoria, London SW1W 0AU, tel: (0171) 730 8235.

By Car

Many drivers are daunted by the thought of a long drive (745 miles/1,200 km from London and over 560 miles/900 km from Paris), before even starting their holiday. Indeed, in high season the roads can become very crowded. For those in a hurry, the autoroute from Paris to Nice (A6, A7, A8) takes about eight hours, but toll fees can add up. For travellers driving from the port of Calais, it is now possible to travel all the way to the Riviera by motorway.

However, if speed is not of the essence and you intend to make the drive part of your holiday, follow the green holiday route signs to your destination – these form part of a national network of *bison futé* routes to avoid traffic congestion at peak periods. You will discover parts of France you never knew existed and are more likely to arrive relaxed. The first weekend in August and the public holiday on the 15th are usually the worst times to travel, so avoid them if you can. For further details about driving in France, *see Getting Around* page 319.

Special Facilities

Doing Business

Business travel is now such an important part of the tourist economy that the French Government Tourist Office in London and Chicago (*see Useful Addresses*) have a department set up just to deal with business enquiries. They will help organise hotels, conference centres and incentive deals for any group, large or small.

On the Côte d'Azur in particular, business tourism is of vital importance to the region's economy, and has been developed alongside its regular tourist industry. Nice, Cannes and Monte-Carlo all attract visitors to the trade fairs and other events that take place annually, and the larger hotels depend on the conference trade for a major part of their business. The international airport at Nice, with direct flights to much of Europe and the US means that it is an ideal venue for top-flight companies who can afford to indulge their higher paid executives.

Cannes, Nice and Monte-Carlo all have huge, modern convention centres, in very attractive locations. The one in Cannes is at the west end of La Croisette and plays host to the annual Film Festival. In Nice, the **Acropolis** is set in splendid gardens studded with statues by famous artists while Monte-Carlo's **Convention Centre and Auditorium** is suspended over the Mediterranean. Most larger hotels also have conference facilities.

For general information about business travel and facilities contact the regional tourist offices (*see Useful Addresses* page 316). Another good source of business information and local assistance, are the **Chambres de Commerce et d'Industrie** in the individual *départements*. Here you can obtain details about local companies, assistance with the technicalities of export and import, interpretation/translation agencies and conference centres – indeed, most chambers of commerce have conference facilities.

There is also a **French Chamber of Commerce** in London (tel: 0171 225 5250) which exists to promote business between the two countries, and at the same address is **French Trade Exhibitions**: 2nd floor, Knightsbridge House, 197 Knightsbridge, London SW7 1RB, tel: (0171) 225 5566.

Travelling with Children

The Riveria is more the kind of place that attracts adults for its glamorous beaches and nightlife than a family resort, and young families could be well advised to stay away from the crowds (and high prices) of the high season. The coastal resorts to the west of the region are more easily approached by car and therefore more attractive to families. To get anywhere near the beaches of Nice or Cannes in August could be a nightmare with young children and their accompanying clutter in tow (remembering the difficulties of parking).

However, the private beaches of the Riviera *do* cater well for children, and have beach clubs providing various amusements (for a fee). Some of the public beaches also have the same kind of facilities (expect to pay a fee for the morning/afternoon session). There are also plenty of other places to take children: **Marineland** in Antibes, the **Museum of Oceanography** in Monaco, to name just two. Consult the *Attractions* section (page 328) for more ideas.

In France generally, children are treated as people, not just nuisances. It is pleasant to be able to take them into restaurants (even in the evening) without heads being turned in horror at the invasion. French children, being accustomed to eating out from an early age, are on the whole well behaved in restaurants so it helps if one's own offspring understand that they can't run wild.

Many restaurants offer a children's menu; otherwise, they will often split a *prix-fixe* menu between two children. If travelling with very young children, you may find it practical to order nothing specific at all for them but request an extra plate and give them tasty morsels to try from your own dish. It is a good introduction to foreign food for them, without too much waste. French meals are generally generous enough (*nouvelle cuisine* excepted) to allow you to do this without going hungry yourself, and you are unlikely to encounter any hostility from *le patron* (or *la patronne*). Another option is to order a single simple, inexpensive dish from the à la carte menu, such as an omelette, which most childen like to eat.

Most hotels have family rooms so

children do not have to be separated from parents and a cot (*lit bébé*) can often be provided for a small supplement, it is a good idea to check availability if booking in advance.

Some of the hotels offer a baby listening or child-minding service.

Travellers with Special Needs

Most disabled travellers will be keen to book accommodation in advance rather than arriving "on spec". Most of the official list of hotels (available from the FGTO or the regional tourist office – *see Useful Addresses* page 316) include a symbol to denote wheelchair access, but it is always advisable to check directly with the chosen hotel as to exactly what facilities are available. Balladins runs a chain of budget-priced hotels throughout France which all have at least one room designed for disabled guests. Restaurants and all other public areas are wheelchair accessible. For a complete list contact Hotels Balladins, 20 rue du Pont des Halles, 94656 Rungis Cedex, tel: 49 78 24 61, fax: 46 87 68 60.

An information sheet aimed at disabled travellers is published by the French Government Tourist Office: for a copy send a stamped addressed envelope. There is a guide – *Oú Ferons Nous Etape?* (in French only) – which lists accommodation throughout France that is suitable for disabled people, including wheelchair users. Once again, if you have specific needs you should double check when booking. It is available for around FF40 by post from the Association des Paralysés, Service Information, 17 Boulevard August Blanqui, 75013 Paris, tel: (1) 40 78 69 00. This organization may also be able to deal direct with specific enquiries and can provide addresses of their branches throughout France. The *Rousseau H Comme Handicapé* guide may also prove useful. It is available from Hachette bookshops or at SCOP, 4 rue Gustave-Rouanet, 75018 Paris, tel: (1) 42 52 97 00.

Michelin's Red Guide *France* for hotels and its *Camping-Caravanning – France* both include symbols for disabled welcome.

The Royal Association for Disability and Rehabilitation (RADAR), 25 Mortimer Street, London W1N 8AB, tel: (0171) 637 5400, has some useful information for tourists, including a guide book, *Holidays and Travel Abroad.* This is a general country-by-country guide and provides information about France as a whole, including hotel chains offering suitable accommodation and tour operators offering specialist holidays.

France's sister organization to RADAR, the Comité National Français de Liaison pour la Réadaptation des Handicapés (CNFLRH) is based at 38 Boulevard Raspail, 75007 Paris, tel: (1) 45 48 90 13. It offers a good information service for visitors with special needs travelling to France, although it does not have any specific information about the regions of France.

The Holiday Care Service offers free information on travel accommodation and counterpart associations in France. Send a large stamped addressed envelope to: 2 Old Bank Chambers, Station Road, Horley, Surrey RH6 9HW, tel: (01293) 774 535, fax: (01293) 784 647, Minicom (for the hearing impaired): (01293) 776 943.

For young people, the Centre d'Information et de Documentation Jeunesse, 101 Quai Branly, 75740 Paris Cedex 15, provides information on services for young disabled travellers. It publishes *Vacances Personnes Handicapées* and annual leaflets on activity and sports holidays for young disabled people. Parents may also find the following organization helpful: Union Nationale des Associations de Parents d'enfants Inadaptés (UNAPEI), 15 Rue Coysevox, 75018 Paris, tel: (1) 42 63 84 33.

The Comité de Liaisons pour le transport des personnes handicapées, Conseil National des Transports, 34 avenue Marceau, 75009 Paris publishes a booklet called *Guide des Transport à l'usage des Personnes à Mobilité Réduite.* This gives brief information on the accessibility and arrangements for less able passengers on all forms of public transport and contacts for special transport schemes throughout France.

Some concessionary ferry fares are available for members of the following organizations. The Disabled Drivers' Association, Ashwellthorpe, Norwich NR16 1EX, tel: (01508) 41449. Disabled Drivers' Motor Club, Coltingham Way, Thrapston, Northants NN14 4PL, tel: (01832) 734 724. The Disabled Motorists' Federation, Unit 2a Atcham Estate, Shrewsbury SY4 4UG, tel: (01743) 761 889.

More information about air and sea travel is available in a guide entitled *Door-to-Door.* For a free copy write to Department of Transport, Door-to-Dooor Guide, Freepost, Victoria Road, South Ruislip, Middlesex HA4 0NZ. There are also copies available on audio cassette for the vision impaired.

In the US, the following offer services to disabled travellers.

Travel Information Service, Moss Rehabilitation Hospital, 1200 West Tabor Road, Philadelphia, PA 19141–3099, tel: (215) 456 9600. General information for would-be travellers.

Society for the Advancement of Travel for the Handicapped (SATH), 26 Court Street, Brooklyn, New York 11242, tel: (718) 858 5483. Advice and assistance in travel matters.

Accessible Journeys, 35 W. Sellers Avenue, Ridley Park, Philadelphia, 19078-2113. Tours using wheelchair-accessible transport in Europe.

In Canada the following organisation may be of help.

Canadian Rehabilitation Council for the Disabled, 45 Sheppard Avenue E., Toronto, Ontario, M2N 5W9, tel: (416) 250 7490. National organization producing some material relating to travel.

Access to Places of Interest

Some places of interest in the area are fitted with a magnetic loop system to help the hearing impaired. These include the **Palais des Festivals** at Cannes, the **Nice Opera** and the **Le Forum Cinema**, also in Nice at 45 Promenade des Anglais. Some museums also have braille aids.

Students & Young People

Students and young people under the age of 26 can benefit from cut-price travel to France and rail cards for getting around the country (for details *see Getting There* page 312).

If you wish a prolonged stay in the region, it may be worth finding out about an exchange visit or study holiday. Several organizations exist to provide information or arrange such visits.

In the UK, the Central Bureau for Educational Visits and Exchanges, Seymour Mews House, Seymour Mews, London WIH 9PE, tel: (0171) 486 5101, produces three books:

Working Holidays (opportunities in France are limited; the grape harvest is still a big draw for young people and employment opportunities are listed here); *Home from Home* (a wealth of useful information about staying with a French family) and *Study Holidays* (details of language courses). Another option, for those with decent French is to approach one of the UK-based camping holiday operators who often employ students as site couriers during the vacation (*see Where to Stay* page 321).

Organizations in the US include:

Council on International Educational Exchange (CIEE), 205 E. 42nd Street, New York, NY 10017, tel: (212) 661 1414 – many services, including travel.

American Council for International Studies Inc., 19 Bay State Road, Bost, Mass. 02215, tel: (617) 236 2051.

Youth for Understanding International Exchange, 3501 Newark Street, NW, Washington DC 20016, tel: (202) 966 6800.

Volunteers are welcome at the workcamps organised on several on the archaeological and cultural sites in Burgundy (mainly during the summer). For information contact the Direction Régionale des Affaires Culturelles, 39 Rue Vannerie, 21000 Dijon, tel: 80 72 53 53. Although unpaid, this is a good way of meeting other young people of all nationalities and an opportunity to learn the language.

There several French tour operators which organize study tours and language courses, some of the more reputable are listed here:

Accueil des Jeunes en France, 119 Rue St Martin, 75004 Paris, tel: (1) 42 77 87 80, fax: (1) 42 77 70 48. Offers French study programmes, inexpensive accommodation (or with a family), and tours for individuals or groups.

Centre des Echanges Internationaux, 104 Rue de Vaugirard, 75006 Paris, tel: (1) 45 49 26 25. Sporting and cultural holidays and educational tours for 15 to 30-year-olds. Non-profit making organization.

Séjours Internationaux Linguistiques et Culturels (SILC), 32 Remparts-de l'Est, 16002 Angoulême, tel: 45 95 83 56.

Union National des Organizations de Séjours Linguistiques (UNOSEL), 293/295 Rue de Vaugirard, 75015 Paris, tel: (1) 42 50 44 99.

A complete list of private language schools is obtainable from regional tourist offices (*see Useful Addresses* page 316).

Souffle is an organization created in 1991 which embraces 11 centres which specialise in teaching French as a foreign language, and have all signed a quality charter. Contact Souffle at BP 133, 83957 La Garde Cedex, tel: 94 21 20 92, fax: 94 21 22 17.

Once in France, students will find a valid student identity card useful to obtain discounts on all sorts of activities. including admission to museums, galleries, cinema and theatre. If you do not have your ID card with you reductions may sometimes be allowed by proving your status with a passport.

The Centre d'Information et Documentation de Jeunesse (CIDJ) at: 101 Quai Branly, 75740 Paris, tel: (1) 45 67 35 85, is a national organization which disseminates information pertaining to youth and student activities. The noticeboard in the Paris office is a mine of useful information regarding accommodation and events.

For individual holidays, the cheapest way to stay is generally under canvas, or in a hostel (expect to pay around FF55 a night without meals).

Gay Life

Gay organisations and social centres are advertised in the local press. More general information is available from the national *Gai Pied Guide* (published in French, sold in the UK). If you need urgent help or information, try the Paris-based gay switchboard (SOS Homosexualité), tel: 16 1-46 27 49 36) with English-speakers.

Note this service is only active Wednesday and Friday from 6pm until midnight.

Useful Addresses

In France

Comité Régional du Tourisme, 55 Promenade des Anglais, 06000 Nice. The tourist authority is very proud of their service, Com'Azur, a single phone number will put you in touch with any of the tourist offices in the region. Tel: 93 37 78 78 for queries to be dealt with in French or English.

Direction du Tourisme et des Congrès de la Principauté de Monaco, 2a Boulevard des Moulins, Monte-Carlo, MC 98030 Monaco Cedex, tel: 92 16 61 16.

Départemental tourist offices (Comité Départemental de Tourisme):

Alpes de Haute-Provence, 19 rue Honorat BP 170, 04005 Digne, tel: 92 32 29 79.

Var, Conseil Général, Boulevard Foch, BP 99, Draguignan Cedex, tel: 94 50 55 50.

Parc National du Mercantour, 23 Rue d'Italie, 06000 Nice, tel: 93 16 78 83. Information about the national park, its flora and fauna, excursions and activities.

Info-Montagne. Tel: 93 87 30 24. A specialist team providing tourist information about the Alps.

Ligue Française pour la Protection des Oiseaux (LPO), La Corderie Royale, BP 263, 17305 Rochefort.

Nice Côte d'Azur International Airport. Tel: 93 21 30 12.

Cannes-Mandelieu International Airport. Tel: 93 90 40 40.

Monaco Heliport, Fontvieille. Tel: 93 30 83 88.

In the UK & Ireland

French Government Tourist Office, 178 Piccadilly, London W1V 0AL, tel: (0891) 244 123, fax: (0171) 493 6594.

Consulat Général de France, 21 Cromwell Road, London SW7 2DQ, tel: (0171) 838 2000, fax: (0171) 838 2001. Visa section: 6a Cromwell Place, London SW7, tel: (0171) 838 2050, fax: (0171) 838 2046.

Consulat Général de France, 11 Randolph Crescent, Edinburgh EH3 7TT, tel: (0131) 225 7954, fax: (0131) 225 8975.

French Embassy, 58 Knightsbridge, London SW1X 7JT, tel: (0171) 201 1000, fax: (0171) 201 1004. Commercial department: 21–24 Grosvenor Place, London SW1X 7HU, tel: (0171) 235 7080, fax: (0171) 235 8598. Cultural department: 23 Cromwell Road, London SW7, tel: (0171) 838 2055, fax: (0171) 838 2088.

Monaco Government Tourist and Convention Office, 3-18 Chelsea Garden Market, Chelsea Harbour, London SW10 0XE, tel: (0171) 352 9962, fax: (0171) 352 2103.

SNCF Rail Shop, 179 Piccadilly, London W1V 0BA, tel: (0891) 515 477 (for information only), (01345) 300 003 (for reservations only)

Air France, 158 New Bond Street, London W1Y 0AY, tel: (0171) 499 9511; 29-30 Dawson Street, Dublin 2, tel: 77 8272 (reservations: tel: 77 8899).

In North America

Maison de la France/French Government Tourist Office, 610 Fifth Avenue, Suite 222, New York, NY 10020-2452, tel: (310) 271 7838; 645 North Michigan Avenue, Suite 630, Chicago, Illinois 60611-2836, tel: (214) 720 4010, fax: (214) 702 0250; Cedar Maple Plaza, 2305 Cedar Springs Road, Suite 205, Dallas, Texas 75201, tel: (214) 720 4010, fax: (214) 702 0250.

Business Travel Division, 610 Fifth Avenue, Suite 222, New York, NY 10020-2452, tel: (212) 757 1125, fax: (212) 247 6464.

Maison de la France / French Government Tourist Office, 1981 Avenue McGill Collège, Tour Esso, Suite 490, Montreal H3A 2W9, Quebec, tel: (514) 288 4264, fax: (514) 845 4868; 30 St Patrick Street, Suite 700, Toronto M5T 3A3 Ontario, tel: (416) 593 4723.

Air France, 666 Fifth Avenue, New York, NY 10019, tel: (212) 315 1122 (toll-free reservations, tel: 1 800 237 2747); 8501 Wilshire Boulevard, Beverly Hills, Los Angeles, CA 90211, tel: (213) 688 9220.

Air France, 979 Ouest Boulevard de Maisonneuve, Montreal, Quebec H3A 1M4, tel: (514) 284 2825; 151 Bloor Street West, Suite 600, Toronto, Ontario M5S 1S4, tel: (416) 922 3344.

For information on railways, contact:

US: Raileurope Inc. at the following locations: 226–230 Westchester Avenue, White Plains, NY 10604; 360 Post Street, San Francisco, CA 94102, tel: (415) 982 1993; 100 Wilshire Boulevard, Santa Monica, CA 90401, tel: (213) 451 5151; IIE Adams Street, Chicago, IL 60603, tel: (312) 427 8691; 800 Corporate Drive, Suite 108, Fort Lauderdale, FL 33334, tel: (305) 776 2729; 6060 N. Central Expressway, Suite 220, Dallas, TX 75206, tel: (214) 691 5573.

Canada: Raileurope Inc. at the following locations: 2087 Dundas East, Suite 100, Mississauga, Ontario L4X IM2, tel: (416) 602 4195; 643 Notre Dame Ouest, Suite 200, Montréal, Quebec H3C 1HB, tel: (514) 392 1311; 409 Granville Street, Suite 452, Vancouver, BC V6C IT2.

For embassy and consulate offices in France, *see Practical Tips.*

Practical Tips

Emergencies

Security & Crime

Take sensible precautions regarding personal possessions. Tourists can be a target for petty thieves, so do not give them an open invitation by leaving valuables lying about on the beach or in hotel rooms. Drivers should follow the rules of the road and always drive sensibly. Heavy on-the-spot fines are given for traffic offences such as speeding, and drivers can be stopped and breathalysed during spot checks. Police are fairly visible on the main roads of France during the summer months.

To report a crime or loss of belongings, visit the local *gendarmerie* or *commisariat de police.* Telephone numbers are given at the front of local directories; in an emergency, dial 17. If you lose a passport, report first to the police, then to the nearest consulate (*see Useful Addresses*). If you are detained by the police for any reason, ask to telephone the nearest consulate for a member of the staff to come to your assistance.

Weights & Measures

The metric system is used in France for all weights and measures, although you may encounter old-fashioned terms such as *livre* (roughly 1 lb weight – 500 grams) still used by small shopkeepers.

For quick and easy conversion, remember that 1 inch is roughly 2.5 cm, 1 metre roughly equivalent to a yard, 4 oz is just over 100 gm and 2 lb is just under 1 kilo. As 5/8 of a mile is 1 kilometre, a handy reckoning whilst travelling is to remember that 50 miles = 80 km, thus 25 miles = 40 km. Accurate conversions are given below:

Weight

1 ounce (oz)	= 28.3 grams (gm)
1 pound (lb)	= 454.0 grams
2.2 pound	= 1.0 kilogram (kg)

Length

1 inch (in)	= 2.5 centimetres (cm)
1 yard (yd)	= 0.914 metres (m)
1 mile	= 1.6 kilometres (km)

Liquid

1 pint	= 0.47 litre (l)
1 Imp. gallon	= 4.54 litres
1 US gallon	= 3.785 litres

Business Hours

Office workers normally start early – 8.30am is not uncommon, but often stay at their desks until 6pm or later. This is partly to make up for the long lunch hours (from noon or 12.30 for two hours) which are still traditional in banks, shops and other public offices. On the Riviera, while the smaller traders still keep to these hours – many closing until 3pm at lunchtime, the larger department stores now tend to stay open. Many companies, too, are beginning to change to shorter lunch-breaks as employees appreciate the advantages of getting home earlier to families in the evening.

Banks on the Riviera are normally open 8.30am–noon and 1.30–5pm, Monday–Friday. However, some bureaux de change are open on Sunday.

Office Provençal, 64 Avenue Jean Médecin, 06000 Nice, tel: 93 13 45 44. Open: 8am–midnight.

Office Provençal, 17 Rue Marechal Foch, 06400 Cannes, tel: 93 39 34 37. Open: 8am–8 pm.

Media

Regional **newspapers**, such as *Nice Matin*, with national and international as well as local news, have a far higher standing here than in the UK and are often read in preference to national dailies such as *Le Monde*, *Libération* and *Le Figaro*. British and American dailies, notably *The Times* and the *International Herald Tribune*, are widely available as are local English-language publications aimed at the tourist and expatriate community. Look out for the *Riviera Reporter* which gives an irreverent, insider's view of the region.

Television viewers in the region can receive two main national channels: TF1 (commercial) and France 2 (state-owned but largely financed by advertising); as well as FR3 which offers regional programmes. French houses are also beginning to be defaced by satellite dishes at about the same rate as their British counterparts. Cable TV provides access to BBC channels.

France Inter is the main national **radio** station (1892m long wave), it broadcasts English-language news twice a day in summer (generally 9am and 4pm). Essential (English) listening is Monte Carlo's Riviera Radio (106.3 and 106.5), 24 hours of world news, regional broadcasts, small ads for jobs, property and so forth.

Postal Services

Provincial post offices – *Postes* or PTTs (pronounced pay-tay-tay) are generally open Monday to Friday 9am–noon and 2–5pm, Saturday 9am–noon (opening hours are posted outside); in Paris and other large cities they are generally open continuously from 8am–7pm. Exceptionally, the main post office in Paris is open 24 hours every day, at 52 Rue du Louvre, 75001 Paris.

Inside major post offices, individual counters are marked for different requirements – if you just need stamps, go to the window marked *Timbres.* If you need to send an urgent letter overseas, ask for it to be sent *par exprès*, or through the Chronopost system which is faster, but very expensive. Stamps are often available at tobacconists (*tabacs*) and shops selling postcards. Letters within France and most of the EU are FF2.80 up to 20g; FF4.30 for airmail to Ireland, the US and Canada; and FF5.10 to Australia.

Telegrams (cables) can be sent during post office hours or by telephone (24-hours); to send a telegram in English dial 1614 233 2111. Expect to pay around FF75 for a minimum of 15 words to the US, Canada or the UK.

For a small fee, mail can be kept *poste restante* at any post office, addressed to *Poste Restante, Poste Centrale* (for main post office), then the town's postcode and name, e.g. 16000 Angoulême. A passport is required as proof of identity when collecting mail. Many post offices have coin-in-slot photocopying machines.

Telephone

Telex, Minitel information service (useful for directory enquiries) and fax facilities are available in the main post office in most major towns.

The French telephone system, once quirky, is now one of the most efficient in the world. That is not to say that you can be guaranteed to find telephone boxes (*cabines publiques*) that are always operational, but most are. Telephone numbers have been rationalised to ten figures, given in sets of two, e.g. 99 44 63 21 17, the only codes necessary are for dialling into or out of Paris or overseas. To dial Paris from the provinces, dial 16 1, then the subscriber's number; to dial out of Paris, just dial 16 then the number.

International calls can be made from most public booths, but it is often easier to use a booth in a post office – ask at the counter to use the phone, then go back to settle the bill – but you have no record of the cost of the call until the end.

Coin-operated phones take most coins and card phones are now very common and simple to use. It is worth purchasing a phone card (*une télécarte* – currently F50 or F120) if you are likely to need to use a public call box, as many are being converted to take cards and in some towns are far more numerous now than coin-operated ones. Cards are available from post offices, stationers, railway stations, some cafés and tobacconists. Several main post offices now also have telephones that can be used with credit cards.

If you use a phone (not a public call box) in a café, shop or restaurant you are likely to be surcharged. Some hotels and cafés now have computerised public telephones whereby the caller receives a printed statement of the details of his call on payment of the bill at the bar – a useful asset for business travellers.

Making calls

To make an international call, lift the receiver, insert the money (if necessary), dial 19, wait for the tone to change, dial the country code, followed by the area code (omitting any initial 0) then dial the telephone number.

International dialling codes: Australia 61; Canada 1; Ireland 353; UK 44; US 1.

Useful numbers: operator services 13; directory enquiries 12.

Note that numbers will be given in pairs of figures, unless you ask for them to be given *chiffre par chiffre* (singly).

If using a US credit phone card, dial the company's access number.

- Sprint, tel: 19 00 87
- AT & T, tel: 19 00 11
- MCI, tel: 19 00 19.

Most main post offices in France have now replaced the traditional telephone directories with the computerised Minitel system. Members of the public can use this free of charge to look up any number in the country. The instructions (in French) are fairly simple to understand, and you simply tap in the name of the town, *département* and person (or company) whose number you seek for it to be displayed on the small screen, connected to the telephone. It can also be used in the same way as yellow pages to find, for example, all the dry cleaners listed in a particular town.

If you need to make a phone call in rural areas, or small villages with no public phone, look out for the blue plaque saying téléphone publique on private houses. This means the owner is officially required to allow you to use the phone and charge the normal amount for the call.

You cannot reverse charges (call collect) in France but you can to countries which will accept such calls. Go through the operator and ask to make a PCV (pronounced pay-say-vay) call. Telephone calls can only be received at call boxes displaying the blue bell sign.

The cheapest times to telephone are weekdays 10.30pm–8am and at weekends after 2pm on Saturday.

Note: The French telephone system was overhauled in 1996. Eight-digit numbers were extended to 10 digits and the following regional telephone numbers gained a prefix: Paris, Ile de France region 01; North West 02; North East 03; South East and Corsica 04, and South West 05.

When dialling Paris from outside France drop the (1).

Embassies & Consulates

The nearest consular service may be in Paris.

American Embassy, 2 Avenue Gabriel, 75382 Paris, Cedex 08, tel: (16) 142 961202; Consulate: 31 Rue Maréchal Joffre, 06000 Nice, tel: 93 88 89 55.

Australian Embassy, 4 Rue Jean-Rey, 75015 Paris, tel: 01 40 59 33 00.

British Consulate, 9 Avenue Hoche, Paris 75008, tel: 1 42 66 91 42; 12 Rue de France, 06000 Nice, tel: 93 82 32 04. **Embassy:** 35 Rue du Faubourg-St-Honoré, 75008 Paris, tel: (16) 1 42 66 91 42.
Canadian Embassy, 35 Avenue Montaigne, 75008 Paris, tel: 1 44 43 29 00. **Consulate:** le Continental, Place des Moulins, Monte-Carlo, tel: 93 25 58 22.
Irish Embassy, 12 Avenue Foch, 75116 Paris, tel: 1 45 00 20 87.

Getting Around

Domestic Travel

Public transport on the Côte d'Azur is quite good and avoids the problem of finding a parking space. It is really only sensible to take a car if you are touring. Roads to and around the main resorts get completely choked up during July and August and you can spend as much time getting to the beach as you spend on it. Parking in the main resorts is costly. Some towns – Cannes, for instance – have no street meters and tickets must be purchased from a machine and displayed.

Car hire is expensive, but bikes are fairly readily available. Most railway stations hire them out and they do not necessarily have to be returned to the same station. Bikes are carried free of charge on buses and some trains *(Autotrains)*; on other, faster services you will have to pay (check before you travel – some services have high charges for carrying cycles). Travelling by a combination of bike and bus or train can be an excellent way of touring and viewing the region.

By Bus

Details of routes and timetables are generally available free of charge. The main source of information for bus travel is available from Agence Sunbus, 10 Avenue Félix Faure, and also from local tourist offices. There are good services from the airport to all the major resorts, but inland services can be infrequent.

By Train

Information on services is available from the Gare SNCF, Avenue Thiers, 06049 Nice Cedex, tel: 93 87 50 50 (information); 93 88 89 93 (bookings). The Metrazur rail network links all the coastal towns.

Further services run inland. If you intend to travel extensively by train it may be worth obtaining one of the rail passes available before leaving home (*see Getting There* page 312). These tickets can be used on any journey, otherwise individual tickets need to be purchased – but check on any discounts available, e.g. the *Carte Couple* for married couples travelling together on off-peak services. Children under 4 travel free, from 4 to 12 for half-fare. All tickets purchased at French stations have to be put through the orange machines at the stations to validate them before boarding the train. These are marked *compostez votre billet*.

The Chemin de Fer de Provence runs from Nice to Digne-les-Bains through some spectacular countryside (up to five services a day in each direction). Information from: Gare du Sud, 33 Avenue Malaussena, 06000 Nice.

By Car

British, US, Canadian and Australian licences are all valid in France and you should always carry your car's registration document and insurance (third party is the absolute minimum, but it is advisable to ask your insurance company to provide additional cover).

Additional insurance cover, which can include a get-you-home service, is offered by a number of organizations including the British and American Automobile Associations and Europ-Assistance, Sussex House, Perrymount Road, Haywards Heath RH16 1DN, tel: (01444) 442211; in the US, Europ-Assistance Worldwide Services Inc., 1133 15th Street, Suite 400, Washington DC 20005, tel: (202) 347 7113. The Automobile Club National is the Umbrella organization of France's 40-odd motoring clubs. It will assist any motorist whose own club has an agreement with it. Details at: 9 rue Anatole-de-la-Forge, 75017 Paris, tel: (1) 42 27 82 00, fax: (1) 40 53 90 52

Rules of the Road

The use of seat belts (front and rear if fitted) and crash helmets for motorcyclists is compulsory. Children under 10 are not permitted to ride in the front seat unless the car has no rear seat.

Priorité à la droite: An important rule to remember is that priority on French roads is always given to vehicles approaching from the right, except where otherwise indicated. In practice, on main roads the major road will normally have priority, with traffic being halted on minor approach roads with one of the following signs:

STOP
Cédez le passage – give way
Vous n'avez pas la priorité – you do not have right of way
Passage protégé – no right of way

Particular care should be taken in towns, where you may wrongly assume you are on the major road, and in rural areas where there may not be any road markings (watch out for farm vehicles).

The French recently changed the rules concerning roundabouts – in theory, drivers already on the roundabout now have priority over those entering it, but beware. Some drivers still insist that priority belongs to the drivers entering a roundabout.

Speed limits: Speed limits are as follows: 130 kph (80 mph) on toll motorways; 110 kph (68 mph) on other motorways and dual carriageways; 90 kph (56 mph) on other roads except in towns where the limit is 50 kph (30 mph). There is now a minimum speed limit of 80 kph (50 mph) on the outside lane of motorways during daylight with good visibility and on level ground. Speed limits are reduced in wet weather as follows: toll motorways: 110 kph, dual carriageways: 100 kph, other roads: 80kph.

On-the-spot fines can be levied for speeding. On toll roads, the time is printed on the ticket you take at your entry point; your average speed can thus be calculated and a fine imposed on exit. Nearly all motorways (*autoroutes*) are toll roads, so you will need to have some cash with you (especially small change) if you intend to use them, although toll booths will now accept payment by Visa and there is always a manned booth.

Autoroutes are designated "A" roads and national highways "N" roads. "D" roads are usually well maintained, while "C" or local roads, may not always be so.

You must carry a red triangle to place 50 metres (164 ft) behind the car in case of a breakdown or accident. In an accident or emergency, call the police (dial 17) or use the free emergency telephones (every 2 km/1 mile) on motorways. It is useful to carry an European Accident Statement Form (obtainable from your insurance company) which will simplify matters in the case of an accident.

Unleaded petrol (*essence sans plomb*) is now widely available in France. If in doubt, a map showing the location of filling stations is available from main tourist offices.

For information about current road conditions, contact: Autoroute, tel: 93 49 33 33; CRIR, tel: 91 78 78 78. In the Alps you may need snow chains, which can be bought cheaply at hypermarkets or hired from garages.

Car Hire

Hiring a car is an expensive business in France, partly because of the high VAT (TVA) rate of 33 percent on luxury items. Some fly/drive deals work out reasonably well if you're only going for a short visit – Air France, for instance, offers a flydrive service to Nice, with daily departures. French Railways offer a good deal on combined train/car rental bookings. Weekly rates are often better than daily hire and it can be cheaper to arrange before leaving for France. Major car hire companies are listed below:

Avis
UK: 0181 848 8733
Nice: 0493 21 36 33

Budget
UK: 0800 181181
France: 0800 10 00 01

Europcar
UK: 0345 222525
Nice: 0493 21 36 44

Hertz
UK: 0181 679 1799
France: 0800 05 33 11

Routes

Following a tourist circuit, or route is a sure way of getting to see the major sites of a region. The *Carte Routière* of the Côte d'Azur is published free by UDOTSI des Alpes Maritimes (*see Useful Adresses* page 316) and gives 11 suggested itineraries. Local tourist offices will help with suggestions, some of the major routes are given below:

Route des Hauts Lieux de Provence: this covers an extensive area, in the west of the region, from Toulon to Fréjus and as far north as Draguignan. It takes in, among other sites, the Cité Episcopale de Fréjus and the Roman Arenas; the Château de Grimaud, the Château d'Entrecasteaux and the Palais des Comtes de Provence à Brignoles.

Côtes de Provence Wine Road: much of this route takes in the same area as the route des Hauts Lieux de Provence. For details of vineyards open to the public and offering tastings, contact the Syndicat des vins Côtes de Provence, 83460 Les Arcs-sur-Argens, tel: 94 73 31 01.

Circuit sans frontière de Nice à Turin: as its name suggests, this road leads all the way to Turin, and its aim is to cover in particular, all the major religious sites en route.

Ramblers

The hinterland behind the coast, the national parks of Mercantour and Luberon and of course, the mountains offer superb opportunities for walkers. There are also a number of coastal paths, for example the Sentier du Littoral which follows the coast south from La Favière (Var), and can easily be achieved in a day's walk. All the main footpaths in France form part of the national network of long distance footpaths (Sentiers de Grandes Randonnées or GR). The major footpaths in the region are the GR5 which goes from Nice all the way up to Amsterdam; the GR51, from Theoule to Castellar, overlooking the coast; the GR52 from Menton to the Vallée des Merveilles and the GR4 to the Gorges du Verdon.

It should be noted both the Parc National du Mercantour and the Vallée des Merveilles enforce a strict code of country behaviour and it is forbidden to enter many of the sites in the latter without an official guide.

The French Ramblers' Association, Fédération Française de la Randonnée Pédestre (FFRP) in Paris publishes Topoguides (guide books incorporating IGN 1:50,000 scale maps) to all France's footpaths, in French. However there is a series of guide books in English published by Robertson-McCarta called *Footpaths of Europe*, which are based on the French topoguides with IGN maps and include information about accommodation along the way. Titles appropriate to the region are: Walking the GR5: Larche to Nice, and peripherally, Walking the GR5: Modane to Larche and Walks in Provence. All these titles are available by mail order from Compass Books.

IGN Blue series maps at a scale of 1:25.000 are ideal for walkers, and they also publish maps of the national parks. Didier-Richard are specialist publishers of walking maps, at a scale of 1:50,000. Useful sheets are No. 1 Alpes de Provence, No. 9 Mercantour, No. 19 Haute-Provence and No. 26 Au Pays d'Azur.

French topoguides are available from all good bookshops in the region.

The Comité Regional pour la Randonnée Pédestre organises a variety of activities throughout the year: guided walks taking a day, a weekend or more; as well as themed walks, flora or wildlife for example. For more information contact: CRRP, M. Chartier, 365 rue des Iris, 83230 Bormes-les-Mimosa, tel: 71 50 38.

For a list of state-qualified guides working in the Alps contact: M. Jacques Raoust, rue Basse, 04170 Saint André-les-Alpes, tel: 92 89 04 19.

Various walking holidays with accommodation either in hotels or under canvas are available. Some are organised through package operators in the UK, others are bookable through the French organisations such as Clés de France, the agency for the French National Parks.

Clés de France, 13 Rue Saint-Louis, 78100 Saint-Germain-en-Laye, tel: (1) 30 61 23 23. For holidays in the Mercantour and Luberon national parks.

Ramblers Holidays, Box 43, Welwyn Garden City, Herts AL8 6PQ, tel: (01707) 331133.

Waymark Holidays, 44 Windsor Road, Slough SL1 2EJ, tel: (01735) 516 477.

Hitchhiking

With sensible precautions, hitchhiking can be an interesting and inexpensive way to get around France. Would-be hitchhikers may be discouraged by the difficulty of getting a lift out of the Channel ports, so it may be worth taking a bus or train for the first leg of your journey. Hitching is forbidden on motorways, but you can wait on slip roads or at toll booths. Allostop is a nationwide organisation which aims to connect hikers with drivers (you pay a registration fee and a contribution towards the petrol). Tel: (1) 42 46 00 66 via Paris, or 0447 700201.

Where to Stay

Accommodation

A wide variety of accommodation exists for the millions who visit the Côte d'Azur every year. Here is an outline of all the different types of place to stay, with specific suggestions.

Hotels

This hotel list names the region's most famous hotels and also suggests others that have a certain interest or distinctive charm. It is by no means exhaustive. It should be noted that prices on the Côte d'Azur tend to be higher than in other regions of France, but it is still possible to find reasonably-priced accommodation. Opening and closing dates and room prices may vary.

Note: hotels are listed in accordance with the order of the *Places* chapters.

Hyeres, Iles D'hyeres & Massif Des Maures

Giens

Relais du Bon Accueil. Tel: 94 58 20 48. A member of the Relais de Silence group. A charming and simple establishment set in beautiful grounds with sea-view. Credit cards: Visa. Rooms from FF350.

Porquerolles

Mas du Langoustier. Tel: 94 58 30 09. An old Provençal *mas* with its own gardens and two tennis courts. Closed: November–April. Credit cards: Amex, Diners, MasterCard, Visa. Rooms: full-board only, from FF1000.

Port Cros

Le Manoir. Tel: 94 05 90 52. A tropical atmosphere with large garden and colonial-style family house. Comfortable rooms, some with balcony. Closed: early October–early May. Credit cards: MasterCard, Visa. Rooms: half-board from FF1000.

Aiguebelle

(just outside Le Lavandou)

Les Roches. Tel: 94 71 05 07. Set on the cliffs with fabulous sea-views, a luxurious modern hotel tastefully decorated and furnished. Private beach, fresh-water swimming-pool. Closed: mid November–mid December and early January–early March. Credit cards: Amex, Diners, MasterCard, Visa. Rooms from FF700.

St-Tropez Region: From La Croix Valmer to Les Issambres

St-Tropez

Bastide de St-Tropez, Route des Carles, tel: 94 97 58 16. The height of luxury in the heart of the vineyards. Some of the rooms and suites with private garden and jacuzzi. Open: all year round. Credit cards: Amex, Diners, MasterCard, Visa. Rooms: FF1,800–3,200.

La Ponche, 3 rue des Remparts, St-Tropez, tel: 94 97 02 53. Once a favourite of Picasso's, this hotel was originally a row of little fishermen's cottages in the old town. Excellent restaurant. Rooms from FF700.

Lou Cagnard, Avenue P. Roussel, 83990, tel: 94 97 04 24. New very reasonably-priced hotel near the port and with a pretty courtyard. No credit cards. Rooms from FF200.

Résidence de la Pinède, Plage de la Bouillabaisse, tel: 94 97 04 21. On the famous Bouillabaisse beach, under the pine trees. The hotel has been refurbished to provide comfortable rooms and suites. A member of the Relais and Châteaux group. Closed: 25 October–20 March. Credit cards: Amex, Diners, MasterCard, Visa. Rooms from FF1000.

Le Yaca, 1 Boulevard d'Aumale, tel: 94 97 11 79. An attractive old Provençal residence in town, tastefully refurbished. Accommodation built around a swimming-pool and gardens. Closed: 15 October–20 December and 10 January–10 April. Credit cards: Amex, Diners, MasterCard, Visa. Rooms from FF1000.

Ramatuelle

La Ferme d'Augustin, Route de Tahiti, tel: 94 97 23 83. An old farm with a beautiful Mediterranean garden. Rustic atmosphere and furniture. All rooms with sea-view. Closed: mid October–end March. Credit cards: Visa. Rooms from FF500.

Grimaud

La Boulangerie, Route de Collobrières, tel: 94 43 23 16. Simple and comfortable, a small friendly hotel quietly situated in the Maures hills. Swimming-pool and tennis courts. Closed: mid October–early April. Credit cards: Visa. Rooms from FF400.

Gigaro

(La Croix Valmer)

Souleias, Plage de Gigaro, tel: 94 79 61 91. Modern hotel in extensive grounds overlooking the unspoilt beach of Gigaro. Spacious rooms, swimming-pool, tennis courts, private yacht. Closed: November–mid March. Credit cards: Eurocard, Diners, Visa.

Ramatuelle

(6 miles from Ste-Maxime)

Mas des Brugassières. Tel: 94 43 72 42. Away from the coast in the Maures hills. A small hotel with rooms on to either the terrace around the swimming-pool or a private terrace. Tennis courts. Open: all year round. Credit cards: Amex, Diners, Visa. Rooms: FF400–600.

St-Raphael, Frejus & Massif De L'esterel

Frejus

Residence du Colombier, route de Bagnols, tel: 94 51 45 92. Separate villas with private terraces surrounded by pine woods. Swimming pool and sports facilities. Rooms from FF400.

Cannes

Carlton Intercontinental, 58 Boulevard Croisette, tel: 04 93 06 40 06. Cannes' world-famous waterfront luxury hotel. The rooms and lobby have recently been completely renovated and are now more splendid than ever. Health centre and casino on the top floor. Open: all year round. Credit cards: Amex, Diners, MasterCard, Visa. Rooms: FF2,000–3,500.

Cap 'Antibes from Golfe Juan to La Brague

Cap d'Antibe

Grand Hotel du Cap, Boulevard Kennedy, tel: 93 61 39 01. Beautifully set on the water's edge in extensive wooded grounds. Recently refurbished, very comfortable rooms. Heated seawater swimming-pool, tennis courts. Closed: end October–end March. Credit cards: Amex, Diners, Mastercard, Visa. Rooms from FF3500.

Antibes

Mas de la Pagane, 15 Avenue du Mas-Ensoleillé, tel: 93 33 33 78. An attractive old Provençal *mas* in surprisingly calm situation close to the town centre. Friendly family atmosphere. Open: all year round. Credit cards: Visa. Rooms: FF250–450.

Juan-les-Pins

Belles Rives, Boulevard Baudoin, tel: 93 61 02 79. Close enough to town to enjoy the lively atmosphere, yet sufficiently far away from the noise and crowds, a former 1930s villa that has retained all the charm of its era, when it was the home of Zelda and Scott Fitgerald. Closed: 10 September–Palm Sunday. Credit cards: Amex, Diners, MasterCard, Visa. Rooms from FF1000.

Garden Beach Hotel, 15–17 Boulevard Baudoin, tel: 93 67 25 25. On the site of the former casino, right in the centre of town and with a nice terrace overlooking the bay. Open: all year round. Credit cards: Amex, Diners, MasterCard, Visa. Rooms from FF500–2000.

Grasse

Mougins

Le Mas Candille, Boulevard Rebuffel, tel: 93 90 00 85. A beautiful 200-year-old farmhouse in the countryside outside Mougins, re-opened after extensive renovations that have respected its character. Swimming-pool, terrace with wonderful views of the Pre-Alps. Open: all year round. Credit cards: Amex, Diners, MasterCard, Visa. Rooms from FF900.

Les Muscadins, 18 Boulevard Courteline, tel: 93 90 00 43. On the edge of the village, an attractive hotel with a good view of the Bay of Cannes. Only 8 bedrooms, each different, all nicely furnished and decorated. Closed: 1 February–1 April and 1–15 December. Credit cards: Amex, Diners, MasterCard, Visa. Rooms from FF900.

Vence, St-Paul, Cagnes & The Var Valley

Cagnes-sur-Mer

(Haut-de-Cagnes)

Le Cagnard, Rue du Pontis-Long, tel: 93 20 73 21. Situated in the little winding back-streets not far from the Grimaldi Castle, a charming hotel with a rustic atmosphere. Wooden beams, low ceilings and attractive old furniture. Member of the Relais et Châteaux group. Open: all year round. Credit cards: Amex, Diners, MasterCard, Visa. Rooms FF550–1500.

Roquefort les Pins

Auberge du Colombier. Tel: 93 77 10 27. A small friendly hotel set away from the coast in a beautiful well-established garden commanding a fine view down to the Mediterranean. Swimming-pool and tennis courts. Closed: 10 January–10 February. Credit cards: Amex, Diners, MasterCard, Visa. Rooms from FF200.

Vence

Château du Domaine St-Martin, Route de Coursegoules, tel: 93 58 02 02. True luxury set on the hills above Vence, with a magnificent view of the coast. Extensive grounds, swimming-pool. A member of the Relais and Châteaux group. Closed: 20 November–10 March. Credit cards: Amex, Diners, MasterCard, Visa. Rooms: FF4000.

La Roseraie, Avenue Henri Giraud, tel: 93 58 02 20. Small friendly hotel in a 1930s villa. Pretty garden and pool. Closed: January. Credit cards: Amex, Visa. Rooms from FF400.

St-Paul

La Colombe d'Or, Place du Général de Gaulle, tel: 93 32 80 02. A lovely old building on the edge of the village, once frequented by artists such as Picasso, Matisse, Miró and Léger, whose works still adorn the walls. Private courtyard and swimming-pool. Closed: mid November–mid December. Credit cards: Amex, Diners, MasterCard, Visa. Rooms from FF950.

Mas d'Artigny, Route de la Colle, tel: 93 32 84 54. Beautifully situated in the woods between St-Paul and la Colle with a splendid 360° view of the sea and the mountains. Open: all year round. Credit cards: Amex, Visa. Rooms from FF600.

Nice

Hotel Négresco, 37 Promenade des Anglais, tel: 0493 166400. The last vestige of Nice's era of splendour at the end of the 19th century with its famous dome dominating the coastline of the Baie des Anges. Period furniture from the 16th and 18th century, and priceless paintings and tapestries. Open: all year round. Credit cards: Amex, Diners, MasterCard, Visa. Rooms from FF1300.

La Pérouse, 11 Quai Rauba-Capéu, tel: 93 62 34 63. At the east end of the Promenade des Anglais, conveniently situated between the old town and the port. The rooms have splendid views of the Baie des Anges. Swimming-pool. Open: all year round. Credit cards: Amex, Diners, MasterCard, Visa. Rooms from FF890.

Hotel Windsor, 11 Rue Dalpozzo, tel: 93 88 59 35. Centrally located, with garden, swimming-pool and fitness room. Spacious, nicely furnished rooms. Open: all year round. Credit cards: Amex, Diners, MasterCard, Visa. Rooms from FF550.

Cap Ferrat & The Golden Triangle

Eze

Château Eza. Tel: 93 41 16 64. Accessible only on foot (baggage carried up by donkey), this 400-year-old castle is perched on top of the cliff and overlooks 250 km (160 miles) of coast. Beautifully decorated rooms with antique furniture, oriental rugs, some with fireplace. Closed: November–March. Credit cards: Amex, Diners, MasterCard, Visa. Rooms: FF1,500–3,500.

Beaulieu-sur-Mer

La Réserve de Beaulieu, 5 Boulevard Leclerc, tel: 93 01 00 01. A luxurious late 19th-century villa, beautifully situated on the coast with private beach and harbour. Swimming-pool in the garden. Closed: mid November–mid December. Credit cards: Amex, Diners, MasterCard, Visa. Rooms from FF1000.

St-Jean Cap Ferrat

Brise Marine, 58, Avenue Jean Mermoz, tel: 93 76 04 36. A small hotel in an attractive terraced garden. Some of the rooms overlook the sea. Closed: end October–1 February. Credit cards: Visa. Rooms: FF250–600.

La Voile d'Or, Yachting harbour, tel: 93 01 13 13. An Italian villa in a garden overlooking the yachting harbour. Rooms of all sizes, attractively decorated. Two pools. Closed: 31 October–1 March. Credit cards: Visa. Rooms from FF1000.

Monaco

Abela Hotel, 23, Avenue des Papalins, Fontvieille, tel: 92 05 90 00. A little way out of the centre, a comfortable modern hotel overlooking the new harbour. Open: all year round. Credit cards: Amex, Diners, MasterCard, Visa. Rooms from FF700.

Hotel Hermitage, Square Beaumarchais, tel: 92 16 40 00. Beautiful Edwardian architecture, spacious comfortable rooms. Swimming-pool and fitness centre. Open: all year round. Credit cards: Amex, Diners, MasterCard, Visa. Rooms from FF1300.

Hotel de Paris, Place du Casino, tel: 92 16 30 00. The most prestigious and famous of Monaco's luxury hotels. Indoor swimming-pool. Open: all year round. Credit cards: Amex, Diners, MasterCard, Visa. Rooms from FF1800.

Menton & Roquebrune

Menton

Chambord, 6, Avenue Boyer, tel: 93 35 94 19. Three-star hotel just off the Promenade du Soleil. Open: all year round. Credit cards: Amex, Diners, MasterCard, Visa. Rooms from FF400.

Hotel de Londres, 15, Avenue Carnot, tel: 93 35 74 62. Small central hotel. Open: 23 December–31 October. Credit cards: Amex, Diners, MasterCard, Visa. Rooms from FF300.

Roquebrune Cap Martin

Vista Palace Hotel, Grande Corniche, tel: 92 10 40 00. A modern luxury hotel set high above Monaco with wonderful views. Light spacious rooms, swimming-pool and fitness centre. Open: all year round. Credit cards: Amex, Diners, MasterCard, Visa. Rooms from FF1000.

Westminster, 14, Avenue Laurent, tel: 93 35 00 68. Closed: early January–early February and end October–25 December. Credit cards: Visa. Rooms from FF900.

Perched Villages

Peillon

Auberge de la Madone. Tel: 93 79 91 17. A simple country hotel, whose rooms offer splendid views of the hilltop village and the valley. Closed: January, early November–20 December, and Wednesdays. Credit cards: not accepted. Rooms from FF430.

Lantosque

L'Ancienne Gendarmerie. Tel: 93 03 00 65. Once a police-station, now a small family inn. Rooms simple but comfortable. Closed: early November–31 December and Mondays. Credit cards: Amex, Diners. Rooms from FF350.

Utelle

Bellevue, Utelle. 06450 Lantosque, tel: 93 03 17 19. Quiet, family hotel with stunning views and swimming pool. Credit cards: not accepted. Rooms: from FF250.

Border Country

Sospel

Hotel de France, 9 Boulevard de Verdun, tel: 93 04 00 01. Friendly family-run hotel overlooking river; restaurant with local specialities. Open: all year round. Credit cards: Amex, Diners, MasterCard, Visa. Rooms: from FF250 for demi-pension.

Hotel des Etrangers, 7 Boulevard de Verdun, tel: 93 04 00 09. Swimming pool on site, English spoken and proprietor is expert on local history. Credit cards: Amex, Diners, MasterCard, Visa. Rooms: from FF300 for demi-pension.

Tende

Le Prieuré, St-Dalmas-de-Tende, tel: 93 04 75 70. Three-star hotel with good restaurant in lovely valley. Organises trips to Vallée des Merveilles. June–September. Credit cards: Amex, Diners, MasterCard, Visa. Rooms: from FF250.

Bed & Breakfast

Apart from members of the Fédération Nationale des Gîtes Ruraux de France who have always offered a few *chambres d'hôtes* (guest rooms), the notion of bed and breakfast is a fairly recent one in France. It has always been so easy to find good, cheap hotels in France, that there has been less demand for this kind of accommodation. Now, however, visitors to the country are more keen to get to know the local people and enjoy their hospitality.

Bookings outside France: 5 Worlds End Lane, Green St-Green, Orpington, Kent BR6 6AA, tel: (01689) 855538. Offer a straightforward bed and breakfast service which can include ferry bookings. Their brochure currently lists just a few homes in the region, but is also useful for touring and overnight stops en route.

Café-Couette, 8 Rue de l'Isly, 75008 Paris, tel: (1) 42 94 92 00. Is a Paris-based organisation offering B&B, or *Hébergement chez l'habitant.*

For details of bed and breakfast accommodation offered by the Fédération des Gîtes Ruraux, write to the Relais, addresses listed under *Self-Catering.*

Self-Catering

France probably has the best network of self-catering cottages anywhere in Europe. The *Fédération des Gîtes Ruraux de France* was set up over 30 years ago with the aim of restoring rural properties (by means of offering grants to owners) on the condition that these properties would then be let as cheap holiday homes for the less well-off town and city dwellers. These gîtes (literally, a place to lay one's head) have now become extremely popular with the British as an inexpensive way of enjoying a rural holiday in France and properties range from very simple farm cottages to grand manor houses and even the odd château.

The properties are all inspected by the Relais Départemental des Gîtes de France (the county office of the national federation) and given an *épi* (ear of corn) classification. Gîtes are completely self-catering (in many cases expect to supply your own bedlinen), but most have owners living nearby who will tell you where to buy produce (and if on a farm, often provide it).

One salutary note: many of these cottages are on farms, and as such, are surrounded by wildlife – so if you are squeamish about the odd mouse in the kitchen, stay in a hotel. The properties should be, and generally are, kept clean and in good order.

As gîtes are, by their nature, rural properties, there are very few to be found on the coast. Most are off the beaten track and a car, or at least a bicycle, is usually essential. Bicycles can often be hired locally or sometimes from gîte owners. Car hire is expensive, but some fly/drive packages still make this a relatively inexpensive way to visit the region, as gîtes can cost as little as F1,200 a week for the whole house.

Gîtes do get very heavily booked in high season, so start the process in the new year. If you wish to deal directly with France, the Relais Départemental will send you a list of all the gîtes in their *département*. Most gîtes in the Alpes-Maritimes are in rural areas away from the coast; as the Var is less built-up, it has a wide selection, with a total of 850 gîtes. Contact: Maison des Gîtes de France, 35 rue Godot-de-Mauroy, 75439 Paris, tel: (1) 49 70 75 75

Tour operators offering package holidays include:
Cresta: (0161 927 7000)
British Airways Holidays: (01293 723100)
Travelscene: (0181 427 8800);
Inghams: (0181 780 7700)
French Life: (0113 239 0077)
French Expression: (0171 431 1312)
VSB: (0124 224 0340).

Club Méditerranée

The Club Med, as it is affectionately known, is almost an institution in France – a kind of upmarket holiday camp with meals (including unlimited wine) and all kinds of sports and leisure facilities laid on. The Club Med site at Opio is one of the most luxurious there is, with accommodation in a de-luxe hotel. For more information, contact the company at 106–110 Brompton Road, London SW3 1JJ, tel: (0171) 581 1161 or (01635) 38450 (brochure service), or in France: 2 Place de la Bourse, 75083 Paris Cedex 02, tel: (1) 42 96 10 00.

Camping

There is a good choice of campsites in the region. The Comité Régional du Tourisme (*see Useful Addresses* page 316) produces a list of all recognised sites, with details of star-rating and facilities.

In the Alpes-Maritimes in particular, the quieter campsites tend to be away from the coast. If you are looking for a young atmosphere with plenty of activity, there are several sites just outside Antibes at La Brague, but choose your pitch carefully to avoid ending up right next to the main road.

As with other types of holiday accommodation, the sites get heavily booked in high season, especially those closest to the coast so advance booking is advisable, if not essential. Members of the Camping Club or Camping and Caravanning Club of Great Britain can make use of their booking services. The *Michelin Camping/Caravanning Guide* lists sites which accept (or insist on) pre-booking. **The Camping Service** at 69 Westbourne Grove, London W2 4UJ, tel: (0171) 792 I944, can book sites either from their own brochure of 3 and 4-star sites or any other you may wish to book. They will also book ferries as part of the package.

A camping carnet is useful (some sites will not accept a booking without one). Available in the UK for members of the AA, RAC or the Camping Clubs mentioned in this section; or from the GB Car Club, PO Box 11, Romsey, Hants SO5 8XX.

Campsites, like hotels, have official classifications from one-star (minimal comfort, water points, showers and sinks) to four-star luxury sites which allow more space to each pitch, and offer above-average facilities, often including a restaurant or takeway food, games areas and swimming-pools. Sites near the coast particularly have a lot to offer families, including children's clubs and entertainment and discos for teenagers. The majority of sites nationwide are two-star, but most of the four-star sites are by the coast.

If you really like to get back to nature and are unimpressed by the modern trappings of hot water and electric power, look out for camp-sites designated *Aire naturelle de camping*, where facilities will be absolutely minimal and prices to match. With a maximum of 25 pitches, they offer the opportunity to stay away from some of the more commercial sites (which can be huge). The FFCC Guide (*see Useful Publications*) lists over 2,000 such sites nationwide.

Do not be tempted to get back to nature by off-site camping. This is strictly forbidden because of the risk of fire.

Some farms offer "official" sites too, under the auspices of the Fédération Nationale des Gîtes Ruraux (*see Self-catering*) – these are designated *Camping à la ferme*. Again, facilities are usually limited but farmers are allowed to have only six pitches and if you are lucky you will get to enjoy the farm life and some of its produce.

Campsites to the west of the region are becoming increasingly popular. They avoid some of the crowds of the fashionable resorts and are often right by the beach. Sites to the east of St-Tropez tend to be further inland, involving a drive from the site to the coast and inevitable parking problems.

Packaged camping holidays are now very popular, as all the camping paraphernalia is provided on the site – you bring only your personal luggage. Many companies now offer this type of holiday, mostly with ferry travel included in the all-in price. Like other package tours, the companies have couriers on the sites to help with any problems. Where such companies have taken over sections of existing sites facilities have improved to meet the demands of their customers and so benefit all campers. Many companies offer good opportunities for sports and leisure, such as wind-surfing or surfing; often the equipment, and sometimes instruction too is covered by the cost of the package. Be warned though that some of the sites are very large, so might not suit those who wish to get away from it all.

A selection of the package operators is listed below, for others check the Sunday press.

Canvas Holidays, 12 Abbey Park Place, Dunfermline KY12 7PD, tel: (01383) 621 000. Pioneers in the field; offers a nanny service.

Eurocamp Travel, Canute Court, Toft Road, Knutsford, Cheshire WA16 0NL, tel: (01565) 626262.

Keycamp Holidays, Ellerman House, 92-96 Lind Road, Sutton SM1 4PL, tel: (0181) 395 4000.

Useful Publications & Addresses

French Federation of Camping and Caravanning Guide (FFCC), lists 11,300 sites nationwide, and also shows which have facilities for disabled campers. Available from Springdene, Shepherd's Way, Fairlight, E. Sussex TN35 4BB; or 78 rue de Rivoli, Paris, tel: 01 42 72 84 08.

Michelin Green Guide – Camping/Caravanning France. Very informative and also lists sites with facilities for the disabled. Published annually in March.

Good Camp Guide for France by Alan Rogers (Deneway Guides) lists 200 inspected sites nationwide, mostly around the coast.

Camping and Caravanning Club, 11 Lower Grosvenor Place, London SW1, tel: 01203 422024.

Caravan Club, East Grinstead House, East Grinstead, Sussex RH19 1UA.

Naturism

With its wonderful climate, the Côte d'Azur is an ideal resort for naturists. Indeed, the world's first nudist centre was established on the Île du Levant in 1931 by two doctors, Gaston and André Durville. The island still attracts naturists and there are many other sites in the region. The following is a selection:

La Grande Terre la Baume, 04120 Castellane, tel: 92 83 64 24. Twenty caravans available and places for 100 tents at the edge of the Grand Canyon of Verdon. Open: Easter to the end of October.

Les Lauzons, 04300 Limans, tel: 92 76 00 60. Twenty mobile homes and 180 camping places, plus a gîte rural at an altitude of 500 metres. Open: all year.

Domaine d'Enriou, 04480 Saint-Laurent-du-Verdon, tel: 92 74 41 02. Four houses to let, plus 100 camping places, at the edge of the Verdon Gorge. Open: mid-May to mid-September.

Nice Nature, 77 Boulevard Virgile Barel, 06300 Nice, tel: 93 55 60 50. Campsite plus chalet and dormitory accommodation in the heart of Nice. Open: all year.

Centre Naturisme Origan, 06260 Puget-Therniers, tel: 93 05 06 00. Fifteen mobile homes and 100 camping places in the region of the gorges by the river Var. Open: 1 May–30 October.

Youth Hostels

Holders of accredited Youth Hostel Association cards may stay in any French hostels which are in fact run by two separate organisations; Fédération Unie des Auberges de Jeunesse (FUAJ), 27 Rue Pajol, 75018 Paris, tel: 01 44 89 37 27, which is affiliated to the International Youth Hostel Federation, and the Ligue Française pour les Auberges de Jeunesse (LFAJ), 38 Boulevard Raspail, 75007 Paris, tel: (1) 45 48 69 84.

There are about half a dozen accredited hostels on the coast and more inland. Information locally about hostels is available from Centre Information Jeunesse Côte d'Azur, 19 Rue Gioffredo, 06000 Nice, tel: 93 80 93 93; fax: 93 80 30 33. Open: Monday–Friday, 8.45am–6.45pm.

Auberges de Jeunesse are open to members of the Youth Hostel Association or holders of a youth card (*carte jeune*).

Tende (06430): Chemin Ste-Cathérine, tel: 93 04 62 74.

The British YHA publishes the International Youth Hostel Handbook, Vol I (revised each March), which includes all the hostels in the region, price £5.99 by post from Youth Hostel Association, 14 Southampton Street, London WC2E 7H7, tel: (0171) 836 8541. They also handle membership queries, tel: (0171) 836 1036.

In the US apply to the American Youth Hostels Inc, PO Box 37613, Dept USA, Washington DC 20013/7613, tel: (202) 783 6161.

Gîtes d'Etapes offer hostel accommodation and are popular with ramblers, climbers and horse riders (some offer stabling). All official gîtes d'étapes come under the auspices of the Relais Départementaux des Gîtes Ruraux (for addresses *see Self-catering*). These are a popular form of cheap accommodation, particularly in the mountain regions. Prices are similar to youth hostels but can be more expensive in the more luxurious establishments which may be on farms offering riding facilities and/or stabling. You do not have to be a member of any organisation to use them.

Eating Out

Where to Eat

As with the hotels, the purpose of this list is to mention some of the region's most famous restaurants, and to recommend others that are particularly attractive or interesting.

Hyères, Iles d'Hyères & Massif des Maures

Aiguebelle, Le Lavandou

Les Roches, 1 Avenue des Trois Dauphins, tel: 93 71 05 07. Beautiful beach setting and good food inspired by the flavours of Provence. Closed: early November–end March. Credit cards: Visa, Amex, Eurocard. Menus FF280 and FF480, à la carte FF550.

St-Tropez Region: From La Croix Valmer to Les Issambres

St-Tropez

La Bouillabaisse, Quartier la Bouillabaisse, tel: 04 94 97 54 00. In an old fisherman's cottage serving excellent fresh fish from the terrace right by the beach, and you can even arrive by boat. Credit cards: Visa, Amex. Menu up to FF180.

La Cascade, 5, Rue de l'Eglise, tel: 94 54 83 46. Lively Caribbean atmosphere and Caribbean specialities. Credit cards: Visa. Menu FF129, à la carte FF200.

L'Olivier, Route des Carles, tel: 94 97 58 16. A country house restaurant serving elegant cuisine based on the flavours of Provence. Closed: mid November–third week December, Monday and Tuesday lunchtimes out of season. All credit cards accepted. Menus: FF200 and FF350, à la carte FF300.

Gassin

Villa de Belieu. Tel: 94 56 40 56. Credit cards: Amex, Visa, MasterCard, Diners. A beautiful setting in a wine domain. Four excellent menus. Menus FF250–600, à la carte FF500–600.

Grimaud

Café de France, Place Neuve, tel: 94 43 20 05. Simple Provençal food, shady terrace set back from the village square. Closed: end October–February, Tuesday. Credit cards: Visa. Menu: FF105, à la carte FF200.

St-Raphael, Fréjus & Massif de l'Esterel

St-Raphael

Pastorel, 54, Rue de la Liberté, tel: 94 95 02 36. Good traditional food with a Provençal touch. Closed: 15 November–15 December, Sunday evenings and Mondays. Credit cards: Visa, Amex, Diners. Menus: FF130, FF190 and FF230, à la carte FF250.

Les Adrets

Auberge des Adrets, Route Nationale 7, towards Mandelieu, tel: 94 40 36 24. Good food in a pleasant setting. Closed: Mondays. Credit cards: Visa. Menu: FF195, à la carte FF350.

Auribeau sur Siagne

Auberge de la Vignette Haute, tel: 93 42 20 01. Rustic setting and romantic atmosphere. The dining room is lit by 400 oil lamps. Credit cards: Visa, Amex, Diners. Menus: FF280–430.

Cannes

La Côte, Hotel Carlton Intercontinental, 58, Boulevard de la Croisette, tel: 93 06 40 06. Elegant dining-room and excellent cuisine. Closed: mid November–end December. Credit cards: Visa, Amex, Diners. Menus: FF190 (weekday lunchtimes), and FF330, à la carte FF450.

L'Eléphant Bleu, 4, Rue Batéguier, tel: 93 38 18 70. Good and imaginative Thai cuisine at reasonable prices, right in the heart of restaurant-land.

La Palme d'Or, Hotel Martinez, 73, Boulevard de la Croisette, tel: 92 98 30 18. Imaginative gastronomic cuisine with a taste of the Mediterranean. One of Cannes' top restaurants, with a view of the Bay and the Lérins Islands. Credit cards: Visa, Amex, Diners. Menus FF280 and FF480, à la carte FF520.

Le Petit Carlton, 93, Rue d'Antibes, tel: 93 39 27 25. This used to be just a bar, but has opened up a very French-style unpretentious restaurant. Typical French food, quick service, very reasonable prices. À la carte around FF100.

La Pizza, 3, Quai St-Pierre, tel: 93 39 22 56. The best-known pizza place in the region, which always has plenty of atmosphere.

Le Royal Gray, Hotel Gray d'Albion, 6, Rue des Etats-Unis, tel: 92 99 79 60. Master chef Jacques Chibois has been voted chef of the year many times. Widely recognised as the best restaurant in Cannes. Credit cards: Visa, Amex, Diners. Menus: FF210 (weekday lunch only), FF340–500, à la carte FF500–700.

Cap D'Antibes, From Golfe Juan to La Brague

Golfe Juan

Le Bistrot du Port, 53, Boulevard des Frères Roustan, tel: 93 63 70 64. Mainly fish dishes. Attractive terrace on the old port. Closed: Sunday evenings and Monday. Credit cards: Visa, Eurocard. Menus FF220 and FF250, à la carte FF300.

Juan-Les-Pins

Belles Rives, Boulevard Baudoin, tel: 93 61 02 79. Set right on the water's edge, once the residence of Scott Fitzgerald. Closed: mid October–mid March. Credit cards: Visa, Amex. Menus: FF280, FF380 and FF480, à la carte FF450.

La Terrasse, La Pinède, Avenue Gallice, tel: 93 61 08 70. Recognised as one of the region's best restaurants. Closed: end October–Easter. Menus: FF320 (lunchtime), FF450 and FF520, à la carte from FF600.

Antibes

Auberge Provençale, Place Nationale, tel: 93 34 13 24. Attractive dining-room and beautiful courtyard in summer. Closed: mid April–mid May, mid November–mid December and Mondays. Credit cards: Visa, Amex, Diners, Eurocard. Menus: from FF135–230.

Bacon, 668 Boulevard de Bacon, tel: 04 93 61 50 02. Celebrated restaurant famous for its fish dishes and in particular its superlative bouillabaisse. Credit cards: Visa, Amex, Diners. Menus from FF250.

La Bonne Auberge, Route Nationale 7, tel: 93 33 36 65. One of the best restaurants in the area. Credit cards: Visa, Amex. Menus: FF390, FF490 and FF560, à la carte FF650.

Don Juan, 17, Rue Thuret, tel: 93 34 58 63. Excellent service, good, reasonably-priced pizzas, Italian and provençal dishes.

Casa Pablo, 1, Rue de la Touraque, tel: 93 34 21 54. An unpretentious, pretty restaurant near the ramparts. Closed: mid January, early November and Mondays. Credit cards: Visa, Amex, Diners. Menu: FF90, à la carte from FF200.

Biot

Les Arcades, 16 Place des Arcades, tel: 93 65 01 04. Classical Provençal cuisine in the dining room of a 15th-century house, which doubles as an art gallery. Menus: FF140 and FF150, à la carte FF200.

Auberge du Jarrier, 30, Passage de la Bourgade, tel: 93 65 11 68. Elegant French cuisine with a Mediterranean flavour. Credit cards: Visa, Eurocard. Menus: FF190–320, à la carte FF400.

Le Café Brun, 44 ter, Impasse St-Sébastien, tel: 93 65 04 83. A typical Dutch "brown café" serving Indonesian dishes. Lively atmosphere. Credit cards: Visa, MasterCard. No menu, à la carte FF200.

Les Terraillers, 11, Route du Chemin Neuf, tel: 93 65 01 59. An elegant restaurant just outside the village in a beautiful vaulted cellar. Attractive terrace in summer. Closed: November and Wednesdays. Credit cards: Visa, Amex, Diners. Menus: FF150, FF220 and FF260, à la carte FF350.

Grasse

Mougins

Le Moulin de Mougins, 424, Chemin du Moulin, tel: 93 75 78 24. The most famous restaurant in this village full of famous restaurants. Roger Vergé's "*cuisine du soleil*" is known worldwide.

Closed: end January–early April, Mondays and Thursday lunchtimes. Credit cards: Visa, Amex, Diners. Menu: FF650, à la carte FF800.

L'Amandier, Place du Commandant Lamy, tel: 93 90 00 91. Roger Vergé's second restaurant, in the old village. Closed: Wednesdays and Saturday lunchtimes. Credit cards: Visa, Amex, Diners. Menu: FF330, à la carte FF500.

Le Bistrot de Mougins, Place du Village, tel: 93 42 05 59. In a beautiful vaulted stone cellar, excellent Provençal cuisine. Closed: December–mid January, Tuesdays and Wednesdays. Menu: FF150.

La Ferme de Mougins, 10, Avenue Saint Basile, tel: 93 90 03 74. A Provençal residence built of stone, set in an idyllic garden. Closed: February, Saturday lunchtimes and Thursdays. Credit cards: Visa, Eurocard, Diners, Amex. Menus: FF230 and FF380, à la carte FF500.

VALBONNE

L'Auberge Fleurie, 1016 Route de Cannes, tel: 93 12 02 80. Excellent value for money. Good desserts. Closed: Wednesdays. Credit cards: Visa. Menus: FF98, FF125 and FF155.

CABRIS

Auberge du Petit Prince, 15, Rue Frédéric Mistral, tel: 93 60 51 40. A country inn with an attractive terrace. Closed: mid November–mid December, Thursday evenings and Fridays. Credit cards: Visa, Amex, Diners. Menus: FF98, FF140 and FF180, à la carte FF250.

Vence, St-Paul, Cagnes & The Var Valley

BAR SUR LOUP

La Jarrerie, Route de Grasse, tel: 93 42 92 92. Traditional, elegant atmosphere and cuisine in a former monastery. Closed: January, Monday evenings and Tuesdays. Credit cards: Visa. Menus: FF135–FF250.

TOURRETTES SUR LOUP

Chez Grand'Mère, Place Mirabeau, tel: 93 59 33 34. Very popular for North African specialities and meats grilled on the open fire. Reservations recommended. Closed: November, Saturday lunchtimes and Wednesdays. Menu: under FF100, à la carte FF150.

Le Petit Manoir, 21, Grand'Rue, tel: 93 24 19 19. Elegant restaurant, fine cuisine. Closed: November and February school holidays, Wednesdays and Sunday evenings (except July and August). Credit cards: Visa, Eurocard. Menus: FF120–200.

VENCE

Le Château des Aromes, 2618 Route de Grasse, tel: 93 58 70 24. The château also houses a perfume museum, where the emphasis is on the essences used to flavour the cuisine. Fragant terrace and beautiful views. Closed: November–February, Sunday evenings. Credit cards: Visa, Amex.

La Roseraie, Avenue Henri Giraud, tel: 93 58 02 20. Specialities from the southwest of France. Beautiful terrace around the swimming-pool.Closed: January, Tuesdays and Wednesdays. Credit cards: Visa, Amex. Menus: FF100 and FF150, à la carte FF200.

ST-PAUL

La Colombe d'Or, 1, Place du Général de Gaulle, tel: 93 32 80 02. The dining-room is hung with the works of Matisse, Picasso, Léger, Delaunay and others, the terrace must be the most beautiful in the region. Good, traditional cuisine. Closed: early November–third week in December. Credit cards: Amex, Diners, Visa. No set menu, à la carte FF350.

COURSEGOULES

L'Escaou, tel: 04 93 59 11 28. Restaurant in a mountain village near the coast, serving rustic Provençal cuisine with superb views from its terrace. Credit cards: Visa. Menus: FF90–180.

LA GAUDE

La Seguinière, tel: 93 24 42 92. An attractive villa with plenty of atmosphere. Jazz on Saturday evenings. Garden in summer. Menu: FF260.

CAGNES-SUR-MER

Le Cagnard, Rue du Pontis Long, Haut-de-Cagnes, tel: 93 20 73 21. The cuisine is elegant and beautifully presented. Charming dining-room in what was once the 14th-century castle's guardroom. Closed: early November–mid December and Thursday lunchtimes. Credit cards: Visa, Amex, Diners. Menus: FF340 and FF430, à la carte FF500.

Entre Cour et Jardin, 102 Montee de la Bourgade, tel: 04 93 20 72 27. Friendly restaurant in a little village street with art exhibitions in the courtyard twice a year. Credit cards: Visa. Menus: up to FF180.

Le Picadéro, 3, Boulevard de la Plage, Cros de Cagnes, tel: 93 22 32 84. Bistrot-style, excellent value for money. Closed: Mondays. Menus : FF170 and FF280, à la carte FF320.

Nice

Auberge de Bellet, St-Roman de Bellet, tel: 93 37 83 84. In Nice's most famous vineyard of the same name. Vintage wines and delicacies such as lobster and pigeon and garlic stew. Closed: end of January and Tuesdays. Credit cards: Visa, Eurocard. Menus: FF195 and FF280, à la carte FF400.

Le Chantecler, Hotel Negresco, 37, Promenade des Anglais, tel: 93 16 64 00. Nice's finest restaurant, in the Negresco hotel. Elegant cuisine with a Mediterranean touch. Closed: mid November–mid December. Credit cards: Visa, Amex, Diners, Eurocard. Menus: FF260 (weekday lunch), FF390 and FF550. A la carte FF600.

Le Safari, 1 Cours Saleya, tel: 93 80 18 44. Big café with outside tables in flower market street. Try the *bagna cauda*, a hot anchovy dip with raw vegetables. Credit cards: Visa, Amex. Menus: FF90–180.

Le Comptoir, 20 rue Saint-Francois-de-Paule, tel: 93 92 08 80. A 1930s-style bar and restaurant, excellent for late-night dining. Credit cards: Visa, Amex, Diners. Menus: up to FF180.

Nissa-Socca, 5, Rue Ste-Réparate, tel: 93 80 18 35. Arrive early or be prepared to wait. Very popular and unpretentious, serving Niçois specialities: fresh pasta, vegetable fritters. Excellent value. Closed: Sundays and Monday lunchtimes. Credit cards not accepted. À la carte: FF60–70.

Cap Ferrat & The Golden Triangle

ST-JEAN CAP FERRAT

Le Provençal, 2, Avenue Denis Semeria, tel: 93 76 03 97. Imaginative, gastronomic cuisine with a Mediterranean flavour. Closed: Sundays. Credit cards: Visa, Amex Menus: FF150 (lunchtime only), FF250 and FF450, à la carte FF400–500.

La Voile d'Or, Yachting harbour, tel: 93 76 11 17. High prices justified by the idyllic setting overlooking the pretty harbour and the exquisite cuisine. Closed: November–March. Credit cards: Visa, Amex. Menus: FF400, FF460 and FF550, à la carte FF700–800.

Beaulieu-sur-Mer

Le Metropole, 15, Boulevard Leclerc, tel: 93 01 00 08. Fish specialities in a discreetly luxurious setting. Closed: November–20 December. Credit cards: Visa, MasterCard. Menus: FF380 and FF450, à la carte FF500.

La Réserve, 5, Boulevard Leclerc, tel: 93 01 00 01. Excellent cuisine in an elegant setting. Emphasis on fish dishes. Credit cards: Visa, Diners, Amex, Eurocard, MasterCard. Menus: FF280–450, à la carte FF500.

Eze

Château de la Chèvre d'Or, Moyenne Corniche Rue du Barri, tel: 92 10 66 66. Light, classical cuisine in a medieval château. Closed: December, January, February and Wednesdays. Credit cards: Visa, Amex, Diners. Menu: FF330 (lunchtime), à la carte: FF600–800.

Chateau Eza, tel: 93 41 12 24. Former residence of the Prince of Sweden, suspended high above the sea. Closed: late October–early April. Credit cards: Visa, Amex, Diners, Eurocard. Menus: FF250 (lunchtime) and FF490, à la carte FF500.

Peillon

Auberge de la Madone, tel: 93 79 91 17. A true Provençal inn offering authentic regional cuisine. Closed: end October–end December and Wednesdays. Credit cards: not accepted. Menus: FF120 and FF280, à la carte FF300.

Monaco

Le Café de Paris, Place du Casino, tel: 92 16 36 36. Recently completely renovated in 1920s style, this deserves a visit as one of the sights of Monte-Carlo. Open: every day for lunch and dinner. Credit cards: Visa, Amex, Diners. No set menu, à la carte from FF250.

Polpetta, 2, Rue Paradis, tel: 93 50 67 84. Offering among the best value for money in Monaco. Italian food. Closed: mid October, late February–mid March, Saturday lunchtimes and Tuesdays. Credit cards: Visa, Eurocard. Menu: FF120, à la carte FF200.

Rampoldi, 3, Avenue des Spélugues, tel: 93 30 70 65. Simple cuisine: grills and Italian specialities. Popular with locals. Closed: November. À la carte: FF300.

Menton & Roquebrune

Roquebrune

Au Grand Inquisiteur, Rue du Château, tel: 93 35 05 37. Restaurant in a medieval setting in the old village. Closed: mid March, mid November–December, Mondays. Credit cards: Visa. Menus: FF125 and FF210, à la carte FF250.

Le Vistaero, Grande Corniche, tel: 93 35 01 50. Fabulous view over Monaco and the coast towards Nice. Credit cards: Visa, Amex, Diners, Eurocard. Menus: FF300 and 490, à la carte FF500.

Menton

L'Oursin, 3, Rue Trenca, tel: 93 28 33 62. Fish specialities. Closed: mid December–mid February and Wednesdays. Credit cards: Visa, Amex. À la carte only: FF250–300.

Perched Villages & Border Country

Labrigue

Le Mirval, Rue St-Vincent Ferrier, tel: 93 04 63 71. Most charming restaurant in La Brigue, outside village, by the river. Local specialties include trout, spinach ravioli and game. Open April –November only. Credit cards: Amex, Diners, MasterCard, Visa.

Breil-sur-Roya

Castel du Roy, Route de Tende, tel: 04 93 04 43 66. Charming riverside restaurant with tranquil tree-shaded terrace serving specialities of the region, such as roasted pigeon. Credit cards: Visa. Menus: up to FF180.

Attractions

Places of Interest

The Côte d'Azur is renowned for its luxurious resorts and glamorous lifestyle. You could spend your whole holiday just lazing on the beach, celebrity-spotting. However, you would be doing yourself and the region an injustice. There are all kinds of different activities on offer and places to visit.

This section covers a variety of activities: technical visits, parks and gardens, *caves* (wine cellars) open to the public and steam railways etc. Some of the venues are particular to the region and are well worth seeking out.

All places listed (in alphabetical order) are open daily, morning and afternoon (not including public holidays) except where otherwise specified. Most close for a long lunch break – noon or 12.30 until 2 or 2.30pm. Expect to pay an entrance fee at most venues. A list of museums and art galleries are in *Culture* (page 331).

Many of the major towns in the region offer guided tours of the town – enquire at the Office de Tourisme or Syndicat d'Initiative.

Antibes

Marineland/Aquasplash, 306 Avenue Mozart, tel: 93 33 49 49. The biggest marine show in Europe with dolphins, whales, sealions, etc. Sea museum and aquaria. Separate entrance fee for the water park (Aquasplash) with waterchutes, wave pool and other attractions. Restaurant. Marineland open: all year; Aquasplash: June–September.

The Marineland complex includes: **La Petite Ferme Provençale.** The recreation of a local farm with animals, an oil mill, displays of honey and a perfumery. Open: 10am–6pm. Also the **Butterfly Jungle**. A vast indoor tropical environment where butterflies can be observed in a "natural" habitat. **Villa Thuret**, has 5 hectares (12 acres) of gardens and an arboretum with 2,000 different species.

Biot

Biot is noted for its traditional earthenware pottery and also for hand-blown glass. There are several ceramics studios all along the Route de la Mer, such as: La Poterie Provençale, le Lavandier, Martine Polisset and Aux Jarres de Provence.

For glassworks visit La Verrerie de Biot, Chemin des Combes, 06410 Biot, tel: 93 65 03 00.

Cannes

The town and its surrounding area have some splendid gardens open to the public: the **Parc de la Croix des Gardes**, set above Le Suquet; **La Roseraie de la Croisette**, thousands of rose trees, right on the seafront; **Forêt Dominiale de l'Ile Sainte Marguerite**, 420 acres of indigenous Mediterranean vegetation with an herbarium and botanic trail; visit too the Cistercian **Abbey of Lérins** on Île St-Honorat where the land is still cultivated by the monks using medieval methods.

Contes

Moulin à Huile, 06390 Contes, tel: 93 79 00 01. Olive oil mill in operation during the grinding period from November to February and open to the public on Saturdays (all year).

Eze

The **Jardin Exotique,** tel: 04 93 41 10 30 and the perfumeries of Gallimard and Fragonard (*see Grasse*) are also worth visiting.

Frejus

Aquatica, on the RN 98. A water park, and nearby, **Aquatigolf.** There are also several formal **gardens** in the town: **Villa Aurélienne**, Route de Cannes; **Villa Marie**, Avenue Aristide Briand; **Parc de Sainte Croix**, Avenue du XVe Corps; and **Jardin Havana**, boulevard Alfred de Musset, Saint Aygulf.

For the younger visitors, the **zoo** – Safari de l'Esterel, Le Capitou, tel: 94 40 70 65.

You can also visit the **nurseries** where exotic plants are produced.

Gonfaron

Village des Tortues, Route des Mayons, les Plaines, tel: 94 78 26 42. Wild tortoise preserve.

Grasse

Grasse is internationally famous for its perfumes, which grew up out of the glove-making and tanning industries. Many of the **perfumeries** offer free guided tours all year round; the most important have their own museums, and of course you are invited to buy the products at the end of your tour. Try any (or all) of the following (please make appointments for group visits). (*See also Museums and Art Galleries* page 331.) Both Fragonard and Gallimard also have perfumeries which can be visited in Èze.

Fragonard, Boulevard Fragonard, Route de Cannes, tel: 93 36 02 71.

Gallimard, 73 Route de Cannes, tel: 93 09 20 00.

Hyeres

Observatoire du Pic des Fées, overlooking the bay de l'Almanarre, just outside the town, the observatory is open to the public every Saturday evening. Allée des Pinson, Le Mont des Oiseaux, 83400 Hyères, tel: 94 38 69 03 (Tuesday evening only).

Magic World, a leisure park with fairground amusements and other attractions; regular firework displays and *son-et-lumière* shows, plus a restaurant and bars. Free entry, open every evening 8pm–1am, June–September. Port de Hyères Les Palmiers. Outside the town is Cave **Gasperini**, a wine cellar, offering tastings of its Côtes de Provence AOC wines, 42 Avenue de la Libération, 83260 La Crau, tel: 94 66 70 01.

La Londe Les Maures

Tropical Bird Garden, Quartier St-Honoré, tel: 94 35 02 15.

Le Lavandou

Parc de Loisirs, a big leisure park with amusements for all ages: practice golf, tennis, adventure playground, big chess boards, Mediterranean garden.

Domaine de l'Anglade, Avenue Vincent Auriol, 83980 Le Lavandou, tel: 94 71 10 89. The wine cellars are open to the public.

Niagara Parc Nautique, just to the north of the town on the D27 Route du Canadel, lies Le Môle, the oldest village in the region, and the Niagara water park whose huge swimming-pool offers many watery amusements, tel: 94 49 58 85.

Menton

Known as the "Lemon Capital", the sedate town of Menton has many **gardens** open to the public: **Parc Gorre; Parc du Pian**, an ancient olive grove; **Jardins Bioves** where citrus fruits are displayed for the International Lemon Festival in February; **Palais Carnoles** with 50 varieties of citrus fruits; **Les Colombières**, the creation of Ferdinand Bac, a Mediterranean garden covering 15 acres and finally the botanical garden of the **Natural History Museum** at Val Rahmeh.

Monaco

The tiny principality has some lovely **gardens** to visit. Apart from those of the casino itself, there is the Jardin Exotique, tel: 93 30 33 65 with its notable collection of cheese plants; **Parc de Fontvieille**, landscaped gardens surrounding the Princess Grace rose garden (150 different varieties) and several new museums; the **Zoological Gardens** at La Condamine; and the pine woods of the **Parc-Promenade du Portier**.

Nice

Confiserie du Vieux Nice, Quai Papacino, tel: 93 55 43 50. Confectioners open to the public for guided tours (in English), sampling and a visit to the shop. Admission: free. Closed: Sundays in winter.

Moulin Alziari, 14 rue St. Francois de Paule, tel: 93 85 76 92. Legendary olive oil shop.

Observatoire de Calern, Centre of Geodynamic and Astronomic Research, offers astronomy shows May–October; tours daily at 3pm in July and August, at other times by appointment. Information from PARSEC, 2 Passage du Petit Parc, 06000 Nice, tel: 93 42 66 16.

Observatoire de Nice, Boulevard Bischoffsheim (Grande Corniche), tel: 93 00 30 11. Visits by appointment and every Saturday at 3pm.

Parc des Miniatures, Avenue Impératrice Eugenie, tel: 93 44 67 74. Fascinating history of Nice in miniature, laid out over more than 7 acres. Restaurant. Open: till dusk.

Nice is famed for its gardens, the oldest being **les Jardins du Monastère de Cimiez**, hardly changed since 1546. Visit too the **Jardin des Arènes de Cimiez**, the olive grove where the

Grande Parade du Jazz takes place each July.

The **Parc du Château** is set in 20 hectares (50 acres), with superb views of the coast.

The **Jardins d'Acropolis** display modern sculpture in 6 acres around the Palais des Congrès. The **Parc Floral** at Phoénix de l'Arénas on the Promenade des Anglais offers many attractions such as an aquarium, astronomical garden, musical fountains and other features particularly appealing to children, tel: 93 18 03 33.

Opio

Moulin d'Opio, 2 Route de Chateauneuf, 06650 Opio, tel: 93 77 23 03. Fifteenth-century olive oil mill offering free guided tours in French. Closed: Sundays and 15 October–15 November; in operation November to March.

St-Cezaire

Les Grottes de St-Cézaire, tel: 93 60 22 35. Spectacular underground caves and also a picnic site with a bar. Closed: October to mid-February except Sunday afternoons.

St-Roman-De-Bellet

Château de Bellet, Château de Bellet, St-Roman-de-Bellet, 06200 Nice, tel: 93 37 81 57. Vineyard open on request and by appointment, situated in a very old wine-growing area, now reduced to just 40 hectares (100 acres).

St-Tropez

Once a pretty little fishing port much beloved of painters and other artists, St-Tropez is now perhaps better known as a playground for filmstars (Brigitte Bardot started the trend) and for its nudist beaches. Visit the two hill-villages nearby (Ramatuelle and Gassin), and the **Annonciade Museum** (*see Museums* page 331).

Vallauris

Vallauris is a magnet for local potters, with many opening their studios to the public. A complete list is available from local tourist offices and also from the Syndicat des Potiers, Espace Grandjean, Avenue du Stade, 06220 Vallauris, tel: 93 64 17 93.

Parfumerie Jean Bouis, 50 bis Avenue G. Clémenceau, tel: 93 64 38 27. Open: all year.

Vence

The medieval town is well worth a visit. At **Château Notre Dame Des Fleurs**, the Foundation Maurice Lavoillet invites visitors to its gardens where plants are grown for the production of perfumes and liqueurs; there is also a **Museum of Perfume** and a restaurant specialising in aromatic cooking. See too the **Matisse chapel** (*see Archaeology/Architecture*).

Excursions

Boat trips are the most obvious excursions that come to mind on the Côte d'Azur and many companies offer trips for a just a few hours or a whole day. However, you may prefer to take a trip on a steam train, a jeep or in the air. Some possibilities are listed below:

Sea

Take a trip to Monaco, the Iles de Lérins (where the "Man in the Iron Mask" was confined in the fortress on Ste-Marguerite Island), the Hyères Islands, or even a day trip to Corsica. Or go out in the evening to watch the fireworks from the sea.

From Lavandou: Compagnie des transports Maritimes, 15 Quai Gabriel Péri, 83980 Le Lavandou, tel: 94 71 01 02.

From Sainte Maxime/St-Tropez: Transports Maritime, Plan de la Tour, 83120 St. Maxime, tel: 94 96 51 00. Saint Raphael/St. Tropez, Bateau Bleu, tel: 94 95 17 46.

Calanques de la Corniche d'Or (Esterel), Departures from St. Raphael, tel: 94 95 17 46.

SNCM **Ferryterranée**, Quai du Commerce, 06005 Nice cedex, tel: 93 13 66 66. Day trips to Corsica with two hours ashore (ports vary).

Photo Safari: Trips from June–October (according to the movements of the whales) from Antibes or Beaulieu-sur-Mer, lasting 10–12 hours. Cost includes boat hire and a two-man crew (maximum 8 passengers). Contact: Guigo Marine, Port Vauban, Avenue du 11 Novembre, 06600 Antibes, tel: 93 34 70 70.

Train

The "Train des Pignes" run by Chemins de Fer de Provence line goes from Nice to Digne and a trip on it is a grand way to take in some of the sights. It climbs as high as 900 metres (2,950 ft) at Saint-André les Alpes. All-inclusive day trips, 150 km (95 miles) each way (Tuesday–Thursday) include a meal, wine and coffee and a guided village tour. On most Sundays from mid-May to mid-October, a steam train runs from Puget-Theniers to Annot and back. Information from Chemins de Fer de Provence, 33 Avenue Malaussena, 06000 Nice, tel: 04 93 88 34 72.

It is also worth taking a trip along the SNCF Nice-Cuneo line which passes through splendidly wild landscapes and also offers sights of spectacular engineering in the form of bridges and viaducts. Information from Nice station or SNCF. Tel: 93 87 50 50.

Overland

Access to many of the sites of the Vallées des Merveilles is now forbidden unless a guide is conducting a tour. One way of getting around is by jeep, although it can be costly – upwards of FF1,000 a day. The Association des Taxis Accompagnateurs des Merveilles will take you up to the Vallée des Merveilles (from late June to late October) for a day trip, including a guided tour of the archaeological site. Information from M. J. Bresso, Place de la Mairie, 06430 Tende, tel: 93 04 60 31.

In the Air

Heli-Air-Monaco operate 10-minute trips every day for up to five people. Héliport de Monaco Fontvieille, 98000 Monaco, tel: 93 21 34 95.

Provence Aéro Service offer tourist flights. RN 8, 83330 Le Castellet, tel: 94 90 79 79.

Héli-Air St-Tropez, helicopter flights. 83990 St-Tropez, tel: 94 97 15 12.

Coach Trips

Day or half-day trips with commentary take in many of the sights along the coast and inland, and are less expensive than going by sea or air. Details of the many coach operators are available from local tourist offices or bus/coach stations.

Culture

Some of the greatest artists of the past two centuries have been drawn to the Côte d'Azur by its sunshine, light, colour and freedom. They have all left their mark and the region now has more than 100 art galleries. And the tradition continues: painters still flock to the area to follow in the footsteps of their idols, and many contemporary studios and galleries are just as exciting as the established national museums.

The range of collections in the region's museums is not confined to works of art. There are equally fascinating exhibitions of the history of the area as well as more particular collections such as the Escoffier Museum of culinary arts in Villeneuve-Loubet and the Museum of Oceanography in Monaco (the eighth most visited museum in the whole of France).

Museums & Art Galleries

Most museums charge an entrance fee; for those that are state-owned expect to pay between FF10 and FF25 (half price on Sundays). Reductions are usually given for children, senior citizens and students – on production of a valid card. Those listed here are open every day, morning and afternoons (except public holidays) except where otherwise specified. Remember, most close for a long lunch, from noon or 12.30 to around 2.30pm.

Municipal museums generally have local exhibits and show the history of the area.

ANTIBES

Musée Picasso, Château Grimaldi, Place du Château, tel: 93 34 91 91. Entirely devoted to the works of Picasso. Closed: Tuesday and public holidays.

BIOT

Musée National Fernand Léger, Chemin du Val-de Pome, tel: 93 65 63 61. Known as the "Cathedral of Modern Art", reopened in 1989 with the addition of a new building, houses modern works, in particular stained glass, mosaics and ceramic. Closed: Tuesday. In the same square is an interesting little **museum of local history**, open Thursday, Saturday and Sunday. Tel: 93 65 05 85.

BREIL-SUR-ROYA

Ecomusée du Haut Pays, tourist information, tel: 93 04 99 76. Exhibitions of the natural environment, history and life of the Roya and Bevera valleys.

CAGNES-SUR-MER

La Maison de Renoir, Les Collettes, tel: 93 20 61 07. The house where Renoir lived for the 12 years before his death in 1919. Since 1989 has had on display 10 of his best works, plus drawings and sculpture. Closed: Thursday and mid October–mid November. Visit too the 6 acres of **gardens**, with ancient olive trees and a rose garden.

Also in the town visit the **civic museum** housed in a former château of the Grimaldi family: among is displays are 40 portraits of the local singer Suzy Solidor by 40 different artists (including Cocteau and Dufy) as well as an exhibition devoted to the olive tree.

CANNES

Musée de la Castre, le Suquet, tel: 93 38 55 26. Exhibitions of modern and primitive art in a former château enjoying splendid views over the bay. Closed: Tuesday. Admission: free Wednesday and Sunday. The town also boasts many small **private galleries**, showing mainly the work of contemporary artists. See too the **Musée de la Mer** on Ste-Marguerite Island. Closed: Tuesday and in January and February.

DRAGUIGNAN

Musée Art Tradition Populaire de Moyenne Provence, 15 Rue Joseph Roumanille, tel: 94 47 05 72. Also at the same address, **Musée Arts et Traditions Populaires**. Museums dedicated to local crafts and rural way of life, the latter has a reconstructed olive mill and displays of provençal cuisine. Closed: Sunday morning and Monday. See too, the **Musée Municipal**, 9 Rue de la République, tel: 94 472880. Closed: Monday. Admission: free.

FRÉJUS

Fondation Templon, ZI du Capitou, tel: 94 40 76 30. This foundation advertises itself as housing one of the best collections of modern art in Europe, principally showing works no more than 30 years old.

GRASSE

Musée International de la Parfumerie, 8 place du Cours, tel: 93 36 80 20. One of only three museums of its kind in the world, explaining the development and techniques of the industry. Closed: Monday, Tuesday and November.

Villa-Musée Fragonard, 23 Boulevard Fragonard, tel: 93 36 02 71. A 17th-century villa surrounded by a park, former home of M. Maubert, glovemaker, where Fragonard took shelter during the Revolution. Staterooms and paintings by the artist. A **Rose Festival** is held in May and a **Jasmine Festival** in August. Closed: most Saturdays and Sundays and November.

Musée de la Marine, Hôtel de Pontèves, 2 Boulevard du Jeu de Ballon, tel: 93 40 11 11. Dedicated to the career of Admiral de Grasse and naval history. Closed: Sunday and November.

HYÈRES

Musée Municipal, Place Th. Lefebvre, tel: 94 35 90 42. Includes collections of archaeology, fine arts, local history and natural history. Closed: Tuesday. Admission: free.

MENTON

Musée Jean Cocteau, Vieux Port, tel: 93 57 72 30. Entirely devoted to the life and works of Cocteau. Closed: Monday and Tuesday. Also worth a visit is the **Salle de Mariages** in the town hall, decorated by Cocteau in 1957–58.

Musée des Beaux Arts, Palais Carnoles, 3 Avenue de la Madone, tel: 93 35 49 71. Situated in the former summer palace of the Princes of Monaco, which itself stands in a magnificent garden (**parc de la Madone**), this museum houses collections dating from the 13th to the 19th centuries, as well as contemporary works. Closed: Tuesday. Admission: free.

Musée de Préhistoire Régionale, Rue Loredan Larchey, tel: 93 35 84 64. Closed: Tuesday. Admission: free.

MONACO TOWN

Musée Océanographie, Avenue Saint-Martin, tel: 93 15 36 00. A million visitors a year are drawn to this exciting museum created in 1901 by Prince Albert who was fascinated by the subject. Exhibits of marine technology are complemented by possibly the best aquarium in Europe.

Palais du Prince, tel: 93 25 18 31 (open to the public when the prince is not in residence).

Monte-Carlo

Musée National, 17 Avenue Princesse Grace, tel: 93 30 91 26. Housed in a fine 19th-century villa by the sea and surrounded by the Princess Grace rose garden, perhaps the most fascinating aspect of this museum is the collection of antique dolls and working automats dating from the 18th century.

Mougins

Musée de l'Automobiliste, Aire des Breguières, Autoroute A8, tel: 93 69 27 80. Appealing to both adults and children alike, a superb collection of cars spanning the century. Easiest access is via the motorway exit between Cannes and Antibes, or from the Vallauris–Le Cannet Road.

Musée de la Photographie, tel: 93 75 85 67. Noted in particular for its display of portraits of Picasso by different photographers. Open: Wednesday–Sunday (daily in July and August), afternoons.

Nice

Right in the centre of Nice stands the new arts and theatre complex which includes the **Musée d'Art Moderne et Contemporain**, Promenade des Arts, tel: 93 62 61 62. It has wide-ranging collections of artists mostly from the 1960s on, as well as sculptures in the surrounding gardens. Also includes a library, shop and café. Admission: free.

Musée d'Archéologie, 160 Avenue des Arènes, tel: 93 81 59 57. Set up in 1989 on the site of the baths dating from the 3rd century, this museum offers a superb evocation of the region's ancient history, as one of the oldest known sites of human habitation. Access is via the archaeological site, Avenue Monte Croce. Closed: Sunday afternoon, Monday and November. For prehistory, visit too the **Musée de Terra Amata**, 25 Boulevard Carnot, tel: 93 55 59 93.

Musée d'Art et d'Histoire, Palais Masséna, 65 Rue de France/35 Promenade des Anglais, tel: 93 88 11 34 or 93 55 15 24. Important collections of decorative and religious art and history of the region. Closed: Mondays and November. Admission: free.

Musée Barla, 60 bis Boulevard Risso. Natural history museum; visit too its fascinating annex the **Galerie de Malacologie** at 3 Cours Saleya (by the flower market), with its fine display of shells and underwater creatures. Main museum closed: Tuesday and mid August–mid September; the Galerie closed: Sunday, Tuesday and November. Admission: free.

Musée des Beaux-Arts, 33 Avenue des Baumettes, tel: 93 44 50 72. Vast collections of European fine arts from the 17th century on, including the impressionists and important collections of Chéret, Ziem and Van Dongen. Closed: Mondays. Admission: free.

Musée International d'Art Naïf Anatole Jakovsky, Château Sainte-Hélène, Avenue Val-Marie, 06200 Nice, tel: 93 71 78 99. A villa once owned by the founder of the casino at Monte-Carlo houses a fine collection of naïve art, established by a gift of the Jakovskys of 600 works, but now much expanded with art from all over the world. Closed: Tuesdays. Admission: free.

Musée Matisse, 164 Avenue des Arènes, tel: 93 81 08 08. With the building of a new extension, this museum houses the personal collection of the celebrated artist who died in Nice in 1954. It covers works from all periods of the painter's career.

Musée National Marc Chagall, Avenue du Docteur-Ménard, tel: 93 53 87 20. Built to house Chagall's "Biblical Message" of which 12 canvases (the Creation) are in one room and the other five (Song of Songs) in another. His other work is also well represented in all its various forms: paintings, stained glass, sculptures, mosaics, tapestries, and so forth. Also a library. Closed: Tuesday.

Musée Naval, Tour Bellanda, Parc du Château, tel: 93 80 47 61. A small museum in a building that is itself an historic monument showing the history of Nice as both a naval and pleasure port. Closed: Tuesday and mid-November to mid-December. Admission: free.

Nice also has a large number of **private galleries**, open to the public for viewing and sales.

Peille

Musée du Terroir, Mairie de Peille, tel: 93 79 90 32. One of three "eco-museums". Open: Wednesday, Saturday and Sunday summer afternoons (winter: Sunday only). Admission: free.

St-Jean Cap Ferrat

Musée Ephrussi de Rothschild, tel: 93 01 33 09. Varied and sumptuous collection which was bequeathed to the nation by Baroness de Rothschild who had the Italianate villa specially designed to house it. The ornamental gardens are worth a visit. Closed: Sunday and Monday mornings and November.

Ste-Maxime

Musée des Traditions Locales, Place des Aliziers, Route du Muy, St-Donat, tel: 94 96 50 52. Closed: Monday and Tuesday.

St-Paul-de-Vence

Fondation Maeght, tel: 93 32 81 63. Just northwest of the town this notable building houses the museum of modern art established in 1964 by art dealer Aimé Maeght. Apart from the works of Chagall, Braque, Bonnard etc. inside, the **gardens** are a backdrop to sculptures and other works, including Miró's fountains.

Musée d'Histoire Locale, Place de la Castre, tel: 93 32 41 13. Costumes and sets showing the history of St Paul.

There are also many private art galleries in the town.

St-Raphael

Musée Archéologique, Place de la Vieille Eglise, tel: 94 19 25 75. Archaeological collections and in particular exhibitions of submarine archaeology. Closed: Tuesday in summer (Sunday mid-September to mid-June).

St-Tropez

Musée de l'Annonçiade, Rue de l'Annonçiade, tel: 94 97 04 01. Housed in a 16th-century chapel, the collection in this museum bears witness to the attraction of St-Tropez and its surrounding area to artists who came specifically to capture its colour and exceptional light. Works by Matisse, Bonnard, Braque, Utrillo and Seurat are among those featured. Closed: Tuesday and November.

Musée Naval de St-Tropez, tel: 94 97 59 43.

Vallauris

Musée National Picasso, Place de la Libération, tel: 93 64 97 42. Similar to the one in Antibes, this museum is dedicated to the life and works of the artist, in particular his work *La Guerre et la Paix* (War and Peace). Closed: Tuesday. More of Picasso's works can be seen in the **Musée Municipal**, Place de la Libération, tel: 93 64 16 05. Also houses a good collection of ceramics. Closed: Tuesday; entry to both museums by the same ticket.

Villeneuve-Loubet

Musée Escoffier, 3 Rue Escoffier, tel: 93 20 80 51. A Museum of Culinary Art, in the house where Escoffier, one of France's most famous chefs, was born. Closed: Mondays and November.

Live Arts

The playground of film stars, musicians and artists, the Côte d'Azur offers a wide variety of live arts: music, from jazz to a programme of opera and symphony concerts; festivals of film and café theatre. In all, the region stages some 500 major cultural events each year.

Diary of Events

January

Cannes: MIDEM (International Disc and Music Publishing Festival)
Menton: Theatre season
Monaco: Monte-Carlo Rally; International Circus Festival
Nice: Festival of Birds

February

Isola 2000: Snow Carnival
Menton: International Lemon Festival
Nice: Carnival and Battle of Flowers

March

Antibes: Café Theatre Festival
Grasse: Carnival
Monte-Carlo: MANCAS (Contemporary and film music festival); Spring Arts Festival (continues until end April).

April

Cannes: MIP-TV (International TV Programmes festival)
Roquebrune-Cap-Martin: Costumed procession of lanterns to the castle on Good Friday.
Monte-Carlo: Biennial of Sculpture (odd numbered years, until end of September).

May

Cannes: Film Festival
Fréjus: Fleuriades – flower festival
Grasse: Expo Roses – international rose show
Monaco: Grand Prix
Nice: May Festival and International Youth Folk Festival; Art Jonction International
St-Tropez: The Bravades festival is in honour of the Roman soldier Torpes from whom St-Tropez takes its name.

June

Antibes: International Young Soloist Festival
Cannes: International Cabaret-theatre Festival
Fréjus: Arênes de l'Automobile: exhibition of collector's cars
Monte-Carlo: Fires of Saint Jean folk festival
Nice: Sacred Music Festival
Roquebrune-Cap-Martin: Theatre Festival.

July

Antibes: International Jazz Festival
Fréjus: Forum des Arts et de la Musique: concerts, classical dance, theatre
Golf Juan: Jean Marais Festival (theatre and music)
Grasse: International Festival of Military Music
Monte-Carlo: Season of concerts in the Princes Palace courtyard; Fireworks Festival and Monaco carnival (both end July until mid-August)
Nice: International Folk Festival; "Grande Parade du Jazz"
Vence: Classical concerts in the cathedral and open-air
Villefranche-sur-Mer: Venetian Festival

August

Antibes: International Fireworks Festival
Fréjus: Fête du Raisin – wine-tasting and feasting
Grasse: Festival of Jasmine (floral procession)
Menton: International Chamber Music Festival
Monte-Carlo: Feast of Saint Roman folk festival
Roquebrune-Cap-Martin: Costumed procession to the castle
Vallauris: Pottery Festival

September

St-Tropez: Grape-picking festival

October

Monte-Carlo: Season of Symphony Concerts

November

Monte-Carlo: 19 November national holiday: parades, ceremonies and spectacles (fireworks the previous evening)

December

Fréjus: Foire aux Santons: some 30 provençal craftsmen and women exhibit their santons – small clay figures of saints used for religious purposes.

Archaeology & Architecture

It has been noted that the Riveria was settled by humans early in its history. Included in this listing therefore are some of the earliest prehistoric sites yet discovered. The later civilisations of the Greeks and Romans are also still very much in evidence and there are some very well preserved sites.

In its more recent history, the region was largely dominated by the Italians, with the result that many of its important buildings are either of original Italian construction, or more latterly, designed in an Italianate style in keeping with their surroundings.

In the hinterland, there is much evidence of rural Provençal architecture: the stone-built hill villages, some still with their defending walls, and the solid farmhouses, or *mas*. Efforts are now being made to not to spoil this rural landscape; in many areas it is forbidden to build new houses unless in traditional fashion, using traditional materials.

In all the listings, opening times are as for museums, unless otherwise specified. Expect to pay an entrance fee (except cathedrals and churches).

Antibes

Although a modern resort, the old town of Antibes still has much of interest. Visit the **Rue Fourmillière**, the "most flowered street in Antibes". By the ramparts stands the medieval **Château Grimaldi**, now housing the **Picasso museum** (*see listing*) and nearby is the **cathedral** built in the 17th century, but housing a fine altarpiece by Louis Bréa (1515). Overlook-

ing the harbour is the 16th-century **Fort Carré**, open to the public in July and August. Also worth a visit, at Cap d'Antibes, is the **Hôtel du Cap d'Antibes** which featured in Scott Fitzgerald's *Tender is the Night*.
Musée d'Histoire et d'Archéologie, Bastian St-André, tel: 92 905435.

Auron

Although a modern ski resort, Auron has a notable Romanesque (12th-century) chapel with striking frescoes. Visit too the **Museum of Religious Art**.

Brignoles

Palais des Comtes de Provence Musée du Pays Brignolais, tel: 94 69 45 18. A 12th-century former palace of the Counts of Provence. Some of it is ruined but what remains is interesting, including a typical provençal kitchen. It houses the local museum which shows the history of bauxite mining in the area. Closed: Monday and Tuesday.
Château de Vins, Vins-sur-Caramy, 83170 Brignoles, tel: 94 72 50 40. Restoration work has been going on for some years now to save this Renaissance castle. Visitors are admitted to parts of it, including the courtyard and terraces.

Cannes

The resort boasts the smartest promenade on the Riviera. **La Croisette** is lined with elegant hotels, among which is the **Carlton**, the ultimate in wedding-cake architecture. The town is overlooked by the 11th-century **Le Suquet tower**, now housing the **Le Castre Museum**, tel: 93 38 55 26.

Collobrières

Ancienne Chartreuse de la Verne, 83610 Collobrières. A charterhouse founded around 1174 in the Maures Mountaines. Green serpentine stone used for ornamental motifs gives its a remarkable appearance. It resumed its original vocation in 1983 and now houses a religious community of Bethlehem monks. Closed: Tuesdays and October.

Entrecasteaux

This tiny, typically provençal village dating back to the Middle Ages boasts a heavily fortified **castle**, which was bought in the 1970s by a Scot, Ian McGarvie-Munn who won awards for its restoration, and installed his rather eccentric collections (including Scottish bagpipes). See too the formal **garden** designed by Le Nôtre, France's answer to Capability Brown, tel: 94 04 43 95.

Eze

This hill village enjoys a fantastic location, perched right above the sea and offering breathtaking views. Visit the **church** with its baroque interior and the **Chapel of the White Penitents**.

Frejus

Amphithéâtre and Arènes, Rue Henri Vadon, tel: 94 17 05 60. Dating back to the end of the 1st or the beginning of the 2nd century, this is one of the largest amphitheatres built in Gaul. Built for the use of the Roman garrison, it can accommodate 10,000 people. Closed: Tuesday.
Cité Episcopal, Rue du Fleury, tel: 94 51 26 30. Episcopal city comprising a palaeo-Christian baptistry, one of the oldest Christian monuments of ancient Gaul, the 18th-century **cathedral** (which includes the remains of an older building and an interesting belltower), and the cloister, noteworthy for its fine gothic columns. Closed: Tuesday. The **Musée Archéologique** on the same site houses the ancient Roman forum.

Grasse

The cathedral, **Notre-Dame-du-Puy**, dates back to the 12th century, although much restored in the 17th century. Of particular note are paintings by Rubens, Bréa and a rare Fragonard. Also the 17th-century **Villa Fragonard** (*see Places of Interest* page 329).

Grimaud

This attractive hill village near St-Tropez is dominated by the ruined **Château de Grimaud**. Built on a Gallo-Roman site, the present castle dates back to the 13th century. Restoration work is being carried out, but its is open to visitors at all times.

Hyères

Settled by both the Greeks and Romans, and then important in the Middle Ages, the old town is still enclosed by fortified ramparts. Of particular note is the 12th-century **Tour St-Blaise** and the **Tour des Templiers** in the market place. Vist too the church of **St-Paul** (1572) on a hill just outside the town, and the ruined **St-Bernard Château** and gardens.

Iles De Lerins

Just off the coast and accessible from many of the small ports (*see Excursions in the Things to do section*), these two islands both have notable buildings. **St-Honorat** is named after a 4th-century monk who founded one of the first monasteries in France on the island. It was acquired by the Cistercians after the Revolution. Its museum is open to the public. On the **Île St-Marguerite** stands a 17th-century fortress built by Richelieu, and famous for the imprisonment of the "Man in the Iron Mask", whose identity is still in question. It is now used as a sports and cultural centre; *son-et-lumière* displays are held in season.

La Brigue

In the upper Roya valley sits this unspoilt medieval village with a Romanesque **church**. Also nearby is the **Sanctuary of Notre-Dame-des-Fontaines**, a small chapel with some fine frescos.

La Turbie

Set behind Monaco, this old town boasts a roman landmark, **la Trophée des Alpes**, which has been partly restored by an American patron. See too the **Museum of Roman Provence**, tel: 93 41 10 11.

Le Thoronet

Abbaye du Thoronet, 83340 Le Thoronet, tel: 94 60 43 90. Set in a verdant valley, this Cistercian abbey was founded in the 12th century, and has been preserved practically in its orginal state. Visit the church, cloister, dormitory and chapter house.

Lorgues

Collégiale St-Martin de Lorgues, 83510 Lorgues, tel: 94 73 92 37. A majestic, classic religious building, remarkable because of its size, built by the town in the 18th century. Admission: free.

Mandelieu-La-Napoule

The 14th-century **castle** was bought in 1918 by the rather eccentric American sculptor, Henri Clews, who restored it and lies buried there. Now a museum, housing much of his work, and a Franco-American cultural centre. The **gardens** are also worth a visit.

Mougins

Just north of Cannes, this old fortified village provides a panoramic view of the coast. Of particular note are the 15th-century **gateway**; the romanesque **Saint Barthélémy chapel** and the **chapel of Notre-Dame-de-Vie** on a hilltop nearby. Picasso spent his last years at the *mas* (farmhouse) of Notre-Dame-de-Vie and died there.

Nice

Many of the town's notable buildings have already been mentioned in the Museums listing. Also of note is the **Opera House** and the **Palais Lascaris**, 15 rue Droite, tel: 93 62 05 54. There are some wonderful Italian baroque churches, as well as the Russian Orthodox **Cathedral of Saint Nicholas**, which once served a sizeable Russian community in Nice. It has sumptuous decorations both inside and out. Also on the hill of Cimiez the old Roman settlement has been excavated, showing in particular, the **temple of Apollo** and the **amphitheatre**.

Roquebrune

The well-restored medieval village is dominated by its feudal **castle** where villages proceed each year in traditional costume to give thanks for being saved from the plague in the Middle Ages.

Saint-Cezaire

The village itself has a **Romanesque chapel**, housing a Roman sarcophagus, but of more interest are the **grottoes**, just north of the village. Discovered in the late 19th century, they have remarkable stalactites and stalagmites.

St-Jean-Cap-Ferrat

The home of many of the Riviera's wealthier residents and thus dotted with elegant villas. The **Villa Mauresque** (not open to the public) was the home of Somerset Maugham; but the most notable building is the Italianate mansion which houses the **Rothschild Museum**.

St-Jeannet

At 2,500 ft (760 metres), this village offers splendid views of the whole coast from the Baou peak (easy access to the viewing table). Also the 17th-century **church** and **Templars' castle**.

St-Maximin-la-Sainte-Baume

Basilique et Couvent Royal de St-Maximin, 83470 St-Maximin, tel: 94 78 00 09. Over a Gallo-Roman crypt containing some richly embellished sarcophagi, Charles II of Anjou built this Gothic basilica, the best of its kind in the region, to serve as the reliquary of Mary Magdalen, patron saint of Provence. At the same time (1295) a vast Dominican monastery was built. See too the **medieval town** below with its arcaded Jewish quarter.

St-Paul-de-Vence

A charming hill village, famous for its modern art collections (*see Museums*). You can still walk around the 16th-century **ramparts**; also of note are the alleyways paved with mosaics and piazzas graced by fountains. Visit too the 12th-century hilltop **church** with its wealth of paintings.

St-Tropez

Citadelle de St-Tropez, tel: 94 97 59 43. High above the town this mighty 16th-century fortress affords a breathtaking view from the Alps to the Maures Mountains and the sea. Now houses a naval museum. Closed: Thursdays.

Valbonne

Well-preserved, picturesque village, its main square is bordered by Romanesque arcades. Also nearby is the **Roman aqueduct** of Claussones and to the south, the modern science park of **Sophia-Antipolis**.

Vence

Chapelle du Rosaire, 466 Avenue Henri Matisse, tel: 93 58 03 26. Just outside the town stands a small chapel, also known as the **Matisse Chapel** as it was entirely designed and decorated by the artist. Open: Tuesday and Thursday, or on request with 24 hours' notice. Closed: November to mid-December. Also worth visiting is the **church** in the medieval town itself which houses a mosaic by Marc Chagall.

Villefranche-sur-Mer

Delightful Italianate houses line the harbour of this old fishing port. Visit the **Chapelle Saint Pierre** (tel: 93 76 90 70), by the harbour, which was decorated by Jean Cocteau.

Nightlife

Apart from Paris, the Côte d'Azur has the most exciting nightlife in France. The casino at Monte-Carlo was the first in the country to open in 1865 (at a time when they were not permitted in the rest of France). It saved the principality from bankruptcy and the rich and famous came flocking to try their luck. What started as a Victorian novelty has now been tinged by a touch of Las Vegas and it has been joined by plenty of other casinos along the coast, some of them incorporating nightclubs or cabarets.

Casinos

Note that entrance to most casinos is around FF50–60 (although some are free) and restricted to those over 21 years of age. Many require you to show your passport. Some of the main casinos are listed below:

Antibes

La Siesta, Route de Bord de Mer, tel: 93 33 01 18. Open: June–September.

Cannes

Carlton Casino Club, Carlton Intercontinental, 58 la Croisette, tel: 93 68 00 33. Open: every day 4pm–4am. Also has restaurants, piano bar and disco.
Casino Municipal, 1 Jetée Albert-Edouard, tel: 93 38 12 11. Open: daily from 11am , plus Le Galaxy nightclub every evening (except Monday) at 11pm.
Palm Beach Casino, Place Franklin D. Roosevelt, tel: 93 43 91 12. Open: daily from 1 June–31 October.

Juan-les-Pins

Eden Casino, Boulevard E Baudoin, tel: 92 93 71 71. Refurbished.

Mandelieu-la-Napoule

Loews Hotel, Boulevard Général de Gaulle, tel: 93 49 90 00. Open: daily 8pm–4am. Also restaurant and floor show with orchestra.

MONTE-CARLO

Casino de Monte-Carlo, Place du Casino, tel: 04 92 16 21 21. The original and still the most famous where formal dress is required. Open: all year: main salon from noon, private rooms from 3pm. Also has a separate cabaret, as does **SBM Loews Casino**, Loews Hotel, Avenue des Spelugues, tel: 93 50 65 00. Less formal than its presitigious older brother, with free admission. Open: from 11am.

NICE

Casino Ruhl de Nice, 1 Promenade des Anglais, tel: 93 87 95 87. Open: daily 5pm–5am (4pm–4am in winter). Also offers a restaurant, disco (from 11pm) and cabaret.

STE-MAXIME

Casino Beach, 13 Avenue De Gaulle, tel: 94 96 12 90.

ST-RAPHAEL

Casino, Square de Gant, tel: 94 95 01 56.

Café Theatres & Piano Bars

If gambling is not your style, you can enjoy your evenings at a café theatre, discothèque or piano bar, or simply by soaking up the atmosphere at a pavement café. There are frequent firework displays during the summer, and everywhere on 14 July. For more cultural entertainments, *see Culture* page 331.

Local tourist offices will keep you up to date with what is going on, as will the local English-language and French papers. Following is a list of cafés/restaurants where you can be entertained as you dine. Many of the luxury hotels also have piano bars. You will need a healthy bank account for most of them.

ANTIBES

La Siesta, Pont de la Brague, tel: 93 33 31 31. Shows June–September.

Le Sucrier, 6 Rue des Bains, tel: 93 34 22 00. Café-theatre with performances Thursday–Saturday.

CAGNES-SUR-MER

Le Liberty, 52 Avenue de la Gare, tel: 93 20 69 17. Piano bar and dancing.

CANNES

Palm Beach, Place Franklin D. Roosevelt, tel: 93 43 91 12. Famous venue. Open: 1 June–31 October.

Les Ambassadeurs, Esplanade Georges Pompidou/La Croisette, tel: 93 39 01 01.

GRASSE

Restaurant les Parfums, Rue Eugene Charabot, tel: 93 36 03 15.

HYÈRES

Cafeteria DM, Centre Commercial du Pyanet, tel: 94 65 79 64. Weekend dinner-dances.

Lord's, Rue Joseph Clotis, tel: 94 35 47 00.

Royal Cocktails Club, 32 Rue de Limans, tel: 94 65 62 20.

ISOLA 2000

Auberge de la Lombard, tel: 93 23 11 67. Open: for the winter sports season, December–May and then from June–September.

STE-MAXIME

Café de Paris, Place du Casino, tel: 93 25 59 60.

Le Cygne, 7 Avenue Princesse Grace, tel: 93 25 59 60. Closed: Sundays and in January.

ROQUEBRUNE-CAP-MARTIN

Le Vista Palace, Grande Corniche, tel: 93 35 01 50. Open: all year. Dinner is served around the pool.

SAINT-LAURENT-DU-VAR

Le Trotteur, Plage de St-Laurent, tel: 93 31 10 76. And the **Cocody Beach**, tel: 93 07 52 10 are right on the seafront.

VENCE

Le Vieux Moulin, 661 Chemin Ste-Colombe, tel: 93 58 96 96. Piano-bar and show. Closed: Sunday.

Discotheques

Those listed are open all year unless otherwise indicated. They mostly open late (10 or 11pm).

ANTIBES

La Siesta, Route du Bord de Mer, tel: 93 33 31 31.

Shock, Avenue du 11 Novembre, tel: 93 33 69 93.

FRÉJUS

La Playa, Boulevard Libération, Fréjus Plage, tel: 94 52 22 98.

L'Odyssée, Boulevard Libération, Fréjus Plage, tel: 94 51 27 54.

JUAN-LES-PINS

Les Pecheurs, Avenue Baudoin, tel: 93 67 30 30.

Voom-voom, Boulevard de la Pinède, tel: 93 61 18 71.

Whisky à Gogo, La Pinède, tel: 93 61 26 40.

MONTE-CARLO

La Boccaccio, 39 Avenue Princesse Grace, tel: 93 30 15 22.

Jimmy'z, Place du Casino, tel: 93 50 80 80. Open: nightly, September–June. Also **Jimmy'z de la Mer**, Avenue Princesse Grace, tel: 92 16 22 77. Open: July and August.

The Living Room, 7 Avenue des Spélugues, tel: 93 50 80 31.

Parady'z, Avenue Princesse Grace, tel: 93 30 71 71. Open: July and August.

Tiffany's, 3 Avenue des Spélegues, tel: 93 30 70 55.

L'X Club, 13 Avenue des Spélegues, tel: 93 30 70 55.

ST-TROPEZ

Les Caves du Roy, Hôtel Byblos, Place des Lices, tel: 94 56 68 00.

Le Papagayo, Résidence du Port, tel: 94 97 07 56.

In the Countryside

Tourists in the mountainous and more rural areas of the region tend not to expect such a glamorous lifestyle. However, visitors staying in country gîtes in the smaller villages and towns will normally be very welcome to join in the local festivities that go on all over France, especially during the summer. Practically every village has its own local fête, which is usually rounded off with a *bal* or fireworks, or both.

Shopping

Shopping Areas

Over the years most major towns in France have made the sensible decision to keep the town centre for small boutiques and individual shops. Many of these areas are pedestrianised and so rather attractive (although beware – some cars ignore the *voie piétonnée* signs). The large supermarkets, hypermarkets, furniture stores and do-it-yourself outlets are grouped on the outskirts of the town, mostly designated as a Centre Commercial. This laudable intent is, however, somewhat marred by the horrendous design of some of these centres – groups of garish functional buildings which make the town's outskirts very unattractive. In the case of Nice, for example, there are vast hypermarkets, out by the airport to the west of the town.

These centres are fine for bulk shopping, for self-catering or for finding a selection of wine to take home at reasonable prices, but otherwise the town centres are far more interesting. It is here that you will find the individual souvenirs that give a taste of the region, alongside the beautifully dressed windows of delicatessens and pâtisseries.

Nice itself has glamorous shopping districts to attract its wealthy tourists. The **Masséna quarter** is a pedestrianised area of chic boutiques, where you will also find the main department stores, Galeries Lafayettes and La Riviera. In **Cannes**, head for the city centre, particularly Rue d'Antibes with its irresistible confectioners and luxury boutiques.

Markets

The heart of every French town is its market, and the markets of the Côte d'Azur and Provence are possibly the most colourful and lively of any in the whole of France. In many towns the market is held every day (except Monday); they mostly start early in the morning and close at midday. The French themselves usually visit early to get the best of the produce.

Some of the best general daily markets are in **Nice** (cours Saleya), **Antibes** (cours Masséna, covered market), **Cannes** (Marché Forville, also the flower market, Jardin des Allées – not Saturday), **Grasse** (Place aux Aires), **Menton** (Esplanade du Carei, and covered market), **Toulon** (Cours Lafayette), **Monte-Carlo** (Place d'Armes), **St-Maxime** (covered market, Rue Fenand Bessy, open all day in summer). Other markets which are well worth a visit, but not held daily are as follows (mornings): **St-Tropez** (Tuesday and Saturday), **Fréjus** (Wednesday and Saturday, Place des Poivriers, also **Fréjus Plage**, Place de la République, Tuesday and Friday, June–September), **Hyères** (Tuesday, Place de la République, Saturday, Avenue Gambetta), **Le Lavandou** (Thursday), **Draguignan** (Wednesday and Saturday), **Ste-Maxime** (Old Town, Thursday; marché du Capet, Avenue Georges Pompidou, Monday).

Another attraction are the specialist markets. All the above have flower stalls, but Nice, where the flower market is open all day, and **Cannes** are especially colourful. Antique and second-hand (*brocante*) markets are also very popular; those listed below are held regularly and open all day unless otherwise indicated.

Antibes: Place Audiberti, Thursday; also Cours Masséna for bric-à-brac and crafts, Tuesday and Friday afternoons.

Cagnes: Place du Château, Sunday.

Cannes: Allées de la Liberté, Saturday.

Menton: Place aux Herbes, Friday.

Nice: Rues A. Gauthier/C. Ségurane/E. Philibert, also the flea market, Place Guynemer, both daily except Sunday; philatelist's market, Square Durandy, Rue Pastorelli, Sunday morning.

Ste-Maxime-sur-Mer: Marché des Artisans (craft market), Thursday.

La Seyne-sur-Mer: Les Sablettes, Saturday, plus a flea market, Place B. Frachon, alternate Sundays except in July.

Vence: L'Ara, Wednesday.

Villefranche-sur-Mer: Place A. Pollonais, Sunday.

There are also antique and craft fairs and *marchés exceptionnels*, held at various points throughout the year, such as harvest times. Check with the local tourist office for details.

Buying Wine Direct

You may be tempted by all the signs you see along the road for *dégustations* – tastings. Many wine producers and farmers will invite you to try their wines and other produce with the aim of making a sale. This is a good way to try before you buy and can sometimes include a visit to a wine cellar. Often farm produce is more expensive to buy this way than in the supermarkets – do not forget that it is freshly produced, and not factory processed. However, this should not be true of wine and it can be more reliable, as well as cheaper to buy something you have tried and know you like. For a selection of wine cellars open to the public, *see Places of Interest*.

Shopping Tips

Food shops, especially bakers, tend to open early; boutiques and department stores open from 9am, but sometimes not until 10am. In town centres, just about everything closes from noon until 3pm apart from the department stores which usually stay open. Most shops close in the evening at 7pm. Out of town, the hypermarkets are usually open all day until 8 or even 9pm. Most shops are closed Monday mornings and large stores generally all day. If you want to buy a picnic lunch, remember to buy everything you need before midday. Good delicatessens (*charcuterie*) have a selection of delicious ready-prepared dishes, which make picnicking a delight.

On most purchases, the price includes TVA (VAT or purchase tax). The base rate is currently l8.6 percent, but can be as high as 33 percent on luxury items. Foreign visitors can claim back TVA paid and this may be worth doing if you spend more than FF4,200 (FF2,000 for non-EC residents) in one place. Some large stores and hypermarkets have information bureaux where you can obtain a refund form. This must be completed to show (with the goods purchased) to customs officers on leaving the country (pack the items separately for ease of access). Then mail the form back to the retailer who will refund the TVA in a month or two. Certain items purchased (e.g. antiques) may need special customs clearance. For more information contact the Service de Détaxe et de la Réglementation, tel: 93 85 27 55.

Complaints

If you have a complaint about any purchase, return it in the first place to the shop as soon as possible. In the case of any serious dispute, contact the Direction Départementale de la Concurrence et de la Consommation et de la Répression des Fraudes.

Sports & Leisure

It has been noted before that the Côte d'Azur is a very privileged region and its vast range of sporting facilities reflects the diversity of its landscape. Whatever sport you wish to pursue, you are likely to find opportunities to do so, whatever the season.

Participant Sports

Water Sports

It is not necessary to be a millionaire and member of the most fashionable yacht club to enjoy the pleasures of the sea. Of course, if you wish to hire a luxury yacht for a week's cruise, being a millionaire might help. You also need money to enjoy some of the beaches. Only 70 percent are open to the public, the rest (nearly 150 beaches) are privately owned (usually by hotels) and an entrance fee is charged. Most of the private beaches have a good range of equipment for hire: windsurfers, dinghies, catamarans, water skiing, parascending etc.

To hire a boat, or a yacht, for a day or longer, all you need really do is stroll around the pleasure ports of the resorts and ask. Another source of information is the local syndicat d'initiative or tourist office (*see Useful Addresses* page 316).

See also the *Excursions* page 330, for scheduled cruises. There are too many operators offering boats for cruising and sailing to list them all here, hence a selection. Most offer them for hire with or without a crew and they are open all year, unless stated otherwise.

Sailing & Windsurfing

Comité Régional de Voile Côte d"Azur, Espace Antibes 2208 Route de Grasse, 06600 Antibes, tel: 93 74 77 05.

Cannes: Station Voile, 9 rue Esprit Violet, tel: 04 92 18 88 87.

Juan les Pins: Nautique 2000, tel: 04 93 61 20 01.

Scuba Diving

Fédération française d'études et de sports Sous-Marins, tel: 93 65 11 64.

Antibes: Sondyle Club 62 allé des Pins du Cap, tel: 93 61 45 45.

Nice Centre inter de Plongée, 2 Ruelle des Moulins, tel: 04 93 55 59 50.

Cannes: Plongé Club de Cannes, 46 rue Georges Clemenceau, tel: 93 38 67 57.

Canoeing & Kayaking

Ligue Régionale Alpes-Provence, 14 Avenue Vincent Auriol, 30200 Bagnols-sur-Ceze, tel: 66 89 47 71.

Freshwater Fishing

Federation Departementale de Pêche, 34 Avenue St-Augustin, Nice, tel: 93 72 06 04 for information.

Sea Fishing

Antibes: Avec Lucien, du Port d'Antibes, tel: 93 64 28 39.

Nice: Atout Pêche, 67 Avenue St-Augustin, tel: 93 71 30 35.

Cannes: Cannes Pêche, 44 rue Georges Clemenceau, tel: 93 39 76 17.

Parascending

Nice: Federation française de Vol Libre, 4 rue de Suisse, tel: 04 93 88 62 89.

Skiing

Club Alpin: 14 rue Mirabeau, Nice, tel: 93 62 59 99.

Downhill Skiing

Auron: Office du Tourisme, tel: 04 93 23 02 66.

Isola 2000: Office du Tourisme, tel: 04 93 23 15 15.

Cross-Country Skiing

Val Casterino, tel: 93 04 73 71.

Le Boréon, St-Martin-de-Vesubie, tel: 93 03 33 77.

Tennis

Nice: Nice Leader Apollo, 66 Route de Grenoble, tel: 04 93 18 00 95.

Antibes: Tennis Club municipal d'Antibes, Avenue Jules Grec, tel: 93 33 74 49.

Tennis municipal de Cannes: Avenue Francis Tonnere, tel: 93 47 05 82.

Golf

Biot: Golfe du Biot La Basride du Roy, tel: 93 65 08 40.

Victoria Golf Club: Domaine du Val Martin, Valbonne, tel: 93 12 23 26.

Cannes: Golf de Cannes, Route du Golf, Mandelieu, tel: 04 93 49 55 39.

Golf de Nice: 198 Route de Grenoble, tel: 93 29 82 00.

Spectator Sports

Probably the most famous event in the whole region is the prestigious **Monte-Carlo Car Rally**, held in January. First staged in 1911, this road trial continues to attract the top names in the sport. Another lesser-known rally is held in November at St-Tropez; the 20 km (12 miles) **Rolls-Royce Rally**. The other big motoring event is the **Monte-Carlo Grand Prix** in May, one of the most decisive contests in the competition for the world motor racing championship.

April is the time for the International Tennis championships in Monte-Carlo, the **Monte-Carlo Open**, which is complemented by another "open", this time the **Golf Tournament** which takes place in early July. Another golfing event is the **Professional Golf Open** at

Mougins (Cannes) which is held every April.

The major horse-racing venue is the **Côte d'Azur Hippodrome** at Cagnes-sur-Mer where meetings are held during the day from December to May and in the evenings in July and August. One of its major events takes place in February. There is also an **international show-jumping competiton** in Cannes during May. Hyères is popular for racing, and meetings are held at the **Hippodrome** there during the spring and autumn. Fréjus hosts a **horse show** in June.

Naturally, being on the coast there are all kinds of sailing and other water-sport events, with most of the major competitions taking place at Mandelieu-la-Napoule, just west of Cannes, including the **Grand Prix de la Corniche d'Or** (April), "**Les Vieilles Ecoutes"** (July), the **International Rowing Regatta** (August) and the **Grand Prix de la Ville** (October). Other events are the **International Marathon** in the Baie des Anges, Nice in April, the **Transgolfe Windsurf Regatta** in St-Tropez in July and the **Royal Regattas** in September in Cannes to coincide with the **International Pleasure Boat Festival**; there is also a **Boat Show** at Beaulieu-sur-Mer in May. Details of other sporting events can be obtained from the nearest tourist office.

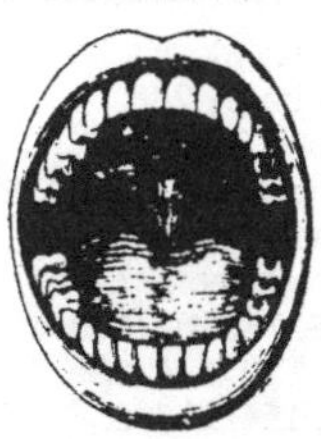

Language

The principal language of the region is, of course, French, although both Italian and English are widely spoken and understood, particularly in the major resorts. The French of the locals is tinged with the twang and somewhat flattened vowel sounds which is general in the whole of the south of France and can take a little while to become attuned to; for instance *pain* becomes *paing, maintenant* becomes *maintenaing*. In Monaco the old dialect of Monégasque can still occasionally be heard spoken by older people, and efforts are being made to revive its study in the local schools.

Further Reading

General

Ardagh, John. *France Today*. London: Secker and Warburg. Up-to-date, hefty tome on modern France.

Braudel, Fernand. *The Identity of France*. Fontana Press.

Cole, Robert. *A Traveller's History of France*. London: The Windrush Press. Slim volume for background reading.

Connolly, Cyril. *The Rock Pool*. Oxford University Press.

Fitzgerald, F. Scott. *Tender is the Night*. Penguin.

Forbes, Leslie. *A Table in Provence*. Webb & Bower. Recipes plus.

Grey-Wilson C. & Blamey M. *The Alpine Flowers of Britain and Europe*. Collins. Comprehensive reference book.

Guinsberg S. & E. *The Perched Villages of the Alpes-Maritimes*. Editions Edisud. Detailed guide to over 90 mountain villages, often ignored by tourists.

Hamilton, Ronald. *A Holiday History of France*. London: The Hogarth Press. Illustrated guide to history and architecture.

Howarth, Patrick. *When the Riviera was Ours*. Century Hutchinson. History of the development of the riveria as a tourist resort.

Sagan, Françoise. *Bonjour Tristesse*. Penguin.

Schonfelder & Schonfelder. *Wild Flowers of the Mediterranean*. Collins. Over 1,000 species described and hundreds of photographs.

Stendhal. *Travels in the South of France*. John Calder. Record of a journey made by the author in 1838.

Tomkins, Calvin. *Living Well is the Best Revenge*. E.P. Dutton.

Zeldin, Theodore. *The French*. How the French live today.

Other Insight Guides

Among the 192 companion **Insight Guides** to this book, the following highlight French destinations: *France, Paris, Normandy, Brittany, Loire Valley, Burgundy, Provence* and *Alsace*.

Apa Publications has two complementary series:

Insight Pocket Guides are specifically designed for the short-stay visitor and contain full-size fold-out maps. Titles in this series include: *Paris, Brittany, Loire Valley, Côte D'Azur, Provence* and *Alsace*.

Insight Compact Guides are handy mini-encyclopedias packed with facts, photographs and cross-referenced maps; titles include: *Paris, Normandy, Brittany, Burgundy* and *Provence*.

Art/Photo Credits

Photography by
Rosemary Bailey 288
Dirk Buwalda 71
Cannes Tourisme 76, 80, 106
Robert Capa/Magnum 101
Douglas Corrance 1, 12/13, 27, 72/73, 74/75, 78, 102/103, 120/121, 126/127, 129, 134, 135, 140, 141, 144, 151, 154/155, 156, 157, 159, 160, 161, 162, 163, 164, 166/167, 169, 171, 173, 175, 176, 178/179, 181, 183, 184, 185, 188, 194, 198/199, 200, 203, 204, 205, 208/209, 210, 211, 213, 214, 217, 220, 221, 222, 227, 232, 233, 234, 235, 244, 245, 249, 252, 253, 265, 267, 270, 271, 272, 277, 292/293, 295, 297, 298, 299, 301, 304, 305, 306, 308
CRT Côte d'Azur 302, 303
Douglas Dickens 289, 290
Rex Features 62/63, 66, 68, 105, 107, 108, 174, 260
Imperial War Museum 54, 55, 56, 57, 59, 61
Catherine Karnow 2, 9, 10/11, 14/15, 16/17, 81, 92, 109, 110/111, 112, 113, 114L, 114R, 115, 118/119, 122/123, 124, 128, 132, 133, 136, 137, 143, 145, 150, 152, 165, 172, 187, 190, 191, 193, 201, 224/225, 236/237, 238, 239, 241, 243, 246/247, 248, 251, 257, 258, 259, 261, 262/263, 264, 268, 269, 273, 278/279, 280, 287, 291, 294, 296, 307
Khachadourian Gallery 28/29
Barry Miles 26, 192, 207, 223, 281, 285
Menton Tourist Authority/Pierre Diot 266
Monaco Tourism 254, 255
Nègre 25, 30, 32, 49
Pictor International 206, 231, 274
Rex Features 104
Sotheby's 242
Spectrum 117, 148, 153, 177, 186
Sygma 67, 79
Topham Picturepoint 38, 65, 82, 83, 87, 89, 189
Bill Wassman 18, 25, 26, 69, 70, 116, 138/139, 146, 147, 168, 180, 195, 216, 218, 219L, 219R, 275, 276

Maps Berndtson & Berndtson

Visual Consultant V. Barl

Index

A B C D E F G I J a b c d e f g h j k l